D0955794

The
UNSCHOOLED
WIZARD

The
UNSCHOOLED
WIZARD

by BARBARA HAMBLY

THE LADIES OF MANDRIGYN
THE WITCHES OF WENSHAR

NELSON DOUBLEDAY, INC.
GARDEN CITY, NEW YORK

CONTENTS

THE
LADIES
OF
MANDRIGYN

To my fellow members of the
West Coast Karate Association
BROAD SQUAD

Anne
Gayle
Helen
Sherrie
Janet
Georgia

With love.

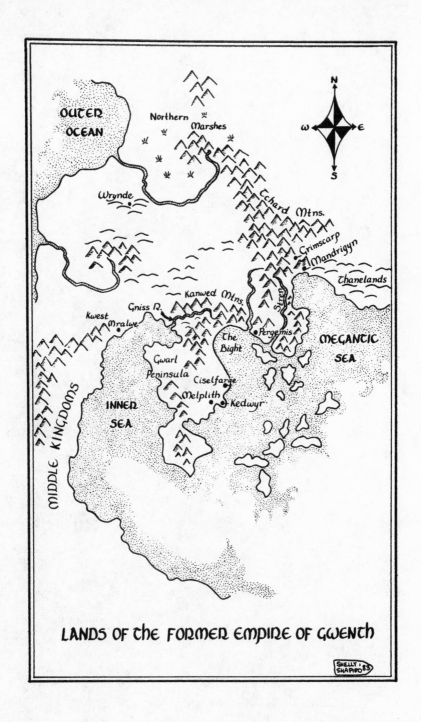

LANDS OF THE FORMER EMPIRE OF GWENTH

CHAPTER

 1

"**W**HAT IN THE NAME OF THE COLD HELLS IS THIS?" SUN Wolf held the scrap of unfolded paper between stubby fingers that were still slightly stained with blood.

Starhawk, his tall, rawboned second-in-command, glanced up from cleaning the grime of battle off the hilt of her sword and raised dark, level brows inquiringly. Outside, torchlight reddened the windy night. The camp was riotous with the noise of victory; the mercenaries of Wrynde and the troops of the City of Kedwyr were uninhibitedly celebrating the final breaking of the siege of Melplith.

"What's it look like?" she asked reasonably.

"It looks like a poxy proposition." He handed it to her, the amber light of the oil lamp overhead falling over his body, naked to the waist and glittering with a light curly rug of gold hair. Starhawk had been fighting under his command for long enough to know that, if he had actually thought it nothing more than a proposition, he would have put it in the fire without a word.

Sun Wolf, Commander of the Mercenaries, Camp of Kedwyr below the walls of Melplith, from Sheera Galernas of Mandrigyn, greetings. I will be coming to you in your tent tonight with a matter of interest to you. For my sake and that of my cause, please be alone, and speak to no one of this. Sheera.

"Woman's handwriting," Starhawk commented, and ran her thumb consideringly along the gilt edge of the expensive paper.

Sun Wolf looked at her sharply from beneath his curiously tufted brows. "If she wasn't from Mandrigyn, I'd say it was the local madam trying to drum up business."

Starhawk nodded in absent-minded agreement.

Outside the tent, the noise scaled up into a crescendo. Boozy cat-calls mixed with cries of encouragement and yells of "Kill him! Kill the bastard!" Between the regular troops of the City of Kedwyr and the City's Outland Militia Levies, a lively hatred existed, perhaps stronger than the feeling that either body of warriors had toward the hapless citizen-soldiers of the besieged town of Melplith. It was a conflict that the Wolf and his mercenaries had stayed well clear of—the Wolf because he made it his policy never to get involved in local politics, and his men because of a blood-chilling directive from their captain on the subject. The noises of drunken murder did not concern him—there wasn't a man in his troop who would have so much as stayed to watch.

"Mandrigyn," Starhawk said thoughtfully. "Altiokis conquered that city last spring, didn't he?"

Sun Wolf nodded and settled himself into a fantastic camp chair made of staghorn bound with gold, looted from some tribal king in the far northeast. Most of the big tent's furnishings had been plundered from somewhere or other. The peacock hangings that separated it into two rooms had once adorned the bedroom of a prince of the K'Chin Desert. The cups of translucent, jade-green lacquer and gold had belonged to a merchant on the Bight Coast. The graceful ebony table, its delicate inlays almost hidden under the bloody armor that had been dumped upon it, had once graced the wine room of a gentlemanly noble of the Middle Kingdoms, before his precious vintages had been swilled by the invading armies of his enemies and he himself had been dispatched beyond such concerns.

"The city went fast," Sun Wolf remarked, picking up a rag and setting to work cleaning his own weapons. "Basically, it was the same situation as we had here in Melplith—factional splits in the parliament, scandal involving the royal family—they have a royal family there, or they did have, anyway—the city weakened by internal fighting before Altiokis marched down the pass. I'm told there were people there who welcomed him as a liberator."

Starhawk shrugged. "No weirder than some of the things the Trinitarian heretics believe," she joked, deadpan, and he grinned. Like most northerners, the Hawk held to the Old Faith against the more sophisticated theologies of the Triple God.

"The Wizard King's Citadel has been on Mandrigyn's back doorstep for a hundred and fifty years," the Wolf continued after a moment. "Last year they signed some kind of treaty with him. I could see it coming even then."

Starhawk shoved her sword back into its sheath and wiped her fingers on a rag. Sun Wolf's talent for collecting and sorting information was uncanny, but it was a skill that served him well. He had a knack for gathering rumors, extrapolating political probabilities from crop prices and currency fluctuations and the most trivial bits of information that made their way north to his broken-down stronghold at the old administrative town of Wrynde. Thus he and his men had been on the spot in the Gwarl Peninsula when the fighting had broken out between the trading rivals of Kedwyr and Melplith. Kedwyr had hired the Wolf and his troop at an astronomical sum.

It didn't always work that way—in her eight years as a mercenary in Sun Wolf's troop, Starhawk had seen one or two spectacular pieces of mistiming—but on the whole it had enabled the Wolf to maintain his troops in better-than-average style, fighting in the summer and sitting out the violence of the winter storms in the relative comfort of the half-ruined town of Wyrnde.

Like all mercenary troops, Sun Wolf's shifted from year to year in size and composition, though they centered around a hard core that had been with him for years. As far as Starhawk knew, Sun Wolf was the only mercenary captain who operated a regular school of combat in the winter months. The school itself was renowned throughout the West and the North for the excellence of its fighters. Every winter, when the rains made war impossible, young men and occasional young women made the perilous journey through the northern wastelands that had once been the agricultural heart of the old Empire of Gwenth to the ruined and isolated little town of Wyrnde, there to ask to be taught the hard arts of war.

There were always wars to fight somewhere. Since the moribund Empire of Gwenth had finally been riven apart by the conflict between the Three Gods and the One, there had always been wars—over the small bits of good land among the immense tracts of bad, over the trade with the East in silk and amber and spices, over religion, or over nothing. Starhawk, whose early training had given her a taste for such things, had once explained the theology behind the Schism to the Wolf. Being a barbarian from the far north, he worshipped the spirits of his ancestors and would cheerfully take money from proponents of either faith. An understanding of the situation had only amused him, as she knew it would. Lately the wars had been over the rising of the Wizard King Altiokis, who was expanding his own empire from the dark Citadel of Grimscarp, engulfing the Thanes who ruled the countryside and such cities as Mandrigyn.

"Will you see this woman from Mandrigyn?" she asked.

"Probably." The noise of the fight outside peaked in a crazy climax of yelling, punctuated by the heavy crack of the whips of the Kedwyr military police. It was the fourth fight they'd heard since returning to the camp after the sacking of the town was done; victory was headier than any booze ever brewed.

Starhawk collected her gear—sword, dagger, mail shirt—preparatory to returning to her own tent. Melplith stood on high ground, above its sheltered bay—one of those arid regions whose chief crops of citrus and olives had naturally turned its inhabitants to trade for their living. Chill winds now blew up from the choppy waters of the bay, making the lampflame flicker in its topaz glass and chilling her flesh through the damp cotton of her dark, embroidered shirt.

"You think it's a job?"

"I think she'll offer me one."

"Will you take it?"

The Wolf glanced over at her briefly. His eyes, in this light, were pale gold, like the wines of the Middle Kingdoms. He was close to forty, and his tawny hair was thinning, but there was no gray either in it or in the ragged mustache that drooped like a clump of yellowbrown winter weeds from the underside of a craggy and much-bent nose. The power and thickness of his chest and shoulders made him seem taller than his six feet when he was standing up; seated and at rest, he reminded her of a big, dusty lion. "Would you go against Altiokis?" he asked her.

She hesitated, not speaking her true answer to that. She had heard stories of the Wizard King since she was a tiny girl—bizarre, distorted tales of his conquests, his sins, and his greed. Horrible tales were told of what happened to those who had opposed him, over the timeless years of his uncanny existence.

Her true answer, the one she did not say aloud, was: *Yes, if you wanted me to.*

What she said was, "Would you?"

He shook his head. "I'm a soldier," he said briefly. "I'm no wizard. I couldn't go against a wizard, and I wouldn't take my people against one. There are two things that my father always told me, if I wanted to live to grow old—don't fall in love and don't mess with magic."

"Three things," Starhawk corrected, with one of her rare, fleeting grins. "Don't argue with fanatics."

"That comes under magic. Or arguing with drunks, I'm not sure which. I don't understand how there could be one God or three Gods or five or more, but I do know that I had ancestors, drunken, lecherous clowns that they were . . . Hello, sweetpea."

The curtain that divided the tent parted, and Fawn came in, brushing the last dampness from the heavy curls of her mink-brown hair. The pale green gauze of her gown made her eyes seem greener, almost emerald. She was Sun Wolf's latest concubine, eighteen, and heartbreakingly beautiful. "Your bath's ready," she said, coming behind the camp chair where he sat to kiss the thin spot in his hair at the top of his head.

He took her hand where it lay on his shoulder and, with a curiously tender gesture for so large and rough-looking a man, he pressed his lips to the white skin of her wrist. "Thanks," he said. "Hawk, will you wait for a few minutes? If this skirt wants to see me alone, would you take Fawn over to your tent for a while?"

Starhawk nodded. She had seen a series of his girls come and go, all of them beautiful, soft-spoken, pliant, and a little helpless. The camp tonight, after the sacking of the town, was no place for a girl not raised to killing, even if she was the mistress of a man like Sun Wolf.

"So you're receiving ladies alone in your tent now, are you?" Fawn chided teasingly.

With a movement too swift to be either fought or fled, he was out of his chair, catching her up, squeaking, in his arms as he rose. She wailed, "Stop it! No! I'm sorry!" as he bore her off through the curtain into the other room, her squeals scaling up into a desperate crescendo that ended in a monumental and steamy splash.

Without a flicker of an eyelid, Starhawk shouldered her war gear, called out, "I'll be back for you in an hour, Fawn," and departed; only when she was outside did she allow herself a small, amused grin.

She returned in company with Ari, a young man who was Sun Wolf's other lieutenant and who rather resembled an adolescent black bear. They bade the Wolf a grave good evening, collected the damp, subdued, and rather pink-cheeked Fawn, and made their way across the camp. The wind had risen again, cold off the sea with the promise of the winter's deadly storms; drifts of woodsmoke from the camp's fires blew into their eyes. Above them, the fires in the city flared, fanned by the renewed breezes, and a sulfurous glow outlined the black crenelations of the walls. The night tasted raw, wild, and strange, still rank with blood and broken by the wailing of women taken in the sacking of the town.

"Things settling down?" the Hawk asked.

Ari shrugged. "Some. The militia units are already drunk. Gradduck—that tin-pot general who commanded the City Troops—is taking all the credit for breaking the siege."

Starhawk feigned deep thought. "Oh, yes," she remembered at length. "The one the Chief said couldn't lay siege to a pothouse."

"No, no," Ari protested, "it wasn't a pothouse—an outhouse . . ."

Voices yelled Ari's name, calling him to judge an athletic competition that was as indecent as it was ridiculous, and he laughed, waved to the women, and vanished into the darkness. Starhawk and Fawn continued to walk, the wind-torn torchlight banding their faces in lurid colors—the Hawk long-legged and panther-graceful in her man's breeches and doublet, Fawn shy as her namesake amid the brawling noise of the camp, keeping close to Starhawk's side. As they left the noisier precincts around the wine issue, the girl asked, "Is it true he's being asked to go against Altiokis?"

"He won't do it," Starhawk said. "Any more than he'd work for him. He was approached for that, too, years ago. He won't meddle with magic one way or the other, and I can't say that I blame him. Altiokis is news of the worst possible kind."

Fawn shivered in the smoky wind and drew the spiderweb silk of her shawl tighter about her shoulders. "Were they all like that? Wizards, I mean? Is that why they all—died out?"

In the feeble reflection of lamplight from the tents, her green eyes looked huge and transparent. Damp tendrils of hair clung to her cheeks; she brushed them aside, watching Starhawk worriedly. Like most people in the troop, she was a little in awe of that steely and enigmatic woman.

Starhawk ducked under the door flap of her tent, and held it aside for Fawn to pass. "I don't know if that's why the wizards finally died out," she said. "But I do know they weren't all evil like Altiokis. I knew a wizard once when I was a little girl. She was—very good."

Fawn stared at her in surprise that came partly from astonishment that Starhawk had ever been a little girl. In a way, it seemed inconceivable that she had ever been anything but what she was now: a tall, leggy cheetah of a woman, colorless as fine ivory—pale hair, pewter-gray eyes—save where the sun had darkened the fine-grained, flawless skin of her face and throat to burnt gold. Her light, cool voice was remarkably soft for a warrior's, though she was said to have a store of invective that could raise blisters on tanned oxhide. It was more believable of her that she had known a wizard than that she had been a little girl.

"I—I thought they were all gone, long before we were born."

"No," the Hawk said. The lamplight sparkled off the brass buckles that studded her sheepskin doublet as she fetched a skin of wine and two cups. Her tent was small and, like her, neat and spare. She had packed away her gear earlier. The only things remaining on the polished wood folding table were the gold-and-shell winecups and a pack of greasy cards. Starhawk was generally admitted to be a shark of poker—with her face, Fawn reflected, she could hardly be anything else.

"I thought that, too," Starhawk continued, coming back as Fawn seated herself on the edge of the narrow bed. "I didn't know Sister Wellwa was a wizard for—oh, years."

"She was a nun?" Fawn asked, startled.

Starhawk weighed her answer for a moment, as if picking her words carefully. Then she nodded. "The village where I grew up was built around the Convent of St. Cherybi in the West. Sister Wellwa was the oldest nun there—I used to see her every day, sweeping the paths outside with her broom made of sticks. As I said, I didn't know then that she was a wizard."

"How did you find out?" Fawn asked. "Did she tell you?"

"No." Starhawk folded herself into her chair. Like everything else in the tent, it was plain, bare, and easy to pack in a hurry. "The countryside around the village was very wild—I don't know if you're familiar with the West, but it's a land of rock and thin forest, rising toward the sea cliffs. A hard land. Dangerous, too. I'd gone into the woods to gather berries or something silly like that—something I wasn't supposed to do. I was probably escaping from my brothers. And—and there was a nuuwa."

Fawn shivered. She had seen nuuwa, dead, or at a distance. It was possible, Starhawk thought, watching her, that she had also seen their victims.

"I ran," the Hawk continued unemotionally. "I was very young, I'd never seen one before, and I thought that, since it didn't have any eyes, it couldn't follow me. I must have thought at first that it was just an eyeless man. But it came after me, groaning and slobbering, crashing through the woods. I never looked back, but I could hear it behind me, getting closer as I came out of the woods. I ran through the rocks up the hill toward the Convent, and Sister Wellwa was outside, sweeping the path as she always was. And she—she raised her hand—and it was as if fire exploded from her fingers, a ball of red and blue fire that she flung at the nuuwa's head. Then she caught me up in her arms, and we ran together through the door and shut and bolted it. Later we found places where the nuuwa had tried to chew through the doorframe."

She was silent; if any of the horror of that memory stirred in her heart, it did not show on her fine-boned, enigmatic face. It was Fawn who shuddered and made a small, sickened noise in her throat.

"It was the only time I saw her do magic," Starhawk continued after a moment. "When I asked her about it later, she told me she had only grabbed me and carried me inside."

Across the rim of the untasted cup, Fawn studied the older woman for a moment more. Rumor in the camp had it that the Hawk had once been a nun herself, before she had elected to leave the Convent and follow the Wolf. Though Fawn had never believed it before, something in this story made her wonder if it might be true. There were elements of asceticism and mysticism in Starhawk; Fawn knew that she meditated daily, and the tent was certainly as barren as a nun's cell. Though a cold-blooded and ruthless warrior, the Hawk was never senselessly brutal—but then, few of the handful of women in Wolf's troop were.

It was on the tip of Fawn's tongue to ask her, but Starhawk was not a woman of whom one asked questions without permission. Besides, Fawn could think of no reason why anyone would have left the comforts of the Convent to follow the brutal trail of war.

Instead she asked, "Why did she lie?"

"The Mother only knows. She was a very old lady then—she died a year or so after, and I don't think anyone else in the Convent ever knew what she was."

Fawn's tapering fingers toyed with the cup, the diamonds of her rings winking like teardrops in the dim, golden light. Somewhere quite close, a drunken chorus in another tent began to sing.

> "All in the town of Kedwyr,
> A hundred years ago or more,
> There lived a lass named Sella . . ."

"I have often wondered," Fawn said quietly, "about wizards. Why is Altiokis the only wizard left in the world? Why hasn't he died, in all these years? What happened to all the others?"

Starhawk shrugged. "The Mother only knows," she said again. As ever, her face gave away nothing; if it was a question that had ever crossed her mind, she did not show it. Instead she slapped the deck of cards before Fawn. "Bank?"

Fawn shuffled deftly despite her fashionably long, tinted fingernails. It was one of the first things she had learned when she'd been sold to Sun Wolf two years ago as a terrified virgin of sixteen—mostly in self-defense, since the Wolf and Starhawk were cutthroat card players.

Watching her, Starhawk reflected how out of place the girl looked here. Fawn—whose name had certainly been something else before she'd been kidnapped en route from her father's home in the Middle Kingdoms to a finishing school in Kwest Mralwe—had clearly been brought up in an atmosphere of taste and elegance. The clothes and jewelry she picked for herself spoke of it. Starhawk, though raised in an environment both countrified and austere, had done enough looting in the course of eight years of sieges to understand the difference between new-rich tawdriness and quality. Every line of Fawn spoke of fastidious taste and careful breeding, as much at odds with the nunlike barrenness of Starhawk's living quarters as she was with the rather barbaric opulence of the Chief's.

What had she been? the Hawk wondered. A nobleman's daughter? A merchant's? Those white hands, delicate amid their carefully chosen jewelry, had certainly never handled anything harsher than a man's flesh in all her life. *The loveliest that money could buy,* Starhawk thought, with a wry twinge of bitterness for the girl's sake—*whether she wanted to be bought or not.*

Fawn laid the cards down, undealt. In repose, her face looked suddenly tired. "What's going to become of him, Hawk?" she asked quietly.

Starhawk shrugged, deliberately misunderstanding. "I can't see the Chief being crazy enough to get mixed up in any affair having to do with magic," she began, and Fawn shook her head impatiently.

"It isn't just this," she insisted. "If he goes on as he's doing, he's going to slip up one day. He's the best, they say—but he's also forty. Is he going to go on leading troops into battle and wintering in Wrynde, until one day he's a little slow dodging some enemy's axe? If it isn't Altiokis, how long will it be before it's something else?"

Starhawk looked away from those suddenly luminous eyes. Rather gruffly, she said, "Oh, he'll probably conquer a city, make a fortune, and die stinking rich at the age of ninety. The old bastard's welfare isn't worth your losing sleep over."

Fawn laughed shakily at the picture presented, and they spoke of other things. But on the whole, as she dealt the cards, Starhawk wished that the girl had not touched that way upon her own buried forebodings.

Sun Wolf felt, rather than heard, the woman's soft tread outside his tent; he was watching the entrance when the flap was moved aside. The woman came in with the wild sea smell of the night.

With the lamps at his back, their light catching in his thinning, dust-colored hair and framing his face in gold, he did look like a sun wolf, the big, deadly, tawny hunter of the eastern steppes. The woman put back the hood from her hair.

"Sheera Galernas?" he asked quietly.

"Captain Sun Wolf?"

He gestured her to take the other chair. She was younger than he had thought, at most twenty-five. Her black hair curled thickly around a face that tapered from wide, delicate cheekbones to a pointed chin. Her lips, full almost to the corners of her mouth, were sensual and dark as the lees of wine. Her deep-set eyes seemed wine-colored, too, their lids stained violet from sleepless nights. She was tall for a woman and, as far as he could determine under the muffling folds of her cloak, well set up.

For a moment neither spoke. Then she said, "You're different from what I had thought."

"I can't apologize for that." He'd put on a shirt and breeches and a brown velvet doublet. The hair on the backs of his arms caught the light as he folded his strong, heavy hands.

She stirred in her chair, wary, watching him. He found himself wondering what it would be like to bed her and if the experiment would be worth the trouble it could cost. "I have a proposition for you," she said at last, meeting his eyes with a kind of anger, defying him to look at her face instead of her body.

"Most ladies who come to my tent do."

Her skin deepened to clay-red along the cheekbones and her nostrils flared a little, like a horse scenting battle. But she only said, "What would you say to ten thousand pieces of gold, to bring your troop and do a job for me in Mandrigyn?"

He shrugged. "I'd say no."

She sat up, truly shocked. "For ten thousand gold pieces?" The sum was enormous—five thousand would have bought the entire troop for a summer's campaign and been thought generous. He wondered where she'd come up with it, if in fact she intended to pay him. The size of the sum inclined him to doubt it.

"I wouldn't go against Altiokis for fifty thousand," he said calmly. "And I wouldn't tie up on a word-of-mouth proposition with a skirt from a conquered city for a hundred, wizard or no wizard."

As he'd intended, it prodded her out of her calm. The flush in her face deepened, for she was a woman to whom few men had ever said no. An edge of ugly rage slid into her voice. "Are you afraid?"

"Madam," Sun Wolf said, "if it's a question of having my bowels pulled out through my eye sockets, I'm afraid. There's no amount of money in the world that would make me pick a quarrel with Altiokis."

"Or is it just that you'd prefer to deal with a man?"

She'd spat the words at him in spite, but he gave them due consideration; after a moment, he replied, "As a matter of fact, yes." His hand forestalled her intaken breath. "I know where women stand in Mandrigyn. I know they'd never put one in public office and they'd never send one on a mission like this. And if you're from Madrigyn, you know that."

She subsided, her breath coming fast and thick with anger, but she didn't deny his words.

"So that means it's private," he went on. "Ten thousand gold pieces is one hell of a lot of tin from a private party, especially from a city that's just been taken and likely tapped for indemnity for whatever wasn't carried off in the sack. And since I know women are vengeful and sneaky . . ."

"Rot your eyes, you—" she exploded, and he held up his hand for silence again.

"They have reasons for fighting underhand the way they do, and I understand them, but the fact remains that I don't trust a desperate woman. A woman will do anything."

"You're right," she said quietly, her eyes burning with an eerie intensity into his, her voice deadly calm. "We will do anything. But I don't think you understand what it is to love your city, to be proud of it, ready to lay down your life to defend it, if need be—and not be allowed to participate in its government, not even be allowed by the canons of good manners to talk politics. Holy Gods, we're not even permitted to walk about the streets unveiled! To see the town torn apart by factionalism and conquered, with all the men who did fight for it led away in chains while the wicked, the venal, and the greedy sit in the seats of power . . .

"Do you know why no man came to you tonight?

"For decades—centuries—Altiokis has coveted Mandrigyn. He has taken over the lands of the old mountain Thanes and of the clans to the southeast of us; he sits like a toad across the overland trade roads to the East. But he's landlocked, and Mandrigyn is the key to the Megantic. We made trade concessions to him, turned a blind eye to encroachments along the border, signed treaties. You know that's never enough.

"His agents stirred up trouble and factions in the city, cast doubt on the legitimacy of the rightful Prince, Tarrin of the House of Her, split the parliament—and when we were exhausted with fighting one another, he and his armies marched down Iron Pass. Tarrin led the whole force of the men of Mandrigyn to meet them in battle, in the deeps of the Tchard Mountains. The next day, Altiokis and his armies came into the city."

Her eyes focused suddenly, an amber gleam deep in their brown depths. "I know Tarrin is still alive."

"How do you know?"

"Tarrin is my lover."

"I've had more women in my life," Sun Wolf said tiredly, "than I've had pairs of boots, and I couldn't for the life of me tell you where one of them is now."

"You'd know best about that," she sneered. "The men were all made slaves in the mines beneath the Tchard Mountains—Altiokis has miles of mines; no one knows how deep, or how many armies of slaves work there. The—girls—from the city sometimes go up there to—do business—with the overseers. One of them saw Tarrin there." The expression of her face changed, suffused, suddenly, with tender eagerness and the burning anger of revenge. "He's alive."

"We'll skip over how this girl knew him," Sun Wolf said. He was gratified to see that tender expression turn to one of fury. "I'll ask you this. You want me and my men to rescue him from Altiokis' mines?"

Almost trembling with anger, Sheera took a grip on herself and said, "Yes. Not Tarrin only, but all of the men of Mandrigyn."

"So they can go back down the mountain, retake the city, and live happily forever after."

"Yes." She was leaning forward, her eyes blazing, her cloak fallen aside to reveal the dark purple satin of her gown, pearled over like dew with opal beads. "No man came to you because there was no man to come. The only males left in Mandrigyn are old cripples, little boys, and slaves—and the cake-mouthed, poxy cowards who would sell their children to feed Altiokis' dogs, if the price were a little power. We raised the money among us—we, the ladies of Mandrigyn. We'll pay you anything, anything you want. It's the only hope for our city."

Her voice rose, strong as martial music, and Sun Wolf leaned back in his chair and studied her thoughtfully. He took in the richness of the gown she wore and the softness of those unworked hands. Supposing the city were taken without sack—which would be to Altiokis' advantage if he wanted to continue using it as a port. Sun Wolf was familiar with the soft-handed burghers who paid other men to do their fighting, but he had never given much thought to the strength or motivations of their wives. Maybe it was possible that they'd raised the sum, he thought. Golden earrings, household funds, monies embezzled from husbands too cowardly or too prudent to go to war. Possible, but not probable.

"Ten thousand gold pieces is the ransom of a king," he began.

"It is the ransom of a city's freedom!" she bit back at him.

Starhawk was right, he thought. *There are other fanatics besides religious ones.*

"But it isn't just the cost of men's lives," he returned quietly. "I wouldn't lead them against Altiokis and they wouldn't go. It's autumn already. The storms will break in a matter of days. It's a long march to Mandrigyn overland through the mountains."

"I have a ship," she began.

"You're not getting me on the ocean at this time of year. I have better things to do with my body than use it for crab food. We'll be a few days mopping up here, and by then the storms will have started. I'm not waging a winter war. Not against Altiokis—not in the Tchard Mountains."

"There's a woman on board my ship who can command the weather," Sheera persisted. "The skies will remain clear until we're safe in port."

"A wizard?" He grunted. "Don't make me laugh. There are no wizards anymore, bar Altiokis himself—and I wouldn't take up with you if you had one. I won't mix myself in a wizards' war."

"And," he went on, his voice hardening, "I'm not interested in any case. I won't take ten thousand gold pieces to buy my men coffins, and that's what it would come to, going against Altiokis, winter or summer, mountains or flatland. Your girlfriend may have seen Tarrin alive, lady, but I'll wager your ten thousand gold pieces against a plug copper that his brain and his soul weren't his own. And a plug copper's all my own life would be worth if I were fool enough to take your poxy money."

She was on her feet then, her face mottled with rage. "What do you want?" she demanded in a low voice. "Anything. Me—or any woman in the city or all of us. Dream-sugar? We can get you a bushel of it if you want it. Slaves? The town crawls with them. Diamonds? Twenty thousand gold pieces . . ."

"You couldn't raise twenty thousand gold pieces, woman. I don't know how you raised ten," Sun Wolf snapped. "And I don't touch dream-sugar. You? I'd sooner bed a poisonous snake."

That touched her on the raw, for she was a woman whom men had begged for since she was twelve. But the rage in her was something more—condensed, like the core of a flame—and it was this that had caused Sun Wolf to speak what sounded like an insult but was, in fact, the literal truth. She was a dangerous woman, passionate, intelligent, and ruthless; a woman who could wait months or years for revenge. Sun Wolf did not rise from his chair, but he gauged the distance between them and calculated how swiftly she might move if she struck.

Then a draft of wild smoky night breathed suddenly through the tent, and Sheera swung around as Starhawk paused in the doorway. For a moment, the women stood facing each other, the one in her dark gown sewn with shadowy opals, with her wild and perilous beauty, the other windburned and plain as bread, her man's doublet accentuating the wide shoulders and narrow hips, the angular face with its cropped hair. Starhawk's rolled-back sleeves showed forearms muscled like a man's, all crimped with pink war scars.

They sized each other up in silence. Then Sheera thrust past Starhawk, through the tent flap, to vanish into the blood-scented night.

The Hawk looked after her in silence for a moment, then turned back to her chief, who still sat in his camp chair, his hands folded before him and his fox-yellow eyes brooding. He sighed, and the tension seemed to ebb from his muscles as much as it ever did on campaign. The door curtain moved again, and Fawn entered, her dark hair fretted to tangles, falling in a soft web over her slender back.

Sun Wolf stood up and shook his head in answer to his lieutenant's unasked question. "May the spirits of his ancestors," he said quietly, "help the poor bastard who falls afoul of her."

CHAPTER

2

S UNLIGHT LAY LIKE A THICK AMBER RESIN ON THE SURFACE OF THE
council table, catching in a burning line on the brass of its inlay work,
like the glare at the edge of the sea. For all the twinge of autumn that
spiced the air outside, it was over-warm up here, and the Council of
Kedwyr, laced firmly into their sober coats of padded and reinforced
black wool, were sweating gently in the magnified sunlight that fell
through the great oriel windows. Sun Wolf sat at the foot of the table
between the Captain of the Outland Levies and the Commander of the
City Guards, his hands folded, the glaring sun catching like spurts of
fire on the brass buckles of his doublet, and waited for the President of
the Council to try and wriggle out of his contract.

Both the Outland Captain Gobaris and the City Commander Breg
had warned him. They themselves fought for Kedwyr largely as a duty
fixed by tradition, and their pay was notoriously elastic.

The President of the Council opened the proceedings with a well-
rehearsed paean of praise for the Wolf's services, touching briefly
upon his regrets at having had to go to war against such a small neighbor as Melplith at all. He went on to speak of the hardships they had
all endured, and Sun Wolf, scanning those pink, sweaty faces and hamlike jowls bulging out over the high-wrapped white neckclothes, remembered the rotten rations and wondered how much these men had
made off them. The President, a tall, handsome man with the air of a

middle-aged athlete run to fat, came to his conclusion, turned to the ferret-faced clerk at his side, and said, "Now, as to the matter of payment. I believe the sum promised to Captain Sun Wolf was thirty-five hundred gold pieces or its equivalent?"

The man nodded in agreement, glancing down at the unrolled parchment of the contract that he held in his little white hand.

"In the currency of the Realm of Kedwyr . . ." the President began, and Sun Wolf interrupted him, his deep rumbling voice deceptively lazy.

"The word 'equivalent' isn't in my copy of the contract."

He reached into the pouch on his belt and pulled out a much-folded wad of parchment. As he deliberately spread it out on the surface of the table before him, he could see the uneasy glance that passed among the councilmen. They had not thought that he could read.

The President's wide smile widened. "Well, of course, it is understood that—"

"I didn't understand it," Sun Wolf said, still in that mild tone of voice. "If I had meant 'gold or local,' I'd have specified it. The contract says 'gold'—and by international contractual law, gold is defined by assay weight, not coinage count."

In the appalled silence that followed, Captain Gobaris of the Outland Levies leaned his chin on his palm in such a way that his fingers concealed the grin that was struggling over his round, heavy face.

The President gave his famous, glittering smile. "It's a pleasure to deal with a man of education, Captain Sun Wolf," he said, looking as if he would derive even greater pleasure from seeing Sun Wolf on board a ship that was headed straight for the rocks that fringed Kedwyr's cliffs. "But as a man of education, you must realize that, because of the disrupted conditions on the Peninsula, assay-weight gold coinage is in critically short supply. The balance of imports and exports must be re-established before our stockpiles of gold are sufficient to meet your demands."

"My demands," Sun Wolf reminded him gently, "were made six months ago, before the trade was disrupted."

"Indeed they were, and you may be sure that under ordinary circumstances our treasuries would have been more than sufficient to give you your rightful dues in absolute-weight coinage. But emergency contingencies arose which there was no way to foresee. The warehouse fires on the silk wharves and the failure of the lemon crops on which so much of our export depends caused shortages in the treasury which had to be covered from funds originally earmarked for the war."

Sun Wolf glanced up. The ceiling of the council hall was newly gilded—he'd watched the workmen doing it, one afternoon when he'd been kept kicking his heels here for an hour and a half trying to see the President about the rations the Council members had been selling them.

Gilding was not cheap.

"Nevertheless," the President went on, leaning forward a little and lowering his voice to a confiding tone, which the Outland Captain had told Sun Wolf meant he was about to tighten up the screws, "we should be able to meet the agreed-upon amount in gold coinage in four weeks, when the amber convoys come in from the mountains. If you are willing to wait, all can be arranged to your satisfaction."

Except that my men and I will not be stuck on the hostile Peninsula for the winter, the Wolf thought dryly. If they were paid promptly and left at the end of this week, they might make it over the Gniss River, which separated the Peninsula from the rolling wastelands beyond, before it became impassable with winter floods. If they waited four weeks, the river would be thirty feet higher than it was now in the gorges, and the Silver Hills beyond clogged with snow and blistered by winds. If they waited four weeks to be paid, many of the men might never make it back to winter quarters in Wrynde at all.

He folded his hands and regarded the President in silence. The moment elongated itself uncomfortably into a minute, then two. The next offer would be for local currency, of course—stipulated at a far higher rate than he could get in Wrynde. Silver coinage tended to fluctuate in value, and right now the silver content wasn't going to be high. But he let the silence run on, knowing the effect of it on men already a little nervous about that corps of storm troops camped by the walls of Melplith.

It was General Gradduck, the head of all the Kedwyr forces who had taken most of the credit for breaking the siege, who finally spoke. "But if you are willing to accept local currency . . ." he began, and left the bait dangling.

They expected the Wolf to start grudgingly stipulating silver content on coinage—impossible to guarantee unless he wanted to have every coin assayed individually. Instead he said, "You mean you'd like to renegotiate the contract?"

"Well—" the President said, irritated.

"Contractually, you're obligated for gold," Sun Wolf said. "But if you are willing to renegotiate, I certainly am. I believe, in matters regarding international trade, the custom in the Peninsula is to impanel a jury of impartial representatives of the other states hereabouts, to determine equivalent local currency values for thirty-five hundred in gold."

The President did not quite turn pale at the thought of representatives from the other Peninsular states setting the amount of money he'd have to pay this mercenary and his men. The other states, already alarmed by Kedwyr's attack on its rival Melplith, would love to be given the opportunity to disrupt Kedwyr's economy in that fashion— not to mention doing Sun Wolf a favor that could be tendered as part of the payment the next time they needed a mercenary troop.

He was clearly sorry he had mentioned it.

A pinch-faced little councilman down at the end of the table quavered, "Of all the nerve!"

The President forced one last smile. "Of course, Captain, such negotiations could be badly drawn out."

Sun Wolf nodded equably. "I realize the drain that's already been put on you by our presence here. I'm sure my men could be put up in some other city in the vicinity, such as Ciselfarge."

It had been a toss-up whether Kedwyr would invade Melplith or Ciselfarge in this latest power struggle for the amber and silk trades, and Sun Wolf knew it. If the President hadn't just returned from swearing lasting peace and brotherhood with Ciselfarge's prince, the remark could have been construed as an open threat.

Grimly, the President said, "I am sure that such a delay will not be necessary."

The bar of sunlight slid along the table, glared for a time in Sun Wolf's eyes, then shifted its gleam to the wall above his head. Servants came in to light the lamps before the negotiations were done. Once or twice, Sun Wolf went down to the square outside the Town Hall to speak to the men he'd brought into the town with him, ostensibly to make sure they weren't drinking themselves insensible in the taverns around the square, but in fact to let them know he was still alive. The men, like most of the Wolf's men, didn't drink nearly as much as they seemed to—this trip counted as campaign, not recreation.

The third time the Wolf came down the wide staircase, it was with the fat Captain Gobaris of the Outland Levies and the thin, bitter, handsome Commander Breg of the Kedwyr City Guards. The Outland Captain was chuckling juicily over the discomfiture of the Council at Sun Wolf's hands. "I thought we'd lose our President to the apoplexy, for sure, when you specified the currency had to be delivered tomorrow."

"If I'd given him the week he'd asked for, he'd have had time to get another run of it from the City Mint," the Wolf said reasonably. "There'd be half the silver content of the current coins, and he'd pay me off in that."

The Guards Commander glanced sideways at him with black, gloomy eyes. "I suspect it's what he did last year, when the city contracts were signed," he said. "We contracted for five years at sixty stallins a year, and that was when stallins were forty to a gold piece. Within two months they were down to sixty-five."

"Oh, there's not much I wouldn't put past that slick bastard." Gobaris chuckled as they stepped through the great doors. Before them, the town square lay in a checkwork of moonlight and shadow, bordered with the embroidered gold of a hundred lamps from the taverns that rimmed it. Music drifted on the wind, with the smell of the sea.

No, Sun Wolf thought, signaling to his men. *And that's why I didn't come to this town alone.*

They left their places in the open tavern fronts and drifted toward him across the square. Gobaris scratched the big hard ball of his belly, and sniffed at the wild air. "Winter rains are holding off," he judged. "They're late this year."

"Odd," the commander said. "The clouds have been piling up on the sea horizon, day after day."

Obliquely, it crossed Sun Wolf's mind that the woman Sheera had spoken of having someone on board her ship who could command the weather. *A wizard?* he wondered. *Impossible.* Then his men were around him, grinning, and he raised his thumbs in a signal of success. There were ironic cheers, laughter, and bantering chaff, and Sheera slipped from the Wolf's mind as Gobaris said, "Well, that's over, and a better job of butchery on a more deserving group of men I've never seen. Come on, Commander," he added, jabbing his morose colleague in the ribs with an elbow. "Is there anyplace in this town a man can get some wine to wash out the taste of them?"

They ended up making a circuit of the square, Sun Wolf, Gobaris, and Commander Breg, with all of Sun Wolf's bodyguard and as many of the Outland Levies as had remained in the town. Amid joking, laughter, and horseplay with the girls of the local sisterhood who had turned out in their tawdry finery, Sun Wolf managed to get a good deal of information about Kedwyr and its allies from Commander Breg and a general picture of the latest state of Peninsula politics.

A cool, little hand slid over his shoulder, and a girl joined them on the bench where he sat, her eyes teasing with professional promise. Remarkable eyes, he thought; deep gold, like peach brandy, lighting up a face that was young and exquisitely beautiful. Her hair was the soft, fallow gold of a ripe apricot, escaping its artful pins and lying over slim, bare shoulders in a shining mane. He thought, momentarily, of Fawn, back at the camp—this girl couldn't be much older than eighteen years.

The tastes of wine and victory were mingled in his mouth. He said to the men he'd brought with him, "I'll be back." With their good-natured ribaldry shouting in his ears, he rose and followed the girl down an alley to her rose-scented room.

It was later than he had anticipated when he returned to the square. A white sickle moon had cleared the overhanging housetops that closed in the alley; it glittered sharply on the messy water that trickled down the gutter in the center of the street. The noise from the square had entirely faded, music and laughter dying away into four-bit love and finally sleep. His men, Sun Wolf thought to himself with a wry grin, weren't going to be pleased at having waited so long, and he steeled himself for the inevitable comments.

The square was empty.

One glance told him that all the taverns were shut, a circumstance that bunch of rowdy bastards would never have permitted if they'd still been around. Dropping back into the sheltering shadows of the alley, he scanned the empty pavement again—milky where the moon struck it, barred with the angular black frieze of the shadows cast by the roof of the Town Hall. Every window of that great building and of all the buildings round about was dark.

Had the President had them arrested?

Unlikely. The candlelighted room to which the girl had led him wasn't that far from the square; if there'd been an arrest, there would have been a fight, and the noise would have come to him.

Besides, if the Council had given orders for his arrest, they'd have followed him and taken him in the twisting mazes of alleys, away from his men.

A town crier's distant voice announced that it was the second watch of the night and all was well.

Much later than he'd anticipated, he thought and cursed the girl's teasing laughter that had drawn him back to her. But no matter how late he was, his men would never have gone off without him unless so ordered, even if they'd had to wait until sunup.

After a moment's thought, he doubled back toward the harbor gates. It was half in his mind to return to the Town Hall and make a private investigation of the cells that would invariably be underneath it. But as much as his first instinct pulled him toward a direct rescue, long experience with the politics of war told him it would be foolish. If the men had merely been arrested for drunken rowdiness—which the Wolf did not believe for a moment—they were in no danger. If they were in danger, it meant they'd been gathered in for some other reason, and the Wolf stood a far better chance of helping them by slipping out of the city himself and getting back to his position of strength in the camp. If he did not return, it would be morning before Starhawk acted and possibly too late for any of them.

His soft boots made no noise on the cobbles of the streets. In the dark mazes of the poor quarter, there was little sound—no hint of pursuit or of anything else. A late-walking water seller's mournful call drifted through the blackness. From a grimy thieves' tavern, built half into a cellar, smoky and mephitic light seeped, and with it came raucous laughter and the high-pitched, shrieking voices of whores. Elsewhere, the bells of the local Convent—Kedwyr had always been a stronghold of the Mother's followers—chimed plaintively for midnight rites.

The harbor gate was a squat, round tower, crouching like a monstrous frog against the starry backdrop of velvet sky. Slipping out that way would mean an extra mile or so of walking, scrambling up the precarious cliff road, but the Wolf assumed that, if the President had men watching for him, they'd be watching by the main land gates.

Certainly there were none awaiting him here. A couple of men and a stocky, plain-looking woman in the uniforms of the City Guards were playing cards in the little turret room beside the closed gates, a bottle of cheap wine on the table between them. Sun Wolf slid cautiously through the shadows toward the heavily barred and awkwardly placed postern door that was cut in the bigger gates—a feature of many city gates, and one that he habitually spied out in any city he visited.

Slipping out by the postern would put him in full view of the guards in the turret for as long as it took to count to sixty, he calculated, gauging distances and times from the dense shadows of the gate arch. If the guards were not alert for someone trying to get out of the city, he could just manage, with luck. For all his size, he had had from childhood an almost abnormal talent for remaining unseen, like a stalking wolf in the woods that could come within feet of its prey. His father, who was his size but as big and blundering as a mountain bear, had cursed him for it as a sneaking pussyfoot, though in the end he had admitted it was a handy talent for a warrior to have.

It served him well now. None of the card players so much as turned a head as he eased the bar from the bolt slots and stole through.

After the torchlight near the gate, the night outside was inky dark. The tide was coming in, rising over the vicious teeth of the rocks below the cliffs to the southwest, the starlight ghostly on the wet backs of the crabs that swarmed at their feet. As he climbed the cliff path, he saw that there were chains embedded in the weedy stones of the cliff's base, winking faintly with the movement of the waves.

He shuddered with distaste. His training for war had been harsh, physically and mentally, both from his father's inclination and from the customs of the northern tribe into which he had been born. He had learned early that an active imagination was a curse to a warrior. It had taken him years to suppress his.

The cliff path was narrow and steep, but not impassable. It had been made for woodcutters and sailors to go up from and down to the beaches when the tide was out. Only an invading troop attacking the habor gate would find it perilous. He was soaked to the skin from the spray when he reached its top, half a mile or so from the walls; the wind was biting through the wet sheepskin of his jerkin. In the winter, the storms would make the place a deathtrap, he thought, looking about him at the flat, formless lands at the top. Windbreaks of trees crisscrossed all the lands between the cliffs and the main road from the city gates, and a low wall of gray stones, half ruined and crumbling, lay like a snake a dozen yards inland of the cliff top, a final bastion for those blinded by wind and darkness. From here the waves had a greedy sound.

He turned his face to the sea again, the wind flaying his cheeks. Above the dark indigo of the sea, he could discern great columns of flat-topped clouds, guarding lightning within them. The storms could hit at any time, he thought, and his mind went back to the rough country of the wastelands beyond the Gniss River. If there was a delay getting those jokers out of the city jail . . .

He cursed his bodyguard as he turned his steps back toward the road that ran from the land gate of the city Melplith. He'd left Little Thurg in charge of them. *You'd think the little bastard would have the sense to keep them out of trouble,* he thought, first bitterly, then speculatively. In point of fact, Little Thurg did generally have the brains to keep out of trouble and, for all his height of barely five feet, he had the authority to keep men under his command out of trouble, too. It was that which had troubled Sun Wolf from the first.

Then, like a soft word spoken in the night, he heard the hum of a bowstring. A pain, like the strike of a snake, bit his leg just above the knee. Almost before he was aware that he'd been winged, Sun Wolf flung himself down and forward, rolling into the low ground at the side of the road, concealed by the blackest shadows of the windbreaks. For a time he lay still, listening. No sounds came to his ears but the humming of the wind over the stones and the slurred voices of the whispering trees overhead.

Shot from behind a windbreak, he thought, and his hand slipped down to touch the shaft that stood out from his flesh. The touch of it startled him, and he looked down. He'd been expecting a war arrow, a killing shaft. But this was short, lightweight, fletched with narrow, gray feathers—the sort of thing children and soft-bred court ladies shot at marsh birds with. The head, which he could feel buried an inch and a half in his leg, was smooth. After the savage barbs he had from time to time hacked out of his own flesh in twenty-five years of war, the thing was a toy.

He pulled it out as he would have pulled a thorn, the dark blood trickling unheeded down his boot. It was senseless. You couldn't kill a man with something like that unless you put it straight through his eye.

Unless it was poisoned.

Slowly he raised his head, scanning the vague and star-lighted landscape. He could see nothing, no movement in the deceptive shadows of the stunted trees. But he knew they were out there waiting for him. And he knew they had him.

They?

If he was going to be trapped, why not in the town? Unless the President was unsure of the loyalty of his city Troops and the Outland Levies? Would Gobaris' men have rioted at Sun Wolf's arrest?

If they'd thought it was the prelude to being done out of their own pay, they would.

Working quickly, he slashed the wound with his knife and sucked and spat as much of the blood as he could, his ears straining for some anomalous sound over the thin keening of the wind. He unbuckled his damp jerkin and used his belt for a tourniquet, then broke off the head of the slender arrow and put it in his pocket in the hopes that, if he did make it as far as the camp, Butcher would be able to tell what the poison was. But already his mind was reviewing the road, as he had studied it time and again during the weeks of the siege, seeing it in terms of cover and ambush. It was well over an hour's walk.

He got to his feet cautiously, though he knew there would be no second arrow, and began to walk. Through the sweeping darkness that surrounded him, he thought he sensed movement, stealthy in the shadows of the windbreaks, but he did not turn to look. He knew perfectly well they would be following.

He felt it very soon, that first sudden numbness and the spreading fire of feverish pain. When the road dipped and turned through a copse of dark trees, he looked back and saw them, a flutter of cloaks crossing open ground. Four or five of them, a broad, scattered ring.

He had begun to shiver, the breath laboring in his lungs. Even as he left the threshing shadows of the grove, the starlight on the plain beyond seemed less bright than it had been, the distance from landmark to landmark far greater than he had remembered. The detached corner of his mind that had always been capable of cold reasoning, even when he was fighting for his life, noted that the poison was fast-acting. The symptoms resembled toadwort, he thought with a curious calm. Better that—if it had to be poison—than the endless purgings and vomitings of mercury, or the screaming hallucinatory agonies of anzid. As a mercenary, he had seen almost as much of politics as he had of war. Poison deaths were nothing new, and he had seen the symptoms of them all.

But he was damned if he'd let that sleek, toothy President win this one uncontested.

He was aware that he'd begun to stagger, the fog in his brain making the air glitter darkly before his eyes. Tiny stones in the road seemed to magnify themselves hugely to trip his feet. He was aware, too, that his pursuers were less careful than they had been. He could see the shadows of two of them, where they hid among the trees. Soon they wouldn't even bother with concealment.

Come on, he told himself grimly. *You've pushed on when you were freezing to death; this isn't any worse than that. If you can make it to the next stand of rocks, you can take a couple of the bastards out with you.*

It wasn't likely that the President would be with them, but the thought of him gave Sun Wolf the strength to make it up the long grade of the road, toward the black puddle of shadow that lay across it where the land leveled out again. He was aware of all his pursuers now, dark, drifting shapes, ringing as wolves would ring a wounded caribou. Numb sleep pulled at him. The shadow of the rocks appeared to be floating away from him, and it seemed to him then that, if he pushed himself that far, he wouldn't have the strength to do anything, once he reached the place.

You will, he told himself foggily. *The smiling bastard probably told them it would be a piece of cake, rot his eyes. I'll give them cake.*

In the shadow of the rocks, he let his knees buckle and crumpled to the ground. Under cover of trying to rise and then collapsing again, he drew his sword, concealing it under him as he heard those swift, light footfalls make their cautious approach.

The ground felt wonderful under him, like a soft bed after hard fighting. Desperately he fought the desire for sleep, trying to garner the strength that he felt slipping away like water. The dust of the road filled his nostrils, and the salt tang of the distant sea, magnified a thousand times, swam like liquor in his darkening brain. He heard the footsteps, slurring in the dry autumn grass, and wondered if he'd pass out before they came.

I may go straight to the Cold Hells, he thought bitterly, *but by the spirit of my first ancestor, I'm not going alone.*

Dimly he was aware of them all around him. The fold of a cloak crumpled down over his arm, and someone set a light bow in the grass nearby. A hand touched his shoulder and turned him over.

Like a snake striking, he grabbed at the dark form bent over him, catching the nape of the neck with his left hand and driving the sword upward toward the chest with his right. Then he saw the face in the starlight and jerked his motion to a halt as the blade pricked the skin and his victim gave a tiny gasping cry. For a moment, he could only stare up into the face of the amber-eyed girl from the tavern, the soft masses of her pale hair falling like silk over his gripping hand.

Under his fingers, her neck was like a flower's stem. He could feel her breath quivering beneath the point of his sword. *I can't kill her,* he thought despairingly. *Not a girl Fawnie's age and frozen with terror.*

Then darkness and cold took him, and he slid to the ground. His last conscious memory was of someone jerking the sword out of his hand.

CHAPTER

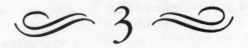

3

"*A*RI SENT YOU AWAY?" STARHAWK LOOKED SHARPLY FROM Little Thurg to Ari, who stood quietly at her side.

Thurg nodded, puzzlement stamped into every line of his round, rather bland-looking countenance. "I thought it funny myself, sir," he said, and the bright blue eyes shifted over to Ari. "But I asked you about it then, and you told me . . ."

"I was never there," Ari objected quietly. "I was never in Kedwyr at all." He looked over at Starhawk, as if for confirmation. They had spent the night with half of Sun Wolf's other lieutenants, playing poker in Penpusher's tent, waiting for word to come back from their chief. "You know . . ."

Starhawk nodded. "I know," she said and looked back at Thurg, who was clearly shaken and more than a little frightened.

"You can ask the others, sir," he said, and a pleading note crept into his voice. "We all saw him, plain as daylight. And after the Chief had gone off with that woman, I thought he met and spoke with Ari. May God strike me blind if that isn't the truth."

Starhawk reflected to herself that being struck blind by God was an exceedingly mild fate compared with what any man who had deserted his captain in the middle of an enemy city was likely to get. The fact that they were in the pay of the Council of Kedwyr did not make that city friendly territory—quite the contrary, in fact. *You can dishonor a man's wife, kill his cattle, loot his goods,* Sun Wolf had often said, *and he will become your friend quicker than any ruling body that owes you money for something you've done for them.*

She settled back in the folding camp chair that was set under the marquee outside Sun Wolf's tent and studied the man in front of her. The sea wind riffled her pale, flyaway hair and made the awning crack above her head. The wind had turned in the night, blowing hard and steady toward the east. The racing scud of the clouds threw an uneasy alternation of brightness and shadow over the dry, wolf-colored hills that surrounded Melplith's stove-in walls on three sides and formed a backdrop of worried calculations, like a half-heard noise, to all her thoughts.

Her silence was salt to Thurg's already flayed nerves. "I swear it was Ari I saw," he insisted. "I don't know how it came about, but you know I'd never have left the Chief. I've been with him for years."

She knew that this was true. She also knew that women, more than once, mistaking her for a man in her armor, had offered to sell her their young daughters for concubines, and the knowledge that there was literally nothing that human beings would not sell for ready cash must have been in her eyes. The little man in front of her began to sweat, his glance flickering in hopeless anguish from her face to Ari's. Starhawk's cold-bloodedness was more feared than Sun Wolf's rages. A man who had taken a bribe to betray Sun Wolf could expect from her no mercy and certainly nothing even remotely quick.

She glanced up at Ari, who stood behind her chair. He looked doubtful, as well he might; Thurg had always proved himself trustworthy and had, as he had said, been with Sun Wolf's troop for years. She herself was puzzled, as much by the utter unlikeliness of Thurg's story as by the possibility of betrayal. In his place, she would have thought up a far better story, and she had enough respect for his brains to think that he would have, also.

"Where did Ari speak to you?" she asked at last.

"In the square, sir," Thurg said, swallowing and glancing from her face to Ari's and back again. "He—he came out of the alleyway the Chief had gone down with that girl and—and walked over to where we were sitting in the tavern. It was getting late. I'd already talked to the innkeeper once about keeping the place open."

"He came over to you—or called you to him?"

"He came over, sir. He said, 'You can head on back to camp,

troops. The Chief and I will be along later.' And he gave us this big wink. They all laughed and made jokes, but I asked didn't he want a couple of us to stay, just in case? And he said, 'You think we can't handle City Troops? You've seen 'em fight!' And we—we came away. I thought if Ari was with the Chief . . ." He let his voice trail off, struggling within himself. Then he flung his hands out. "It sounds like your grandfather's whiskers, but it's true! Ask any of 'em!" Desperation corrugated his sunburned little face. "You've got to believe me!"

But he did not look as if he thought that this was at all likely.

They said in the camp that Starhawk had not been born—she'd been sculpted. She considered him for a moment more, then asked, "He came out of the alley, came toward the tavern, and spoke to you?"

"Yes."

"He was facing the tavern lamps?"

"Yes—they were behind me. It was one of those open-front places —I was at a table toward the edge, out on the square, like."

"And you saw him clearly?"

"Yes! I swear it!" He was trembling, sweat trickling down his scar-seamed brown cheeks. Behind him, just outside the rippling shade of the awning, two guards looked away, feeling that electric desperation in the air and not willing to witness the breaking of a man they both respected. Frantic, Thurg said, "If I'd sold the Chief to the Council, you think I'd have come back to the camp?"

Starhawk shrugged. "If you'd thought you could get me to believe you thought you were talking to Ari, maybe. I've seen too many betrayals to know whether you'd have sold him out or not—but I do find it hard to believe you'd have done it this stupidly. You're confined to quarters until we see whether the Council sends out the money they promised."

When the guards had taken Little Thurg away, Ari shook his head and sighed. "Of all the damned stupid stories . . . How could he have done it, Hawk? There was no way he had of knowing that I wasn't with ten other people—which I was!"

She glanced up at him, towering above her, big and bearlike and perplexed, the slow burn of both anger and hurt visible in those clear, hazel-gray eyes. "That's what inclines me to believe he's telling the truth," she said and got to her feet. "Or what he thinks is the truth, anyway. If I'm not back from Kedwyr in three hours, hit the town with everything we've got and send messages to Ciselfarge . . ."

"You're going by yourself?"

"If they're hiding what they've done, I'm in no danger," she said briefly, casting a quick glance at the piebald sky and picking up her sheepskin jacket from the back of her chair. "I can fight my way out alone as well as I could with a small bodyguard—and if the Council doesn't know the Wolf's missing, I'm not going to tell them so by going in with a large one."

But on the highroad from the camp to the city gates, she met a convoy of sturdy little pack donkeys and a troop of the Kedwyr City Guards, bearing the specified payment from the Council. Thin and morose, like a drooping black heron upon his cobby little Peninsular mare, Commander Breg hailed her. She drew her horse alongside his. "No trouble?" she asked, nodding toward the laden donkeys and the dark-clothed guards who led them.

The commander made the single coughing noise that was the closest he ever came to a laugh. The day had turned cold with the streaming wind; he wore a black cloak and surcoat wound over the shining steel back-and-breast mail, and his face, framed in the metal of his helmet, was mottled with vermilion splotches of cold. "Our President came near to an apoplexy and took to his bed with grief over the amount of it," he told her. "But a doctor was summoned—they say he will recover."

Starhawk laughed. "Ari and Penpusher are there waiting to go over it with you."

"Penpusher," the commander said thoughtfully. "Is he that yak in chain mail who threw the defending captain off the tower at the storming of Melplith's gates?"

"Oh, yes," Starhawk agreed. "He's only like that in battle. As a treasurer, he's untouchable."

"As a warrior," the commander said, "he's someone I would not much like to try and touch, either." A spurt of wind tore at his cloak, fraying the horses' manes into tangled clouds and hooning eerily through the broken lines of windbreak and stone. He glanced past Starhawk's shoulder at the gray rim of the sea, visible beyond the distant cliffs. The sky there was densely piled with bruised-looking clouds. Over the whining of the wind, the waves could occasionally be heard, hammerlike against the rocks.

"Will you make it beyond the Gniss," he asked, "before the river floods?"

"If we get started tomorrow." It was her way never to give anyone anything. She would not speak to a comparative stranger of her fears that they would not, in fact, reach the river in time for a safe crossing. It was midmorning; were it not for Sun Wolf's disappearance, they would have been breaking camp already, to depart as soon as the money was counted. With the rapid rise of the Gniss, hours could be important. As the wind knifed through the thick sheepskin of her coat and stung the exposed flesh of her face, she wondered if the commander's words were a chance remark or a veiled warning to take themselves off before it was too late.

"By the way," she asked, curvetting her horse away from the path of the little convoy, "where does Gobaris keep himself when he's in town? Or has he left already?"

The commander shook his head. "He's still there, in the barracks behind the Town Hall square. It's his last day in the town, though— he's getting ready to go back to his farm and that wife he's been telling us about all through the campaign."

"Thanks." Starhawk grinned and raised her hand in farewell. Then she turned her horse's head in the direction of the town and spurred to a canter through the cold, flying winds of the coming storms.

She found Gobaris, round, pink, and slothful, packing his few belongings and the mail that no longer quite fitted him, in the section of barracks reserved by the Council for the Outland Levies during their service to the town. Few of them were left; this section of the barracks, allotted to the men of the levies, was mostly empty, the straw raked from the bunks and heaped on the stone floor ready to be hosed out, the cold drafts whistling through the leak-stained rafters. The walls were covered with mute and obscene testimony of the rivalry between the Outland Levies and the City Troops.

"I don't know which is worse," she murmured, clicking her tongue thoughtfully, "the lack of imagination or the inability to spell a simple four-letter word that they use all the time."

"Lack of imagination," Gobaris said promptly, straightening up in a two-stage motion to favor the effect of the coming dampness on his lower back. "If one more man had tried to tell me the story about the City Trooper and the baby goat, I'd have strangled the life out of him before he'd got past 'Once upon a time.' What can I do for you, Hawk?''

She spun him a tale of a missing soldier, watching his puffy, unshaven face closely, and saw nothing in the wide blue eyes but annoyance and concern that the man should be found before the rest of the troop left without him. He let his packing lie and took her down to the city hall, shouting down the regular guards there and opening without demur any door she asked to see the other side of. At the end, she shook her head in assumed disgust and sighed. "Well, that rules out trouble, anyway. He'll be either sodden drunk or snugged up with some woman.'' It took all her long self-discipline and all the inexpressive calm of years of barracks poker to hide the sick qualm of dread that rose in her and accept with equanimity the Outland Captain's invitation to share a quart of ale at the nearest tavern.

She was reviewing in her memory the other possible ways to enter the jail by stealth and search for other cells there when Gobaris asked, "Did your chief get back to the camp all right, then?''

She frowned, resting her hands around the mug on the rather grimy surface of the tavern table. "Why would he not?''

Gobaris sighed, shook his head, and rubbed at the pink, bristly rolls of his jaw. "I didn't like it myself, for all that Ari's a stout enough fighter. If the President had wanted to make trouble, he could have trapped the two of them in the town. It was dangerous, is all.''

Starhawk leaned back in her chair and considered the fat man in the cold white light that came in through the open tavern front from the square. "You mean Ari was the only man he had with him?'' she asked, playing for time.

"Only one I saw." He threw back his head, revealing a grayish crescent of dirty collar above the edge of his pink livery doublet, and drank deeply, then wiped his lips with an odd daintiness on the cuff of his sleeve. "He might have had others up the alley, mind, but none whom I saw.''

"Which alley?'' she asked in a voice of mild curiosity, turning her head to scan the half-empty square. No booths or other tavern fronts opened into that great expanse of checked white and black stone today —a rainsquall had already dappled the pavement, and the fleeting patches of white and blue of the sky were more and more obscured by threatening gray.

"That one there." He pointed. From this angle, it was little more than a shaded slot behind the keyhole turrets of an elaborately timbered inn front. "We were at that alehouse there, the Cock in Leather Breeches, waiting for your chief to get back. Then Ari came out of the alley, walked slap up to the bodyguard, and sent 'em off back to camp. I thought it wasn't like the Wolf to be that careless, but nobody asked me my opinion."

"You knew it was Ari."

Gobaris looked surprised. "Of course it was Ari," he said. "He was standing within a yard of me, wasn't he? Facing the lamps of the inn."

Ari was waiting for Starhawk at Sun Wolf's tent when she came back from the city. The camp was alive with the movement of departure, warriors calling curses and jokes back and forth to one another as they loaded pack beasts with their possessions and loot from the sacking of Melplith. Starhawk, being not by nature a looter, had very little to pack; she could have been ready to depart in half an hour, tent and all. Someone—probably Fawn—had begun to dismantle Sun Wolf's possessions, and the big tent was a chaos of tumbled hangings, their iridescence shot with gold stitching, of disordered camp furniture and cushions, and of mail and weapons. In the midst of it, on the inlaid ebony table where their armor had rested last night, sat a priceless rose porcelain pitcher in which slips of iris had been rudely potted. Beside it was a small leather sack.

Starhawk picked up the sack and weighed it curiously in her hand. She glanced inside, then across at Ari. The bag contained gold pieces.

"Every grain of gold he contracted for was delivered," Ari said somberly.

The Hawk stripped off her rain-wet coat and threw it over the back of the staghorn chair. "I'm not surprised," she said. "Gobaris says he saw you, too. Though if it were a setup . . ."

Ari shook his head. "I had the tents of all the men on that detail searched. Little Thurg wasn't the only one, either . . ." He leaned out the tent door and called, "Thurg!" to someone outside. The doorway darkened and Big Thurg came in, making the small room minuscule by his bulk.

Big Thurg was the largest man in the Wolf's troop, reducing Sun Wolf, Ari, and Penpusher to frailty by comparison. The absurd thing about him was that, although he and Little Thurg came from opposite ends of the country and were presumably no relation to each other, in face and build they were virtually twins, giving the general impression that Little Thurg had somehow been made up from the scraps left over from the creation of his immense counterpart.

"It's true, sir," he said, guessing her question, looking down at her, and scratching his head. "We all saw him—me, Long Mat, Snarky, everyone."

"A double?" Starhawk asked.

"But why?" Ari threw out his hands in a gesture of angry frustration. "They paid us!"

Outside, someone led a laden mule past, the sound of the creaking pack straps a whispered reminder that time was very short. Big Thurg folded enormous hands before his belt buckle, his bright eyes grave with fear. "I think it's witchery."

Neither Starhawk nor Ari spoke. Starhawk's cold face remained impassive, but a line appeared between the thick fur of Ari's brows.

Big Thurg went on. "I've heard tell of it in stories. How a wizard can take on the form of a man, to lie with a woman the night, and her thinking all the time it's her husband; or else put on a woman's shape and call on a nurse to ask for a child. When the true mother shows up, the kid's long gone. A wizard could have seen you anywhere about the camp, sir, to know who you were."

"But there aren't any wizards anymore," Ari said, and Starhawk could hear the fear in his voice. Even among the mercenaries, Ari was accounted a brave man, for all his youth—brave with the courage of one who had no need for bravado. But there were very few men indeed who did not shudder at the thought of dabbling in wizardry. She and Ari both knew for a fact that there was only one wizard alive in the world—Altiokis.

Starhawk said, "Thank you, Thurg. You can go. We'll have the guards let Little Thurg go, with our apologies." The big man saluted and left. When she and Ari were alone, she said quietly, "The Chief got an offer the other night to go against Altiokis at Mandrigyn."

Ari swore, softly, vividly, hopelessly. Then he said. "No. Oh, no, Hawk." Around them, the camp was a noisy confusion, but the steady pattering of the rain against the leather tent walls and in the puddles beyond the door came through, like a whispered threat. It would be a long, beastly journey north; there could be no more waiting. Ari looked at her, and in his eyes Starhawk saw the grief of one who had already heard of a death.

She continued in her usual calm voice. "It would explain why the President sent us our pay. He knows nothing of it. The woman who came and spoke to the Wolf here was from one of Altiokis cities."

For a time Ari did not speak, only stood with his head bowed, listening to the noises of the camp and the rain and her soft-spoken words of doom. The fading afternoon light laid a gleam like pewter on the creamy brown of his arm muscles; it winked on the gold stitching of his faded, garish tunic and on the jewels among the braided scalps that decorated his shoulders. His gold earrings flashed against his long, black hair as he turned his head. "So what are we going to do?"

Starhawk paused and considered her several courses of action. There was only one of them that she knew she could follow. Knowing this, she did not inquire of herself the reasons why. "I think," she said at last, "that the best thing would be for you to get the troop back to Wrynde. If Altiokis had wanted the Chief dead, he would have killed him here. Instead, it looks as if he spirited him away somewhere." A dozen tales of the Wizard King's incredible, capricious cruelty contradicted her, but she did not give Ari time to say so. She knew that, if she accepted that explanation, she might just as well give Sun Wolf up for dead now. She went on. "I don't know why he took him and I don't know where, but the Citadel of Grimscarp in the East is a good guess. I know the Wolf, Ari. When he's trapped by a situation, he plays for time."

Ari raised his head finally, staring at her in horrified disbelief. "You're not going there?"

She looked back at him impassively. "It's either assume he's there and alive and can be rescued—or decide that he's dead and give him up now." Seeing his stricken look at the coldness of her logic, she added gently, "I don't think either of us is ready to do that yet."

He turned from her and paced the tent in silence. On the other side of the peacock hangings, Fawn could be heard moving quietly about, preparing for departure. Sun Wolf's armor and battle gear still hung on their stand at one end of the room, a mute echo of his presence; the feathers on the helmet's widespread wings were translucent in the pallid light from the door.

Finally Ari said, "He could be elsewhere."

She shrugged. "In that case, it's short odds that he can get himself out of trouble. If Altiokis has him—which I believe he does—he'll need help. I'm willing to risk the trip." She hooked her hands through her sword belt and watched Ari, waiting.

"You'll go overland?" he asked at last.

"Through the Kanwed Mountains, yes. I'll take a donkey—a horse would be more trouble than it was worth, between wolves and robbers, and it wouldn't add anything to my time. I can always buy one when I reach the uplands." Her mind was leaping ahead, calculating the campaign details that could be dealt with—road conditions, provisions, perils—to free herself from the fear that she knew would numb her heart.

There's nothing you can do right now to help him, she told herself coldly, *except what you are doing. Feeling fear or worry for him will not help either him or you.* But the fear smoldered in her nevertheless, like a buried fire in the heart of a mountain of ice.

Ari asked, "Whom will you take with you?"

She raised her brows, her voice still calm and matter-of-fact. "Who do you think could be trusted with the news that we might be messing with Altiokis? I personally can't think of anyone."

As he crossed the room back to her, she could see the worry lines already settling into his face—the lines that would be there all winter, maybe all his life. Morale in the troop was going to be hard enough to maintain in the face of the Wolf's disappearance, without dealing with the added panic that the Wizard King's name would cause, and they both knew it.

She went on. "A lone traveler is less conspicuous than a small troop, especially in the wintertime. I'll be all right."

The echo of a hundred nursery tales of Altiokis was in Ari's voice as he asked, "How will you get into the Citadel?"

She shrugged again. "I'll figure out that part when I get there."

Ari was the only one to see her off that night. She had delayed her departure until after dark, partly to avoid spies, partly to avoid comment in the troop itself. Her close friends in the troop—Penpusher, Butcher the camp doctor, Firecat, and Dogbreath—she had told only that she was going to help the Chief and that they'd both be back at Wrynde in the spring. Altiokis was not spoken of. After packing most of her things to be sent back to Wrynde, she had spent the afternoon in meditation, preparing her mind and heart for the journey in the silence of the Invisible Circle, as they had taught her in the Convent of St. Cherybi.

Ari was quiet as he walked with her down the road toward the dark hills. By the light of his torch, she thought, he looked older than he had this morning. He was in for a hellish winter, she knew, and wondered momentarily if she ought not, after all, to remain with the troop, for she was the senior of the two lieutenants and the one who had more experience in dealing with the town council of Wrynde.

But she let the thought pass. Her mind was already set on her quest, with the calm single-mindedness with which she went into battle. In a sense, she had already severed herself from Ari and the troop; and in any case, she was not sure that her own road would not be the harder of the two.

"Take care of yourself," Ari said. In the sulfurous glare of the torch, the coat of black bearskin he wore gave him more than ever the look of a young beast. The hills stood before them, tall against the sky; above the sea to their backs, the clouds rose in vast pillars of darkness, the winter storms still holding uncannily at bay.

"You, also." She took the donkey's headstall in her left hand, then turned and put her right hand on Ari's shoulder and kissed him lightly on the cheek. "I don't know who's in for a worse time of it."

"Starhawk," Ari said quietly. The wind fluttered at his long hair; in the shadows she could see the sudden jump of his tensed jaw muscles. "What am I going to do," he asked her, "if someone shows up sometime this winter, without you, claiming to be the Chief? How will I know it's really him?"

Starhawk was silent. They were both remembering Little Thurg, speaking to Ari's double in the square of Kedwyr.

Sweet Mother, she thought, *how will I know it's the Chief when I find him?*

For a moment, a shiver ran through her, almost like panic; the fear of magic, of wizards, of the uncanny, threatened to overcome her. Then the face of Sister Wellwa returned to her, withered in its frame of black veils; she saw the hunched back and tiny hands and herself, as a curious child, helping to sort dried herbs in the old nun's cell and wondering why, of all the nuns in the Convent of St. Cherybi, Wellwa alone, the oldest and most wrinkled, possessed . . .

"A mirror," she said.

Ari blinked at her, startled. "A what?"

"Put a mirror somewhere, in an angle of the room where you can see it. A mirror will reflect a true form, without illusion."

"You're sure?"

"I think so," she said doubtfully. "Or else you can take him out to the marshes on a night when there are demons about. As far as I know, Sun Wolf is the only man I've ever met who could see demons."

They had both seen him do it, in the dripping marshes to the north of Wrynde, and had watched him following those loathsome, giggling voices with his eyes through the ice-bitten trees.

"It may be that a wizard can see demons, too, by means of magic," Ari said. "It was said they could see through illusion."

"Maybe," she agreed. "But the mirror will show you a fraud." It occurred to her for the first time to wonder why Sister Wellwa had kept that fragment of reflective glass positioned in the corner of her cell. Whom had she expected to see in it, entering the room disguised as someone else she knew?

"Maybe," Ari echoed softly. "And what then?"

They looked into each other's eyes, warm hazel into cold gray, and she shook her head. "I don't know," she whispered. "I don't know."

She turned away from him and took the road into the darkness of the hills. Behind her and to her left lay the dim scattering of lights visible through the broken walls of Melplith and the collection of red sparks that was the mercenary camp. By dawn tomorrow, the camp would be broken and gone. Kedwyr's Council had smashed its rival's pretensions, and the overland trade in furs and onyx would return to Kedwyr, high tariffs or no high tariffs. Melplith would sink back to being a poky little market town like those farther back in the hills, and what had anybody gained? A lot of people were dead, including one of Gobaris' brothers; a lot of mercenaries were richer; a lot of women had been raped, men maimed, children starved. The wide lands north of the Gniss River were still a burned-over wasteland in which nuuwa and wolves wandered; demons still haunted the cold marshes in whistling, biting clusters; abominations bred in the southern deserts, while the cities of the Peninsula fought over money and those of the Middle Kingdoms fought over religion.

The raw dampness of the wind stung Starhawk's face and whipped at her half-numbed cheeks with the ends of her hair. She'd meant to crop it before leaving, as she did before the summer campaigns every year, but had forgotten.

She wondered why Altiokis had wanted the Chief. Sun Wolf had obviously sent Mandrigyn's emissary packing—and had himself vanished without a trace the following night.

Revenge? She shuddered inwardly at the tales of Altiokis' revenges. *Or for other reasons? Will Ari, during the course of the winter, find himself faced with a man who claims to be Sun Wolf?*

On the hillside to her left, the slurring rush of the wind through the bracken was cut by another sound, a shifting that was not part of the pattern of harmless noise.

Starhawk never paused in her step, though the burro she led turned its long ears backward uneasily. In this country, it would take a skilled tracker to follow in silence, even on a windy night. The ditches on either side of the hard-packed dirt of the highroad were filled with a mix of gravel and summer brushwood, and the sound of a body forcing passage anywhere near the road was ridiculously loud to the Hawk's trained ears. When the track wound deeper into the foothills, the ditches petered out, but the scrub grew thicker. As she walked on, the Hawk could identify and pinpoint the sound of her pursuer, thirty feet behind her and closing.

Human. A wolf would be quieter; a nuuwa—if there were such things this close to settled territory—wouldn't have the brains to stalk at all. The thought of Altiokis' spies drifted unpleasantly through her mind.

To hell with it, she told herself and faked a stumble, cursing. The scrunching in the brush stopped.

Limping ostentatiously, Starhawk hobbled to the side of the track and sat down in the dense shadows of the brushwood. Under cover of fiddling with her bootlaces, she tied the burro's lead to a branch. Then she slithered backward into the brush, snaked her way down the shallow, overgrown ditch, and climbed up onto the scrubby hillside beyond.

The night was clouding over again, but enough starlight remained to give her some idea of the shape of the land. Her pursuer moved cautiously in the scrub; she focused on the direction of the popping of cracked twigs. Keeping low to better her own vision against the lighter sky, she scanned the dark jumble of twisted black trunks and the mottling of grayed leaves.

Nothing. Her shadow was keeping still.

Softly her fingers stole over the loose sandy soil until they found what they sought, a sizable rock washed from the stream bed by last winter's rains. Moving slowly to remain as quiet as she could, she worked it free of the dirt. With a flick of the wrist she sent it spinning into the brush a few yards away.

There was a satisfactory rustling, and part of the pattern of dark and light that lay so dimly before her jerked, again counter to the general restless movement of the wind. The vague glow of the sky caught the pallid reflection of a face.

Very good, the Hawk thought and eased her dagger soundlessly from its sheath.

Then the wind changed and brought to her, incongruous in the sharpness of the juniper, the sweet scent of patchouli.

Starhawk braced herself to dodge in case she was wrong and called out softly, "Fawn!"

There was a startled shift in the pattern. The shape of the girl's body was revealed under the voluminous folds of a mottled plaid cloak—the dull, almost random-looking northern plaid that blended so deceptively into any pattern of earth and trees. Fawn's voice was shaky and scared. "Starhawk?"

Starhawk stood up, clearly startling the daylights out of the girl by her nearness. They stood facing each other for a time on the wind-swept darkness of the hillside. Because they were both women, there was a great deal that did not need to be said. Starhawk remembered that most of what she had said to Ari had been in Sun Wolf's tent; of course the girl would overhear.

It was Fawn who spoke first. "Don't send me away," she said.

"Don't be foolish," Starhawk said brusquely.

"I promise I won't slow you down."

"You can't promise anything of the kind and you know it," the Hawk retorted. "I'm making the best time to Grimscarp that I can, over some damned dirty country. It's not the same as traveling with the troop from Wrynde to the Peninsula or down to the Middle King-doms and back."

Fawn's voice was desperate, low against the whining of the wind. *"Don't leave me."*

Starhawk was silent a moment. Though a warrior herself, she was woman enough to understand the fear in that taut voice. Her own was kinder when she said, "Ari will see that you come to no harm."

"And what then?" Fawn pleaded. "Spend the winter in Wrynde, wondering who's going to have me if Sun Wolf doesn't come back?"

"It's better than being passed around a bandit troop and ending up with your throat slit in a ditch."

"You run that risk yourself!" And when Starhawk did not answer, but only hooked her hands through the buckle of her sword belt, Fawn went on. "I swear to you, if you won't take me with you to Grimscarp, I'll follow you on my own."

The girl bent down, the winds billowing the great plaid cloak about her slender body, and picked up something Starhawk saw was a pack from among the heather at her feet. She slung it over her shoulder and descended to where the Hawk stood, catching at the branches now and then for balance, holding her dark, heavy skirts out of the brambles. Starhawk held out a hand to her to help her down to the road. The Hawk's grip was like a man's, firm under the delicate elbow. When they reached the road together, Fawn looked up at her, as if trying to read the expression in that craggy, inscrutable face, those transparent eyes.

"Starhawk, I love him," she said. "Don't you understand what it is to love?"

"I understand," Starhawk said in a carefully colorless voice, "that your love for him won't get you to Grimscarp alive. I elected to search for him because I have a little—a very little—experience with wizards and because I believe that he can be found and rescued. It could easily have been any of the men who came. I can hold my own against any of them in battle."

"Is that all it is to you?" Fawn demanded passionately. "Another job? Starhawk, Sun Wolf saved me from—from things so unspeakable it makes me sick to remember them. I had seen my father murdered—" Her voice caught in a way that told Starhawk that the death had been neither quick nor clean. "I'd been dragged hundreds of miles by a band of leering, dirty, cruel men, I'd seen my maid raped and murdered, and I knew that the only reason they didn't do the same to me was because I'd fetch a better price as a virgin. But they talked about it."

Her face seemed to burn white in the filmy starlight, her body trembling with the hideous memories. "I was so terrified at—at being sold to a captain of a mercenary troop that I think I would have killed myself if I hadn't been watched constantly. And then Sun Wolf bought me and he was so good to me, so kind . . ."

The hood of her cloak had blown back, and the stars glinted on the tears that streaked her cheeks. Grief and compassion filled Starhawk's heart—for that distant, frightened child and for the girl before her now. But she said, with deliberate coldness, "None of that means that you'll be able to find him safely."

"I don't want to be safe!" Fawn cried. "I want to find him—or know in my heart that he's dead."

Starhawk glanced away, annoyed. She had never questioned that she should look for the Chief—her loyalty to him was such that she would have undertaken the quest no matter what Ari had said. Her own unquestioned prowess as a warrior had merely been one of the arguments. Her native honesty forced her to recognize Fawn's iron resolution as akin to her own, regardless of what kind of nuisance she'd be on the road.

The older woman sighed bitterly and relaxed. "I don't suppose," she said after a moment, "that there is any way I could prevent you from coming with me, short of tying you up and dragging you back to camp. Besides losing me time, that would only make the two of us look ridiculous." She stared coldly down her nose when Fawn giggled at the thought. "You know, don't you, that you might cause the troop's departure to be delayed if Ari takes it into his head to search the town for you?"

Fawn colored strangely under the starlight. She bent to pick up her pack again and start toward where the burro was still tethered, head-down against the wind. "Ari won't look for me," she said. "For one thing, you know he wouldn't delay the march north. And besides . . ." Her voice faltered with shame. "I took everything valuable of mine. Clothes, jewels—everything that I would take if I were running off with another man. And that's what he'll think I did."

Unexpectedly, Starhawk grinned. Fawn might not be able to reason her way past their arguments, but she certainly had found a matter-of-fact means of discouraging pursuit. "Don't tell me you have all that in that little pack?"

Startled at the sudden lightening of the Hawk's voice, Fawn looked quickly up to meet her eyes, then returned her smile ruefully. "Only the jewels. I thought we could sell them for food on the way. The rest of it I bundled up and dropped over the sea cliffs."

"Very nice." Starhawk smiled approvingly, reflecting that she was evidently not the only person in the troop to hold possessions lightly. "You have a good grasp of essentials. We'll make a trooper of you yet."

CHAPTER

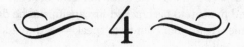

WHEN SUN WOLF WAS A BOY, HE HAD BEEN STRICKEN BY A
fever. He had concealed it from his father as long as he could, going
hunting with the other men of the tribe in the dark, half-frozen
marshes where demons flitted from tree to tree like pale slips of phosphorescent light. He had come home and hidden in the cattle loft.
There his mother had found him, sobbing in silent delirium, and had
insisted that they call the shaman of the tribe. It all came back to him
now, with the memory of parching thirst and restless pain: the low
rafters with their red and blue dragons almost hidden under the black-
ening of smoke; the querulous voice of that dapper, busy little charlatan with the holy bones and dangling locks of ancestral hair; and his
father looming like an angry, disapproving shadow beside the reddish,
pulsing glow of the hearth. The Wolf remembered his father's growl-
ing voice. "If he can't throw it off himself, he'd better die, then. Get
your stinking smokes and your dirty bones out of here; I have goats
who could work better magic than you." He remembered the shaman's offended sniff—because, of course, his father was right.

And he remembered the awful agony of thirst.

The dream changed. Cool hands touched his face and raised the rim
of a cup to his lips. The metal was ice-cold, like the water in the cup.
As he drank, he opened swollen eyelids to look into the face of the

amber-eyed girl. The fear that widened her eyes told him he was awake.

I tried to kill her, he thought cloudily. *But she tried to kill me—or did she?* His memory was unclear. Mixed with the perfume of her body, he could smell the salt flavor of the sea; the creak of wood and cordage and the shift of the bed where he lay told him he was aboard a ship. The girl's eyes were full of fear, but her arm beneath his head was soft. She raised the cup to his cracked lips again, and he drained it. He tried to stammer thanks but could not speak—tried to ask her why she had wanted to kill him.

Abruptly, Sun Wolf slid into sleep again.

The dreams were worse, a terrifying nightmare of racking, helpless pain. He had a tangled vision of darkness and wind and rock, of being trapped and left prey to things he could not see, of dangling over a tossing abyss of change and loss and terrible loneliness. In the darkness, demons seemed to ring him—demons that he alone could see, as he had always been able to see them, though to others—his father, the other men of the tribe, even the shaman—they had been only vague voices and a sense of terror. Once he seemed to see, small and clear and distant, the school of Wrynde, shabby and deserted beneath the sluicing rain, with only the old warrior who looked after the place in the troop's absence sweeping the blown leaves from the training floor with a broom of sticks. The smell and feel of the place cried to him, so real that he could almost touch the worn cedar of the pillars and hear the wailing of the wind around the rocks. Then the vision vanished in a shrieking storm of fire, and he was lost in spinning darkness that cut at him like swords, pulling him closer and closer to a vortex of silent pain.

Then that, too, faded, and there was only white emptiness that blended slowly to exhausted waking. He lay like a hollowed shell cast up on a beach, scoured by sun and salt until there was nothing left, cold to the bone and so weary that he ached. He could not find the strength to move, but only stared at the timbers above his head, listening to the creak and roll of the ship and the slap of water against the hull, feeling the sunlight that lay in a small, heatless bar over his face.

They were in full ocean, he judged, and heading fast before the wind.

He remembered the mountains of clouds, standing waiting on the horizon. If the storms hit and the ship went to pieces now, he would never have the strength to swim.

So it would be the crabs, after all.

But that cold, calm portion of his mind, the part that seemed always to be almost detached from his physical body, found neither strength nor anger in that thought. It didn't matter—nothing mattered. The sway of the ship moved the chip of sunlight back and forth across his face, and he found that he lacked the strength even to wonder where he was—or care.

An hour passed. The sunlight traveled slowly down the blanket that covered his body and lay like a pale, glittering shawl over the foot of the bunk. Like the blink of light from a sword blade, the chased gold rim of the empty cup on the table beside him gleamed faintly in the moving shadows. Footsteps descended a hatch somewhere nearby, then came down the hall.

The door opposite his feet opened, and Sheera Galernas stepped in.

Not the President of Kedwyr, after all, he thought, still with that eerie sense of unconcern.

She regarded him impassively from the doorway for a moment, then stepped aside. Without a word, four women filed in behind her, dressed as she was, for traveling, in dark, serviceable skirts, quilted bodices, and light boots. For a time none of them spoke, but they watched him, lined behind Sheera like acolytes behind a priestess at a rite.

One of them was the amber-eyed girl, he saw, her delicate, curiously secretive face downcast and afraid and—*what? Ashamed?* Why *ashamed?* The rose-tinted memory of her room in Kedwyr slid through his mind, with the warmth of her scented flesh twined with his. She was clearly a professional, for all her youth . . . *Why ashamed?* But he was too tired to wonder, and the thought slipped away.

The woman beside her was as pretty, but in a different way—certainly not professional, at least not about that. She was as tiny and fragile as a porcelain doll, her moonlight-blond hair caught in a loose knot at the back of her head, her sea-blue eyes marked at the corners with the faint lines of living and grief. He wondered what she was doing in the company of a hellcat like Sheera . . . in the company of any of those others, for that matter.

Neither of the other two women had or would even make the pretense of beauty. They were both tall, the younger of them nearly

Sun Wolf's own height—a broad-shouldered, hard-muscled girl who reminded him of the women in his own troops. She was dressed like a man in leather breeches and an embroidered shirt, and her shaven skull was brown from exposure to the sun. So was her face, brown as wood and scarred from weapons, like that of a gladiator. After a moment's thought, Sun Wolf supposed she must be one.

The last woman stood in the shadows, having sought them with an almost unthinking instinct. The shadows did nothing to mask the fact that she was the ugliest woman Sun Wolf had ever laid eyes on— middle-aged, hook-nosed, her mouth distorted by the brown smear of a birthmark that ran like mud down onto her jutting chin. Her eyes, beneath a single black bar of brow, were as green, as cold, and as hard as jade, infused with the bitter strength of a woman who had been reviled from birth.

They looked from him to Sheera, and on Sheera their eyes remained.

Though he was almost too tired to speak, Sun Wolf asked after a time, "You kidnap my men, too?" There was no strength in his voice; he saw them move slightly to listen. There was a gritty note to it, too, like a streak of rust on metal, that he knew had not been there before. An effect of the poison, maybe.

Sheera's back stiffened slightly with the sarcasm, but she replied steadily, "No. Only you."

He nodded. It was a slight gesture, but all he had strength for. "You going to pay me the whole ten thousand?"

"When you're done, yes."

"Hmm." His eyes traveled over the women again, slowly. Part of his mind was struggling against this paralyzing helplessness, screaming to him that he had to find a means to think his way out of this, but the rest of him was too tired to care. "You realize it will take me a little longer to storm the mines single-handedly?"

That stung her, and those full red lips tightened. The porcelain doll, as if quite against her will, grinned.

"It won't be just you," Sheera said, her voice low and intense. "We're bringing you back to Mandrigyn with us as a teacher—a teacher of the arts of war. We can raise our own strike force, release the prisoners in the mines, and free the city."

Sun Wolf regarded her for a moment from beneath half-lowered lids, reflecting to himself that here was a fanatic if ever he saw one—

crazy, dangerous, and powerful. "And just whom for starters," he inquired wearily, "are you planning on having in your strike force, if all the men of the city are working in the mines?"

"Us," she said. "The ladies of Mandrigyn."

He sighed and closed his eyes. "Don't be stupid."

"What's stupid about it?" she lashed at him. "Evidently your precious men can't be bothered to risk themselves, even for ready cash. We aren't going to sit down and let Altiokis appoint the worst scoundrels in the city as his governors, to bleed us with taxes and carry off whom he pleases to forced labor in his mines and his armies. It's our city! And even in Mandrigyn, where it's as much as a woman's social life is worth to go abroad in the streets unveiled and unchaperoned, there are women gladiators like Denga Rey here. In other places women can be members of city guards and of military companies. You have women in your forces yourself. Fighting women, warriors. I saw one of them in your tent that night."

Against the sting of her voice, he saw Starhawk and Sheera again, cool and wary as a couple of cats with the torch smoke blowing about them. Wearily, he said, "That wasn't a woman, that was my second-in-command, one of the finest warriors I've ever met."

"She was a woman," Sheera repeated. "And she isn't the only woman in your forces. They said in the city that you've trained women to fight before this."

"I've trained warriors," the Wolf said without opening his eyes, the exhaustion of even the effort to speak weighting him like a sickness. "If some of 'em come equipped to suckle babies later on, it's no concern of mine, so long as they don't get themselves pregnant while they're training. I'm not going to train up a whole corps of them from scratch."

"You will," Sheera said quietly. "You have no choice."

"Woman," he told her, while that lucid and detached portion of his mind reminded him that arguing with a fanatic was about as profitable as arguing with a drunk and far more dangerous, "what I said about Altiokis still goes. I'm not going to risk getting involved in any kind of resistance in a town he's just taken, and I sure as hell won't do it to train a troop of skirts commanded by a female maniac like yourself. And ten thousand poxy gold pieces, or twenty thousand, or whatever the hell else you'll offer me isn't about to change my mind."

"How about your life?" the woman asked, her voice uninflected, almost disinterested. "Is that reward enough?"

He sighed. "My life isn't worth a plug copper at this point. If you want to chuck me overside, there's surely no way I can stop you from doing it."

It was a foolish thing to have said, and he knew it, for Sheera was not a woman to be pushed and she was clearly supreme on this ship, as shown by the fact that she'd gotten its captain to put out to sea at this time of the year at all. It struck him again how absolutely alone he was here and how helpless.

He had expected her to fly into a rage, as she had done in his tent. But she only folded her arms and tipped her head a little to one side, the glossy curls of her hair catching in the stiff embroidery of her collar. Conversationally, she said, "There was anzid in the water you drank."

The shock of it cut his breath like a garrote. He opened his eyes, fear like a cold sickness chilling the marrow of his bones. "I didn't drink anything," he said, his mouth dry as the taste of dust. He had seen deaths from anzid. The worst of them had taken two days, and the victim had never ceased screaming.

The ugly woman spoke for the first time, her low voice mellow as the notes of a rosewood flute. "You woke up thirsty from the arrow poison, after dreams of fever," she said. "Amber Eyes gave you water to drink." The long slender hand moved toward the empty cup beside the bed. "There was anzid in the water."

Horror crawled like a tarantula along his flesh. Sheera's face was like a stone; Amber Eyes turned away, cheeks blazing with shame, unable to meet his gaze.

"You're lying," he whispered, knowing that she was not.

"You think so? Yirth has been a midwife, a Healer, and an abortionist long enough to know everything there is to know about poisons—it isn't likely she'd have made a mistake. If you hesitate to join us out of fear of Altiokis, I can tell you now that nothing the Wizard King might do to you if our plan fails would be as bad as that death. You have nothing further to lose by obeying us now."

Weak as he was, he had begun to shake; he wondered how long it took for the symptoms of anzid to be felt. How long had it been since he had been given the poison? It flashed through his mind to take Sheera by that round, golden throat of hers and strangle the life out of her. But weakness held him prisoner; in any case, it would not save his life. And besides that, there was not even sense in cursing her.

When he had been silent for a time, the woman Yirth spoke again, her cold, green eyes looking out from the concealing shadows, clinical and detached. "I am not the wizard that my master was, before Altiokis had her murdered," she said. "But it still lies within my powers to arrest the effects of a poison from day to day by means of spells. When we reach Mandrigyn, I shall place a bounding-spell upon you, that the poison shall not lay hold of you so long as you pass a part of each night within the walls of the city. The true antidote," she continued, with a hint of malice in that low, pure voice, "shall be given to you with your gold when you depart, after the city is freed."

The shaking had become uncontrollable. Fighting to keep panic from his voice, he whispered, "You are a wizard yourself, then. The woman who controls the winds."

"Of course," Sheera said scornfully. "Do you think we'd have dared consider an assault on Altiokis' Citadel without a wizard?"

"I don't think there's anything you're crazy enough not to dare!"

It was on his lips to curse her and die—but not that death. He lay back against the thin pillows, his eyes closing, and the trembling that had seized him passed off. He felt as bleached and twisted as a half-dried rag; even the fear seemed to trickle out of him. In the silence, he could hear the separate draw and whisper of each woman's breath and the faint splash and murmur of water against the hull.

The silence seemed to settle around his heart and brain, white, empty, and somehow strangely calming. He knew he would die, then, hideously, one way or the other. Having accepted that, his mind began to grope fumblingly for ways of playing for time, of getting himself out of this, of fighting his way back to life. *Not,* he told himself with weary savagery, *that I really think there's a chance of it. Old habits die hard.*

And by the spirits of my ancestors freezing down in the cold waters of Hell, I'm going to die a great deal harder.

He drew a tired breath and let it drain from his lips. Something stirred within him, goaded back to feeble and unwilling life, and he opened his eyes and studied the women before him, stripping them with his eyes, judging them as he would have judged them had they turned up, en masse, at the school of Wrynde, wondering if there was muscle as well as curving flesh under Sheera's night-blue gown and which of them was a good enough shot to hit a man with a birding arrow at fifty yards.

"Damn your eyes." He sighed and looked at Sheera again. "So who am I supposed to be?"

She blinked at him, startled by the sudden capitulation. "What?"

"Who am I supposed to be?" he repeated. Tiredness slurred his voice; he tried to garner his waning energy and felt it slip like fine sand through his fingers. His voice had grown weaker. As if some spell of distance had been broken, the women gathered around him, Amber Eyes and the porcelain doll going so far as to sit on the edge of his bunk. Sheera would not let herself so unbend; she stood over him, her arms still folded, her curving brows drawn heavily down over the straight, strong nose.

"If Altiokis has dragged all the men away in chains," he continued quietly, "you can't just have a strange man turn up in your household. Am I your long-lost brother? A gigolo you picked up in Kedwyr? A bodyguard?"

The porcelain doll shook her head. "We'll have to pass you off as a slave," she said, her voice low and husky, like a young boy's. "They're the only men whose coming into the city at this time of the year can well be accounted for. There won't be any merchants or travelers in winter."

She met the angry glitter in his eyes with cool reasonableness. "You know it's true."

"And in spite of the fact that you find it demeaning to be a woman's slave," Sheera added maliciously, "you haven't really got any say in the matter, now, have you, Captain?" She glanced at the others. "Gilden Shorad is right," she said. "A slave can pass pretty much unquestioned. I can get the ship's smith to put a collar on you before we reach port."

"What about Derroug Dru?" Amber Eyes asked doubtfully. "Altiokis' new governor of the town," she explained to Sun Wolf. "He's been known to confiscate slaves."

"What would he want with another slave?" Denga Rey the gladiator demanded, hooking her square, brown hands into the buckle of her sword belt.

Gilden Shorad frowned. "What would Sheera want with one, for that matter?" she asked, half to herself. Close to, Sun Wolf observed that she was older than he had at first thought—Starhawk's age, twenty-seven or so. Older than any of the others except the witch Yirth, who, unlike them, had remained in the shadows by the door, watching them with those cool, jade eyes.

"He can't simply turn up as a slave without any explanation for why you bought him," the tiny woman clarified, tucking aside a strand of her ivory hair with deft little fingers.

"Would you need a groom?" Amber Eyes asked.

"My own groom would be suspicious if we got another one suddenly," Sheera vetoed.

She looked so perplexed that Sun Wolf couldn't resist turning the knife. "Not as easy as just hiring your killing done, is it? You married?"

A flush stained her strong cheekbones. "My husband is dead."

He gave her a stripping glance and grunted. "Just as well. Kids?"

The flush deepened with her anger. "My daughter is six, my son, four."

"Too young to need an arms master, then."

Denga Rey added maliciously, "You don't want anyone in that town to see you with a sword in your hand anyway, soldier. Old Derroug Dru suspects anybody who can so much as cut his meat at table without slitting his fingers. Besides, he's got it in for big, buff fellows like you."

"Wonderful," the Wolf said without enthusiasm. "Leaving aside where this strike force of yours is going to practice, and where you're going to get money for weapons . . ."

"We have money!" Sheera retorted, harried.

"I'll be damned surprised if you'll be able to find weapons for sale in a town that Altiokis has just added to his domains. How big is your town place? What did your late lamented do for a living?"

By the bullion stitching on her gloves, the poor bastard couldn't have been worth less than five thousand a year, he decided.

"He was a merchant," she said, her breast heaving with the quickening of her anger. "Exports—this is one of his ships. And what business is it of yours—"

"It is my business, if I'm going to be risking what little is left of my life to teach you females to fight," he snapped. "I want to make damned sure you don't get gathered in and sent to the mines yourselves before I'm able to take my money and your poxy antidote and get the hell out of that scummy marsh you call a town. Is your place big enough to have gardens? An orangery, maybe?"

"We have an orangery," Sheera said sullenly. "It's across the grounds from the main house. It's been shut up for years—boarded up. It was the first thing I thought of when I decided that we had to bring you to Mandrigyn. We could use it to practice in."

He nodded. There were very few places where orange trees could be left outdoors year-round, yet groves of them were the fashion in all but the coldest of cities. Orangeries tended to be large, barnlike buildings—inefficient for the purpose of wintering fruit trees for the most part, but just passable as training floors.

"Gardeners?" he asked.

"There were two of them, freedmen," she said and added, a little defiantly, "They marched with Tarrin's army to Iron Pass. Even though they had not been born in Mandrigyn, they thought enough of their city's freedom to—"

"Stupid thing to do," he cut her off and saw her eyes flash with rage. "There a place to live in this orangery of yours?"

In a voice stifled with anger, she said, "There is."

"Good." Tiredness was coming over him again, final and irresistible, as if argument and thought and struggle against what he knew would be his fate had drained him of the little strength he had. The wan sunlight, the faces of the women around him and their soft voices, seemed to be drifting farther and farther away, and he fought to hold them in focus. "You—what's your name? Denga Rey—I'll need you for my second-in-command. You fight during the winter?"

"In Mandrigyn?" she scoffed. "If it isn't pouring sideways rain and hail, the ground's not fit for anything but boat races. The last fights were three weeks ago."

"I hope you were trounced to within an inch of your life," he said dispassionately.

"Not a chance, soldier." She put her hands on her strong hips, a glint of mockery in those dark eyes. "What I wonder is, who's going to look after all those little trees so it looks as if there's really a gardener doing the job? If Sheera buys one special, somebody's going to get suspicious."

Sun Wolf looked up at her bleakly. "I am," he said. "I'm a warrior by trade, but gardening is my hobby." His eyes returned to Sheera. "And I damned well better draw pay for it, too."

For the first time, she smiled, the warm, bright smile of the hellcat girl she hadn't been in years. He could see then why men had fought for her hand—as they must have done, to make her so poxy arrogant. "I'll add it in," she said, "to your ten thousand gold pieces."

Sun Wolf sighed and closed his eyes, wondering if it would be wise to tell her what she could do with her ten thousand gold pieces. But when he opened them again, he found that it was dark, the afternoon long over, and the women gone.

CHAPTER

*T*HEY SAILED INTO MANDRIGYN HARBOR IN THE VANGUARD OF the storms, as if the boat drew the rain in its wake.

Throughout the forenoon, Sun Wolf had stood in the waist of the ship, watching the clouds that had followed them like a black and seething wall through the gray mazes of the islands draw steadily closer, and wondering whether, if the ship went to pieces on the rocky headlands that guarded the harbor itself, he'd be able to swim clear before he was pulped by the breakers. For a time, he indulged in hopes that it would be so and that, other than himself, the ship would go down with all hands and Sheera and her wildcats would never be heard from again. This thought cheered him until he remembered that, if the sea didn't kill him, the anzid would.

As they passed through the narrow channel between the turret-guarded horns of the harbor, he turned his eyes from the dark, solitary shape of Yirth, standing, as she had stood on and off for the past three days, on the stern castle of the ship; he looked across the choppy gray waters of the harbor to where Mandrigyn lay spread like a jeweled collar upon its thousand islands.

Mandrigyn was the queen city of the Megantic Sea, the crossroads of trade; even in the bitter slate colors of the winter day, it glittered like a spilled jewel box, turquoise, gold, and crystal. Sun Wolf looked upon Mandrigyn and shivered.

Above the town rose the dark masses of the Tchard Mountains, the huge shape of Grimscarp veiled in a livid rack of purplish clouds, as if the Wizard King sought to conceal his fortress from prying eyes. Closer to, he could identify the trashy gaggle of markets and bawdy theaters as East Shore—the suburb that Gilden Shorad had told him lay outside the city's jurisdiction on the eastern bank of the Rack River. The colors of raw wood and cheap paint stood out like little chips of brightness against the rolling masses of empty, furze-brown hills that lay beyond; the Thanelands, where the ancient landholders still held their ancestral sway.

A gust of rain struck him, cold and stinging through the drab canvas of his shirt. As he hunched his shoulders against it like a wet animal, he felt the unfamiliar hardness of metal against his flesh, the traditional slave collar, a slip-chain like a steel noose that the ship's aged handyman had affixed around his neck.

He glanced back over his shoulder, hatred in his eyes, but Yirth had vanished from the poop deck. Sailors, at least half of them women or young boys, were scrambling up and down the rigging, making the vessel ready to be guided into the quays.

There was little activity in the harbor, most shipping having ceased a week ago in anticipation of the storms. Of the sailors and stevedores whom Sun Wolf could see about the docks, most were older men, young boys, or women. The city, he thought, had been hard hit indeed. As the rain-laden gusts of wind drove the ship toward the wharves, he could hear a ragged cheer go up from the vast gaggle of unveiled and brightly clad women who loitered on the pillared promenade of the long seafront terrace that overlooked the harbor. Friends of Denga Rey's, he guessed, noting the couple of nasty-looking female gladiators who swaggered in their midst.

Well, why not? Business is probably damned slow these days.

At some distance from that rowdy mob he picked out other welcoming committees. There was a tall girl and a taller woman whose ivory-blond hair, whipped by the wind from beneath their desperately clutched indigo veils, proclaimed them as kin of Gilden Shorad's. With them was a lady as tiny, and as fashionably dressed, as Gilden—*family,* he thought, no error.

Farther back, among the pillars of the windswept promenade, a couple of liveried servants held an oiled-silk canopy over the head of a tiny woman in amethyst moire, veiled in trailing clouds of lilac silk and glittering with gold and diamonds. *With that kind of ostentation*, he thought, *she has to be a friend of Sheera's.*

No one, evidently, had come to meet Yirth.

A voice at his elbow said quietly, "We made it into harbor just in time."

He turned to see Sheera beside him, covered, as befitted a lady, from crown to soles, her hands encased in gold-stitched kid, her hair a mass of curls and jewels that supported the long screens of her plum-colored veils. She held a fur-lined cloak of waterproof silk tightly around her; Sun Wolf, wearing only the shabby, secondhand shirt and breeches of a slave, studied her for a moment, fingering the chain around his neck, then glanced back at the vicious sea visible beyond the headlands. Even in the shelter of the harbor, the waters churned and threw vast columns of bone-white spray where they struck the stone piers; no ship could make it through the channel now. "If you ask me, we cut that a little too close for comfort," he growled.

Sheera's lips tightened under the blowing gauze. "No one asked you," she replied thinly. "You have Yirth to thank that we're alive at all. She's been existing on drugs and stamina for the last three days to hold off the storms until we could make port."

"I have Yirth to thank," Sun Wolf said grimly, "that I'm on this pox-rotted vessel to begin with."

There was a momentary silence, Sheera gazing up into his eyes with a dangerous tautness to her face. By the look of it, she hadn't gotten much more sleep in the last several days than Yirth had. Sun Wolf returned her gaze calmly, almost mockingly, daring her to fly into one of her rages.

When she spoke, her voice was almost a whisper. "Just remember," she said, "that I could speak to Yirth and let you scream yourself to death."

Equally softly, he replied, "Then you'd have to find someone else to train your ladies, wouldn't you?"

Sheera's next words were forestalled by the arrival of Gilden, veiled diaphanously and preceding a whole line of porters bearing enough luggage for a year in the wilds. She said quietly to Sheera, "Yirth's in her cabin. She'll wait until the crowds have thinned off a bit, then slip away unnoticed. The ship's coming in this way ahead of the storm will have attracted enough notice as it is; we don't want any of Derroug's spies reporting to Altiokis that Yirth was on board."

Sheera nodded. "All right," she agreed, and Gilden moved off, slipping back effortlessly into the role of an indefatigably frivolous, middle-class globe-trotter amid the welter of her luggage.

They had come in among the quays now, the crew making the ship fast to the long stone wharf. The wet air crackled with orders, curses, and shouts. Farther up the rail, Denga Rey and Amber Eyes were leaning over to wave and call to their cronies on the dock. The fitful, blowing gusts of rain beaded the gladiator's shaven scalp and the courtesan's soft, apricot-colored mane of unveiled hair; both Gilden and Sheera, as was proper for women of their station and class, ignored them totally.

The gangplank was let down. A couple of sailors, a woman and a boy, brought up Sheera's trunk. After a single burning, haughty stare from Sheera, Sun Wolf lifted it to his shoulder and carried it down the cleated ramp at her heels.

The wharves of Mandrigyn, as the Wolf had seen from the deck of the ship, were connected at their landward end by a columned promenade, undoubtedly a strolling place in the heat of the summer for the fashionable of the town. In the winter, with its elaborate topiary laid naked by the winds and its marble pillars and statues stained and darkened by flickering rain, it was drafty and depressing. At a score of intervals along its length, it was broken by brightly tiled footbridges that crossed the mouths of Mandrigyn's famous canals; looking down through the nearest bridge's half-hexagon archway, the Wolf could see a sort of sheltered lagoon there, where half a dozen gondolas rocked on their moorings. Beyond these rainbow-colored, minnowlike boats, the canal wound away into the watery city between the high walls of the houses, the waters shivering where they were brushed by squalls of rain. Everything seemed dark with wetness and clammy with moss. Against this background, the tiny lady who emerged from beneath her oiled-silk canopy to greet Sheera seemed incongruously gaudy.

"Sheera, I was terrified you wouldn't make it into the harbor!" she cried in a high, rather light voice and extended tiny hands, gloved in diamond-speckled confections of white and lavender lace.

Sheera took her hands in greeting, and they exchanged a formal kiss of welcome amid a whirl of wind-torn silk veils. "To tell you the truth, I was afraid of that myself," she admitted, with a smile that was the closest Sun Wolf had seen her get to warm friendliness in all their short acquaintance. Sheera was evidently fond of this woman—and, by her next remark, very much in her confidence.

"Did you find one?" the tiny lady asked, looking up into Sheera's face with a curiously intent expression, as if for the moment, Sheera and Sheera alone existed for her. "Did you succeed?"

"Well," Sheera said, and her glance flickered to Sun Wolf, standing stoically, the trunk balanced on his shoulder, a little way off. "There has been a change in plans."

The woman frowned indignantly, as if at an affront. "What? How?" The wind caught in her lilac-colored veils, blowing them back to reveal a delicate-complected, fine-boned face, set off by beautiful brown eyes under long, perfectly straight lashes. For all that she was as overdressed as a saint in a Trinitarian cathedral, she was a well-made little thing, Sun Wolf judged, both dainty and full-breasted. No girl, but a woman of Sheera's age.

Sheera introduced them quietly. "Drypettis Dru, sister to the governor of Mandrigyn. Captain Sun Wolf, chief of the mercenaries of Wrynde."

Drypettis' eyes, originally dark with indignation at being presented to a slave, widened with shock, then flickered quickly back to Sheera. "You brought their commander *here?*"

From the direction of the ship, the whole gaudy crowd of what looked like prostitutes and gladiators came boiling past them, laughing and joking among themselves. At the sight of Sun Wolf, they let fly a volley of appreciative whistles, groans, and commentary so outspoken that Drypettis Dru stiffened with shocked indignation, and blood came stinging up under the thin skin of her cheeks.

"Really, Sheera," she whispered tightly, "if we must have people like that in the organization, can't you speak to them about being a little more—more seemly in public?"

"We're lucky to have them in our organization, Dru," Sheera said soothingly. "They can go anywhere and know everything—and we will need them all the more now."

The limpid brown eyes darted back to Sheera. "You mean you were asked for more money than you could offer?"

"No," Sheera said quietly. "I can't explain here. I've told Gilden to spread the word. There's a meeting tonight at midnight in the old orangery in my gardens. I'll explain to everyone then."

"But . . ."

Sheera lifted a finger to her for silence. From the direction of the nearest lagoon, a couple of elderly servants were approaching, bowing with profuse apologies to Sheera for being late. She made a formal curtsy to Drypettis and took her leave, walking toward the gondola moored at the foot of a flight of moss-slippery stone stairs without glancing back to see if Sun Wolf were following. After a moment, he did follow, but he felt Drypettis' eyes on his back all the way.

While one servitor was making Sheera comfortable under a canopy in the waist of the gondola, Sun Wolf handed the trunk down the narrow steps to the other one. Before descending, he looked back along the quay, deserted now, with the masts of the ships tossing restlessly against the scudding rack of the sky. He saw the woman Yirth, like a shadow, come walking slowly down the gangplank and pause at its bottom, leaning upon the bronze bollard there as if she were close to stumbling with exhaustion. Then, after a moment, she straightened up, pulled her plain frieze cloak more tightly about her, and walked away into the darkening city alone.

From his loft above the orangery, Sun Wolf could hear the women arriving. He heard the first one come in silence, her footfalls a faint, tapping echo in the wooden spaces of the huge room. He heard the soft whisper of talk when the second one joined her. From the loft's high window, he could see their catlike shapes slip through the postern gate at the bottom of the garden that gave onto the Leam Canal and glide silently from the stables, where, Sheera had told him, there was an old smugglers' tunnel to the cellar of a building on the Leam Lagoon. He watched them scuttle through the shadows of the wet, weedy garden, past the silhouetted lacework of the bathhouse pavilion, and with unpracticed stealth, into the orangery itself.

He had to admit that Sheera had not erred in her choice of location. The orangery was the farthest building from the house, forming the southern end of the quadrangle of its outbuildings. A strip of drying yard, the property wall, and the muddy, greenish canal called Mothersditch separated it from the nearest other building, the great laundries of St. Quillan, which closed up at the third hour of the night. There was little chance they would be overheard if they practiced here.

He lay in the darkness on his narrow cot, listened to the high-pitched, muted babble in the room below, and thought about women.

Women. Human beings who are not men.

Who had said that to him once? Starhawk—last winter, or the winter before, when she was explaining something about that highly individual fighting style of hers . . . It was something he had not thought of at the time. Now it came back to him, with the memory of those gray, enigmatic eyes.

Human beings who are not men.

Even as a child, he had understood that the demons that haunted the empty marshlands around his village were entities like himself, intelligent after their fashion, but not human. Push them, and they did not react like men.

He had met men who feared women and he understood that fear. Not a physical fear—indeed, it was this type of man who was often guilty of the worst excesses during the sacking of a city. This fear was something deeper. And yet the other side of that coin was the yearning to touch, to possess, the desire for the soft and alien flesh.

There was no logic to it. But training this troop wasn't going to be like training a troop of inexperienced boys, or of men, none of whom weighed over a hundred and thirty pounds.

The day's rain had broken after sundown. A watery gleam of moonlight painted the slanted wall above his head. With the cold wind, voices from the garden blew in—Sheera's, speaking to those wealthier women who had come, as if to a party, in their gondolas to the front door of her great, marble-faced townhouse. Women's voices, like music in the wet night.

Was it training, he wondered, that made women distrustful of one another? The fact that so much was denied them? Maybe, especially in a city like Mandrigyn, where the women were close-kept and forbidden to do those things that would free them from the tutelage of men. He'd seen that before—the hothouse atmosphere of gossip and petty jealousies, of wrongs remembered down through the years and unearthed, fresh and stinking, on the occasions of quarrels. Would women be different if they were brought up differently?

Would men?

His father's bitter, mocking laughter echoed briefly through his mind.

Then he became aware that someone was standing by the foot of his bed.

He had not seen her arrive, nor heard the petal-fall of her feet on the floorboards. Only now he saw her face, floating like a misshapen skull above the dark blob of the birthmark, framed in the silver-shot masses of her hair. He was aware that she had been standing there for some time.

"What the . . ." he began, rising, and she held up her hand.

"I have only come to lay on you the bounding-spells to hold the poison in your veins harmless, so long as you remain in Mandrigyn," she said. "As I am not a true wizard, not come to the fullness of my power, I cannot work spells at a distance by the mind alone." Like a skeleton hand, her white fingers moved in the air, and she added, "It is done."

"You did it all right on the ship," he grumbled sullenly.

One end of that black line of eyebrow moved. "You think so? It is one of the earliest things wizards know—how to come and go unnoticed, even by someone who might be looking straight at them." She gathered her cloak about her, a rustling in the darkness, preparing to go. "They are downstairs now. Will you join them?"

"Why should I?" he asked, settling his shoulders back against the wall at the bed's head. "I'm only the hired help."

The rosewood voice was expressionless. "Perhaps to see what you will have to contend with? Or to let them see it?"

After a moment, he got to his feet, the movement of his shoulders easing a little the unaccustomed pressure of the chain. As he came closer to her, he saw how ravaged Yirth's face was by exhaustion. The black smudges beneath her eyes, the harsh lines of strain, did nothing for her looks. The last days of the voyage were worn into her face and spirit as coal dust wore itself into a miner's hands—to be lightened by time, maybe, but never to be eradicated.

He paused, looking into those cold, green eyes. "Does Sheera know this?" he asked. "If, as you say, you aren't a true wizard—if you haven't come to the fullness of your power—it's insanity for you to go against a wizard who's been exercising his powers for a hundred and fifty years—who's outlived every other wizard in the world and seems to be deathless. Does Sheera know you're not even in his class?"

"She does." Yirth's voice was cool and bitter in the darkness of the room. "It is because of Altiokis that I have not—and will never—come to the fullness of my power as a wizard. My master Chilisirdin gave me the knowledge and the training that those who are born with a mage's powers must have. It is that training which allows me to wring the winds to my commanding, to hold you prisoned, to see through the illusions and the traps with which Altiokis guards the mines. But Chilisirdin was murdered—murdered before she could give to me the secret of the Great Trial. And without that, I will never have the Power."

Sun Wolf's eyes narrowed. "The what?" he asked. In the language of the West, the word connoted a judicial ordeal as well as tribulation; in the northern dialect, the word was sometimes used to mean death as well.

The misshapen nostrils flared in scorn. "You are a man who prides himself on his ignorance of these things," she remarked. "Like love, you can never be sure when they will cross your life, will or nil. Of what the Great Trial consisted I never knew—only that it killed those who were not born with the powers of a mage. Its secret was handed down from master to pupil through generations. I have sought for many years to find even one of that last generation of wizards, or one of their students, who might know what it was—who might have learned how one did this thing that melds the power born into those few children with the long learning they must acquire from a master wizard. But Altiokis has murdered them all, or driven them into hiding so deep that they dare not reveal to any what they are—or what they could have been. That is why I threw in my lot with Sheera. Altiokis has robbed us all—all of us who would have been mages and who are now condemned to this half-life of thwarted longings. It is for me to take revenge upon him, or to die in the trying."

"That's your choice," the Wolf said quietly. "What I object to is your hauling me with you—me and all those stupid women downstairs who think they're going to be trained to be warriors."

The voices rose to them, a light distant babbling, like the pleasant sounds of a spring brook in the darkness. Yirth's eyes flashed like a cat's. "They also have their revenge to take," she replied. "And as for you, you would die for the sake of the two pennies they will put upon your eyes, to pay the death gods to ferry you to Hell."

"Yes," he agreed tightly. "But that's my choice—of time and manner and whom I take with me when I go."

She sniffed. "You have no choice, my friend. You were made what you are by the father who spawned you—as I was made when I was born with the talent for wizardry in my heart and this mark like a piece of thrown offal on my face. You had no more choice in the matter than you had about the color of your eyes."

She gathered the dark veil about her once again, to cover her ugliness, and in silence descended the stairs.

After a moment, Sun Wolf followed her.

A few candles had been lighted on the table near the staircase, but their feeble light penetrated no more than a dozen feet into the vast wooden vault of the orangery. All that could be seen in that huge darkness was the multiplied reflection in hundreds of watching eyes. Like the wind dying on the summer night, the sound of talking hushed as Sun Wolf stepped into the dim halo of light, a big, feral, golden man, with Yirth like a fell black shadow at his heels.

He had not expected to see so many women. Startled, he cast a swift glance at Yirth, who returned an enigmatic stare. "Where the hell did they come from?" he whispered.

She brushed the thick, silver-shot mane back over her shoulders. "Gilden Shorad," she replied softly. "She and her partner Wilarne M'Tree are the foremost hairdressers in Mandrigyn. There isn't a woman in the city they cannot speak to at will, from noblewomen like Sheera and Drypettis Dru down to common whores."

Sun Wolf looked out at them again—there must have been close to three hundred women there, sitting on the worn and dusty pine of the floor or on the edges of the big earth tubs that contained the orange trees. Smooth, beardless faces turned toward him; he was aware of watching eyes, bright hair, and small feet tucked up underneath the colors of the long skirts. Whether it was from their numbers alone, or whether the hypocaust under the floor had been fired, the huge, barnlike room was warm, and the smell of old dirt and citrus was mingled with the smells of women and of perfume. The rustle of their gowns and of the lace on the wrists of the rich ones was like a summer forest.

Then silence.

Into that silence, Sheera spoke.

"We got back from Kedwyr today," she said without preamble, and her clear, rather deep voice penetrated easily into the fusty brown shadows of the room. "All of you know why we went. You put your money into the venture and your hearts—did without things, some of you, to contribute; or put yourselves in danger; or did things that you'd rather not have done to get the money. You know the value of what you gave—I certainly do."

She stood up, the gold of her brocade gown turned her into a glittering flame, the stiff lace of her collar tangling with the fire-jewels in her hair. From where he stood behind her, Sun Wolf could see the faces of the women, rapt to silence, their eyes drinking in her words.

"All of you know the plan," she continued, leaning her rump against the edge of the table, her gem-bright hands relaxed among the folds of her skirts. "To hire mercenaries, storm the mines, free the men, and liberate the city from Altiokis and the pack of vultures he's put in charge. I want you to know right away that I couldn't hire anyone.

"Maybe I shouldn't have been surprised," she went on. "Winter's coming. Nobody wants to fight a winter war. Every man's first loyalty is to himself, and nobody wanted to risk Altiokis' wrath, not even for gold. I understand that."

Her voice rose a little, gaining strength and power. "But for them it's only money. For us it's our lives. There isn't a woman here who doesn't have a man—lover, husband, father—who either died at Iron Pass or was enslaved there. And that was every decent man in the city; every man who had the courage to march in Tarrin's army in the first place, every man who understood what would happen if Altiokis added Mandrigyn to his empire. We've seen it in other cities—at Racken Scrag, and at Kilpithie. We've seen him put the corrupt, the greedy, and the unscrupulous into power—the men who'll toad-eat to him for the privilege of making their own money out of us. We've seen him put such a man in charge here."

Their eyes went to Drypettis Dru, who had come in with Sheera and taken her seat as close to the table as she could, almost literally sitting at her leader's feet. Throughout the speech, she had been silent, gazing up at Sheera with the passionate gleam of fanaticism in her brown eyes, her little hands clenched desperately in her lap; but as the women looked at her, she sat up a bit.

"You have all heard the evil reports of Derroug," Sheera said in a quieter tone. "I think there are some of you who have—had experience with his—habits." Her dark eyes flashed somberly. "You will know that his own sister has turned against him and has been like my right hand in organizing our cause."

"Not turned against him," Drypettis corrected in her rather high, breathless voice. "My brother's actions have always been deplorable and repugnant to me. He has disgraced our house, which was the highest in the city. For that I shall never forgive him. Nor for his lewdness toward you, nor—"

"Nor shall any of us forgive him, Drypettis," Sheera said, cutting short what threatened to turn into a discursive catalog of the governor's sins. "We have all seen the evil effects of Altiokis' rule starting here in Mandrigyn. If it is to be stopped, we must stop it now.

"*We* must stop it," she repeated, and her voice pressed heavily on the words. "We are fighting for more than just ourselves. We all have children. We all have families—or had them." A murmur stirred like wind through the room. "Since we can't hire men, we have to learn to do what we can ourselves."

She looked about her, into that shadowy, eye-glittering silence. The candlelight caught in the stiff fabric of her golden gown, making her flash like an upraised sword blade.

"We've all done it," she said. "Since Iron Pass, you've all stepped in to take over your husbands' affairs, in one way or another. Erntwyff, you go out every day with the fishing fleet. Most of the fleet is now manned by fishermen's wives, isn't it? Eo, you've taken over the forge . . ."

"Had to," said a big, cowlike woman, whose whips of ivory-fair hair marked her as a relation of Gilden Shorad's. "Woulda starved, else."

"And you've taken Gilden's daughter Tisa for your apprentice, too, haven't you? Sister Quincis, they tell me they've even been appointing women as provisional priests in the Cathedral, something they haven't done in hundreds of years. Fillibi, you're running your husband's store—and running it damned well, too . . . And nobody cares whether any of you wears a veil or not, or has a chaperon. Business is business.

"Well, our business is defending the city and freeing the men. We've all proved women can work as well as men. I think they can fight as well as men, too.

"I think all of you know," she continued, her voice growing grave, "that if you put a woman with her back to the wall, fighting, not for herself, but for her man, her children, and her home, she's braver than a man, tougher than a man—hell, she's tougher than a cornered rat. And, ladies, that's where we are."

If she asked for volunteers, they'd turn out to a woman, the Wolf thought. *She has a king's magic; that magic of trust.*

Damned arrogant bitch.

Sheera's voice was low; a pin could have been heard dropping in the breathing silence of the orangery. "No," she said, "I couldn't hire men to do it. But I hired one man—to come here and teach us to do it ourselves. *If* we're willing to fight. There's a difference between just giving money, no matter how much money, and picking up a sword yourself. And I tell you, ladies—now is the time to see that difference."

They could not applaud, for the sound would carry, but the silence was a magic crown on those dark curls. *Point them the way*, Sun Wolf thought cynically, *and they'd march to the mines tonight, the silly bitches, and be dead by morning.* Like too many rulers, Sheera had the quality of making others ready to go out and fight without ever asking themselves what it would cost them.

He gave himself a little shove with his shoulder against the doorframe and walked to where she stood before them in that aura of candle flame, flamelike herself in her golden gown. At this movement, she turned her head, surprised. *Maybe she didn't think I'd speak*, he thought, with a prickle of anger at that certainty of hers. He turned to the devouring sea of eyes.

"What Sheera says is true," he agreed quietly, the gravelly rumble of his voice pitched, as a leader must know how to pitch it, to the size of his troop. "A woman fighting for her children—or occasionally for a man—will fight like a cornered rat. But I've driven rats into corners and killed them with the toe of my boot, and don't think that can't happen to you."

Sheera swung around, the whole of her body glittering with rage. He caught her gaze and silenced her, as if he had laid a hand over her mouth. After a moment, his eyes returned to the women.

"So all right, I agreed to teach you, to make warriors out of you; and by the spirits of my ancestors, I'll do it, if I have to break your necks. But I want you all to understand what it is you're doing.

"War is serious. War is dead serious. You are all smaller, lighter, and slower on the run than men. If you expect to beat men in combat, you had damned well better be twice as good as they are. I can make you twice as good. That's my job. But in the process, you're going to get cut up, you're going to get hurt, you're going to get shouted at and cursed, and you'll crawl home so exhausted you can hardly stand up, because that's the only way to get good, especially if you're little enough for some man to lift and carry away under his arm." His eyes

CHAPTER

6

"*T*HIS IS A SWORD," SUN WOLF SAID. "YOU HOLD IT BY THIS end."

He glared at the dozen women who stood in a line before him, all of them wheezing with the exertion of an hour of warming-up and tumbling exercises that had convinced them, as well as their instructor, that they'd never be warriors.

"You." He pointed to Gilden Shorad's partner-in-crime, the tiny, fragile-looking Wilarne M'Tree. She stepped forward, bright, black eyes raised trustingly to his, and he tossed the weapon to her hilt-first. She fielded it, but he saw by the way she caught herself that it was heavier than she'd been ready for.

He held out his hand and snapped his fingers. She threw it back awkwardly. He plucked it out of the air with no visible effort.

"You're going to be working with weighted weapons," he told them, as he'd told the two groups he had worked with last night and would tell another group later on tonight. "That's the only way you can build up the strength in your arms."

One of the women protested, "But I thought we—"

He whirled on her. "You *ask* for permission to speak!" he snapped.

Her face reddened angrily. She was a tall, piquant-faced woman with the red-gold hair of a highlander, her breasts small under their leather binding, her legs rather knock-kneed in her short linen draw-

picked the diminutive Gilden Shorad out of the crowd and met a hard, challenging, sea-blue stare.

"So if you don't think you can finish the race, don't waste my time by starting it. Whenever I get a batch of new recruits, I end up shaking out about half of them, anyway. You don't have to be tough to start— I'll make you tough. But you have to stay with it. And you have to be committed to killing people and maybe losing a limb or losing your life. That's war."

His eyes raked them, gleaming like a gold beast's in the dimness: the whores, sweet as all the spices of the East with their curled hair and painted eyes; the brown laborer women, prematurely old, like bundles of dowdy serge; the wives of merchants, now many of them merchants themselves, soft and well cared for in their lace and jewels.

"You decide if you can do it or not," he said quietly. "I want my corps here tomorrow night at this time. That's all."

He turned and met Sheera's eyes. Under her lowered lids he could see the speculation, the curiosity and reevaluation, as if she were wondering what she had brought to Mandrigyn.

ers, the marks of past pregnancies printed on the muscleless white flesh of her belly. After a moment, she said in a stifled tone, "Permission to speak, sir."

"Permission granted," he growled.

Permission to speak, he had found, was one of the best ways to break the first rush of hasty words. Most recruits didn't know what they were talking about, anyway.

It worked in this case. Her first outburst checked, the woman spoke in sullenness rather than in outrage. "I thought we were training for a —a surprise attack. A sneak attack."

"You are," Sun Wolf said calmly. "But if something goes wrong, or if you're trapped, you may have to take on a man with a sword—or several men, for that matter. You may have to hold off attackers from the rest of the party or maintain a key position while the others go on. You won't just be fighting for your own life then, you'll be fighting for everybody's."

The woman stepped back, blushing hotly and greatly discomfited. With instinctive tact, the Wolf turned to the other women. "That goes for all of you," he told them gruffly. "And for anything I teach. I was hired because I'm a warrior—I know what you're going to run up against. Believe me, everything I teach you has a purpose, no matter how pointless it seems. I can't take the time to explain it to you. Do you understand?"

Cowed, they nodded.

He bellowed at them, "Don't just stand there bobbing your heads up and down! I can't hear your brains rattle at this distance! Do you understand?"

"Yes, sir," Gilden and Wilarne hastened to reply.

He glared at the group of them. "What?"

All of them chorused this time. "Yes, sir."

He nodded brusquely. "Good." He jerked his thumb at the weapons that lay amid a pile of sacking in one corner of the dimly lighted orangery. "There are your weapons. Along the wall you'll find posts embedded in the floor." He pointed to where he had set the posts himself earlier that day, where they would be easily concealable among the old tree tubs and stacks of clay pots. "I want to see your exercise—backhand, forehand, and down, just those three strokes. First just to get the hang of your sword, then as hard as you can, as if you had a man in front of you, out to slice off your heads."

A few of them looked squeamish at the idea; others started eagerly for the weapons. Sun Wolf roared, "Get back into ranks!"

They did—quickly. The tall woman looked as if she might speak, but thought better of it.

"Nobody breaks ranks until I give the order," he barked at them. "If you were my men, I'd smarten you up with a switch. As it is, all I can do is throw you out on your pretty little arses before you endanger the rest of the troop by failure to obey orders. If I tell you to stand in ranks and then I walk out of the room and take a nap, I'd better find you still in ranks and on your feet when I get back, even if it's the next morning. You understand?"

"Yes, sir," they sang out.

"Now go!" He clapped his hands, and the echoes of it were still ringing in the high rafters as the women scattered to obey.

Behind him, a woman's voice remarked, "You're being nice to them."

He glanced back and met Denga Rey's dark, sardonic eyes. Like him, and like most of the women, the gladiator was stripped for exercise, and her brown body was marked with scars of varying age. The feeble lamplight flashed on the bald arch of her skull.

He grunted. "If you call that 'nice,' you have a different standard of it than I do, woman."

"After the gladiators' school," the warrior returned equably, "you're a lover's caress—and I think we've got the same standard, soldier."

He studied her in silence for a moment. She was younger than he'd first thought, probably not more than twenty-one or twenty-two, a big, dark mare of a girl with belly muscles as ridged and ripply as a crocodile's back. In her alternation of silence and mockery on the voyage, he had sensed her animosity toward him and had wondered what he would do if his only possible second-in-command hated him because she was not first. He knew himself to be an intruder to the organization, whether against his will or not. Sheera was still clearly in command, but he had usurped a spot only slightly below hers; no matter how much they needed him, there was bound to be ill will. He had just been wondering whether it would come down to a physical confrontation between himself and the gladiator when, for reasons of her own, she had apparently decided to accept him; but occasionally he still caught her watching him with a strange gleam in her dark eyes.

"There's no point in taking it out on them because I was dragooned into this lunacy," he said at last. Then, nodding toward them, he asked, "What do you think of them?"

She grinned. "They're rather sweet," she said. "Six months ago, you'd never have got a sword into their dainty little mitts. But since the men have been gone, they've been learning that they can work—not just these women, or the women in the conspiracy, but all of them. They're running the shops, the farms, and the banking and merchant concerns as well. I think some of them, like our Gilden, even enjoy having a blade in their hands."

He admitted grudgingly, "I will say this for them—they did turn out. That surprised me. Most people will put up all the money you want, from a safe distance."

She shrugged her shoulders, the muscles of them shining like brown hardwood. "They did put up a phenomenal amount of money, you know," she remarked. "For all that little Drypettis gets under my skin, she's a damned good organizer when it comes to the tin side of an operation. She was responsible for that end of it."

"Was she?" His eyes traveled down the line of sweating women, hacking doggedly at their posts, as he searched out Sheera's pint-size disciple.

"Of course. She's still the one who holds the purse strings of the operation. When it was just a question of hiring you and your men, she was Sheera's number two person. It's Dru who's kept that damned brother of hers off our backs, too," she added, flicking a speck of dust from the worn black leather of her breast guard. "She's done one hell of a lot for the organization—but damn, that pinch face of hers sticks in my craw. If Sheera hadn't pointed out to her that what we were doing was a military operation, I don't think she'd ever have spoken to me."

His eyes narrowed as they returned to that straight, rigid back and the long tail of thick brown hair that dangled between those slender shoulders.

Not Denga Rey. It was Drypettis whom he had supplanted.

From what he'd seen of her, she wasn't likely to take kindly to being ousted from her place as Sheera's advisor and relegated to mere trooper—the more so because she was not that good a trooper. He remembered her expression on the wharf when Denga Rey, Amber Eyes, and their rowdy friends had rioted past, whistling at him like a crowd of sailors ogling a girl—an expression not only of embarrassed rage but also almost of pain at having to associate with such people at all.

Politics makes strange bedfellows and no error, he thought and wondered again how these disparate women had ever come together in the first place.

"And what about you?" he asked Denga Rey as the gladiator stood, scarred arms folded, surveying their joint charges. "How'd a nice girl like you end up in a place like this?"

Her eyes mocked him. "Me? Oh, I'm in this only for the sake of the one I love."

He stared at her in surprise. "You have a man up in the mines?" It was the last thing he would have expected of her.

The curved, black eyebrows shot up; then she burst into a whoop of delighted laughter. "A *man?*" she choked, her eyes dancing. "You think I'd do this for a *man?* Oh, soldier, you kill me." And she swaggered off, chuckling richly to herself.

Sun Wolf shook his head and turned his attention back to the laboring women. The hard maple of the practice posts was barely chipped —none of them seemed to have any idea how to hold or use a sword. He rolled his eyes briefly heavenward, as if seeking advice from his ancestors—not, he reflected, that any of the lunatic berserkers whose seed had spawned him had ever found themselves in the position of teaching a bunch of soft-bred and lily-handed ladies the grim arts of war. Then he went patiently down the line, correcting grips that would surely have cost the wielders their weapons at the first blow, if they didn't break their wrists in the bargain.

Most of the young men who had come to him in Wrynde, singly or in small troops, were not novices. They had handled swords, if only in the more gentlemanly arts of dueling or militia training. Their muscles were hardened from the sports of boys or from work. A fair number of these women—the wealthier ones especially—had very clearly done neither sports nor work since childhood. Their bodies, as he viewed them with a critical eye that brought blushes to the cheeks of those who noticed the direction of his gaze, might be trim enough, but their flesh was slack.

He shook his head again. And they expected to be able to storm the mines! He only hoped to be far along the road to Wrynde when they tried it.

He went back along the line, patiently correcting strokes.

Many of them shied from his touch, having been trained to walk veiled and downcast in the presence of men. The tall woman who had challenged him was red-faced and missish; Gilden Shorad, coldly businesslike; Wilarne M'Tree, grave and trusting. Drypettis jerked violently from his correcting hand, and for a moment he saw in her eyes not only a jealous hatred but terror as well. *A virgin,* he thought. *It figures. And likely to remain that way, for all her prettiness.*

Gently, he held out his hand for the sword and demonstrated the proper way to use it. Those huge, pansy-brown eyes followed the movements of his hand devouringly, without once straying to either his body or his face. Her cheeks were scarlet, as if scalded.

For all that she was a tough little piece, and grittily determined to do well, she was another one, Sun Wolf thought, whom he'd have to watch.

It was only at Sheera's insistence that she had been included in the troop at all.

The first muster of women had yielded over a hundred, of whom he had cut almost half on the spot. Some of them had been dismissed purely for physical reasons—fatness, or that telltale pallor of internal pain that marked old childbirth injuries. Many of them he'd cut because of the obvious signs of drunkenness or drug addiction. Four girls he had rejected simply because they were thirteen years old, though they had sworn, with tears, that they were fifteen and their mothers knew where they were. Three women he had dismissed, as tactfully as he could, because his instincts and a very short observation told him that they were quarrelsome, people who fomented discord either for their own amusement or simply unconsciously, as if they could not help it. The female version of this was less physical than that of the male, but the result was the same. In a secret command, troublemakers were not to be tolerated.

The women who were left were mostly young, the wives of craftsmen and laborers, though there was a fair sprinkling of merchants' wives of varying degrees of wealth. About a dozen were whores, though privately, Sun Wolf did not expect most of them to stay the course. Enormous experience in the field had taught him that most women who sold themselves for a living lacked either discipline or the strength to control their lives—and he suspected this to be true even of those whom he had not rejected out of hand for drinking or drugs. One of the women in the final group that remained was a nun, an elderly woman who'd been the Convent baker for twenty years and had a grip like a blacksmith's. He thought of Starhawk and smiled.

Those who were left he had divided into four groups, with instructions to report on alternate nights, either a few hours after sunset or at midnight. With luck, this arrangement would keep Sheera's townhouse and grounds from being obviously the center of activity, for there were three or four ways into the compound, and others were being devised. Yirth had sworn a death curse upon betrayal from within, and the women had sworn fellowship with one another and loyalty to Sheera.

They were as safe as they could be, given the appalling circumstances, but Sun Wolf looked down the line of those white, sweating, sluglike bodies with no particularly sanguine hopes of success.

The women slipped quietly away from the bathhouse at the bottom of the grounds nearly two hours later, gowned once more as the respectable matrons or maidens they had been before they took up the study of arms. From the dark door of the orangery, Sun Wolf watched them, brief shadows against the dull, reddish glow from the pavilion's windows, seeking passages, posterns, plank bridges over the canals, and the narrow back streets that would lead them to gondolas tied up in secluded courtyard lagoons. Light rainfall pattered on the bare, gray stems of the deserted garden. Beyond the walls, the lapping of the canals formed the murmurous background music to all life in that watery city.

The water clock in the dim room behind him told him that it would shortly be midnight. The women of the next group would appear soon.

The cold dampness bit into the bare flesh of his shoulders and legs, and he turned back into the silent wooden vaults of the orangery itself.

Sheera was there, wrapped in a shawl of flame-colored wool whose fringes brushed her bare feet. She was dressed for training in short drawers and leather guards, and her dark eyes were angry.

"Do you have to run them so hard?" she demanded shortly. "Some of them are so exhausted they can hardly stagger."

"You want to ask 'em whether they'd rather be exhausted now or slaughtered to the last woman later on?"

Her face reddened. "Or are you trying to run them all out, in the hopes that I'll give up my plans to free the men from the mines?"

"Women, I've learned by this time it's no use hoping you'll give up any plan that you've come up with, no matter how witless it is," he snapped at her, walking over to the room's single brazier of charcoal to rub his hands over the molten glow of the blaze. "If those women can't take it, they'd better get out of the army. We don't know what kind of resistance you'll meet with up in the mines. Since you've made me the instructor, I'm damned well going to prepare those women for anything."

"There's no need to—" she began hotly.

"There is, unless they train more than a couple of hours every other night!" He swung back to face her, the reflection of the fire edging him in a line of gold. "And considering that you couldn't come up with more than fourteen swords . . ."

"We're doing what we can about that!" she retorted. "And about finding somewhere else to practice during the daytime. But the first thing Derroug Dru did when he came to power was collect every weapon in the city—"

"I told you that in the beginning."

"Shut up! And he has spies everywhere within the walls."

"Then meet outside the city."

"Where?" she lashed out viciously.

With silky sweetness he replied, "That's your affair, madam. I'm only your humble slave, remember? But I'm telling you that if those women don't get more training than they're getting, they'll never be soldiers."

"Do you sometimes wonder if Sheera is crazy?" he asked Amber Eyes, much later, as the pale glow of the sinking moon broke through the clouds to filter through the loft window and touch the fallow gold of her hair. It lay like a river of silk over his arm and chest, almost white against the brown of his skin.

She considered the matter for a moment, a grave look coming into those usually dreamy, golden eyes. *Bedroom eyes,* he called them, gentle and a little vulnerable, even when she was wielding a sword. At length she said, "No. At least, no crazier than the rest of us."

He shifted his shoulders against the pillow. "That isn't saying much."

She turned her head, where it lay in the crook of his arm, and studied him for a moment, a tiny frown creasing her brow. The moonlight glimmered on the thread-fine chain of gold that encircled her throat, its shadow like a delicate pen stroke where it crossed the tiny points of her collarbone and vanished into the softer shadows of her hair.

The night of the first meeting in the orangery, when he had come up the stairs, she had been here, waiting, sitting on the edge of the narrow bed, clothed only in that heavy golden mane. Never one to question opportunity, Sun Wolf had taken her—that night and on the two nights since. He occasionally wondered why she had come to him, since she was obviously afraid of him; but aside from the love talk of her trade, she was a silent girl, enigmatic and evasive when he spoke to her.

Tonight was the first time she had treated him like a partner in the same enterprise, rather than a customer.

The orangery below them was silent now, and the garden still but for the incessant whisper of the canal beyond the walls. After a final, inconclusive quarrel with Sheera, Sun Wolf had gone to the bathhouse, dark after the departure of the women, its only light the soft, red pulsation under the copper boilers. By this dim glow, he'd stripped, left his clothes on the baroque, black and gilt marble bench in the antechamber, washed, and then swum for a time in the lightless waters of the hot pool.

It had eased his muscles, if not his feelings.

When Amber Eyes had been too long silent, he said, "She's crazy if she thinks she's going to rescue this Prince Tarrin safe and sound. Oh, I know someone's supposed to have seen him alive, but they always say that of a popular ruler."

"Oh, no." She sat up a little, those gold kitten eyes very earnest in the wan moonlight. "I've seen him. In fact, I delivered a message to him only a few weeks ago, the last time I was up in the mines making maps."

Sun Wolf stared at her. "What?"

"Oh, yes," she said. "We've all seen him—Cobra, Crazy-red . . ." She named two of the other courtesans in the troop. "Plus a lot of the girls you cut—the pros, I mean. How else could we let him know what's going on here?"

"You mean," Sun Wolf said slowly, "you've been in communication with the men all along?"

"Of course." Amber Eyes sat up with a swift, compact lightness and shook out the splendid pale gold mane around shoulders that gleamed like alabaster in the shadows. She seemed to forget the languid grace of a courtesan and hugged her arms around her knees. "I expect Sheera didn't want to tell you about it," she added frankly, "but that end of the organization was set up—oh, long before we went to fetch you."

The disingenuous phrase made him smile. For all her shy appearance, when she wasn't hiding behind what Sun Wolf thought of as her professional manner, Amber Eyes could be disarmingly outspoken. He'd seen it in her dealings with other women in the troop. It was as if she showed to men—to her customers—only what they thought they wanted to see.

"Did Sheera set that up?" he wanted to know.

She shook her head. "This was before Sheera and Dru got into it. It came about almost by chance, really. Well, you know that the city was very hard hit, with the men gone. We—the pros—didn't feel it emotionally so sharply, except for those who had regular lovers who had marched with Tarrin. But I remember one afternoon I went to Gilden's hairdressing parlor—all of us who can afford the prices go to Gilden and Wilarne—and she said that her own husband had been killed, but that Wilarne didn't know whether Beddick—her husband —was alive or dead. Gilden said that many others were in the same situation. Wilarne was half distracted by grief—not that Beddick was anyone to compose songs about, mind you—and I said I'd see what I could learn. So I went riding in the foothills near one of the southern entrances to the mines that looks out onto Iron Pass and I let my horse get away from me and pretended to sprain my foot—the usual." She smiled with remembered amusement. "The superintendent of that end of the mines was very gallant.

"After that it was easy. The next time I went up, I brought friends. The superintendents of the various sections of the mines and the sergeants of the guards don't get into town often. It's forbidden to them to have women up to the barracks, but who's going to report it? Gilden and I were able to set up a regular information service that way, getting news of who was dead and who was alive—Beddick the Bland for one, and, eventually, Tarrin."

Her face clouded in the veiled moonlight. "That was how Sheera came into it in the first place. She'd heard that there was a way of getting news. She got word to me through Gilden. By that time we had girls going up almost every day and we were starting to pass messages in code. Tarrin, it turned out, was starting to organize the miners already, passing messages from gang to gang as they were taken here and there to different work sites in the mines. The men are taken from one place to another in darkness, so they haven't any clear idea of where they are in the tunnels; if a man wanders away from his gang, he can wander in the deeper tunnels until he dies. The tunnels are gated, too, and locked off from one another. But they were starting to work up maps by the time we got in touch with them. On our end, we'd already begun to make maps of the mine entrances, the guardrooms, and where the main barracks are that guard the tunnels from the mines up into the Citadel of Grimscarp itself."

Sun Wolf frowned. "There are ways from the Citadel down into the mines?"

"That's what the miners say. It's because the Citadel's so inaccessible from the outside—it's very defensible, of course, but because of the way it's placed, on the very edge of the cliff, the road from Racken Scrag—the Wizard King's administrative town at the other end of Iron Pass—has to tunnel through a shoulder of the mountain itself even to get to the gates. Since it was so expensive to bring food up the Scarp, they connected that tunnel directly with the mines; now they haul the food straight up from Racken through the mountain itself. The ways into the Citadel from the mines are said to be heavily guarded by magic and illusion."

"But if you women storm the mines," the Wolf said grimly, "Altiokis can send his troops right down on top of you directly from the Citadel. Isn't that right?"

"Well . . ." Amber Eyes said unhappily. "If we strike quickly enough . . ."

"Wonderful." He sighed and slumped back against the pillows. "More battles have been lost because some fool of a general was basing his plans on 'if this or that.'"

"We do have Yirth, though," the girl said defensively. "She can protect us against the worst of Altiokis' magic and spot his illusions."

"Yirth." He sniffed, his fingers involuntarily touching the metal links of his chain. "That's how she got into this, isn't it?"

"Well, yes." Amber Eyes looked down at her hands, restlessly pleating a corner of the sheet between her fingers. Outside, a wind-tossed branch scratched like a ghoul's fingers at the roof. The lantern on a passing gondola reflected in a watery smear of dark gold against the window's rippled glass.

"It was Sheera who brought Yirth into it," she said at length. "We all knew Yirth, of course—I don't think there's a woman in the city who hasn't gone to her for contraceptives, abortions, love philters, or just because she's the only doctor in the city who's a woman. Sheera was one of the very few who knew she was a wizard. She never had anything to do with the organization when all we did was pass information back and forth.

"But when Sheera came into it—she changed it. Before, it had all been so hopeless. What was the point in communicating with the men in the mines, even if they were men you loved, if there was no hope of their ever getting out? If something went wrong here—if your property was confiscated, or your friends arrested—you couldn't tell them of it, really, because it would only add to their misery. But Sheera was the one who said that where information could be exchanged, plans could be formed. She gave us hope.

"And then Dru figured out a way that we could get money from the treasury, and they started raising funds to hire mercenaries. And . . ." She spread her hands, her fine fingers almost translucent in the ivory moonlight. "Our organization became a part of theirs—and Tarrin's. Tarrin and the men are still getting us information on the mines, sending it through the skags . . ."

"The what?" The word was familiar to him from mercenary slang; he knew it to mean the cheapest sort of women who'd sell themselves to hide tanners and garbagemen for the price of a cup of inferior wine.

"The skags." She widened those soft, mead-colored orbs at him. "You know—the ugly women or the fat ones or the old, flabby ones. The guards think it's hilarious to throw them to a gang of miners. Some of the slaves down there have been in the mines so long they're almost beasts themselves." The delicate lips tightened into momentary hardness, and an anger that he had never seen before flashed in those kitten eyes. "They'll drag one of these women down and toss her into a slave barracks, say, 'Have at her, boys,' and then leave."

She was silent for a moment, looking out into the distance, drawing the edge of the sheet over and over through her fingers. Outwardly her face was calm, but her rage against the men who had the power to do this—and perhaps against all men—was like a heat that he could feel through her silken skin where it touched his shoulder. And who was he to argue? he wondered bitterly. The memory of things that he himself, or men he had known, had considered funny while half drunk and sacking a city silenced him before her anger.

Then she shrugged and put the anger aside. "But it's the skags who communicate from gang to gang of the men. Mostly Tarrin's orders keep them from being abused. The superintendents keep mixing the newcomers, the men of Mandrigyn, in with older miners—there are thousands of them down there—to prevent the men from plotting among themselves. But they only spread the plot. And the rest of us— the ones most of these men wouldn't let their wives talk to before the war—have gotten maps of the mines and wax impressions of the keys to the gates—you know Gilden's sister Eo is a smith? She copies the keys—and details of where the armories are."

He settled his back against the wall and regarded her almost won- deringly in the shadows. Outside, the moonlight was dimming, and the smell of rain blew in through the window like a cold perfume. Limned by the faint light, the girl's face looked young, almost child- like; he remembered her by candlelight in the rose-scented room in Kedwyr, laughing that soft, throaty, professional laugh as she drew him into the conspiracy's trap. He realized that it was a compliment to him that she showed him her other face—frank, open, without artifice, the face she showed her women friends. Undoubtedly, it was the face she showed her lover. He found himself wondering if she had a lover, as opposed to a "regular"; or if he, like Gilden's nameless husband, like Beddick M'Tree, like so many others, had followed Tarrin of the House of Her on that last campaign up to the Iron Pass.

The warm weight of her settled against his shoulder, a gesture of intimacy that was less sexual than friendly, like a cat deciding to settle on his knee. "We've been talking too much," she said, and her profes- sional voice was back, soft and teasing.

"One more question," he said. "Why are you here?"

She smiled.

He intercepted her reaching hand. "You're afraid of me, aren't you?"

He felt her body shift in the circle of his arm; when she answered, her voice was that of a girl of nineteen, scarred by what she was, but frank and without artifice. "I was," she said. Moonlight tipped her lashes in silver as she looked up at him. "But I didn't think it was fair for you not to know how things stood with the organization. Dru and Sheera said that the less you knew, the less you could tell anyone. But as for your question . . ." Her lips brushed his in the darkness. "I have my secrets, too."

He drew her to him. As he moved, the links of the chain around his neck jangled faintly in the silence of the dark loft.

CHAPTER

*T*HE PROBLEMS OF WEAPONS AND OF A SECONDARY PLACE TO practice by daylight, away from Derroug Dru's spies, were solved, not by Sheera's ingenuity, but by fate, guided presumably by Sun Wolf's deceased and uproariously amused ancestors.

The Thanelands that lay to the east of Mandrigyn had long been under the governorship of Altiokis; indeed, the haughty and old-fashioned Thanes of the clans that held them had been the first to swear allegiance to the Wizard King. But Altiokis' realm had spread to the richer cities of the coastlands and had drawn upon the slave-worked veins of gold and silver in the mountains for its wealth. The Thanelands were left, as they had always been, as a useless and sparsely populated backwater. The roads winding into those gray hills from the jumble of taverns and dives of East Shore led nowhere. After the sheep that grazed on the scraggly grass and heather had been folded in for the winter, the Thanelands lay utterly empty.

So it was an easy matter for the women to slip across the Rack River in the predawn darkness of a rainy morning and be away from all sight of the city by sunup, to run in the wilderness of whin and peat bogs unobserved.

Freezing wind blew another squall of rain over Sun Wolf's bare back. In the low ground between the drenched, gray hills, the water lay like hammered silver, just above the freezing point; on the high ground, the rocks made the easiest going, for the wet, bare, winter-tough brambles could scratch even the most liberally mud-armored flesh.

Ahead of him, the main pack of the running women bobbed through the colorless light of the wan afternoon. They were clearly flagging.

Those who hadn't braided their hair up wore it in slick, sodden cloaks down over their backs. Just ahead of him, a slender woman raised her arms to gather up a soaked blond coil that reached almost down to her shapely backside, her pace slackening as she did so. Sun Wolf, overtaking her in the slashing rain, bellowed, "You going to mess with your poxy hair in battle, sweetheart?"

She turned a startled, flowerlike face upon him, now haggard with fatigue; others, as guilty as she, looked also. He raised his voice into a cutting roar, meant to be heard over the din of battle. "Next person who touches her hair, I'm going to cut it off!"

They all buckled to and ran harder, arms swinging, knees pumping, leather-bound breasts bouncing, drawers sticking wetly to their bodies in the rain. They had all come to the conclusion, in the course of the last week, that there was not a great deal that Sun Wolf would not do.

And that, he thought grimly as he increased his own pace and forged easily ahead through the pack, was as it should be.

Very few of the women ran well. Tisa did—Gilden Shorad's leggy fifteen-year-old daughter. So did whatever her name was—a rangy, homely mare of a fisherman's wife—Erntwyff Fish. So did Denga Rey. The rest of them had been soft-raised, and even the hardiest had neither the wind nor the endurance for sustained fighting.

A few of them, Sun Wolf was amused to note, still suffered agonies of self-consciousness about being near naked in the presence of a man.

He passed Sheera, laboring exhaustedly in the rear third of the field. Her black hair was plastered to her cheeks where it had come out of its braids; she was muddy, wet, gasping, and still enough to stir a man's blood in his veins. He hoped viciously that she was enjoying training as a warrior.

On the whole, Sun Wolf was surprised at how many had lasted that first week.

A week's hard training had cut their numbers down to fifty, and it spoke well for their determination that any had remained at all. All of them—maidens, matrons, and those who were neither—had been subjected to the most taxingly rigorous physical training that Sun Wolf could devise: tumbling to train the reflexes and identify the cowards; weights and throwing to strengthen the arms; hand-to-hand fighting, wrestling, or dueling with blunted weapons; running on the hills. These were preliminaries to the more vicious arts of infighting and sneaky death to come.

Women whom the Wolf would have sworn would make champions with the best had dropped out; half-pints like Wilarne M'Tree and maladroits like Drypettis Dru were still with them. He could see those two from where he ran, laboring along a dozen yards behind the rest of the pack.

Sun Wolf was rapidly coming to the conclusion that he did not and never would understand women.

Starhawk . . .

He had always thought of Starhawk as different from other women, even from the other warrior women of his own troop. It was only now, when he was surrounded by women, that elements of her personality fell into place for him, and he saw her as both less and more enigmatic, a woman who had rejected the subjugation these women had been trained in—had rejected it long before her path had crossed his own.

Briefly the memory of their first meeting flitted through his mind; how cold the spring sunlight had been in the garden of the Convent of St. Cherybi, and how strong the smell of the new-turned earth. He saw her again as the tall girl she had been, ascetic, distant, and cold as marble in the dark robes of a nun. He'd forgotten why he'd even been at the Convent—probably extorting provisions from the Mother there —but he remembered that moment when their eyes met and he knew that this woman was a warrior in her heart.

He had never believed that he would miss her as much as he did. Amber Eyes was sweet-natured and supremely beddable, exactly the kind of girl he liked—or had liked, anyway—but it was Starhawk for whom he reached, as a man in danger would reach for his sword. He had never quite gotten over not having her there at his side.

His front runners were cresting the final hill above the copse of woods where they had gathered that morning. They'd covered about two and a half miles—not bad for a first run, for women untrained to it, he thought as he slacked his pace and let himself fall back through the pack once more. He yelled a curse at Gilden, who was flagging, her face the bright fuschia hue that extremely fair women turned in exhaustion; she staggered into a futile but gratifying attempt at a burst of speed. He cursed them as he would have cursed his men, calling them cowards, babies, sluts. As he fell back farther in the group, to run beside the grimly stumbling Sister Quincis, he yelled, "I've seen Trinitarian heretics run faster than that!"

They broke over the crest of the hill in a spilling wave. Below them, the land lay barren and grayish brown under the sluicing rain, the long snake of silver water in the bottom of the vale reflecting the colorless sky. The brush around it was black, dead with winter. Sun Wolf slowed his pace still further to round in the last of the stragglers. Denga Rey, her hard brown muscles shining with moisture, had already reached the mere below.

He yelled after them, "Run, you lazy bitches!" and collected a look from Drypettis that could have been bottled and sold to remove the veneer from furniture. He was almost standing still as Wilarne M'Tree staggered past. He hurried her on her way with a swat on her little round rump.

By the time he reached the growing group around the water, two or three of them had recovered enough breath to begin throwing up.

"You do that in the woods under the leaves where it's not going to be seen by an enemy scout!" he roared at the green-faced and retching Eo. "You want Altiokis' spies to follow the stink of you to your hideout? I mean it!" he added as she started to double over again and, seizing her by the back of the neck, he shoved her toward the trees. Others had begun to stumble in that direction already.

To Sheera, for whom it was too late, he ordered, "Clean that up."

Without a word, for she was far past speech, she gathered up leaves to obey him.

"And the rest of you start walking," he ordered curtly. "You'll get chilled if you stand around, and I'm not going to have the lot of you sniveling and fainting on me at practice tonight."

"Very nice!" A voice, deep and harsh as a crow's, laughed from the sheltering darkness of the nearby woods. "I had been told that any excuse for a red-blooded male in Mandrigyn had been sent to the mines. I am pleased to see that the reports were exaggerated."

Sun Wolf swung around. White-faced, Sheera got to her feet. A tall bay horse stepped from the tangled brambles of the thickets. The woman on its back sat sidesaddle, her body straight as a spear. In the shadows of a green oilskin hood, hazel-gray eyes flashed mockingly. The cloak covered most of her, except for the hem of her gown and her gloves, and these were of such barbaric richness as to leave little doubt about her station. The bay's bridle had cheekpieces of brass, worked into the shape of flowers.

"Marigolds," Sheera said quietly. "The emblem of the Thanes of Wrinshardin."

The old woman turned her head with a slow, ironic smile. "Yes," she purred. "Yes, I am Lady Wrinshardin. The Thane's mother, not his wife. And you are, unless I am much mistaken, the legendary Sheera Galernas, in whose honor my son once wrote such puerile verse."

Sheera's chin came up. The thick curls of her black hair plastered wetly to her cheeks, and the rain gleamed on her bare arms and shoulders, which had already turned bright red with cold and gooseflesh. "If your son is the present Thane of Wrinshardin who courted me when I was fifteen," she replied coolly, "I am pleased to see that your taste in poetry so closely parallels my own."

There was a momentary silence. Then that mocking smile widened, and Lady Wrinshardin said, "Well. At the time, I presumed that, like most town-bred hussies, you had turned down the chance of wedding decent blood out of considerations of money and the boredom of country life. I am pleased to see that you acted rather from good sense." The sharp, faded old eyes casually raked the scene before her, taking in the exhausted, bedraggled women and the big man with the chain about his neck who had not the eyes of a slave.

"I don't suppose I have ever seen a man chase this many women since my husband died," she remarked in her harsh, drawling voice. "And even he never did so fifty at a time. Is running about the hills naked in the wintertime a new fad in the town, or could it be that there is a purpose behind this?"

"Not anything anyone's likely to hear of."

Lady Wrinshardin turned her head slowly at the sound of Denga Rey's voice, as if she had just noticed the big gladiator. The wrinkled eyelids drooped. "Do I detect a threat in that rather cryptic utterance?" she inquired disinterestedly.

The horse flung up its head with a squeal of fear. From the wet underbrush of the woods, a ring of women materialized behind and around Lady Wrinshardin, some of them a little pale, but all as grim-faced as bandits.

One eyebrow slowly ascended that corrugated forehead. "Goodness," she murmured to herself. Then, with a quick tweak of the reins, she wheeled the horse and spurred through the line, heading for open country.

"Stop her!" Sheera barked.

Hands grabbed at the bridle, the horse rearing and lashing out at the women who crowded so close around it. Denga Rey caught the bit, dragging its head down while the animal twisted violently to get free. "Enough!" Lady Wrinshardin said sharply, keeping her seat on that pirouetting saddle with the aplomb of a grandmother riding her rocking chair. "You've proved your courage; there's no need to be redundant about it to the point of damaging his mouth."

The dark woman released her pressure on the bit, but did not step back. Tisa clung grimly to the rein on the other side, her hair in her eyes, looking absurdly young. The haughty noblewoman gazed about at the women hemming her in, and the mocking, amused smile returned to her wrinkled face.

Abruptly she extended her hand to Tisa. "You may help me down, child."

Startled, the girl held out her clasped hands to make a step. With a single lithe movement, Lady Wrinshardin stepped to the ground and crossed the wet grass to where Sheera stood. She had the haughty and self-centered carriage of a queen.

"Your troops are well trained," she remarked.

Sheera shook her head. "Only well disciplined." Alone of the women, she did not appear to be awed by that elegant matriarch. Even Drypettis, whose family—as she hastened to remind anyone who was interested—was among the highest in the city, was cowed. After a moment, Sheera added, "In time, they will be well trained."

The eyes flickered to Sun Wolf speculatively, then back to Sheera again. "You were wise not to wed my son," the lady said, putting back the oilskin hood to reveal a tight-coiled braid of white hair pinned close about her head. "He has no more courage than a cur dog that suffers itself to be put out into the rain and fed only the guts of its kills. He is like his father, who also feared Altiokis. Have you met Altiokis?"

Sheera looked startled at the question, as if meeting the Wizard

King were tantamount to meeting one's remoter ancestors, Sun Wolf thought—or meeting the Mother or the Triple God in person.

The lady's thin lip curled. "He is vulgar," she pronounced. "How such a creature could have lived these many years . . ." Under their creased lids, her eyes flickered, studying Sheera, and her square-cut lips settled into their fanning wrinkles with a look of determination. Sun Wolf was uncomfortably reminded of an old aunt of his who had kept all of his family and most of the tribe in terror for years.

"Come with me to the top of the hill, child," she said at last. The two women moved off through the wet, winter-faded grass; then Lady Wrinshardin paused and glanced back, as if as an afterthought, at the Wolf. "You come, too."

He hesitated, then obeyed her—as everyone else must also obey her —following them up the steep slope where granite outcrops thrust through the shallow soil, as if the body of the earth were impatient with that thin and unproductive garment. Greenish-brown hills circled them under the blowing dun rags of the hoary sky.

"My great-grandfather swore allegiance to the Thane of Grimscarp a hundred and fifty years ago," Lady Wrinshardin said after they had climbed in silence for a few moments, with the tor still rising above their heads, vast as an ocean swell. "Few remember him or the empire that he set out to build, he and his son. In those days, many rulers had court wizards. The greater kings, the lords of the Middle Kingdoms in the southwest, could afford the best. But those who served the Thanes were either the young, unfledged ones, out to make their reputations, or the ones who hadn't the ability to be or do anything more. They were all of a piece, pretty much—my great-grandfather had one, the Thanes of Schlaeg had one . . . and the Thanes of Grimscarp, the most powerful of the Tchard Mountain Thanes, had one.

"His name was Altiokis.

"This much I had from my grandfather, who was a boy when the Thane of Grimscarp started setting up an alliance of all the Thanes of all the great old clans, the ancient warrior clans here, in the Tchard Mountains, and down along the Bight Coast, where they hadn't been pushed out by a bunch of jumped-up tradesmen and weavers who lived behind city walls and never put their noses out of doors to tell which way the wind was blowing. This was in the days before the nuuwa began to multiply until they roamed the mountains and these hills like foul wolves, the days before those human-dog-things, those abominations they call ugies, had ever been heard of. The old Thane of Grim wanted to get up a coalition of the Thanes and the merchant cities and he was succeeding quite nicely, they say.

"But something happened to him. Grandfather couldn't remember clearly whether it was sudden or gradual; he said the old Thane's grip seemed to slip. A week, two weeks, then he was dead. His son, a boy of eighteen, ruled the new coalition, with Altiokis at his side. None of us was ever quite sure when the boy dropped out of sight."

The steepness of the hill had slowed their steps, the old woman and the young one leaning into the slope. Glancing back, the Wolf could see the other women moving about down below, their flesh bright against the smoky colors of the ground. Tisa and her aunt, Gilden's sister, the big, bovine Eo, were holding the horse still and stroking its soft nose; Drypettis, as usual, was sitting apart from the others, talking to herself; her eyes were jealously following Sheera.

The freshening wind cracked in Lady Wrinshardin's cloak like an unfurling sail. The wry old voice went on. "Altiokis' first conquest was Kilpithie—a fair-sized city on the other side of the mountains; they wove quite good woolen cloth there. He used its inhabitants as slaves to build his new Citadel at the top of the Grim Scarp, where he'd raised that stone hut of his in a single night. They said that he used to go up there to meditate. From there he raised his armies and founded his empire."

"With the armies of the clans?" Sheera asked quietly.

They had paused for breath, but the climb had warmed her again, and she stood without shivering, the wind that combed the hillcrests tangling her black hair across her face.

"At first," the lady said grimly. "Once he began to mine gold from the Scarp and from the mountains all about it, he could afford to hire mercenaries. They always said there was another evil that marched in his armies, too—but maybe it was only the sort of men he hired. He pollutes all he touches. Strange beasts multiply in his realm. You know ugies? Ape-things—the Tchard Mountains are stiff with them, though they were never seen before. Nuuwa—"

"Altiokis surely didn't invent nuuwa," Sun Wolf put in. He shook his wet hair back, freeing it of the chain around his neck; he was aware of the old lady's sharp eyes gauging him, judging the relationship between the chain and Sheera against the sureness and command in his voice. He went on. "You get nuuwa turning up in records of one place or another for as far back as the records go. They're mentioned in some of the oldest songs of my tribe, ten, twelve, fifteen generations ago. Every now and again, you'll just get them, blundering around the wilderness, killing and eating anything they see."

The fine-chiseled nostrils flared a little, as if Lady Wrinshardin were unwilling to concede any evil for which Altiokis were not responsible. "They say that nuuwa march in his armies."

"I've heard that," the Wolf said. "But if you know anything about nuuwa, you'd know it's impossible. For one thing, there just aren't that many of them. They—they simply appear, but their appearances are few and far between."

"Not so few these days," she said stubbornly. She pulled her oilskin cloak more tightly about her narrow shoulders and continued up the hill.

"And anyway," the Wolf argued as he and Sheera fell into step with her once more, "they're too stupid to march anywhere. Hell, all they are is walking mouths . . ."

"But it cannot be denied," the lady continued, "that Altiokis spreads evil to what he touches. The Thanes served him once out of regard for their vows to the Thane of Grim. Now they do so from fear of him and his armies."

They stopped at the crest of the hill, while the winds stormed over and around them like the sea between narrow rocks. Below them on the other side, the Thanelands rolled on, silent and haunting in their winter drabness, possessed of a weird spare beauty of their own. The dead heather and grass of the hills of slate-gray granite gleamed silver with wetness. Twisted trees clung to the skyline like bent crones and shook flailing fists at the heavens.

Far off, in a cuplike depression between three hills, a single, half-ruined tower pointed like a broken bone end toward the windy void above.

"What you're doing is foolish, you know," the lady said.

Sheera's nostrils flared, but she said nothing. *Quite a tribute,* the Wolf thought, *to the old broad's strength of character, if she can keep Sheera quiet.*

"I suppose there's some scheme afoot in the city to free Tarrin and the menfolk and retake Mandrigyn. As if, having beaten them once, Altiokis could not do so again."

"He beat them because they were divided by factions," Sheera said quietly. "I know. My husband was the first man in Derroug Dru's party and had more to do than most with Altiokis' victory. Many of the men who supported Altiokis' cause—the poorer ones, whose favor he did not need to buy—were sent to the mines as well. And my girls, the whores who go up to the mines, tell me that there is another army of miners, from all corners of Altiokis' realm, who would fight for the man who freed them."

"Your sweetheart Tarrin."

Color blazed into Sheera's face, her red lips opening to retort.

"Oh, yes, my girl, we've heard all about your Golden Prince, for all that his family were parvenus who made their money off a salt monopoly and from draining the swamps to build East Shore. Better blood than your precious husband's, anyway." She sniffed.

"My husband—" Sheera began hotly.

Lady Wrinshardin cut her off. "You really think this pack of white-limbed schoolgirls can be taught to overcome Altiokis' mercenaries?"

Sheera's lips tightened, but she said nothing.

The lady glanced down into the vale behind them, as haughty as if she reviewed her own troops. Her hands, in their crimson and gold gloves, stroked the oilskin of her cloak.

"I'll tell you this, then. If you succeed in what you aim, don't return to the city. The tunnels of the mine connect with the Citadel itself. Cut off the serpent's head—don't go back to hide behind her walls and wait for it to get you."

Eyes widening with alarm, Sheera whispered, "That's impossible. Those ways are guarded by magic. Altiokis himself is deathless . . ."

"He wasn't birthless," Lady Wrinshardin snapped. "He was born a man and, like a man, he can be killed. Attack the Citadel, and you'll have the Thanes on your side—myself, Drathweard of Schlaeg, and all the little fry as well. Wait for him to put the city under siege again, and he'll fall on you with everything he's got."

She jerked her chin toward the rolling valleys and distant tower. "That's the old Cairn Tower. The Thanes of Cairn ran afoul of the fifteenth Thane of Wrinshardin, God rest what passed in them for souls. The place hasn't been inhabited since. It is a good run," she added with a malicious glitter in her eyes, "from here."

And turning, she moved back down the hill, straight and arrogant as a queen of these wild lands. Sheera and Sun Wolf marked the location of the tower with their eyes and followed her down.

While she was mounting her horse beside the mere again, the lady said, as if as an afterthought, "They used to say that weapons were stored there. I doubt you'll find any of the old caches, but you are welcome to whatever you come across."

She settled herself in the saddle and collected the reins with a spare economy of movement that spoke of a life lived in the saddle. "Come out of that web-footed marsh to visit me, if you will," she added. "We need to further our acquaintance."

So saying, she wheeled her horse and, ignoring the other women as if they had not existed, rode through them and away over the moors.

After that they met mornings and evenings, rotating the groups—by daylight in the ruins of the old Cairn Tower, by lamplight in the boarded-up orangery. Sun Wolf announced that running to and from the peasant hut where they frequently hid their cloaks would provide the conditioning necessary for wind and muscles, and thereafter seldom took the women on a general run. Within a week he could tell which ones ran to and from the tower and which walked.

The ones who walked—there were not many—were cut.

And all the while, he could feel them coming together as a force under his hand. He was beginning to know them and to understand the changes he saw in them, not only in their bodies but in their minds as well. With their veils and chaperons, they had—timidly at first, then more boldly—discarded the instinctive notion that they were incapable of wielding weapons, even in their own defense. Since his conversation with Amber Eyes, Sun Wolf had often wondered what went on in the minds of those pliant, quiet ones, the ones who had been raised to tell men only what they wanted to hear. These women looked him in the face when they spoke to him now, even the shyest. He wondered whether that was the effect of weapons training or whether it was because, when they weren't learning how to fight, they were running the financial life of the city.

He had to admit to himself that, after a discouraging start, they were turning out to be a fairly good batch of warriors.

The weapons they found cached in the Cairn Tower were old, and their make cruder and heavier than was general among the expert metalworkers of Mandrigyn. Gilden's sister Eo and young Tisa set up a forge at the tower to lighten them as much as they could without losing the weight necessary to parry and deliver killing strokes. Denga

Rey, watching the practice at the tower one day, suggested that the half-pints of the troop use halberds instead.

"A five-foot halberd can be used in battle like a sword," she said, watching Wilarne laboring to wield her weapon against a leggy black courtesan named Cobra. The roofless hall of the old fortress made a smooth-floored, oval arena some forty feet in length, and the women were scattered across it, wrestling, fighting with weapons, practicing the deadlier throws and breaks of sneak attacks. For once it was not raining, and, except in the low places, the floor was dry. The Wolf had worked them here on days when mud coated them so thickly that it was only by size and the way they moved that they could be distinguished.

From where he and the gladiator stood on what must have been the old feasting dais, they could look out across the sunken floor of the room to the steps and the empty triple arch of the doorway and to the moors beyond. There must have been a courtyard of some kind there once—now there was only a flattened depression in the ground and little heaps of stones covered with lichens and weeds. And below him, between him and the door, the women were busy.

He wondered what the Hawk would make of them.

Denga Rey continued. "Most of the little ones are using swords that are as light as possible for effective weapons—and they are still having troubles. In a pitched fight, a man could outreach them."

Sun Wolf nodded. With luck, they would surprise the guards at the mines and free and arm the men from the guards' armories without the need for a pitched battle. But long experience had taught him never to rely on luck.

The only problem with having the smaller women use halberds in battle came from Drypettis, who took it as a personal affront that the Wolf would make allowances for her size. In a tight voice, she told him, "We can succeed on your own terms, Captain. There is no need to condescend."

He glanced down at her, startled. At times she sounded like an absurd echo of Sheera, without Sheera's shrewdness or her sense of purpose. Patiently, he said, "There's only one set of terms to measure success in war, Drypettis."

That tight little fold at the corners of her mouth deepened. "So you have told us—repeatedly," she retorted with distaste. "And in the crudest possible fashion."

Behind her, Gilden and Wilarne exchanged a glance; the other small women—Sister Quincis and red-haired Tamis Weaver—looked uneasy.

"Have I?" the Wolf rumbled quietly. "I don't think so.

"Success in war," he went on, "is measured by whether or not you do what you aim to—not by whether you yourself live or die. The success of a war is not measured in the same terms as the success of a fight. Succeeding in a war is getting what you want, whether you yourself live or die. Now, it's sometimes nicer to be alive afterward and enjoy what you've fought for—provided what you've fought for is enjoyable. But if you want it badly enough—want others to have it—even that isn't necessary. And it sure as hell doesn't matter how nobly or how crudely you pursue your goal, or who makes allowances or who condescends to you in the process. If you know what you want, and you want it badly enough to do *whatever you have to,* then do it. If you don't—forget it."

The silence in that single corner of the half-ruined tower was palpable, the shrill grunts and barked commands in the hall beyond them seeming to grow as faint and distant as the keening of the wind across the moors beyond the walls. It was the first time that he had spoken of war to them, and he felt all the eyes of this small group of tiny women on him.

"It's the halfway that eats you," he said softly. "The trying to do what you're not certain that you want to do; the wanting to do what you haven't the go-to-hell courage—or selfishness—to carry through. If what you think you want can only be got with injustice and getting your hands dirty and trampling over friends and strangers—then understand what it will do to others, what it will do to you, and either fish or cut bait. If what you think you want can only be got with your own death or your own lifelong utter misery—understand that, too.

"I fight for money. If I don't win, I don't get paid. That makes everything real clear for me. You—you're fighting for other things. Maybe for an idea. Maybe for what you think you ought to believe in, because people you consider better than you believe in it, or say they do. Maybe to save someone who fed and clothed and loved you, the father of your children—maybe out of love and maybe out of gratitude. Maybe you're fighting because somebody else's will had drawn you into this, and you'd rather die yourself than tell her you have other goals than hers. I don't know that. But I think you'd better know it—and know it real clearly, before any of you faces an armed enemy."

They were silent around him, these half-pints, these small and delicate women. Wilarne's eyes fell in confusion, and he saw rose flush up under her wind-bitten cheeks.

But it was Drypettis who spoke. "Honor demands—"

"To hell with honor," the Wolf said shortly, understanding that she had not heard one word he had said. "Women don't have honor."

She went white with anger. "Maybe the women you habitually consort with do not—"

"Captain!" Denga Rey's voice cut across the scuffling, sharp and uneasy. "Someone coming!"

Every sense suddenly snapped alert. He said briefly, "Hide." All around them, at the sound of the gladiator's words, the women had been fading from sight, seeking the darkness of the arches that had once supported a gallery around the hall, now a ruin of scrub and shadow; they were concealing themselves in the hundred bolt holes afforded by ruined passages and half-collapsed turrets whose stones were feathered with dry moss and fern. Gilden and Wilarne clambered up inside the monstrous flue of the hall's old chimney as if trained from childhood as climbing boys.

Only Drypettis stood where she was, rigid with anger. "You can't . . ." she began, almost stifling with rage.

Sun Wolf seized her arm impatiently and half threw her toward a droop-eyed hollow of a broken doorway. "Hide, rot your eyes!" he roared at her and ran to where only Sheera and Denga Rey stood, visible on either side of the triple arch of the raised door.

From here, the valley in which the Cairn Tower was situated could be seen in one sweep of trampled brown grass and standing water. Desolately empty, it lay hemmed in by the stone-crested hills and the gray weight of cloud cover, a solitude unbroken save by a few barren and wind-crippled trees. Then, in that solitude, something moved, a figure running toward the tower.

"It's Tisa," Sheera said, surprise and fear in her voice. "She was on watch at Ghnir Crag, keeping an eye on the direction of town."

Denga Rey said, "There's something else moving down there, too. Look, in the brush along the side of the crag."

The girl plunged, stumbling, up the ruined steps and into Sun Wolf's arms. She was panting, unable to catch her breath—not the measured wind of a racer, but the panic gasps of one who had fled for her life.

"What is it?" Sun Wolf asked, and she raised her face to stare into his with widened eyes.

"Nuuwa," she choked. "Coming here—lots of them, Captain."

"More than twenty?"

She nodded; her flesh was trembling under his hands at what she had so narrowly escaped. "I couldn't count, but I think there were more than twenty. Coming from all sides . . ."

"Pox rot the filthy things. Turn out!" he bellowed, his voice like thunder in the weed-grown walls. "We're under attack! Nuuwa—lots of 'em!"

The shadows blossomed women. Just under half the strength of the troop was there that day, eighteen women counting Sheera.

"Twenty nuuwa!" Denga Rey was saying. "What the hell are that many nuuwa doing in the Thaneland? That's ridiculous! You never see more than a few at a time, and never . . ."

But as she was cursing she was gathering up her weapons. Women were running all around, leaping up the crazy walls under Sheera's shouted commands. Some of them had bows and arrows; others had the heavy, old-fashioned swords. All of them had daggers.

But if you are close enough to use a dagger on a nuuwa, Sun Wolf thought, *it is far too late.*

He could see them now, moving out in the hills. Slumped bodies were creeping along the road, or emerging from the brushy slopes between the hills with a deceptively quick, shambling lope. He felt his hair prickle at the numbers of them. By the First Ancestor of the World, how many were there?

"Somebody make a fire," he ordered, and went scrambling up the slumped remains of a gallery stair to the broken platform above the door. The view from the top turned him sick with dread.

The nuuwa had broken cover from the hills all around and were converging on the tower. Eyeless heads wagged loosely on lolling necks; shoulders were bent so that the creatures' big, claw-nailed hands flopped, twitching, around their knees. The hollows of those eaten-out eye sockets swayed back and forth, as if they still sighted through the scarred-over, fallen flesh. If it were not for the way the nuuwa moved—dead straight, with no consideration for the rise and fall of the ground—they might almost have been mistaken for true men.

Sun Wolf counted almost forty.

From here, he could look down upon all of the Cairn Tower. What remained of the curtain wall that had once surrounded the place lay in a sloppy ring around the oval tower itself. Wall and tower were not concentric—the tower stood at one end, so that its triple-arched doorway, empty of any defensive barrier, looked straight out into the valley. Below him, he could see the women fanning out along the broken top of the curtain wall, the bare flesh of their shoulders and the colors of their hair very bright against the winter drabness of lichenous stone and yellowed weeds and heather. No need to conceal themselves, for nuuwa did not track their prey by sight. No need for strategy, for the nuuwa understood none.

All they understood—all they sought—was flesh.

From the wall, he heard the whining *thwunk* of bowstrings and saw two of the advancing creatures stumble. One of them lumbered to its feet again and came on, the arrow sticking through its neck like a hatpin through a doll; the other staggered a few steps, spouting blood from a punctured jugular, then fell, its grotesquely grown teeth snapping in horrible chewing motions as it tried to wallow its way along. Another of the creatures tripped over it in its advance, then got up and shambled on. Nuuwa—in common with all other predators—would not touch the flesh of nuuwa. The ground was prickled with arrows. Most of the women had terrible aim.

Smoke stung his eyes. Below him in the court, he could see that Gilden had got a fire going—Tisa was gathering up branches, sticks, anything that could be used as torches. Sheera and Denga Rey both had fire in their hands as they stood in the open arches of the door. Nuuwa had just enough instinct to fear the heat of fire. From his vantage point, the Wolf could see that in some fashion they knew that there was no wall at the doorway. Half a dozen were shambling toward the two women who stood in that gap.

He came down from the platform at a run.

Wet mud and pits of last week's thin snowfall scummed the crazy steps. The entire curtain wall must have the same vile footing, he thought. Then he heard it, beyond the higher ruins of the tower. From along the wall, now out of his sight, came the slithering crash of dislodged stone and falling bodies, the hooting grunts of the nuuwa, and the soft, smacking *thunk* of steel biting naked flesh.

He had a torch in one hand and a sword in the other as he sprang up the steps to the empty gateway instants before the nuuwa came lolloping, gape-mouthed, to meet the women. Sheera made the mistake of slashing at the widest target—the breast—and the creature she cut fell on her with a vast, streaming wound yawning in its chest, eyeless face contorted, mouth reaching to bite. The Wolf had decapitated the first creature within range; he spun in the next split second and hacked off both huge hands that gripped Sheera's arm, allowing her to spring back out of range and slash downward on the thing's neck. It was all he had time for—nuuwa were pressing up toward them, heedless of the cut of the steel; spouting blood drenched them, hot on the flesh and running down slippery underfoot. Beside him, he was vaguely aware of Denga Rey, fighting with the businesslike brutality of a professional with sword and torch.

He felt something gash and tear at his ankle, then saw that a fallen nuuwa had sunk its teeth into his calf. He slashed downward, severing the head as it tore at his flesh. Clawed hands seized his sword arm, and he cut at the eyeless face with his torch, setting the matted hair and filthy, falling beard aflame. The creature released him and began shrieking in a rattling, hoarse gasp, blundering against its fellows and pawing at the blaze. Denga Rey, freed for an instant, kicked it viciously back, and it went rolling down the steps, face flaming, howling in death agonies as others stumbled over it to close in on the defenders.

Through the confusion of that hideous fight and the searing agony of the head still clinging doggedly to his calf, Sun Wolf could hear the distant chaos of cries, hoarse grunts, and shrill shouts. He heard a scream, keening and horrible, rising to a fever pitch of rending pain and terror, and knew that one of the women had been overcome and was being killed. But like so many things in the heat of battle, he noted it without much interest, detached, grimly fighting to avoid a like fate himself. Another scream sounded closer, together with a slithering crash of bodies falling from the wall. From the corner of his eye, he saw locked forms writhing on the icy clay of the hall floor, a tangle of threshing limbs and fountaining blood. Eo the blacksmith sprang forward with one of those huge two-handed broadswords upraised as if it were as light as a willow switch. He saw no more; filthy hands and snapping, slobbering mouths pressed close around him. For a moment, he felt as if he were being engulfed in that horrible mob, driven back into the shadow of the empty gateway and wondering where the drop of the steps was.

Then steel zinged near him; as he decapitated one of the things grabbing and biting at him, Denga Rey's sword sliced the spine of another, and it fell, rolling and spasming, at his feet. Those were the last of the immediate attackers. He swung around and saw that the steps were piled knee-deep in twitching bodies, from which a thick current of brilliant red ran down to pool among the rocks. Behind him, the tower was silent, save for a single voice raised in a despairing wail of grief.

The nuuwa were all dead.

He looked down to where the severed head still locked on his calf with a death grip. Fighting a surge of nausea, he bent down and beat at the joint of the jawbone with the weighted pommel of his sword until the jaw broke and he was able to pull the thing off by its verminous hair. Hands shaking, he knelt on the slimy steps and held out his hand for Denga Rey's torch, since his own had been lost in the fight. Reversing it, he drove the flaming end into the wound. Smoke and the stink of burning meat assailed his nostrils; the pain went through his body like a stroke of lightning. Distantly, he was aware of the sound of Sheera's being sick in a corner of the hall.

He flung the torch away and collapsed on his hands and knees, fighting nausea and darkness. It wasn't the first time he had had to do this, from nuuwa or from other wounds, but it never got any easier.

Footsteps pattered on the clay floor. He heard the murmur of voices and opened his eyes to see Amber Eyes binding up Denga Rey's bloody arm with someone's torn, gold-embroidered scarf.

Both women hastened to his side, and Amber Eyes knelt to bandage his wounds. Her hands were sticky with gore. When he had breath to speak, Sun Wolf asked them, "You bitten anywhere?"

"Few slashes," the gladiator said shortly.

"Burn 'em."

"They're not deep."

"I said burn 'em. We aren't talking about sword cuts in the arena; nuuwa are filthier than mad dogs. I'll do it for you if you're afraid."

That got her. She damned his eyes, without malice, knowing he was right. Under her swarthy tan, even she looked pale and sick.

After a quick, brutal cauterization, he helped her to her feet, both of them leaning a little on Amber Eyes for support. They were joined in a moment by a very pallid Sheera, her hair in wet black strings before her eyes. Like theirs, her limbs were plastered in gore. Sun Wolf shook himself clear of Denga Rey and limped to put a gentle hand on her shoulder.

"You all right?"

She was quivering all over, like a bowstring after its arrow was spent. He sensed that it was touch and go whether she would fall on his shoulder in hysterics; but after a moment she drew a deep breath and said huskily, "I'll be all right."

"Good girl." He slapped her comfortingly on the buttock and was rewarded with the kind of glare generally reserved for the humbler sort of insects in their last moments before a servant was called to swat them. He grinned to himself. She'd obviously got over the first shock.

There were no other women in the empty hall. Slowly, limping with the pain of their wounds, the four of them staggered to the narrow postern that let them into the ruined circle of the curtain wall. Like the steps, the ground there was littered with the bodies of dead nuuwa with severed heads and hands and feet. Dark blood dripped down the stones and soaked into the winter-hard ground. At the far end of the court, the women stood in a silent group, staring in nauseated fascination at a tall, rawboned woman named Kraken, who was kneeling, her face buried in her hands, over the dismembered and half-eaten body of sharp, little, red-haired Tamis Weaver. Kraken was rocking back and forth and wailing, a desolate moaning sound, like a hurt animal.

After a moment Gilden and Wilarne moved in, bitten and painted with the blood of their dead enemies, and gently helped Kraken to her feet and led her away. She moved like a blind woman, half doubled over with grief.

Sun Wolf looked around at those who were left. He saw women with scared faces, gray with shock and nausea, the ends of their tangled hair pointy with blood. Some of them had been bitten, clawed, chewed—there'd be more work, burning the wounds, the agonizing aftermath of war. The place stank with that peculiar battleground smell, the vile reek of blood and vomit and excrement, of death and terror. Some of them, like Erntwyff Fish, looked angry still; others, like Sister Quincis and Eo, seemed burned out, as if only cold ash remained of the fire that had carried them alive through battle. Others looked merely puzzled, staring about in confusion, as if they had no idea how they had come to be wounded, exhausted, cold, and sick in this slaughterhouse place. More than one was crying, with shock and grief and relief.

But none of them looked, or would ever again look, quite as they had.

The Wolf sighed. "Well, ladies," he said quietly, "now you've seen battle."

CHAPTER

8

T HE RAIN THAT SLASHED AGAINST THE BOLTED SHUTTERS OF THE Brazen Monkey made a far-off, roaring sound, like the distant sea. With her boots extended toward the enormous blaze that was the only illumination in the shadowy common room, Starhawk scanned the few travelers still on the roads in this weather and decided that she and Fawn would take turns sleeping tonight.

Inns in this part of the mountains were notorious in any event, but during the dry season, when the caravans from Mandrigyn, Pergemis, and the Middle Kingdoms filled even this vast common room to capacity, there was some degree of safety. Most merchants were decent enough fellows, and no traveler would suffer to see another robbed, if only from the knowledge that it could happen to him next. During the rains it was different.

Opposite her, on the other worn and narrow plank bench, an unshaven little man with a loose mouth and a looser eye kept glancing over at Fawn, who stood at the far end of the long room, haggling with the innkeeper. Two others were hunched over pewter mugs of beer and the remains of a haunch of venison at one of the tables, oblivious to their surroundings. The Hawk wasn't prepared to bet on any of their help, if there were trouble.

In a businesslike fashion, she began reviewing exits from the common room and escape routes from the inn.

Down at the other end of the room, Fawn was still nodding, the occasional sweetness of her low voice punctuating the innkeeper's ingratiating whine. They'd been haggling about the price of rooms, food, and supplies for the last fifteen minutes, a protracted process that Fawn was capable of continuing for upward of an hour without ever losing her air of grave interest. The heat of the room was drying her great plaid cloak; in the smoky amber of the firelight, Starhawk could see the steam rising from it, like faint breath on a snowy night.

From Kedwyr, they'd journeyed through the olive and lemon groves of the brown hills to the poorer inland cities of Nishboth and Plegg. Those cities had long ago knuckled under to Kedwyr's dominance and had shrunk to little better than market towns, with their decaying mansions of stone lace and the crumbling ruins of their mosaic cathedrals dreaming of better days. After two days on the road, the rains had hit, freezing winds roaring in from the sea and torrents of black water pouring from the skies, flooding the roads and turning innocuous streams in the barren foothills behind Plegg into boiling, white millraces.

They had climbed toward Gaunt Pass and the wide road that twisted through the gray spires of the Kanwed Mountains from the East to the Middle Kingdoms. Snow had caught them three days from the pass itself, and for days they had plowed and floundered their way through that icy world of winds and stone, discouraged, exhausted, making sometimes as little as five miles a day. From the pass, they had taken the road along the rim of the mountain mass, with the tree-cloaked shoulders of the main peaks towering thousands of feet above them, invisible in the gray turmoil of clouds.

Through it all, Fawn had never complained and had done her loyal best to keep up with Starhawk's surer pace. For all that she had spent the last two years in the soft living of a concubine, she was tough, and the Hawk had to admit that the girl was less trouble than she had at first feared. In Plegg, where they'd sold her jewels, she'd gotten a far better price than Starhawk had expected that sleepy, half-deserted town could have paid; and she'd shown an unexpected flair for bargaining for food, lodging, and fodder for the donkey along the way. Starhawk didn't see how she did it—but then, like most mercenaries, the Hawk had always paid three times the local rate for everything and had never been aware of the difference.

She had asked Fawn about it one night, when they'd been camped in a rock cave above Gaunt Pass, with a fire lighted at the entrance to frighten away wolves. Blushing, Fawn had admitted, "My father was a merchant. He always wanted me to learn the deportment of a lady, to better myself through an elegant marriage, but I knew too much about the cost of things ever to appear really well bred."

The Hawk had stared at her in astonishment. "But you're the most ladylike person I've ever met," she protested.

Fawn had laughed. "It's all the result of the most agonizing work. I'm really a storekeeper at heart. My father always said so."

Fawn came back across the room now, the fire picking smoky streaks of red from the close-braided bands of her dark hair. The greasy little rogue in the inglenook looked up at her, and even the two blockheads at the table raised their noses from their beer mugs as she passed.

"You want to bet you get an offer of free room?" Starhawk asked as Fawn seated herself on the worn, blackened oak of the bench at her side.

"I've already had one, thanks," the girl replied in a low voice and glanced across at the greasy man, who met her eyes and gave her a broken-toothed leer. She looked away, her cheeks even redder than the firelight could have made them. "I've paid for supper, bed, breakfast, bait for the donkey, and some supplies to go on with."

Starhawk nodded. "He have any idea how far to the next inn?"

"Fifteen miles, he says. The Peacock. After that there's nothing until Foonspay, twenty-five miles beyond, and that's a fair-sized village."

The Hawk did some rapid mental calculations. "Tomorrow night in the open, anyway," she said. "Maybe the night after, depending on the road. If this rain turns to snow again, it's going to be hell's own mess."

Movement caught her eye. The greasy little man had shuffled over to the bar, where he stood talking in a low voice to the innkeeper. Starhawk's eyes narrowed.

"Did you ask for the supplies tonight rather than in the morning?"

Fawn nodded. "He said yes, later."

She sniffed. "We'll make damned sure of it, then. I'm going out to the stables to collect the packs. I don't want there to be any reason we couldn't get out of here in the middle of the night if we wanted to."

Fawn looked unhappy, but Starhawk's wariness was legendary in the troop and had more than once saved the lives of scouting parties under her command. She left the common room as quietly as possible, crossing the soup of mud, snow, and driving rain in the yard only after she was fairly certain of the whereabouts of the innkeeper and the slattern who did his cooking. The Brazen Monkey boasted no stableman. Inspecting the interior of the big stone stables built into the cliff that rose from the muck of the inn yard, the Hawk thought the place rather too well stocked and kept for the little traffic they must have had in the last few weeks before these late rains.

She collected all the supplies and equipment except the actual pack-saddle itself, slinging them by straps over her arms and shoulders, and waited in the darkness of the big arched doorway until she saw both the innkeeper's shadow and the woman's cross the lamplight of the half-open door. They'd be going to the common room, with supper for Fawn and herself. Picking her footing carefully, she slipped back into the inn by way of the shadows along the wall and up the twisting stairs to their room.

Seeing the damp and bug-infested mattresses on the two narrow cots, she was just as glad she'd brought up their own bedding. The room itself was freezing cold, and the roof leaked in two places. Nevertheless, she wrestled the bolt of the shutters back and looked out into the streaming darkness of the night. A foot or so below the sill of the window, the thatch of the kitchen roof was swimming like a hay meadow in a flood, steam rising from it with the heat below. Satisfied, she closed the shutters again, but did not bolt them; she checked the door bolt, shoved the supplies well under the beds, and went downstairs.

The greasy little man was leaning against the table, talking to an unhappy-looking Fawn. Starhawk crossed the room to them, looked him up and down calmly, and asked, "You invite this cheesebrain to supper, Fawnie?"

The man started to sputter some kind of explanation. Starhawk looked him in the eyes, calculating, fixing his features in her mind to know again. His eyes shifted. Then he ducked his head and hastily left the room, the rain blowing in from the outside door as it opened and shut again behind him.

Starhawk slid onto the bench opposite Fawn and applied herself to venison stew and black bread.

Fawn sighed. "Thank you. I couldn't seem to get rid of him . . ."

"What did he want?" the Hawk asked, around a mug of beer.

"He came over and offered to tell me about the road ahead. And I —I thought he sounded as if he knew what he was talking about, but I couldn't be sure."

"More likely he's trying to find out which way we're going and where we'll be by dark tomorrow night. How much did that robber want for the kennel he's stuck us in?"

As Starhawk hoped, Fawn cheered up at that. She'd talked the inn-keeper down to half the asking price; recounting it brought a sparkle to her soft eyes. They spoke of other inns and innkeepers, of bargaining and prices, swapping stories of some of the more outrageous payments that Sun Wolf or other mercenaries they'd known had either asked or been offered. Neither spoke of their destination or of what they would do when they reached the impenetrable walls of Altiokis' Citadel; by tacit consent, each kept her own hope and her own fear to herself.

In time, another man came down from upstairs, a wizened, spade-bearded little cricket in black who looked like a decayed gentleman from one of the more down-at-heels cities of the Peninsula with his starched neck ruff and darned, soot-gray hose. He settled himself beside the two blockheads in the padded coats who were drinking ale and talking in quiet voices; eventually they all went upstairs to bed.

Starhawk became uncomfortably aware of how her voice and Fawn's echoed in the empty common room and how dark were the shadows that clotted under its smoke-blackened rafters. Outside, the wind groaned louder over the rocks. Its sound would cover that of anyone's approach.

She was glad enough to leave the hall. By the light of a feeble tallow dip, she and Fawn climbed the narrow corkscrew of stairs to the cold room under the rafters.

"Well, these beds will have a use, after all," she commented wryly as she dropped the door bolt into its slot. Fawn laughed and pulled one end of the heavy log frame away from the wall. "Not like that— here. We'll lift. No sense telling that old cutthroat downstairs what we're doing."

It was a struggle to barricade the door quietly. Halfway through their task, a sound arrested the Hawk's attention; she held up her hand, listening. The inn walls were thick, but it sounded as if others in the place had the same idea.

Fawn unrolled her bedding along the wall where the bed had been, carefully arranging it to avoid the major leaks in the roof. "Do you really think they'll try to rob us in the night?" Her voice had gotten very quiet; her eyes, in the flickering light of the already failing dip, had lost the ebullience they'd shown downstairs. Her face looked shadowed and tired. Starhawk reflected that for all her bright courage, Fawn did not travel well. She looked worn down and anxious.

"I almost hope so," the Hawk replied quietly. She blew on the flame, and the room was plunged into inky darkness. "I'd far rather deal with it here than on the road tomorrow."

Silence settled over the inn.

Between her travels, wars, and the long watches of ambush, the Hawk had developed a fairly clear estimate of time. At the end of about three hours, she reached over and shook Fawn awake, talked to her in the darkness for a few minutes to make sure that she *was* awake, then lay back and dropped at once into the light, wary, animal sleep of guard dogs and professional soldiers. She surfaced briefly when the rain lightened an hour and a half later; she heard the drumming of it fade to a soft, restless pattering in the dark, like tiny feet running endlessly across the leaky thatch, and, below that sound, the soft murmur of Fawn's voice, whispering the words of an old ballad to herself to keep awake and pass the time. Then she slept again.

She wakened quickly, silently, and without moving, at the urgent touch of Fawn's hand on her shoulder. She tapped the knuckles lightly to show herself awake and listened intently for the sounds that had alerted the girl to danger.

After a moment, she heard it: the creak of a footstep on the crazy boards of the hall. It was followed by the sticky squeak of wet leather and the clink of a buckle. But more than any single clue, she could sense, almost feel, the weight and warmth and breath gathered in the darkness outside their door.

Starhawk sat up, reached to where her sword lay beside her on the dirty floor, and drew its well-oiled length without a sound. With luck, she thought, Fawn would remember to have her dagger ready; she wasn't going to warn anyone that they were awake by asking aloud.

A single crack of light appeared in the darkness, a thin chink from the yellowish glow of a tallow dip. In the utter darkness, even that dim gleam was bright as summer sun. Then she heard the scraping of a fine-honed dagger being slid through the door crack under the bolt, pushing it gently up. There was a soft, distinct *plunk* as it dropped backward out of its slot. Then came another long and listening silence.

Fawn and the Hawk were both on their feet. Fawn moved back toward the window, as they had previously agreed; Starhawk stepped noiselessly toward the barricaded door. The slit of light widened, and bulky shadows became visible beyond. There was a jarring vibration, followed by a soft-voiced curse, rotting their eyes for a pair of impudent sluts. A heavy shoulder slammed against the wood, and the barricading bed grated and tipped back as the huge shape of a man slid sideways through the narrow gap.

The door opened inward and to the right. The intruder had to enter left shoulder first. Killing him was as easy as sticking a frog. He gasped as the sword slid in, and his knees buckled; there was the stink and splatter of blood, and Starhawk sprang back as others slammed and pushed the door in, cursing furiously, falling over the body and the bed, and dropping the light in the confusion. The Hawk went in silently, hacking and thrusting; voices shouted and cursed. Steel bit her leg. She thought there were three still living, blundering around in the darkness like blind pigs in a pit.

Then she heard Fawn scream, and a man's heavy rasp of breathing where she guessed the girl would be. A body tangled with hers, hands grappling her legs and pulling her off balance. A hoarse voice yelled, "Over here! I got one!" She cut downward at the source of the voice, then swung in a wide circle with her sword and felt its tip snag something that gasped and swore; the man pulled her down, clutching and grappling, too close now for the sword to be of use. She dropped it, hacking with her dagger; then light streamed in over them, and more men came thundering in from the hall.

The light showed the raised knife of the man who clutched her thighs, and Starhawk cut backhand as he turned his head toward the newcomers, opening both windpipe and jugular and spraying herself in a hot fountain of blood. The first man through the door tripped over the corpse there, then the bed; the second man clambered straight up over all three, his huge bulk blotting the light, and threw himself like an immense lion on the only bandit left standing. He knocked the man's blade aside with a backhand blow that would have stunned a horse, caught him by the throat, and slammed his head back against the stone wall behind with a hideous crunch. Then he swung around, his square, heavy-jawed face pink and sweating in the faint gleam of brightness from the hall, as if seeking new prey. Past him, Starhawk saw Fawn standing flattened against the wall by the shuttered window, her face white and her disheveled clothing smeared with dark blood. There was a dagger in her hand and a gutted robber still twitching and sobbing at her feet.

The big newcomer relaxed and turned to the jostling scramble of his companion in the doorway. "Don't drop the light, ye gaum-snatched chucklehead," he said. "We're behind the fair." One step took him to Fawn. "Are you hurt, lass?"

The man who'd tripped unraveled himself from the trampled remains of the collapsed bed and stumbled again over the dead bandit in his hurry to reach Starhawk, who was still sitting, covered with blood and floor-grime, beneath her slaughtered assailant. He knelt beside her, an even bigger man than the first one, with the same lock of brown hair falling over grave, blue-gray eyes. "Are ye hurt?"

Starhawk shook her head. "I'm fine," she said. "But thank you."

Much to her surprise, he lifted her to her feet as if she'd been a doll. "We'd have been sooner," he said ruefully, "but for some shrinking violet's wanting to barricade our door . . ."

"Violet yourself," the other man retorted, in the burring accent of the Bight Coast. "If we'd been the first ones they attacked, you'd have been glad enough for the warning and delay—if the sound of their shoving over the bed had waked you at all."

The bigger man swung about, like a bullock goaded by flies. "And what makes you think any bandit in the mountains is something you and I together couldn't handle without even troubling to wake up?"

"You sang a different tune night before last, when the wolves raided—"

"Ram! Orris!" a creaky voice chirped from the doorway. The two behemoths fell silent. The scrawny little gentleman in the starched ruff whom Starhawk had seen briefly down in the common room came scrambling agilely over the mess in the doorway, holding aloft a lantern in one hand. The other hand was weighted down by a short sword, enormous in the bony grip. "You must excuse my nephews," he said to the women, with a courtly salaam appallingly incongruous with the gruesome setting. "Back home I use them for a plow team, and thus their manners with regard to ladies have been sadly neglected."

He straightened up. Bright, black eyes twinkled into Starhawk's, and she grinned at him in return.

"Naagh . . ." Ram and Orris pulled back hamlike fists threateningly at this slur on their company manners.

The little man disregarded them with sublime unconcern. "My name is Anyog Spicer, gentleman, scholar, and poet. There is water in the room next to us, since I'm sure ablutions are in order . . ."

"First I'm going to find that damned innkeeper, rot his eyes," Starhawk snapped, "and make sure he doesn't have any other bravos hiding out around here." She looked up and saw that Fawn's face had gone suddenly from white to green. She turned to the immense man who still hovered at her side. "Take Fawn down to your room, if you would," she said. "I'll get some wine when I'm in the kitchen."

"We've wine," the big man—Ram or Orris—said. "And better nor what this place stocks. I'll come with you, lassie. Orris, take care of Miss Fawn. And see you don't make a muff of it," he added as he and Starhawk started for the door.

Orris—the handsomer of the two brothers and, Starhawk guessed, the younger by several years—raised sharply back-slanted dark eyebrows. *"Me* make muff of it?" he asked as he gently took Fawn's arm and removed the dagger that she still held in her nerveless hand. "And who fell over his own big feet blasting into the room like a bull through a gate, pray? Of all the gaum-snatched things . . ."

"Be a fair desperate gaum would take the time to find your wits to snatch 'em . . ."

Starhawk, who sensed that the brothers would probably argue through battle and world's end, caught Ram's quilted sleeve and pulled him determinedly toward the door.

There were no more bandits at the inn. They found the innkeeper, disheveled and groaning, in the room behind the kitchen, amid a tangle of sheets in which he said he had been tied after being overpowered. But while he was explaining all this at length to Ram, Starhawk had a look at the torn cloth and found no tight-bunched creases, such as were made by knots. The woman said sullenly that she had locked herself in the larder from fear of them. Both looked white and shaken enough for it to have been true, but Starhawk began to suspect that by killing the bandits, she had demolished the couple's livelihood. She smiled to herself with grim satisfaction as she and Ram mounted the stairs once more.

"You're no stranger to rough work, seemingly," Ram said, his voice rather awed.

Starhawk shrugged. "I've been a mercenary for eight years," she said. "These were amateurs."

"How can you tell?" He cocked his head and gazed down at her curiously. "They looked to me as if they were born with shivs in their fists."

"A professional would have put a guard on your door. And what in the hell does 'gaum-snatched' mean? That's one I never heard before."

He chuckled, a deep rumble in his throat. "Oh, it's what they say to mean your wits have gone begging. Gaums are—what you call?— dragonflies; at least that's what we call 'em where I come from. There are old wives who say they'll steal away a man's wits and let him wander about the country until he drowns himself walkin' into a marsh."

Starhawk nodded as they turned the corner at the top of the stair and saw light streaming out of one of the rooms halfway down the hall. "In the north, they say demons will lead a man to his death that way—or chase him crying to him from the air. But I never heard it was dragonflies."

They came to the slaughterhouse room. By the light of the lamp she'd appropriated from the kitchen, Starhawk saw that the greasy little man who'd spoken to Fawn was the one Orris had brained. It was a good guess, then, that the innkeeper had indeed been in league with them. Ram jerked his head toward the door as they passed it. "What about them?"

"We'll let our host clean up," Starhawk said callously. "It's his inn— and his friends."

Orris and Uncle Anyog had moved the women's possessions to their own room while Ram and the Hawk were reconnoitering. Beds had been made up on the sagging mattresses. Fawn was asleep, her hair lying about her in dark and careless glory on the seedy pillow. By the look of his boots, Uncle Anyog had been investigating the stables. He reported nothing missing or lamed.

"Meant to do that after we'd been settled," Starhawk said, collecting spare breeches, shirt, and doublet from her pack and preparing to go into the next room to wash and change. "Maybe they didn't mean to take you three on at all. If you asked after the two of us, the innkeeper could always tell you we'd departed early."

"Hardly that," Orris pointed out. "Else we'd overtake you on the road, wouldn't we?"

"Depends on which direction you were going in."

In the vacant room, she took a very fast, very cold damp-cloth bath to get the dried blood out of her flesh and hair, cleaned the superficial gash on her leg with wine and bound it up, and changed her clothes. When she returned to the brothers' room, Uncle Anyog was curled up asleep on the floor in a corner; Ram and Orris were still talking quietly, arguing over how good a bargain they'd really gotten on some opals they'd bought from the mines in the North. Starhawk settled herself down with a rag, a pan of water, and a bottle of oil, to clean her weapons and leather before moving on. The night was far spent and she knew she would sleep no more.

Orris finished pointing out to his brother some facts about the fluctuation in the price of furs and how opals could be held for a rise in prices—neither argument made any sense to Starhawk—and turned to her to ask, "Starhawk? If you don't mind my asking—which direction were you bound in, you and Miss Fawn? It's a rotten time to be on the roads at all, I know. Where were you headed?"

"East," the Hawk said evasively.

"Where east?" Orris persisted, not taking the hint.

She abandoned tact. "Does it matter?"

"In a way of speaking, it does," the young man said earnestly, leaning forward with his hands on his cocked-up knees. "You see, we're bound for Pergemis, with a pack train of fox and beaver pelts and opals and onyx from the North. We've met trouble on the road before this—the man we took with us was killed five nights ago by wolves. If there's more trouble with bandits along the way, we stand to lose all the summer's profits. Now, I make no doubt you're a fighter, which we could do with; and neither of us is so bad at it himself, which Miss Fawn could do with. If you were bound toward the south . . ."

Starhawk hesitated a moment, then shook her head. "We aren't," she said. Pergemis lay where the Bight washed up against the feet of the massive tablelands that surrounded the Kanwed Mountains, far to the southwest of Grimscarp. She continued, "But our road lies with yours as far as Foonspay. That will get us out of the mountains and out of the worst of the snow country. If you have no objection, we'll join you that far."

"Done," Orris said, pleased; then the light died from his honest, slab-sided face, and his eyes narrowed. "You're not ever bound for Racken Scrag, are you, lass? It's a bad business, all through that country, mixing with the Wizard King."

"So I've heard," Starhawk replied noncommittally.

When she said no more, but returned to cleaning the blood from the handle of her dagger, Orris grew fidgety and went on. "Two girls traveling about alone . . ."

"Would probably be in a lot of danger," she agreed. "But it happens I've killed quite a few men in my time . . ." She tested the dagger blade with her thumb. "And since I could probably give you five years, I'd hardly qualify as a lass."

"Yes, lass, but . . ."

At this point, Ram kicked him—no gentle effort—and the two brothers relapsed into jovial bickering, leaving Starhawk to her silent thoughts.

In the days that followed, she had cause to be thankful for their partnership, for all that the brothers periodically drove her crazy with their fits of chivalry. Orris never ceased trying to find out the women's destination and objectives, not from any malice but, what was worse, out of the best of intentions to dissuade them from doing anything foolish or dangerous. Starhawk admitted to herself that their journey was both foolish and dangerous, but that fact did not make it any less necessary, if they were going to find and aid Sun Wolf and learn what, if any, designs Altiokis had toward the rest of the troop. Orris' automatic assumption that, having met them only a day or so ago and being completely in ignorance of the reasons for their quest, he was nevertheless better qualified than they to judge its rightness and its possibilities of success alternately amused Starhawk and irritated her almost past bearing.

Likewise, the brothers' good-natured arguments and insults could be carried far past the point of being entertaining. When they weren't poking fun at each other's appearance, brains, or social manners, they joined verbally to belabor Uncle Anyog for his habit of reciting poetry as he walked, for his small size, or for his flights of rhetorical eloquence, all of which Anyog took in good part. Around the campfires in the evenings, the brothers listened, as enthralled as Fawn and the

Hawk were, to the little man's tales of heroes and dragons and to the silver magic of his songs. Years in the war camps had given Starhawk an enormous tolerance for the brothers' brand of bovine wit, but she found herself more than once wishing that she could trade either or both of them for a half hour of absolute silence.

But, she reasoned, hers was not to choose her companions. Noisy, busy blockheads like the brothers and the hyperloquacious Anyog were far preferable to travelling through the mountains in winter alone.

The Peacock Inn, when they reached it, was deserted, with snow drifting through the windows of its shattered common room. In the stable, Starhawk discovered the bones of a horse, chewed, broken, and crusted with frost, but clearly fresh; the splintered shutters and doors of the ground floor had scarcely been weathered. With thick powder snow squeaking under her boots, she waded back across the yard. In the common room, she found Fawn and Uncle Anyog, huddled together, looking uneasily about them and breathing like dragons in the fading daylight. Orris and Ram came down the slippery drifts of the staircase.

"Nothing abovestairs," Orris reported briefly. "The door at the top's been scratched and pounded, but no signs that it was forced. Whatever's done this, it's gone now; but we'd probably be safer spending the night up there."

"Will the mules go up the steps?" Starhawk asked. She told them what she'd found in the stables. There were six mules, besides her own little donkey.

Orris started to object and lay out a schedule for double watches on the stable, but Ram said, "Nay, we'd best have 'em up with us. If any ill fell to 'em, we'd be fair put to it between here and Foonspay, never mind leaving behind the pelts and things."

It was a stupid and ridiculous way to spend an evening, Starhawk thought, shoving and coaxing seven wholly recalcitrant creatures up into the chambers usually reserved for their social superiors. Uncle Anyog helped her, with vivid and startlingly elaborate curses—the elderly scholar was more agile than he looked—while Orris and Ram set to with shovels to clear a place around the hearth for cooking, and Fawn gathered straw bedding in the stables and kindling in the yard.

As night settled over the frozen wastes of the mountains and they barricaded themselves into the upper storey of the inn, Starhawk found herself feeling moody and restless, prey to an uneasy sense of danger. The brothers' boisterousness did nothing to improve her temper, nor did the grave lecture Orris gave her on the necessity for them all to keep together. As usual, she said nothing of either her apprehension or her irritation. Only Ram glanced up when she left early for her watch. Fawn and Orris were too deeply immersed in a lively discussion of the spice trade to notice her departure.

The silence of the dark hallway was like water after a long fever. She checked the mules where they were stabled in the best front bedroom, then followed the feeble glow of the tallow dip to the head of the stairs, where Uncle Anyog sat before the locked door.

His bright eyes sparkled as he saw her. "Ah, in good time, my warrior dove. Trust a professional to be on time for her watch. Are my oxen bedded down?"

"You think Orris would shut his eyes when he has an audience to listen to his schemes for financing a venture to the East?"

Though she spoke with her usual calm, the old man must have caught some spark of bitterness in her words, for he smiled up at her wryly. "Our pecuniary and busy-handed child." He sighed. "All the way from Kwest Mralwe, through the woods of Swyrmlaedden, where the nightingales sing, through the golden velvet hills of Harm, and across the snow-shawled feet of the Mountains of Ambersith, he favored me with the minutest details of the latest fluctuations of the currency of the Middle Kingdoms." He sighed again with regret. "That's our Orris. But he is very good at what he is, you know."

"Oh, I know." Starhawk folded her long legs under her and sat beside him, her back braced against the stained plaster of the wall. "To make a great deal of money, a person has to think about money a great deal of the time. I suppose that's why, in all the years I've been paid so handsomely, I'm never much ahead. No mercenary is."

The salt-and-pepper beard split in a wide smile. "But you are far ahead of them in the memory of joy, my dove," he said. "And those memories are not affected by currency fluctuations. I was an itinerant scholar all over the world, from the azure lagoons of Mandrigyn to the windy cliffs of the West, until I became too old and they made me be an itinerant teacher, instead—and I've been paid fortunes by universities of Kwest Mrawle and Kedwyr and half the Middle Kingdoms. Now here I am, returning in my old age to be a pensioner in my sister's house in Pergemis, to stay with a girl whose only knowledge ever lay in how to add, subtract, and raise big, wayfaring sons." He shook his head with a regret that was only partially self-mockery. "There is no justice in the world, my dove."

"Stale news, professor." The Hawk sighed.

"I fear you're right." Uncle Anyog extended one booted toe to nudge the stout wood of the door. "You saw the marks on the other side?"

She nodded. Neither Ram nor Orris had identified them. She herself had seen their like only once before, as a small child. "Nuuwa?"

He nodded, the stiff white petals of his ruff bobbing, catching an edge of the light like an absurd flower. "More than one, I should say. Quite a large band, if they were capable of breaking into the inn."

Starhawk's face was grave. "I've never heard of them running in bands."

"Haven't you?" Anyog leaned forward to prick up the tallow dip that sat in a tin cup between them on the floor. His shadow, huge and distorted, bent over him, like the darkness of some horrible destiny. "They get thicker as you go east—didn't you know? And they've been seen in bands since early last summer in all the lands around the Tchard Mountains."

She glanced sideways at him, wondering how much he knew or guessed of her destination. Down below in the inn, she could hear the soft scrabbling noises of foxes and weasels quarreling over the garbage of dinner. For some reason, the sound made her shudder.

"Why is that?" she asked, when the silence had begun to prickle along her skin. "You're a scholar, Anyog. What are nuuwa? Is it true that they used to be men? That something—some sickness—causes them to lose their eyes, to change and distort as they do? I hear bits and pieces about them, but no one seems to know anything for certain. The Wolf says that they used to appear only rarely and singly. Now you tell me that they're coming out of the East in big bands."

"The Wolf?" The little man raised one tufted eyebrow inquiringly.

"The man I'm—Fawn and I—are seeking," Starhawk explained unwillingly.

"A man, is it?" the scholar mused, and Starhawk unaccountably felt her cheeks grow warm.

She went on hastily. "In some places I know, they say that a man has only to walk out in the night air to become a nuuwa; I think your nephews' tale about gaums—dragonflies—may have something to do with it. Not true dragonflies, but perhaps something that looks or moves like them. But no one knows. And I'm beginning to find that fact in itself a little suspicious."

He looked sharply across at her, his dark eyes suddenly wary. Starhawk met his gaze calmly, wondering why she had the momentary impression that he was afraid of her. Then he looked away and folded his fine little hands around his bony knees. "A wizard might know," he said, "were there any left."

The memory came back to her of the eyeless, mewing thing that had beaten and chewed at the Convent gates; she remembered Sister Wellwa, flinging fire from her knotted hands, and a sliver of mirror angled in the corner of a room. She recalled Little Thurg's speaking to a man who was not what he seemed.

"Anyog," she said slowly, "in all of your travels—have you ever heard of other wizards besides Altiokis?"

The silence stretched, and the flickering gleam of the tallow dip outlined the scholar's profile in an edge of gold as he continued to look steadily away from her into the darkness. At length he said, "No. None whom I have ever found."

"Are there any yet alive?"

He laughed, a soft, cracked little chuckle in the dark. "Oh, there are. There are said to be, anyway. But those who are born with the Power have more sense than to say so these days. If they learn any magic at all, they're careful to make their staffs into little wands that can be hidden up their sleeves, if they're men, or concealed as broom handles. There's even a legend about a wizard who hired herself out as governess to a rich man's children and who kept her staff hidden as the handle of her parasol."

"Because of Altiokis?" Starhawk asked quietly.

The old man sighed. "Because of Altiokis." He turned back to her, the dim, uncertain glimmer making his face suddenly older, more tired, scored with wrinkles like the spoor of years of grief. "And in any case, there are fewer and fewer wizards who have crossed into the fullness of their power. They have the little powers, what they can be taught by nature or by their masters, if they have them—or so I've heard. But few these days dare to attempt the Great Trial—even such few as are left who remember what it was."

He got to his feet, dusting the seat of his breeches, his scrawny body silhouetted against the dim light from the room where Ram and Orris

were arguing over the time it took to sail from Mandrigyn to
Pergemis in the summer trading.

"And what was it?" Starhawk asked curiously, looking up at Anyog
as he flicked straight the draggled lace at his cuffs.

"Ah. Who knows? Even to admit knowledge of its existence puts a
man under suspicion from Altiokis' spies, whether he knows anything
about wizardry itself or not."

He strolled off down the hall, wiry and awkward as some strange
daddy longlegs, whistling an air from some complex counterpoint so-
nata in the dark.

CHAPTER

 9

"*I* DON'T LIKE IT." STARHAWK FROWNED AS SHE STUDIED THE town below her.

Beside her, Ram folded his great arms against him for warmth. In his wadded layers of purple quilting, he looked immense, his blunt, homely face reddened by the cold. "It all seems quiet," he objected doubtfully.

Starhawk's gray gaze slid sideways at him. "Very quiet," she agreed. "But not one of those chimneys is smoking." She pointed, and a stray flake of mealy snow, shaken from the pine boughs overhead, settled into the fleece of her cuff. "This snow fell two nights ago, and nothing's tracked it since—not in the street, nor from any of those houses to the sheds behind."

Ram frowned, squinting. "You're right, lass. Your eyes are keener than mine, but 'twas stupid of me not to look. There are tracks round about the walls, aren't there?"

"Oh, yes," Starhawk said softly. "There are tracks." She turned back, scrambling down from the promontory that overlooked the little valley in which lay the village of Foonspay. Her feet slid in the slick powder of the snow; even though she stepped in her own tracks, the going was rough. Ram lost his balance twice, falling amid great clouds of billowing powder; nevertheless, he offered her his arm for support with dogged gallantry at every swell of the ground.

—

Snow had fallen the night they had spent at the Peacock Inn, then rain and more snow. The road, such as it was, had become crusted and treacherous, and they had lost most of a day floundering through it, exhausted by the mere effort of taking a step. Around them, the woods had lain in silence, a silence that prickled along Starhawk's nerves. She had found herself listening, seeking some sound—any sound. But no squirrel had dislodged snow from the green-black branches of the somber pines overhead; no rabbit had squeaked in the teeth of a fox. For two nights, not even wolves had howled; in her scouting to both sides of the buried road, Starhawk had seen no track of any bird or beast.

There was something abroad in the woods, something before which even the wolves ran silent.

The others felt it, too. Up ahead, she could see the six mules and the donkey as dark blobs on the marble whiteness of the snow, the vivid blue of Orris' quilted jacket, Anyog's rusty black, and Fawn's green and brown plaid—a tight little cluster of colors, huddled together in fear. They all jumped when she and Ram emerged through the trees.

"The town's deserted," she said as she came near.

"The buildings are standing, but the Mother only knows what's prowling around them. Let's get into the open. Then I'll take Ram and go ahead to scout the place."

The brothers nodded their agreement, but she saw the doubt in their faces—Orris because, deep down in his heart, he believed that he should be giving the orders, in spite of the fact that he knew Starhawk to be his superior in matters of defense, Ram because he knew it, too, and considered it an unseemly thing for a woman to be.

She supposed, as she led the way cautiously down the gentle slope of the road, that most women would have been pleased and flattered by the big man's protectiveness. She merely found it irritating, as if he assumed her to be unable to protect herself—and all the worse because it was both unconscious and well meaning. Sun Wolf, she reflected, glancing over her shoulder at the unnaturally silent woods, would help her out of trouble, but assumed that she could hold up her end of the fight just fine.

She scanned the sky, which was darker than the time of day could account for, then looked over her shoulder again—a habit she'd picked up these days. Ahead of them, the stone walls and snow-laden roofs of the town grew larger, and she ran her eye over them, searching for some sign, some mark. Her back hackled with nervousness. The shutters of several buildings had been broken and scratched, the marks yellow against the gray of weathering. She stumbled, her feet sliding and breaking through the crusts of the snow, and she gripped the headstall of the mule she led for balance. Behind her, the others were doing the same. The world was silent but for the hiss of Orris' cursing and the crunching of hooves and boots in the snow. The dark buildings seemed to stare at them with shadowy eyes through the mauve-tinted twilight.

Orris' voice sounded hideously loud. "You want to scout that great house there in the center of town? The door's shut and the shutters are intact. There'll be room for us there and for the beasts as well."

"Looks good," Starhawk agreed. "Ram—"

The mule beside her jerked its head free of her hold and reared up with a piercing squeal. Starhawk swung around, scanning the silent crescent of trees at their backs.

It came lumbering from the woods with that queerly staggering gait, the eyeless head lolling on the weaving neck. Starhawk yelled, "Nuuwa!" even as Orris cried out, pointing—pointing as three more shambling forms dragged themselves from the crusted brush of the surrounding woods. Starhawk swore, though she had known from what Anyog had said at the Peacock that there might be several of them, and flung Anyog the lead rein of the mule. "Make for the big house!" she called to the others. "And for God's sake . . ."

Then she saw something else, a floundering in the brush all around the edges of the woods, and she heard Anyog whisper, "Holy Three!"

Fawn screamed.

Starhawk had never seen that many nuuwa together. There were twenty at least, floundering through the snow at a jagged lope, their misshapen arms swinging for balance. She plunged after the rest of the party, moving as fast as she dared, her boots breaking through the buried crusts of the snow, panic heating her veins like cheap brandy. Her memories threw up at her the child she had been, fleeing screaming toward the Convent walls with the groaning, mouthing thing slobbering at her heels—merging with the creatures that pursued her now. There was a hideous slowness to the flight, like running in a dream. The nuuwa fell and rose and fell again, lunging toward them with a terrible inexorability. As in a dream, she could see every detail of them with preternatural vividness—the deformed, discolored teeth in the gaping mouths, the rotted eye sockets seared over with dirty scar tissue, the running sores that blotched the flabby flesh.

Ahead of her, Fawn fell for the tenth time; Ram dragged her to her feet and fell himself. Starhawk, stopping to let them remain ahead of her, cursed them for a pair of paddle-footed oafs and calculated that, if they slowed the flight much more, none of them would make it to safety.

The walls bulked up like cliffs; she could see the scattered bones of humans and animals half covered with snow in the streets. She guessed that the nearest nuuwa, the ones lumbering directly behind her, were some hundred feet to the rear, their groaning yammer and the slurpy bubble of their breath seeming to fill her ears. She thought of turning and fighting. Once she stopped, she'd draw them, and the others would go on . . .

Rot that, she thought indignantly. *I'm not a piece of meat to be thrown to wolves . . .*

Great Mother, but I know what is!

She yelled, "Anyog, stop! Stop!"

Not only the old man but the whole train checked, the mules plunging and screaming on their leads. Fawn slipped again and fell to her knees in the deep snow. Starhawk yelled, "The rest of you go on! Anyog, bring back one of those mules! *Now!*"

"What is it you're after doing . . ." Orris began.

Arguing, Great Mother! Starhawk thought with what horrified indignation was left her. "Rot your eyes, *get running!*" she screamed at them.

"But . . ."

"MOVE!"

Anyog was already beside her, hauling one of the screaming, pitching animals by its lead. For a moment, it was touch and go whether Orris would get them all killed by continuing the discussion, but the closing ring of nuuwa around him seemed to decide him. He threw his whole weight against the headstalls of the mules he led. Ram dragged Fawn to her feet, fighting their way along like a pair of wallowing drunks.

Gasping, his face under its little spade beard as white as his bedraggled ruff, Anyog managed to get the mule within Starhawk's range. The nearest nuuwa were thirty feet away, howling as they slithered in the snow, drool foaming from their lips. The Hawk stabbed her sword point-down in the snow, whipped the dagger from her belt, and grabbed the mule's headstall. Anyog realized what she was doing and added his own weight to bring the thrashing head down. The mule reared, and the steel bit deep into the great vein of the neck.

She'd shoved the gory dagger back into its sheath and pulled her sword free before the beast even fell. It rolled to the ground, heaving in its death agony, crimson spouting everywhere, searingly bright against the snow. She and Anyog plunged back in the direction of the town, Anyog going like a gazelle for two steps before he outraced his own balance and went down in a sprawling heap of bones.

Starhawk saw him fall from the corner of her eye; at the same time she saw the first nuuwa fall slavering on the screaming mule. The stink of the fresh blood drew the creatures; they were already tearing hunks of the live and steaming flesh from the mule where it lay. Anyog scrambled to his feet, neither calling out to her nor asking her to stop, and floundered after her. They were past the time when one could wait for the other. That would only mean that they would die together.

She heard the nuuwa mewing and wheezing behind her and the scrunch of those staggering feet in the snow. She caught them in her peripheral vision—one near enough to overtake her before she reached the black cliff of the building, two others farther back. She braced her feet and whirled, her sword a flashing arc in the wan twilight.

The nuuwa fell back from the slicing blade, blood and guts dripping down from the slit in its abdomen. Then it flung itself on her again, mouthing and grabbing and tripping over its own entrails, as another came lumbering up from the side. Others were close, she thought as she dispatched the first one. An instant's delay would have them all on her. Two fell upon her simultaneously. As she severed the head of the one in front, the weight of the second struck her back, the stink of it overwhelming her as the huge teeth ripped at the leather of her coat. She twisted, hacking, fighting the frenzy of panic at the slobbering thing that rode her. Distantly, she could hear Anyog's despairing screams. The clawing weight on her back bore her down, unreachable by her sword blade. The hissing, foaming mouth grated on the back of her skull. With a final writhe, she slithered free of her coat, springing clear and running frantically between the houses.

The gray bulk of the largest house in town loomed before her, broken by a black mouth of door with a mill of terrified mules around it. Scrunching footfalls seemed to fill her ears, staggering behind her with whistling gasps of breath. The steps of the house tripped her feet. Orris' voice bawled curses at the mules, and from the corner of her eye, she glimpsed her nearest pursuer—not a nuuwa at all, but Anyog, with one of the foul things clutching at him, clinging and dragging.

It felled him on the steps, almost at Starhawk's feet, the greedy, filthy mouth tearing gouts of flesh from his side. Starhawk sprang down toward them, her sword blazing in the gray murk of dusk, cleaving down like an axe on those writhing bodies. The rest of the nuuwa were six or eight paces behind; she dragged the old man up and flung him to the blurred purple bulk that she knew was Ram. Snapping jaws peeled three inches of leather from her boot-heel as she made it through the door. The slamming of it was like thunder in the empty building.

The nuuwa screamed outside.

They laid Anyog down beside the fire that Fawn managed to kindle in the great hearth of the downstairs hall. As Starhawk had suspected, the place had been the principal inn of Foonspay, and there were signs that much of the population of the village had lived here for several days, crowded together, for protection. While she worked over Anyog with what makeshift dressings she could gather, with needles and thread, boiling water, and cheap, strong wine, she wondered how many of them had been killed before they'd managed to get away, and if they'd made it to safety elsewhere, or had been killed on the road.

Ram and Orris took brands from the raised brick hearth to light their way as they explored the pitch-darkness of the inn corridors while Fawn went to find a place for the mules. Dimly, the hooting grunts of the nuuwa could be heard beyond the thick walls and heavy shutters. Within, all was deathly silent.

It had been said once that wizards were Healers—that their power could cleanse the hidden seeds of gangrene, close the bleeding for the flesh to heal. As she worked, bloodied to the elbows, Starhawk knew that it would take such power to save the old man's life. Against the darkness of his beard, Anyog's face was as colorless as wax, pinched and sunken. Long experience had given her intimate knowledge of the death marks, and she saw them here.

How long she worked she did not know, nor how long, afterward, she sat at the old man's side, watching the colors of the fire play over the colorless flesh of his face. She had no idea where the others were, nor, she thought to herself, did it particularly matter. They had their own concerns, merely in staying alive; it wasn't for her to trouble them with stale news. They must all have known, when they carried the old man in, that he would die.

In time, the thin, cold fingers under hers twitched, and Anyog's creaky voice whispered, "My warrior dove?"

"I'm here," the Hawk said, her voice carefully neutral in the still, firelighted dimness of the room. To hearten him, she said, "We'll turn you over to your sister yet."

There was a thin whisper of laughter, instantly followed by an even thinner gasp of pain. Then he murmured, "And you, my dove?"

She shrugged. "We're going on."

"Going on." The words were no more than the hissing of his breath. "To Grimscarp?"

For a long moment she was silent, sitting with her back to the chipped brickwork of the raised hearth, looking down at the shrunken form that lay among the huddle of stained blankets before her. Then she nodded and said simply, "Yes."

"Ah," he whispered. "What other destination would you hide with such care from our ox team? But they are right," he murmured. "They are right. Do not go there, child. Altiokis destroys that which is bright and pure. He will destroy you and the beautiful Fawnie, for no other reason than that you are what you are."

"Nevertheless, we must go," she said softly.

Anyog shook his head, his dark eyes opening, fever-bright in the firelight. "Don't you understand?" he whispered. "Only another wizard can enter his Citadel, unless to come in as his captive or his slave. Only a wizard can hope to work against him. Without magic of your own, you are helpless before him; he will trap you with illusion and trick you to your own destruction. His power is old; it is deep; it is not the magic of humankind. An evil magic," he murmured, the lids sliding shut once again over the glassy eyes, the flesh around them stained dark and mottled with the sinking of his flesh. "Not to be defied."

Something rustled in the darkness. Starhawk looked up sharply, the cool tension of battle leaping to her heart, but she saw nothing in the impenetrable shadows that loomed in every corner of the vast room. As lightly as a mother who wished not to disturb the sleep of her child, she slipped her hands from beneath Anyog's and stood up, her sword springing almost of itself to her grip, the reflex of long years of war. Yet when she reached the stone archway that led into the hall, she found nothing and heard no sound in the passage beyond.

When she returned to his side, Anyog was asleep, the little white hands that had never done work harder than the making of music or the writing of poems lying as motionless as two bunches of crushed sticks upon the sunken chest. She satisfied herself that a thread of breath still leaked through those white lips, then sat where she had been and gradually let the silence surround her in a kind of despairing peace. She knew that Anyog was right—without the help of a wizard, she could not hope to enter the Citadel or to rescue the Wolf from the Wizard King's toils. In a way, she supposed that she and Fawn had both known it from the first, though neither of them had been willing to admit it; neither had been willing to give Sun Wolf up.

From that silence, she sought the deeper stillness and peace of meditation, focusing her mind upon the Invisible Circle, upon the music that no one could hear. Many of the nuns had looked into fire to begin it; Starhawk was too good a warrior to night-blind herself that way, but she had learned, in her long years as a mercenary, that she could find the starting place in her mind alone.

The fire crackled and whispered in the grate, its unimaginable variations of color playing like silk over the edges of brick and wood and flesh. Starhawk became slowly aware of the air that stirred through the winding corridors of the dark inn, of the stress and weight of the beams where they joined overhead, and of the moldering thatch above, cloaked by the frost-silver of the moon. Her awareness spread out, like water over a flood plain—of the mules, sleeping in the darkness of what had become their stable, of Fawn weeping there, of the weighty tread of the brothers as they explored the inn, of the nuuwa prowling and yammering outside; and of the stars in the distant night.

She was aware when the still air of the room was touched by magic.

It came to her as faint as a thread of half-heard music, but clear, like the scent of a single rose in a darkened room. She had not thought that magic would feel like that. It was nothing like the blaze of thrown fire or the deadly webs of illusion woven by the Wizard King and spoken of in four generations of terrified whispers. It was a very simple thing, like the aura of brightness that had sometimes seemed to cling about old Sister Wellwa—akin to meditation, but moving, rather than still.

She heard the faint, trembling voice of Uncle Anyog, whispering spells of healing in the darkness.

In time, she came out of her meditation. Anyog's muttering voice ran on a bit, then stilled. Without the shift in her consciousness, in her awareness, she might have thought only that he raved with fever, and perhaps he had counted on this. He lay motionless, his open eyes reflecting the embers of the fire like candles in a darkened room. She moved toward him and rested her hand upon his.

"You are a wizard," she said softly, "aren't you?"

A hoarse rattle, like a sob, escaped his throat. "Me? Never." The dry fingers twitched beneath hers, lacking the strength to grip. "At one time I thought—I thought . . . But I was afraid. Afraid of Altiokis—afraid of the Great Trial itself. I ran away—left my master—pretended to love other things more. Music—poems—going in fear lest any suspect. Garnering little pot-bound slips of power, consumed by the dreams of what I might have had."

The fever-bright eyes stared up into hers, brilliant and restless. Overhead, the boards creaked with the brothers' heavy stride. Somewhere in the darkness, a mule whuffled over its fodder. "My warrior dove," he whispered, "what is it that you seek of the Wizard King? What is this dream that I see in your eyes, this dream you will follow to your own destruction in his Citadel?"

Starhawk shook her head stubbornly. "It is not a dream," she replied, her voice low. "He is my chief—Altiokis has him prisoner."

"Ah." The breath ran thinly from the blue lips. "Altiokis. My child, he does not lightly loose what he has taken. Even could you find a wizard—a true wizard—to aid you, you would not live long enough to die at your captain's side."

"Perhaps not," Starhawk said quietly and was silent for a time, staring into the sunken glow of the hearth; the flames were gone, and only the deep, rippling heat of the coals was left, stronger than the fire, but unseen. At length she asked, "And did giving up your dream bring you happiness with your safety, Anyog?"

The withered face worked briefly with pain, then grew still. She thought that he slept, but after a long silence, his lips moved. His voice was thin and halting. "This man whom you seek," he murmured. "You must love him better than life."

Starhawk looked away. The words went through her mind like the grinding of a sword blade in her flesh, shocking and sudden, and she understood that Anyog had spoken the truth. It was a truth that she had hidden from the other warriors of Sun Wolf's troop, from Sun Wolf himself, and from her own consciousness; yet she felt no surprise in knowing that it was true. For years she had told herself that it was the loyalty a warrior owed to a chosen captain, and that, at least, had spared her jealousy toward the Wolf's numerous concubines. From her girlhood, she had known herself plain, and the Wolf had his pick of beautiful girls.

But she was not the only one who loved him better than life.

She closed her teeth hard upon that bitterness and stared dry-eyed into the darkness. Once the thing had been brought into the open, she could not unknow it, but she understood why she had worked to deceive herself almost from the first. Anything was better than the chasm of this despair.

Ram's voice echoed in the inn kitchen, through the half-open door that led into the common room where Starhawk sat. He was saying something to Orris—something about wedging the windows there tighter shut—and Starhawk sighed. Whether her feelings toward Sun Wolf were a soldier's loyalty or a woman's love, whether he ever knew it or was even still alive to care, didn't alter the more immediate fact that she was trapped in an inn with the nuuwa yammering and chewing at the brickwork outside. *First things first,* she told herself wryly, getting to her feet. *There'll be time to mess with love—and magic—if you're alive this time tomorrow.*

She found the brothers conferring in the shadows beside the vast, cold kitchen hearth, the light of Orris' torch throwing reflections like the gleaming eyes of dragons on the copper bottoms of the pans and on the drinking water in the stone basin nearby. The nuuwa could be heard from outside, scratching and mouthing at the window frames, their grunting moans occasionally broken by long, piercing wails. "How is he?" Orris asked.

Starhawk shook her head. "Tougher than he looks," she replied. "I'd have bet he'd be dead by now—and lost my money. All secure here?"

They both looked deeply surprised. Orris recovered himself first and gave his opinion that the shutters would hold. "We've driven wedges in some of the downstairs ones," he added. "God knows there are axes and wedges aplenty in the wood room, though little enough wood. But as to how we're going to get cut of this hole . . ."

"We'll manage," Starhawk said. "If worst comes to worst, we can pack Uncle Anyog on one of the mules and leave the rest of them as bait."

"But the pelts!" Orris protested, horrified. "And the stores! All this summer's trading . . ."

"Mother will kill us," Ram added.

"She'll have to stand at the end of a long line," Starhawk reminded him, jerking her thumb toward the shuttered windows. "Where's Fawnie?"

She found Fawn in the parlor they'd converted to a stable, huddled in the shadows among the unloaded packs of furs, her face buried in her hands. The strangled sounds of her weeping were what had drawn Starhawk, for the room was lightless and the long corridor from the common room almost so. The Hawk stood hidden by the black arch of the doorway, listening to that horribly muffled sound, her instinct to go and comfort the girl's fears forestalled by the new awareness that Anyog's words had brought into consciousness within her mind.

She loved Sun Wolf. Loved him not as a warrior loved a leader, but as a woman loved a man; and she could conceive of loving no man but him.

Her childhood had taught her that love meant the subjection of the will to the will of another. She had seen her mother invariably bow to her father's wishes, for all the love that had been between them. She remembered those girls who had competed in subservience to become her brothers' humble wives, baking their bread, cleaning their houses, giving up the brightness of their youth to bear and care for their sons. She had seen Fawn—and all those other soft, pliant girls before her— girls who had been Sun Wolf's slaves, whether bought with money or not.

There had been times when the Wolf had asked her to do things she did not like. But his requests had never been without a reason, and his reasons had always been honest. From being his student, she had become his friend, perhaps the closest friend he had. For all his easy camaraderie with his men, there was a part of himself that he kept hidden from them, the part of him that argued theology on long winter evenings, or arranged and rearranged rocks in a garden until they fitted his sense of stillness and perfection. To her he had shown that part of himself—to her only.

Yet this girl was his woman.

My rival, Starhawk thought, with a tang of bitter distaste. *Is that what we'll come to, I and this woman with whom I've shared a dozen campfires over the mountains? My companion in danger, who split watches with me and bargained with the innkeepers? Are we going to end up hair-pulling, like a couple of village girls fighting over the affections of one of the local louts?*

The thought was ugly to her, like the base and soiling memories of her older brothers' sweethearts and their cheap subterfuges to gain dances with them at the fairs.

And, for that matter, what has Fawn taken from me? Nothing that I ever would have had. I broke my vows for Sun Wolf and broke my body to learn from him the hard skills of war. I'll never regret doing either of those things— but from the first, he never wanted me for his woman.

Isn't it enough to be counted as his friend?

The woman in her remembered how Fawn had rested her small hands so lightly on the broad shoulders and kissed the thin place at the top of his hair. No, it wasn't enough.

Yet she saw also, with curious clarity, that Fawn had all the things that she herself lacked—gentleness, the capacity to receive love without distrusting the motives of its giver, the yielding softness that complemented the Wolf's overwhelming strength, and the magic garment of her beauty that made her precious in his eyes.

It would be easier, she reflected, *if Fawnie were a spoiled, grasping little bitch. Then, at least, I would know what to feel.* But then, of course, the Wolf would not have chosen her for his own. And she would certainly not have sold all that she had and left safety and comfort to seek him among the dangers of Altiokis' Citadel.

Fawn was eighteen, wretched, and very frightened; it was this, rather than any consideration of Sun Wolf one way or the other, that finally drew the Hawk to her side, to comfort her in awkward and unaccustomed arms.

In spite of her exhaustion, Starhawk slept badly that night after her watch. Anyog's words returned to her, again and again: *You must love him better than life . . . Only another wizard can enter his Citadel . . . Only a wizard . . . His power is old; it is deep . . . An evil magic, not to be defied . . .*

Never fall in love and never mess with magic . . .

In her dreams, she found herself stumbling through tortuous, shadow-haunted hallways, where the trunks of trees forced apart the stones of the crumbling walls and weeds trailed in the water that pooled across the slimy floors. She was seeking for someone, someone who could help her, and it was desperately important that she find him before it was too late. But she had never sought anyone's help before this; her battles she had always fought alone—she did not know the words to call out. In the darkness, she heard Sister Wellwa's neat little footfalls retreating from her, saw the pale gleam of Anyog's starched, white ruff. And behind her from the vine-choked turnings of the corridors, other sounds came to her—blundering bodies and harsh, snuffling breath. She struggled to break the grip of the dream, but she was too tired; the slobbering, mewing sounds in the dark seemed to come closer.

With a great effort, she opened her eyes and saw Fawn sitting on the raised hearth, bending over to catch the words that Uncle Anyog was whispering. The redness of the sunken fire outlined her face in an edge of ruby; her lips looked taut and set. The air of the room was stuffy. Through the muzziness of half sleep, Starhawk heard Ram and Orris making their rounds elsewhere in the inn—soft, blundering noises, bickering voices. Uncle Anyog fell silent, and Fawn reached down to wipe the sweat that beaded his sunken cheeks.

Then she got to her feet and gathered her plaid cloak around her over the white shift that was all that she wore. Her unbound hair glinted with slivers of amber and carnelian in the dying light. Starhawk asked her cloudily, "Where are you going?"

"Just to get some water," Fawn said, putting her hand to the kitchen door.

There was a basin there, Starhawk remembered, her tired mind moving slowly. She'd seen it when she'd spoken to Ram and Orris, standing next to the monstrous darkness of the overhanging chimney . . . the chimney . . .

Her shout of "No!" was drowned in Fawn's scream as the door opened.

She thought, later, that she must have been on her feet and moving even as Fawn cried out. She caught up the blanket as a shield; that and the thick folds of the cloak that Fawn still clutched around her body were enough to entangle the first nuuwa and save Fawn from its ripping rush. The second and third blundered over the struggling, howling monster on the threshold. Starhawk decapitated one even as it plunged at her, then whirled to hack at the other as it ripped a mouthful of flesh from Fawn's arm. The head went bouncing and rolling, the bloody mouth still chewing, the hands clutching at the girl as if it could devour her still.

Starhawk kicked shut the kitchen door and slammed the bolt, catching a vague glimpse of other movement, struggling and flopping, in the vicinity of the hearth.

When she turned back, Ram and Orris were already cutting loose the thing that gripped Fawn. By the light of Ram's torch, it could be seen to be covered with soot that made a blackish muck, mingled with its spouting blood. Fawn was unconscious. For a sickening instant, Starhawk thought that she was dead.

The Wolf will never forgive me . . .

My rival . . .

Was I deliberately slow?

Great Mother, no wonder he says it's unprofessional to love! It makes hash of your fighting instinct!

"They're coming down the chimney," she said. Ram was just standing up. It could not have been more than sixty seconds from the time Fawn had opened the kitchen door. "They'll be all over the roof."

With a quickness astonishing in so huge a man, Ram was at the nearest window, peering through a knot in the shutter at the thin moonlight outside. From within the kitchen, there was a crashing and a vast yammer of sounds; the great bolts of the door sagged suddenly under the heaving weight of bodies.

"Can we break for it?" he demanded, turning back. The dot of moonlight lay like a little coin on his flat-boned, unshaven cheek.

"Are you mad?" Orris demanded hoarsely. "They'll be off the roof and on our backs—"

"Not if we torch the inn."

"Look, you gaum-snatched cully, they'll have left some to guard the doors—"

"No," the Hawk said. She'd rushed to the other side of the room to open the shutter there a crack. The chink of air showed the white snow of the street empty between the blackness of the buildings. "They don't even have the brains to work in concert, as wolves do. Having found a way into the inn, they'll all take it. Listen, they don't even know enough for them all to throw themselves against the door at once or to use the table in there for a ram."

Orris got to his feet, with Fawn limp and white in his arms, except for the spreading smear of crimson on her shift. "By the Three, creatures more witless than my brothers!" he cried. "I never thought to find them."

"You'll find as many of them as you can do with, if you don't stir those moss-grown clubs you've been calling feet all these years," Ram snapped, making a run for the mules' parlor. Starhawk was seizing torches and throwing together bedding, one ear turned always to listen to the growing din in the kitchen. She raked what was left in the woodbox against the kitchen door and picked up a torch from the blaze on the hearth.

"What about Anyog?" Orris demanded, and knelt at the old man's side. "We can't make a litter, nor even a travois . . ."

"Pack him like killed meat, then," the Hawk retorted, having been taken off battlefields that way herself. "He'll die, anyway, if he's left here." Already she could see the hinges of the kitchen door moving under the thrashing weight. Orris stared at her, gape-mouthed with horror. "Rot you, do as I say!" she shouted, as she would at a trooper in battle. "We haven't time to waste!"

Orris scrambled to obey her. *If Anyog is a wizard*, she thought, *Altiokis or no Altiokis, he'll put forth what power he has to stay alive. That's all we can hope for now.*

But just as she was a professional soldier, the brothers were professional merchants and could pack five mules and a donkey with the lightning speed acquired in hundreds of emergency disencampments. In moments, it seemed, the mules were squealing and kicking in the hall, with Orris cursing them and lashing at them with a switch. Ram came running back to Starhawk's side, an axe and wedges from the wood room like toys in his great hands. From the tail of her eye, Starhawk had a glimpse of the long, muffled bundle that was Uncle Anyog tied over the back of one mule and of Fawn, somehow on her feet and wrapped in the old man's rusty black coat, stumbling to open the great outside doors.

Icy air streamed in on them. The ululations of the creatures in the kitchen had grown to fever pitch. The doors were sagging as she and Ram made the rounds of the other parlors. Flame licked upward over the rafters and blazed in the mules' straw that they'd scattered across the floor. The kitchen door was breaking as she flung her torch at it, then raced back through the furnace of the common room to where Ram waited for her, framed against the snowy night beyond.

Half a dozen wedges sealed the doors. As they sprang down the steps to where Orris waited with the mules, the Hawk glanced back to see, silhouetted against the roof flames, the black shapes of the nuuwa, shrieking and screaming like the souls of the damned in the Trinitarian hells.

Nothing challenged them as they made their way from the town. As they wound their way up the road into the mountains beyond, they could see the light behind them for a long time.

CHAPTER

10

"**M**OTHER'S CRYING."

Sun Wolf glanced up at this new, soft voice intruding into the solitude of the rain-wet garden. Sheera's daughter, Trella, who was sitting beside him with the trowel and handrake in her small grip, said automatically, "She isn't either."

The tiny boy who had brought this news picked his way through the damp, turned ground to where the Wolf and the little girl sat on a huge rock; he seemed infinitely careful about not getting mud on his black slippers and hose. Trella, who was six and had been assisting Sun Wolf in his duties as gardener since he had come to Sheera's townhouse, had no such considerations. Her black wool skirts were kilted up almost to her thighs, and two little legs in wrinkled black stockings stuck out over the edge of the rock like sticks.

The boy said nothing, only stared at them both with Sheera's beautiful, pansy-brown eyes.

"Mother never cries nowadays. And Nurse says you're not supposed to suck your thumb like a baby," Trella added, as a clinching argument.

He removed thumb from mouth, but held onto it with his other hand, as if he were afraid it would fall off or dry out if not protected. "She cried when Father died," he said defensively. "And Nurse says you're not supposed to sit on rocks and play with the slaves."

"I'm not playing with him, I'm helping him work," Trella said with dignity. "Aren't I?"

"Indeed you are," Sun Wolf replied gravely, but there was a glitter of amusement in his beer-colored eyes as he regarded Sheera's children.

He seldom saw Graal Galernas, age four; though the boy was physically a miniature Sheera, he was soft, rather timid, and stood very much upon his dignity as the head of the House of Galernas. Trella presumably favored their deceased father; she was a sandy-haired, hazel-eyed, snub-nosed child who stood in awe of no one but her beautiful mother. Sun Wolf had met the two when they'd sneaked away from their nurse to play in the orangery, as was evidently their wont. It was a custom Sheera had never mentioned, and he wondered if she knew. Graal had bored quickly of gardening, but Trella had helped him build the succession houses along the south orangery wall, in the course of which project she had provided him with a surprising and varied assortment of information about Sheera herself.

Now Graal said, "She did too cry when Father died."

Trella shrugged. "She was crying before that. She cried when the messengers came to the house about the battle and she was crying when she got back from Lady Yirth's later that day. And I heard her crying down in the kitchen when she was mulling some wine for Father."

"She never did that," her brother contradicted, still hanging onto his thumb. "We've got servants to mull wine." He was shivering, despite the silver-laced velvet of his tiny doublet; though it had stopped raining some hours ago, the day was cold and the air damp. In the barren drabness of the empty garden, he looked like a dropped jewel against the dirt.

"Well, she did too," Trella retorted. "I was playing in the pantry and I heard her. And then she went up to her room and cried and cried and she was still up there when Father got stomach cramps and died, so there."

Tears flooded the boy's soft eyes, and his thumb returned to his mouth. Around it he mumbled wretchedly, "Nurse says you're not supposed to play in the pantry."

"That was months and months and months ago, and if you tattle, I'll put a snail in your bed." Just to be prepared, she hopped down from the rock and began to hunt for the promised snail. Graal backed hastily away and fled crying toward the house.

Sun Wolf sat, his knees drawn up, on the river-smoothed stone and watched the child go. Then he glanced back at the little girl, still grubbing purposefully about in the loose, turned earth of the rock garden bed he'd been preparing. "He loved your father, didn't he?"

She straightened up, flushed and sullen. "He's just a baby." That, evidently, settled father and brother both.

If they knew so much, the Wolf wondered whether they knew about their mother and Tarrin as well.

He himself would no more have told a child that her father was a collaborator or her mother a slut than he would have whipped a puppy for something it did not do, and for pretty much the same reasons. He looked upon children as young animals, and neither Graal nor Trella seemed to mind this offhand treatment. But his own childhood had taught him that there was very little that men and women would not do to their children.

He wondered what it was that Sheera had gotten from Yirth to put in her husband's mulled wine.

Wind stirred the bare branches of the hedges above the hollow where they worked; silver droplets of rain shook loose over them. Sun Wolf paid the drops no heed—he'd been wet and cold a good portion of his life and thought nothing of it—and Trella, who had been consciously imitating him for some weeks, ignored them as well. The smell of the earth mingled with the damp, musty silence as he arranged and rearranged the smooth, bare bones of the rocks, seeking the indefinable harmony of shape, and it wasn't until much later that Trella broke the silence.

"She isn't crying," she declared. After a moment she added, "And anyway, it's just because that man's here to see her."

"That man," Sun Wolf knew, was Derroug Dru, Altiokis' governor of Mandrigyn.

Sure enough, a short while later he saw the dapper little figure of the governor emerge from the orangery and stroll along the path with a servant to hold a gilt-tasseled umbrella over his head. The family resemblance to Drypettis was marked; both were tiny, but where Drypettis was slender, Governor Derroug Dru was a skinny, crooked little runt, the haughty set of whose head and shoulders dwindled rapidly to weak and spindly legs. One leg was nothing more than a twisted bone cased in silken hose whose discreet padding accentuated, rather than hid, its deformity; he walked with a cane, and Sun Wolf had seen how all of his entourage slowed their steps to match his, not out of courtesy, but out of fear. His thinning brown hair was suspiciously bright around the temples, and his eyes, brown and dissipated, were carefully painted to hide the worst marks of excess. Right now, he had only the one servant with him, but the Wolf knew he usually traveled with a whole shoal of hangers-on and several bodyguards. He was not a man popular in Mandrigyn.

Amber Eyes had told the Wolf that before Altiokis had taken the town, she and her friends used to draw straws, the short straw having to take Derroug. Since he had become governor, his vices had become more open.

Sun Wolf bent his head, smoothing the damp earth around the stones. He heard the tap of the cane and the slightly dragging stride pause on the flagstoned path; he felt the man's eyes on him, hating him for his height. Then Derroug passed on. It was beneath the dignity of the governor of Mandrigyn to notice a slave seriously.

At his elbow, Trella's voice whispered, "I hate him!"

He glanced from the little girl to the elegant figure ascending the terrace steps, a splash of white fur and lilac silks against the mottled grays and moss-stained reds of the back of the house and the startling white of the marble of pavement and pilaster. Sheera never spoke of the governor, but he had come to see her several times since the Wolf had been there, and never when Drypettis was present. Sun Wolf guessed that the little woman ran interference between her brother and her friend—which, totally aside from her former position in the conspiracy, might explain Sheera's attachment to her.

It had begun to rain again. The children's nurse came bustling along the path to scold Trella for being out without a maidservant, for not wearing her veils, for getting her hands dirty, and for consorting with a rough and dirty man. "Speaking to a man alone . . . a fine little trull people will take you for!" she clucked, and Trella hung her head.

Sun Wolf wiped his hands on his patched breeches and said dryly, "I've been accused of a lot of things in my time, woman, but this is the first anyone's ever thought I'd try to corrupt a six-year-old." He did not like the nurse.

She elevated her well-shaped little nose to a slightly more lofty angle than usual and retorted, "It is the principle. A girl cannot learn too young what is beyond the lines of propriety. It appalls me to see what is happening in the town these days—women going barefaced and sitting right out at the counters of public shops like prostitutes in their windows . . . and consorting with prostitutes, too, I shouldn't wonder! That hussy who was here earlier actually had paint on her face! What my old lord would have said . . ."

She retreated down the path, holding the unwilling child close to her skirts, clucking and fluttering to herself about the city's fall from virtue.

Sun Wolf shook his head and gathered up his tools. The rain was the fine, blowing, fitful sort that heralded a heavier storm come nightfall; it plastered his long hair down over his shoulders and soaked quickly through the coarse canvas of his shirt. Still, he stood for a time, studying the rocks where he'd settled them—the smooth granite boulder buried half heeled over, so that the long fissure in its side was visible and it formed a sort of cave underneath, protected by the four smaller stones. The lines of it were right, making a sort of music against the starkness of the liver-colored earth, but he thought that he would have liked to have Starhawk's opinion.

In a way it troubled him, how often that thought had crossed his mind.

He had always known she was a good lieutenant. Not only her skill in taking on and defeating much larger men but also the inhuman cold-bloodedness that she habitually showed the troops put them in awe of her, and that was as it should be. As a leader, he had valued her wary painstakingness and her lucidness in defining problems and solutions. As a man set apart by his position as chief, he had valued her company.

It wasn't until now that he realized how much he simply valued her. On campaign, days or weeks might go by without his seeing her, but he had known she was always there. Now sometimes he would waken in the night and realize that if something went wrong—which he had no doubt that it would—he would never see her again. He had half expected to die in Mandrigyn, but he had never before thought of death in those terms.

It was a dangerous thought, and he pushed it from his mind as he entered the vast brown shadows of the orangery. It was, he thought, what his father had meant when he spoke of going soft—a blurring on the hard edge of a warrior's heart. And why, damn it all? Starhawk wasn't even pretty.

Not what most fools would call pretty, anyway.

Rain beat on the portion of the orangery roof that was not covered by the loft. The great room echoed softly with its dull roaring. In the now-familiar darkness, the few trees that had not been moved out into the succession houses were grouped like sleeping trolls in a corner, concealing the practice hacking-posts. The table still stood at the end of the room near the door that led to his narrow stairs. On an over-turned tub, her head in her hands, staring blindly at the gray boards of the wall, sat Sheera, the heavy wool of her crimson gown falling like a river of blood about her feet.

Her son had been right. She had clearly been crying.

Her eyes, when she raised them as he passed, were red-rimmed and swollen, but he saw her force hardness into them and calm into her face. She said, "How soon can the women be ready to attack the mines?"

"With or without a wizard to help?" he countered.

The tiredness in her face turned to anger, like a flash of lighted blasting powder, and she opened her mouth to snap something at him.

"A real wizard, not the local poison monger."

The red lips closed, and the hard lines that he had lately seen so often carved themselves from the flared nostrils to the taut corners of her mouth. "How long?"

"A month—six weeks."

"That's too long."

He shrugged. "You're the commander—Commander."

He turned to go, and she surged to her feet and seized his arm, thrusting him around to face her again. "What's wrong with going in now?"

"Nothing," he said. "As long as you don't care that all of your friends who've been loyal enough to you—and to their patriotic and pox-rotted cause—to half kill themselves and put their families in danger by learning how to soldier are going to die because you lead them into battle half prepared."

Her hand dropped from his arm as if his flesh had turned to a serpent's scales. But he saw in her anger a lurking fear as well, the desperation of a woman fighting fate and circumstance with dwindling reserves of strength.

"Don't you understand?" she asked, her voice trembling with weariness and rage. "Every day we wait, *he* gets stronger; and every day we wait, the chances double that Tarrin will be hurt or put to death in the mines. They already suspect him of organizing trouble there; he has been whipped and racked for it, then thrown back onto the chain to do his full share of the work with his limbs half dislocated. One day word of it will get back to Altiokis. But without him, the men's resistance would crumble—he is all their hope, and the brightness of his courage all that stands between their minds and the numbing despair of slavery.

"I know," she whispered. "He is a born leader, a born king; and he has a king's magic, to draw the hearts of his followers unquestioningly. I loved him from the moment we met; from the instant we laid eyes on each other, we knew we would be lovers."

"And does that keep you from playing along with the courtship of Derroug Dru?" the Wolf demanded snidely.

"Courtship?" She spat the word at him scornfully. "Pah! Is that what you think he wants? Marriage or even an honorable love? You don't know the man. Because I was the wife of his chief supporter, the most important and richest man of his faction in the town, he held off. But he would always follow me with his eyes. Now he comes around like a dog when the bitch is in season . . ."

Sun Wolf leaned his broad shoulders against one of the rude cedar pillars that held up the roof, "Then I guess poisoning your husband was a little hasty on your part, wasn't it?"

Her eyes flashed at him like a beast's in the gloom of the vast hall. "Hasty?" she snarled at him. "Hasty, when that pig had pretended to go over to Tarrin's faction, during the feuding before Altiokis' attack; when he encouraged every man loyal to Tarrin, every man loyal to his city, to join Tarrin's army, already knowing what would happen to them at Iron Pass? There was nothing he did not deserve for what he did that day."

She was striding back and forth, the faint sheen from the windows rippling like light on an animal's pelt, her face white against the bloody color of her gown and the blackness of her hair. "What he did that day has cut across my life, cut across the life of every person in this city. It has left us uprooted, robbed us of the ones we love, and put us in continual peril of our lives. What did he deserve, if not that?"

"I don't know," Sun Wolf said quietly. "Considering that's exactly what you did to me, without so much as a second thought, I can't give a very fair answer to that question." He left her and mounted the dark, enclosed stairway to his loft, the rain beating like thunder around him and over his head.

CHAPTER

❧ 11 ❧

*I*T WAS RAINING IN PERGEMIS. THE HARD, LEADEN DOWNPOUR BEAT
a fierce tattoo on the peaked slate roofs of that crowded city with a
sound almost like the drumming of hail. The cobblestones of the sloping street, three storeys below the window where Starhawk sat, were
running like a river; white streams frothed from the gutters of the
roofs. Beyond the close-angled stone walls, the distant sea was the
same cold, deep gray as the sky.

Starhawk, leaning her forehead against the glass, felt it like damp
ice against her skin. Somewhere in the tall, narrow house she could
hear Fawn's voice, light and bantering, the tone she used to speak to
the children. Then her footfalls came dancing down the stairs.

She is on her feet again, the Hawk thought. *It is time to travel on.*

The thought pulled at her, like a load resumed before the back was
fully rested. She wondered how many days they had lost. Twenty?
Thirty? What might have befallen the Wolf in those days?

Nothing that she could have remedied, she thought. And she could
not have left Fawn.

By the time they had reached the crossroads, where the southward
way to the Bight Coast parted from the highland road that led to
Racken Scrag and eventually to Grimscarp, the mauled flesh of Fawn's
arm and throat had begun to fester. Starhawk had done what she could
for it. Anyog, whose hurts by chance or magic remained clean, was far

too ill to help her. There had been no question of a parting of the ways.

By the time they had reached Pergemis, Fawn had been raving, moaning in an agony of pain and calling weakly for Sun Wolf. In the blurred nightmare of days and nights that had followed, in spite of all that the lady Pel Farstep could do, the girl had wandered in desperate delirium, sobbing for him to save her.

During those first four or five days in the house of the widowed mother of Ram and Orris, Starhawk had known very little beyond unremitting tiredness and fear and remembered clearly meeting no one but Pel herself. The mother of the ox team was ridiculously like her brother Anyog—small, wiry, with hair as crisp and white-streaked as his beard. She had taken immediate charge of Fawn and Starhawk both, nursing the sick girl tirelessly in the intervals of running one of the most thriving mercantile establishments in the town. Starhawk's memories of that time were a blur of stinking poultices that burned her hands, herbed steam and the coolness of lavender water, exhaustion such as she had never known in war, and a bitter, guilty wretchedness that returned like the hurt of an old wound every time she saw Fawn's white, drawn face. The other members of the household had been only voices and occasional faces peering in at the door.

Her only clear recollection of the events of that time had been of the night they had cut half a handful of suppurating flesh from Fawn's wound. She had sat up with Fawn afterward, the girl's faint, sleeping breath the only sound in the dark house. She had meditated, found no peace in it, and was sitting in the cushioned chair beside the bed, staring into the darkness beyond the single candle, when Anyog had come in, panting with the exertion of having dragged himself there from his own room on the other side of the house. He had shaken off her anxious efforts to make him sit; up until recently he had been worse off than Fawn and still looked like a corpse in its winding sheet, wrapped in his draggled bed robe.

He had only clung to her for support, gasping, "Swear to me you will tell no one. Swear it on your life." And when she had sworn, he had sat on the edge of the bed and clumsily, with the air of one long out of practice, worked spells of healing with hands that shook from weakness.

Pel Farstep had remarked to Starhawk after this that her brother's sleep seemed troubled. In his nightmares, he could be heard to whisper the name of the Wizard King.

In addition to Pel, the family consisted of her three sons—Imber was the oldest, splitting the headship of the Farstep merchant interests with her—Imber's wife Gillie, and their horrifyingly enterprising offspring, Idjit and Keltie. Idjit was three, alarmingly suave and nimbletongued for a boy of his years and masterfully adept at getting his younger sister to do his mischief for him. In the spring, Gillie expected a third child. "We're praying for another lassie," Imber confided to Starhawk one evening as she played at finger swords with Idjit before the kitchen hearth, "given the peck of trouble this lad's been."

The household further boasted a maid, a manservant, and three clerks who slept in the attics under the streaming slates of the roof, plus two cats and three of the little black ships' dogs seen in such numbers about the city. Pel ruled the whole concern with brisk love and a rod of iron.

It was a house, Starhawk thought, in which she could have been happy, had things been otherwise.

There would be no glory here, she mused, gazing out into the dove-colored afternoon rain; none of the cold, bright truth of battle, where all things had the shine of triumph, edged in the inky shadow of death. There was none of the strenuous beauty of the warrior's way here and no one here who would understand it. But life in more muted colors could be comfortable, too. And she would not be lonely.

Loneliness was nothing new to Starhawk. There were times when she felt that she had always been lonely, except when she was with Sun Wolf.

These days of rest had given her time to be alone and time to meditate, and the deep calm of it had cleared her thoughts. Having admitted her love to herself, she did not know whether she could return to being what she had been; but without the Wolf's presence, she knew that it would not much matter to her where she was or what she did. There was the possibility—the probability after so much time —that he was dead and that her long quest would find only darkness and grief at its end.

Yet she could not conceive of abandoning that quest.

It was nearing lamplighting time. The room was on the south side of the house, facing the sea, and brightness lingered on there when, in the rest of the house, Gillie and the maid Pearl began to set out the fat, white, beeswax candles and the lamps of multicolored glass. The hangings of the bed—the best guest bed that she had shared with Fawn for the last week, since Fawn's recovery—were a rich shade of red in daylight, but in this half-light they looked almost black, and the colors of the frieze of stenciled flowers on the pale plaster of walls had grown vague and indistinguishable in the shadows. Opposite her, above the heavy carved dresser, a big mural showed some local saint walking on the waters of the sea to preach to the mermaids, with fish and octopi meticulously depicted playing about his toes.

Sitting in the window seat, Starhawk pulled the thick folds of her green wool robe closer about her. Her hair was damp from washing and still smelled of herbed soap. She and Ram had taken Idjit and baby Keltie down walking on the stone quays after lunch, as the gulls wheeled overhead piping warnings of the coming storm. The expedition had been a success. Idjit had induced Keltie to fetch him crabs from one of the tide pools at the far end of the horn of land that lay beyond the edge of the docks, and Starhawk had had to slop to the rescue, with Ram hovering anxiously about, warning her not to be hurt. *A most satisfying day for all concerned,* she thought and grinned.

For a woman who had spent her entire life in the company of adults —either nuns or warriors—she was appalled at how idiotically fond she was of children.

It would not be easy, she knew, to leave this pleasant house, particularly in light of what she and Fawn must face.

Yet the days here had been fraught with guilty restlessness; nights she had lain awake, listening to the girl's soft breath beside her, wondering if the days she spent taking care of Fawn were bought out of Sun Wolf's life.

But she could not abandon her among strangers. And this knowledge had made Starhawk philosophical. There had been entire days in which she had been truly able to rest and peaceful evenings in the great kitchen or in the family room, listening to Gillie play her bone flute and talking of travel and far places with Ram. When Fawn was able to come haltingly down the stairs, she joined them. Starhawk was amused to see that she had won Orris' busy heart with her quick understanding of money and trade.

For Starhawk, at such times, it was as if she had refound her older brothers. After Pel and Fawn and Gillie had taken themselves off to bed, she had spent evening after evening drinking and dicing with the three big oxen, telling stories, or listening to them speak of the north-eastward roads.

"You aren't the only ones who've spoken of the nuuwa running in bands these days," Imber said, tucking his long-stemmed pipe into the corner of his mouth and gazing across the table at Starhawk with eyes that were as blue, but much quicker and shrewder, than those of either of his brothers. "After these gomerils left for the North, we had word of it, before the weather closed the sea lanes. I had fears they'd come to grief in the mountains."

Orris frowned. "You mean, others have seen bands as big?"

"Eh—twice and three times that size." Imber leaned forward to his carved chair and pushed his glass toward Ram, who had charge of the pitcher of mulled wine. "Fleg Barnhithe told me some sheepman from the Thanelands said there'd been a band there numbered near forty . . ."

"Forty!" the others cried, aghast.

"They're breeding up in the mountains somewhere." Imber sighed, shaking his head. "It's made fair hash of the overland roads. Them and other things, other kinds of monsters . . ."

Starhawk frowned, remembering her words with Anyog in the half darkness of the corridor of the deserted Peacock Inn. "Breeding?" she said softly. "Now, I've heard tell they're men—or were once men."

"That's impossible," Orris stated, a little too quickly. "Blinding's a punishment that's practiced everywhere, and those who are blinded don't even lose their reason, much less turn into—into those. And anyway, a blinded man doesn't follow the way they do. Nor has any man that kind of—of insane strength."

But his eyes flickered as he spoke, and there was a touch of fear in his voice; if the nuuwa had once been men, the hideous corollary was that any man stood in danger of becoming a nuuwa.

"I've seen men close to that kind of strength in battle," Starhawk objected. She folded her long, bony hands on the waxed oak of the table top. "I've met men you'd have to kill to stop—men driven by necessity for survival out of all bounds of human strength."

"But if it was a thing that—that happened, as if it were a sickness, wouldn't it happen to women, too? I don't think anyone's ever seen a woman of 'em."

"But that goes double for them breeding," Ram pointed out, filling the glasses with the wine like molten gold in the gleaming lamplight. "Anyroad, they'd never reproduce—they'd eat their own young, as they do everything else they come on."

"The Mother doesn't mold them out of little clay bits," Starhawk said.

Orris laughed. "You'll never convince our Ram of it."

"Nah, just because he didn't have no schooling, bar what the wardens of the jail could give him . . ." Imber teased, his eyes sparkling with mischief.

"Better nor what the kennelman gave you," Ram retorted with a broad grin, and the discussion degenerated into the rough-and-tumble kidding that Starhawk had grown used to in that boisterous house.

But the memory of that evening came back to her now as she thought of taking the road again. She shivered and drew up her knees under the soft folds of the robe, resting her chin on her crossed wrists. Neither she nor Fawn had spoken to any of them of their destination; not for the first time, she was thankful for the brothers' collective denseness that prevented them from guessing what Anyog had known. She had no desire to deal with the overwhelming rush of protectiveness that even the suspicion would have brought out in them.

From somewhere below, she caught Fawn's voice, like a drift of passing perfume; ". . . if that's the case, then keeping a fortified post in the North open year-round would pay, wouldn't it?"

Pel's brisk tones replied, "Yes, but the returns on the trade in onyx alone . . ."

It must have been years, the Hawk thought, since Fawn had been in company with the kind of people she had grown up with, years since she had heard that clever, practical language of finance and trade. Starhawk smiled a little to herself, remembering Fawn's shamefaced admission that she was a merchant at heart. Her father—whose bones had been lying these two years, bleached where the robbers had scattered them—had tried to make a great lady of her; Sun Wolf had made a skilled and practiced mistress of her; it was only now, after trial and struggle and desperate adventure, that Fawn was free to fly her own colors. In spite of what she knew to be their rivalry for the same man, Starhawk was proud of her.

Heavy footfalls creaked in the hallway. Ram's, she identified them, and realized that the room had grown dark. She got to her feet and lighted a spill from the embers of the glowing hearth. She was touching the light to the wick of a brass lamp in the shape of a joyous dolphin when the footsteps paused, and Ram's hesitant knock sounded at the door.

"Starhawk?" He pushed it shyly open. He, too, was sleek and damp from his bath, the sleeves of his reddish-bronze tunic turned back from enormous forearms, the thin, gold neck chain he wore like a streak of flame in the lamplight.

She smiled at him. "The infants all bathed?"

He laughed. "Aye, for all that Keltie wailed and screamed until I'd let her bathe with Idjit and me. It was a fine, wet time we had in the kitchen, let me tell you. It's like high tide on the floor, and the steam like the fogs in spring."

Starhawk chuckled at the thought, noticing, as she smiled up at him, how the rose-amber of the light put streaks of deep gold in his brown hair and tiny reflections in his eyes. She saw the graveness of his face and her laughter faded.

"Starhawk," he said quietly, "you spoke this afternoon of moving on. Going away to seek this man of Fawnie's. Must you?"

. . . *this man of Fawnie's.* She looked away, down at her own hands, spangled with the topaz reflections of the lamp's facets. *Trust Ram,* she thought, *to go protective on me . . .* "I'll have to go sooner or later," she replied. "It's better now."

"Must it be—sooner or later?"

She said nothing. The oil hissed faintly against the cold metal of the lamp; the smell of the scented whale oil, rich and faintly flowery, came hot to her nostrils, along with the bland smells of soap and wool. She did not meet his eyes.

"If the man's been missing this long, he's likely dead," Ram persisted softly. "Starhawk, I know you have vows of loyalty to him as your chief and I respect that, I truly do. But—could you not stay with us?"

The drumming of the rain on the slates crept into her silence, and the memory of the bleak cold of the roads. She felt the bitter, weary knowledge that she would have to find a wizard somewhere, if she wanted to have any chance at the tower of Grimscarp at all, and that the going would be harder now, with maybe only that final grief at the end.

If it's this hard for me, she thought, *what will it be for Fawn, alone?*

Doggedly, she shook her head, but could not speak.

"In the spring . . ." he began.

"In the spring, it will be too late." She raised her head and saw his face suddenly taut with emotion, the big square chin thrust out and the flat lips pressed hard together.

"It's too late now," he said. "Starhawk—must you make me write it all down, and me no good hand with words? I love you. I want to marry you and for you to stay here with me." And with awkward passion, he folded her in his great arms and kissed her.

Between her shock that any man would ever say those words to her and the rough strength of his grasp, for a moment she made no move either to yield or to repulse. The two affairs she had had while in Sun Wolf's troop had been short-lived, almost perfunctory, a clumsy seeking for something she knew from the start that she would never find. But this was different. He was offering her not the warmth of a night, but a life in this place at his side. That, as much as the shape and strength of a man's body in her arms, drew her.

He must have felt her waver, unresponsive and uncertain, for his arms slacked from around her, and he drew back. There was misery in his face. "Could you not?"

Shakily and for the first time, she looked at him not as a traveler like herself nor as an amateur warrior to her professionalism, but as a man to her womanliness. It had been comforting to rest her head on that huge barrel of a chest and to feel the massive arms strong around her, a comfort like nothing else she had known. She found herself thinking, *He is very much like the Chief . . .* and turned away, flooded with a helpless sense of shame, bitterness, and regret.

Silently she damned Anyog for doing this to her, for making her aware of herself as a woman and of his nephew, that good, deserving ox, only in terms of the man she truly wanted and could never hope to have.

She heard the rustle of his clothing and stepped away from his hand before he could touch her again. "Don't," she murmured tiredly and looked up, to see the hurt in his eyes.

"Could you not give up the way of the warrior, then?" he asked softly, and the guilt that burned her was all the sharper for the fact that she had never spoken to him of another love. The very genuine liking she had for him made it all the worse.

But she loved him no more than she loved Ari; and she could not conceive of herself marrying a lumpish, earnest merchant and having to deal with his clumsy efforts to protect her and to rule her life.

"It wouldn't be fair to you," she said.

"To take me a warlady to wife?" A faint smile glimmered in his eyes. "But you'd no longer be a warrior then, would you? I'd be the mock of my brothers, maybe, but then you could protect me and lay about them for me, you see."

And when she said nothing, the flicker of mischief died from his face.

"Eh, well," he said after a time. "I'm sorry I spoke, Hawk. Don't feel you need leave this house before you wish, just to get clear of my ardor. I'll not speak again."

She lowered her eyes, but could find nothing to say. She knew she should speak, and tell him that, though she did not love him, she liked him hugely, better than either of his brothers; tell him that were she not struggling with a love as hopeless as it was desperate, she would like nothing better than to join his loud and brawling family . . . But she could not. There was no one, in fact, whom she could speak to of it—there was only one person whom she trusted with her feelings enough to tell, and he was the one person who must never know.

. . . *this man of Fawnie's.*

She changed her clothes and went downstairs to supper. She had little idea of what she ate or of the few things she replied to those who spoke to her. Ram was there, pale and quiet under the gibes of his brothers. Though she was past noticing much, Starhawk was aware that Fawn, too, had very little to say. Pel Farstep's sharp, black eyes flicked from face to face, but the shrewd little merchant made no mention of their silence and was seen to kick her youngest son under the table when he bawled a question to Ram, asking, was he in love, that he couldn't eat?

They always said that love affects women this way, Starhawk thought, fleeing the convivial clamor in the supper room as soon as she decently could. *Great Mother, I've eaten hearty dinners after sacking towns and slitting the throats of innocent civilians. Why should saying "No" to one lumpish burgher whom I don't even love make whatever it was that Gillie spent her time and sweat in the kitchen for taste like flour paste and ash? The Chief would kill me.*

No, she thought. *The Chief would understand.*

She paused before the mirror in her room and stood for a long time, candle in hand, studying the pale, fragile-boned face reflected there.

She saw nothing that anyone by any stretch of courtesy would call pretty. For all the delicacy of the cheekbones and the whiteness of the fair skin, it was a face cursed with a chin both too long and too square, with lips too thin, and with a nose that was marked with that telltale, bumpy crookedness that was the family resemblance of fighters. Fine, pale hair caught the candle's light, which darkened it to the color of corn silk—in sunlight it was nearly white, tow and flyaway as a child's. It had grown out some in her journeying, hanging wispy against the hollows of her cheeks. Sunlight, too, would have lightened her eyes almost to silver; in this light, they were smoke-colored, almost as dark as the charcoal-gray ring that circled her pupils. Her lashes were straight and colorless. There was a scar on her cheek, too, like a rudely drawn line of pink chalk. In her bath, she had noted again how the line of it picked up again at her collarbone and extended for a hand-span down across pectoral muscle and breast.

She remembered a time when she had been proud of her scars.

Who but Ram, she wondered, would offer to take a warlady to wife? Certainly not a man who had his choice of fragile young beauties like Fawn.

The door opened behind her. The liquid deeps of the mirror showed her another candle, and its sheen rippled over a gown of brown velvet, tagged with the pale ecru lace such as the ladies of the Bight Islands made, with a delicate face lost in shadow above.

She turned from the mirror. "How do you feel?" she asked.

Fawn shrugged and set the candle down. "Renewed," she replied quietly. "As if—oh, as if spring had come, after a nightmare winter." She crossed to the small table that stood beside the window and picked up her hairbrush, as was her nightly wont. But she set it down again, as she had set down untasted forkfuls of flour paste and ash at tonight's supper. In the silky, amber gleam of candle and lamp, her fingers were trembling.

"Ready to take the road again?" the Hawk asked, her voice ringing tinnily in her own ears. *This man of Fawnie's,* Ram had said. But that, she told herself, was nothing that she had to burden Fawn with. It was no doing of hers that she had been stolen away from her family and had taken Sun Wolf's fancy. The Wolf was lost and in grave danger, and Fawn had put her life at risk to find him.

Fawn was silent for a long moment, staring down at the brush, her face turned away. In a muffled voice, she finally said, "No." She looked up with wretched defiance in her green eyes. "I'm not going on."

Even Ram's unexpected proposal of marriage had not struck Starhawk with such shock. For a moment, she could only stare, and her first feeling was one of indignation that this girl would abandon her quest for her lover. "What?" was all she could say.

Fawn's voice was shaking. "I'm going to stay here," she said haltingly, "and—and marry Orris."

"What?" And then, seeing the girl's eyes flood with tears of shame and wretchedness, Starhawk crossed the room in two quick strides and caught her in a swift hug, reassuring her while her own mind reeled in divided confusion. "Fawnie, I—"

Fawn began sobbing in earnest. "Starhawk, don't be angry with me. Please don't be angry with me. Sun Wolf was so good to me, so kind— he saved me from I don't know what kind of slavery and misery. But —but Anyog was right. I was there at the inn when he said we would never enter the Citadel without the help of a wizard—I was listening in the hall. And he's right, Hawk. We can't go against Altiokis by ourselves. And there are no wizards anymore. He's the last one left, the only one . . ."

Not if I can put the screws to Anyog in some way, he's not, Starhawk thought grimly. But she only said, "We'll find one." Her honesty drove her to recognize Fawn's love for the Wolf to be as valid as her own, even as it had driven her to allow the girl to accompany her in the first place.

"No," Fawn whispered. "Hawk, even if we could—it isn't only that." She drew back, looking earnestly up at the older woman with those wide, absinthe-green eyes. "Starhawk, it isn't enough. I want a home; I want children of my own. Even if we find him, even if he's not dead, I don't want to live as a mercenary's woman. I love Sun Wolf—I think I'll always love him. But I won't go on being a glorified camp follower. I can't."

Her trembling fingers gestured at the dim room, with its curtained bed and softly shining lamps, its stiff-robed, ridiculous saint preaching to the mermaids in the sea, with their weedy hair flowing down over their breasts. "This is the sort of house that I grew up in, Hawk. This is the life I know. I belong here. And believe me," she added with a wry smile, "marrying into a firm of spice merchants is a better thing, in the long run, than being mistress to the richest mercenary in creation."

Flabbergasted, Starhawk could not speak, but only look in puzzlement at that beautiful, secretive face and wonder that anyone who actually had Sun Wolf's love could give it up for a bustling, pompous busybody like Orris Farstep.

Fawn disengaged herself quietly from Starhawk's grasp and walked to the window. The lace at her throat almost covered the bandages that remained over the wounds that the nuuwa had left; like Starhawk, she would carry scars to the end of her days. Her voice was soft as she went on. "I spoke to Pel about it this afternoon. I know Orris is fond of me. And I—I want this, Hawk. I want a home and a family and a place; I want to know that my man isn't going to get himself killed in a war next week or discard me for someone else next year. I love this place and I love these people. Do you understand?"

"Yes," the Hawk said, her voice so low that she was almost not sure that it could be heard over the clamoring sounds in her own heart and mind. "Yes, I understand."

Fawn's back was a shape of darkness against the deep well of the window's shadow; the candle threw a little wisp of light along the edge of the lace and on the halo of her hair. "What will you do?" she asked.

Starhawk shrugged. "Go on alone."

She took her leave of them next day. Pel, Orris, Gillie, and the children went with her to see her off at the city's land gate, wrapped in oilskins to keep off the rain. Anyog, though he was able now to get about, had remained at home, as had Ram and Fawn, each for a different, personal reason.

All the way through the steep-slanted cobbled streets of the town, Orris had kept up a worried stream of caution and advice regarding the roads through the Stren Water Valley that would take her northeast to Racken Scrag, about the bandits who were said to haunt them, and concerning the dangers of Altiokis' lands. "It isn't only the bandits stealing your horses you'll have to worry about, lass," he fretted—Pel had given Starhawk a riding mare and a pack mule. "That Altiokis, he's hiring mercenaries, and the countryside's stiff with them. They're dangerous fellows . . ."

The Hawk sighed patiently, glancing sideways at Orris from beneath her streaming hood. "I know all about mercenaries that I need to."

"Yes, but—"

"Leave the poor woman alone," Pel ordered briskly. "By God, how she put up with you all the way from Foonspay I'll never know." Her smile flashed white in the gypsy brown of her face. Her hood was of the fashionable calash type—under its boned arch, the piled braids of her widow's coif gleamed faintly in the rainy daylight. She quickened her step to where Starhawk walked in front of the little cavalcade of led horses and took the Hawk's hand in her own little square one.

In a softer voice, she said, "But we're all glad that you have been here, child. Your staying made all the difference to Fawn. In the pinch, it may even be that it saved her life to know that she had not been abandoned in a strange place."

Starhawk said nothing. She felt uncomfortable about Fawn, almost guilty. But her impassive face showed nothing of the turmoil within her as she looked around at the bright-painted walls of this rain-drenched, fish-smelling town. Pel seemed to accept her silence for what it was and moved along briskly beside her, keeping her heavy black skirts lifted above the runnels that trickled among the cobblestones.

Orris persisted. "But mercenaries—they're a bad breed, Starhawk, begging your pardon for saying so. And they say the Dark Eagle whom Altiokis has put in charge of all his mercenaries is the worst . . ."

"The Dark Eagle?" Starhawk raised her dark, level brows.

"Aye. He's a wicked man, they say . . ."

"Oh, bosh," Pel retorted. "Our girl's probably served with him; haven't you, child?"

"As a matter of fact, I have," she admitted, and Orris looked shocked.

From the saddle of the riding mare, Idjit announced, "I be goin' with the Hawk."

"Say, 'I *am* going with the Hawk,' " corrected Gillie, who was leading the mare. "And in any case, you aren't, laddie."

"Then I maun't say't," the boy retorted in the broad Bight Coast dialect that his mother was laboring diligently to erase from his speech. Keltie, perched amid the packs on the mule, watched her brother with worship in her round, blue eyes.

Their mother looked annoyed with this challenge, but Starhawk only said, "That's all right, Gillie. Even if I could take a child along— which I can't—I wouldn't have one with me who talked like a fisherman."

At this rebuke from his hero, Idjit subsided, and Pel hid a grin. They had reached the squat towers of the city gate. Amid the crowds of incoming countryfolk and local farmers, they said good-by, Starhawk lifting the children down and mounting in Idjit's place, leaning from the saddle to clasp their hands. She missed them already— and more than these who had come to see her off, she missed Ram and Anyog and Fawn. But there was nothing that she could have said to them in parting. What could she say to a man she was leaving to seek another, or to the woman who had abandoned that quest? And though in the end she had not had the heart to speak to Anyog of her desperate need for even a cowardly and unfledged wizard's aid, she knew that Anyog knew it. She did not blame him for his fear, but she knew that he blamed himself.

"The Stren Water Valley will be in flood this time of year," Orris advised. "Best go up it by the foothills."

The mare shied, more offended than afraid, as a market woman chivied a herd of geese through the gate; in the shelter of the gatehouse eaves, a boy was selling roast chestnuts out of a brazier full of coals, his thin, monotonous song rising above the general din. Light and steady, rain drummed on the shining slates and on Starhawk's black oilskin cloak. The sound of rain and the smell of fish and the sea would always be twined in her mind with these people—with the two children hanging onto Gillie Farstep's hands, with the monumental Orris, fussing at her to watch what inns she put up at, and with Pel Farstep, like a little brown sparrow, reaching up to take her hands in farewell.

"Keep yourself safe, child," she said gently. "And remember, wherever you are, there is a home here for you if you need one."

Starhawk bent from the saddle and kissed the brown cheek. Then she turned the horse's head; the mule stretched out its neck to the full extent of the lead before it followed. She left the Farsteps in the crowded shadows of the noisy gate and did not look back.

You have parted from so many people, she told herself, to still that treacherous ache in her heart. *In time, you got over all but one and you'll get over these.*

She made herself wonder if the Dark Eagle would take her on as a mercenary; that would get her into the Citadel, without the need to search for a wizard to aid her. From things Ram and his brothers had said, most people didn't believe in the existence of wizards anymore—only in Altiokis, inhuman, deathless, undefeatable, coiled in the darkness of the Tchard Mountains like a poisonous snake beneath the kitchen floor.

The wet wind lifted her cloak. Shreds of white cloud blew, unveiling the distant foothills of those mountains and the rolling uplands, stony and deserted, that guarded all approaches to them on this side. How long would it be, she wondered, before Altiokis turned his energies toward the Bight Coast, as he had turned them toward Mandrigyn and the straits of the Megantic?

Once she would have watched the proceedings with interest, as Sun Wolf did, gauging the proper time to apply for work amid the chaos. She had burned and looted many cities—this was the first time, she realized, she had dwelt in one in peace. Pel, Ram, and Orris were the burghers she and her men had helped kill; Idjit and Keltie were the children who had been sold into slavery to pay them.

She shook her head, forcing those thoughts into the background of her mind. *One thing at a time,* she told herself, *and the thing now is to figure out what I'm going to do when I reach the Citadel walls.* The Dark Eagle would know of her unshakable loyalty to the Wolf—he'd seen them work together when they'd all been fighting in the East. Even if she came up with a story of disaffected loyalties, the timing, with the Wolf, being a prisoner in the Citadel, would give the game away.

She had to find a wizard—one who was not too terrified of Altiokis to admit his powers, preferably one who had passed this Trial that Anyog had spoken of. But there was all the Mother's green earth to search in and all the days that she had lost in Pergemis pressing on her, reminding her how little time it took for a man to die.

Damn Fawnie, anyway, she thought, exasperated, and then felt a twinge of guilt. She did not rationally expect that the girl would have known at the outset that she would not be going on from Pergemis; and in any case, Pel Farstep might very well have been right. It would be easy to die, lying friendless among strangers. Yet knowing Fawn for her rival, Starhawk could never have abandoned her to her death.

Hooves clattered on the hard surface of the highroad. Starhawk swung around in the saddle, the freshening wind blowing the hood back from her hair. It was a single rider, wrapped like herself in a black oilskin poncho, the folds of it whipping like the horse's black, tangled mane and tail in the moist chill of the air. They drew up beside her, horse and rider steaming with breath.

Starhawk said, "Are you out of your lint-picking mind?"

"I suspect so." Uncle Anyog was panting, clinging to the pommel of the saddle for balance, his face white against the darkness of his salt-and-pepper beard. "But I couldn't let you go on, my warrior dove. Not alone."

She regarded him from beneath lowered lids. "You going to start calling me 'lass,' as Ram does?"

He grinned. She reined her mare around and started up the road for the foothills and the way to the Tchard Mountains, Anyog jogging at her side.

"For that matter, did Ram put you up to this?" she asked suddenly.

"It would do my wits greater credit if I said he'd threatened me with a horrible death if I didn't go to your aid." The old man sighed. "But alas, in old age one learns to take credit for one's own follies. None of them knows a thing, my child. I left Pel a note."

"It must have covered three pages," she remarked.

Anyog was recovering his breath a little. She could see, under the oilskin, that he was dressed as he always was—as a gentleman—in his drab and sober black, the starched white lace of his ruff like petals around his face. "In the finest iambic pentameter," he amplified. "My dove, I know why you refused our Ram's hamlike but gold-filled hand —and I suspect I know why you left the Convent." Her head swiveled sharply around, her gray eyes narrowing. "Oh, yes—I have seen you meditate and I know you didn't learn that as a mercenary . . . But why did you become a Sister to begin with?"

She drew rein, meeting that bright, black scrutiny with cold reserve. "I never turn down an offer of help," she said. "And now that you have offered, I won't send you back, because I need you. But that doesn't mean I won't gag you and pack you up to Grimscarp, the way we packed you into Pergemis, if you ask after things that are none of your affair."

She clucked to the mare and moved off.

"But it is my affair, my dove," the little man said, wholly unperturbed. "For I think we are more alike than you know. You became a Sister, I suspect, for the same reasons that you later became a warrior —because you would not tolerate the slow breaking of your spirit to the yoke of a house and a child and some man's whims, and any life seemed preferable to that—because you need a life of the brighter colors, because you prefer lightning-edged darkness to an eternal twilight. My child," he said softly, urging his bay mare up beside hers on the narrow road, "I could no more have remained a pensioner in my estimable sister's house than I could become a warrior like yourself.

"I have lived with my fear a long time," he continued, drawing the oilskin closer about his body as the wind turned chill once again. "Not until now had I realized how it had come to rule me."

CHAPTER

12

*S*UN *WOLF PAUSED IN HIS PACING, HEARING THE SOUND OF SOFT,* approaching footfalls in the darkness. *From the stairs,* he thought. His sigh was deep and bored, and he shifted his weight as a man would do on a long stint of guard. The pattering steps halted. Around him, the vast, chilly darkness was lambent with breath.

Somewhere a board creaked. Then weight struck his shoulders and the back of his knee—light, muscled weight, like a cat's, vicious and controlled. At the first breath of impact, he twisted, slithering free of the smooth arms that sought his neck. In the darkness, he reached back and expertly tweaked the short little nose that snorted with exertion so close to his ear.

He felt his assailant step away. With an oily hiss of hot metal, someone uncovered a dark-lantern. Behind him, Gilden stood panting, regarding him with injured chagrin.

All around the room, their hair tight-braided and their smooth arms traced in the shadows with the faint, clear lines of muscle definition, the ladies of Mandrigyn watched him, a sea of aggrieved eyes.

"You're pulling with your shoulders," he told Gilden, looking down into those long-lashed, sea-blue eyes. "Your center of balance is lower than a man's—that's why you women have hell's own time throwing each other. It's one of your advantages against a man. Throw from the hips—like this—lever me down. Somebody your size, trying to use brute force against someone my size, is more than stupid—she's suicidal."

Gilden colored, but said, "Yes, sir. Thank you, sir."

"And I heard you coming."

She said something else then, sotto voce and obviously picked up from Crazyred's vocabulary.

He glanced at the assembled ladies. "Next?"

Behind him, he heard Gilden's swift hiss of intaken breath, a voiceless protest. When he turned and raised one shaggy brow at her, she asked, "Couldn't I try again?"

"No," he said gently, "because you had only one chance, and now you're dead. Go sit down."

She returned without a word to her place on the edge of one of the upturned tree tubs between Wilarne and her daughter, Tisa. Sun Wolf, for the tenth time so far that evening, walked over to the little potting room that opened off the main orangery, so that he would neither see nor hear—supposedly—where his next assailant would begin her attack. The single dark-lantern that illuminated the vast room threw his shadow, huge and grotesque and swaying, across the gray boards of the wall; he heard Denga Rey fuss with the lantern slide and curse when she scorched her fingers. As he closed the door behind him, he heard the soft rise of talk. Gilden, glib as always, had informed him that this was to cover any noise that the next attacker might make in taking her place, but Sun Wolf suspected that it was simply because the women liked to talk.

It was something he'd found was true even of Starhawk, though there wasn't a man in the troop who'd believe that. So far as he knew, he was the only one she talked to freely, not with the inconsequential small talk of war and the camp, but of things that really concerned her, the past and the future, gardening, theology, the nature of fear. In an odd way, he had felt curiously honored when he had realized that this was true, for Starhawk's facade was one of the coldest and most distant that he had ever seen. Most of the men were a little afraid of her.

He himself had been appalled by the realization that he loved her.

For one thing, one of the most fatal mistakes any commander could make was to fall in love with one of his captains, whether man or woman. It always became known, and he had never seen a time when trouble had not come of it.

For another thing, Starhawk was heart and bones a warrior; logical, emotionless, and ruthless with anything that came in the way of her chosen course. The affairs she had had with other members of the troop had been terminated the minute the men had interfered with her training. Sun Wolf was not entirely certain what her reaction would be if he should return to Wrynde and tell her, "I love you, Starhawk."

And yet, he found himself very much looking forward to returning to Wrynde and finding her there, grave, homely, sarcastically demanding if he'd been kidnapped by all those women for stud.

There was a respectful tap at the door. He came out and signaled Denga Rey to kill the lamp again. Then he began to walk, with a slow pace like a sentry's, the length of that empty darkness, listening for his next student in this lesson in how to take out and kill a man.

It was Eo, not quite as heavy and not nearly as clumsy as she had been. She acquitted herself well, timing her footsteps against his and remembering to throw from the hip, not the shoulders. He hit the floor hard and tapped her arm as the bone of her wrist clamped his windpipe shut. She released him instantly, and the light went up to show her bending anxiously over him, afraid she had done him real harm. He sat up, rubbing his throat and grinning; it was very much like the blacksmith to knock a man senseless and beg his pardon contritely when he came to.

That was something he had found quite common to the women, this concern for one another's bruises. Curse and revile himself blue in the face as he might, he could seldom get even the smallest aggression toward one another out of them. Their technique was good. Most of them understood the leverage their small size needed and, between running and strenuous, night-and-morning training, they were developing the reflexes necessary to put them even with larger and heavier opponents. But he was forever seeing someone at sword practice get in a really telling wallop on her opponent, then immediately lower her weapon and make sure the other woman wasn't hurt before going on. It drove Sun Wolf nearly crazy; if he hadn't seen them fight against the nuuwa, he would have tried—unsuccessfully, he presumed—to wash his hands of the whole affair.

He had found out many things about women in the last few weeks.

He had learned that women, among themselves, could carry on conversations whose bawdiness would have set any mercenary of the Wolf's acquaintance squirming. He'd learned this the evening he'd gone to soak himself in the hot tub, partitioned from the main bath-house, after training, when the women were in the main part of the baths and had assumed he'd gone up to bed. It had been a startling and eye-opening experience for a man raised on the popular masculine myth of feminine delicacy. *"I* wouldn't even tell jokes like that," he'd said later to Amber Eyes, and she had dissolved into disconcerting giggles.

Another alarming thing about the women was their prankishness. The ringleaders in everything from ambushing him as he emerged, pink and dripping, after his bath to sending him anonymous and hor-rific love letters were Gilden Shorad and Wilarne M'Tree, outwardly as gracious and poised a pair of matrons as ever a man made his bow to in the street.

But the main thing that he had found was their strength—dogged, ruthless, and, if necessary, crueler than any man's. It had an animal quality to it, forged by years of repression; for all their beauty and sweetness, these were fifty people who would do whatever it was nec-essary to do, and the single-mindedness of it sometimes frightened him.

He thought of it now, sitting at last alone in the potting room, warming his hands over a brazier of coals, listening to the women depart. The rain had resumed, pattering noisily on the roof overhead, murmuring in the waters of the canals. Most mornings, the lower islands of the city were flooded, the great squares before its floating miracles of churches and town hall transformed to wastes of water crossed with crude duckboards. The damp cold ate at his bones. The women were wrapped like treacle-cured hams in leather and oiled silk, their voices a soft music in the semidark.

The next class would be starting soon. Through the slits of the shuttered window of the potting room, he watched their shadows flicker against the lights of the house and smiled a little at the thought of them. They'd come a long way—from veiled, timid creatures blush-ing at the presence of a man—even the ones who had children and had presumably conceived them somehow—to cool and deadly fighters. If what Gilden and others told him was true, they'd become hardheaded, matter-of-fact businessmen and shopkeepers as well.

The men of Mandrigyn, he thought wryly, were in for one hell of a surprise when they finally got home.

The potting room was dark, but for the poppy-red glow of the brazier; shadowy shapes of trowels, rakes, and sprouted bulbs lurked gold-edged in the shadows. The smells of the place were familiar to him—humus, compost, cedar mast, the wetter, rockier scent of gravel, and the faintly dusty smell of the half hod of sea coal in the corner. From the door, he caught Sheera's voice, low and tense, speaking to someone outside, then Drypettis' high, piercing tones. He heard Tarrin's name spoken—that lost Prince and golden hope, slaving to organize the mines—and then Drypettis' voice again.

"But he is worthy of you, Sheera," she said. "Of all of them, he is the only man in the city worthy of your love—the greatest and the best. I have always thought it."

"He is the only man in the city whom I have ever loved," Sheera replied.

"That's what infuriates me; that you and he should be enslaved and humiliated—he by the mines and the lash, you by the base uses of the barracks. That you should stoop to using a—a violent clodhopper who can keep neither his eyes nor his hands off those who are fighting for their city . . ."

"I assigned Amber Eyes to him," Sheera corrected diplomatically. "She didn't object."

"He could have had the decency to have left her alone!"

Sheera laughed. "Oh, really, Dru! Think how insulted she would have been!"

He could almost see the sensitive lips pinch up. "I'm sure that was his only consideration," Drypettis retorted with heavy sarcasm, and a moment later he heard the soft boom of the closed door. Then Sheera's footfalls approached, slow and tired, and she stood framed in the darkness of the potting room doorway.

Sun Wolf hooked a stool from under the workbench and pushed it toward her with his foot. She looked worn and stretched, as she always did these days when one of the girls from the mines brought her news of Tarrin. She ignored the proffered seat.

"If she hates me that much," the Wolf said, holding his hands to the luminous coals, "why does she stay? She's free to quit the troop and she'd be no loss."

Sheera's mouth tightened, and an angry glint flickered in her eyes. Stripped for training, she held an old blanket wrapped about her shoulders, its thick folds muffling the strong shape of her body. "I suppose that you, as a mercenary, would judge everyone by your own standards," she retorted. "It's inconceivable to you that, no matter what someone's personal feelings about her leadership are, she could remain out of loyalty to a higher goal. Like me—like all of us." She jerked her head back toward where the half-seen shapes of Denga Rey and Amber Eyes could be distinguished, talking quietly at the far end of the room. "Drypettis is a citizen of Mandrigyn. She wants to see her city proud and free—"

"The fact that she's the governor's sister couldn't have anything to do with her staying, could it?" Sun Wolf rasped.

Sheera sniffed scornfully. "Derroug could find a hundred better spies."

"Whom you trust?"

"Who are more acceptable to your tastes, anyway," Sheera snapped back at him. "She may be a hideous snob; she may be unreasonably obstinate; she may be rigid and vain and prudish beyond words; but I've known her all my life, since we were girls in school together. She wouldn't betray us."

"She could betray us by being too self-involved to know what she's doing." He moved his shoulders, rubbed the aching muscles of his neck, and encountered, as he did a dozen times a day, the steel of the slip-chain that lay around his throat like a noose.

"Whatever else she is, she isn't stupid."

"She's a weak link."

"Not in this case."

He swung back toward her. "In any case," he snapped. "You all have weaknesses of one kind or another. It's a commander's business to know what they are and take them into account. A single unstable member could wreck the whole enterprise, and I say that woman is about as unstable as any I've ever seen."

"It would be an insult to throw her out of the troop at this point without cause," Sheera retorted hotly. "When it was only a matter of organization, she was virtually second in command . . ."

"Or is it that you just like having a faithful disciple?"

"As much as you hate not having one." She was angry now, carnelian reflections of the fire leaping in her eyes. "She's been loyal to me, not only as a conspirator but as a friend."

"As commander—"

Her voice gritted. "May I remind you, Captain, that *I* am the commander of this force."

The silence between them was as audible as the twang of an over-strained rope. In the ruddy light, her eyes seemed to burn with the reflected fires of the brazier. But whatever words would have next passed between them were forestalled by the opening of the orangery doors and the joking voices of Crazyred and Erntwyff Fish. "So he says, 'What cheap bastard gave you only a copper?' And she says, 'What do you mean? They *all* gave me a copper.' "

The women were coming in for the second class. After a long moment, Sheera turned on her heel, her blanket swirling like a cloak with her steps, and went to speak to them, leaving Sun Wolf standing silent in the potting room, looking out at her through the frame of the dark door.

The next morning he left the house at dawn to seek the witch Yirth in the city.

He had the impression of having seen Yirth several times since they had spoken in his loft on the night of that first meeting, but he would have been hard pressed to say precisely where or when. She was a woman adept at making herself unnoticed. *No small feat,* he thought rather crudely, *for someone that ugly,* forgetting that, for all his size, he, too, had a talent for staying out of sight. He had hesitated to seek her out, knowing that it was in truth her hand, not Sheera's, that held the choke rein on his life. Moreover, he was not entirely certain that he would be able to find her.

As soon as curfew lifted, he went out, leaving Amber Eyes curled unstirring in his bed, and took one of the secret exits of the women out of the grounds. The night's rain had ceased, and the canals lay as opaque as silver mirrors among the moss-streaked walls; the dripping of the rooftrees upon the narrow footpaths and catwalks that bordered the water fell hollow into the stillness of the morning, like the intermittent footsteps of drunken sprites.

He had taken care not to go about in the city too often; Altiokis used mercenary troops as part of the city garrison, and there was always a chance that he would be recognized by one of them. But more than that, there was something in any captured town that made the Wolf uneasy—a sense of being spied upon, a sense that, if he called for help when in trouble, no one would come. The battle at Iron Pass had indeed, as Sheera had said, stripped the city of all that was healthy and decent, and the men whom he met in the streets were mostly cripples, addicts—for Mandrigyn was one of the key ports in the dream-sugar traffic from Kilpithie—or else had a furtive air of shame and deceit about them that made them obviously unsuitable. Even the slaves he saw in the town were a bad crop, the stronger ones having been confiscated as part of the indemnity after the battle and sent with their masters to labor in the mines. Sun Wolf's health and his size made him conspicuous—and matters were not helped by the several women who had sent unequivocally worded notes to Sheera, requesting a loan of his—unspecified—services.

He crossed through the spiderweb windings of twisting streets and over plank bridges that spanned canals he could have jumped, had there been room on those jammed islets for a running start. On catwalks that paralleled the canals or circled the courtyard lagoons along the second or third storey of the houses that fronted them, crones and young girls were already appearing, to shake out bedding in the damp air and call gossip back and forth across the narrow waters. In the black latticework of alleys, ankle-deep in icy water on the lower islands, he saw the lights going up in kitchens and heard the rattle of ironware and the scrape of metal on stone as ashes were raked. Crossing a small square before the black and silent fortress of a three-spired church, he smelled from somewhere the waft and glory of bread baking, like a ghost's guiding glimpse of the heaven of the saints.

In the silvery light of morning, the city market was a riot of colors: the rain-darkened crimson of the servants of the rich and the wet blue of country smocks; the somber viridians of spinach and kale and the crisp greens of lettuces; the scarlets and golds of fruits; and the prodigal, cloisonné brightness of pyramids of melons, all shining like polished porcelain under their beading of rain. The smells of sharp herbs and fishy mud smote him, mixed with those of clinging soil and the smoky tang of wet wool; he heard girls' voices as sweet as the hothouse strawberries they cried and old countrymen's half-unintelligible patois. Raised as he had been in the barbaric North, Sun Wolf had been a grown man before he had ever seen a city marketplace; and even after all these years, the impact of kaleidoscopic delight was the same.

From a countrywoman in a stall where game birds hung like great feathered mops, he asked the direction of the woman Yirth; and though she gave him a suspicious look from dark old eyes, she told him where Yirth could be found.

The house stood on the Little Island, tall, faded, and old. Like most of the houses there, it was of the old-fashioned style, half timbered and lavishly decorated with carving, every pillar, doorpost, and window lattice encrusted with an extravagant lacework of saints, demons, and beasts, wreathed about with all the flowers of the fields. But the paint and gilding had long since worn off them. Standing before the door, Sun Wolf had the impression of being on the edge of a dark and carven wood, watched from beneath the trellised leaves by deformed and malevolent elves. Yet the house itself was severely clean; the shutters that were hinged to every window of its narrow face were darkly varnished, and the worn brick of the step was washed and scraped. He heard his own knock ring hollowly in the fastnesses of the place; a moment later, he heard the light, soft touch of the wizard's approaching stride.

She stepped aside quickly to let him in. Sun Wolf guessed that few people lingered on that step.

"Did Sheera send you?" she asked.

"No." He saw the flicker of suspicion cross the sea-colored eyes. "I've come on my own."

The single dark bar of brow deepened in the middle, over the hooked nose. Then she said, "Come upstairs." On the lower isles, none but the very poorest used the ground floors of their houses for anything except storage.

Yirth's consulting room was dark, long, and narrow, the tall window at its far end looking out over the greenish light of a canal. Plants curtained it, crowding in pots or hanging like robber gangs all from the same gallows, and the light that penetrated was green and mottled. Around him, the Wolf had a sense of half-hidden things, of clay crocks containing herbs lining the dark shelves, of books whose worn bindings gleamed with wax and gold, and of embryos preserved in brandy and herbs hung in dried and knobby bunches from the low rafters. Unknown musical instruments slept like curious monsters in the corners; maps, charts in forgotten tongues, and arcane diagrams of the stars lined the pale plaster of the walls. The place smelled of soap, herbs, and drugs. He felt the curious, tingling sense of latent magic in the air.

She turned to face him in the tabby shadows. "What did you want?" she asked.

"I want to know what I can give you, or what I can do for you, to have you set me free." It came to him as he spoke that there was, in fact, nothing that he could give her, for he had quite literally no possessions beyond his sword. *A hell of a spot,* he thought, *for the richest mercenary in the West.*

But Yirth only considered him for a moment, her hands folded over the gray web of her shawl. Then she said, "Kill Altiokis."

His hand slammed down on the long table that divided the room, making the glass bottles there jump, and his voice crackled with anger. "Curse it, woman, that wasn't your price on the ship!"

The black brow moved; the eyes did not. "It is the price I claim to set you free now," she responded coolly. "Otherwise, your bargain with Sheera stands. You shall be freed—and paid—when the strike force marches."

"You know as well as I do that's insane."

She said nothing, using her silence against him.

"Damn your eyes, you know that lunatic woman's going to get every skirt in that troop killed!" he stormed at her. "I've worked on those women and I've taught them, and some of them will be damned fine warriors in about two years' time, if they live that long, which they won't if they go into battle with a green captain. But if she's stubborn enough to do it, then all I want is to be out of here—to have nothing further to do with it or with her!"

"I fear you have no choice about that," Yirth replied calmly. She rested her hands on the dark wood of the table; the wan light picked out their knots and sinews, making them hardly human, like the strange, folded shapes of an oak burl. "Men go to war for their own entertainment, or for some other man's—women, only because they must. Altiokis, now—Altiokis is deathless and, being deathless, he is bored. It amuses him to conquer cities. Have you seen what happens to a city under his rule?"

"Not being suicidal," the Wolf rumbled irritably, "I've avoided cities under his rule."

"Not being a merchant, or the father of children, or a tradesman needing to make his living, you can do that, I suppose," Yirth returned. "But Tarrin—Tarrin fought for the men who were, and for the generation of men who would not see their children grow up under Altiokis' rule. He and Sheera seek to free Mandrigyn. But my goal is different. I seek to see the Wizard King destroyed, rooted out, as he rooted out and destroyed the other wizards. We are not insane, Captain—the insane ones are those who let him live and grow."

"You don't even know he can be killed," Sun Wolf said. "He's been a wizard since before you were born. We don't even know if he's a man or a demon or what he is."

"He's a man," she lashed out, coldly bitter.

"Then why hasn't he died?" the Wolf demanded. "All the magic in the world won't prolong a man's life—not for a hundred and fifty years! Else we'd have an army of superannuated wizards from all the ages in the past crawling down the walls like ants. But demons are deathless . . ."

"He's a man," she insisted. "Swollen and corrupt on his own immortality. His desires are a man's desires—power, lands, money. His caprices are a man's caprices, not a demon's. He has found a way—some way—of prolonging his life, indefinitely for all we know. Unless he is stopped, he will continue to grow, and all that he touches will rot." She turned and strode to the glimmering window, the light catching the pale streaks in her hair, like wood ash in a half-burned fire. "It is his death I seek, whatever the cost."

"Pox rot you, you're not even a wizard yourself!" he yelled at her. "You've never even gone through this bloody Great Trial I keep hearing about; you haven't got the strength to blow out his bedroom candles! You're as big a fool as Sheera is!"

"Bigger," she bit out, whirling to face him, and Sun Wolf could feel the tension smoking from her, like mist from a pond on a freezing night. "Bigger—because Sheera fights with hope, and I have none. I know what Altiokis is—I know just how great is the gap between his powers and mine. But if he can be drawn into battle, there is a chance, however slim. I will use the might of a freed Mandrigyn to destroy him, as he destroyed my master—as he destroyed my future. If I can do so, I shall be satisfied, though it costs me my life. As a wizard in a town under his rule, I know that it will only be a matter of time before he learns of my existence, and my life would be forfeit then, no matter what I did."

"And what about the cost to the others?" he stormed at her. "What about their lives that Altiokis will destroy?"

"I thought you cared only about your own, Captain," she jeered at him. "We all have our motives, as you yourself have said. Without me, they would still fight. Without you, without Sheera, without Tarrin. Without them, I would have found another weapon to wield against the Wizard King. Depend upon it, Captain, you are a part of us, your flesh and your fate sealed to ours. You can no more desert us now than the string can desert the bow. The others do not fully see this; even Sheera understands it only in terms of her own need, as they all do. But late or soon, the Wizard King must be met. And willing or unwilling, knowing or unknowing, you, Sheera, Tarrin, every man in the mines, and every woman in Mandrigyn will play a part of that meeting."

Sun Wolf stared at her for a moment, silent before her deadly bitterness. Then he said again, "You're insane."

But she only looked at him with those eyes like jade and polar ice. She stood like a black-oak statue, framed in the trailing greenery of the window, wrapped in the misty and terrible cloak of her power. She made no move as his storming footfalls retreated down the sounding well of the stair, nor when the door banged as he let himself out into the narrow street.

In black anger, Sun Wolf made his way through the streets of Mandrigyn. He saw now that, even in the unlikely event that he could talk or coerce that hellcat Sheera into releasing him, Yirth would never let her do it. He had heard women called vacillating and fickle, but he saw now that it was only in such matters as were of little moment to them. Given a single target, a single goal, they could not be shaken. It was a race now, he thought, to finish the training of the strike force before someone in the city learned of what was happening.

He traversed the Spired Bridge and turned aside through the Cathedral Square to avoid the dissolving throngs in the market. Morning was still fresh in the sky, the air cold and wet against his face and throat, and the sea birds crying among the heaped pillows of clouds, warning of storms to come. On two sides of the square, bright-colored clusters of silks and furs proclaimed the patrons of the bookbinders' stalls there; on the third side, a small troop of Governor Derroug's household guards stood watch over his curtained litter beside the Cathedral steps. The usual sycophants were there. The Wolf recognized Stirk, the harbor master, looking like a dressed-up corpse at a Trinitarian funeral, and the fat brute who was Derroug's captain of the watch. Above them, the Cathedral rose, its gold and turquoise mosaics glimmering in the pale morning, buttress and dome seeming to be made of gilded light.

As he passed the steps, a voice beyond him called out, "Captain!"

He knew the voice, and his heart squeezed in his breast with fear and fury. He kept walking. If anyone was within earshot, he had best not stop.

Thin and clear as a cat's mew, Drypettis' voice called out again. "Captain!"

A quick glance showed him no one close enough to hear. He turned in his tracks, hearing the approaching footsteps down the church's tessellated ascent and the restive jittering of tangled gold.

Fluttering with veils, like a half-furled pennoncel pinned with gems, the little woman came scurrying importantly up to him. "Captain, I want you to tell Sheera—" she began.

Sun Wolf caught her by the narrow shoulders as if he would shake the life from her. "Don't you ever," he said in a soundless explosion of wrath, "don't you *ever* address me as captain in public again."

The prim-mouthed face went white with rage, though she must have known that she was in the wrong. Under the thread-drawn saffron of her puffed sleeves, he felt the delicate muscle harden like bone. "How dare you!" she snarled at him. With a wrench she freed herself of his grip. "How dare you speak to *me . . .*"

Anger crackled into him—an anger fed by Yirth's mocking despair, by Sheera's stubbornness, and by the dangers that he had long sensed closing around him. Impatiently he snapped, "You're bloody right I'll speak to you, if you're ever stupid enough to . . ."

She shrank from his pointing finger, pale, blazing, spitting like a cornered cat. The rage in her eyes stopped him, startled, even before she cried, "Don't you touch me, you lecherous blackguard!"

The clipped, mincing accents of Derroug Dru demanded, "And what, pray, is this?"

Altiokis' governor had just emerged from the great bronze doors of the Cathedral and was standing at the top of the steps, twisted and elegant against his backdrop of clients. From where he stood, he could look down upon Sun Wolf. "Unhand my sister, boy."

The guards who had been around the litter were already approaching at a run.

CHAPTER

13

*T*HE SLAVES' CELL OF THE JAIL UNDER THE CITY RECORDS OFFICE
was damp, filthy, and smelled like a privy; the straw underfoot crawled
with black and furtive life. For as many people as there were chained
to the walls, the place was oddly quiet. Even those lucky enough to be
fettered to the wall by a long chain—long enough to allow them to sit
or lie, at any rate—had the sense to keep their mouths shut. Those
who, like Sun Wolf, had had their slave collars locked to the six inches
or so of short chain could only lean against the dripping bricks in
exhausted silence, unable to move, to rest, or to reach the scummy
trough of water that ran down the center of the cell.

The Wolf wasn't certain how long he'd been there. Hours, he
thought, shifting his cramped knees. Like most soldiers, he could relax
in any position; it would be quite some time before the strain began to
tell on him. Others were not so fortunate, or perhaps they had been
here longer. There was a good-looking boy of twenty or so, with a soft
mop of auburn hair that hung over his eyes, who had fallen three
times since the Wolf had been there. Each time he'd been brought up
choking as the iron slip-collar tightened around the flesh of his throat.
He was standing now, but he looked white and sick, his breathing
labored, his eyes glazed and desperate, as if he could feel the last of his
strength leaking away with every minute that passed. The Wolf wondered what crime the boy had committed, if any.

Across the room, a man was moaning and retching where he lay in the unspeakable straw—the opening symptoms to full-scale drug withdrawal. Sun Wolf shut his eyes wearily and wondered how long it would be before someone got word to Sheera of where he was.

Drypettis would do that much, he told himself. She had been in the wrong to call him by his title rather than by his name; but much as she might hate to admit she'd made a mistake, and much as she hated him for supplanting her as Sheera's right hand in the conspiracy, she wouldn't endanger Sheera's cause for the sake of her own pride—at least he hoped not.

The far-off tramp of feet came to him. Iron rattled. He heard Derroug's rather shrill voice again, coldly syrupy. The Wolf remembered the jealous, bitter glare the little man had given him as the guards had dragged him down here. The footsteps came clearer now, the clack of the cane emphasizing the uneven drag of the crippled foot.

Sun Wolf sighed and braced himself. The fetid air was like warm glue in his lungs. Across the room, the drug addict had begun to whimper and pick at the insects, both visible and invisible, that swarmed over his sweating flesh.

There was a smart slap of saluting arms and the grate of a key in the lock. Sun Wolf opened his eyes as torchlight and a sigh of cooler air belched through the open door; he saw figures silhouetted in the doorway at the top of the short flight of steps. Derroug stood there, one white hand emerging like a stamen from a flower of lace to rest on the weighted gold knob of his cane. Sun Wolf remembered the cane, too—the bruise from it was livid on his jaw.

Beside Derroug was Sheera, topping him by half a head.

"Yes, that's him," she said disinterestedly.

He thought he saw the little man's eyes glitter greedily.

A guard in the blue and gold livery of the city came down the steps with the keys, followed by another with a torch. They unlocked his neck chain from the wall, but left his hands manacled behind him, and pushed him forward down the long room, the torchlight flashing darkly from the scummy puddles on the floor. At the bottom of the steps, they stopped, and he looked up at Sheera, haughty and exquisite in heliotrope satin, amethysts sparkling like trapped stars in the black handfuls of her hair.

She was shaking, like a too tightly tensioned wire before it snapped.

"You insulted my sister," Derroug purred, still looking down at the taller man, though Sun Wolf had the odd feeling that it was not he who was being spoken to, but Sheera. "For that I could confiscate you and have you cut and put to work cleaning out latrines for the rest of your life, boy."

I'd kill you first, Sun Wolf thought, but he could feel Sheera's eyes on him, desperately willing him to be humble. He swallowed and kept his attention fixed on the pearl-sewn insets of lace around the flounced hem of her gown. "I know that, my lord. I am truly sorry—it was never my intention to do so." He knew if he looked up and met those smug eyes, something of his own desire to ram those little white teeth through the back of that oily head might show.

"But after consulting with your—mistress—" The cool voice laid a double meaning upon the term of ownership, and Sun Wolf glanced up in time to see Derroug run his eyes appraisingly over Sheera's body. "—my sister has agreed to forget the incident. You are, after all, a barbarian, and I am sure that my lady Sheera could ill spare your—services."

He saw Sheera's cheeks darken in the torchlight and Derroug's insinuating smile.

He made himself say, "Thank you, my lord."

"And since you are a barbarian," Derroug continued primly, "I am positive that your education has been so far neglected that you are not aware that it is customary to kneel when a slave addresses the governor of this city."

Sun Wolf, who was perfectly conversant with the laws of servitude, knew that the custom was nothing of the kind—that this little man merely wished to see a bigger one on his knees before the governor. Awkwardly, because his hands were still bound behind him, he knelt and touched his forehead to the stinking clay of the dirty steps. "I am sorry, my lord," he murmured through clenched teeth.

Sheera's voice said, "Get up."

He obeyed her, schooling his face to show nothing of the rage that went through him like the burning of fever, wishing that he had Starhawk's cool impassivity of countenance. He saw Derroug watching him intently, saw the little pointed tip of a pink tongue steal out to lick his lips.

"But I'm afraid, Sheera darling, that you are partly at fault for not having schooled him better. I know these barbarians—the lash is all they understand. But as it happens, I have—something better." The governor's glinting brown eyes slid sideways at her, his gaze traveling slowly over her, like a lingering hand. "Would you object to my dispensing a salutary lesson?"

Sheera shrugged and did not look in Sun Wolf's direction. Her voice was carefully unconcerned. "If you think it would benefit anyone."

"Oh, I'm sure it would." Derroug Dru smiled. "I think it will be of great benefit to you both. Lessons in the consequences of willful disobedience are always worth watching."

As the guards conducted them down the narrow corridors under the Records Office, Sun Wolf felt the sweat making tracks in the grime of his face. A lesson in the consequences of disobedience could mean anything, and Sheera was evidently quite prepared to let him take it. Not, he reflected in that grimly calm corner of his mind, that there was anything she could do about it. Like him, she had the choice of trying to fight her way out of it now and very likely implicating and destroying all the others in the troop in the resulting furor or going along and gambling on her bluff. Among the lurching shadows of the ever-narrowing halls, her back was straight and uncommunicative. The gleam of the torch flame spilled down the satin of her dress as she held it clear of the filthy flagstones; Derroug's hand, straying to touch her hip, was like a flaccid white spider on the shining fabric.

"Our Lord Altiokis has recently sent me—ah—assurances that can be used to punish those who are disobedient or disloyal to me as his governor," he was saying. "In view of the recent upheavals, such measures are quite necessary. There must be no doubt in my mind of the loyalty of our citizens."

"No," Sheera murmured. "Of course not."

Behind her, Sun Wolf could see she was trembling, either with rage or with fear.

A guard opened a door, the second to the last along the narrow hall. Torchlight gleamed on something smooth and reflective in the darkness. As he stepped aside to let Sheera precede him into the room, Derroug asked the sergeant of the guards, "Has one of them been let loose?"

"Yes, my lord," the man muttered and wiped his beaded face under the gold helmet rim.

The little man smiled and followed Sheera into the room. Other guards pushed Sun Wolf down the two little steps after them. The door closed, shutting out the torchlight from the hall.

The only light in the room came from candles that flickered behind a thick pane of glass set in the wall that faced the door. It showed Sun Wolf a narrow cell, such as commonly contained prisoners important enough to be singly confined, its bricks scarred by the bored scrapings of former inmates. The room was small, some five feet by five; it hid nothing, even from that diffuse gleam. The reflections of the candles showed him Sheera's face, impassive but wary, and the greedy gleam in the governor's eyes as he looked at her.

"Observe," Derroug purred, his hand moving toward the window. "I have been privileged to see Altiokis' cell like this, built in the oldest part of his Citadel; I have been more than privileged that he has—ah —sent me the wherewithal to establish one of my own. It is most effective for—disloyalty."

The room beyond the glass was clearly another solitary cell. It was only a little larger than the first, and utterly bare of furniture. Candles burned in niches close to the ceiling, higher than a man could reach. It contained four or five small lead boxes; one of them had been opened. The cell door, clearly the last door along the hall down which they had passed, was shut, but the Wolf could hear more guards approaching along the corridor. Mixed with their surer tread, he could distinguish the unwilling, shuffling step of a prisoner's feet.

Something moved in the semidark of the room beyond the window. For a moment, he thought it was only a chance reflection in the glass, but he saw Sheera's head jerk to catch the motion as well. In a moment there was another flicker, bright and elusive. There was something there, something like a whirling flake of fire, drifting and eddying near the ceiling with a restless motion that was almost like life.

Sun Wolf frowned, following it with his eyes through the protective window. Whether it was bright in itself or merely reflective of chance flames, he could not tell. It was difficult to track its motions, for it skittered here and there, almost randomly, like a housefly on a hot day or a dragonfly skimming on the warm air over the marshes; it was a single, moving point of bright flame in the murk beyond the glass.

There was a fumbling noise in the corridor. With astonishing quickness, the door visible in the other room opened and slammed shut again behind the man who had been thrust inside—the red-haired young slave who had stood opposite Sun Wolf in the jail. The prisoner stumbled, throwing his unbound hands wide for balance; for an instant he stood in the center of the room, gaping about him, baby-blue eyes wide and staring with fear.

The boy swung around with a startled cry.

Like an elongating needle of light, the flake of fire—or whatever it was—struck, an instantaneous vision of incredible quickness. The young man staggered, his hands going to cover one of his eyes as if something had stung it. The next instant, his screaming could be heard through the stone and glass of the wall.

What followed was sickening, horrifying even to a mercenary inured to all the terrible fashions in which men slew one another. The boy bent double, clutching his eye, his screams rising to a frenzied pitch. He began to run, clawing blindly, ineffectually, at his face, falling into walls. The Wolf saw the thread of blood begin to drip from between the grabbing fingers as the boy's knees buckled. He registered, with clinical awareness, the progress of the pain by the twisting jerks of the boy's body on the floor and by the rising agony and terror of the shrieks. Sun Wolf noted how the frantic fingers dug and picked, how the helpless limbs threshed about, and how the back writhed into an arch.

It seemed to take forever. The boy was rolling on the floor, screaming . . . screaming . . .

Sun Wolf could tell—he thought they all could tell—when the screams changed, when the fire—poison—insect—whatever it was—ate its way through to the brain. Something broke in the boy's cries; a deafening, animal howl replaced the human voice. The body jerked, as if every muscle had spasmed together, and began to roll and hop around the cell in a grotesque and filthy parody of life. Glancing at Sheera, Sun Wolf saw that she had closed her eyes. Had she been able to, she would have brought up her hands to cover her ears as well. Beyond her, Derroug's face wore a tight, satisfied smile; through his flared nostrils, his breathing dragged, as if he had drunk wine.

Sun Wolf looked back to the window, feeling his own face, his own hands, bathed in icy sweat. If there were ever a suspicion, ever a question, about the troop, the governor had only to show the suspect what he himself had just seen. There was no doubt that person would tell everything—the Wolf knew that he would.

The screaming continued, a gross, bestial ululation; the body was still moving, blood-splotched hands fumbling at the stones on the floor.

Derroug's voice was a soft, almost dreamy murmur. "So you see, my dear," he was saying, "it is best that we ascertain, once and for all, who can—demonstrate—their loyalty to me." And his little white hand stole around her waist. "Send your boy home."

"Apologize to Drypettis?" Sun Wolf paused in the act of pouring; the golden brandy slopped over the rim of the cup and onto his hand. The pine table of the potting room was pooled with red wine and amber spirits; the laden air reeked of them, heavy over the thick aromas of dirt and potting clay. His eyes were red-rimmed, bloodshot, and unnaturally steady. He had been drinking methodically and comprehensively since he had returned home that morning. It was now an hour short of sunset, and Sheera had just returned. His voice was only slightly thickened as he said, "That haughty little snirp should never have called me captain in public and she knows it."

Sheera's mouth looked rather white, her lips pressed tight together, her dark hair still sticking to her cheeks with the dampness of her bath. The Wolf was half tempted to pull up a chair for her and pour her a glass—not that there was much left in any of the bottles by this time. He had never seen a woman who looked as if she needed it more.

But Sheera said, "She says she never called you captain."

He stared at her, wondering if the brandy had affected his perception. "She what?"

"She never called you captain. She told me she called out to you and told you to take a message to me, and you refused and told her you were no one's errand boy . . ."

"That's a lie." He straight-armed the brandy at one shot and let the glass slide from his fingers. Then rage hit him, stronger than any drink, stronger than what he had felt for Derroug while on his knees before the governor in the prison.

"Captain," Sheera said tightly, "Dru spoke to me just before I left the palace. She would never have called you by your title in public. She knows better than that."

"She may know better than that," Sun Wolf said levelly, "but it's possible to forget. All right. But that's what she called me, and that's why—"

The controlled voice cracked suddenly. "You're saying Dru lied to me."

"Yes," the Wolf said, "that's what I'm saying. Rather than admit that she was in the wrong." It crossed his mind fleetingly that he should not be arguing—not drunk as he was, not this afternoon, not after the kind of scene he was fairly certain had taken place with Drypettis immediately after what amounted to rape. He could see the lines of tension digging themselves tighter and tighter into Sheera's face, like the print of ugly memories in her tired flesh, and the sudden, uncontrollable trembling of her bruised lips. But her next words drove any thought from his mind.

"And what would you rather do than admit you're wrong, Captain?"

"Not lie about one of my troops."

"Hah!" She had picked up a small rake, turning it nervously in fingers that shook; now she threw it back to the table with ringing violence. "Your troops! You'd have tossed her out from the start—"

"Damned right I would," he retorted, "and this is why."

"Because she was never to your taste, you mean!"

"Woman, if you think all I've had to do in the last two months has been to put together a harem of assassins for myself—"

"Rot your eyes, what else have you been doing?" she yelled back at him. "From Lady Wrinshardin to Gilden and Wilarne—"

"Let's not forget the ones who were assigned," he roared, pitching his voice to drown hers. "If you're jealous . . ."

"Don't flatter yourself!" she spat at him. "That's what sickens you, isn't it? You can't stand to teach women the arts of war because those are your preserve, aren't they? The only way you can take it is if you make them your women. They have your permission to be good so long as you're better, and the ones who get to be the best you make damned sure will love you too much ever to beat you!"

"You don't know what the hell you're talking about and you sure aren't warrior enough to know what it means!" he lashed back at her, hurling the brandy bottle at the opposite wall, so that it shattered in an explosion of alcohol and glass. "The best of the women I know is better than any man—"

"Oh, yes," the woman sneered furiously. "I've seen that best one of yours, and she looked at you the way a schoolgirl looks at her first beau! You've never given two cow patties together for anything about this troop! You wouldn't care if we were all destroyed, so long as you aren't threatened by anyone else's excellence!"

"You talk to me about that when you've been a warrior anywhere near as long as I have—or the Hawk has!" he stormed at her. "And no, I don't give two cow pats together for you and your stupid cause. And yes, part of it's because of the ladies whom I don't want to see get their throats cut in your damfool enterprise—"

"Tarrin—"

"I'm damned sick of hearing about pox-rotted Tarrin and your reeking cause!" he roared.

Red with rage, she shouted over his voice, "You can't see any higher than your own comforts—"

He yelled back at her, "That's what I've said from the beginning, rot your poxy eyes! I'd have washed my hands of the whole flaming business, and of you, too—stubborn, bullheaded hellcat that you are! I'm through with you and your damned tantrums!"

"You'll stay and you'll like it!" Sheera raged. "Or you'll die screaming your guts out a day's journey from the wall, and that's the only choice you've got, soldier! You'll do what I tell you or Yirth may not even give you that choice!"

She whirled in a flame-colored slash of skirts and veils and stormed from the little room, slamming the flimsy door behind her. He heard her footsteps stride into the distance, crashing hollowly, and at last heard the thunderous smash of the outer door. Through the window, he saw her stride up into the twilight of the garden toward the house, past the rocks he had settled among the bare roots of juniper, and past the dark pavilion of the bathhouse. She was sobbing, the dry, bitter weeping of rage.

Deliberately, Sun Wolf picked up a wine bottle from the table and hurled it against the opposite wall. He did the same with the next and the next and the next—and all the others that he had consumed in the course of the day, since he had returned from seeing what it was that Derroug had hidden beneath his palace. Then he got up and made his way with a perfectly steady stride to the stables, saddled a horse, and rode out of Mandrigyn by the land gate, just as the sun was setting.

He rode throughout the night and on into morning. The alcohol burned slowly out of his blood without lessening in him the determination to thwart Sheera, once and for all. Anzid was just about the last choice he would have taken, had he been allowed to pick his own death, but horrible death of some sort would come to him for certain if he remained in Mandrigyn. Today he had seen at least one that was worse than anzid. And in any case, he would die his own man, not Sheera's slave.

He turned the horse's head toward the west, traversing in darkness the half-flooded fields, spiky with sedge and with the bare branches of naked trees. Before midnight, he reached the crossroads where the way ran up to the Iron Pass and the greater bulk of the Tchard Mountains and out over the uplands to pass through the rocks of the Stren Water Valley down to the rich Bight Coast. It had been in his mind to ride north up the pass, knowing that Sheera would never think to seek him on Altiokis' very doorstep. And seek him she would, of that he was certain. She would never endure this last defiance from him. He had vowed that he would not give her the satisfaction of ever finding his body, of ever knowing for certain that he was dead.

Besides, if she found him before the anzid killed him, it might be possible for her to bring him back.

But in the end, he could not take the Citadel road. He turned the mare's head westward where the roads crossed and spurred on through the dripping silence of the dark woods.

He wondered if the Hawk would understand what he was doing.

Ari, he knew, would have apologized to Drypettis with every evidence of sincerity and a mental vow to take it out of that pinch-faced little vixen later. And the Hawk . . . The Hawk would have told them at the outset that she would die and be damned to them—or else have found a way to avoid the entire situation.

What had Sheera meant about the way the Hawk had looked at him? Was it simply Sheera's jealousy or her hate? Or did she, as a woman, see things with a woman's different eyes.

He didn't think so, much as he would have liked to believe that Starhawk had looked at him with something other than that calm, businesslike gaze. In his experience, love had always meant demands —on the time, on the soul, and certainly on the attention. Starhawk had never asked him for anything except instruction in their chosen craft of war and an occasional daffodil bulb for her own garden.

It was Starhawk, in fact, who had defined for him why love was death to the professional, on one of those long winter evenings in Wrynde when Fawn had gone to sleep, her head on his lap, her curls spilling over his thigh. He and the Hawk had sat up talking, half drunk before the white sand of the sunken hearth, listening to the rain drumming on the cypresses of the gardens outside. It was he who had spoken of love, who had quoted his father's maxim: *Don't fall in love and don't mess with magic.* Love was a crack in a man's armor, he had said. But the Hawk, with her clearer insight, had said that love simply caused one to cease being single-minded. For a warrior, to look aside from the main goal of survival could mean death. He could not love, if his goal was to survive at all costs.

Could a woman who loved speak of love with such clear-eyed brutality?

Could a woman who didn't?

Dawn came, slow and gray through the wooded hills. Yellow leaves muffled the road in soaked carpets; overhanging branches splattered and dripped on the Wolf's back. He rode more slowly now, scouting as he went, taking his bearings on the crowding hills visible above the bare trees. South of the road, those hills shouldered close, massive and lumpy, stitched with narrow ravines and a rising network of ledges, half choked in scrub and wild grape. Here and there, he heard the frothing voices of swollen streams, booming among the rocks.

Wind flicked his long hair back over his shoulders and laid a cold hand on his cheek. He had forgotten how good it felt to be alone and free, even if only free to die.

It was midafternoon when he let the horse go. He sent it on its way along the westward road with a slap on the rump, and it trotted off gamely, leaving tracks that Sheera was sure to follow. With any luck, she'd trail it quite a distance and never find his body at all. It would rot that hellcat's soul, he thought with a grim inward smile, to think that he might, by some miracle, have eluded her—to think that, somewhere in the world, he might still be alive and laughing.

He was already beginning to feel the anzid working in his veins, like the early stirrings of fever. He struck back through the woods in an oblique course toward the rocks of the higher hills and the caves that he knew lay in the direction of Mandrigyn. It was a long way, and he went cautiously, covering his tracks, wading in the freezing scour of the streams, and finding his way over the rocky ground by instinct when the daylight faded again into evening.

He had always had sharper senses in the dark than most men; he had had that ability as a child, he remembered, and it had been almost uncanny. Even in the cloud-covered darkness and rising wind, he made out the vague shapes of the trees, the ghostly birches and leering, gargoyle oaks. His nose told him it would rain later, destroying his tracks; wind was already tugging at his clothes.

The ground underfoot grew steep and stony, rising sharply and broken by the outcropped bones of the earth. He found that his breath had begun to saw at his lungs and throat, a cold sharpness, as if broken glass were lodged somewhere inside. Still the ground steepened, and the foliage thinned around him; vague rock shapes became visible above, rimmed with a milky half-light that only the utter darkness of the rest of the night let him see at all. Weakness pulled at him and a kind of feverish pain that had no single location; nausea had begun to cramp his stomach like chewing pincers.

The first wave of it hit him in the high, windy darkness of a broken hillside, doubling him over, as if a drench of acid had been spilled through his guts. The shock of it took his breath away and, when the pain faded, left him weak and shaking, feeling sickened and queerly vulnerable. After a time, he got to his feet, hardly daring to move for fear the red agony would return. Even as he staggered on, he felt it lying in wait for him, lurking behind every fiber of his muscles.

It took him another hour to find the kind of place that he sought. He had been looking for a cave deep in the hills, so far from the road that, no matter how loudly he screamed, no searchers would hear. What he found was a ruined building, a sort of chapel whose broken walls were wreathed and hung with curtains of winter-brown vines. In the crypt below it was a pit, some twenty feet deep and circular, ten or fifteen feet across. Thrown pebbles clinked solidly or rustled in weeds; the little light that filtered through the blowing branches above him showed him nothing stirring but wind-tossed heather.

By now he was sweating, his hands trembling, a growing pain in his body punctuated by lightning bolts of cramps. Cautiously, he hung by his hands over the edge, then let himself drop.

It was a mistake. It was as if his entire body had been flayed apart; the slightest shock or jar pierced him like tearing splinters of wood. The sickening intensity of the pain made him vomit, and the retching brought with it new pains, which in turn fed others. Like the first cracking of a sea wall, each new agony lessened his resistance to those mounting behind it, until they ripped his flesh and his mind as a volcano would rip the rock that sealed it. Dimly, he wondered how he could still be conscious, or if the agony would go on like this until he died.

It was only the beginning of an endless night.

Sheera found him in the pit, long after the dawn that barely lightened the blackness of the rainsqualls of the night. Wind tore at her wet riding skirts as she stood looking down from the pit's edge and snagged at the dripping coils of her hair. Though it was his screaming which had drawn her, his voice had cracked and failed. Through the rain that slashed her eyes, she could see him still moving, crawling feverishly through the gross filth that smeared every inch of the pit's floor, groaning brokenly but unable to rest.

In spite of the rain, the place smelled like one of the lower cesspools of Hell. Resolutely, she knotted the rope she had brought with her to the bole of a tree and shinned down. Her lioness rage had carried her through the night hunt, but now, seeing what was left after the anzid had done its work, she felt only a queer mingling of pity and spite and horror. She wondered if Yirth had been aware that the death would take this long.

From fever or pain, he had thrown off most of his clothes, and the rain made runnels through the filth that smeared his blue and icy flesh. He was still crawling doggedly, as if he could somehow outdistance the agony; but as she approached, he was seized with a spasm of retching that had long since ceased to bring up anything but gory bile. She saw that his hands were torn and bloody, clenched in pain so tightly she thought the force of it must break the bones. After the convulsion had ceased, he lay sobbing, racked by the aftermath, the rain trickling through the stringy weeds of his hair. His face was turned aside a little from the unspeakable pools in which he half lay, and the flesh of it looked sunken and pinched, like a dying man's.

There were no sounds in the pit then, except for the dreary, incessant rustle of falling water and his hoarse, wretched sobbing. That, too, she had not expected. She walked a step nearer and stood looking in a kind of horrible fascination at the degraded head, the sodden hair thin and matted with slime, and the broken and trembling hands. Quietly, she said, "You stupid, stubborn bastard." Her own voice sounded shaky to her ears. "I've got a good mind to go off and leave you, after all."

She had not thought he'd heard. But he moved his head a little, dilated eyes regarding her through a fog of pain from pits of black-ened flesh. She could tell he was almost blind, fighting with every tormented muscle of his body to bring her into focus, to speak, and to control the wheezing thread of his scream-shattered voice into some-thing that could be heard and understood.

He managed to whisper, "Leave me, then."

Her own horror at what she had done turned to fury, fed by the weariness of her long night's terrified searching. Through darkness and clouds of weakness, Sun Wolf could see almost nothing, but his senses, raw as if sandpapered, brought him the feel of her rage like a wave of heat. For a moment, he wondered if she would kick him where he lay or lash at him with the riding whip in her hands.

But then he heard her turn away, and the splash of her boots re-treated through the puddles that scattered the pit's floor in the rain. For an elastic time he lay fighting the unconsciousness that he knew would only bring him the hideous terror of visions. Then he heard the rattle of her horse's retreating hooves, dying away into the thundering clatter of the rain. He slipped again into the red vortex of delirium.

There was utter loneliness there and terrors that reduced the pain ripping through his distant body to an insignificant ache that would merely result in his eventual death. Worse things pursued and caught him—loss, regret, self-hate, and all the spilling ugliness that festered in the bottommost pits of the mind.

And then, after black wanderings, he was aware of moonlight in a place he had never been before and the far-off surge of the sea. Blink-ing, he made out the narrowing stone walls of one of those beehive chapels that dotted the rocky coasts of the ocean in the northwest, the darkness around the Mother's altar, and the shape of a warrior kneel-ing just beyond the uneven circle of moonlight that lay like a tiny carpet in the center of the trampled clay floor.

The warrior's clothing was unfamiliar, the quilted, shiny stuff of the Bight Coast. The scarred boots he knew, and the sword that lay with the edge of its blade across the moonlight, a white and blinding silver. The bent head, pale and bright as the moonlight, he could have mis-taken for no other.

She looked up, and he saw tears glittering on the high cheekbones, like rain fallen on stone. She whispered, "Chief?" and got haltingly to her feet, her eyes struggling to pierce the gloom that separated them. "Chief, where are you? I've been looking for you . . ."

He held out his hand to her and saw it, torn and filthy, as he had seen it lying in the slime of the pit. She hesitated, then took it, her lips like ice against it, her tears scalding the raw flesh.

"Where are you?" she whispered again.

"I'm in Mandrigyn," he said quietly, forcing the scorched remains of his voice to be steady. "I'm dying—don't look for me further."

"Rot that," Starhawk said, her voice shaking. "I haven't come all this way just to—"

"Hawk, listen," he whispered, and she raised her eyes, the blood from his hand streaking her cheek, blotched and smeared with her tears. "Just tell me this—did you love me?"

"Of course," she said impatiently. "Wolf, I'll always love you. I always have loved you."

He sighed, and the weight settled heavier over him, the grief for what could have been. "I'm sorry," he said. "I wasted the time we had —and I'm sorry for what that did to you."

She shook her head, even the slight brushing movement of it tearing at the rawness of his overtaxed body. He shut his teeth hard against the pain, for he could feel himself already fraying, his flesh tugged at by the winds of nothingness.

"The time wasn't wasted," Starhawk said softly. "If you'd thought you loved me as you loved Fawnie and the others, you would have kept me at a distance, as you did them, and that would have been worse. I would rather be one of your men than one of your women."

"I see that," he murmured, for he had seen it, in the twisting visions of the endless night. "But that speaks better of you than it does of me."

"You are what you are." Her voice was so quiet that, over it, he could hear the distant beat of the sea on the rocks and the faint thread of the night wind. Her hands tightened like icy bones around the broken mess of his fingers, and he knew she could feel him going. "I wouldn't have traded it."

"I was what I was," he corrected her. "And I wanted you to know."

"I knew."

He had never before seen her cry, not even when they'd cut arrowheads from her flesh on the battlefields; her tears fell without bitterness or weakness, only coursing with the loneliness that he had himself come to understand. He raised his hand to touch the white silk of her hair. "I love you, Hawk," he whispered. "Not just as one of my men

—and not just as one of my women. I'm sorry I did not know it in time."

He felt himself slip from her, drawn back toward that bleak and storming darkness. He knew his body and his soul were breaking, like a ship on a reef; all his garnered strength sieved bleeding through the wreckage of spars. All the buried things, the loves and hopes and desires that he had derided and forgotten because he could not bear to see them denied him by fate, poured burning from their cracked hiding places and challenged him to deny them now.

They were like ancient dreams of fire, as searing as molten gold. He heard his father's derisive jeers through the darkness, though the voice was his own; the old dreams burned like flame, the heat of them greater than the pain of the anzid burning through his flesh. But he gathered the dreams into his hands, though they were made of fire, of molten rage, and of wonder. The scorching of their power seared and peeled the last of his flesh away, and his final vision was of the stark lacework of his bones, clutching those forgotten fires.

Then the vision disappeared from him, as his own apparition had faded from Starhawk's grasp. He opened his eyes to the slanted wood of the loft ceiling, fretted with the wan sunlight that filtered through the bare trees of Sheera's courtyard. He heard the murmur of Sheera's voice from below in the orangery and Yirth's terse and scornful reply.

Yirth, he thought and closed his eyes again, overborne by horror and despair. All his efforts of that long day to hide his trail from Sheera—and she had only to ask Yirth to speak his name and look into standing water. The night he had spent in the pit, the pain, and the unnamable grief had been for nothing.

Weak and spent, there was nothing of his scoured flesh or mind that would answer his bidding; had he had the strength to do so, he would have wept. The women had won. He was still alive and still their slave. Even had he been able to find a way to elude Yirth's magic, he knew he would make no further attempt at escape. He would never have the strength to go through that again.

CHAPTER

～ 14 ～

HAD SUN WOLF BEEN ABLE TO, HE WOULD HAVE AVOIDED Yirth's care, but he could not. For two days he lay utterly helpless, drinking what little she gave him to drink, feeling the shadows shrink and rise with the passage of the cloudy days, and listening to the rain drum on the tiles or trickle, gossiping, from the eaves. In the nights, he heard the women assemble below, the thud of feet and the sharp bark of Denga Rey's voice, Sheera's curt commands, and mingling of voices in the gardens, as they came and went from the bathhouse. Once he heard a hesitant tread climb the stairs toward his loft, pause just below the turn that led to his door, and wait there for a long time, before retreating once again.

He slept a great deal. His body and mind both felt gutted. Sometimes the women who came—Amber Eyes, Yirth, occasionally Sheera —would speak to him, but he did not remember replying. There seemed to be no point in it.

On the third day, he was able to eat again, a little, though meat still nauseated him. In the afternoon, he went down to the potting room and repaired the damage that neglect had done to his bulbs and to the young trees in the succession houses. Like a spark slowly flickering to life against damp tinder, he could feel himself coming back to himself, but the weariness that clung to his bones made him wary of even the slightest tax on either his body or the more deeply lacerated ribbons of his soul. When he heard Sheera come into the orangery in the changeable twilight at sundown, he avoided her, fading back into the shadows of the potting room when she entered it and slipping unseen out the door behind her.

After the women had come and gone that night, he went to lie in the hot water and steam of the bathhouse, listening to the wind that thrashed the bare branches overhead, feeling, as he had felt as a child, that curious sense of being alive with the life of the night around him.

He returned to a sleep unmarred by dreams.

Voices in the orangery woke him, a soft, furtive murmuring, and the swift patter of bare feet. During his illness, though she had nursed him by day, Amber Eyes had not spent the night there. He wondered whether she had had another lover all along while Sheera had assigned her to keep him occupied. The room was empty as he rolled soundlessly to his feet and stole toward the stairway door.

He could hear their voices clearly.

". . . silly cuckoos, you should never have tried it alone! If you'd been taken . . ."

It was Sheera's voice, the stammering tension giving the lie to the anger in her words.

"More of us wouldn't have done any good," Gilden's huskier tones argued. "It would have just made more to be caught . . . Holy God, Sheera, you weren't there! I don't know what it was! But . . ."

"Is she still there, then?" Denga Rey demanded sharply.

Gilden must have nodded. After a moment, the gladiator went on roughly. "Then we'll have to go back."

"But they'll know someone's trying to rescue her now." That was Wilarne's voice.

By the spirits of my ancestors, how the hell many of them are in on it, whatever it is? Sun Wolf asked himself.

Exercising every ounce of animal caution he possessed, trusting that whatever noise they were making down in the orangery would divert their minds, if the stairs creaked—though it shouldn't, if their training had done them any good!—he slipped down the stairs, stopping just behind where he knew his body would catch the light.

There were five of them, grouped around the seed of light that glowed above the clay lamp on the table. A thread of gold reflection outlined the sharp curve of Denga Rey's aquiline profile and glistened in her dark eyes. Beside her, Sheera was wrapped in the cherry-red wool of her bed robe, her black hair strewed over her shoulders like sea wrack. The three women before them were dressed—or undressed —for battle.

From his hiding place, Sun Wolf noted the changes in those delicate-boned bodies. The slack flesh had given place to hard muscle. Even Eo, towering above the two little hairdressers, had a taut sleekness to her, for all her remaining bulk. Under dark cloaks, they wore only the leather breast guards of their training outfits, short drawers, and knife belts. Their hair had been braided tightly back; Wilarne's had come half undone in some kind of struggle and lay in an asymmetrical rope over her left shoulder, the ends tipped and sticky with blood.

Sheera's women, he thought, had gone to battle before their commander was ready for it. He wondered why.

Sheera was saying, "When was she arrested? And why?"

Eo fixed her with cold, bitter blue eyes. "Do you really need to ask why?"

Sheera's back stiffened. Gilden said, with her usual diplomacy, "The reason was supposedly insolence in the street. But he spoke to her yesterday outside Eo's forge . . ."

Eo went on bitterly. "Well, he can hardly seriously suspect a fifteen-year-old girl of treason."

"We had to act fast," Wilarne said, dark almond eyes wide with concern. "That's why we weren't in class tonight."

"You'd have done better to come and get help," Denga Rey snapped.

In the darkness of the stairs, Sun Wolf felt sudden anger kindle through him, startling and cold. *Tisa,* he thought. *Gilden's daughter— Eo's niece and apprentice.* A girl whose adolescent gawkishness was fading into a coltish beauty. He wondered if she, too, had been given an opportunity to prove her "loyalty" to Derroug and had been arrested for rebuffing him.

Gilden was saying, "We went in over the wall near the Lupris Canal. We took out two guards, weighted the bodies, and dumped them. But —Sheera, the guards in the palace compound itself! I swear they see in the dark. There was no light, none, but they saw us and came after us. We could hear them. One of them caught Wilarne . . ."

"I don't understand it," Wilarne whispered. Her hands, fine-boned and as little as a child's, clenched together in the memory of the fight and the fear. "He—he didn't seem to feel pain. Others were coming

—I hurt him, I know I hurt him, but it didn't stop him, it didn't do anything. I barely got away . . .''

"All right," Sheera said. "I'll send a message to Drypettis, tell her what's happened, and see if she can get us into the palace."

"She'll be watched," Sun Wolf said. "And you couldn't get a message to her tonight."

It was the first time that he had spoken in three days, and they swung around, startled, not even knowing that he had been there watching them. Having spoken to Starhawk from the pit, he was no longer surprised at what remained of his voice, but he saw the frown that folded Sheera's brow at the rasping wheeze of it, the worry in Eo's broad, motherly face, and the flood of joy and relief in the eyes of Gilden and Wilarne. They had, he realized, been truly frightened for him.

Sheera was the first to speak. "Derroug doesn't suspect Dru . . ."

"Maybe not of treason, but he knows she'd do just about anything you bade her. Whether he understands that there's some kind of connection between you and Gilden, I don't know . . . But in any case, we've got to get Tisa out of there before he tries to lay hands on her."

He intercepted a look from Gilden and realized that, for all her briskly matter-of-fact attitude about her daughter, she was not quite the offhand mother she seemed. He also realized that she had not expected him to agree with her. Gruffly, he amplified. "If Derroug tries to force her, she'll fight—and she'll fight like a trained warrior, not a scared girl. Then the cat's really going to be out of the bag. So when did you take out the guards, Gilden?"

Gilden stammered, recovering herself, "About two hours ago," she said. "They were starting their watch—the watches are four hours."

"We'll need a diversion, then." He glanced across at Sheera. "Think you can find Derroug's sleeping quarters again?"

Her face scarlet, she said, "Yes," in a stifled voice.

"Change your clothes, then, and bring your weapons. Denga, you stay here. I'm not surprised the little bastard's guards saw you skirts in the dark if you didn't blacken your flesh."

Gilden, Wilarne, and Eo looked at one another in confusion.

"But never mind, you're lucky you weren't killed, and we'll leave it at that. I don't know if you've made any provision for the plot being blown, Sheera, but it's too late to make one now. You know that if anyone's captured, she'll talk. You were in that cellar, too."

At the memory of the red-haired young slave's screams, Sheera went pale, her face drained of color as quickly as it had suffused.

"Myself, I'd sit tight and try to bluff it out. But if we're not back by morning, Denga, you can assume that you're in command and Derroug knows everything. Take whatever steps you think you need to."

"All right," the gladiator said.

"We'll get Tisa to Lady Wrinshardin's. Derroug know she's your daughter?" This last was addressed to Gilden, who shook her head.

"Good." He stood for a moment, studying his two half-pints, dainty little assassins with blood in their hair. "One more thing. As I said, we'll need a diversion. You two are so good at coming up with pranks —by the time I come back, I want you to think of a real good one."

And the interesting thing was that, when he came downstairs five minutes later, wearing only a short battle kilt, boots, and his weapons, they had thought of one.

"There they go." Turning his face slightly to keep his nose out of the muddy roof tiles, Sun Wolf glanced down into the barracks court-yard of the governor's palace, then across at Sheera, who lay spread-eagled in the shadows of the ornamental parapet at his side. She raised her head a little; the view from the roof of the counting house that backed the barracks court was excellent. Men could be seen pouring out of the barracks, sleepily pulling on their blue and gold livery or rubbing unshaven faces and cursing. In their midst, solicitously supported by the fat captain, minced the veiled forms of Gilden and Wilarne, dressed to the eyebrows in a fashion that would have done Cobra and Crazyred proud.

He heard the faint breath of Sheera's laughter. "Where on earth did Gilden get that feather tippet?" she whispered. "That's the most vulgar thing I've ever seen, but it must have cost somebody fifty crowns!"

Strident and foul, Gilden's voice carried up to them in a startlingly accurate rendering of a by-no-means carefully bred courtesan's tones. "The bastard said something about burning the records—that all his Highness' troops wouldn't do him a speck of good without records."

Sheera whispered, "The Records Office is in the northeast corner of the palace. Derroug's quarters are at the southwest."

"Right." Moving carefully, Sun Wolf slid down the sharp slant of the roof, edged around a lead gargoyle, and lowered himself down to the oak spar of a decorated beam end that thrust itself out into space, a dozen feet above the dark slot of the alley that separated counting house from barracks wall. The gap was negligible, though the landing was narrow—eighteen inches at the top of the parapet. In this corner of the old defense works that had once surrounded this part of the grounds, the stonework looked neglected and treacherous. He jumped, out and down, his body flexing compactly as it hit the top of the crenelations, and he sprang neatly down to the catwalk a few feet below.

He looked back up to the roof. Sheera had the sense to keep moving, smoothly and swiftly, once she broke cover. The windy darkness of the night was such that everything seemed to be moving—it would have been difficult to distinguish the movement as human. Since his ordeal in the pit, Sun Wolf was aware that he could see clearly now in darkness—he thought that his sense of direction, always excellent, had improved as well. In the shadows, he could see Sheera's face, tense and watchful, as she reached the edge of the roof. She lowered herself over, her feet feeling competently for the beam, her blackened arms momentarily silhouetted against the paler plaster of the house.

A cat-leap, and she was beside him. Silently, she scanned the dark bulk of the palace before them, then pointed southwest.

Thanks to the alarm, the barracks were empty. They descended from the wall by the turret stair of the guardhouse itself, ducking through the stable wing that Sheera knew, from her acquaintance with Drypettis, ran the length of the west side of the grounds, merging with the kitchens on the southwest corner. As they dodged along the walls, in the darkness Sun Wolf could sense the restlessness of the horses in their stalls, excited by the winds and by the far-off turmoil from other quarters of the palace. At the first opportunity, he drew Sheera through the postern of the carriage house and thence up a ladder to the lofts that ran continuously over the long rows of boxes. Twice they heard the voices of grooms and sleepy, grouchy stableboys below them, but no one associated the uneasiness of the animals with anything but the wind.

Certainly the guards, running here and there throughout the rest of the palace grounds in search of unspecified anarchists out to burn the Records Office, never thought to look for them among the governor's cattle.

From the loft, they climbed to the roof of the kitchens and over the tall, ridged backbone of the rooftree. Lights milled distantly, clustering around the tall, foursquare shapes of the northern administrative wing. To their left lay the south wall of the palace enclosure, hiding the Grand Canal behind its marble-faced stone; the lights of the great houses on the other side glittered few and faint at this hour, and their reflections thrown by the waters rippled over the stone lacework like moire silk.

Something was moving about in the dark space of the kitchen gardens. *Dogs?* the Wolf wondered. *But in that case, there would be barking.* Still, the noise was animal, not human.

From where he lay flattened on the slanted roof, he could make out the little postern and water stairs, through which Gilden, Wilarne, and Eo had said they'd entered, and the empty catwalk above it.

He heard quick, slipping movement on the tiles, and then warm flesh stretched out beside him. Sheera whispered, "Can we cross the garden without being seen?"

"There's something down there," the Wolf replied, barely above a breath. "Animals, I think—hunting cats or dogs." He edged sideways, keeping his head below the final, crowning ridge of the kitchen roof, a sharp friezework of saints and gargoyles, green with age where they were not crusted into unrecognizable lumps of white by long communion with the palace pigeons. The tiles were warmer under his bare flesh as he slipped around a great cluster of chimney pots and raised his head again.

"There," he murmured. "The covered walkway from the kitchens into the state dining room. You said yourself, the times you've eaten with the governor, the food arrived three-quarters cold."

"To be dropped on gold plates to complete the chilling," Sheera agreed, quietly amused. "Yes, I see. That lighted window above and to the left will be the anteroom to his bedchamber. That one there is the window that lights the end of the hall."

"Good." Booted toes feeling for breaks in the tiles, he eased himself backward down the slant of the roof. Below him, the stable courts were a maze of rooftrees and wells of darkness. Wind flickered over his skin, stirring the long wisps of his hair. The tiles, offensive with moss and droppings, were rough under his groping hands, still only partially healed. At the bottom of the roof, a sort of gutter ran the length of the kitchens, and he slipped along it, moving swiftly, to the peaked end of the building that overlooked the edge of the gardens on the canal side. The wind was stronger here, channeled by the walls;

it carried on it the fish smell of the sea and the high salt flavor of the wind. Down below him, the gardens were a restless murmuration of skeletal trees and brown, wiry networks of hedge, an uneasy darkness broken by anomalous shufflings.

Bracing himself on the gutter, the Wolf worked loose a tile. The noise of the wind that streamed like cool water over his body covered the scraping sounds of his task—indeed, they almost covered the sounds of the voices. He heard a man curse and froze, flattening himself on the uneven darkness of the roof and praying that the mix of lampblack and grease that covered his body hadn't scraped off in patches to show the paler flesh beneath.

From below, he heard a guard's thorough, businesslike cursing. A second voice said, "Nothing out here."

"Any sign of Kran?"

Evidently a head was shaken; the Wolf pressed his face to the filthy tiles, wondering how long it would be until one or the other of them looked up.

"Damned funny, him missing a match-up with the guard on the next beat like that . . . If them troublemakers came in from this side . . ."

"When they're out to burn the Records Office? Not qualified likely. Good thing them two sluts got us word of it . . ."

"So why check the stables? Rot that sergeant's eyes . . ."

Then, with a curious, almost atavistic sensation, Sun Wolf knew that it was within his power to prevent the guards from looking up. It was nothing he had ever experienced before, but it tugged at him; an overwhelming knowledge of a technique, a shifting of the mind and attention, that he could not even define to himself. It was as natural as slashing after a parry, as ingrained in him as footwork; yet it was nothing he had done or even conceived of doing before. It was akin to the way he had always been able to avoid people's eyes—but never from a position of complete exposure.

Without moving, without even looking down, he consciously and deliberately prevented either of them from looking up, as if he drew that thought from their minds by some process he had never known of, except in his childhood dreams. Whether it was for this reason, or because the night was cold and windy and the men disgruntled, neither *did* look up.

"Let's get on, mate, I'm poxy freezing. There's nothing here."

"Aye. Rot his eyes, anyway . . ."

A door closed. The Wolf lay for a moment on the windswept tiles, counting the retreat of their footfalls, until he was sure they were gone. Then he hefted the lump of loose tiles in his hand, leaned around the edge of the gable, and threw them down into the dark corner of garden beyond.

The tiles crashed noisily in the dry hedges below. The Wolf ducked back around the corner of the roof as more crashes answered, and whatever had been below—dogs or sentries—bounded to investigate. Hidden from them by the angle of the roof, he slid along the gutter and made his way, swift as a tomcat, up the slope to where Sheera lay. He could see movement flicker around the corner at the far end of the kitchens as he scrambled up beside her; in that short span of bought time, he half rose to climb over the uneven teeth of the roof ridge and down to the top of the walkway.

The walkway top was flat—a stupid thing, in as rainy a town as Mandrigyn. *Probably leaks like a sieve all winter,* he thought, crawling flat on his belly along it. A quick glance showed him Sheera directly behind, her body as grazed and filthy as his own; another quick glance showed him the gardens below, still empty. He addressed a brief request to his ancestors to keep them that way and scanned the available windows.

"Captain!" Sheera whispered.

He glanced back at her. The wind veered suddenly and he smelled smoke.

As a man adept at the starting of fires, he recognized it as new smoke, the first springing of a really commendable blaze. Looking, he saw it rolling in a formidable column from the north end of the palace, streaming in huge, white-edged billows in the wind. Voices were shouting, feet racing; everyone who had been turned out for the original alarm was dashing toward the fire, and everyone who had not was following close behind.

Gilden and Wilarne were nothing if not thorough.

Scrambling to the nearest window sill, Sun Wolf drove his boot through the glass.

It was, as Sheera had said, the end window of a long corridor, dimly lighted with lamps of amber glass and muffled by carpets of blue Islands work and iridescent silk. He ducked through the nearest door into an antechamber, searching for the way into the bedroom; then a noise behind him in the hall made him swing around. He saw Sheera, frozen in the act of following him into the doorway, black and filthy as a demon from one of the dirtier pits of Hell; and before her in the hall, his crippled body clothed in a lavish robe of crimson brocade and miniver and his prim face wearing an expression of profound and startled astonishment, was Derroug Dru himself.

For one instant, they faced each other; from the tenebrous ante-chamber, Sun Wolf saw the jump of the governor's chest and the leap of breath in his throat as he inhaled to shout for the guards . . .

He never made a sound. Sheera was taller than he and heavier; training day after day to the point of exhaustion had made her light-ning-fast. For all his power to bend others to his will, Derroug was a cripple. Sun Wolf saw the dagger in Sheera's hand but doubted that Derroug ever did. She caught the body and was dragging it into the anteroom, even as blood sprayed from the slashed arteries of the throat. The room stank of it, sharp and metallic above the suffocating weight of balsam incense. Her hands glistened in the faint reflection of the corridor lamps.

"Throw something over him," Sun Wolf whispered as she pushed the door to behind her. "That cuts our time—pray Tisa really *is* here and we don't have to go hunt for her."

As Sheera bundled the body into a corner, he was already crossing the anteroom to the bolted door on the other side. He slammed back the bolts and stepped through. "Tisa . . ."

Something hit his shoulders and the back of his knee; cold and slim, an arm locked across his windpipe, and small hands knotted below the corner of his jaw in a strangle. Reflex took over. He rolled his shoul-ders forward, ducked, and threw. Incredibly light weight went sailing over his head, to slam like a soaked blanket into the deep furs of the floor.

Under the softness of the carpets was hard tile, and a thin little sob was wrenched from her, but Tisa was rolling to her feet as he caught her wrists. She'd kept her head clear of the impact, but tears of terror and pain streamed down her face. Then she saw who he was and turned her face away, ashamed that he should see her weep.

It was no time, the Wolf thought, to be a warrior—especially if one was fifteen and the victim of a powerful and cruel man. He gathered her into his arms. She was shaking with silent terror, burying her small, pointed face in the grimy muscle of his hard chest. Sheera stood silent in the doorway, her hands red to the elbows, watching as he stroked Tisa's disheveled ivory hair and murmured to her as a father might to a child frightened by a nightmare.

"He's dead," he said softly. "It's all right. We've come to get you out, and he's dead and won't come after you."

The girl stammered, "Mother . . ."

"Your mum's out burning down the other side of the palace," the Wolf said, in the same comforting accents. "She's fine—"

Tisa raised her head, her cheek all smutched with blacking, green moss stains, and bird droppings. "Are you kidding me?" she asked, laughter and suspicion fighting through her tears.

The Wolf made wide eyes at her. "No," he said. "Did you think I was?"

She wiped her eyes and swallowed hard. "I'm not crying," she explained, after a moment.

"No," he agreed. "I'm sorry I hurt you, Tisa."

"You didn't hurt me." Her voice was shaky; the breath had been very soundly knocked out of her, if nothing else.

"Well, you damned near strangled me," he returned gruffly. "You think you can swim?"

She nodded. She was wearing, he now saw, a kind of loose white robe, clearly given to her by Derroug. It was slightly too large for her and sewn over with white sequins and elaborate swirls of milky, opalescent beads. Against it, he saw her transformed, no longer a coltish girl, but a half-opened bud of womanhood. Her eyelids were stained dark with fatigue and terror, her hair pale against the silk, almost as light as Starhawk's in the shimmer of the bedroom lamp. The gown was cut so as to reveal half her young bosom. Before taking her post to attack, she'd prosaically pinned the robe with a ruby stickpin that glowed beneath her collarbone like a huge bead of blood.

She was as light as a flower in his hands as he lifted her to her feet. Her eyes lighted on Sheera and widened at the sight of the blood.

Sun Wolf whispered, "Let's go. They'll be looking for him, now that the fire's started."

As they slipped back through the anteroom and out the window, Tisa breathed, "What happened to your voice, Captain? And I thought . . ."

"Not now."

Obediently, she gathered handfuls of her voluminous skirts and followed Sheera down onto the roof of the walkway. Even to his sharper eyes, the gardens below looked deserted. He could see, vague against the deeper dark of the shadowed wall, the shape of the postern gate.

"Wait here till I signal," he said softly. "A whistle like a nightjar. Then keep to the shadows along the wall. If it's locked, we'll have to go up the steps to the parapet and dive."

Sheera gauged the height of the wall. "Thank God it's the Grand Canal. It's the deepest one in the city."

Sun Wolf slithered down the side of the walkway and into the gardens below.

The overcast was growing thicker with the night winds that fanned the blaze on the north end of the palace. The din was audible over the moaning of the wind. *It should keep them all busy for at least another hour,* he calculated and began to move, slowly and cautiously, along the wall toward the inky wells of shadow that lay between him and the gate.

The blackness here was almost absolute; a month ago he would have been able to see nothing. As it was, he was aware of shapes and details with a sense that he was not altogether certain was sight—an effect of the anzid, he guessed, as well as that curious ability to prevent people from looking at him.

That would come in handy, he thought. Come to think of it, he realized he had used it twice before tonight—when he'd evaded Sheera almost unthinkingly in the narrow confines of the potting room, and earlier this evening, when he had first come down the stairs to hear the war council in the orangery. The professional in him toyed with ways of developing that strange talent; but deep within him, a tug of primitive excitement shivered in his bones, as it had done when he had first known that he could see demons and others could not.

The postern was unguarded, but locked. He glanced around the blackness under the gate arch and found the narrow stair to the parapet above. The garden behind him still appeared deserted, but a tension, a premonition of danger, had begun to prickle at the nape of his neck. The brush and hedges seemed to rustle too much, and the wind, laden with smoke and shouting, seemed somehow to carry the scent of evil to his nostrils. He whistled softly, like a nightjar, and saw swift movement near the covered walk, then the flash of Tisa's almost luminous white gown.

They were halfway across the garden when something else moved, from around the corner of the kitchen building.

The things were armored like men, but weaponless. From where he stood at the bottom of the parapet stair, the Wolf could see that they walked steadily, oblivious to the darkness that made the fugitive women's steps so halting and slow. They moved so softly that he wasn't sure Sheera and Tisa were aware of them, but his own sharpened vision showed them clearly to him. There were four, wearing the fouled liveries of Derroug's guards, their eyeless heads swinging as if they also could see in darkness.

They were nuuwa.

Realization hit him, and horrible enlightenment, as if pieces of some huge and ghastly puzzle had fallen into place. Rage and utter loathing swept over him, such as he had never felt toward anyone or anything before. The nuuwa began to lope. Sheera swung around, hearing the steps on the grass, but her eyes were unable to pierce the utter darkness.

Sun Wolf bellowed, "Run for it! Here!"

His sword whined from its sheath. Unquestioning, the women ran, Tisa stripping out of her billowing white robe as it caught on the dead limbs of a thorn hedge. They ran blindly, stumbling, blundering through soft earth and gray tangles of vine and hedge, and the nuuwa plunged soundlessly after. He yelled again, a half-voiceless croaking that was answered by wild commotion in the windows of the palace behind them. Tisa hit the stairs first, with Sheera a few strides behind. The nuuwa were hard on their heels, running sightlessly with the drool glistening on those gaping, deformed mouths.

Sword naked in his hand, Sun Wolf followed the women up the steps, the foremost of the pursuers not three feet behind. At the top of the wall, Tisa dived, plunging down into the dark murk of the canal; Sheera's dark-stained, gleaming body outlined momentarily against the reflected lamps in the villas across the way as she followed. When the Wolf reached the parapet, huge hands dug into his flesh from behind, and he writhed away from the fangs that tore like great wedges of rusty iron into his shoulder. He turned, ripping with his sword, knowing he had only seconds until they were all on him, literally eating him alive. As the blade cleaved the filthy flesh of the nuuwa's body, the misshapen face was inches from his own, the huge mouth still rending at him, flowing with blood, the empty eye sockets scabbed wells of shadow.

Then he was plunging down, and the freezing, salty, unspeakably filthy waters of the canal swallowed him. The nuuwa, nothing daunted, flung themselves over the wall after their prey. Weighted in their armor, too blind and too stupid to swim, they sank like stones.

In her usual silence, Yirth gathered up her medicines and glided from the dim confines of the loft. Sun Wolf lay still for a time, staring up at the slant of the ceiling over his head, as he had stared at it four mornings ago, when he had awakened to know that Sheera had indeed won.

But there was no thought of Sheera now in his mind.

He was thinking now of Lady Wrinshardin, of Derroug Dru, and of Altiokis.

He felt weak from loss of blood, woozy and aching from the pain of Yirth's remedies. Against his cheek on the pillow, his hair was damp, and his flesh chilled where the lampblack and grease had been sponged off it. Sheera, in her velvet bed, and Tisa, safe at the Thane of Wrinshardin's castle, would both be striped like tigers with bruises and scratches from that last crashing flight through the gardens.

He himself scarcely felt the pain. Knowledge still burned in him, and the heat of fury that knowledge had brought; deformed, hideous, the face of the nuuwa returned to his thoughts, no matter what he did to push it aside. The grayish light beyond the window grew broader, and he wondered if he had best get up and go about his business for the benefit of whatever servants of the household might be questioned by Derroug's successors.

Weakness weighted his limbs. He was still lying there when the door of the orangery opened and shut, and he heard the creak of light feet on the steps, the soft, thick slur of satin petticoats, and the stiff rubbing of starched lace.

He turned his head. Sheera stood in the doorway, where she had so seldom come before. Cosmetics covered the scratches on her face; but below the paint, he thought she looked pale and drawn. In that crowded and terrible night, he realized, she had avenged herself on Derroug. But it had been a businesslike, almost unthinking revenge.

"I came to thank you for last night," she said tiredly. "And—to apologize for things that I said. You did not have to do what you did."

"I told you before," Sun Wolf rasped, his new voice still scraping oddly in his ears. "All it would have taken was for our girl to tackle Derroug the way she tackled me for there to have been a lot of questions asked. And as for the other business—you were tired and I was drunk. That should never have happened."

"No," Sheera said. "It shouldn't have." She rubbed her eyes, the clusters of pearl and sardonyx that decorated her ears and hair flickering in the wan light of morning. "I've come to tell you that you're free to leave Mandrigyn. I'm going to speak to Yirth—to have her give you the antidote to the anzid—to let you go. For what you did . . ."

He held out his hand. After a moment's hesitation, she stepped forward, and he drew her to sit on the edge of his bed. Her fingers felt like ice in his.

"Sheera," he said, "that doesn't matter now. When you march to the mines—when you free the men—what are you going to do?"

Taken off guard, she stammered, "I—we—Tarrin and I will lead them back here . . ."

"No," he said. "Lady Wrinshardin was right, Sheera. Yirth is right. Don't wait for Altiokis to come to you. Those ways from the mines up to the Citadel itself—could Amber's girls find them?"

"I suppose," she said hesitantly. "Crazyred says she's seen one of them. But they're guarded by magic, by traps . . ."

"Yirth will have to deal with that," he told her quietly. "She'll have to find some way to get you through them—and she will, or die trying. Sheera, Altiokis has to be destroyed. He's got an evil up there worse than anything I imagined—and he's breeding it, creating it, calling it up out of some other world, I don't know. Lady Wrinshardin guessed it; Yirth knows it. He has to be destroyed, and that evil with him."

Sheera was silent, looking down at her hands where they rested among the folds of her gown. Once she might have triumphed over his admission that she was right and he wrong—but that had been before the pit, and before the garden last night.

Watching her eyes, he realized that, since she had spoken with Lady Wrinshardin, she had known in her heart that they would have to storm the Citadel.

He went on. "Those were nuuwa that pursued us from Derroug's gardens last night. Nuuwa under the control of Altiokis, I would guess —as nuuwa under his control are said to march in his armies. When he's done with them—as he was after the battle of Iron Pass—he turns most of them out, to overrun the conquered lands; or else he gives them over to his governors as watchdogs. I think they deform, they deteriorate, in time—and that's why Altiokis and Derroug have to go on creating new ones."

"Creating?" She raised her head quickly; he could see in her face the hideous comprehension knocking on the doors of her mind, as it had knocked on his last night.

"You remember that room in Derroug's prison? That—that thing that looked like a flake of fire, or a shining dragonfly?"

She glanced away, nauseated by the memory. After a moment, the thick curls of her hair slipped across her red satin shoulder as she nodded. He felt her cold fingers tighten over his.

"That red-haired boy became the creature who tore up my shoulder last night," he told her.

CHAPTER

 15

*F*ROM PERGEMIS, THE ROAD WOUND NORTHEAST, FIRST THROUGH the rich croplands and forests of the Bight Coast, then through mist-hung, green foothills, where snow lay light upon the ground, printed with the spoor of fox and beaver. In the summer, it would have been possible to take a ship from the port, around the vast hammer of cliff-girt headlands and through the gray walls of the Islands, to the port city of Mandrigyn below the walls of Grimscarp itself. But the world lay in the iron grip of winter. Starhawk and Anyog made their way into the Wizard King's domains slowly, overland, as best they could.

In the higher foothills, the rains turned to snow, and the winds drove down upon them from the stony uplands above. When they could, they put up at settlements—either the new villages of traders and hunters or the ancient clan holds of the old Thanes, who had once ruled all these lands and now lived in haughty obsolescence in the depths of the trackless forests.

Starhawk found the going far slower than she had anticipated, for Anyog, despite his uncomplaining gameness, tired easily. In this weather, and in this country, an hour or two of travel would leave the little scholar gray-faced and gasping, and the time span shortened steadily as they pressed on. She would have scorned the weakness in one of her own men and used the lash of her tongue to drive him. But she could not do so. It was her doing that the old man had undertaken the hardships of a winter journey when he should have been still in bed, letting his wounds heal. Besides, she admitted to herself, she'd grown to be extremely fond of the old goat.

Never before had she found that her personal feelings toward someone bred tolerance of his weakness. *Have I grown soft,* she wondered, *those weeks in Pel Farstep's house? Or is this something love does for you—makes you kinder toward others as well?*

Dealing with the irrationalities of love that she found in her own soul frightened her. Her jealousy of poor Fawn had been as senseless as was her stubbornness in pursuing a hopeless quest for a man who was almost certainly already dead and who had never spoken to her of love in the first place. She knew herself to be behaving stupidly, yet the thought of turning around and retracing her steps to Pergemis or Wrynde was intolerable to the point of pain. Meditation cleared and calmed her mind, but gave her no answer—she could find herself within the Invisible Circle, but she could not find another person.

No wonder the Wolf had always steered clear of love. She wondered how she could ever find the courage to tell him that she loved him and what he would say when or if she did.

And with love, she found herself involved in magic as well.

"Why did you never go on to become a wizard?" she asked one evening, watching Anyog as he brought fire spurting to the little heap of sticks and kindling with a gesture of his bony fingers. "Was it fear of Altiokis alone?"

The bright, black eyes twinkled up at her, catching the glittering reflection of the sparks. "Funk—pure and simple." He held out his hands to the blaze. The light seemed to shine through them, so thin they were. The white ruffles at his wrists, like those at his throat, were draggled and gray.

Starhawk eyed him for a moment, where he hunched like a cricket over the little blaze, then half glanced over her shoulder at the dark that always seemed to hang over the uplands to the north.

He read her gesture and grinned wryly. "Not solely of our deathless friend," he explained. "Though I will admit that that consideration loomed largest in my mind when I deserted the master who taught me and took the road for sunnier climes in the south.

"My master was an old man, a hermit who lived in the hills. Even as a little boy, I knew I had the Power—I could find things that were lost or start fires by looking at bits of dried grass. I could see things that other people could not see. This old man was a mystic—crazy, some said—but he taught me . . ." Anyog paused, staring into the shivering color of the blaze. "Perhaps he taught me more than he knew.

"I tasted it then, you see." He glanced up at her, standing above him, across the leaping light; the fire touched in his face every wrinkle and line of gaiety and dissipation. "Tasted glory—tasted magic—and tasted what that glory would cost. He was a shy old man, terrified of strangers. I had to hunt for him for two weeks before he would even see me. He distrusted everything, everyone—all from fear of Altiokis."

Starhawk was silent, remembering that whitewashed cell in the distant Convent and the mirror set in an angle of its walls. Somewhere in the woods an owl hooted, hunting on soundless wings. The horses stamped at their tethers, pawing at the crusted snow.

The dark eyes were studying her face, wondering if she understood. "It meant giving up all things for only one thing," Anyog said. "Even then I knew I wanted to travel, to learn. I loved the small, bright beauties of the mind. What is life without poetry, without wit, without music? Without the well-turned phrase and the sharpening of your own philosophy upon the philosophies of others? My master lived hidden—he would go for years without seeing another soul. If I became a wizard like him, it would mean the same kind of life for me."

The old man sighed and turned to pick up the iron spits and begin setting them in their place over the fire. "So I chose all those small beauties over the great, single, lonely one. I became a scholar, teacher, dancer, poet—my *Song of the Moon Dog and the Ocean Child* will be sung throughout the Middle Kingdoms long after I am gone—and I pretended I did not regret. Until that night at the inn, when you asked me if my safety had bought me happiness. And I could not say that it had."

He looked away from her and occupied himself in spitting pieces of the rabbit she had shot that afternoon on the long iron cooking spike. Starhawk said nothing, but hunted through the mule's packs for barley bannocks and a pan to melt snow for drinking water. She was remembering the warm safety of Pel Farstep's house and how she had not even thought twice about leaving it to pursue her quest.

"And then," Anyog continued, "I feared the Great Trial. Without passing through that, I could never have come to the fullness of my power in any case."

"What is it?" Starhawk asked, sitting down opposite him. "Could you take it now, before we reached Grimscarp?"

The old man shook his head; she thought the withered muscles of his jaw tightened in apprehension in the flickering firelight. "No," he said. "I never learned enough magic to withstand it, and what I learned . . . It has been long since I used that. The Trial kills the weak, as it kills those who are not mage-born."

She frowned. "But if you passed through it—would it make you deathless, like Altiokis?"

"Altiokis?" The winged brows plunged down suddenly over his nose. For an instant she saw him, not as a half-sick and regretful little old man, but as a wizard, an echo of the Power he had passed by. "Pah. Altiokis never passed the Great Trial. According to my master, he never even knew what it was. My master knew him, you see. Vain, lazy, trifling . . . the worst of them all."

He might have been a classical poet speaking of the latest popular serenade writer. She half smiled. "But you've got to admit he's up there and you're down here, hiding from him. He's got to have acquired that power from somewhere."

Anyog's voice sank, as if he feared that, this close to the Citadel of the Wizard King, the very winds would hear. "He has," he told her quietly.

Her glance sharpened, and she remembered the smoky darkness of the inn at Foonspay and the old man's raving quietly before the sinking fire, with Fawn standing quiet, hidden in the shadows of the corridor. "You spoke of that before," she said.

"Did I? I didn't mean to." He poked the fire, more for something to do than because it needed stirring. The wind brought the voices of wolves from the hills above, sweet and distant upon the hunting trail. "My master knew it—but very few others did. If Altiokis ever found out that it was known, he would guess that my master had taught others. He would find me."

"Where does Altiokis get his power?"

Anyog was silent for a time, staring into the fire, and Starhawk wondered if he would answer her at all. She had just decided that he would not when he said softly, "From the Hole. Holes in the world, they are called—but I think Holes *between* worlds would be more accurate. For it is said that something lives in them—something other than the gaums that eat men's brains."

"Gaums . . ." she began.

"Oh, yes. My nephews call them after dragonflies, but they're things—whatever they are—that come out of the Holes. They are mindless, and they eat the minds of their victims, so that their victims become mindless, too—nuuwa, in fact. The Holes appear—oh, at intervals of hundreds of years, sometimes. My master said they were ruled by the courses of the stars. Sunlight destroys them—they appear at night and vanish with the coming of dawn."

Something moved, dark against the mottled background of broken snow and old pine needles; Anyog looked up with a gasp, as if at an enemy footfall, and Starhawk, following his gaze, saw the brief green flash of a weasel's eyes. The old man subsided, shivering and rubbing his hands.

At length he continued. "The Holes vanish with sunlight—as do the gaums, if they don't find a victim first. But this Hole Altiokis sheltered. He is said to have built a stone hut over it in a single night, and from that time his powers have grown. It animates his flesh, giving him life—but he has changed since then. I don't know." He shook his head wearily, a harried, sick old man once more. "He had only to wait for the great mages of his own generation to die and to kill off those who followed before they came to greatness. As he will kill me."

His voice was shaky with exhaustion and despair; looking at him across the topaz glow of the fire, Starhawk saw how white he looked, how darkly the crazy eyebrows stood out against the pinched flesh. As if he'd been a boy trooper, funked before his first battle, she said hearteningly, "He won't kill you."

They left the magical silence of the foothills, to climb the Stren Water Valley.

Fed by the drowning rains on the uplands above, the Stren Water roared in full spate, spreading its channels throughout the narrow, marshy country that lay between the higher cliffs, cutting off hilltops to islands, and driving those farmers who eked their living from its soil to their winter villages on the slopes above. Starhawk and Anyog made their way along the rocky foothills that bordered the flooded lands, always wet, always cold. Anyog told tales and sang songs; of wizardry and Altiokis, they did not speak.

They made a dozen river crossings a day—sometimes of boggy little channels of the main flood, sometimes of boiling white streams that had permanent channels. At one of these, they lost the packs and almost lost the mule as well. Starhawk suspected that the struggle with the raging waters had broken something within Anyog; after that, he had a white look about the mouth that never left him and he could not travel more than a few miles without a rest.

She had always been a blisteringly efficient commander, using her own supple strength to drive and bully her men to follow. But she found that her fears for Sun Wolf, though unabated, left room for a care for the old man, who she was sure now would never be able to help her, and she broke the journey to give him a day's rest while she hunted mountain sheep in the high rock country to the northwest.

She was coming back from this when she found the tracks of the mercenaries.

It had been a small band—probably not more than fifteen, she guessed, studying the sloppy trail in the fading afternoon light. Their mere presence in the valley told her they were out of work and had been so for at least three months, since the rains had begun, holed up somewhere, living off the land by hunting or pillage—too small a group to be hired for anything but tribal war between the Thanes; and most of the Thanes in these parts hadn't the money to hire, anyway, and wouldn't go to war in the winter if they could.

Starhawk cursed. Her experience with out-of-work mercenaries was that they were always a nuisance and generally robbers to boot; she would have to trail them to make sure where they were headed and what they were up to before she would feel safe returning to camp.

She had shot a sheep in the high rocks, one of the small, shaggy crag jumpers, and was carrying the carcass over her shoulders. She hung it from the limb of a tree to keep it from wolves and hung her coat up with it; she might want her arms free. Then she transferred her sword from her back, where she'd been carrying it on the hunt, to her hip, restrung her bow, and checked her arrows. She had been a mercenary for a long time—she was under no illusions about her own kind.

The trail was fresh; the droppings of the few horses still steamed in the cold evening. She found the place where they'd turned aside from the main trail through the hills at the sight of Anyog's campfire—she could still see the smoke of it herself, rising through the trees from the wooded hollow where she'd left him. As she clambered cautiously down the rocks that skirted the downward trail, she began to hear their voices, too, and their laughter.

She muttered words that did greater credit to her imagination than to her convent training. They wanted horses, of course. She hoped to the Mother that Anyog had more sense than to antagonize them—not that anything would be likely to help him much, if they were drunk—which, by the sound of it, they were.

She'd chosen the campsite carefully—a wooded dell surrounded by thin trees with a minimum of large boulders, difficult to spy into and impossible to sneak up on. She pressed her body to the trunk of the largest available tree and looked down into the dell.

There were about a dozen men, and they were drunk. One or two of them she thought she recognized—mercenaries were always crossing one another's paths, and most of them got to know one another by sight. The leader was a squat, hairy man in a greasy doublet sewn over with iron plates. It was before him that Anyog knelt on hands and knees, his gray head bowed and trickling with blood.

At this distance it was hard to hear what the leader was saying, but it was obvious the robbers had already appropriated the livestock. Starhawk could see the two horses and the mule among the small cavy of broken-down nags at the far edge of the clearing; the camp was strewn with cooking gear, and a couple of snaggle-haired camp followers stood among the half circle of men with her and Anyog's bedrolls. She barely felt her anger in the midst of her calculations. The horses were unguarded at the rear of the cavy, since most of the men were up front, watching the fun with Anyog. The animals would provide better cover if she could get to them.

More laughter burst from the circle of men; a couple of them jostled for a better position. She saw the leader's hand move, and Anyog began to crawl, evidently after something thrown into the muddy pine needles. Bawling with laughter, the mercenary captain reached out his boot and kicked the old man in the side, sending him sprawling. Doggedly, Anyog got back to his hands and knees and continued to crawl.

Starhawk was familiar with the game; paying for the horses, it was called. A player threw coppers at greater and greater distances and made the poor bastard crawl after them while everyone kicked him over. The game was on a par with ducking the mayor of the village, or forcing his wife to clean the captain's boots with her hair—the sort of thing that went on during the sacking of a town. It was hilariously funny if a person was drunk, of course, or had just survived a battle that could have left him feeding the local cats on his spilled guts.

But sober, and watching it played on a man who had done her nothing but kindness, she felt both anger and distaste. It was, she saw, akin to rape; and like rape, it could easily get out of hand and end with the victim dead as well.

She began to edge her way through the trees toward the far side of the cavy. The gathering darkness helped her—it had been blackly overcast all day, with snow falling lightly in the high country where she had hunted; the world smelled of rain and frost. The men, more-over, aside from being drunk, were totally engrossed in their game. Anyog was kicked down again and lay where he had fallen. It was hard to tell in the twilight, but Starhawk thought he was bleeding from the mouth. She decided then that, whether or not they offered him further injury, she would kill them. One of the camp followers, a slut of sixteen or so, walked over to the old man and kicked him to make him get up; Starhawk saw his hands move as he struggled to rise.

The mercenaries closed in around him.

It took her a few extra seconds to cut the reins of the horses from the tether rope; the men were yelling and laughing and never saw her until she was mounted. She fired into their midst, calmly and without rage; her first arrow took the captain straight through the throat, above the iron-plated doublet; her second pinned the camp follower between the breasts.

She was mounted; the height and the weight of the horse gave her an edge over their numbers, though later she suspected that she would have taken on the twelve of them, even had she been afoot. She came plowing in among them from the darkness, the last light flashing from her sword blade as from the sickle of the Death Goddess of ancient days—silent, inhuman, merciless as the Plague Star. She killed two before they even had their weapons drawn, and the horse accounted for a third, rearing as they closed around it and smashing the man's skull with an iron-shod hoof. Another man seized her leg to pull her down and she took his hands off at the wrists. She left him standing, screaming, staring at the spouting stumps, as she turned and beheaded the other camp follower and another man who was grabbing at her from the opposite side. Two men had the bridle, dragging and twist-ing to pull the horse down; she dug in her heels and drove the animal straight ahead over them, so that they had to release their grip or be trampled. One of them she hacked through the shoulder as she went by, and he crumpled, screaming and kicking in the plowed, wet pine mast.

All this she did calmly, without feeling. She was a technician of death and good at her job; she knew what she wanted to do. The men were running in all directions, drunk and confused. Someone got to the packs; a moment later, an arrow embedded itself in the saddletree a few inches from her leg. She wheeled the horse and rode at the man. Another shaft sang wide beside her, his aim erratic from panic or from cheap gin; then he dropped his bow and ran, and she cut him through the spine as she overtook his flight.

The men who were chasing the fleeing horses she brought down with arrows, as if they were hares. Only the last stood and fought her, sword to sword, when her arrows were spent; and though she was dismounted by this time and he was both larger and heavier than she, she had the advantage of speed.

She pulled her grating sword blade from his ribs, wiped it on his clothes, and turned back to where Anyog lay in the trampled slush. The cold brightness of battle still clung to her; she looked down at the crumpled body and thought, *Another deader.*

Then the grief hit her, like the howling of a wolf at the moon.

She looked around her at the bodies that lay like dark lumps of mud against the slightly lighter blur of the pine needles. The air smelled heavy with blood, like a battlefield; already foxes were creeping from the woods, sniffing at the carrion. In the night, there would be wolves. She saw that at least one of the mercenaries had been a woman, something that she hadn't noticed in the heat of the fight. And none of their deaths would bring Anyog back.

Gently, she knelt beside him and turned him over. His breath caught in a gasp of pain; she saw that he was not, in fact, dead; but he would have to be a powerful wizard indeed to pull himself back from the darkness now. Around her, the trees began to whisper under the falling of rain.

Starhawk worked through the night, rigging a shelter for him and for the fire she built, and making a travois. Beyond the circle of the firelight, she was conscious of continual movement, of faint snarlings and growls, and huge green eyes that flashed with the reflected light. The single horse she had salvaged—one of Pel Farstep's—snorted with fear and jerked at its tether, but nothing threatened them from the rainy blackness. The kill was fresh and enough to glut a pack.

The sodden dawn was barely glimmering through the trees when she moved on. She collected what little food the mercenaries had carried, plus several skins of raw liquor—Blind White, it was called— and all the arrows she could recover. As she was tying Anyog to the travois, the dark eyes opened, glazed with pain, and he whispered, "Dove?"

"I'm here," she said gruffly. "Uncle, I'm sorry. I . . ."

His voice was a thread. "Couldn't let you face . . . Altiokis . . . alone . . ."

He coughed, bringing up blood. Starhawk stood up and went to hang the rest of their meager supplies over the various projections of the saddle, fighting the guilt that came from bitter enlightenment and the sudden understanding of why Anyog had joined her in her hope-less quest. She stood for a moment, leaning her throbbing head against the horse's withers while the rain streamed down through her pale, dripping hair. Ram had taken his courage in his hands, as he had said, and spoken to her; and having spoken, had been turned down. Perhaps it was Anyog's age that had robbed him of the courage to speak, or perhaps it was the prior knowledge that his love for her would not be returned. But it was the old man, not the young, who had come with her to his death.

Starhawk sighed. She had learned a long time ago that crying only wasted time. They had a long road to go.

It was almost nightfall before they came to shelter. Because she could not scout the countryside, Starhawk backtrailed the mercenaries, hoping that they had spent the previous night in a place not too ex-posed to the elements. The rain had lightened through the afternoon, but the cold was deeper, and she began to fear snow. The road led them up the hard, rocky tracks into the higher foothills, skirting the deep flood meres and the sour bogs that surrounded them. In the end, it led her to a high valley, a sort of bay wedged among the tall cliffs, where a chapel had been built, looking like something that had grown of itself from the lichened stones.

The chapel was filthy. It had clearly served as a stable, and its altar had been further defiled by all the gross usages of which drunken and violent men were capable when they grew bored. Starhawk was used to this kind of thing and had moreover been raised to believe that the worship of the Triple God was an intellectualized heresy; nevertheless, she was angered that men would treat holy things so, simply because they were holy.

Still, the roof was intact, and the single doorway narrow enough to forbid the entrance of wild beasts, if a fire were kindled there. She cleared a place among the mess to lay Anyog down and set about gathering damp brushwood, then barked her knuckles with flint and steel lighting it.

It snowed in the night, with bitter wind keening around the open chapel door. By dawn, it was obvious to Starhawk that Uncle Anyog would never recover.

Yet he was too tough to die quickly. He lingered on the cloudy borderlands of death, sometimes in a cold sleep that she would have mistaken for death, had it not been for the painful wheezing of his breath, other times weeping and raving feebly of Altiokis, of the nuuwa, of his sister, or singing snatches of poems and songs in a cracked little voice like the grating of a rusty hinge. Occasionally he was lucid enough to recognize her cropped hair and brass-studded doublet as the marks of a trooper and struggled with feeble determination against the gruel she fed him or the water she washed him with.

On the third night of this, it crossed her mind that the sensible thing to do would be to kill him and go with her quest. There was no hope of his recovery—even if what remained of the little wizardry he had been taught was strong enough to pull him back from death, it would be long before he could embark on another journey by travois. One way or the other, she would have to free Sun Wolf from the Citadel of the Wizard King alone, without the aid of a wizard—without the hope now of ever finding one.

It was better that she got on with it and did not delay further.

Yet she stayed. The cold deepened over the high peaks, and the snow locked its grip on the valley tighter. Daily the Hawk trudged to the few tufts of birch and aspen at the lower end of the little valley by the spring to cut firewood. She saw in the snow the marks where deer had pawed at the crust to feed on the dead grasses underneath; she hunted, and the calm absorption of it eased her heart. During the night she meditated, contemplating in the stillness of the Invisible Circle the truths of her own violent soul. In spite of her own faith in the Mother, she tended the altar of the Triple God, ridding the chapel of its pollutions and cleansing the stone with ritual fire; and in that, too, she found comfort.

Night after night she sat listening to Anyog's quiet murmuring and staring out into the still darkness of the silent valley and the flooded lands beyond.

What had happened to her, she wondered, those weeks in Pel Farstep's tall stone house? She did not want to become like them, like the busy, bustling Pel or the placid Gillie. So why did her mind keep returning to that peaceful place and the small beauties of everyday things?

Would she even love the Wolf when she met him again, or would she find that he was like the men she had killed, brutish, dirty, and crass?

The Mother knew, she'd seen him perform worse outrages than that when they'd sacked cities.

But her own experience with the wild, careless arrogance of victory prevented her from thinking that what one did during a sack was what one would do in cold blood.

Would it be better if she found that she did not love him, for that matter? Had Fawnie had the right idea, to marry a well-off man who would cherish her?

If the Wolf was a mercenary like the others, why did she still love him enough to seek him? And if she still loved him with that same determination, why did she not kill Anyog, who was dying anyway, bury him, and leave?

From there she would settle herself into meditation; but the answers that she found within its stillness were not the answers that she sought.

One night the wind changed, squalling down over the mountains in a fury of driving, intermittent rain. Droplets hissed loudly in the little fire; Starhawk could hear its fitful beating against the stone walls of the chapel, but within the hollow darkness at the far end of the holy place, the altar lights burned with a steady, hypnotic glow. Her mind focused upon them, drawing them into herself, and the light and darkness merged and clarified into one entity—rain and earth, wind and silence, that which was known and that which was yet to be—the single Circle of Is.

She found herself in another wind-sounding darkness, hearing the far-off beating of the sea. She knew the place well—the Mother's chapel on the cliffs, part of the Convent of St. Cherybi, which she had left to follow Sun Wolf to learn the ways of war. She had heard of other nuns doing this, for each point of the Invisible Circle was each point, everywhere, and it was possible, she had heard, to step from one to another. Moonlight shone down through the sky-hole, the only illumination in that dark place, a blinding sliver on the edge of her drawn sword. Peace filled her, as it had always done here. She wondered if this were a dream of her past, but knew, even as she formulated the thought, that it was not so. There were small changes from what she had known—weather stains on the floor and the walls, slight shifts in the way the vessels stood upon the bare stone of the shadow-obscured altar—which told her that she was truly there, and this did not surprise her.

When she saw Sun Wolf, standing in the darkness near the door, she knew that he, too, was truly there—that he had come there to find her . . .

She had never cried as an adult. But when she returned to the barren darkness of the chapel in the Stren Water Valley, tears were icy on her face, and exultation and bitter grief warred in her heart.

I'm sorry I did not know it in time, he had said. And yet, when he lay dying in Mandrigyn, he had contrived to come to her.

So near, she thought. *Had I not stayed in Pergemis with Fawn . . .*

But she knew she could not have deserted the girl.

Grief and defeat and exhaustion weakened her; long after her sobbing had ceased, the tears ran down from her open eyes. She had followed him for years to war, and they had saved each other's life a dozen times, almost casually. She must have known, she told herself, that he was going to die sometime.

Was this grief because she had always expected to be at his side when it happened? Or because of this stupid, cursed, miserable condition that people called love, which had broken her warrior's strength and given her nothing in return?

She wondered what she would do, now that he was dead.

The gray house in Pergemis came to her mind, with the booming of the sea and the mewing of the wheeling gulls. Pel Farstep had said that Starhawk would always have a home with them. Yet it would be shabby treatment of so good a man as Ram to make him forever her second choice; and shabbier still to live in that house, but not as his wife. Though the peace that she had felt there called to her, she knew in her heart that their way—to count money, and raise children, and wait for ships to come in—was not her way.

Wrynde? It was peace of another sort, the rainy quiet of the winters and the mindless violence and glory of campaign. Her friends among the mercenaries returned to her mind, along with the bright joys of battle and war. But what was known could never be unknown. One day, she thought, she might become a warrior again. But having lived among her victims, she knew that she could never ride to the sacking of a town.

The altar lights flickered. As she walked through the darkness of the chapel to trim them, she automatically made the sign of respect, although it was a holy place of the Three, not of the One—the worship of the Triple God had always struck her as rather sterile and business-like; and in any case, she knew that ritual was for the benefit of the worshipper and not from any need of the God's.

As she stood in the deep silence beside the altar stone, it came to her that she could remain here.

The chapel's guardian had been chased away or killed by the merce-naries who had camped here, but the building had been recently in-habited. Even in the depths of the holy place, the crying of the wind came to her, and the sporadic flurries of rain; it was close to dawn, the valley around the chapel an empty darkness, inhabited only by winds, wolves, and deer. To have this life, this peace . . . this place of medi-tation and solitude . . . a place to find her own road . . .

She stepped down from the altar and crossed the darkness once again, to the wall niche where Anyog slept, like a corpse already awaiting burial.

He, too, had loved her, she thought. It seemed that Sun Wolf's father had been right, after all; love brought nothing but grief and death, as magic brought nothing but isolation.

But as Anyog had found—and as she, to her grief, was finding—the lack of them brought something infinitely worse.

Why Mandrigyn? she wondered suddenly.

He had said Mandrigyn, not Grimscarp . . . What was the Wolf doing in Mandrigyn?

Distantly, the woman's face returned to her—the dark-haired woman she had seen so briefly in Sun Wolf's tent the night he had shown her the letter. *Sheera Galernas of Mandrigyn . . . a matter of interest to you . . .*

She stopped still in the darkness of the chapel, her mind suddenly leaping ahead. *Sweet Mother, he didn't change his mind and accept her proposal, after all, did he?*

Why wouldn't he have told anyone? Why the illusion of Ari? He'd never have left the troop to find its own way home . . .

How the illusion of Ari, for that matter?

Was there another wizard in it, after all? Or a partial wizard, like Anyog —one who had never passed through the Great Trial?

What the hell was the Wolf doing in Mandrigyn?

From the darkness, she heard Anyog whisper, "My dove . . ."

The chapel was tiny; a step brought her to his side, and she bent down to take his cold hands in hers. Anyog seemed in the last few days to have shrunk to a tiny skeleton, wrapped in a suit of withered skin. His features were the features of a skull; from dark hollows, black eyes stared up at her, clouded with fever and fear. She whispered, "I'm here, Uncle," and the thin lips blew out a pettish sigh.

"Leave you . . ." he murmured, ". . . face him alone."

She stroked his clammy forehead. "It's all right," she assured him quietly.

Outside, a rainy morning was struggling with the wind-torn rags of the sky. Through the door, she saw that much of the snow had melted; the long stretch of the valley below the chapel looked dirty and sodden, like the earth in the first forewhispers of spring.

Skeletal little fingers tightened weakly over hers. "Never the courage," he breathed, "to grasp . . ."

Her love? she wondered. *Or the Great Trial, the fearsome gate to power?*

"What was it?" she asked him and brushed his sunken cheek gently with her scarred hand.

"Secret . . . from master to pupil . . . So few know now . . . No one remembers. Not Altiokis . . . no one."

"But you must know it, if you feared it," she said, wondering, in the back of her mind, if the knowledge could be used. If there were an untried wizard in Mandrigyn who had had something to do with the Wolf's death . . .

He shook his head feebly. "Only the mageborn survive it," he murmured. "Others die . . . and even for those who survive . . ."

"But what was it?" she asked him.

His breath leaked out in a little gasp, and the dark eyes closed. Then he whispered, "Anzid."

CHAPTER

16

"*A*LTIOKIS IS COMING."

"To Mandrigyn?"

Sheera nodded. "Wilarne had it from Stirk the harbor master's wife this morning." Above the frame of her starched lace collar, her jaw muscles were settled into a hard line.

Sun Wolf rested his shoulders against the cedar upright that supported the roof of the potting room and asked, "Why? To replace Derroug?"

"Partly," she assented. "And partly to make a show of force against the rumors of insurrection in the city. Wilarne said he was supposedly bringing troops." She leaned against the doorpost and looked down at her hands, clasped in the wine-colored folds of her skirts. Like most of the women, she had abandoned wearing rings—a warrior's habit. In a quieter voice, she began, "If I hadn't killed Derroug . . ."

"He'd have had every guard in the palace down on us," Sun Wolf finished for her. Still she did not meet his eyes. "Does Drypettis know?"

Sheera shook her head, then glanced up, weary hardness in those brown eyes. "No," she said. "In fact, I had the impression that his death really didn't concern her one way or the other. It—it was almost as if she didn't know about it."

The Wolf frowned. "You think that might be the case?"

"No," Sheera said. She moved her shoulder against the doorframe; the light glimmered on the swirls of opal and garnet that armored her bodice and festooned her extravagant sleeves. "I went to see her the day after it happened, and she did mention it. But—in passing. Almost for form's sake. The rest of our talk that day was about—other things." Her mouth tightened a little at the memory. "And I'm inclined to think you were right about her, after all."

He was silent for a moment, studying her face. Her eyelids were stained with weariness and, he saw now, had begun to acquire those sharp, small creases that spoke of character and responsibility, which men claimed ruined a woman's looks. "What did she say?"

"Not much to the point." She shrugged. "Why did I take your part over hers? Why did I let you poison my mind against her? Were you my lover?"

"What did you tell her?"

She looked down again. "That it wasn't her affair."

"She'll take that for a 'Yes.' "

"I know." Sheera shook her head tiredly. "But she'd have taken 'No' for a 'Yes.' "

"Very likely," he agreed.

Sheera occupied herself for a long moment in rearranging the folds of the lace that cascaded from her cuffs over her hands. Sun Wolf noticed what Gilden had pointed out to him only yesterday—that Sheera, along with most of the women in the troop and scores of women who were unaware of its existence, had gone over to what they called the "new mode" of dressing, without the stiff boning and lacing-in and padded panniers. Though as elaborate and ostentatious as the old style had been, it allowed for more comfort and quicker movement. Privately, the Wolf thought it was more seductive as well.

She raised her eyes to his again. "What do you think of her?" she asked.

He considered the question for a moment before replying. "What do *you* think of her?"

"I don't know." She began to pace, her restless movement somehow feral, like that of a caged lioness. "I've known her from the time we were girls in school together. She said I was the only person who was ever good to her. Good to her! All I ever did was extend her common courtesy and keep the other girls from teasing her because she was proud and solitary and talked to herself."

He smiled. "In other words, you were her champion."

"I suppose. One goes through a stage of being someone's champion —or at least, I did. And I know one goes through a stage of being in love with another girl—oh, perfectly innocently! It's more a—a domination of the personality. A 'pash,' we called it—a 'rave.' And it seldom goes beyond that. But—I suppose you could say Dru never outgrew her 'pash' for me." She shrugged again. "Dru was such a precocious child, but socially she was so backward."

"She still is a precocious child," the Wolf pointed out, "at the age of twenty-five."

Sheera's eyes flashed suddenly, and he saw in her again the head girl of the school, beautiful and imperious at the age of ten, taking under her wing the wealthiest, proudest, and most miserable child in her class. She had always, he thought, been a champion, even as she was now. "It doesn't mean Dru would betray us," she said defiantly.

"No," he agreed. "But what it does mean is that there's no knowing which way she'll go if she's pushed. With most things—men or women, horses, demons, dogs—you know at least to some degree what they'll do if you push them—get angry, break down, stab you in the back. Drypettis . . ." He shook his head. "The bad thing is that we've given her a certain amount of power."

"You wouldn't have," Sheera said glumly.

The Wolf shrugged. "I wouldn't have given you power, either," he returned. "I've been wrong before."

Absurdly, color flushed up under that thin, browned skin. "Do you really mean that?"

"Am I in the habit of saying things I don't mean?" he inquired. The yellow fox eyes glinted curiously in the gloom of the potting room. "You're a fine warrior, Sheera, in spite of the fact that you're crazy; and if it weren't for the sake of another warrior who's both finer and also crazier than you, I might just be tempted to fall in love with you. Though the thought makes me shudder," he added.

"Good grief, I should hope so!" she said, genuinely appalled at the idea.

Sun Wolf laughed. It was a horrible sound, like the scraping of rusty iron, and he stopped, coughing. Sheera had the grace to look unhappy. The loss of his voice was her doing, and she knew it.

"Listen, Sheera," he said after a moment. "How long would it take the mining superintendents' comfort brigade to find out how many men Altiokis is bringing with him?"

Sheera frowned. "I think Amber Eyes can get a report within a day. Why?"

"Because it occurs to me that this may be our time to strike, while Altiokis and a lot of his troops aren't in the Citadel at all. Yirth says that the tunnels from the mines up to the Citadel are guarded with illusion and magic—but if Yirth is going to be the one to try and break the illusions, it would probably be better if she did it when Altiokis was gone."

Sheera was staring at him, her dark eyes blazing with sudden fire. "You mean—strike now? Free the men now?"

"When Altiokis comes to Mandrigyn, yes. Can you?"

She took a deep breath. "I—I don't know. Yes. Yes, we can. Eo's made copies of the keys to most of the weapons stores and gates in the mines . . . Amber Eyes can get word to Tarrin to be ready . . ." She was shivering all over with suppressed excitement, her hands clenched in the velvet of her skirts. "Lady Wrinshardin can get word to the other Thanes," she continued after a moment. "They can be ready to strike once we've freed the men."

"No," the Wolf said. "The Thanes are always ready to fight, anyway —we won't give Altiokis the warning of a rumor. He's here to investigate the rumors Gilden and Wilarne started the night they burned the Records Office. How soon will they arrive?"

A meeting was called that evening in the orangery, the heads of the conspiracy arriving secretly, slipping across the canals and through the tunnels to assemble in the vast cavern of the dim room. Amber Eyes came in with Denga Rey, their constant company in the last few days since Amber Eyes had parted from the Wolf explaining a lot of things about the gladiator's commitment to the cause. Gilden and Wilarne arrived by separate routes—a different sort of friendship, the Wolf thought; probably closer, for all its lack of a physical or romantic element. Having waded through the morass of their jokes, verbal and otherwise, he had developed a hearty sympathy for his half-pints' respective husbands.

After a few minutes of the swift crossfire conversation among those four, Sun Wolf saw Yirth arrive, fading soundlessly from the shadows of the door and moving like a cat to take her place in the darkness beyond the single candle's flicker. She'd been there almost ten minutes before any of the others noticed her, listening, her crooked mouth smiling; Denga Rey's expression when she finally did see her was almost comical. But when they heard the sound of the door closing again, and all eyes turned—as they always did—to watch Sheera stride into the circle of the candle's light, Sun Wolf felt the witch's gaze, brief and speculative, touch him.

Sheera sat down among them, and her look traveled from face to face. "Well?"

"Eo says the keys are ready," Gilden reported.

"Yirth?"

"I have read and studied," the witch said softly, "everything that my master left me on the subject of Altiokis and upon illusion. I am as prepared as any can be who has not crossed through the Great Trial."

Sheera smiled and reached across the table to clasp the long, heavy-knuckled hands. "It's all we ask of you," she said. "Amber Eyes?"

"Cobra just got back from the mines," the girl reported in her low, sweet voice. "She says they expect a force of about fifteen hundred with Altiokis, leaving about that many in the Citadel. Cobra says Fat Maali was going to see if she could find Tarrin himself. She'll come to us directly here."

Sheera's face was half in shadow, half edged in the primrose softness of the dim light. Sun Wolf, watching her, saw the change in her eyes at the mention of Tarrin's name, saw the champion, the war leader, the woman who would be Queen of Mandrigyn, change suddenly for a fleeting second to a girl who heard her lover's name. In spite of all she had done to him, his heart went out to her. Like Starhawk, she was seeking, with single-minded brutality, to find and free the man she loved.

Then she was all business again. "Captain Sun Wolf?" she asked. "Would you say the women are ready?"

"I'd rather have another two weeks," he said, the harsh scrape of his voice startling in the gloom. "But I think Altiokis' absence and fewer troops make up for the lack. I have only one request of you, Sheera."

She nodded. "I know," she said. "Yirth, I was going to ask you—"

"No," Sun Wolf said. "It isn't that. I want to lead the troops myself."

The silence was as echoing as the silence that followed thunder. The women were staring at him, openmouthed with astonishment. In that silence, his eyes met Sheera's, defying her to refuse to let him shove his nose in her right to command.

"You may be a decent commander," he said after a moment, "and you may even be good, in about another five years. But I've trained these women and forged them into a weapon; and I don't want that weapon being broken by inexperience. If you're taking on Altiokis, you'll need a seasoned leader."

Sheera's eyes were wide and dark in the candlelight; surprise and relief at having a seasoned general and fighter like the Wolf struggled with resentment at being supplanted and relegated to second place. After a moment of silence, she breathed, "Would you? I mean—I thought—" The resentment faded and vanished, and the Wolf smiled to himself.

"Well, we both thought a lot of different things," he growled. "And if I'm going to mess around with magic, anyway, I want to make sure the job gets done right."

It was a momentary stalemate whether the leadership of the resistance forces of Mandrigyn would behave like grim and serious conspirators or like thrilled schoolgirls; and regrettably, instinct won out. Wilarne flung her arms around Sun Wolf's neck and planted an enthusiastic kiss on his mouth, followed in quick succession by Gilden, Sheera, Amber Eyes, and a bone-crushing hug from Denga Rey. Sun Wolf fought them off with a show of disgust. "I knew this would happen when I went to work for a bunch of skirts," he snarled.

Gilden retorted, "You hoped, you mean."

He was conscious again of Yirth's watching him from the shadows, of the puzzlement in the sea-green eyes. He glowered at her. "What's the matter? You never seen a man change his mind before?"

"No," the witch admitted. "Men pride themselves on their inflexibility."

"I'll get you for that," he promised and saw, for the first time, an answering sparkle in the sardonic depths of her eyes.

Then the sparkle vanished, like a candle doused by water; she swung around, even as he raised his head, hearing the sound of footfalls on the wet gravel of the garden path. A moment later the orangery's outer door opened, and the woman they called Fat Maali came in.

Fat Maali was clearly one of Amber Eyes' skags, the lowest type of camp follower, of the class of women whom mercenaries referred to by a name as descriptive as it was unrepeatable. She could have been thirty-five, but looked fifty, immense, blowsy, and strong, with a hard face that had never been beautiful and was now ravaged by poverty and debasement. Her eyes were limpid blue and cheerful. Sun Wolf wouldn't have wanted to be drunk in her company, if she knew he had any money on him.

She was dressed in a filthy green gown with clearly nothing underneath. Brass-colored curls tumbled down over her shoulders like a young girl's. The effect was almost as horrible as the stench of her perfume.

She said, "I've seen Tarrin."

Sheera was on her feet, her face alive with eagerness. "And?"

"He says don't do it."

Sheera sagged back as if struck, shock and disbelief parting her lips without words.

It was Amber Eyes who spoke. "Did he say why?" she asked quietly.

Fat Maali nodded, and her eyes were downcast. "Yes," she said softly. "He says—and I—I agree with him—that if we attacked the Citadel while Altiokis and his men were in the town, he's afraid of what would happen to the people here. The ones who didn't have anything to do with any of it, who just want to be let alone. He says the old bastard would massacre 'em, sure." She looked up, her eyes troubled but unwavering. "And he would, Amber. Y'know he would."

There was silence, the fat woman's gaze going worriedly from Amber Eyes to Sheera, and to the faces of the others in turn—Denga Rey, Gilden, Wilarne, Yirth, Sun Wolf. It was Sun Wolf who broke the silence. "He's right," he said.

"M'lord Tarrin—" Maali said hesitantly. "M'lord Tarrin said he wouldn't buy his freedom or the city's at that cost. He said he'd die a slave first."

Two days later, on orders from Acting Governor Stirk, the larger portion of the population of Mandrigyn turned out along the Golden Street, which led into the town from the tall land gate, to welcome Altiokis of Grimscarp, Wizard King of the Tchard Mountains. Though the crowds that lined the way were thick—troopers of the governor were going from house to house to make sure of it—they were silent.

Even those who had welcomed the soldiers who had put an end to the succession troubles in the city ten months before in Altiokis' name no longer cheered.

In the thick of the crowd, dressed in his patched brown gardening things, with Gilden and Wilarne brightly veiled and giggling on either arm, Sun Wolf watched the Wizard King ride in.

"He never came after Iron Pass," Gilden whispered, her calmly businesslike tone belying the caressing way she rubbed her cheek on his arm. "The captain of his mercenaries—the Dark Eagle, his name is —led his troops into the city, with Derroug and Stirk and some of the other chiefs of the council who'd been exiled by Tarrin. Amber Eyes tells me . . ."

A harsh blare of trumpets rose over the deeper drone of the battle horns, cutting off her words. The Wolf raised his head, the sounds prickling his spine. Rolling like thunder down the wide, tree-lined street, the deep boom of the kettledrums was picked up and flung from wall to marble-fronted wall. Sun Wolf and the girls had taken their positions in the last straight reach of the Golden Street, where it ran down to the Great Landing; beyond the crowds, the gilding of the ceremonial barge flashed in the wan sunlight. Across the way, on a balcony draped with pennons, one of Amber Eyes' girls sat combing her hair, preparing to tally the number of troops as they passed.

"There," Wilarne whispered.

Around the corner of the lane they appeared, a mass of black-mailed bodies, their measured tread lost in the sonorous crash of the drums. Antlike heads, faceless behind slit-eyed helmets, stared out straight ahead. Sun Wolf wondered, with a prickle of loathing, whether the eye slits were functional or merely to keep the populace from suspecting. Like the nuuwa in the palace gardens, these soldiers marched unarmed.

"Altiokis' private troops," Wilarne breathed, under cover of the Wolf's drawing her closer to him as if to protect her. *Though his ancestors help the man who thought this sloe-eyed scrap of primordial mayhem needed protection!* "That's Gilgath at their head, riding the black horse. He's the Captain of Grimscarp, Commander of Altiokis' Citadel."

The Wolf considered the inhuman, mailed bulk with narrowed eyes. Like his men, Gilgath was masked and hidden by his armor. Men at his sides led beasts on chains—huge, strange beasts, like slumped dog-apes with chisel teeth and mad, stupid eyes—ugies, Lady Wrinshardin had called them.

More of them walked with the black-mailed guards around the Wizard King's ebony litter. The people in the street had fallen utterly silent; the only sounds now were the blows of the drums, steady and inescapable as doom.

At the sight of the litter, the Wolf felt his flesh crawl. It was borne by two black horses, their eyes masked with silver, led by the black-armored guards. Pillars of twisted ebony, whose capitals flashed with opal and nacre, supported dead-black curtains; where the curtains had been drawn back, the interior of the litter was masked by heavy lattices of carven blackwood. Sun Wolf, who stood taller than anyone around him in that chiefly female crowd, craned his neck, but could see nothing of the wizard within, except for a still, dark shadow, unmoving against the blackness of the cushions.

And yet, at the sight of it, something stirred in Sun Wolf, anger and an emotion deeper than anger; revulsion and an implacable hate. The impact of his feelings startled him, with the awareness that he looked upon pollution. And behind that came the horrible and revolting certainty that he had sometimes felt in the haunts of the marsh demons of the North—the certainty that he looked upon that which was not entirely human.

This was not a demon, he knew, edging his way forward through the crowd to follow the litter with his eyes. But something . . .

He pushed ahead to the front edge of the packed throng as the litter descended to the landing stage and the waiting barge. No snake, no spider, no foul and creeping thing had ever affected him with such cold loathing, and he struggled for a glimpse of the thing that would emerge. Distance and the angle confused his line of sight; Gilgath, the Commander of the Citadel, was deploying his soldiers across the covered tunnel of the Spired Bridge, to line the canal route toward the governor's palace. Behind him, other marching footsteps echoed in the narrow street as the rest of Altiokis' force approached.

Then the Wolf heard a single deep voice call out, "Arrest that man." Turning, he found himself staring up into the face of the Dark Eagle, captain of Altiokis' mercenary forces.

The Eagle hadn't changed since they'd campaigned together in the East. The sardonic blue eyes still held their expression of bitter amusement as Sun Wolf turned to flee.

He found himself hemmed in by the civilians at his back and the City Troops that were running toward him from all sides. Gilden and Wilarne had melted away into the crowd, already heading in opposite directions to get the news to Sheera. The Eagle spurred his black mount forward toward him, bowmen clustering around his stirrups— if the Wolf remembered the Dark Eagle's specialties, there wasn't much chance they'd miss. Civilians were crowding away from him, panic-stricken. Someone grabbed his arm from behind and shoved a sword blade against his ribs; he ducked and feinted. An arrow shaft burned his shoulder as it buried itself in the body of the man behind him.

The Wolf grabbed the sword from the slacking grip and spun to meet his would-be captors, throwing another one of them into the path of the second arrow and darting for the mouth of the nearest alley. A man in his way cut at him with a halberd; he parried, slashed along the shaft, and jumped over the falling weapon. The crowd milled and scattered before him. The Eagle's mercenaries and the City Troops broke ranks to pursue.

He was closed in, he saw. He cut another man's face open and turned to strike a third. Though battle concentrated his mind, he was somehow peripherally aware of movement near the landing, of a stirring in the black curtains . . .

Something, he did not know what, like a smoky and confusing cloud, struck at his face, and he turned to slash at it. His sword cleaved it like air, haloed in a splattering of red lightning. In the last second in which he realized that it was merely an illusion sent to break his concentration, something hit him on the back of the head, and darkness closed around him.

CHAPTER

~ 17 ~

"*CAPTAIN SUN WOLF.*"

The voice that penetrated the blackness of his mind seemed to come from a great distance away. It was the Dark Eagle's, he recognized, obscured by the buzzing roar that filled his skull.

"And in such clothes, too. Open your eyes, you barbarian; I know you can hear me."

The Wolf pried one grit-filled eye open and squinted against the burning glare of yellow light.

"They say when you hire out your sword, you meet acquaintances in all corners of the world," the Eagle went on, "but I hardly expected to see an old friend here."

Sun Wolf blinked painfully. The light that had blinded him a moment ago resolved itself into the smoldering fireball at the end of a torch stuck in a greasy iron wall sconce, just behind the Dark Eagle's shoulder. He became slowly aware of the burning ache in his arms; when he tried to move them, he found that they were, in fact, supporting the weight of his limp body. The short chain that joined his wrists had been thrown over a hook a few feet above his head. He was hanging with his back to the stone wall of a room which he guessed was underground—under what was left of the Records Office, presumably—and the memory of another small underground room and the drifting sparkle of unknown fire on the air brought sweat to his stubbled face. He got his feet under him and stood, glaring at the mercenary chief, who was, for the moment, the only other man in the room.

"The least you could have done was keep your flapping mouth shut," he growled hoarsely.

The Dark Eagle frowned. He was a stocky man of medium height, his black hair falling forward over his bright eyes. "Lost your tongue?"

"A lady poisoned me, and I lost my voice over it," the Wolf answered quite truthfully, hearing, as he said the words, the metallic rasp of the sound.

The flicker of concern that had glimmered behind the blue eyes fled. The mercenary chief laughed. "I hope you had your revenge. The reason I took you in is that I'm paid to keep order in Altiokis' domains. Why ever you've decided to winter in this lovely town, I'd have to clean up the mess sooner or later. Where are your men?"

"At Wrynde."

"I didn't mean your troops, I mean the men you're leading. And believe me, Wolf, I'm not going to accept that you're in this town to no purpose. What men are you at the head of?"

Sun Wolf sighed, leaning his head back against the rough rock of the wall behind him. "None," he said. "No one."

"You put up one hell of a fight for a man with a clear conscience."

"You wouldn't know a clear conscience if you found one in your bed. What in the name of all your sniveling ancestors are you doing serving that demon?"

The Dark Eagle frowned. "Demon?"

"Whatever was in that litter, it wasn't human. I'll take oath on that."

The blue eyes narrowed to slits. "You always could spot them, couldn't you? But Altiokis is no demon. I've seen him summon demons and I've seen him handle the things they dread to protect himself against them."

"He's no demon, but—I don't know what he is."

A white grin split the swarthy countenance, and the uneasy look vanished. "He's the greatest wizard of the world—and a man of uncommon appetites to boot." The smile faded. "Why do you say he isn't human?"

"Because he isn't, dammit! Can't you tell it? Can't you feel it?"

The blue eyes hardened. "I think we hit you harder than we intended, my friend," the Eagle said. "Or maybe your light-skirt's poison addled your never-very-stout brains. Altiokis is a man—and a man who can afford to pay damned well to keep trouble out of his lands. As you shall see."

He moved toward the cell door, then paused, his hand on the handle. In a quieter voice, he said, "I'd advise you to tell him whatever you're in, Wolf."

He opened the door and stepped aside.

Altiokis entered.

Two impressions, spiritual and physical, seemed to overlap for a second in Sun Wolf's brain.

The spiritual was the impression of a half-rotted tree, leprous with age, its cancered bark still standing but enclosing another entity, a black and lucid fire that showed through the cracks.

The physical was the sight of a man of medium height, impossibly obese from eating rich foods, with bad skin, the suspicion of a shadow of stubble on his pouchy jaw, and too many rings embedded in the flesh of his fat fingers. Contact with merchants' wives had sharpened Sun Wolf's appreciation of the value of cloth; the black velvet that formed the underpinning of the jewel-beaded embroidery of the immense doublet sold for fifty silver crowns a yard. The jeweled belts that supported the overhanging rolls of fat would have purchased cities.

In the back of his mind, the Wolf heard Lady Wrinshardin's acid voice saying, "He is vulgar."

And he knew, watching the Dark Eagle's face and the faces of the gaunt harbor master, Stirk, and of Drypettis, who stood in the shadows of the corridor behind him, that the physical being was all anyone ever saw.

He wanted to scream at them, "Don't you see it? Don't you understand what he is?" But he did not understand himself.

Sunk in their pouches of fat, the cold little eyes gleamed with smug amusement. The Wizard King stepped forward, raising his staff. Like the pillars of his litter, it was carved of ebony in twisting patterns, its ornate tip flickering with the ghostly gleam of opal and abalone. The touch of it on Sun Wolf's neck was like ice and fire, a searing dart of pain, and he flinched from it with a stifled cry.

A satisfied little smile decorated the puffy lips.

"So you're the man who thought he could go against me?"

Sun Wolf said nothing. After the ordeal of the anzid, pain had changed its meaning for him, but the shock of being touched by that staff had taken his breath away. He was aware of Drypettis, standing in the doorway, like some monstrous orchid in her orange gown and veils; he could see her huge brown eyes watching him with an unreadable mixture of coldness and hatred and spite. He wondered if she had thought to tell Sheera where he was being held and what good it would do anyone if she had.

Or was she waiting to see if he broke, to slip away and warn the others when he did?

Altiokis' voice went on. "Who hired you, Captain?"

The Wolf swallowed and shook his head. "He never told me his name," he whispered. "He said he'd pay me to spy out the city, the gates, and the canals and to lay out a siege plan . . ."

"Probably one of the Thanes." Altiokis yawned. "They're always stirring up trouble—and it's time they were put down."

"Where did he meet you, this man?" the Dark Eagle asked.

In a stifled voice, the Wolf replied, "In the Peninsula, after the siege of Melplith. He arranged a meeting with me, three weeks from now, in East Shore. I was to come here, which I did, overland, and lay out my plans . . ."

"Yes, yes," Altiokis said in a bored voice. "But who was he?"

"I tell you, I don't know." The Wolf glanced from the Eagle to Altiokis and back again, sensing that the Wizard King didn't really much care who had hired him. Was he that confident of his own powers and of the magic that protected the Citadel? Or had he, as a result of his endless life, merely reached the point of bored carelessness with everything?

"The man chose an expensive spy," the Dark Eagle commented thoughtfully. "The world abounds in cheaper ones."

The Wolf flashed him what he hoped was an angry dagger of a glance. "Would you hire a cheap one?"

Then he flinched in agony from the glowing tip of the Wizard King's staff.

"Remember to whom you're talking, barbarian," Altiokis said, with a kind of quiet relish. He brought the staff toward Sun Wolf's face, the white metal of its tip seeming to glow with an unholy luminescence. The Wolf drew back from it, feeling the sweat that poured down his cheeks, staring as if hypnotized at the star-flash of the opals and at the twined jaws of the inlaid serpents that held them. Something that was not heat seemed to smoke from the jeweled tip, like a cold promise of unbearable pain.

"I am Altiokis," the Wizard King said softly. "No one has the temerity to speak thus to my servants."

The burning jewels were within a half inch of the Wolf's eyes when he whispered, "I'm sorry, my lord."

Past the opals, he saw the little smirk appear and wrenched his head aside as the staff touched him again. A cry of pain escaped him, and he felt the flesh along his cheekbone sear and curl, the shock of it piercing his whole body like a sword.

Savoringly, Altiokis said, "I could chip you away, piece by piece, until you begged for the chance to tell what you know and the mercy of a cut throat. I may do it yet, merely to amuse myself."

Sun Wolf made no reply to this. For a time, speech was beyond him. Sickened with the pain, he hung from the chain above his head, trying to regather his thoughts, telling himself that, no matter how bad it was, the anzid had been far worse. But beyond that, he was conscious of both anger and outrage that a man with the powers of the Wizard King should use them so, like a cruel child pulling the wings from a fly. He had met enough men in his time who were amused by pain. He had not expected a man who had mastered the hard disciplines of wizardry to be one of them.

"Governor Stirk . . ." Altiokis said, and Stirk looked up, the surprised gratification on his face reminding Sun Wolf of a dog that hoped for a pat. The tall harbor master came forward, almost wagging his tail. In the doorway, Drypettis stiffened with outraged indignation. Stirk actually went down on his knees and kissed the Wizard King's jewel-crusted shoe. Altiokis almost purred.

"Did the interrogation chamber survive the fire?" the wizard asked.

The new governor's face fell. "Alas, no, my lord," he said, rising and unobtrusively dusting his knees. "The upper level of the prisons was gutted by the fire the night Governor Derroug was murdered."

My ancestors, the Wolf thought, through the raw anguish that seemed to be pouring into his flesh from the open burn on his face, *are looking out for me, after all.*

There was a pout in the fruity voice. "Then he shall go with me to the Citadel in the morning. When I depart, Governor Stirk, I shall leave a force of men here under the command of General Dark Eagle, to be billeted in the houses of citizens as you choose. Do not think that in the event of these disruptions, the annual tribute from this city will be excused. Moreover, I feel sure that you are moved to make some suitable show of gratitude for your elevation to your new position."

Stirk almost fell over himself agreeing; Sun Wolf wondered what Altiokis could possibly want with more wealth.

"As for this—arrogant barbarian . . ." The butt end of the staff licked out and cracked sharply on the side of Sun Wolf's knee. Beside the agony of his seared face, he hardly noticed. "I scarcely feel that he is telling us all the truth; but in time, we shall learn from him the names of the men ill-intentioned enough to hire such a person to spy out my city. From my Citadel, I can see all. No army can approach without my knowledge. But it will save trouble to know whom to punish."

The words were rhetorical, and Sun Wolf knew it. Altiokis didn't much care whom he punished or why; to a man a hundred and fifty years old and of no great mental resources to begin with, the infliction of pain was one of few amusements left. Sun Wolf's eyes followed the fat wizard as he waddled toward the door, with Stirk bowing along at his heels. The Dark Eagle, his face a smooth and cynical blank, brought up the rear.

Did others wonder about this, too? the Wolf asked himself, watching them mount the few steps to the hall. *How could something that trivial, that spiteful and vicious, have acquired this kind of power?*

Didn't any of them see?

"One more thing."

Altiokis turned back, the torchlight from the hall outside streaming over his jewels like a spent wave over a barnacle-encrusted hull. He snapped his fingers. Past him, the Wolf saw the guards in the hallway startle, heard Drypettis give a sharp squeak of alarm.

Two nuuwa entered the cell.

Sun Wolf felt his heart stop, then pound to life with a surge of terror that momentarily drowned out all things else. He cast one quick glance at the hook that held his chained hands helpless above his head, calculating whether he could get free before they began ripping at his flesh, then stared back at them, knowing he was trapped. Altiokis' smile broadened with delight.

"You like my friends, eh?" he asked.

Both waggling heads turned toward Sun Wolf, as if they could see him or smell the blood in his veins. Drool glistened on the misshapen chins, and they champed their impossibly grown teeth and fidgeted as the wizard laid companionable hands on the sloped backs. Their uniforms—foul, torn, and crawling with lice—were so filthy the Wolf wondered how anyone could bring himself to touch even those, let alone the mindless, unclean flesh beneath.

"You'll be quite safe." Altiokis smiled. "As long as you make no attempt to get away, they shall curb their appetites and be content with —ah—contemplation. But believe me, should you try to get away, I'm sure they could chew off quite large portions of you before your screams brought the guards—if any guards would be willing to try to separate them from their victim."

That pleased smile widened still more at the thought, and the most powerful wizard in the world paused thoughtfully to excavate a nostril with his jeweled finger. He wiped it fastidiously on Stirk's sleeve. Stirk gave a fatuous smile.

"I hope I shall see you in the morning."

The door shut behind him.

For a long time Sun Wolf stood, his twisted shoulders racked and aching from the drag of his body against the chain, his mind chasing itself blindly from thought to thought.

The most powerful wizard in the world! His stomach turned at the thought of that power and that waste.

But the power came from nothing within Altiokis himself. He was a man half rotted from the inside by something else; the power was not of his own finding. That first, fleeting impression was all the Wolf had to go on; afterward, he had seen the wizard only as others saw him— obese, omnipotent, and terrifying. Sun Wolf felt as he had in his childhood, frantically insisting to his father and to the other men of the tribe that he could see the demons whose voices taunted them from the marsh mists and being sharply told to shut up and follow. He had been right then, he knew. And he knew now that there was something in Altiokis that was neither human nor clean nor sane.

Tomorrow he would be taken up to the Citadel. He'd seen enough torture to harbor no illusions about his own abilities to withstand it for any protracted period of time. Altiokis was right—the threat of being given anzid again, or of being put into a room with whatever it was that could transform a man into a nuuwa, would have him selling off all these women he had come to be so fond of without a moment's hesitation.

Except, he thought, that it probably would not save him, anyway. Even upon short acquaintance, he knew Altiokis too well for that.

His eyes returned to the nuuwa. Altiokis had left a torch, burning in its bracket on the other side of the room. The nuuwa wore the uniforms of Altiokis' troops, but they were already ragged and fouled, for the creatures were too brainless to change them or even unsnag them if they caught on something. It occurred obliquely to the Wolf, in the one corner of his mind not occupied by horror, that what undoubtedly became of nuuwa, if they weren't killed, was that they simply rotted away from self-neglect. One of these already had what looked like a badly festered gash on its leg, visible through the torn and soiled breeches.

Now that he had seen them made from men, the Wolf could tell that one of these was more recent than the other—the one eye seared out and scarred over, the other rotted out from within and already scarring. The second nuuwa was older, the bones of the face changed and deformed, the shoulders more slumped. It was impossible to tell through which eye the flame-creature had bored.

They stood unmoving, watching him from eyeless holes, their reek filling the cell. Sometimes one of them would shift from foot to foot, but neither stirred itself to brush away the roaches that crawled over its feet in the straw. Once Sun Wolf looked cautiously over his head at the chain and hook again, and they grew restless, snuffling and fidgeting.

He gave up the attempt.

His mind returned to that windowed cell in the burned-out wing of the prison. The flake of flame, the young slave screaming as he clutched his bleeding eye . . . Altogether it had taken nearly a minute, the Wolf calculated, between the time the thing had got the boy and the time it had bored through to the brain. Had he known what would happen to him in those endless, racking seconds? Or had the pain been too great?

The Wolf shuddered with the memory of it. In his heart, he already knew what was intended for him, whether he revealed any plans or not.

The anzid had changed his tolerance for pain, which was already higher than most men's, but it had given him a hearty appreciation of how bad pain could get. And even with the blessing of ignorance, without the knowledge that one's scooped-out husk would be ruled by

Altiokis' foul will, the sixty seconds or so that it took for the thing—fire, insect, or whatever—to bore its way inward would be like the distilled essence of the deepest Hells.

He glanced at the nuuwa and then back up at the chains.

It would be possible, he saw now, to stretch his body and arms enough to lift the manacles up over the top of the hook that held them. The hook was positioned for a slightly shorter man—few of the men of Mandrigyn topped six feet—and he thought that he could manage with a struggle. But it would take a short while; in the meantime, his body would hang exposed and helpless before those mindless things drooling in their corner.

He wondered how far his own abilities of nonvisibility went.

He'd experimented with them since the night he'd first called them into use on the roof of the palace kitchens, the night he and the women had rescued Tisa. With a little practice, he had found that he could, within certain limits, avoid the eyes of someone entering a fairly small and well-lighted room, provided he did nothing to call attention to himself. The nuuwa had no eyes—it stood to reason that they saw with their minds. But if that were the case, his nonvisibility should work better on them, since it was, in fact, avoidance of the attention.

It might be worth a try.

In any case, he was aware that, objectively, in the long run, he would not be worse off. Being devoured alive by them would be a messy and hideous way to die, but he wondered whether it would be worse than becoming a nuuwa himself.

It was a choice he had no desire to put to the test.

Hesitantly, he groped his mind out toward theirs, shifting their attention past him, toward the stones of the wall and the crawling straw at his feet, letting them look through him, around him, turning that intentness toward trivial things, and making them forget that he was there. He found himself sweating with the effort of it, trickles of moisture running down his aching arms and down his face and his body. He made himself relax into the effort, becoming less and less important in their minds against their general awareness of the cell and occupying their attention, their senses, with the crackle of insect feet in the straw, the smell of the torch smoke . . .

He braced his body, then began to reach upward, rising on his toes and stretching his stiff back and shoulders toward the iron hook.

The nuuwa stared stolidly at the walls to either side of him.

Delicately, he hooked the tips of his half-numbed fingers under the short links that joined the metal bracelets. He strained to lift them toward the tip of the hook, loosening his back muscles against the shooting fire of cramps that raced down them from their long inactivity. The sweat burned in the raw flesh of his opened cheek, and his arms trembled at the effort of movement. The tip of the hook seemed impossibly high. One of the nuuwa belched, the sound sharp as an explosion in the silent room; half hypnotized by the effort of concentration, the Wolf never took his mind from the illusion of nonvisibility that he held with his whole attention, despite the physical strain that occupied his limbs. He had been trapped once by having his concentration broken. Even if they tore him to pieces, he would not do so again.

The metal slipped over metal. The slacking of the hook's support was abrupt, as the links slid over it. The Wolf felt as if all the weight of his body had dropped suddenly upon his exhausted muscles. He could have collapsed in a thankful heap on the fetid straw, but he forced himself to remain upright, lowering his arms slowly to his sides, shaking all over with the effort. The separate agonies of the day were swallowed in an all-encompassing wave of anguishing cramps in arms and back.

The nuuwa continued to look at the wall.

As soon as he was satisfied that his legs would support him, Sun Wolf took a cautious step forward.

There was no reaction.

His mind held their attention at bay, but the concentration required most of his strength, and he knew he could not keep it up for long. He took another step and another, without either of them appearing to notice . . . *No mean feat,* he thought in that clear cynical corner of his mind, *to keep a nuuwa from going after ambulatory food.*

The door was bolted with an iron dead bolt, not merely a wooden drop that could be lifted with a card. He glanced over his shoulder at the nuuwa, the nearest of which stood, a stinking lump of flesh, less than six feet from him.

He decided to risk it.

"Dark Eagle!" he yelled, lifting his raw voice to as carrying a pitch as he could manage. "Stirk! I'll tell you what you want to know! Just keep them off me!"

His concentration pressed against the nuuwa, a sheer physical effort, like that of trying to hold up a falling wall. The nuuwa shifted, scuffling around the cell, arms swinging, lolling heads wagging, as if seeking for what they could not find. *Rot your eyes, you poxy corridor guard,* he thought, *don't you want to be the first with the news that your prisoner's broken?*

He yelled again. "I'll tell you anything! Just get me out of here! I'll tell you what you want!"

Running footsteps sounded in the corridor. One man, he guessed from the sound, hesitating outside the door. *Open it, you cowardly bastard!* the Wolf demanded silently. *Don't call your chief . . .*

The bolt shot back.

Sun Wolf came slamming out of the cell, throwing his full weight on the door, heedless of any weapon the man might have had. The guard's drawn short sword jammed in the wood of the door and stuck; the man had his mouth open, too startled to scream, showing a wide expanse of dirty teeth. Sun Wolf grabbed him by the neck and hurled him bodily into the arms of the advancing nuuwa.

He sent the door crashing shut and shot the bolt against the man's screams, pulled the sword free, and ran up the empty corridor as if heading for the half-closed doors of Hell.

CHAPTER

∽ 18 ∽

"*A*ND YOU TURNED THEIR MINDS ASIDE?"

Sun Wolf nodded. Yirth's drugs could ease pain without dulling the mind, but the release of concentration acted almost like a drug in itself. Lying in the fading light of her tiny whitewashed attic room, he felt as exhausted as he did after battle. The smell of the place, of the drying herbs that festooned the low rafters in strings, filled him with a curious sense of peace, and he watched her moving around, gaunt and powerful, and wondered how he had ever thought of her as ugly. Stern and strong in her power, yes. But the marring birthmark no longer drew his eyes from the rest of her face, and he saw her now as a harsh-faced woman a few years older than he, whose life had been, in its way, as strenuous as his own.

As if she felt his thoughts, she turned back to him. "How did you do this thing?" she asked.

"I don't know," he replied wearily. "It was the anzid, I think." He saw her sudden frown and realized it wasn't much of an explanation.

"I think the anzid did something to me—besides half killing me, that is. Since I was brought back, I've been able to see in the dark, and I've had this—this ability to avoid people's sight. I've always been good at it, but now it's—it's uncanny. I used it the first time when we rescued Tisa, and I've been practicing since then. I used to—"

She held up her hand against his words. "No," she said. "Let me think."

She turned from him, pacing to the narrow window that looked out over the wet, red roofs of Mandrigyn. For a long moment she stood, her dark head bent, the gray light gleaming in the pewter streaks that frosted her hair. Outside, the plop and splash of a gondola's pole could be heard in the canal, and the light tapping of hooves over the bridge nearby. Yirth's cat, curled at the foot of Sun Wolf's narrow cot, woke, stretched, and sprang soundlessly to the floor.

Then Yirth whispered, "Dear Mother." She looked back at him. "Tell me about the night you spent in the pit," she said.

He returned her gaze in silence, unwilling to share the extent of grief and pain and humiliation. Only one person knew the whole and, if she were even still alive, he did not know where she was now. At length he said, "Sheera had her victory over me. Isn't that enough?"

"Don't be a fool," the witch said coldly. "There was no anzid left in your system when she led us back to you."

He stared at her, not comprehending.

"Did you have visions?"

He nodded mutely, his body shaken with a fit of shivering at the memory of those dreams of power and despair.

She put her hands to her temples, the thick, streaky hair springing over and through her fingers, like water through a sieve of bone. "Dear Mother," she murmured again.

Her voice sounded hollow, half stunned. "I found it among her things when she was killed," she said, as if to herself. "Chilisirdin—my master. I didn't think . . . In our business there are always poisons. We deal in them—poisons, philters, abortifacients. Sometimes a death is the only answer. I never thought anything else of it."

"What are you talking about?" he whispered, though it was coming to him, in a kind of unveiling of horror, what she meant.

Her face, in the deepening shadows, seemed suddenly very young, its stony self-possession stripped away by fear and hope. "Tell me, Captain—why did you become a warrior and not a shaman among your people?"

Sun Wolf stared at her for as long as it would take to count to a hundred, stunned at the truth of her question, struck as he had been during the tortured visions in the pit, with the memory of his black and icy childhood and of all those things of beauty and power that he had set aside in the face of his father's bleak mockery. In a voice very unlike his own, he stammered, "The old shaman died—long before I was born. The one we had was a charlatan, a fake. My father . . ." He was silent, unable to go on.

For a time neither spoke.

Then he said, "No." He made a movement, as if thrusting from him the thought that he could have what he had known from his earliest childhood was his birthright. "I'm no wizard."

"What are you, then?" she demanded harshly. "If you hadn't been born with the Power, the anzid would have killed you. I was surprised that it didn't, but I thought it was because you were tough, were strong. It never crossed my mind otherwise, even though my master had told me that the Great Trial would kill any who were not mageborn to begin with."

Cold and irrational terror rose in him. His mouth dry, he whispered, "I'm no wizard. I'm a warrior. My business is war. I stay out of that stuff. My life is war. Starhawk . . ." He paused, uncertain what he had meant to say about Starhawk. "I can't change at my age."

"You *are* changed," Yirth said bitterly. "Like it or not."

"But I don't know any magic!" he protested.

"Then you had best learn," she rasped, an edge of impatience stinging into her voice. "For believe me, Altiokis will come to know that there is another proven wizard in the world, another who has passed through the Great Trial. Most of us undergo the training first, and the Trial when we have the strength to endure it. You had the strength— either from your training as a warrior or because the magic you were born with is strong, stronger than any I have heard tell of. But without training in the ways of it, you are helpless to fight the Wizard King."

Sun Wolf lay back on the cot. The smart of his arms and shoulders and the raw places on his wrists where the spancel had been removed bitterly reinforced his memory of the Wizard King. "He'll follow me wherever I go, won't he?" he asked quietly.

"Probably," Yirth answered. "As he hounded my master Chilisirdin to her death."

The Wolf turned his eyes toward her in the dark. The daylight had faded from the attic, but among themselves, wizards had no need of light. "I'm sorry," he said. "I was just given for free what you would have sold everything you owned to possess; and here I am complaining because I don't want it. But I was raised to steer very clear of magic, and I—I'm afraid of the Power."

"You should be," she snapped. In a quieter voice, she went on. "It is unheard of for an untrained mage to pass through the Great Trial. You must leave Altiokis' domains, and quickly; but if you take my advice, you must seek out another wizard as fast as you can. You do not know the extent of your powers; without the teaching and the discipline of wizardry, you are as dangerous as a mad dog."

Sun Wolf chuckled softly in the darkness. "I know. I've seen it a thousand times in my own business. When a boy comes to me to be trained in arms, he's the most dangerous between the fourth month and the twelfth. That's when he's learned the physical power, but not the spiritual control—and he hasn't quite grasped the fact that there's anyone alive who can beat him. That's the age when someone—myself or Starhawk or Ari—has to trounce the daylights out of him, to keep him from picking fights with everyone else in the troop. If a boy survives the first year, he has the discipline and the brains to be a soldier."

He heard her small, faint sniff, which he rightly interpreted as laughter. "And to think I once despised you for being a soldier," she said. "I will teach you what I can while you are hidden here, until we can get you out of the city. But you must find a true wizard—one who has had the fullness of his power for many years and who understands in truth what I know only in theory."

"I would do that in any case," Sun Wolf said quietly. "I know that my days as a warrior are done."

Clear and sharp, the vision returned to him of his own hands seared to the bone from grasping the molten fire of his dreams. It hurt to let the old life go, to release what he had striven for and taken pride in since he was a boy old enough to wield a child's sword. It left him with a stricken feeling of emptiness, as if with the sword he had given up an arm as well. Ari would take the troop and the school at Wrynde. Starhawk . . .

He looked up. "There'll be a woman coming here," he said, knowing that with the Hawk's stubbornness, even his vision manifesting itself to her in a dream and telling her to give up the search would not be sufficient to turn her aside. *Stubborn female!* he added to himself. "She's looking for me. Tell her . . ."

Tell her what? That he'd gone on, searching for a wizard in a world long bereft of such things? That she should follow him once again?

"Tell her to meet me in Wrynde, before the summer's end. Tell her I swear that I will come to her there." He paused, picturing her with sharp and painful clarity in the quiet of the stone garden below the school. He had not walked its paths in summer for nearly twenty years. "Tell her what became of me," he added quietly.

The deformed mouth quirked suddenly into a wry smile, showing teeth white as snow in the gloom. "A long way to travel," she remarked. "Shall I teach you how to find this woman yourself?"

He saw what must have been his own expression reflected in the one of deepening amusement in her eyes and grinned ruefully. "If I'm going to go back to being a schoolboy at my age," he said, "I'm certainly developing the reactions of one."

"That, Captain, is only because you have never before this particularly cared where anyone else was, or if that person lived or died," Yirth replied calmly. "The relationships of the body are the business of women like Amber Eyes—the relationships of the heart are mine. I have made as many love philters as I have made poisons and abortifacients. They all tell me why. They are driven to tell; I do not ask. There is nothing that I have not heard.

"And do you know, Captain, that I have heard men sneer at—what do they call? A respectable man of full age—suddenly discovering what it is to love another person. Doubtless you yourself know what they say."

Sun Wolf had the grace to blush.

"But if a man who has been crippled from childhood is healed at the age of forty, will he not jump and dance and turn cartwheels like a young boy, scorning the dignity of his years? The mockers are those who themselves are still crippled. Think nothing of it." She shook back the thick mane of hair from her shoulders, her face framed in it like the white blur of an asymmetrical skull in the gloom. "Will you sleep?"

He hesitated. "If you're tired, yes," he said. "If you're willing, I'd rather spend the night learning whatever you have to teach me about my new trade."

And Yirth laughed, a faint, dry, little sound that Sun Wolf reflected he was probably the first member of the male sex to have heard.

"What I have to teach is meager enough," she said. "I have the learning, but my powers are very small."

"Will they increase when you yourself pass through the Trial?"

She hesitated, the indecision in her green eyes, the fear robbing her of her years of experience, making her look again like a thin, bitter, ugly young girl—like the duckling in that rather comforting fable, who knew that she would never grow into a swan. "They should," she said at length. "And I will read and learn all that I can about it before I take the anzid myself, so that I may meet Altiokis as a proven wizard when Sheera and Tarrin agree that it is time to attack. And that must be soon. Altiokis has long suspected there is another person born with the powers of wizardry here in Mandrigyn; after the Trial, it will be harder to hide."

In the darkness, he heard her move, stepping to the narrow window that overlooked the slimy alley outside, the reflected light from the other houses that crowded the Little Island touching the hooked aquiline profile and the spider threads of silver in the dark masses of her hair as she turned back to face him once more. "As for the Trial itself, I think that my strength is sufficient to carry me through it alive," she went on. "For thirty years, since I came to my powers as a child, I have felt them in me, chafing and twisting at the walls that flesh and mind set against their exercise. I know they are strong—there have been times when I have felt like a woman in travail with a dragon's child, unable to give it birth."

She was silent again, only the ragged draw of her breath audible in the cool, herb-smelling darkness of the bare attic room. Seeing her clearly in the darkness, the Wolf could see also the girl that she had been, like a young tree girdled with steel as a sapling, warping a little more each day as it strove despairingly toward a destiny not permitted it—*And ugly,* he thought, *to boot.* He knew now that the limitations that beauty set upon a woman were far pleasanter, at least at the time, than the ones ugliness placed—and he knew from bitter personal memory how cruel the world could be to women who were not pleasing to men's eyes.

But he only said, "At least you knew why you were in pain. I never did."

"Knowing why only made it worse," she whispered.

"Maybe," the Wolf said, sitting up a little in the narrow bed and bracing his shoulders against the dry, smooth wood of the wall. "I'm

not sure whether it would have been better to know I'd been robbed
or to grow up trying to hide from everyone—particularly my father—
the fact that I suspected that I was mad."

Against the reflected window lights, he saw her head turn sharply
and felt the touch of her green eyes on him. He wondered suddenly
how long it had been between the time she had realized her own
powers and the time she had found someone who understood what
they were.

When she spoke again, her voice was quieter, and the edge of bitter
mockery was gone from it, leaving it sweet in the darkness, like the
sweetness of the smell of drying rosemary. "I should look to the Trial
as a gate to freedom—freedom from all that I have been—even if it is
only freedom to challenge Altiokis and die. But—I saw you when we
brought you up out of the pit, Captain."

Then she turned away, covering her fear of pain with brusqueness,
as the Wolf had seen warriors curse rather than weep when their bones
were set. "Come. If you intend to learn tonight, we had best start."

Twenty-five years of hard soldiering had not given Sun Wolf much
background in wizardry or love, but they had taught him discipline
and the concentration to set aside physical weariness and apply himself
to what must be done. As he worked under Yirth's guidance through
the dark hours, he was constantly aware that it might be months or
years before he found another teacher. *I will sleep,* he told himself,
when I get on the road.

One of the first things that she taught him were the spells to hold
back the need for sleep and rest and the drugs to reinforce them. He'd
been familiar already with the drugs—most mercenaries were.

But this was only a beginning.

As with the body, there were exercises of the mind and spirit, without which large portions of wizardry would be impossible to comprehend, even for those born with its seeds within them. Those exercises
she also taught him, in the shadowy dimness of that long workroom
with its arcane charts, its age-worn books, and its phials of poisons and
philters—things that in a year, or two years, or five years would come
to fruition, if he meditated daily and practiced and learned the com-
plexities of mathematics and music which were as much a part of
wizardry as drugs and illusion. At one point, she stopped in her teaching and regarded him across the cluttered table, her long hands resting
tranquilly among the diagrams that strewed its waxed surface.

"You are certainly the most cooperative student I have ever heard of," she commented. "At this point, I was in tears, arguing with my master. I hated the mathematics part."

He grinned ruefully and pushed the lank, sweat-damp strands of his hair back from his stubbled face. "Mathematics has always been a closed book to me," he admitted. "I know enough about trajectories to get a rock over a wall with a catapult, but this . . ." He gestured in amazement at the abstruse figures that covered the yellowed parchments. "I'm going to have to take a couple of hours and memorize it by rote, in the hopes that one day it will make sense to me. By the spirits of all my drunken ancestors, it sure doesn't now!"

She sat back, a wry expression on her craggy face. "For a warrior, you're certainly peaceable about accepting things on faith."

"I accept that you know more about it than I do," he told her. "In fact, that's exactly what made teaching those wildcats of Sheera's so easy. To teach men, I have to prove to them that I'm capable of whipping the daylights out of them—and I have to go on proving it. Women don't care." He shrugged. "That was the most surprising thing about it. Women are a pleasure to teach the arts of war."

Her white teeth glimmered again in a smile. "For the sake of your self-esteem I shall not pass that along to Sheera. But I tell you this also —it is a pleasure to teach this . . ." The spare movement of her hand took in not only the charts but the whole of the long room, the gold gleam of the book bindings in the brown shadows, the jungles of hanging plants, and the skeletal shapes of the instruments that read the stars. ". . . to a mind that has already grasped the concept of discipline. That is what I myself found hardest to learn."

It was the discipline of a warrior that carried him through that night. Toward morning, he snatched an hour or so of sleep, abovestairs, in the little whitewashed attic where Yirth had cared for so many exhausted mothers, but rest eluded him. When the witch descended the stairs to her workroom at dawn, she found him already up and dressed in the shabby, brown smock of Sheera's gardener, as still as stone over the mathematical exercises, memorizing their incomprehensible patterns.

Sheera came after sundown that evening. He could tell by the way she spoke to him that she had heard what had happened to him; when she thought he was not looking, he caught the glimpse of something in her eyes that was almost fear.

"Altiokis left for the Citadel this morning," she reported, settling wearily onto the carved X of a folding chair in Yirth's long study. She rubbed her eyes in a way that told the Wolf that she had had hardly more sleep than he. He himself had dozed a little in the afternoon, but always the pressure was nagging at his mind—that he must learn, must absorb all that he could, before he left this stern and clear-hearted teacher. Yirth had spoken to him of what her own master Chilisirdin had told her many years ago, and he knew that it might take years of searching before he could find another wizard with even Yirth's limited education to continue his training. And in those years, Altiokis would be searching for him.

"According to Drypettis, the Dark Eagle has orders to remain with the troops here in Mandrigyn and hunt for you. The gates of the city are double-guarded. There are far too many for a couple of girls and a phial of laudanum to account for."

"I'll get out," Sun Wolf said.

Yirth raised one of her straight brows. "Illusion is a thing that comes only with long study," she said. "This nonvisibility I cannot do —I must look like someone, not no one. You can elude the guards, if you move quietly and keep from drawing attention to yourself. Once men see you, you cannot vanish. But get through locked gates you cannot, without calling down their eyes upon you."

"I'll leave at dawn, when they unlock the land gates."

"There'll be a horse waiting for you in the first woods," Sheera said. "There will be gold in the saddlebags . . ."

"Ten thousand pieces?" Sun Wolf inquired, with mild curiosity, and saw Sheera flush. "I'll let you owe me," he temporized with a smile.

She hesitated, then rose from her chair and went around the end of the table to lay her hands on his broad shoulders. "Captain, I want to say thank you—and, I'm sorry."

He grinned up at her. "Sheera, it has been far from pleasurable to know you; but, like dying in the pit, it's something I think I'm glad I did. Take care of my ladies for me."

"I will." Behind the graveness in those brown eyes, he could read the same grim purpose that he had seen four months ago in his tent below the walls of Melplith. But the wildness in them had been tempered by experience and by the knowledge of her own limitations. She bent gravely, to touch her lips to his.

"Makes me sorry I never bothered to seduce you," he murmured and was pleased to see her bristle with her old rage. "When are you going to hit the mines?"

"Two weeks," she replied, swallowing her angry words at him with difficulty. "We'll send word to Lady Wrinshardin to start an insurrection in the Thanelands, and draw Altiokis out of his Citadel that way. By then, Yirth will have had time to go through the Great Trial herself and to recover from it. Tarrin . . ."

"You know, I'll always be sorry I never met Tarrin," Sun Wolf mused.

Sheera was touched. "He would have been honored . . ." she began.

"It isn't that. It's just that I've heard so much about his perfection, I'm curious to see if he really is seven feet tall and glows in the dark."

"You—" she flared, and he caught her drawn-back fist, laughing, and kissed her once again.

"I wish the poor bastard joy with you." He grinned. "Be careful, Sheera."

There was fog the next morning. It had begun to creep in from the sea during the night; the Wolf had seen Yirth sitting alone in the shadows of her study, surrounded by her herbs and her charts of the sky, stirring at the surface of the water in her ancient pottery bowl, watching as the liquid within grew gray and clouded. He had not bidden her good-by, not wanting to break her concentration and knowing that she would understand.

The Golden Gate loomed before him through the slaty darkness, like the bristling back of a sleeping dragon. Sun Wolf moved quietly from shadow to shadow, hearing and feeling around him the faint noises of the awakening city, wary as an animal going down to drink. Distantly, the lapping of the canals came to his ears and the far-off mewing of the gulls in the harbor.

He wondered if he would ever see any of these people again.

It was not something that had ever troubled him before; in twenty years, he had left so many cities behind! He wondered whether this was an effect of Starhawk's influence on him or simply that he was forty now instead of twenty; or because he was a solitary fugitive, with no idea of where he would go. Three days ago, from this street, he'd been able to look beyond the walls to the dark crags of the Tchard Mountains; they were hidden now in fog, and the Wizard King was within them. If Sheera's plan succeeded, he would be able to return to Mandrigyn eventually. If it did not—if she and her Tarrin met defeat and death—he would be hounded by Altiokis to the ends of the earth.

They would need a wizard on their side to emerge victorious.

Yirth's face returned to him, and the fear in her eyes as she'd said, "I saw you when they brought you up out of the pit." She had to want her power very badly, if she proved willing to seek it in the racking of her body and the lightless pits of her mind. He did not doubt that she would do it, but he understood her fears.

Would I go through that voluntarily, if I knew?

He didn't know.

Like a ghost, he drifted into the looming shadows of the turreted gates.

There were soldiers everywhere, and the gold of the torchlight within the passage under the overspanning gatehouse flashed on polished mail and leather. The great gates were still shut, barred, bolted, and studded with iron. A group of the Dark Eagle's mercenaries loitered around the winch that would raise the portcullis; others were dicing in an archway opposite, their gleaming steel breastplates catching the red firelight, silhouetting them against the impenetrable dark beyond.

Sun Wolf melted himself back into the shadows of another of the numerous arches that supported the gatehouse overhead and waited. It wouldn't be long. Already he could hear the market carts assembling on the other side of the gates, bringing in produce from the countryside. It would be easy enough to drift out in the confusion.

And yet . . . The memory returned to him of the fight in the street, when the Dark Eagle had taken him, and of the illusion that had broken his concentration. In the heat of battle it took very little to break a defensive line; and once an army began to flee in panic, there was little hope of its rallying. Was that how Altiokis had defeated them, up at Iron Pass?

Would Sheera be able to handle that, even with Yirth at her side? She had the courage of a lioness, but she was inexperienced—as inexperienced as Yirth would be against Altiokis' greater magic.

The red-haired slave boy in the prison came back to his thoughts, and the obscene thing that had raped the boy's mind. What of that?

It was Altiokis' doing that Sun Wolf would have to search the earth for someone to teach him to handle the powers he had. If the women met defeat in the mines and the Citadel, it was Altiokis who would pursue him.

Beside their bonfire, one of the soldiers cracked a rude joke and got a general laugh. Outside the gates, farmers' voices could be heard. The gray mists in the wide street behind were paling. He thought of Starhawk, hunting for him somewhere, thought of telling her that he was a warrior and her captain no longer, but that he was a fugitive, neither wizard nor warrior, doomed to wander.

He thought again of Altiokis.

Very softly, he turned and started back toward the streets of the town.

Like the flare of a far-off explosion, amber light sprang into view in the darkness of a pillared arch. Curiously hard-edged, a glint of light fell like a round hand from there onto his shoulder, and the Dark Eagle's voice said, "Good morning, my barbarian."

The chief of Altiokis' mercenaries materialized from the shadows. In one hand he held a sword; in the other, a mirror.

A faint, steely rattle sounded and men stepped from behind pillars, from around the turrets and gargoyles, and from the black pockets of shadow behind the columns of the gatehouse stair. Flattened back into a niche, Sun Wolf found himself facing a battery of arrows, the bows straining at full draw. He let his sword hand fall empty to his side.

"No, no, by all means, draw your weapon," the Eagle chided. "You can throw it here at my feet." When Sun Wolf did not move, he added, "When you've lost enough blood to pass out, we can always take it from you, I suppose. My lord Altiokis will not be pleased to receive you in a damaged condition—but believe me, my barbarian, he will receive you alive."

The blade clattered on the stone pavement. The Dark Eagle snapped his fingers, and a man ran warily out to fetch it.

The mercenary captain flashed the mirror in the torchlight, his eyes glinting pale and bright under the dark metal of his helmet. "We were warned you'd grown trickier. You can fool the eyes of a man, my friend, but not a piece of glass. Hold your arms out to the sides, shoulder-high. If you touch the men who are going to put the bracelets on you, you may find yourself conducting your interview with my lord Altiokis from a stretcher on the floor. So."

"Who told you I'd be here?" Sun Wolf asked quietly as the irons were locked to his wrists. He shivered at their touch—there were spells forged into the metal of the bracelets and into the five feet of chain that joined them.

The Dark Eagle laughed. "My dear Wolf—your secret is how you've acquired your wizard tricks, mine is how we learned where and when you would make your break. Ask your precious ancestors about it. You'll be seeing them soon, but not, I daresay, soon enough."

CHAPTER

 19

*S*TARHAWK HEARD THE HOOFBEATS OF THE CAVALCADE LONG
before they emerged from the gray mists. She was in the open country
of stubble fields, not far from the walls of Mandrigyn; there was but
little cover beyond the fog itself. Still, they sounded to be in a hurry.

She scrambled down the dead and matted vines of the roadside
ditch and curled herself half under a tangle of gray and web-spun ivy
just above the brim of the ice-cold water. Yesterday the water in the
ditches had been scummed with ice and every leaf rimmed with a
white powder of frost, but the weather seemed to have turned. In a
few more weeks it would be spring.

Pebbles thrown from the hooves of the horses clattered around her.
She heard the brisk jingling of mail and the rattle of weapons and
trappings. She estimated the force to be a largish squadron, between
fifteen and twenty riders. Yesterday at the crossroads, where the wide
trade road from the Bight Coast joined the Mandrigyn Road up to the
Iron Pass, she'd found the unmistakable spoor of a huge force going
from the Citadel to the city and the marks, not many hours old, of a
smaller force returning. Yet this road was also marked with cart traffic,
farmers taking vegetables to town, so at least the place wasn't under
siege.

Starhawk lay with her head down under the wiry thicket of the vines, listening to the riders pass, and wondered what she would do when she reached Mandrigyn.

Seek out Sun Wolf? He had said he was dying.

Seek out Sheera Galernas?

May his ancestors help the poor bastard, Sun Wolf had said, *who falls afoul of her.*

The memory of the vision came back, the aching confusion of misery and despair and a weird, deep-seated peace. She had been right in her love for him, right to seek him, as, at the end, dying, he had sought her. But she had been too late—after months of journeying, she had missed him by less than a week.

And now he was dead.

She remembered his face, pain-ravaged and exhausted, and how warm the blood on his hands had been in contrast with the coldness of his flesh. What had happened to him in Mandrigyn?

Had Altiokis done that to him?

He said that he loved me.

She had tried to hate Fawnie for delaying her, but it had not been Fawn's fault. All she had done was what the Hawk herself had done—sought for the man she loved. That she had been injured doing so was only due to the difference in their training; that she had found another sort of happiness altogether was something that the Hawk could not pretend couldn't just as easily have happened to herself.

None of it changed the fact that she had been too late.

Anyog had lived for three days after the night of her vision, sinking gradually into deeper and deeper delirium. At first he had raved about the Hole, about Altiokis, about the spirit that dwelt in that sunless gap between worlds. Between tending him and hunting in the woods, she had had little time for other thought, or to wonder why she wanted to make this final conclusion to her quest.

When Anyog had died, she had buried him in the birch grove at the bottom of the valley, with tools she had found in the cell of the chapel's former guardian. Whether because of the old man's love for her, or because Sun Wolf's death had broken some last wall of resistance within her soul—or simply because, she thought without bitterness, she had, after all, grown soft—she had wept over Anyog's grave and had been unashamed of her tears. Tears might be a waste of time, she had thought, but she now had time; and the tears had been a medicine to her chilled soul.

The hoofbeats faded into the distance. Starhawk got to her feet, brushing the damp ivy from her buckskin breeches and from the quilted sleeves of her much-stained black coat. It only remained for her to make her way to Mandrigyn and seek out Sheera Galernas, to ask her why and particularly how she had been able to carry off a full-grown and presumably protesting captain of mercenaries—and what had become of him.

The woman in the marketplace from whom she asked directions looked askance at Starhawk's sword belt and brass-buckled doublet, but directed her without comment to the house of Sheera Galernas. It stood upon its own island, like so many of the great townhouses of that checkerboard city; from the mouth of the narrow street that debouched into the canal just opposite it, Starhawk studied its inlaid marble facade. Carved lattices of interlocking stone quatrefoils shaded the canalfront arcades; red and purple silk banners, their bullion embroidery gleaming wanly with the lifting of the morning's white mist, made stripes of brilliant color against the black and white starkness of the stone. Two gondolas were already moored at the foot of the black marble steps—a curious thing, the Hawk thought, at so early an hour.

She followed the narrow wooden catwalk that formed a footpath for a few dozen yards above the waters at the edge of the canal, crossing eventually by a miniature camelback bridge that led into the maze of alleys on the next islet. It was difficult to maintain any kind of sense of direction here, for the high walls of that crowded district cut her off from any glimpse of the roofline of Sheera's house; but by dint of much backtracking over tiny bridges and through the twisting streets, she was eventually able to circle the grounds. From the catwalk along the wall of the nearby church-owned public laundry, she could look down into the grounds themselves and guessed that, with so much waste space, Sheera Galernas must be rich indeed. Behind the house stretched elaborately laid-out gardens, fallow and waiting for the rains to end, a big, boarded-up orangery and a string of new, glass-roofed succession houses, and a stable court and what looked like a pleasure pavilion or a bathhouse, brave with pillars of colored porphyry.

It occurred to Starhawk that there were an unnatural number of entrances to those grounds.

She glimpsed movement in an alleyway on an adjacent island and pressed herself back against the uneven brick of the laundry's high wall. A stealthy figure descended the few steps that led from the alley's mouth to the opaque green waters of the canal and glanced quickly to the right and left. From where she stood on the catwalk above, Starhawk could see the woman—for it was a woman, wrapped in a dark cloak—go to the cellar door of the last house on the alley and from it produce a plank, which she laid across the canal to a disused-looking postern door in Sheera's back wall. In spite of the postern's dilapidated appearance, it did not seem to be locked, nor, the Hawk noticed, did the hinges creak. The woman crossed, pulled the plank after her, and shut the door.

Curious, Starhawk swung down the rickety flight of steps and wound her way through the alleys to where the woman had been. The cellar door wasn't locked; in the muddy-floored room lay quite a few planks.

Intrigued, Starhawk returned to the mouth of the alley. It led straight down into the dirty canal water, about two feet below. The stones of the alley were uneven, slimy and offensive with moss; she guessed this was the neighborhood dumping ground for chamber pots. Leaning around the corner of the tall house beside her, she could see the backs of all the houses along the curve of the canal; women were laying out bedding over the rails of makeshift balconies to air, and someone was dumping a pan of dishwater from a kitchen doorstep directly into the murk a few feet below. A couple of the houses had little turrets, with long green smears of moss on the walls below them to announce their function.

A quiet place, altogether, she thought, glancing back at the deep-set little door in the wall. It wasn't the regular kitchen entrance—that was visible down at the far end of the wall, a double door and a kind of little step for deliverymen unloading from gondolas.

The Hawk had another careful look around, then fetched a plank from the cellar, as she had seen the furtive woman do. It just reached from the pavement to the doorsill; Starhawk realized that all these planks had been cut to the same length. She drew her sword, took a final look around, and slipped across.

The postern was unlocked. It opened directly onto a thicket of laurel bushes, which masked it from the main house. There was no one in sight.

Starhawk pulled in her plank and added it to the three that already lay concealed under the laurels. The ground here was trampled and grassless. As Ari would say, somebody had more up the sleeve than the arm.

Well, of course Sheera was involved in a cause—meaning a conspiracy. But whether she'd been able to involve Sun Wolf in it . . .

The Hawk moved soundlessly around the edge of the laurel thicket and stopped, startled by what she saw.

The gardens were empty, the brown, formal hedges marching in elaborate patterns away toward the distant terrace of the main house. But here someone had quite recently half built, half excavated, a pocket-sized wilderness in one corner of those formal beds, the rocks settled like the bones of the sleeping earth, waiting for their attendant vegetation.

Sun Wolf had laid out those rocks.

She knew it, recognized his style in the shaping of them, the lie of the colored fissure in the granite, and the latent tension between large shapes and small. How she knew it she was not sure—the aesthetics of rock gardening was a subject she knew only through him—but she was as certain of it as those who could look upon a painting or hear a tune and say "This was created by that person."

The warrior in her remarked, *He was here, then,* while some other part of her throbbed with a deep and unexpected ache, as if she had found his glove or his dagger.

And then, an instant later, an absurd thought crossed her mind: *I knew good gardeners were hard to find, but this . . . . !*

She knew from working with him on the one at Wrynde that rock gardens like this were the work of days, sometimes weeks.

Steam billowed from the laundry quarters at the back of the house, drifting across the brown beds of the gardens. Voices came to her, like distant bird song.

A high, twittering voice insisted, "I've told you, he's learned all he wants to know! There's no danger! He's looking for men, and looking in the Thanelands . . ."

Among the bare white stems of the ornamental birch, Starhawk saw two people descending the terrace steps—a black-haired woman in purple and sables, with amethysts snagged in the dark curls that lay scattered across her shoulders, and a small, curiously childish shape pattering at her side, rattling with incongruous masses of heavy, jingling jewels, a king's ransom in bad taste.

The dark-haired woman she recognized at once as Sheera Galernas.

"We don't know that," Sheera said.

The smaller woman said, "We do! I do. I heard them talk of it. Altiokis has no interest in questioning him. And Tarrin says—"

"Tarrin doesn't know the situation here."

The little woman looked shocked. "But he does! You've kept him informed . . ."

"For God's sake, Dru, that isn't the same as being here!"

The women passed through the door of the orangery. As it shut behind them, Starhawk glimpsed other forms moving about inside.

Who, she wondered, had Altiokis taken for questioning—or not for questioning, as the case might be? The hoofbeats of the passing caval-cade returned to her with new meaning. Greatly interested, she slipped cautiously across the open space that separated her from the orangery and glided along its wall until she found an open window that let into a sort of potting shed built out of one wall. It was empty. She found it a simple matter to force the catch with her dagger and climb in unheard. The women in the main, boarded-up section of the building were talking far too intently to hear the small sounds of her feet.

Sun Wolf had been here. Looking about her in the gloom, she was virtually certain of it. He had been here and had worked here. She knew the way he habitually laid out things at his workshop back in Wrynde too well to think that another could have his same order of putting up those mysterious little medicines to succor ailing plants.

But—it made absolutely no sense. Holy Mother, had Sheera *really* kidnapped him to do her gardening? And why—and how, for that matter?—had he appeared to Starhawk in a dream, and how and why had he died? Her hand tightened over the worn hilt of her dagger. *That, at least, Sheera Galernas will tell me. And if it was her doing . . .*

Starhawk stopped. She had far too much experience with the moti-vations of sudden death to make an unequivocal threat, even in the privacy of her mind. It was perfectly possible that Sun Wolf had asked for the fate he got—and in fact, knowing the Wolf as she did, more than likely.

She pressed her ear to the door.

A confusion of voices came to her, the high, strident twitter of the little woman called Dru, insisting over and over again that they were safe. Starhawk found a knothole in the door just as a tiny, golden-haired lady snapped impatiently, "Oh, button it, Dru!"

Dru swung around, blazing with self-righteous wrath. "You dare speak that way to me—" she began furiously. Then she caught Sheera's disapproving eye and relapsed into red-faced and stifled silence.

Sheera said to another woman, "What about it, Amber Eyes?"

Starhawk had noticed her before, a slender girl of about Fawn's age, standing almost shyly in the circle of her big, dark-eyed friend's arm. But the moment she spoke, the Hawk realized that the helpless shyness was only an illusion—she was clearly the stronger of the partners.

She said, "It's true we don't know where Tarrin and the other leaders are working today. But Cobra and Crazyred have both been all over the mines, as I have, and we've all made maps. We can get you to the armories, to the passages up to the Outer Citadel, and to the storerooms where they keep the blasting powder. There's enough blasting powder to destroy half the Citadel, if it could be placed. It doesn't need magic to be ignited, just a slow match."

"What if he's talked already?" her friend demanded worriedly. "Altiokis might question him up at the Citadel—from what Dru told us, it's in the wizard's power to put him to what no man could stand. They could be lying in wait for us when we get there."

"I tell you—" Dru began in her high, hissing voice.

Then from the dark doorway of the potting room, Starhawk spoke. "If that's the case, you'd better chance it and strike now."

All eyes swiveled to her. The women were shocked into silence as she stepped forth from the shadows. To do them credit, they weren't frozen with astonishment—three of them were already moving to flank her as she emerged. Sheera Galernas was frowning at her, trying to place her, knowing they had met before.

Starhawk went on. "Waiting won't buy you anything if your friend breaks."

"We could get out of the city—" someone began.

A thin little woman in the dark robes of a nun asked, "Do you really believe Altiokis would not hound us over the face of the earth, once he knew who we were?"

Starhawk rested her hands on the buckle of her sword belt and surveyed the group quietly. "It isn't any of my affair, of course," she said, surprised at how easily she fell back into her habit of command, then accepting the way they listened to her, somehow knowing her for a commander. "I'm only here to speak to Sheera Galernas." From the

tail of her eye, she saw Sheera startle as the memory returned. "But if
your friend was the one who passed me under escort this morning, I'd
say strike, if you think he has any kind of strength to hold out against
questioning."

The little blonde murmured, "He has the strength."

"They won't reach the Citadel until after noon," the Hawk continued. "That gives you maybe an hour or two hours to gamble on
whatever you plan to do. It all depends on how tough you think your
friend is."

She saw their eyes, exchanging glances, questioning. As a rule, she
had found that women vastly overestimated a man's stamina against
torture, as men underestimated women's. That seemed to be the case
here—none of them appeared to be in much doubt, except Sheera
herself. To her, Starhawk said, "I won't trouble you now, if you're
going into battle. But there's something you owe me to speak of when
you're done."

Sheera's eyes met hers, and she nodded, understanding. But a taller
woman, harsh-faced and ugly, who had stood in the shadows, spoke
up. "He said there would be a woman coming to seek him." The
voice was as low and soft as a rosewood flute, the green eyes like sea-
light in the dimness. "You are she?"

There was no need to ask who "he" was. Starhawk said, "I am."

"And your name?"

"Starhawk."

There was a pause. "He has spoken of you," the beautiful voice
said. "You are welcome. I am Yirth." She came forward and held out
long slender hands. "He told me to tell you what became of him."

"I know what became of him," Starhawk replied grimly. On all
sides of them, the women watched silently, amazed both at her presence and at the fact that this dark, lanky woman seemed to have expected her. To them, the exchange between Yirth and Starhawk must
be cryptic, half intelligible; but none asked for an explanation. The
tension in the room was too electric; they feared to break it.

Starhawk said, "I know that he died. What I want to know is how
and why."

"No," Yirth said quietly. "He did not die. He is a wizard now."

Shock left Starhawk speechless. She could only stare at Yirth in
blank astonishment, scarcely aware that her surprise was shared by all
but a very few of the other women in the room.

Yirth added, "And he is Altiokis' prisoner."

"And I don't think there is any question," Sheera put in, her voice suddenly hard and cutting as a sword blade, "that Altiokis' mercenaries knew where to look for him."

She swung around, her eyes going from face to face—browned faces, darkened from exposure, some of them with the bruises of training hidden under carefully applied cosmetics. There were pretty faces, faces plain or homely, but none of them weak, none of them afraid. "Starhawk is right," she said quietly. "We must strike and strike now."

Drypettis caught her petaled sleeve. "Don't be a fool!" she cried. "Do you know how many men there are in Grimscarp now?"

"Fifteen hundred less," purred a red-haired woman in a prostitute's thin, gaudy silks, "than there were a week ago."

"And Altiokis!" the little woman squeaked.

"And Altiokis," Sheera echoed. She turned back to Yirth, who still stood at Starhawk's side. "Can you do it, Yirth? Can you fight him?"

Yirth shook her head. "I can lead you through illusion," she said, "and to some degree protect you from the traps of magic that are set to guard the ways to the Citadel from the mines. But my wizardry is knowledge without the Great Power, even as the captain's is Power without the knowledge of how to use it. We are equally helpless before Altiokis' might, though he is stronger than I. But as I see it, neither I nor any of us has a choice. It is now or never, prepared or unprepared."

"Don't be fools!" Drypettis cried hysterically. "And you *are* fools, if you let yourselves be stampeded this way! Altiokis doesn't care about information. All he wants is Sun Wolf's death! I know—I overheard Stirk and the mercenary captain speak of it! If we rush in now, before Yirth has a chance to gain the power she needs, before we can coordinate with Tarrin, we will cast away everything!"

"And if we wait," Gilden lashed, "Sun Wolf is going to die."

"He would have let the lot of us die!" Drypettis retorted, her face suddenly mottled with red blotches of rage. "Even those of you he made his sluts!"

Gilden's hand came up to strike her; but with a curiously practiced neatness, an equally tiny lady standing behind Gilden caught her wrist before she could deliver the blow. Drypettis stood before her trembling, her face white now but for the spots of color that stood out like rouge on her delicate cheekbones.

In a cold voice, Sheera said, "He was brought here against his will, Dru. And as for the rest, that is hardly your affair."

The little woman whirled on her in a hurricane of jangling metal and tangled veils. "It *is* my affair!" she cried, her brown eyes blazing with shame and rage. "It is exactly my affair! How is the good and the decent in this city to triumph, if it debases itself to the level of its enemies to defeat them? How are we to face the men whom we wish to free, if we make trollops of ourselves to free them? That is precisely what this captain of ours has done. He has debased us all. Debased us? Seduced us into debasing ourselves, rather, with this lure of success at any cost! We should have suffered the evils that befell us and learned to work around them, before we turned ourselves into coarse and dirty soldiers like this—this—" Her jerking hand waved violently toward the startled and silent Starhawk. "—this camp follower of his!"

Her tone changed, became wheedling. "You are worthy of the Prince, Sheera, worthy to wed the King of Mandrigyn and to be its Queen. And I would have supported you in this, given everything to you for it—my wealth and the honor of the most ancient House in the city! I would have given you my life, gladly. But to have given these, only to see you turn them and the cause itself over to such a man as that—to transform an ideal of decency and self-sacrifice into a base, athletic exercise in brute muscle and sneakiness—"

Sheera strode forward, caught the hysterical woman's shoulders in powerful hands, and shook her with terrible violence. All the ridiculous jewelry jangled and rattled, catching in the sudden tumble of unraveled brown hair. She shook her until they were both breathless, her eyes burning with fury; then she said, "You told them."

"I did it for your sake!" Drypettis screeched. "I have seen what one man's influence can do—how far one man's influence can defile everything that he touches! You are worthy—"

"Be quiet," Sheera said softly. "And sit down."

Drypettis obeyed, staring up at her in silence, tears of fury pouring down her round, red-stained cheeks. Watching their faces, Starhawk was conscious of that curiously concentrated quality to Drypettis' gaze, as if Sheera and Sheera alone had any reality for her, as if she were literally unaware that she had enacted a lovers' quarrel in the presence of some fifty other people. For her, they did not exist. Only Sheera existed—perhaps only Sheera ever had.

Very slowly and quietly, Sheera said, "Drypettis, I don't know whether or not you ever wanted yourself to be queen of Mandrigyn, rather than me, as the ancient lineage of your House might qualify you to be. I never questioned your loyalty to me, or your loyalty to my cause."

"I was never disloyal to you," Drypettis whispered in a thin voice, like the sound of a crack running through glass. "It was all for you—to purge the cause of the evil in it that could destroy it and you. To make it pure again, as it was before that barbarian came."

"Or to get rid of a man of whom you were jealous?" Sheera's hands tightened over the slender shoulders. "A man who took it away from being your cause, operated by your money and your influence, and threw it open to all who were willing to fight for it, no matter how rough their origins, how crass their motives, or how inelegant and dirty their methods might be? A man who changed the whole game from something that was bought to something that was done? A man who put commoners on the same level with yourself? Who treated you like a potential soldier instead of a lady? Is that why?" she asked, her voice low and harsh. "Or do you even know?"

Drypettis' face seemed to soften and melt like wax with grief, the exquisite brown eyes growing huge in the puckering flesh. Then she crumpled forward, her face buried in her hands, sobbing bitterly. The faint, silvery light from the high windows danced like expensive glitter over the incongruous riot of ornaments strewn through her hair. "He has done this to you," she keened. "He has made you like him, thinking only of victory, no matter how dishonorable you become in the process."

Sheera straightened up, her mouth and nostrils white, as if with sickness. "Defeat will only make us dead," she said, "not honorable. I will never say anything to anyone about what has happened here, and no one else in this room ever will, either; not even to one another. That's not an order," she added, looking about her at the stunned, silent circle of women. "That's a request, from a friend, that I hope you will honor." She turned back to the bowed form of Drypettis, now rocking back and forth in the straight-backed chair where she herself had sat, during that first meeting in the orangery, the night Sun Wolf had come to Mandrigyn. "I will never speak of this," she repeated, "but I do not ever want to see you again."

Her face still hidden in her hands, Drypettis got slowly to her feet. The women made way for her as she stumbled from the room;

through the orangery door, they could see the colors of her clothes, a gaudy fluttering of whalebone and panniers, veils and jewels, against the liver-colored earth of the garden, until she vanished into the shadows of the house.

Sheera watched, her face white and tears glittering like beads of glass upon her wind-burned cheeks; the grief in her eyes was like that on the face of Drypettis, the grief of one who had lost a close friend. At her sides, her sword-bruised hands were clenched, the knuckles white under the brown of the skin.

Not what she needed, Starhawk thought dryly, *with her first battle before her;* and if for nothing else, she cursed the woman for that selfishness.

That was first; and then the anger came—anger at the petty jealousy of Drypettis, at her own slow realization that the man whose capabilities to resist torture they had been speaking of was, in fact, the Wolf himself, still alive—but in horrible danger. She had missed him by hours. He had passed within a dozen feet of her as she lay hiding in the roadside ditch, the stones of his horse's hooves showering her with pebbles . . .

He was alive! Whatever else had happened to him, would happen to him, he was alive now, and that knowledge went through her like a living heat, kindling both blood and spirit.

But, with her customary calm, she turned to the woman beside her, the woman who still gazed, with her jaw set, out into the now-empty garden, grief and the bitterness of betrayal marked onto her face like a careless thumbprint on cooling bronze. A sister in the fellowship of arms.

The women around them were silent, not knowing what to say or how to speak of that betrayal.

It was Starhawk who broke the silence, her natural habit of command laying the course for all the others to follow. Sheera's grief was her own; Starhawk understood, and was the first of them not to speak of it. She laid a hand on the woman's shoulder and asked in her most businesslike voice, "How soon can your ladies be ready to march?"

CHAPTER

 20

*I*F WHAT LADY WRINSHARDIN HAD SAID WAS TRUE—AND SUN WOLF could think of no reason for her to have lied—the fortress of the Thanes of Grimscarp had once stood at the base of that rocky and forbidding knee of stone which thrust out of the mountain above the Iron Pass. The siegecraft that had been bred into his bones picked out the place, even as the Dark Eagle and his men took him past it—a weed-grown rubble of stones, just past where the road divided. There was no signpost at the fork, but Amber Eyes and her girls had told him that the right-hand way went up to the southward entrances of the mines below the Citadel, then wound around the base of the mountain to the main, western entrances above Altiokis' administrative center at Racken Scrag; the left-hand way twisted up the rock face, toward the Citadel itself.

Weary from two days with little sleep and from half a day's hard ride up the rocky Iron Pass, his wrists chafed and raw from the weight of some thirty pounds of iron chain, Sun Wolf looked up through the murk of low-lying cloud at the Citadel, where the Wizard King awaited him, and wondered why anyone in his right mind would have made the place the center of his realm.

There was the legend Lady Wrinshardin had quoted about the stone hut that Altiokis had raised in a single night—the stone hut that was supposed to be still standing, the buried nucleus of the Citadel's inner core. But why Altiokis had chosen to do so made no sense to the Wolf, unless, as he had begun to suspect, the Wizard King were mad. Perhaps he had built the Citadel in such an impossible, inaccessible place simply to show that he could. Perhaps he had put it here so that no city could grow up around his walls; Racken Scrag perforce lay on the other side of the mountain.

The Gods knew, the place was defensible enough. The impossible road was overlooked at every turning by overhanging cliffs; if Yirth were right about Altiokis' powers of far-seeing, he would be able to detect any force coming up that road, long before it got within sight of the Citadel, and bury it under avalanches of stone or landslides of burning wood. But when they reached the narrow, rocky valley before the Citadel's main gate, Sun Wolf understood why it was cheaper and simpler to haul the food for the legions up through the mines, for here Altiokis' fears had excelled themselves.

Most of the works in the valley were new, Sun Wolf judged; with the expansion of his empire, the Wizard King had evidently grown more and more uneasy. The Citadel of Grimscarp had originally been built between the cliff edge that looked northward over the wastes of the Tchard Mountains and a great spur of rock that cut it off from the rest of the Scarp on which it stood; its main entrance had tunneled straight through this unscalable knee of rock. Now the floor of the valley below the gate had been cut with giant pits, like a series of dry moats; slave gangs were still at work carving out the nearer ones as the Dark Eagle and his party emerged from between the dark watchtowers that overhung the little pass into the vale. While they paused to breathe the horses after the climb, Sun Wolf could see that the rock and earth within these long moats were charred. If an enemy managed to bridge them—if any enemy could get bridges up that winding road —the ditches could be floored with some flammable substance and ignited at a distance by the magic of the Wizard King.

They were bridged now by drawbridges of wood and stone, things that could easily be torn down or destroyed. The bridges did not lie in a direct line with the gate, which was cut directly into the cliff face at the other side, without turrets or outworks. The Wolf knew instinctively that it was the kind of gate that could be concealed with illusion; if Altiokis willed it, travelers to that Citadel would see nothing but the stark and treeless gray rock of the Scarp as they reached the head of the road.

He was coming to understand how a man such as the Wizard King had built his empire, between unlimited wealth and animal cunning, between hired strength and the dark webs of his power.

The men who held the reins of Sun Wolf's horse led him on, down the slope toward the bridges and the iron-toothed, forbidding gate. The hooves of the horses echoed weirdly in the smooth stone of the tunnel walls. Guards in black armor held up smoky torches to look at them. The Dark Eagle repeated passwords with a faint air of impatience and led them onward. The tunnel itself reeked with evil; its stone walls seemed to drip horror. The air there was fraught with latent magic that could be turned into illusions of unspeakable fear. Great gates led into wide, downward-sloping ways, the lines of torches along the walls fading into blackness at the end. The warm breath that rose from these tunnels stank of muddy rock, of illusion, and of the glittering, nameless magic of utter dread. It was as if Altiokis' power had been spread throughout his Citadel, as if his mind permeated the tunnels, the darkness, and the stone.

Sun Wolf whispered, almost unaware that he spoke aloud, "How can he spread himself so thin?"

The Dark Eagle's head snapped around. "What?"

There were no words to express it to someone not mageborn; it was a concept impossible to describe. The closest the Wolf could come to it was to say, "His spirit is everywhere here."

White teeth flashed in the gloom. "Ah. You've felt that, have you?"

The Wolf could see that the mercenary captain thought that he spoke in admiration, or in awe. He shook his head impatiently. "It's everywhere, but it isn't in himself. He's put part of his power in the rocks, in the air, in the illusions at the bottom of the mine shafts—but he has to keep it all up. He has to hold it together somehow, and—how can there be anything left back at the center of him, the key of his being, to hold it with?"

The Dark Eagle's smile faded; that round, swarthy countenance grew thoughtful; in the darkness, the blue eyes seemed very bright. "Gilgath, Altiokis' Commander of the Citadel, has said that my lord has been slipping—he's been with Altiokis far longer than I." His voice was low, excluding even the men who rode about them. "I never believed it until about two years ago—and what you say makes sense." He shrugged, and that wary look left his face. "But even so, my barbarian," he continued, as slaves came to take their horses, and they passed through the courtyards of the heavily defended Outer Citadel, "he has power enough to crush his enemies to dust—and money enough to pay his friends."

Other guards surrounded them, men and a few women in the bright panoplies of the mercenary troops. They were escorted through the courts and gateways of the Outer Citadel, up to the massive gatehouse that loomed against the sky, guarding the way into the Inner Citadel. The Dark Eagle strode now at Sun Wolf's side, the chain mail of his shirt jingling, the gilded spike that protruded through the dark, fluttering veils of his helmet crests flashing in the wan daylight.

"Wait until you come into the Inner Citadel, if you think his power has thinned."

They entered the darkness of the gatehouse, two men holding the chain that joined Sun Wolf's wrists, the rest of the troop walking with drawn swords behind him. All the while the Wolf was concentrating, his mind calm and alert as in battle, waiting for his chance to escape and reviewing the way down the mountain.

Daylight blazed ahead. Like a huge mouth, a gate opened around them. As they stepped from the dense shadows, Sun Wolf saw that it led onto a kind of causeway that spanned the long, stone-walled ditch separating the Outer Citadel from the Inner. At the center, the causeway was broken by a railless drawbridge. The pit itself crawled with nuuwa.

In spite of the day's cold, the carrion stink of them rose in a suffocating wave. Halfway across the drawbridge itself, the Wolf stopped. Turning, he saw that the Dark Eagle had his hand on his sword hilt. "Don't try it," the mercenary said quietly. "Believe me, if I went over, I guarantee that you'd go, too."

"Would it make that much difference?"

The Dark Eagle cocked a sardonic eyebrow. "That depends on what you think your chances of escaping from the Inner Citadel are."

Below them, the nuuwa had begun to gather, their grunting ululations shattering the air. Sun Wolf glanced at the men holding his chain, then back at the Eagle. He could see that the sheer wall of the Inner Citadel was broken by two gates, one fairly close and one several hundred feet away, with steps leading down into the pit of the nuuwa, plus the heavily guarded gate on their own level that let onto the causeway. There were gates into the pit from the Outer Citadel as well. It was a good bet that those were all heavily barred.

It was a gamble—to die horribly now, or to risk an uglier fate against an almost nonexistent chance of escape.

Compared with this, he thought bitterly as he moved off again toward the looming maw of the Inner Citadel's gates, the choice Sheera had given him on the ship appeared monumental in its opportunities. But he would not give up when the chance remained to play for time.

The nuuwa's screams followed them, like derisive jeers.

"You'll be down there soon enough," the Dark Eagle remarked at his elbow. "It's a pity, for no one knows as well as I how fine a soldier you are, my barbarian. But I know that's what my lord Wizard does with those who go against him. And after that thing gets through gnawing your brains out, you won't much care about the accommodations."

Sun Wolf glanced back at him. "What is it?" he asked. "What are those—those flame-things? Does he create them?"

The mercenary captain frowned, as if gauging the reasons for the question and how much he would give away in his answer. Then he shook his head. "I don't know. There's a—a darkness in the room at the bottom of the Citadel, a cold. They come out of that darkness; usually one or two, but sometimes in flocks. Other times there'll be days, weeks, with nothing. He himself won't go into the room—I think he fears them as much as anyone else does. He can't command them as he does the nuuwa."

"Can he command the darkness they come from?"

The Dark Eagle paused in his stride, those swooping black brows drawing together beneath the crested helmet rim. But all he said was, "You have changed, my barbarian, since we rode together in the East."

The black doors of the Inner Citadel opened. Its shadows swallowed them.

The dread of the place, the eerie terror that permeated the very air, struck Sun Wolf like a blow in the face as he crossed the threshold. Like a dog that would not pass the door of a haunted room, he stopped, his breath catching in his lungs; the men dragged him through by the chain on his wrists, but he could see that their faces, too, were wet with sweat. Fear filled the shadowy maze of tunnels and guardrooms on the lower level of the Citadel, as if a species of gas had been spread upon the air; the men who surrounded him with a hedge of drawn swords looked nervously about them, as if they were not certain in which direction the danger lay. Even the Dark Eagle's eyes darted from shadow to shadow, the only restlessness in his still face.

But more than the fear, Sun Wolf could feel the power there, cold and almost visible, like an iridescent fog. It seemed to cling to the very walls, as it had pervaded the tunnel of the gate—a strength greater than that of Altiokis, all-pervasive and yet tangible. He felt that, if he only knew how, he could have gathered it together in his hands.

They ascended a stair and passed through a guarded door. It shut behind them, and Sun Wolf looked around him in sudden, utter amazement at the upper levels of the tower, the inner heart of the Citadel of Altiokis, the dwelling place of the greatest wizard on the face of the earth.

Quite factually, Sun Wolf said, "I've seen better taste in whorehouses."

The Dark Eagle laughed, his teeth and eyes bright in his swarthy face. "But not more expensive materials, I daresay," he commented and flicked with a fingernail the gold that sheathed the inner side of the great doors. "A house, as my lord Wizard is fond of saying, fit for a man to live in."

Sun Wolf's eyes traveled slowly from the jeweled garlands that embroidered the ivory panels of the ceiling, down slender columns of pink porphyry and polished green malachite twined with golden serpents, to the tastelessly pornographic statues in ebony, alabaster, and agate that stood between them. Gilding was spread like butter over everything; the air was larded with the scent of patchouli and roses.

"A man, maybe," he said slowly, realizing it was only a gross exaggeration of the kind of opulence he would have gone in for himself, not too many months ago. Then he understood what had shocked him in his soul about the place and about all the fortress of the Wizard King. "But not the greatest of the wizards; not the only wizard left on the face of the earth, damn it." He looked back at the Dark Eagle, wondering why the man did not understand. "This is obscene."

The captain chuckled. "Oh, come now, Wolf." He gestured at the shamelessly posturing statues. "You're getting squeamish in your old age. You've seen worse than this in the cathouses in Kwest Mralwe—the most expensive ones, that is."

"I don't mean that," the Wolf said. He looked around him again, at the gilded archways, the embroidered hangings, and the bronze lampstands on which burned not flames, but round, glowing bubbles of pure light. In his mind, he was comparing the garish waste with Yirth's shadowy workroom, with its worn and well-cared-for books, its delicate instruments of brass and crystal, and its dry, muted scent of medicinal herbs. "He is deathless, he is powerful; he has command over magic that I would trade my soul for. He can have anything he wants. And he chooses this—trash."

The Dark Eagle cocked an amused eyebrow up at the Wolf and signaled his men. They jerked on the chain and rattled their swords, leading Sun Wolf on through the wide, softly lighted halls of the upper levels, their feet scuffing over silken rugs or whispering over carved jade tiles. "I remember you almost cut my throat fighting over trash very much like this when we looted the palace at Thardin," he reminded the Wolf with a grin.

Sun Wolf remembered it. He could not explain that that had been before the pit and the ordeal of the anzid; he could not explain, could not make the Eagle understand, the monstrousness of what Altiokis was. He only said, "How could a mind that trivial achieve this kind of power?"

The Dark Eagle laughed. "Whoa! Teach him a few tricks and he knows all about wizardry and power, does he?"

Sun Wolf was silent. He could not say how he knew what he knew, or why it seemed inconceivable to him that a man with a mind whose greatest ambitions rose no higher than dirty statues and silk rugs could have gained the power to become deathless, could have made himself the last, most powerful wizard on the earth. He understood, then, Yirth's anger at his frightened rejection of his power; he felt it reflected in his own outrage at a man who would not only so waste his own vast potential but destroy everyone else's as well.

Doors of white jade and crystal swung open. The room beyond them was black—black marble floor and walls, pillars of black marble supporting a vaulted ceiling of shadow. A ball of pale bluish light hung over the head of the man who overflowed the huge chair of carved ebony between the columns at the far end of the room, and the light picked out the details of the sculpted dragons and gargoyles, of the writhing sea life and shining insects, that covered the chair, the pillars, and the wall. The incense-reeking darkness seemed filled with magic; but with a curious clarity of the senses, Sun Wolf saw how flawed it was, like a prostitute's makeup seen in the light of day. Whatever Altiokis had been, as the Dark Eagle had said, he was slipping now. Having destroyed everyone else's power, he was letting his own run to seed as well.

Looking at him as he squatted, obscenely gross, in his ebony chair, for a moment the Wolf felt, not fear, but angry disgust. Not even unlimited evil could give this man dignity. Sun Wolf's captors pushed him forward until he stood alone before the Wizard King, his shoulders dragged down by the weight of his chains.

Altiokis belched and scratched his jewel-encrusted belly. "So," he said, in a voice thick with brandy, "you think the palace of Altiokis, the greatest prince this world has known, looks like a whorehouse?"

His wizard's senses had spread throughout that tawdry palace; he had heard every word that they had said. The Dark Eagle looked frightened, but Sun Wolf knew how it was done, though he himself could not do it. He only looked at the Wizard King, trying to understand what unlimited life, unlimited power, and unlimited boredom had done to this man, this last and most powerful wizard.

"You poor ass, did you really think you could get away from me that easily?" Altiokis asked. "Did you really have any idea of what you'd be up against when you accepted the commission of that fool, whatever his name was—the man who hired you? One of the Thanes, I think we said. Not that it matters, of course. I know who my enemies are. We'll have them gathered in . . ."

The Dark Eagle's bright blue eyes widened with alarm. "My lord, we don't know—"

"Oh, be silent," Altiokis snapped pettishly. "Cowards—I am surrounded by cowards."

"My lord," the Dark Eagle grated, "if you arrest without proof, there'll be trouble among the Thanes . . ."

"Oh, there's always trouble among the Thanes," the Wizard King retorted angrily. "And there always has been—we needed only the excuse to put them down. Let them come against me—if they dare. I will crush them . . ." The dark, little eyes glittered unnaturally bright in the gloom. ". . . as I will crush this slave."

He had risen from his chair, his eyes holding Sun Wolf's, and the Wolf saw in the wizard what had struck him before. There was very little that was human left of the man. The fire within was eating it away, his soul literally rotting, like the minds of the nuuwa. Like them, the Wolf realized, Altiokis existed almost solely to devour.

Sun Wolf fell back a step as the Wizard King raised the staff with its evil, gleaming head. At a distance of several feet, he could already feel the searing pain that radiated like waves of heat from the metal. Altiokis raised it, and the Wolf retreated until he felt the sword points of the guards press his back.

"Are you stupid," the Wizard King whispered, "or only a nerveless animal? Or don't you believe what could happen to you here?"

"I believe you," Sun Wolf said, keeping a wary eye on the staff, which hovered a foot or so in front of his throat. His voice was a dry rasp, the only sound in that hushed darkness of perfume and sweat. "I just don't believe that anything I can say will stop you from doing what you choose."

It was as polite a way as any he could think of to say that he made it a policy never to argue with a crazy man.

A sneer contorted the greasy face. "So it has wisdom, after all," the wizard said. "Pity you did not exercise it sooner. I have lived longer than you know. I am versed in the art of crushing the soul from the body, while leaving the brain time for—reflection. I could put the blood worms on you, until a month from now you would be nothing but a crawling mass of maggots, begging me for the mercy of death. Or I could blind and cripple you with drugs and find a job for you hauling bath water for my mercenaries—eh? Or I could wall you into a stone room, with only a cup of water, and that water filled with anzid, and leave you to choose between slow death from poison and slower from thirst."

Sun Wolf fought to keep his expression impassive, knowing full well that the fat man had both the power and the inclination to mete out any one of those fates, merely for the entertainment of seeing him die. But, sickened as he was by horror, two things remained very clear in the back of his brain.

The first was that Altiokis had never passed the Great Trial. He clearly had no idea that anzid was anything other than a particularly loathsome poison. And that meant that he had derived his power from some other source.

It would explain some things, the Wolf thought, his mind struggling to grasp that awareness. The power that pervaded the lower level of the tower and that filled the mines was then not entirely from Altiokis' attenuated personality. It was something else, something foul and filthy, not like Yirth's academic sorcery, nor what the Wolf felt of the wild magic that seemed to fill his own soul. Was the power only channeled through the Wizard King from the darkness that the Eagle had spoken of, the darkness that dwelt in the innermost room of the tower? A power that had no ambitions, but that Altiokis had seized upon to fulfill his own?

The second thing Sun Wolf realized was that, like a cruel child, Altiokis was simply telling him this, not to learn any information, but in order to see him break. He knew from his own experience that a screaming victim was more satisfactory to watch. He did not doubt for a moment that they would get down to the screaming sooner or later, but he was damned to the Cold Hells if he'd give the Wizard King that pleasure now.

Altiokis' face changed. "Or I could give you worse," he snarled. He snapped his fingers for the Dark Eagle and his men. "Downstairs," he ordered. "With me."

The mercenaries closed in around Sun Wolf, dragging at his wrist chains, thrusting from behind with their swords. A door opened in the wall, where no door had been; the blue brimfire that floated over Altiokis' head illuminated the first steps of a stair that curved down into darkness. The Wolf balked in sudden terror at the power, the evil, that rose like a nauseating stench from the pit below. The blackness seemed filled with an alien, hideous chill, like that from the demons he had seen in the marshes of his childhood—a sensation of seeing something that had risen from unknowable gulfs of nothingness, a sensing of something that was not of this earth.

Someone shoved a blade against his ribs, pushing him through the door. The soldiers seemed unaware of what lay below; they could not know what he knew and still be willing to go that way themselves. He almost turned to fight them in the doorway, but Altiokis reached forward with his staff and used the glowing head of it to drive the Wolf forward down the stairs. The men surrounded him again, and the eldritch cold rose about them as they descended.

The descent was less far than he had thought. The stair made one circle, then leveled out; the floor, he saw, was rock and dirt. They must be at ground level, at what had been the top of the crag, close to the cliff's edge. At the end of the short, lightless vault of the hallway was a small door. Even as his soul shrank from it, he thought, *I have done this before.*

The room beyond was like the one Derroug Dru had shown him in the prison below the Records Office in Mandrigyn. It was small and dank, furnished with a huge, carved chair whose black velvet cushions boasted bullion tassels. The white glow of the witchlight gleamed oilily on the wall of glass before the chair. The only difference from that other chamber was that there was a door beside the wide window that looked into darkness.

Something like a restless flake of fire moved in that dark beyond the glass.

Sun Wolf had known this was coming to him, all the long road up the mountain. In a way, he had known it since Derroug Dru had first shown the abominations that Altiokis had given him, in the cell beneath the Records Offices. Horror went through the Wolf like a sword of ice; horror and despair and the terrified consciousness that in that room, not in the fat man chuckling throatily beside him, lay the centerpoint of the evil power that pervaded the Citadel. Whatever was in there, it was the source, not only of the creatures that turned men into nuuwa, but of the power that had let Altiokis become the swollen and abominable thing that he was.

Behind the glass, the bright flake of fire zagged idly in the air, leaving a thin fire trail in the stygian dark. It was waiting for him, waiting to devour his brain, to make him one of the mewing, slobbering things that were filled, like the dead stones of the Citadel, with Altiokis' perverted will.

Swords pressed into Sun Wolf's back, forcing him toward the narrow door. All of his senses seemed to have dulled and concentrated; he was conscious of no sound but the frantic hammering of his own heart and of no sensation but the cold of sweat pouring down his face and breast and arms. The sharpness of the steel was driving him forward. His vision had shrunk to that idle flake of fire, to the dark door, triple-barred with iron, and to the hands of the men unbarring it.

Cold and evil seemed to flow forth from the black slot of the opening. With curious, instantaneous clarity, he saw the round stone walls of Altiokis' original hut, the weeds that lay dead and tangled about the edges, and the scuffed, fouled dirt within. But all that was peripheral to the awareness of that black pit at the center, a boundaryless, anomalous, and utterly hideous vortex of absolute darkness that seemed to open in the air of the room's center. It was a Hole, a gap of nothingness that led into a universe beyond the ken of humankind. Through it flowed the power that filled the Citadel, filled the nuuwa, and filled Altiokis' corrupted, deathless flesh and rotting brain.

But worse than the awareness of the power was the knowledge of the mind of the Entity that lived within the Hole, of the Thing that was trapped there, its thoughts reaching out to him, as shocking as ice water flowing over his naked brain.

Not human, nor demon . . . demons were of this world, and quite ordinary and comforting compared with that ice-cold, streaming black fire. Yet it was alive, and it reached to fill him.

Hands thrust him, unresisting, forward to the threshold of that tiny room. Unaware that he spoke aloud, he said, "It's alive . . ." And in the last second, as the guards shoved him in, he turned his head, meeting Altiokis' startled, dilating eyes with a sudden knowledge of where he had seen that Thing before. He said, "It gave you your power."

The Wizard King was on his feet, shrieking. "Bring him out of there! Shut the door!" His voice was frenzied, almost in panic.

The guards wavered, uncertain whether they had heard aright. The Dark Eagle grabbed Sun Wolf by the arm and pulled him backward, slamming the door to with a kick; Sun Wolf staggered, as if he had been released from a chain that held him upright, and found there was no strength left in him. He clutched the door bolts for support.

Altiokis was screaming, "Get him out of here! Get him away from here! He sees it! He's a wizard! Get him away!"

"Him?" the Eagle said, rather unwisely. "He's no wizard, my lord . . ."

Altiokis strode forward, swinging his staff to knock Sun Wolf's hands from the door bolts, as if he feared the Wolf would throw the door open and fling himself inside. Ignoring his captain of mercenaries, Altiokis clutched with his fat, jeweled hands at the grubby rags of what remained of Sun Wolf's tunic, his face white with hatred and fear.

"Did you see it?" he demanded in a stinking blast of liquor and rich food.

Exhausted, leaning against the stone wall at his back for support, Sun Wolf whispered, "Yes, I did. I see it now, in your eyes."

"It might choose to call another wizard," the fat man gasped hoarsely, as if he had not heard. "It could give him its power, if he were lucky, as I was lucky . . ."

"I wouldn't touch that power!" the Wolf cried, the thought more sickening to him than the horror of that flake of fire boring steadily through his eye.

Again the Wizard King appeared not to have heard him. "It could even give him immortality." The black, lifeless eyes stared at Sun Wolf, desperate with jealousy and terror. Then Altiokis whirled back to his guards, screaming, "Get him out of here! Throw him to the nuuwa! Get him out!"

Like the tug of a fine wire embedded in his flesh, Sun Wolf felt the touch of that black Entity in the Hole, whispering to his brain.

Furiously, he thrust it aside, more frightened of it than of anything he had yet seen, in the Citadel of Altiokis or out of it. He fought like a tiger as they half dragged, half carried him along the maze of corridors to where a shallow flight of steps led downward to a broad double door. Altiokis strode at their heels, screaming incoherently, reviling the Eagle for bringing this upon him, and cursing his own means of divination that had not shown him this new threat. One of the guards ran ahead to peer through the judas in the door, and the faint yellow bar of light from the westering sun picked out the scars on his face as he looked. He called, "There are few of them out there now, me lord. They're mostly gone in their dens."

"Open their dens, then!" the Wizard King shrieked in a paroxysm of rage. "And do it quickly, before I throw you out to keep him company!"

The man darted off, his footfalls ringing on the stone of the passage-way. Sun Wolf twisted against the hands that gripped him, but far too many men were holding him to give him purchase to fight. The doors at the bottom of the steps were flung open, and sunlight struck him as the Dark Eagle shouted a command. He was flung bodily down the steps, the harsh granite of them tearing at and bruising his flesh as he rolled.

The filthy reek of the nuuwa was all around him. As he heard the doors clang shut above him, the shrill howls began to echo from all sides. He saw that he was in the long ditch between the inner and outer walls. From various points in the shade of the looming wall, a dozen nuuwa and two or three of the apelike ugie-beasts were lol-loping toward him, heads lolling, dripping mouths gaping to slash.

Sun Wolf knew already that there was no further hope of escape. The walls of the ditch were too steep to climb. It was only a matter of time before he would be overpowered, torn apart, and eaten alive. He flung himself back up the few steps to where the embrasure of the door made a kind of hollow in the bald face of the wall, taking advantage of the only cover in sight. He put his back to the massive, brass-bound wood, gathered the five feet of chain that joined his manacled hands, and swung at the first of the things that hurled itself upon him. Brains and blood splattered from the burst skull. He swung again, slashing, the heavy chain whining through the screaming, stinking air. Anything to buy time—minutes, seconds even.

The chain, close to thirty pounds of swinging iron, connected again, flinging the creature that it hit back against two of its fellows. He brained one of them while they were fighting each other; the remaining monstrosities turned on him, spitting mouthfuls of rotted flesh, and he slashed, swinging desperately, keeping them off him as long as he could, praying to his ancestors to do something, anything . . .

You can control them, that black slip of fire whispered in his brain. *Turn them aside. Make them do your bidding.*

Chain connected with flesh. His wrists were scraped raw from the iron, and the smell of the blood was driving the nuuwa to madness. He could feel himself tiring, instant by instant, and knew to within a moment how long his strength would last. All the while, the thought of the Entity he had seen, that black intelligence glimpsed in the Hole and in the Wizard King's possessed eyes, whispered to him the promise of the life that it could give him.

The world had narrowed, containing nothing but blood-mouthed, eyeless faces, ripping hands, pain and sweat and the foul reek of the air, screaming cries and that terrible, nagging whisper of uncertainty in his brain. He was aware of other sounds somewhere, distant noises in the Outer Citadel, a far-off howling like the din of a faraway battle.

An explosion jarred the ground. Then another, heavier, louder, nearer, and he thought he heard, through the shrieking of the mindless things all around him, the triumphal yells of men and the higher, wilder keening of women.

He was aware that no new attackers were running toward him. He swung grimly at those that remained, half conscious of things happening elsewhere in the long ditch—of fighting somewhere—*on the causeway?*—of fire . . .

Teeth slashed at his leg and he stomped, breaking the neck of the ugie that had crawled up below the arc of the swinging chain. Whatever else was happening was only a distraction, a break in his concentration that could cost him his life.

Another explosion sounded, this time very near, and it took all his will not to look. The chain crushed a final skull, the last nuuwa fell, wriggling and snapping at its own flesh, and he stood gasping in the doorway, looking up to see the causeway drawbridge fall in flames.

The top of the outer wall was a friezework of struggling men. A rear guard of black-armored soldiers was being cut to pieces on the causeway itself. What looked like an army of black and filthy gnomes was pouring through the causeway gate and down makeshift ladders into the ditch, brandishing picks, adzes, and weapons stolen from the armories in the mines. The blood of their wounds gleamed bright through the rock dust, and their screams of triumph and anger shook the air.

Then he heard a voice pitched as only a warrior's could be to carry over the roar of battle—the one voice that, of all others, he would have given anything he had ever possessed to hear again.

"DUCK, YOU OAF!"

He ducked as an axe splintered into the wood of the door where his head had been. He saw the advancing forces of the Dark Eagle's mercenaries pouring down from the other side of the causeway to meet the miners in battle in the ditch. With a great scraping of bolts, the doors behind him were thrown open, and reinforcements poured through in a mixed tide of mercenaries, regulars, and nuuwa. The battle was joined on the corpse-strewn steps around him.

Somehow, Starhawk was there, where he knew she always should be, fighting like a demon at his side.

"I thought I told you to go back!" he yelled at her over the general chaos. His chain smashed the helmet and skull of a mercenary before him.

"Rot that!" she yelled back. "I've quit the troops and I'll look for you as long as I bloody well please! Here . . ." She stooped to wrench a sword free from the dead fingers that still grasped it and thrust the bloody hilt at him. "This will get you farther than that silly chain."

"Cheap, rotten, general-armory issue," he grumbled, testing the edge on the neck of an advancing nuuwa. "If you were going to get me a sword, you might at least have made it a decent one."

"Gripe, gripe, gripe, all you ever do is gripe," she retorted, and he laughed, teeth gleaming white through the filthy stubble of his beard, joyful only to be with her again.

They were silent then, except for the wordless yelling of battle, merging with the dirty mob of the advancing forces. But he was conscious of her at his side, battle-cold and bright, filled with concentrated fire, and he wondered how he had ever thought her plain.

The men now around him were gaunt as wolves but rock-muscled from hard labor, their dusty hides striped with the scars of beatings. He knew they were the husbands, the lovers, or the brothers of those crazy and intrepid wildcats he'd spent the winter training. There were more of them than he'd thought; the long ditch was rapidly filling with men. The gate at the top of the steps was disgorging more and more of Altiokis' troops. The mêlée was deafening. A momentary sortie drove the miners down the blood-slick steps, and he heard a woman's voice —Sheera's voice—raised in a piercing rallying cry.

Someone came running up behind him, and he swung around, sword ready, heavy chain rattling. A dusty little man yelled, "Are you Sun Wolf?"

"Yes." Under the grime, he saw that the man's hair was flame-gold, the mark of the royal House of Her, and he asked, "Are you Tarrin?"

"Yes."

"Does one of your people have the key to this mother-loving chain?"

"No, but we've got an axe to cut the links free. We'll get rid of the bracelets later."

"Fine," the Wolf said. Eo loomed up out of the confusion of the fight, half a head taller than Tarrin and brandishing an enormous axe. Tarrin positioned the chain over a corner of the stone steps; they all winced as the axe blade slammed down.

"You girls make it in all right?" the Wolf asked, after Eo had whacked the chain free of the bracelet on his other wrist.

Her reply was drowned in the renewed din of the fighting, the sounds of the struggle rising like a voiceless howling, elemental as a storm. More men were pouring from the doors, impossible numbers of them—the Wolf had not thought there were that many in the fortress. He caught up his sword and plowed back into the fray on the steps at Tarrin's heels. Eo followed with her axe. Battle separated them. Sun Wolf pressed upward, fighting his way to the shadow of the gate, where the line of defenders was weakening. Freed of the chain's weight, he felt he could fight forever.

He slashed and cut, until the sword embedded in flesh and bone. He looked down to pull it loose and froze in nauseated horror at what he saw. The flesh of his arms was white with leprosy.

He didn't see the enemy sword that slashed at his neck until Starhawk's blade deflected it, so frozen was he by sickened despair. She yelled at him, "It's an illusion! Wolf! Stop it! It isn't real!"

He looked up at her, his face gray with shock. She, too, had momentarily stopped fighting, though the battle raged on all sides of them.

"It's an illusion, rot your eyes! Do you think leprosy takes hold that fast? That's how he won at Iron Pass. We've already been through six things like this coming out of the mines!"

Her own face was blotched with it, like lichen on stone. But as he blinked at her, his mind coming back into focus, he saw that what she said was true. As with the seeing of demons, he became aware that by changing his perceptions slightly, he could see the whole flesh under the superimposed illusion of rot. Blood and anger slammed, raging, back into his veins. The men and women struggling all around him didn't have his power to see through, or Yirth's power to combat, illusions—but they had seen the Wizard King's illusions before. And now they were too angry to care.

Cursing like a bullwhacker, the Wolf threw himself back into the fray. He could see through the gate to the corridors beyond, clogged with Altiokis' troops; and, as if the realization that the leprosy was an illusion had somehow cleared a block from his eyes, he saw that three-quarters of these new warriors were illusion as well. By the way they cut at them, the others could not tell the difference, and he knew himself to be fighting as a wizard would fight, and seeing as a wizard would see. Starhawk, at his side, slashed at one of the insubstantial figures as a real warrior cut at her with a halberd. Sun Wolf hacked the man's head off before the blow landed and wondered how many others would fall to just such a fraud.

Behind him, he heard a man cry out in terror.

He whirled, looking into the darkness of the Citadel gate. There was something there, visible behind the backs of the retreating sortie, a shapeless shape of luminous horror, a coldness that ate at the bones. Altiokis' men were retreating through the doors. Tarrin and his miners were unwilling to follow, frozen by the coming of that horrible fog and what was within it. They fell back toward the sunlight of the ditch, and the doors began to swing shut, as if of themselves.

Sun Wolf, left momentarily alone with Starhawk by the ebbing forces, scanned the darkness, searching it with his mind rather than with his eyes . . . and finding nothing but the shape of Altiokis, far back among those glowing wraiths, his hands weaving the illusion from the air.

He bellowed, "It's an illusion, dammit! Don't let them close the gate!" He plunged forward, hearing Starhawk's footfalls at his heels. He heard her voice somewhere in back of him, calling out to the others, and heard them follow. Then he heard the gate slam behind him.

The luminous fog vanished. His arms, as he glimpsed them, swinging his sword at the men who crowded toward him, were clean again. There were few of Altiokis' men still around the gate, the rest having gone to the fighting on the walls, and those few he dispatched or drove away. Then he plunged after the retreating shape of the Wizard King.

The darkness beneath the Citadel seemed thicker than it had before, defeating even his abilities to pierce it. He tore a torch from its holder, and the smoke of it streamed like a banner in his wake. Altiokis' fruity laugh taunted him from the black hole of a corridor arch; Sun Wolf sensed a trap and advanced cautiously, the curious perception that detected reality from illusion showing him the ghostly outlines of the spiked pit in the floor beneath the illusion of damp flagstones. He edged past it on the narrow walkway that the Wizard King had used; but by then his quarry was out of sight.

He seemed to be caught in a maze of twisting rooms and corridors, of doors that opened to nowhere, and of traps in the walls and floor. Once nuuwa attacked him in a room that had seemed empty—purposefully, controlled by another mind, as the nuuwa had fought in the battle. He cut at them with sword and fire, wedging himself into a niche in the wall. As he split skulls and burned the dirty hair and rotted flesh, he felt again that eerie little whisper at the back of his consciousness.

You can control them yourself. You only have to give a little part of your mind to that cold, black fire, and you can control them . . . and other things as well.

Turn away, and what can you offer this woman you want except a battered and poverty-stricken wanderer? Do you really think Ari will give up the troop to you?

He remembered the sightless blaze burning in the rotted remains of Altiokis' failing brains and fought grimly, humanly, bloodily, exhaustedly. He killed two of the nuuwa, and the rest of them drew back, retreating into the stone mazes away from his torchlight, dodging through the stone walls like bats.

Altiokis, he reflected, *must be running out of nuuwa if he's started conserving them.*

Grimly, he pursued.

There was a trap of some kind in one guardroom. His hypersensitive sense of direction let him pick out a way around it, seeking the source of the fat man's wheezing breath. He saw Altiokis then, fleeing up a dark corridor. The torchlight bounced crazily over the rough stone of the walls as the Wolf ran. It glittered on the blood that smeared his arms and on the far-off glint of the jewels on the Wizard King's doublet. He heard the gasping of Altiokis and the stumbling, clumsy footsteps. Ahead, he saw a narrow door, bound and bolted with steel. A darkness, a last illusion, confused his sight, but he heard the door open and shut.

He flung himself at it, tore it open, and plunged through, holding the torch aloft to see. As he passed through the door, he realized that the wall in which it was set was the same as the wall of that tiny, windowed chamber—the rough stone wall of the original hut that Altiokis had built in a night.

And he knew that Altiokis had never come through that door.

It crashed shut behind him, and he heard the bolts slam home. He turned, gasping, his lungs stifling with terror. Black and empty, the Hole of darkness lay before him, absorbing and drowning the light of the flames. On the far side of the Hole, he could make out the window to the observation room and the narrow door beside it—the door, as he recalled, that Altiokis had not bolted when he'd ordered Sun Wolf out of the room.

But the width of the room lay between it and the Wolf, and the ugly, evil, screaming depths of that silent blackness lay between. The sword dropped from his nerveless fingers at the thought of having to walk past it; he could see the light of the torch wavering over the shadowy walls with the shaking of his hand. He stood paralyzed, conscious of the Entity that he would have to pass and of the mindless intelligence of fire and cold trapped these hundreds of years between this universe and whatever arcane depths of unreason it called its home.

Something bright flickered in the corner of his vision, like a spark floating on the air. Too late, he remembered the other danger, the horror that even the Entity that wanted his mind could not prevent. As he wrenched his face away, fire exploded in his left eye, a numbing, searing blast followed by the horrible wash of pain. From his eye, it seemed to be spreading throughout every muscle of his body. He could hear himself screaming, and his knees were buckling with agony. With a curiously clear sliver of the remains of rational thought, he knew exactly how many seconds of consciousness he had left, and the single thing that he must do.

CHAPTER

~ 21 ~

*T*HE DOOR OF THE WINDOWED OBSERVATION ROOM WAS PUSHED carefully open. Altiokis, Wizard King of the greatest empire since the last rulers of Gwenth had retired in a huff to their respective monasteries, peeked cautiously around the doorjamb.

The big mercenary lay face-down on the floor a few feet away. He must, Altiokis thought, have gotten through the door somehow—a glance showed that it wasn't bolted—in his final agony. A trickle of blood ran out from beneath his head.

Altiokis relaxed and smiled with relief. His earlier panic had been absurd. *Drink is making me foolish,* he thought with a self-indulgent sigh. *I really should take less.* He had always suspected that the Entity in the Hole had no real control over the gaums, and it was for that reason that he had never gone near it unprotected. But there was always the risk that some other wizard would know the secret of destroying them—if there was a secret.

He frowned. There was so much that his own master—whatever the old puff-guts' name had been—had never told him. And so much that he had been told had not made sense.

He padded into the little room, two nuuwa shuffling at his heels. Really, it had only been sheerest luck that he hadn't become a nuuwa himself, he thought, looking down at that huge, tawny body at his feet. All those years ago . . . How many had it been? There seemed to be so many periods of time that he couldn't quite recall. It was only by sheerest chance that the men he'd been out with that night—the old Thane's men, silly old bastard!—had their eyes burned out and their brains destroyed, while he hid in the brush and watched. Oh, he'd heard of the Holes, but he'd never thought to see one. And he'd never realized that Something lived in them.

Something, that is, other than gaums.

That was another thing old—old—whatever his name was—had never bothered to tell him.

Altiokis bent down. *A wizard!* After all these years, he'd hardly expected that any dared to oppose him still. But there were those he hadn't accounted for, over the years, and perhaps they'd had students. That was the big advantage, he'd found about living forever, as the Entity in the Hole had promised him he might do.

Well, not promised, exactly. He couldn't recall. Nevertheless, he had won again, and he gave a delighted little giggle at the thought as he bent down to examine his newest recruit to the ranks of the mindless.

A hand closed around his throat like a vise of iron. With bulging eyes, Altiokis found himself staring down into a face that was scarcely human; the one eye socket was empty and charred with fire, but the other eye was alive, sane, and filled with livid pain and berserker rage.

The fat wizard let out one gasping squeak of terror. Then Sun Wolf found himself holding, not a man, but a leopard by the throat.

Claws raked his back. His hands dug through the soft, loose flesh of the white-ruffed throat. Even shape-changed, Altiokis was a fat, old animal. The Wolf rolled to his feet, dragging the twisting, snarling thing toward the narrow door of the room where the Hole waited. Peripherally, his single eye caught the bright movement of more of the fire-flecks beyond the glass, and the smoldering yellow glow of the torch where it lay, burning itself out on the stone floor. The leopard must have known, too; for its struggles redoubled, then suddenly changed, and Sun Wolf found himself with nine feet of cobra between his hands.

It was only for a moment. The tail lashed at his legs, but the poisonous head was prisoned helplessly in his grip.

The next thing was horrible, something he had never seen before, bloated and chitinous, with clawed legs and tentacles raking at him like whips. He yanked open the door.

The nuuwa stirred uneasily, held still by the tangle of forces in the room. The Wolf could feel Altiokis' mind drawing them, and blocked it with his own. With the door open, the whispering in the thoughts was overwhelming. Past the shrieking mouths and flailing antennae of that horrible head between his hands, he could see the movement in the darkness, surrounded by the mindlessly devouring motes of flame. The thing in his hands twisted and lashed, and the blood ran fresh from his clawed shoulders and from the ruined socket of his eye. The monster was hideously strong; he felt the muscle and sinew of his arm cracking under the weight of it, but he refused to release his strangling grip.

As they struggled on the threshold of that vile room, Altiokis became once again a fat man, crazy and sweating with fear. Sun Wolf slung the man inside and crashed the door shut with all his strength. It heaved under the weight thrown against it. He shot the bolts and stood hanging onto them, as he had done before, feeling them jerk and pull under his hands with desperate spells of opening. The two nuuwa jiggled from foot to foot, and he threw the barriers of his mind against them, keeping them from understanding, wondering if it would be worth it, just this once, to yield to the drag in his mind and order them away.

Then the screaming started. The fight to free the door bolts ceased; he heard Altiokis blundering around the room, shrieking with agony, hitting the wall, and falling. Sun Wolf leaned against the door, sickened by the sound, remembering those endless seconds and counting them down.

He had been in enough dirty fighting to know how to gouge out an eye. He doubted that Altiokis had the knowledge and the resolution to do it or the determination needed to sear the bleeding socket with fire. The brutal action had saved him, but he was sure that he would never—could never—erase from his mind the long seconds that it had taken him to nerve himself to do it.

He knew by the screaming and by the change in the behaviour of the nuuwa when what remained of Altiokis' mind was gone. He turned the nuuwa's attention to the opposite walls and walked nonvisible, between them and out into the Citadel.

The black flames tittered in his mind.

Hearing the yelling confusion that came to him from every corner, he guessed that the nuuwa, released from control, had become as they were outside Altiokis' domains—randomly rampaging, turning on the troops beside whom they had fought. He plunged down the corridors, finding his way back to the entrance into the ditch from whence he had come.

The doors were barred. He could hear the slam of a battering rams against them and, faintly, Tarrin's ringing voice. But the defenders, clutched in a corner, fighting the small swarm of nuuwa that had suddenly turned upon them, were in no shape to prevent him from dragging back the bars.

Two of the nuuwa broke away from the main group and shambled toward him, groaning and slavering, as the first blazing crack of daylight opened through the doors. He started to order them away and stopped himself. His brain seemed to be swimming in dark, murmuring liquid, his thoughts struggling against insistent, alien urges.

Men poured through the gate around him. He found himself clutching the doorposts for support. Then hands were gripping his arms. A voice called him back to himself.

"Chief! What in the name of the Mother happened to you?"

He clutched Starhawk's shoulders, holding to her as if to the last spar of sanity in the sea in which he felt himself sinking. "That Thing —the Thing in the room . . ."

"The Hole?"

His eye focused. He noted distantly, automatically, that his depth perception was gone and that he'd have to retrain to compensate. The slanted light of late afternoon that streamed through the gate showed him Starhawk's face, grimy, bloody, and unsurprised. Her gray eyes were clear, looking into his. Though there was no reflection of it in her face, he realized that he himself must have been a choice sight. *Trust the Hawk*, he thought, *not to ask stupid questions until there's time to answer them.*

"How did you know?"

"The wizard Anyog told me," she said. He realized he hadn't seen her in four months; it only seemed like yesterday. "Where is it?"

"Back there. Don't go near it. Don't go in that room with it . . ."

His hands left patches of bloody dirt where they rested on her shoulders. She shook her head. "Is there any room near it? Around it —to put blasting powder from the mines? We were bringing some up to take care of the gate."

"Blasting powder?" The draw on his mind was growing stronger. He wasn't sure he had heard.

"To blow out the walls," she explained. "Daylight will destroy it." She put a hand to his face, slimy with the scum of battle, gentle as a lover's. "Wolf, are you all right?"

She wasn't asking about his eye or the claw marks and sword cuts that covered his body as if he had rolled in broken glass. She knew his physical toughness. Her fears for him went deeper than that.

"Daylight," he said thickly. "Then . . . The hut was built at night."

"Yes, I know," she said.

He didn't bother to ask her how she knew. A darkness seemed to be edging its way into his thoughts, and he shook his head, as if to clear it. "Altiokis' forces are still holding that part of the Citadel," he said. "You'll have to fight your way in."

"Is the room itself guarded?"

He shook his head.

"Then we'll make it. We can leave a long fuse . . ."

Others had come up to them. The battle was raging past into the corridors. Sheera's voice gasped, "Chief! Your eye!" Amber Eyes' hand on his arm was suddenly motherly in spite of the fact that her arms were smeared with blood to the shoulders. A viselike grip that he recognized as Denga Rey's closed over his elbow, offering support.

Starhawk gave them a rapid précis of what needed to be done. The women nodded, evidently on terms of great friendliness with her. Sun Wolf wondered suddenly how Starhawk happened to be there in the first place, then discarded the thought as irrelevant. It was true that in the crisis of battle, the most appalling coincidences were commonplace.

Amber Eyes said, "We can't leave a long fuse, though. It would have to be long enough to let us get clear of the Citadel. In that time, someone would find it."

"You're right," the Hawk agreed.

"Could we wait until the battle's over?" Sheera asked. "By nightfall we should have the place. Altiokis' forces are holed up in the upper part of the tower—once they got clear of their own nuuwa, that is. Then we could—"

"No," Sun Wolf said hoarsely. The Thing—the voice, the urge, whatever it was—he could feel it tearing at the fraying edges of his mind, growing stronger as final exhaustion took its toll on his body. Sunrise tomorrow seemed hideously far away. "It has to be before sunset tonight."

Amber Eyes and Denga Rey looked at him, deeply troubled, but Starhawk nodded. "He's right," she said. "If there's some kind of living thing, some kind of intelligence in the Hole, we can't give it the night to work in."

"We've only got about an hour and a half until sunset," Denga Rey observed doubtfully.

"So we have to work fast. We can stack powder around it. Damned good thing Tarrin had it brought up from the mines to blow the gate or we'd be forever getting it."

"Yirth could light it from a distance," Amber Eyes said suddenly. "I've seen her light torches and candles just by looking at them. If we could get her out here, then she could light the powder . . ."

"Get her," Sheera said.

The lovers vanished in opposite directions. He leaned back against the wall behind him, suddenly weak, his mind drifting. The roar of battle seemed to sink to an unreal whispering.

"Chief!"

He blinked into Starhawk's frightened face. Somehow, Amber Eyes and Denga Rey were back, and Yirth was with them, standing with Sheera, grouped around him as they had been on the ship. He thought for a moment that he had fainted, but found he was still on his feet, leaning against the stone arch of the gate, the long fosse with its carpet of trampled dead stretching away to both sides.

He shook his head, with a sensation of having lost time. "What happened?"

"I don't know," Starhawk said. By the pale light that came through the gateway beside him, her scarred, fine-boned face looked as calm and cold-blooded as ever, but he could hear the fear in her voice. "You were—you were gone. I talked to you, but it was as if you were listening to something else."

"I was," he said grimly, suddenly understanding. "Yirth, can you set fire to something at a distance without having seen it first?"

The witch's dark brows plunged in a startled frown. She alone of them, though she wore a man's doublet and breeches for convenience, bore no marks of physical fighting. But under the crown of her tight-braided hair, her harsh face was set with fatigue, the ugly smear of the birthmark appearing almost black against her pallor. She looked older, the Wolf thought, than she had before she'd led the women through the traps into the Citadel. All her scars would be upon the fabric of her mind. "I cannot set fire to anything at a distance," she said. "I must see it to bring fire."

The others stared at her, shocked at the limitation; the Wolf was puzzled. "You can't—can't bring fire to a place that you know in your mind?" he asked. "Can't form it in your mind?" The act of bringing fire seemed so easy to him, though he had never done it—like turning away the minds of those who sought him, or changing the way he saw things, to pierce another wizard's illusions.

She shook her head, clearly not understanding what he meant. "You can, perhaps," she said. "But it lies beyond my power."

So it was Sun Wolf, after all, who had to lead the small crew through the winding mazes, toward the Hole once again. Yirth followed them, though he had warned her against entering the observation room of the Hole itself; two or three of the freed miners helped carry the sacks of blasting powder. To Sun Wolf's ears, the fighting was far off in the upper part of the tower and, by the sound of it, it was turning into the grim, messy business of mopping up, fighting in pockets here and there—the bloody scrag ends of battle.

Closer and more real in his own mind was the buzzing darkness that ate at the corners of his consciousness, demanding, insistent as a scarcely bearable tickling. He rested his hand on Starhawk's shoulder for support and saw, almost disinterestedly, that his fingers were trembling. He was conscious in a half-detached way of the sun sliding down the outside walls of the Citadel, changing colors as it approached the ragged horizon; though, when he mentioned to Yirth this awareness of things he could not actually see, she shook her head and looked at him strangely with her jade-colored eyes. The Entity whispering in his mind was more real to him than his own body, more real than the stone halls through which he stumbled like a mechanical thing—more real than anything except the sharp bones of the shoulder beneath his hand and the cold, pale silk of hair that brushed the backs of his fingers when Starhawk turned her head.

Through the little window of the observation room, they could see that Altiokis was still moving. Rolling, flopping grotesquely, he would occasionally stagger to his feet or mouth at the window glass. The jewels of his clothing had caught on the rough walls and ripped as he'd moved, and fat, white flesh bulged through the rents. One eye was gone, the other already being eaten away from within; his face was starting to change, as the faces of nuuwas did. Sheera made a gagging noise in her throat and looked away.

Sun Wolf scarcely saw. He remained by the door while the sacks of powder were stacked in the room and in the hall beyond, where Yirth waited. There was enough powder to blow out the whole western wall of the Citadel. His gaze went past the window, past the darkness, to deeper darkness, where he could see the Thing moving.

The giggling, scratching sensation in his brain was almost unendurable. It knew him. Threads of it permeated every fiber of his consciousness; he had a momentary, disturbed vision of himself, visible in the shadows through the thick, black glass of the window, his half-naked body clawed and filthy, his wrists still weighted with the iron bracelets, the blood from the ripped flesh of them slowly dripping down his fingers; his left eye was a charred and gory pit in a face white with shock and strain. The other people in this vision were mere puppets, grotesque, jerking, and unreal as they stumbled about their meaningless tasks. The Entity—whatever it was—could no more see them than they could see it. They were only half-guessed shapes, more like monkeys than human beings.

He watched as one of the shapes shambled up to him and reached a fiddling, picking hand out to touch him.

He closed his eyes, and the vision dissolved. When he opened them, Starhawk was looking worriedly into his face. "Chief?"

He nodded. "I'm all right." His voice sounded like the faint rasp of a fingernail scraping metal. He looked around him, fixing the room in his mind—the stone walls, the shadows, the grayish-white cotton of the sacks that he knew the flames would lick over when he called them, and the carved ebony chair, shoved unceremoniously into a corner.

Starhawk and Denga Rey supported him between them as they led him from the room.

"You sure this is going to work?" Sheera asked nervously.

"No," the Wolf said.

"Could Yirth . . ."

"No," Starhawk said. "We have enough problems without its getting its claws into another wizard."

They turned a corner and followed a narrow passage toward the gate. With the smoothness of a door closing before them, the way was suddenly filled with armed men in black mail. The Dark Eagle stood at their head.

"I thought," he said, smiling, "that we would still find you wandering around here. And Starhawk, too . . . You did bring your men, after all." The Eagle's swarthy face was grimed with blood and dirt in the torchlight, the swirling, petal-edged crests of his helmet torn and hacked with battle, their dark blue edges black in places and dripping; but through it all, his grin was no less bright.

"Let us out of here," Sun Wolf said in a voice that shook. "This is no time for fighting."

"No?" One black brow lifted. "The nuuwa seem all to have gone crazy, but we should be able to drive them off the walls without much trouble. Altiokis should be pleased to hear—"

"Altiokis is dead," the Wolf whispered, fighting to keep his thoughts clear and to keep the words that he spoke his own and not those that crowded, unbidden and unknown, to his throat. His harsh voice had turned slow and stammering, picking at his words. "His power is broken for good—there's no need to fight—just let us out . . ."

The mercenary captain smiled slowly; one of his men laughed. Sheera made a move to draw her sword, and Starhawk caught her wrist, knowing it would do no good.

"Quite a convincing tale," the Dark Eagle said. "But considering that I have here my lord Tarrin's lady—no uncommon general, I might add, my lady—not to mention the witch who led the miners through the traps and into the Citadel—*if* my lord is dead, which I have yet to believe, the power he wielded will be up for the taking. We can—"

"If you can touch the power he had, it will snuff your brains out like a candle flame," the Wolf said harshly. "Go down the corridor and through the door. Look through that pox-rotten glass of his—look at what you see. Then come back, and we'll talk about power!" His voice was trembling with strain and rage, his brain blinded with the effort of holding itself together against those tearing, muttering, black roots that were thrusting it apart. "Now let us the hell out of here, unless you want that Thing in there to take root in my brain as it did in his!"

The Dark Eagle stood for a moment, staring up into Sun Wolf's face, into the hagridden, half-mad, yellow eye that stared from the mass of clotted cuts, stubble, and filth. The captain's own face, under the soot and grime of battle, was smooth, an unreadable blank. Then without a word, he signed to his men to let Sun Wolf and the women pass. The Dark Eagle turned and walked down the corridor toward Altiokis' observation room.

Sun Wolf had no recollection of passing the gate of the Inner Citadel or crossing the causeway over the fosse that was littered with the bodies of the slain. The men the Dark Eagle had sent to guard them halted at the far end of the causeway, and the Wolf slumped down in the shadows of the turreted gates, with his back against the raw, powder-burned stone. Looking back, he could see the towers of the Inner Citadel alive with men and nuuwa, fighting in the corridors or looting the gilded halls. The shrieking came to him in a vast, chaotic din, and the shivering air was rank with the smoke of burning. The sinking sunlight gilded huge, billowing clouds of smoke that poured, black or white, from the tower windows. Heat danced above the walls, and now and then a man or a nuuwa would come running in flames from some inner hall, to fall screaming over the parapet, gleaming against the sunset like a brand. In the direction of the distant sea, torn rags of cloud covered the sky. It would be a night of storm.

Wind touched his face, the breath of the mountains, polluted by the stinks of battle. Everything seemed remote to him, like something viewed through a heavy layer of black glass. He wondered idly if that had been how things appeared to Altiokis—unreal, a little meaningless. No wonder he had sought the grossest and most immediate sensations; they were all he could feel. Or had his perceptions changed after he had given up?

Darkness seemed to be closing in on Sun Wolf. He reached out blindly, not wholly certain what it was that he sought, and a long, bony hand gripped his. The pressure of Starhawk's strong fingers helped clear his mind. His remaining eye met hers; her face appeared calm under the mask of filth and cuts; the sunset light was like brimstone on her colorless hair. Against the grime, her eyes appeared colorless, too, clear as water.

Beyond her, around them, the women stood like a bodyguard, their own blood and that of their enemies vivid on their limbs against the rock dust of the mines. He was aware of Yirth watching him, arms folded, those sea-colored eyes intent upon his face; he wondered if, when his mind gave up and was drowned in blackness, she would kill him.

He hoped so. His hand tightened over Starhawk's.

There was a brief struggle on the far end of the causeway. A sword flashed in the sinking light; one of the soldiers at that end, in the armor of Altiokis' private troops, went staggering over the edge into the ditch.

The Dark Eagle came striding back, sheathing his sword as he picked his way carefully across the makeshift of rope and pole that had been thrown up to replace the burned drawbridge. Under the tattered wrack of his torn helmet crests, his face was green-white and gray about the mouth, as if he had just got done heaving up his farthest guts. The dying sunlight caught on the gilded helmet spike as on a spear.

When he came near, he asked, "How do you mean to destroy it?"

"Light the powder," Sheera said. "Tarrin and the men are clear of the place now."

"There are nuuwa all over the corridors," the Eagle informed her, speaking as he might speak to any other captain. And so she looked, Sun Wolf thought, with her half-unraveled braids and black leather breast guards, her perilous beauty all splattered with blood. "By God and God's Mother, I've never seen such a hell! You'll never get back to put a fuse to it. And even if you did . . ."

"The Wolf can light it," Starhawk said quietly. "From here."

The Dark Eagle looked down curiously at the slumped figure propped among the women against the wall. His blue eyes narrowed. "His Nibs was right, then," he said.

Sun Wolf nodded. Fire and cold were consuming his flesh; voices echoed to him, piping and far away. The shadow of the tower already lay long over the fosse and touched him like a finger of the coming darkness.

Fumblingly, as if in a drugged nightmare, he began to put together the picture of the observation room in his mind.

He could not see it clearly—there were nuuwa there, shambling over everything, blundering into walls, shrieking at their mindless brother and maker, who clawed and screamed through the black glass. He formed the shadows in his mind, the shapes of the powder sacks, the harsh lines of the broken chair . . .

The images blurred.

Suddenly sharp, he saw them from the other side of the window.

He pushed the image away with an almost physical violence. It intruded itself into his mind again, like a weapon pushed into his hands. But he knew if he grasped that weapon, he would never be able to light the flame.

Both images died. He found himself huddled, shaking and dripping with sweat, in the blue shadow of the tower, the cold wind licking at his chilled flesh. He whispered, "I can't."

Starhawk was holding his hands. Trembling as if with fever, he raised his head and looked at the setting sun, which seemed to lie straight over the mountain horizon now, glaring at him like a baleful eye. He tried to piece together the image of the room and had it unravel in his hands into darkness. He shook his head. "I can't."

"All right," the Hawk said quietly. "There's time for me to go in with a fuse."

It would have to be a short fuse, he thought . . . There were nuuwa everywhere . . . If she didn't get out by the time it went off . . .

There would be no time for her to get out before the sun set. And it was quite possible that she knew it.

"No," he whispered as she turned to go. He heard her steps pause. "No," he said in a stronger voice. He closed his eyes, calling nothing yet, losing himself in a chill, sounding darkness. He heard her come back, but she did not touch him, would not distract him.

Small, single, and precise he called it, not in pieces but all at once— room, shadows, chair, powder, window, nuuwa, darkness. He summoned the reality in his mind, distant and glittering as an image seen in fire, and touched the gray cotton of the sacks with a licking breath of fire. The nuuwa, startled by the sudden heat, drew back.

The thunderous roar of the explosion jerked the ground beneath him. The noise of it slammed into his skull. Through his closed eyes, he could see stones leaping outward, sunlight smashing into the centuries of darkness . . . light ripping where that darkness had taken hold of his brain.

He remembered screaming, but nothing after that.

CHAPTER

22

"*T*HERE ISN'T THAT MUCH MORE TO TELL.*"* STARHAWK crossed her long legs and tucked her bare feet up under the tumble of sheets and flowered silk quilts at the end of the bed. Against the dark embroidery of her shirt and the gaily inlaid bedpost at her back, she looked bleached, clean as crystal, remote as the winter sky, with her long, bony hands folded around her knees. "Amber Eyes had a picked squad of the prettiest girls—Gilden and Wilarne were two of them— and they tarted themselves up and went in first, to slit the throats of the gate guards before they knew what was happening. The alarm was out after that, but it was too late to keep the troop out of the mines; once we'd made it to the first of the armories and Tarrin got his men rallied, it was easy."

Sun Wolf nodded. From long professional association, he understood what Starhawk meant by easy. The women all bore wounds of hard fighting. Twelve of the fifty had died in the darkness of the mines, never knowing whether their cause would succeed or not. But the fight had been straightforward, with a clear goal. He doubted whether either Starhawk or Sheera had ever questioned their eventual victory.

He leaned back against the silken bolsters and blinked sleepily at the primrose sunlight that sparkled so heatlessly on the diamond-paned windows. Waking in this room, he had not been certain of his surroundings. It turned out that this was Sheera's best guest room, and that amused him. Never in his stay in Sheera's household had he been permitted inside the main house. He had half expected to wake up in the loft over the orangery again.

Sheera had not yet come.

"She'll be at the coronation," Starhawk said. "It killed me to miss it, but Yirth said she'd rather not have you left alone. Yirth stayed with you yesterday when I went to the wedding—Sheera and Tarrin's, I mean. There was a hell of a dust kicked up over it with the parliament, because Tarrin and Sheera insisted that they be married first and then crowned as joint rulers, rather than have Tarrin crowned King and then take Sheera as Queen Consort." She shrugged. "Parliament's meeting this afternoon, and there'll be a town-wide gorge on free food and wine all night to celebrate. Tomorrow, if you're up to it, you'll be received by Tarrin and Sheera in the Cathedral Square."

He nodded, identifying at last the faint wisps of noise that had formed a background to the room. It was music and cheers, coming from the direction of the Grand Canal. If the town had found time to reorganize itself for celebrations, he realized, he must have been unconscious for longer than he had thought.

He smiled, picturing to himself the jewel-box vaults of the Cathedral of the Three and Sheera in a gown of gold. Drypettis had been more right than she knew. Sheera was worthy to be Queen—but Queen on her own terms and not on any man's. He was glad she'd achieved it, no matter what the hapless Tarrin had felt on the subject.

"What do you think of her?" he asked. "Sheera, I mean."

Starhawk laughed. "I love her," she said. "She's the damnedest woman I've ever met. She's a good general, too, you know, easily better than Tarrin. She always had her forces at her fingertips—always knew what was going on. Even in the worst of it, getting through the traps that guarded the ways up to the Citadel, she never batted an eye. Yirth showed her the true way, and she followed, through illusion and fire and all hell else. The rest had no choice but to do the same."

Sun Wolf grinned and reached up to touch the bandage over his eye that would soon be replaced by the patch that he would wear for life. "Even a man's deepest fear of magic," he said in his hoarse voice, "isn't strong enough to make him admit that he's afraid to follow where a woman leads."

One of those dark, strong eyebrows moved up. "You think I

haven't capitalized on that ever since you made me a squad captain? One memory I'll always cherish is the look on the face of Wilarne M'Tree's husband when they met in the battle in the tunnels. It was a toss-up whether he'd die of a stroke induced by outrage or I'd die laughing. She all but hacked the arm off a mine guard who had him cornered—she's wicked with that halberd of hers—and he looked as indignant, when he finally recognized her, as if she'd made a grab at him in the street."

Sun Wolf laughed. "I suspected Sheera would be a good fighting general," he said. "But sending her green into her first battle—and an underground one involving magic at that—in charge of fifty other people, would be one hell of an expensive way to find out I was wrong."

"You know," Starhawk said thoughtfully, "I always did suspect you were a fraud." The gray eyes met his, wryly amused. "The hardest-headed mercenary in the business . . ."

"Well, I was," he said defensively.

"Really?" Her voice was cool. "Then why didn't you sneak off to Altiokis first thing and offer to trade information about the whole organization for the antidote? It would have got you out."

Sun Wolf colored strangely in the pale, butter-colored sunlight. In a small voice, he answered her. "I couldn't have done that."

She extended her foot like a hand and patted the lump of his knee under the covers. "I know." She smiled, got to her feet, and walked to the window. The shadows of the lattice crisscrossed her face and her short, sulfurous hair. Over her shoulder, she said to him, "The Dark Eagle says there's going to be years' worth of pickings, with Altiokis' empire broken up. Tarrin told me this morning they'd gotten news of a revolt in Kilpithie. You know they lynched Governor Stirk—the man Altiokis appointed here in Derroug Dru's place. There's already war in the North between Altiokis' appointees in Racken Scrag and the mountain Thanes. With the fortune Altiokis amassed in a hundred and fifty years, the money will be incredible."

Her back was to him, only a part of her face visible, edged in the colors of the window; her quiet voice was neutral.

Sun Wolf said, "You know I can't go back, Hawk."

She turned to face him. "Where will you go?"

He shook his head. "I don't know. To Wrynde, at first. To let Ari know I'm alive and to turn the troop over to him. To give Fawn money."

"To pay her off, you mean?"

There was a time when he would have lashed back at those words, no matter who had said them, let alone Starhawk, who had never criticized his dealings with women before. Now he only looked down at his hands and said quietly, "Yes." After a moment, he raised his head and met her eyes again. "I didn't treat her badly, you know."

"No," the Hawk said. "You never treated any of them badly."

It was the first time he had heard bitterness—or any other emotion, for that matter—in her voice. It both stung him and relieved him, to let him know where she stood.

"Do you blame me for it?" he asked.

"Yes," Starhawk said promptly. "Completely illogically, since I was the one who never told you that I loved you—but yes."

Sun Wolf was silent, trying to choose his words carefully. With any of his other women, he would have fallen back on the easier ploys of charm, or excused himself on the grounds of his own philandering nature. But this woman he knew too well to believe that her love for him would keep her by his side if he was anything other than straightforward with her. With any of his other women, he realized that it had not much mattered to him whether they stayed by him or not. The last several months had taught him that he did not want to live without Starhawk in his life.

At last, finding no adequate way to excuse himself, he only said, "I'm sorry I hurt you. I wouldn't have done it knowingly." He hesitated, fumbling for words. "I don't want to have to do this to Fawn, because I know she is fond of me—"

"Fawn," Starhawk said quietly, "loved you enough to leave the troop and come with me to look for you. She traveled with me as far as Pergemis. She loved you very much, Wolf."

He heard her use the past tense and felt both sadness for that gentle girl and shame. Shame because he had, in fact, loved Fawn no more than a kitten, no more than he had loved the others—Gilden, Wilarne, Amber Eyes, or any of his concubines before. "What happened in Pergemis?" he asked.

"She married a merchant," Starhawk replied calmly.

Sun Wolf looked up at her, the expression of hurt vanity on his face almost comical.

Starhawk continued. "Farstep and Sons, spices, furs, and onyx. She said she would rather marry into a firm of merchants than be the mistress of the richest mercenary in creation, and to tell you the truth, I can't say that I blame her. I was asked to stay there myself," the Hawk went on in a softer voice. "I thought about it. We had lost so much time, I don't think she ever thought you'd come out of this alive."

"She wasn't alone in that opinion," the Wolf growled. "Will he be good to her?"

"Yes." Starhawk thought of that tall stone house near the Pergemis quays, of Pel Farstep in her tall hood and elaborately wrought widow's coif, and of Ram and Imber and Orris, smoking and arguing in front of the hearth, amid a great brangle of children and dogs. *Anyog should never have left there,* she thought, and then wondered whether he would have been any happier living among them constantly than she would have been, had she given up her quest and accepted Ram's love.

She realized she had been too long silent. Sun Wolf was watching her, curious and concerned at the change that had come over her face. She said to him, "They are good people, Wolf. They're the kind of people whose homes we've looted and whose throats we've slit for years. I can't go back to our old life in Wrynde any more than you can."

She walked back to the bed and leaned her shoulder against the gay carvings of the inlaid pillar, her long fingers lying among the curved patterns of ivory and gold, like something wrought there of alabaster, the strong knuckles and wrinkled, pink war scars like the work of a master craftsman against the alternation of abalone and ebony. "So here we are," she said ironically. "Your father was right, Wolf. We've been spoiled for our trade by love and magic."

He shrugged, leaning back against the shadowy silk of the many pillows. "Looks as if we'll have to seek a new trade. Or I will, anyway."

He reached up and touched the eye bandage again. As he suspected, his depth perception was completely gone. He'd have to retrain himself with weapons to compensate, if he ever wanted to fight again. "Sheera told you what happened to me that night in the pit?" he asked.

Starhawk nodded, without comment.

"Yirth was right. I need to find a teacher, Hawk. I feel the Power within me; there are things that I know I can do, but I dare not. I don't want to become like Altiokis. I need to find someone to teach me to use my powers without destroying everyone and everything I touch. And the damned thing is, I don't know where to look. Yirth was cut off from the line of her master's masters—Altiokis managed to wipe out most of the lines. I'll have to search—and I have no idea where that search will take me."

He paused, studying that calm, unexpressive face that watched him in the shadows of the bed canopy. He scanned the strength of its bone structure under the straight reddish mark of a war scar, where once her cheek and jaw had been laid open to the bone, fighting to get him off a battlefield when he'd been wounded, and the cool, smoke-gray eyes that seemed to look at all things—including his soul and hers—with such lucid calm.

Then he gathered all his courage into his hands and asked, "Will you come with me? It will be a long search. It could take years, but . . ."

"Wolf," she said softly, "years with you is all I've ever wanted."

She came quietly around the end of the bed and into his arms.

He was received by Tarrin and Sheera in a public ceremonial in the Cathedral Square the following day.

The cold and rains of winter had changed, seemingly overnight, into the first breath of spring. The windless balminess of the morning had a frost-edge sparkle to it, but the crowds that filled the square before the Cathedral of the Three all seemed to be wearing flowers on their shoulders, bosoms, and hatbands, like the pledge of beauty to come. Sun Wolf saw that most of the women wore what had come to be called the new mode, the flowing and easy-moving lines introduced by the fighting women. The men, laced into whaleboned and padded doublets, looked as if they were far thinner than they had been when they had worn that finery last. The faces of the men were pale; those of the women, brown.

The thirty-odd surviving members of Sheera's corps, he saw, were standing in a body at the foot of the Cathedral steps, about where Drypettis had gotten him arrested the morning he had gone to ask Yirth to give him his freedom. Drypettis was not among them, though Starhawk had told him last night that the woman who had betrayed him had come to make her bow to Tarrin at the new King's official reception into the city. She was, after all, the last representative of the most ancient and honorable House in Mandrigyn.

"I was half afraid she would kill herself," he had said when Starhawk had told him, remembering the numerous, ugly scenes he had witnessed and heard of between Dru and Sheera. "Not that she didn't deserve thrashing—but it wouldn't have done Sheera any good. She was fond of the little snirp."

Starhawk had shaken her head with a wry grin. "Drypettis is far too vain to kill herself," she'd said. "In fact, I'm not entirely certain she's even conscious that she did wrong. She still looked upon war as something that gentlefolk—particularly women—hired the ruder classes to do for them, not go out and do themselves. She honestly thought that Sheera had sullied herself and prostituted her soul by becoming a soldier. No, Drypettis will go to her grave believing herself ill-done-by, walling herself tighter and tighter into her own world of the past glories of her House, and exulting in her reputation as one of the original conspirators to the end."

On the way to the square, the gondola in which Sun Wolf and Starhawk were riding had passed the House of Dru, the only one of those marble-fronted palaces of the old merchant nobility to be undecorated and without a hundred watchers on every one of its tiered, trellised balconies. As Sheera's servants had poled the graceful boat past, they had heard music played in one of the rooms above; a single harpsichord, pure, lilting, and disinterested.

The other women were there, massed together as they had been that first night in the orangery, their eyes bright as they followed Sun Wolf's movements. He saw Wilarne M'Tree with Gilden, Eo, and Tisa. Across the square, he saw a man whom he vaguely recognized as Wilarne's husband with their stiff-necked, twelve-year-old son, looking haughty and uncomfortable. He thought Wilarne looked worn, her eyes stained with the blue smudges of fatigue. Here was one, at least, whose reunion had been less than peaceful. But she still stood with the women rather than with her family, and her menfolk did not look happy about this in the least.

There were others of the women who looked the same. But Amber Eyes and Denga Rey were like newlyweds in black velvet. Denga Rey glittered in her new panoply as Captain of the City Guards.

Yirth was there, too, standing a little to one side, her bony hands tucked into the star-stitched sleeves of her night-blue gown, her dark hair braided back, her face showing fully in daylight for the first time since the Wolf had known her—perhaps for the first time in her life. Even at a distance, before he realized what had changed about her, he knew she had passed through the Great Trial, sometime while he had been ill, and had grasped the wider understanding of such magic as she had been taught. The change was clear in her carriage and in her sea-colored eyes. Sun Wolf was quite close to her before he realized that the birthmark which had marred her face was gone, leaving only a faint shadow of a scar. It was, he thought, probably the first thing that she had done when she had the Power.

Near the women were the Thanes, and he glimpsed Lady Wrinshardin among them, haughty as an empress in her barbaric splendor, with marigolds in her white hair. Her gaze crossed his, and she winked at him, to the evident scandal of a podgy young man at her side who was obviously her son.

On the other side of the Cathedral steps, the dark-robed members of the parliament were banked, most of them still with the pale complexions and calloused hands of their former trade of deep-rock gold miners. Between the women and the parliament, Tarrin and Sheera stood like snow and flame, blazing with the pride of their love and triumph.

Clothed in the white silk majesty of his office, Tarrin of the House of Her, King of Mandrigyn, was no longer a dusty, quick-moving little man in a grimy loincloth, but a very elegant prince indeed. Against the miner's pallor of his face, his hair was a golden mane, a shade darker than Amber Eyes'; but of very much the same texture, rough and springing; his eyes were vivid blue. The festoons of lace that fell from his sleeves covered the shackle galls on his wrists. Beside him, Sheera was an idol in bullion-stitched gold, her high, close-fitting lace collar not quite concealing the bandages underneath. Sun Wolf remembered seeing the sword cut on her shoulder and breast when they'd been together in the Citadel and thinking that she would carry the scar to her grave.

Most of the women who had been at the storming of the mines would bear such scars.

Sun Wolf and Starhawk came forward to the foot of the steps. Carpets of eastern work had been laid down on the pavement and on the steps above, crimson and royal blue, scattered with roses and daffodils.

The roaring of voices silenced as the rulers of Mandrigyn descended the steps; a hush fell over the square.

Tarrin's face was set and expressionless as he held out his hands to Sun Wolf. In his right hand was a parchment scroll, the seals of the city dangling from it by purple ribbons; he made no other gesture of welcome.

Sun Wolf took the scroll doubtfully, then glanced at Tarrin, puzzled.

"Read it," the King said, then swallowed.

Sun Wolf unrolled it and read. Then he looked up from the parchment, too incredulous even to be shocked.

"You *what?*" he demanded.

Starhawk looked around his shoulder quickly. "What is it?"

Sun Wolf held it out to her. "It's an order of banishment."

"It's *what?*" She took it, scanned it over, then looked up disbelievingly at the Wolf, at Tarrin, and at Sheera, who stood looking off into the distance, her face an expressionless blank.

Sun Wolf's single eye glittered, yellow and dangerous; his raw voice was like metal scraping. "I did not ask to come here," he said quietly to Tarrin, "and in the course of this winter I have lost my eye, I have lost my voice, and I have damned near lost my life five times over." His voice was rising to an angry roar. "All for the sake of saving your lousy city. And you have the unmitigated and brass-faced nerve to banish me?"

To do him credit, Tarrin did not flinch in front of what ended as a harsh vulture scream of outrage; when he spoke, his voice was quiet. "It was voted upon yesterday in parliament," he said. "I'm afraid the —the original measure was much more punitive."

The paper read:

By Order and Fiat of the Parliament of Mandrigyn, Month of Gebnion, First Year of the Reign of Tarrin II of the House of Her and Sheera, his wife:

Be it herein proclaimed that the bounds and gates of Mandrigyn are closed to one Sun Wolf, wizard and formerly captain of mercenaries, residing at one time in Wrynde in the North; that as from this day he is banished from the City of Mandrigyn and all the lands appertaining to that City, and all the lands that hereinafter will become sway of that City, in perpetuity.

This by reason of his flagrant violation of the laws of the City of Mandri-

gyn, and for his wanton corruption of the morals of the ladies of Mandrigyn.

Be it known that hereafter from this day, if he sets foot upon the lands of
the City of Mandrigyn, he will become liable for the full penalties for
these his crimes.

TARRIN II, KING
SHEERA, HIS WIFE

"It means," Starhawk said, with quiet amusement, into Sun Wolf's
dumbfounded silence, "that you taught the ladies of Mandrigyn to
bear arms."

The Wolf glanced at her and back at the King. Tarrin was looking
deeply embarrassed.

"If I hadn't taught your ladies to bear arms," the Wolf said in a
tight, deadly voice, "you and all the members of your pox-rotted parliament would still be tapping great big rocks into wee small rocks in
the dark at the bottom of Altiokis' mines, without hope of seeing the
sunlight again."

"Captain Sun Wolf," Tarrin said in his light voice, "believe me,
your deeds toward the City of Mandrigyn have earned the gratitude of
our citizens, down through many generations. I am sure that once the
present social disruptions arrange themselves, the order will be re-
scinded, and I will be able to welcome you as befits—"

"Social disruptions?" the Wolf demanded.

Behind him, he heard Starhawk give a very unwarriorlike chuckle.
"He means," she said, "that the ladies won't turn back control of the
city, or of the businesses, or go back to wearing veils, and the men
aren't pleased about that at all."

Tarrin went on. "The social order of Mandrigyn is built upon generations of traditions." There was a thread of desperation in his voice.
"The—repercussions—of your action, laudable and necessary though
it was, have brought nothing but chaos and confusion to every household in the city."

Starhawk's voice was amused. "I think the men are out for your
blood, Chief. And I can't really say that I blame them."

"That's ridiculous!" the Wolf said angrily. "There weren't above
fifty women in the poxy troop! And the women had started to take
over running the businesses of the city from the minute the men
marched off to fight their witless war! Hell, most of the crew of the

ship that brought me here were skirts! And anyway, it wasn't my idea . . ."

"The fact remains," Tarrin said, "that it was you who schooled the women in these—" He glanced at the glowering members of his parliament. "—unseemly arts; and you who encouraged them to consort with gladiators and prostitutes."

Sun Wolf's voice was a croaking roar of rage, *"And I'm being banished for that?"*

"Not only for that," Sheera said quietly. Under the rose and gold of her painted lids, her eyes were touched with something that was not quite sadness, but not quite cynicism either. "And it isn't only the men who want to see you go, Captain. Do you have any concept of what has happened in this city? We were all of us raised to participate in a dance—the men to cherish, the women to be cherished in return, the men to rule and work, the women to be protected and sheltered. We knew what we were—we had harmony in those times, Captain.

"We have all passed through a hell of terror and pain, of toil and despair. We—Tarrin and I, and every man and every woman—fought not only for our city but for the dream of that way of life, that dance. We thought that with victory, all that old comfort of being what we were raised to be would be restored. But the men have returned to find the dream that sustained them in the mines forever broken. The women—" She paused, then went on, her voice level and cool. "Most of those women who did not fight did not even want what has happened. They wanted to be free of Altiokis, but not at the price that we have forced them to pay. We have pushed chaos and struggle into their lives without their consent. You yourself, Captain, and your lady, know that you cannot unknow what you know. And even those who fought find victory an ambiguous fruit to the taste."

As if against his will, the Wolf's eyes went to where Wilarne's husband and son stood without her, their eyes both sullen and confused. How many others of the troop, he wondered, would meet with that mingling of outrage and incomprehending hurt? Not only from those close to them, he now saw—not only from the men. Most of the women in the crowd were silent and looked across at him and at the ladies he had trained with wariness and disapproval, with the anger of those who had something taken from them without their consent and who did not want what was offered in return. The seeds of bitterness were sown and could not be picked out of the soil again.

And, logically, he saw that he was the only one they could banish. He was not the disrupter of the dance, but he was the only one of those new and uneasy things that they could dispose of without tearing still further the already riven fabric of their lives.

He looked back at the young man before him, clothed in the stiff white ceremonial garb of the ruler of the city, and felt an unexpected stab of pity for the poor devil who would have to sort out the ungodly mess. At least he and Starhawk could get on their horses and ride away from it—and there was a good deal to be said simply for that. He grinned and held out his hand. Tarrin, who had been watching his face with some trepidation visible beneath his own calm expression relaxed and returned the smile and the handclasp with broken-knuck-led, pick-calloused fingers.

"Along with the curses of parliament," Tarrin said quietly, "I give you my personal thanks."

"Of the two, that's what matters." The Wolf glanced over his shoulder at the sound of hooves clicking on the pavement behind them. The crowd opened in a long aisle, from the steps where they stood to the flower-twined stone lacework of the Spired Bridge, which led toward the Golden Gate of the city and to the countryside beyond. Down it, a couple of pages in the livery of the city were leading two horses, with saddlebags already packed and the Wolf's and Starhawk's weapons strapped to the cantles. One of the pages, it amused him to see, was Sheera's daughter, Trella.

With a mercenary's typical preoccupation, Starhawk gave one of the saddlebags an experimental prod. It clinked faintly, and Sun Wolf asked, "All ten thousand there?" That was a patent impossibility; no horse in creation could have carried the unwieldy bulk of that much gold.

"The rest of the money will be forwarded to you at Wrynde, Captain," Sheera said, "as soon as it can be raised by parliament. Have no fear of that."

Looking from her calmly enigmatic face to the disgruntled countenances of the members of parliament, the Wolf only muttered to Starhawk, "Where have we heard that before?"

She swung lightly into the saddle, her fair hair catching the sunlight like pale silk. "What the hell does it matter?" she asked. "We're not going back there, anyway."

The Wolf thought about that and realized that she was right. He had sold his sword for the last time—like the women, like Starhawk, he was no longer what he had been. "No," he said quietly. "No, I don't suppose we are." Then he grinned to himself, mounting, and reined back to where Tarrin and Sheera still stood at the foot of the steps. Sun Wolf held out his hand. "My lady Sheera?"

Sheera of Mandrigyn came forward and raised her lace-gloved hand for his formal kiss. In former days he would have asked the permission of Tarrin, but the King said no word, and the glance Sheera cast them silenced the parliament, like a spell of dumbness. For the first time since he had seen them together, Sun Wolf noticed that Sheera stood an inch or so taller than Tarrin.

He bent from the saddle and touched her knuckles to his lips. Their eyes met—but if she had any regrets, or wished for things between them to be or to have been other than they were, he could find no trace of it in that serene and haughty gaze. She was Sheera of Mandrigyn, and no one would ever see her with mud and rain and sweat on her face again.

He said softly, "Don't let the men get your ladies down, Commander."

She elevated a contemptuous eyebrow. "What makes you think they could?"

The Wolf laughed. He found that he could take a great deal of pleasure in seeing those he loved behave exactly like themselves. "Nothing," he said. "May your ancestors bless you, as you will bless those who follow you with blood and spirit."

He reined his horse away; but as he did so, Starhawk rode forward and leaned to take Sheera's hand. A few words were exchanged; then, in a very unqueenly gesture, Sheera slapped Starhawk's knee, and Starhawk laughed. She rode back to him at a decorous walk; the crowd moved aside again to let them ride from the city.

As they moved under the flamboyant turrets of the Spired Bridge, Sun Wolf whispered, "What did she say to you?"

Starhawk glanced at him in the shadows, her wide, square shoulders and pale hair silhouetted against the rainbow colors of the throng they had just left. Past her, the Wolf could still see Tarrin and Sheera, two glittering dolls beneath the scintillating bulk of the Cathedral of Mandrigyn.

"She told me to look after you," the Hawk said.

Sun Wolf's spine stiffened with indignation. "She told *you* to look after *me* . . . ?"

Her grin was white in the gloom of the covered bridge. "Race you to the city gates."

To those standing in the great square of the Cathedral, all that could be heard of the departure of Sun Wolf and Starhawk from the town was the sudden thunder of galloping hooves in the tunnel of the enclosed bridge and, like an echo, a drift of unseemly laughter.

THE
WITCHES
OF
WENSHAR

For Lester

AUTHOR'S NOTE

The word "witch" is a connotative and emotionally charged term. It implied different things at different places and times, and to different groups of people—and, for that reason, has been so used here.

The particular implications of the word as it is used in this story —specifically the different connotations of the words "wizard" and "witch" in the shirdane language—are drawn from the sixteenth/seventeenth century view of witches and witchcraft, and from that view *only.* No more is meant by it than would be meant by my using various connotative words to describe persons of African descent, if I were writing from the viewpoint of a white Southerner in the 1920's. They do not represent my personal opinion or any blanket definition of witches (and indeed, have not been so used in other books of mine). Nor do they have anything to do with the implications of "witches" and "witch-craft" in medieval times, in the nineteenth century, in more conventionalized fairy tales, or at the present day.

What came to be known as European witchcraft was originally simply the worship of the old nature-deities, combined with the herbal medicine practiced by that faith's adherents, as seen through the distorting eye of a paranoid and intolerant medieval Church. The current Wiccan religion, whose devotees term themselves "witches," is a harking-back to this ancient faith, whose chief tenets were responsible use of white magic and love of the nature from which that power springs.

To those good-hearted and sincerely God-loving witches, I extend my apology. I hope I have made it clear in terms of the story itself that the word "witch" is only a word (like "love," or "god," or "Christian") that it is in fact what people do with that word, or do because of what they think of that word, that causes good or ill.

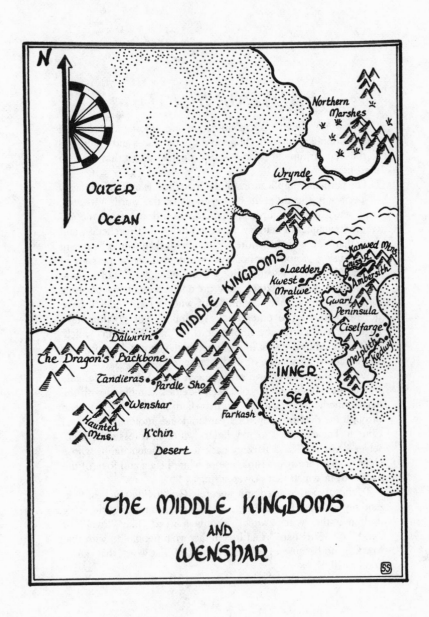

THE MIDDLE KINGDOMS
AND
WENSHAR

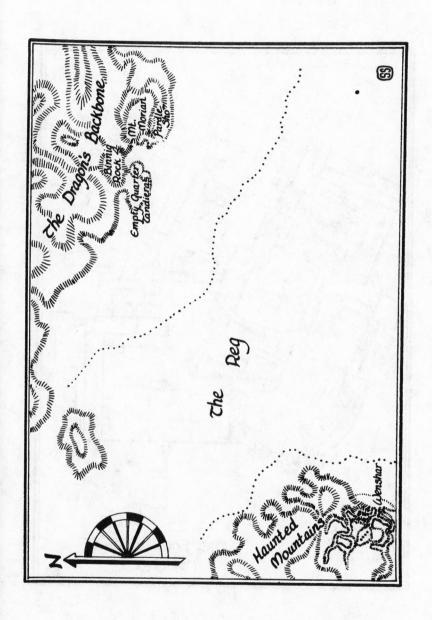

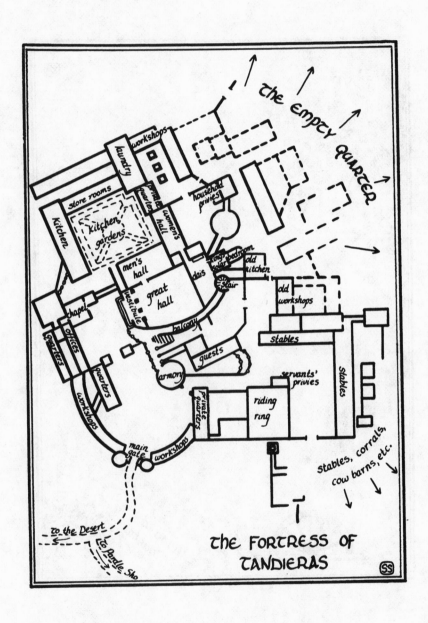

THE FORTRESS OF
TANDIERAS

CHAPTER

 1

"*Y*OU MAY BE A WIZARD, MY LADY," SUN WOLF SAID, TUCK-ing his big hands behind the buckle of his battered sword belt, "but you're also the biggest damn fool I've ever met in my life."

Every man has a gift, Starhawk sighed to herself. *Why do I choose to travel with a man whose gift is to be able to talk audibly with his foot in his mouth up to the knee?*

For one instant the sun-blasted garden with its small citrus trees and hard, clayey red soil was utterly silent. Beneath the sharp black lattice shadows of the bare arbor, the face of the Lady Kaletha, the White Witch of Wenshar, went rigid with an indignation that was three parts shock that anyone, let alone some roving barbarian in a dusty sheep-skin doublet and scarred boots, would dare speak so to her. Her face paled against the dark red coils of her hair, and her protuberant blue eyes blazed, but for the first moment she was literally speechless. One of the little cluster of her ostentatiously black-clothed disciples, misin-terpreting, opened her mouth. Kaletha waved her silent.

"You barbarian pig." She had a voice like the clink of a dropped gold coin upon stone. "Are you slandering me out of fear of what I am —or jealousy of what I have?"

Behind her, her disciples murmured, nodding wisely to one an-other. The gardens of Pardle Sho were public, occupying the grounds of what had been the Governor's Palace back when the land of Wenshar had been ruled by the Lords of the Middle Kingdoms; across the vast open square of sand, two children chased each other through the zebra shadows of the cloister, their voices shrill as birds in the hot air.

After a moment Sun Wolf said, "I fear what you are, Lady."

She drew breath to make some final point, but he cut in over her words in a voice like the rasping of a rusted-out kettle. "What you are is an armed idiot—if you're not simply a liar."

Turning, he walked away. The dark lacework of the vine shadows rolled like the foam pattern on a wave along the lion-colored leather of his doublet, and the Lady Kaletha was left with the uncomfortable choice of giving him the last word or shouting her own rebuttal in an undignified fashion after his retreating back.

Thumbs hooked in her sword belt, Starhawk followed him down that hot, shaded colonnade and across the gardens to the street.

"You know, Chief," she remarked later, coming over with two tin tankards of beer to the intense gloom of a corner of the Longhorn Inn's common room, "sometimes your facility with words leaves me breathless."

His single eye, amber as a tiger's under a long, curling tuft of fading red-gold brow, flicked suspiciously up at her as she stepped casually over the back of the chair next to his and settled into it. The leather patch that covered the empty socket of his other eye was already scuffed and weathered to the same shade as his sun-gilded skin, but the telltale groove of years had not yet been worn across his forehead by its buckskin thong.

Starhawk's face, as usual, was inscrutable as she handed him his beer; features that would have been delicate, had not her original uncomeliness of a long jaw and a square chin been added to, in the course of nine years as a mercenary soldier, by a broken nose and three inches of whitening scar that decorated one high, fragile cheekbone. For the rest, she was a tall, rangy cheetah of a woman, dressed in a man's leather breeches, embroidered shirt, and sheepskin doublet. Her baby-fine blond hair was cropped short and, like Sun Wolf's thinning red-gold mane and faded mustache, bleached out by the sun of the K'Chin Desert, along whose northern edge they had been traveling for four days.

Sun Wolf grumbled, correctly suspecting that what lay behind those water-gray eyes was a deep and private amusement. "The woman is a fool." His voice was like the wheezy creak of an unoiled hinge, as if his vocal chords had all the flesh stripped from them, leaving nothing but bare wire.

Starhawk took a sip of her beer. It was bitter, like all the beer in the Middle Kingdoms, the color of mahogany, and very strong. "She's also the only thing we've seen that remotely resembles a wizard since we left Mandrigyn," she reminded him after a moment. "And since we can't go back to Mandrigyn . . ."

Sun Wolf brushed aside the reminder of his banishment from the city that was known as the Jewel of the Megantic Sea. "The Wizard King Altiokis lived and ruled for a hundred and fifty years," he growled. "He destroyed any wizard with even a guess of the power that might have challenged him. If this Kaletha woman has the powers she claims, he'd have destroyed her, too."

Starhawk shrugged. "She could have kept them hidden until his death. That was only nine months ago. Altiokis got much of his silver from the mines of Wenshar—it's a sure bet Pardle Sho and every little mining town along the cordillera was riddled with his spies. She has to have remained silent, like Yirth of Mandrigyn did, in self-defense."

Sun Wolf wiped the beer foam from his thick, raggedy mustache and said nothing.

Though the air in the common room was hot, still, and strangely dense-feeling, no one of the half-dozen or so miners and drifters there made a move to leave its indigo shadows for the striped black-and-primrose shade of the awning of peeled cottonwood poles outside. It was the season of sandstorms, as autumn drew on toward winter. In the north, sailors would be making fast their vessels till spring opened the sea roads again, and farmers *rechinking* the thatch of their roofs. Throughout the north and west and on to the cold steppes of the east, all life came to a standstill for four months under the flail of those bitter storms. Here in Wenshar, the southernmost of the Middle Kingdoms on the borders of the desert, even the few hardy herds of cattle grazing the patches of scrub that passed for oases were chivvied in to closer pastures near the foothill towns, and the silver miners strung lines of rope from their dwellings to the pitheads, lest the burning sand-winds rise while they were between one point and another, and the darkness come on so swiftly that they would be lost.

Deceptively idle-seeming, Starhawk scanned the room.

Like half the buildings in Pardle Sho, the Longhorn was adobe brick and about fifty years old. Its low roof, thirty-five feet long and less than ten from side to side, was supported by rafters of stripped scrub pine whose shortness gave every adobe building in the town the appearance of a hallway. The older buildings of the town, erected of stone when Pardle Sho was the administrative center through which the Lords of Dalwirin ruled the Desert Lords of the wastelands beyond, were spacious and airy. According to Sun Wolf, who knew things like that, the smallest of those stone houses fetched seven times the price of any adobe dwelling in the town. Looking up at the blackened lattices of rafter and shadow over her head, Starhawk had to concede that the buyers had a point. Adobe was cheap and fast. The men and women who'd come over the mountains, first as slaves, then as free prospectors, to work the silver mines and eventually to wrest them and the land of Wenshar from those who had held them before, often could afford no better.

One of the first wars Starhawk had fought in, she recalled, had been some border squabble between Dalwirin, closest of the Middle Kingdoms north of the mountains, and Wenshar. She remembered being a little surprised that, approached by both sides, Sun Wolf had chosen to take Wenshar's money. She'd been twenty-one then, a silent girl only a year out of the convent which she'd abandoned to follow the big mercenary captain to war; a few weeks of defending the black granite passes of the Dragon's Backbone had shown her the wisdom of taking defense rather than attack on such terrain.

Sipping her beer, she remembered she hadn't had the slightest idea what to do with the prize money after the campaign. Sun Wolf, if she recalled correctly, had used his to buy a silver-eyed black girl named Shadowrose who could beat any warrior in the troop at backgammon.

She glanced across at the man beside her, his gold-furred forearms stretched before him on the table, picturing him then. Even back then, he'd been the best and certainly the richest mercenary in the length and breadth of the old boundaries of the fallen Empire of Gwenth. He'd had both his eyes then and a voice like a landslide in a gravel pit; the thin spot in his tawny hair had been small enough that he could deny its existence. His face had been a little less craggy, the points of bone on the corners of his bearlike shoulders a little less knobby. The deep silences within his soul had been hidden under the bluster of crude sex and physical challenge, which some men used to conceal their vulnerabilities from other men.

He sat now with his back to the corner of the room, as usual, his blind left eye toward her. She was the only person he allowed to sit on that side. Though she saw no more of his face than the broken-nosed profile against the brilliance of the open door, she could feel the thought moving through him, the tension in those heavy shoulders. "Face it, Chief. If this woman Kaletha doesn't teach you how to use your powers, who will?"

He moved his head a little, and she had a glimpse of the amber glint of his eye. Then he turned away again. "She's not the only wizard in the world."

"I thought we'd just established there weren't any at all."

"I don't like her."

"When you had the school at Wrynde, did the people who came to learn the arts of war from you need to like you?" When he didn't answer, she added, "If you're starving, do you need to like the baker from whom you buy your bread?"

He looked back at her then, a deep flame of annoyance in his eye that she'd read the truth in him. She drank off her beer and set the tankard down; her forearms, below the rolled sleeves of her blue-and-white embroidered shirt, were muscled like a man's, marked with the white scars of old wars. Across the common room under the glare of the bar lamps, a couple of women in the dusty clothes of miners were flirting with a lovely young man in brown silk, their voices a low mixture of sound, like a perfume of roses and musk.

"If you want to move on, you know I'll ride with you. You know I don't understand wizardry, or the needs of power. But you called Kaletha an armed idiot for having power and not using it wisely. What does that make you?"

Anger flared in that slitted yellow eye—she was reminded of a big, dusty lion baited in its lair and about to growl. But she met his gaze calmly, challenging him to deny what she said, and, after a moment, it fell. There was a long silence.

Then he sighed and pushed his half-finished tankard from him. "If it was battle, I'd know what to do," he said, very quietly, in a voice she seldom heard him use to her and never to anyone else. "I've been a soldier all my life, Hawk. I have an instinct of fighting that I trust, because it's been borne out in battle after battle. But I'm mageborn. Whether I like it or not, there's a wizard inside of me—not buried and whispering, as it is with the mageborn when their powers first stir, but grown and wild as a dragon. I passed through the Great Trial into the fullness of power without getting even the teaching that most mageborn managed to pick up in secret from the local grannies when Altiokis was alive and killing off wizards. It's like being born, not as a baby, but as a man—having no more mind than a baby, but wanting what a man wants."

Broodingly, he cradled the tankard between his blunt-fingered hands. Away from the lamplight near the bar, the shadows were darkening; the wind that ghosted through the door was cooler now than the trapped, stuffy-smelling heat, scented with dust and the wildness of the desert evening.

"There are times when the want consumes me. In the nine months since I came to the power, it's been like a fire inside me, burning me up. That patchwork of learning I was able to pick up in Mandrigyn before I was banished makes no sense to me. I have instincts shouting at me that mean nothing to me, and I don't know whether they're right or will lead me to a quick death and the Cold Hells. Sometimes I wish by all the spirits of my ancestors I'd been born like my father, just a great crafty beast; and other times . . ." He shook his head, with the nearest admission to helplessness Starhawk had seen from him in all the years since they had met.

Impulsively, she leaned across to him and put her hand on his; his fingers closed warm and rough around hers, accepting a comfort neither of them would even have considered a year ago. His hoarse voice was like the scrape of blown sand in the gloom. "There's a vision in me of myself, from long before I came to my powers—one I had as a child, though I couldn't speak of it then. But it's come back to me since I passed through the Great Trial. It's a vision of looking at a great blazing fire and wanting to grasp the core of the flame in my bare hand, knowing it will hurt—but knowing that when the flesh is all burned off, I'll be able to wield that core like a sword."

Behind the long bar of sleeve-polished pine, the owner of the Longhorn was lighting candles—dented tin lusters throwing back a rancid light. Outside, shadows of the spur-ranges of the Dragon's Backbone had covered the town, the hem fringe of the garment of night. Miners, townsmen, and those who rode herd on the tough, long-horned cattle were coming in, dusty and cursing from work. They were mostly the fair-skinned, blond, or red-haired stock of the north, whence the Middle Kingdoms had acquired their slaves, but with a fair sprinkling of the dark-haired people of the Middle Kingdoms themselves, and the black folk of the long, golden coastlines of the southern Megantic. Among them, striking in their white robes and head veils, were the swarthy shirdar, the desert dwellers, who recognized not the King of Wenshar, but the Ancient Houses of the old Desert Lords. Voices jostled in the warm dimness against the smells of old sweat of work-soiled garments, of white or amber liquor, and of the milky sweetness of beeswax. A round-shouldered little black man in his sixties, the tracks of some ancient battle overlying old ornamental scarring on his face, his body hard as twisted ebony from work in spite of the richness of his clothes, ordered drinks for everyone in the place to thunderous applause.

As the owner's boy and girl began circulating with a tray of beer and whiskey, the little man raised his hands. Candle flame caught on his rings. Starhawk, though never much of a looter in her years as a mercenary, had acquired a professional soldier's quick eye; she reckoned each of them at five gold pieces, a staggering sum to be carrying around on one's hands, particularly on the cordillera. In a voice several times the size of his tough little body, the man bellowed, "This drink is for the honor of the Princess Taswind! We'll serve it and we'll fight for it, come what may!"

Though Starhawk had no idea who the Princess Taswind was, she took a blunt pottery cup of liquor the color of henna from the tray the barboy offered her. Sun Wolf shook his head at the offer of another beer. After passing through the Great Trial, it had been months before he'd been able to touch alcohol at all. There was a chorus of cheers, some woman's raucous whoop riding up over them like a descant. Beside the bar one of the brown-faced shirdar warriors pushed back his head veils and raised his cup as the noise subsided a little. "And drink also to her lord and husband to be, Incarsyn of Hasdrozaboth, Lord of the Dunes!" Under the veils, black hair, long and thick as a woman's and braided against the dust, framed a hawk-thin face that was handsome, proud, and very young.

The three warriors with him—all young men *and none of them over twenty*, Starhawk thought—put aside their veils and lifted their cups. Their piercing cry rang against the sudden silence of the room like the discordant clatter of a dropped tray.

The silence in the room was so complete Starhawk could hear the jingle of bridle bits from the horses tied outside. The young man looked around him, his face scarlet with fury and shame. A few feet away at the bar, the tough little black man leaned against the railing, his brown eyes hard with derisive challenge.

Furious, the young man drank off his cup and hurled it at the wall behind the bar. The barkeep ducked aside—the cup itself, harder-fired than the adobe brick, did not even shatter. Silently, the four young shirdar stalked from the room, their white cloaks swirling against the jambs of the open doors as they vanished into the dusk outside.

"Norbas, one of these days you're going to buy yourself a shiv between the ribs," sighed a voice, deep and half-drunken, from the next table. The black man, stepping away from the bar, whirled in surprise. Then his scarred face broke into a blazing white grin as he saw the big man sitting there.

"What the hell are you doing here, Osgard?" He crowded his way over, followed by two or three others, wearing like him the clothes of wealthy townsmen: boned doublets and stiffened linen collars of gaudier hues than were considered good taste north of the mountains, breeches and boots rather than the more sophisticated long hose. The man at the next table was dressed the same way, though with the slight untidiness that spoke, like his slurring voice, of someone who had been drinking since just past noon.

"Can't a man slip out for a drink now and then?" Like Sun Wolf, the man Osgard was big, a thumb-breadth shorter than the Wolf's six feet, fairer than the Wolf and going gray. Like the others, under the richness of his clothes, his body was the body of a man who has both worked and fought. In his broad, unshaven face his green eyes glinted with annoyance. "Maybe I knew I'd meet you here. The match has been made, Norbas, like others before it. I tell you, let it be."

Norbas sniffed scornfully and stiff-armed a pottery cup brimming with the murderous white liquid known locally as Panther Sweat. "I never trusted those sneaky heathens and I never will," he stated flatly. "I bought the round to drink to Tazey's happiness, not to that of some barbarian she has to marry."

"You have a right to think as you please, but you'll come to grief carrying on about it in bars," the man Osgard said a little grimly. "It's for the good of the land; I've told you that before . . ." And like the wash of a sea wave, the noise of other conversations covered theirs.

"It's a clever choice on somebody's part," Sun Wolf rumbled, half to himself, half to Starhawk. "It's sure as pox what I'd do if I ruled Wenshar." He contemplated the man Osgard for a moment against the blurred candlelight with a narrowed eye. "Most of the shirdar lords are fallen into decay—none of them ever ruled more than a couple handfuls of people in all their hundreds of miles of sand, anyway. With one mud-walled city, a string of oases, and a couple hundred goats and camels, Hasdrozaboth's not terribly powerful, but it's ruinously old, like all the Houses of the Desert Lords. But it's an in to the kin network that Wenshar could call on if Dalwirin or Kwest Mralwe invaded them again from the north."

Starhawk nodded, accepting this information without inquiring how Sun Wolf knew it. Back in the days when Sun Wolf had been a mercenary captain and she his second-in-command, part of his success had been due to his minute knowledge of the politics and economics of every kingdom and principality likely to hire his troops. The habit had stayed with him—he gossiped like an old woman with every tale-telling merchant they'd met on the roads. His aim these days was principally to find rumor of a wizard to teach him to use the powers so suddenly arisen within him, but he managed to pick up a good deal of knowledge of other things in the process. Curious, she asked, "If they never had more than a couple hundred warriors, why do you say they're in decay? Decay from what?"

"From ruling the southern trade routes through the desert to the gold mines of Kimbu," he replied promptly. "The Lords of Wenshar—not the King now, but the Ancient House of the old Lords of Wenshar—ruled the whole desert, back when the Empire of Gwenth was still around in the north for Kimbu to trade with."

"Silly me," apologized Starhawk ironically, and Sun Wolf gave her a grin, half-embarrassed at his own sudden show of erudition, and squeezed the fingers still lightly clasped in his own.

They ordered dinner; through it Sun Wolf alternated between watching the increasing crowd in the tavern and particularly around the next table, where Osgard and Norbas were holding a sort of court for what looked like the wealthier miners, and relapsing into his own thoughts. By the look on his face, Starhawk thought he didn't care much for them, but she had learned long ago when to keep her silence. Full dark fell outside; Osgard and his friends departed singing; the local Children of Joy, youths as well as girls, began to make their appearance. Pergemis silks of rose and violet shimmered softly in the ochre lamplight, and painted eyes teased. When the tavern girl came to clear up, Sun Wolf signed to her to stay. "Where would I find the house of the Lady Kaletha? The wizard?"

The girl hastily sketched in the air the sign against evil. "She'll be up at the Fortress of Tandieras," she mumbled. "But if you need a healer or something, go to Yellow Sincress in Leatherworker's Row. He's . . ."

"Tandieras?" asked Sun Wolf, surprised to hear her name the fortress of the King.

The girl nodded, her dark eyes avoiding his. She was fourteen or so, gawky and plain, with the hawk features of the shirdar in the frame of her straight black braids. "Yeah. She's part of the King's Household." She gathered the pottery dishes with their vivid glazes of yellow and blue onto her tray and prepared to go. Sun Wolf dug into his pouch and dropped a quarter of a silver bit into the empty bread plate. The dark eyes raised to his, startled and shining.

"And where is the Fortress?" Sun Wolf got to his feet, readjusting the set of the sword at his hip.

"You're not gonna go *tonight*?" There was sudden, baffled fear in the girl's plunging brows. "She's a *witch*!" She used the shirdar word for it, and there was loathing in her voice.

"Funny," Starhawk remarked later, as they walked up Main Street, leaning into the steep slope of the hill upon which the town was built. "Most of the people we've met on the road figured wizards are something that died out a long time ago, if they ever existed to begin with. But she was afraid."

With the final sinking of the sun, the hot blast of the desert daylight had given way to dry and bitter cold. Dust hung in the air, the smell of it a constant with which they had lived for days; it blurred the lights of the inns and houses they passed, twinkling amber-gold in the ultramarine darkness. They'd added sheepskin coats to their doublets and still felt the thin lance of the desert night. They had left their horses behind at the inn—it had been a long journey, and the beasts were badly overridden.

Above them, thready moonlight touched the gilded turrets of the Cathedral of the Triple God, triumphant fingers stretching from the highest peak of the town. Higher still, the jagged peaks of the Dragon's Backbone loomed, massive granite domes and sugarloaves, with here and there unscalable plugs of black basalt—dry teeth goring at the stars.

Sun Wolf nodded thoughtfully as they turned along the face of the hill. Ahead of them, a mile or so from the town, the lights of the Fortress of Tandieras winked against the rocky bulk of the spur-range on which it was built. Like a moat, darkness lay before it where the road dipped from the flank of Pardle Hill, a long stretch of gully, boulder, and sand. From the dense shadows, the topmost twigs of a desiccated acacia tree reached up into the moonlight like crooked reeds above spring floods—for the rest it was pitchy dark. Starhawk's every nerve came alert. It was a patch of road made for robbers.

"There may be a reason for it," Sun Wolf said after a few moments. "But I'd fear Kaletha for different reasons. She's arrogant. She's young, Hawk, younger than you. I'm not saying no wizard that young can hold the kind of power she claims to hold, but, if one did, I think I'd feel it." The rock shadows loomed darkly around them. Starhawk's fingers touched the comforting hardness of her sword. Half her mind turned from the Wolf's scratchy wheeze to the soft whisper of shadow sounds. "She should still be a student, not claiming to be able to teach the secrets of the universe to a bunch of fatuous disciples."

"If she teaches you anything," Starhawk pointed out, "she'll have . . ."

Sun Wolf's hand tapped her shoulder for silence a split instant before she heard, faint and muffled, a man's cry and smelled the drift of kicked dust and blood on the night wind. Then there was the ringing whine of a drawn sword, and a voice thick with liquor yelled, "Rot your eyes, you scum-sucking swine . . . !"

The Wolf was already scrambling up over the rocks in the darkness.

Without a word passing between them, Starhawk knew what the plan was and moved forward at a soundless run toward the barely visible bend in the dark road. From the other side of the overhanging rocks, she heard the searing ring of steel on steel and a man's voice shouting, "Help! MURDER!" The scrub along the edge of the road would give more away by its noise than it would conceal in that pitchy dark; Starhawk felt, rather than actually saw, the wide bay between the boulders to her right, sensed violent movement somewhere in the Stygian blackness, and heard the sounds of struggle.

A white blur on the ground turned out to be the face and hands of a dead man amid a stench of spilled blood. She sprang noiselessly over him. Ahead of her, another man was backed to the gray-black front of a massive boulder—pale face, pale hands, the white V of a shirt visible through an unlaced doublet. Ill-defined forms danced before him. Starlight glinted on steel. Starhawk ran one of his black-cloaked attackers through the body before the man had time to realize what was happening. He let out a gasping death scream, and the other assailants turned upon her in a body.

Then, from the top of the rocks, there was a berserker howl, and Sun Wolf was among them. Starhawk caught barely a glimpse of him as he dropped into the darkness. She found by instinct the shoulder of another dark form near to her, caught the thick cloth of his cloak, and shoved her sword up under his ribs as he turned toward the new threat. As she pulled the blade clear in a sticky gush of hot blood over her hand, she glimpsed the white robe beneath the cloak, already staining with the welling blood. Shirdar, she thought, turning and ducking the slash of a curved tulwar, cutting at breast level, and parrying steel that whined within inches of her face. The victim of the ambush had sailed into the fray, fighting like a drunken man with yells of fury. From the road behind them, hooves thudded and lanterns swayed in the darkness; reflected light showed Starhawk the gleam of a sword, and she cut in the darkness where the body would be. Her blade met nothing; the man had turned, and she heard the scrunch of his soft boots on gravel as he fled.

Beside her, the man they'd rescued was yelling, "Here! To me!"—with, Starhawk thought wryly, considerable optimism about whose side the reinforcements were on. A blue burst of witchlight flared in the darkness, the ghostly blaze turning Sun Wolf's craggy features and gore-slimed sword blade into a hashish vision of some barbarian berserker god. He had evidently decided that darkness was no longer to his advantage. By the faint St. Elmo's fire, Starhawk could see the last attackers fleeing into the shadows of the rocks, leaving their dead stretched upon the thin dust of the ground. Men and women in some kind of dark green livery studded with smoked steel were urging their horses down from the road, springing from their saddles to dart in pursuit, until their captain raised his hand and called them back.

"It's useless—don't get yourselves killed over it!" He reined up before Starhawk and the man beside her, the man she now recognized as Osgard from the tavern. The horseman stepped from his saddle with surprising grace for a man of his bulk. "Are you hurt, my lord?"

"By the Three, that was fighting!" Osgard flung an approving arm around Sun Wolf as he came up to them, the heavy sheepskin of his jerkin marked with a sword slash, but apparently unwounded himself. "You never saw the like, Nanciormis! This bastard had them running like rats—like rats!" Standing that close to him, Starhawk could smell, under the reek of the blood that smeared them all, stale alcohol in his sweat.

As tall as Osgard and Sun Wolf, the rider Nanciormis had the swarthy skin and aquiline features of the shirdar. What had once been a hawk-like beauty was blurred by a padded layer of fat. "My lord . . ." The other riders were closing in around them, and the torches they bore threw glints of gold on the clips that held back his waist-length black hair. "I've warned you before about going about the town so, unprotected and with no state . . ."

"State, hell," grumbled Osgard, bending to wipe his sword on the black robe of one of the fallen bandits and sheathing it at his side. His voice had lost its drunken slur—there's nothing like fighting for your life, thought Starhawk, to induce instant sobriety. "It wasn't state that got me crowned King of Wenshar."

Starhawk's glance cut sharply to Sun Wolf. She saw that he wasn't surprised.

"It was men like Norbas Milkom and Quaal Ambergados—miners and fighters, men who know the land. Men like . . ." Osgard turned and regarded Sun Wolf with an arrested eye. "I know you," he said.

Sun Wolf nodded. "Likely you do, your Majesty."

"Not just from the tavern . . ." The green eyes narrowed. "You're Sun Wolf. The mercenary of Wrynde. We hired you—what . . . ?"

"Last war but one with Dalwirin," Sun Wolf provided. "Old Shilmarne was leading her forces down the passes . . ."

"By the Three, that was it!" The King slapped Sun Wolf enthusiastically on the back, then staggered. He'd taken a thigh wound, and blood was still tracking stickily down the leg of his breeches. Sun Wolf and Starhawk caught him as his knees gave way, Nanciormis springing belatedly to help.

Osgard made an impatient move to push them off. "I'm fine . . ."

"The hell you are," Sun Wolf rasped. He pulled from some inner pocket the silk scarf he'd long ago learned to keep handy and tied it around Osgard's leg above the wound. With the hilt of one of the hideout daggers in his boot, he twisted it tight. In the yellow glare of the torchlight, the King's face had gone suddenly waxen as the heat of battle died from his veins. "There a sawbones up at the fortress?"

Nanciormis nodded. "Can you sit a horse, my—"

"Of course I can sit a horse!" Osgard blustered furiously. "Just because I took a little scratch doesn't mean I'm going to go to pieces like some sniveling, weakling coward . . ." His sandy eyebrows stood out darkly against his gray flesh, and, like a candle being blown out, he fainted.

"Good," Sun Wolf grunted, as they eased him gently back to lay him on the sand. "With luck he'll stay unconscious and won't argue about his pox-rotted manhood all the way up to the Fortress."

The guards looked shocked, but, in the commander Nanciormis' eye, he caught the flicker of an appreciative grin.

CHAPTER

2

*I*N THE FORTRESS OF TANDIERAS SUPPER WAS OVER, THE TRESTLE TA-
bles in the Great Hall put away, and the chairs and benches pushed
back against the walls of the vast, granite room which was the old
castle's heart. Like the Longhorn Inn, it was lit chiefly by wall sconces
whose polished metal reflectors threw back the soft beeswax glow into
the room, but here the height of the ceiling, though it added to the
cold, at least relieved the smoke. In addition, a huge fireplace
stretched along one side of the feasting-dais at the far end, around
which carved chairs were clustered, and two chandeliers dangled—
unlit, massive, ominous iron wheels—in the dense shadows overhead.

But Sun Wolf's first impression, as he stepped through the triple
archway that led from the vestibule into the Hall, was one of color,
gaiety, and movement. Since it was the season of sandstorms, the big
wooden shutters that guarded the line of tall windows on the room's
southern wall had been closed nearly to for the night. Servants in drab
shirts and breeches, gently born retainers in colorful broadcloth and
white ruffs, and guards in dark green leather were grouped around the
sides of the Hall, clapping in time to the music of pipes, flutes, and the
fast, heartbreaking throb of a hand-drum; in the center of the Hall, lit
by hand-held lamps and torches all around her, a girl was doing a war
dance.

It was one of the old war dances of the Middle Kingdoms, done these days for the sheer joy of its violent measures. A young man and a girl in guard's uniforms stood aside, sweat-soaked and panting, having clearly just finished their turn. As the dancer's shadow flickered across them, the blades below her glinted. They were using live weapons. But for all the concern on her face, the girl might have been dancing around and over a circle of wheat sheaves; her feet, clad in light riding boots under a kilted-up skirt, tapped at will, now this side, now that side, of the blued edges of the upturned swords. She looked to be about sixteen; her sand-blond hair, mixed fair and dark, caught the light on its thick curls; the torches were not brighter than her eyes.

Beside him, Sun Wolf was aware of Nanciormis striding through the arch into the room, his mouth open to call out the ill news. Sun Wolf caught the man's thick arm and said softly, "Don't startle her."

The guards' commander saw what he meant and checked, then blustered, "No, of course I wasn't going to." He signaled one of the pages to come over and whispered hasty instructions to the boy. The young face paled in the torchlight with shock. "Go on!" Nanciormis ordered, and the page went slipping off through the crowd toward the little knot of gentlemen-in-waiting who stood between the fireplace and the door that led from the dais to the King's solar beyond. Nanciormis glanced defensively back at Sun Wolf. "We can't let his Majesty remain out in the cold court!"

At that moment the music skirled to its circling conclusion; the girl stood panting and radiant in the tawny halo of the lights. A woman hastened down to her from the crowd on the dais, skinny and flustery, her narrow, white face framed unbecomingly in tight-pulled, black hair. She dressed in black, too; the harshness of the color triggered something in Sun Wolf's memory. She had been one of Kaletha's disciples in the public gardens that afternoon. She touched the girl's arm and said something. Stricken, the girl turned eyes wide with shock and green as absinthe toward the doorway; without a word she strode toward them, the black-clothed governess hurrying behind like a skinny ewe sheep who has fostered a gazelle.

"Uncle, is Father all right?" she demanded as soon as she got near enough to Sun Wolf and Nanciormis to speak. "Anshebbeth says—"

"Your father's fine, Tazey."

"You ought to send at once for the Lady Kaletha," the black-clothed woman panted, fussing up behind them. "She can—"

"We already did, Anshebbeth."

"I could go look for her—I know right where she is . . ."

"It's been taken care of." Nanciormis' voice was soothing. Ansheb-beth's long white fingers clasped and unclasped nervously; her huge, dark eyes darted to Nanciormis' face, then to Sun Wolf's body—a look that was covert but unmistakable—then back again, her cheeks color-ing slightly. Sun Wolf wondered whether the blush was because he was aware of the thoughts behind that look or simply that she was. Unaware, Nanciormis went on easily, "Captain Sun Wolf—my niece, the Princess Taswind—her governess the Lady Anshebbeth."

Guards were carrying the unconscious King into the hall. Gentle-men and ladies hurried to open the door through to the solar and to kindle lamps there; Tazey sprang after them, catching up her skirts as if impatient with their weight. Sun Wolf observed the lace trim of her petticoat and the slim strength of her calf in its soft boot before the sharp jab of a bony knee in his thigh made him look around; but Starhawk, who had materialized at his side, was looking around the room, innocently impassive.

Down in the hall, one of the underservants, a thickset hag with puffy ankles showing under a kilted-up skirt and black eyes glinting through a straggling pelt of gray hair, called out in a screechy voice, "Slow getting out the back window, was he, when the husband came home? Hard to run with his breeches around his ankles!"

Tazey didn't even check her stride, but Anshebbeth stopped, stiff with rage and indignation, torn for a moment between staying to take issue with the old woman and remaining with her nurseling. Then, as if she realized she would not come off the better in any battle of words, she spun and hurried after Tazey into the narrow solar door.

"Did you see who they were?" Nanciormis asked quietly, as he led Sun Wolf and the Hawk toward the carved chairs on the dais near the fire. A servant girl came up to take his heavy white cloak and returned his smile with a saucy wink; Sun Wolf, as he and Starhawk divested themselves of their scarred sheepskin coats, observed that Nanciormis drew the admiring eyes of several of the women of the Household. Though corpulent, he was a good-looking man still; but beyond that, Sun Wolf guessed he was the type of man whose vitality would attract women, no matter how fat he became. Even on short acquaintance and in spite of his carelessness about breaking into the delicate concentra-tion needed for the war dance, Sun Wolf found the man likable.

He made a mental note to take that into account.

"Your people, it looked like."

Nanciormis checked his stride. His long hair, braided down from the temples and hanging in a loose mane of black curls behind, caught the sheen of the lamps as he jerked his head around.

"The shirdar—the desert folk," the Wolf went on. "There was a little trouble at the Longhorn—four of 'em proposed a toast to the Princess Taswind's prospective husband—I take it the match is about as popular as maggots in the beer hereabouts. A man named Norbas Milkom was the cause of it, though why they attacked the King . . ."

The commander groaned, and all wariness fled from his eyes. "I should have known. No, the match isn't a popular one." He grinned ruefully and took a seat in one of the chairs by the hearth—heavy ebony from the forests of Kimbu in the south, recushioned with local work of red leather. "Beyond a doubt, they attacked the King because he was foolish enough to walk back alone—unlike our canny Norbas. It's known throughout the desert they've been friends for forty years —if indeed they were the same shirdar as the ones at the Longhorn."

A servant came up—the same who had taken their coats—with an intricately worked brass tray of wine cups and dates in a hammered silver bowl. Sun Wolf saw now that she, like Nanciormis and, he guessed, Anshebbeth also, was of the shirdar, though without the reserved dignity of their ways. Along the foothills, they must have been living among and marrying with the ex-slaves of the north for generations. When she thought no one was looking, she mouthed a kiss at Nanciormis; he received it with a suppressed smile and a dance of pleasure in his pouchy dark eyes.

He went on, "They may have been merely bandits—there are a lot of them along the cordillera—or they may have been operating by the same logic used by the men of Wenshar when they kill Hasdrozidar of the Dunes or Seifidar of the White Erg in retaliation for Regidar slave-raids, not troubling to inquire the truth. All of our people here are looked upon with mistrust by those who came from the north of the mountains."

"With reason," a quiet voice said at his elbow. Sitting with his back to a corner and his blind side to Starhawk, Sun Wolf had seen the slender old man approach them—he would, indeed, have been difficult to miss. He was wearing what Starhawk irreverently described as the undress uniform of Trinitarian bishops, and his scarlet surcoat and gold tabard picked up the torchlight on their bullion embroidery as if the old man were netted all over with a spiderweb of flame. Garnet and rock crystal flashed from the worked medallions of sacred signs; even the sleeves of his white under-robe were stitched with tiny seed pearls. Under all that finery, the old man would have been as pretty as a girl before he grew his beard; full, slightly pouting red lips showed beneath the silky white mustaches; the eyes with their snowy lashes were the clear blue of morning sky.

In a soft, light voice, the Bishop went on, "It is fellowship of worship that binds men together in trust, Nanciormis. You have converted to the true faith of the Triple God, but can the same be said of the shirdar in the guards? It can not. They cling to their old superstitions, their familial cults and wind djinns. How can any true worshiper believe their oaths?"

"I'm sure they can't," Starhawk remarked, lying half-slouched in her chair and regarding him with mild gray eyes. "But the question's rather academic, isn't it, since the Doctrines of Calcedus say that true worshipers aren't obliged to keep oaths made to the followers of untrue gods."

The old Bishop spread his hands deprecatingly. "We are doves in the midst of serpents, Warlady," he explained. "We need such subterfuge to survive."

She studied the obvious wealth and power reflected in those splendid robes and glanced over at Sun Wolf. "I never met a Trinitarian yet who didn't have a good explanation for everything."

The Bishop inclined his white head. "It is because all truths are revealed to us by Holy Scripture."

There was a stirring in the shadows beyond the fireplace; Sun Wolf had already, in his automatic identification of every potential exit from the room, seen the narrow door half-hidden beside the blackened granite of the mantle. Now Kaletha stepped through into the light, followed by another one of her disciples, the only one that afternoon who had not, like her, worn black. Since what he did wear was the blue and gold habit of a Trinitarian novice, he was naturally taken aback when he saw the Bishop. He said, rather loudly, "As I told you, my Lady Kaletha, the King is in his bedchamber beyond the solar."

"Thank you, Egaldus." Kaletha inclined her head graciously and moved toward the dais in a queenly swishing of homespun black robes. After a second's hesitation, the young man, fair-haired and rather nervous looking, turned with clearly manufactured decisiveness and went bustling away in the other direction. Sun Wolf's glance slid to the Bishop, but the old man didn't seem to suspect anything; he was watching Kaletha's approach with a disapproving eye.

"A pity," he said, "that the only healer in the fortress should be a witch."

Kaletha paused on the outside of the ring of firelight, regarding them with an expression that could have nipped spring flowers in their buds. Sun Wolf, feeling that frigid glance pause for a moment on him before passing on, was suddenly conscious of the dust in his clothes and hair and the bruises from the fight that marked his face; Kaletha looked away, as if to say one could have expected to find Sun Wolf on hand in the aftermath of a brawl. To the Bishop she said, "We've been over it time and again, Galdron. It's scarcely likely that your condemnation of my powers one more time will cause me to go against what I know to be my destiny and my duty."

"It is scarcely likely," agreed the little man mildly, "but, as Bishop of Wenshar and responsible for the salvation of your soul from the sulfurous hells reserved for witches, I can yet hope."

The answer was so pat that Sun Wolf was barely able to stifle a snort of laughter; Kaletha's eye flicked to him, like a chilly draft, and then away again. *If wishes were horses*, Sun Wolf thought wryly, *there'd be hoofprints all over my hide* . . .

"Excuse me, Commander, Captain," the Bishop said, as Kaletha turned and crossed the dais to the doorway of the King's solar. "I should probably be present when she attends to the King."

"I take it she's the only sawbones you could get?" the Wolf asked, as the Bishop, like a glittering little doll, hastened to follow the tall, red-haired woman through the door. In the hall before them, things were quieting down. The gray-haired hag, in the midst of a gaggle of grooms and laundresses, was recounting some story to snickers of ribald laughter. The Trinitarian novice, Sun Wolf observed, had in truth had no other business—he was still hanging around the archways into the vestibule, talking with two others of Kaletha's disciples: a fattish boy of sixteen or so and a thin, worried-looking young woman, both dressed, like Kaletha and Anshebbeth, in black.

"On the contrary," Nanciormis said, sipping the wine the servant had left and offering Sun Wolf the hammered bowl of dates. "Kaletha's only recently come to that position, in the absence of anything better. Since she's decided she's going to be a wizard, she evidently considers it a part of her much-vaunted 'destiny.' But she's always been part of the Household."

"Has she?" the Wolf asked thoughtfully. *It would account*, he thought, *for that bitter defensiveness.* It was said that no prophet was without honor except in their own home village. Even he, when he'd announced to his former mercenary troops on his brief visit to Wrynde that spring that he'd become a wizard, had at least done so after going away and coming back. The Wizard King Altiokis had brooked no competition; Kaletha could not have so much as hinted at her powers while he was still alive. She'd had to announce it cold, to people who'd known her all her life. His too-ready imagination framed the notion of claiming wizardy in the village where he'd been raised, and his soul cringed from the thought.

Nanciormis shrugged casually. "She was lady-in-waiting to my sister, Osgard's wife, the Lady Ciannis. When Ciannis died, Osgard kept her on in the Household as librarian, since she had a turn for it. It wasn't until news came of the Wizard King's death that she declared herself to be mageborn and began to teach others."

He laughed, shortly and scornfully. "Not that anything's ever come of it that I've been able to see. Oh, she claims to be able to teach magic, but who are her disciples? A lot of soured spinsters and frustrated virgins who haven't anything better to do with their lives."

"You don't believe her power's real, then?" It must have been the reaction of most of the people in the fortress.

Nanciormis waved a deprecating hand, chubby but strong with its ancient rings of worn gold. "Oh, I'll admit the woman has magic—perhaps some of those poor fools who follow her do as well. But why pursue it? What can it buy you that money cannot? It's been a hundred and fifty years since the old city of Wenshar in the desert was destroyed because of the witcheries practiced there, but, believe me, the local feeling toward it hasn't changed."

Sun Wolf cocked his head a little, remembering the way the girl in the inn had made the sign against evil. *But she's a witch*, she had said. "Why is that?" he asked. "What happened in Wenshar?"

The doors of the solar opened, and Tazey emerged without her governess, looking anxious and preoccupied. Nanciormis glanced at the dark doorway behind her and said softly, "Least said of that is best. Have you paid for rooms in town, Captain? Osgard will want to see you in the morning, I'm sure. We can offer you bunks in the Men's

Hall . . ." He gestured toward a wide arched door halfway down the Hall. ". . . and the Women's." His nod took in the narrow entrance beyond the hearth. "Or if you choose, we can give you a cell to share down near the stable courts, in the empty quarter of the fortress. It's mostly old workshops, kitchens, and barracks, but the closer rooms still have roofs and they're shuttered against storms, should one rise in the night."

Sun Wolf recognized by the inquiring gleam in the commander's eye that the offer was prompted as much by curiosity as by hospitality; he said, "We'll take the room out by the stables," and saw the big man nod to himself, as if he'd satisfied in his mind the relationship between the two partners and how he must deal with them.

From the solar door, the Bishop Galdron emerged, looking fastidious and disapproving; behind him came Kaletha, the gold lamplight deepening the lines of tiredness and disapproval on her fine-boned face, showing up her age, which the Wolf guessed at a year one side or the other of thirty. Anshebbeth fussed at her heels, as if Kaletha's comfort, not Tazey's, was her primary concern. But Tazey, standing near her uncle Nanciormis' chair, said nothing—evidently she understood her governess' discipleship. From across the room, the two other disciples hurried toward their teacher's side, only the novice keeping his watchful distance.

Pointedly ignoring Sun Wolf, the little group made for the doors.

Sun Wolf sighed. He had wanted to put this off until they were not in public, but his sense of timing warned him that to do so would only make the situation worse. There were some things which had to be done at the first available opportunity. He got to his feet and said, "Lady Kaletha."

Her step wavered. She was debating, he thought, whether to make him call out to her and follow her. *If she does,* he thought grimly, with a momentary vision of shaking her until her pearly teeth rattled . . . Then he let it go. Whatever she had, it was what he desperately needed. He would have to ask for it, in whatever fashion she dictated. *Stubborn, cake-mouthed female . . .*

Kaletha took another step, then seemed to change her mind, and stopped. She turned back, chin elevated, cornflower blue eyes regarding him as if he were a beggar.

He'd had runs up to enemy seige towers under fire that he'd enjoyed more. "My lady," he said, his raw, rasping voice neither loud nor furtively quiet, "I'm sorry. I had no right to say what I said to you today, and I ask your forgiveness for speaking stupidly." He forced his single eye to meet hers, aware of the stares of her disciples and of the others—servants, grooms, laundresses, guards, Taswind, and Nanciormis—in the Hall. He felt as he had during the Rites of Manhood in his village in the north long ago, stripped before the eyes of the tribe and obliged to take whatever abuse the shaman chose to give him. Only in that case, he thought dryly, at least those who watched him approved of what he sought to gain by the humiliation. That had been the last time, he realized, that he had ever asked for anything.

The chilly sweetness of her voice was as he remembered it from the gardens. "Do you say that because you are truly sorry," she asked, "or because you know that I will not share my wisdom with you unless you apologize?"

Sun Wolf took a deep breath. At least she had answered him, and spoken to him as if she would listen to what he said. "Both," he said.

It took away any possibility of an accusation of untruth and left her momentarily nonplussed. Then her blue eyes narrowed again. "At least you're honest," she said, as if sorry to learn of it. "That is the first thing you'll have to learn about the arts of wizardry, if you pursue them, Captain. Honesty is almost as important to the study of wizardry as is purity of the body and the soul. You must be honest—utterly honest—at all times, and you must learn to accept the honesty of others."

"You weren't too pleased about my honesty this afternoon."

She didn't miss a beat. "Those were not your true feelings. If you look into your heart, I think you'll find that it was your jealousy of me speaking what you wished to see, not what you actually saw."

With great effort Sun Wolf stifled the first words that came to his lips. *She can teach me,* he reminded himself grimly. *She's the only one I have found to teach me. The rest of it is none of my affair.* But he couldn't resist saying, carefully keeping the irony from his voice, "I expect you'd know more about that than I would, my lady."

From the corner of his eye he saw the impassive Starhawk put her tongue in her cheek, raise her eyebrows, and look away. But Kaletha nodded gravely, accepting his words on their face value and taking them as a deserved tribute to her clarity of insight. "It is something that comes when one has achieved a certain level of understanding." Behind her, her disciples nodded wisely, like a well-trained chorus.

"You must learn to accept discipline, to understand self-control. They may be alien to you . . ."

"I've been a warrior all my life," Sun Wolf said, annoyed. "There *is* discipline involved in that, you know."

"It isn't at all the same thing," she responded serenely, and he bit back, *How the hell would you know?*

Patronizingly, she went on, "I've studied long and hard to achieve my power, Captain. It is my destiny to teach. With meditation and with spells, I can reach the deepest parts of the mind. The mind is all, if the body is pure—all magic comes from the purified intellect. I can wake powers in anyone, even in those who are not mageborn, if they are willing, honest, and pure." She cast another chilly look up and down his big, heavily muscled form, as if seeing through his dusty clothes and disapproving of what she saw. Her glance moved past him, touched Starhawk, and the lines of disapproval pinched a little deeper at the corners of her mouth. "That's something you'll have to learn to accept, if you wish to enter into your powers."

Anger heated in him, as she had no doubt meant it to; words crowded to his lips about frustrated spinsters who made a virtue of the fact that no man would tumble them on a bet. But, with a physical effort, he closed his muscles around those words like a fist. *To buy the bread,* he thought, *you couldn't insult the baker*—and in any case, what she thought about magic was none of his business.

But he'd be damn lucky, he thought dourly, looking at that pale, fine-boned face in the torchlight, if he didn't end by strangling the woman with her own long, red hair.

In his long silence, she studied him appraisingly. She had expected, he realized, some other reaction. After a moment she went on, "If you feel you have the strength and willingness to follow that path, come to me where I teach in the public gardens tomorrow afternoon."

She inclined her head with a graciousness that made Sun Wolf long to slap her and prepared to move off. Down in the Hall, the old laundress called out to her, "I'll bet you're pleased to have him join you—as a change from boys and women!"

Kaletha's face flushed with anger as she turned. Around the dirty old hag, the other laundresses and grooms were bellowing with laughter. As in the garden that afternoon, Kaletha was momentarily speechless with anger. In a flash of insight, Sun Wolf realized that, having no sense of humor, she was unable to slide from beneath this kind of indignity, unable even to understand it. And she must, he thought, have had to put up with it daily since she had announced her wizardry to the world.

All this went through his mind in an instant; as Kaletha drew breath to stammer some reply, he cut in over her words, "It's the sow in rut that squeals the loudest."

The old crone and her friends went into even louder guffaws. "Come down to the laundry and see, you old boar!"

He gave an elaborate shrug. "I haven't got all night to stand in the line."

The laundress laughed so hard he could easily have counted her teeth, had she possessed any. He turned back to Kaletha and said quietly, "I'll be there tomorrow, my Lady, after I've seen the King."

As he and Starhawk walked from the hall, he was aware of Kaletha's speculative gaze upon his back.

The empty quarter of the fortress of Tandieras lay beyond the stables, a picked gray skeleton in the wan monochromes of dawn. From where he lay on the wide bed of waffle-crossed latigo and cottonwood poles, Sun Wolf could see through the half-open shutters of the window a broken labyrinth of crumbling adobe walls, fallen roofs, and scattered tiles—what had once been garrison quarters for the troops of Dalwirin, seige housing for the population of their administrative town, and barracoons for hundreds of slave miners. It was deserted now, covering several acres of ground; among the many things his father had considered unmanly for a warrior to possess had been an aesthetic sense, and Sun Wolf seldom admitted to anyone that he found such things as the stripped shapes of rock and wall or the sculpted dunes carved by the will of the wind beautiful.

Extending his senses, as he had learned to in the meditations Starhawk had taught him, he could feel life stirring in the ruins still. Somewhere desert rats scrabbled over crumbled bricks; somewhere snakes lay dreaming in old ovens, waiting for the sun to warm their cold blood. He felt the quick, furtive flick of a jerboa heading for its burrow. Though it was light enough now to make out the fallen bricks, the dun-colored walls with their drifts of piled sand, and the thrusting black spikes of camel-thorn and bullweed against them, there was not yet any sound of birds.

Traveling along the hem of the desert, he had grown familiar with all of them—sand warblers and wheatears and the soft, timid murmur of rock doves. The wells in the empty quarter should have drawn them by the hundreds.

He frowned.

Against his shoulder, Starhawk still slept, all her cheetah deadliness loosened and her thin face peaceful, her short crop of white-blonde hair ruffled and sticking up like a child's. The Wolf liked to think of his relationship with this woman whom he had known so long as one of equals, warriors of matched strength and capability. But at times like this, he was conscious of feeling toward her a desperate tenderness, a desire to shelter and protect, wholly at odds with their daytime selves or the lion-like lusts of the deep night. He grinned a little at himself— Starhawk was probably the least protectable woman he'd ever encountered.

I'm getting old, he thought ruefully. There was no fear in it, though a year ago it would have terrified him; he felt only amusement at himself. *Old and soft.*

Like the ruins, Starhawk's was a beauty of rocks and bones and scars. Moving his head a little, he kissed the delicate curve of bone on the outer corner of her eye.

Still there was no sound of birds.

His sleep had been unrestful, troubled by inchoate dreams. His anger at Kaletha had bitten deep; he realized that the anger was also at fate, at his ancestors, and at the fact that he'd had to go cap-in-hand to a woman and swallow her self-righteous insults, because only she could give him what he needed. In Wrynde, he remembered, it had been whispered that, like the mad God of the Bards, he had traded his eye for wisdom—he only wished that had been the case.

Yet he knew that Starhawk had been right, as she usually was. What angered him most about Kaletha—her arrogant assumption that she needed no teacher and that she herself was qualified to judge her own progress and that of others—was precisely what he himself was doing in refusing to accept her tutelage.

Beside him, Starhawk moved in her sleep, her arm tightening around his ribcage as if she found reassurance in the touch. He stroked her shoulder, the skin silky under his hand, and gazed out at the pink reflections warming the upper edges of the ruined walls. A stir of wind brought him the warm smell of the stables and the drift of baking bread from the palace kitchens.

Then the wind shifted, and he smelled blood.

Whether Starhawk smelled it, too, and reacted with the hair-trigger reflexes of a warrior in her sleep, or whether she simply felt the stiffening of his muscles, he didn't know, but a moment later her gray eyes were blinking up into his. She'd been in deep sleep a moment ago, but she neither moved nor spoke, instinctively keeping silence against any possible threat.

"Do you smell it?" he asked softly, but the wind had shifted again. There were only the scents of burning wood and baking bread from the kitchens. *So it isn't just the smell of chicken-killing for tonight's dinner*, he thought to himself.

She shook her head. All the childlike helplessness of sleep had dissolved into what it really was—his own fancies—and the woman who had curled so trustingly into his shoulder had a knife in her hand, ready for anything. Starhawk, the Wolf reflected with a grin, was the only person he knew who could be stark naked and still produce a concealed weapon at a second's notice.

"It's probably nothing," he said. "I heard jackals and pariah-dogs out in the empty quarter last night . . ." He frowned again and closed his eye, stilling his mind as he had often done scouting, listening as a wizard listens. The empty quarter was silent. No murmur of the doves that must nest there, no shrill cries of swifts, though it was time and past time when birds called their territories. Though the red trace of blood touched his nostrils again, he could hear no stealthy pad of jackal feet, no querulous snarls of scavenger rats. In the stables nearby a horse nickered softly over its morning feed; a girl began to sing.

Soundlessly, the Wolf rolled out of bed, found his boots and the buckskin trousers he'd worn down from Wrynde, his shirt and doublet, and his belt with sword and daggers. When Starhawk moved to join him, he shook his head and said again, "I don't think it's anything. I'll be back."

The cold was sharp on his face and throat as he stepped out of the little room, a cell in a line of low cells that could have been workshops, guest rooms or makeshift prisons along a narrow, sandy court just off the stables. A storm last week had drifted sand deep against the eastern walls; the adobe faces of the buildings showed marks where pebbles and flying chunks of stone had gouged the softer brick. The other cells of the court were deserted. A pack rat went flicking around the doorpost of one to the shelter of the shadows within.

Cautiously, Sun Wolf moved into the empty quarter. He found the place quite quickly, stalking through the silent maze of empty rooms and fallen beams, caved-in cellars and old wells shrouded thick in greedy vegetation. He had been expecting something, from the smell, but, even so, what he saw filled him with a loathing he could not explain.

The door of the little adobe workshop had been torn off years ago by the killer sandstorms of the desert; most of the roof tiles had blown away, though rafters barred the open, warming sky. The walls were streaked with years' worth of dove droppings, where they were not painted over with splashes of blood.

White and gray feathers were stuck in it and in the puddles on the floor that were still slick and only tacky-dry. From where he stood in the doorway, the Wolf could see the curled, pink feet and torn-off heads of the birds thrown into the corners, already half-invisible under swarming clots of ants.

He made a move to step into the room, but then drew back. There was something loathesome here, foul and utterly evil—a psychic stench that drove him back in fear, although he knew that whatever had done this was gone. He had sacked cities from the Megantic Sea to the Western Ocean and, when it was necessary to make his point, had cut men and women up alive. He did not know why that small cube of adobe-walled dawnlight and rafter-crossed sky, silent but for the persistent humming of flies, should turn him sick.

Only three or four doves were dead, less than he'd eat for supper. It was, he reminded himself, no business of his who had killed them, or why.

But he was a good enough tracker to see, with even the most cursory examination, that there were no footmarks, either entering the room or leaving it.

CHAPTER

3

"*DAMNED WOMAN." OSGARD ANTIVAR, KING OF WENSHAR* and nominal Lord of all the K'Chin Desert, propped himself up on the low ebony divan and impatiently shoved aside the blue silk pillow from beneath his left knee. "Says she won't be responsible if the wound opens up again. Damn her, *I'll* be responsible! I'm not going to lie here like a maiden lady with the vapors all day!" The tray of silver-traced copper on the delicate, jointed shirdar camp table beside the couch contained a decanter of wine, but, pointedly, only one wine cup.

The King fished beneath the divan's pillows and produced a second one, which he slopped full. "Sit down, Captain, and drink up. You can, even if I'm not supposed to. Damned woman." Against the vivid reds and blues of the loose bed-robe he wore over shirt and breeches, he still looked gray from loss of blood, save for where the slight flush of fever colored his pouchy cheeks. "I could stand her when she was just the damn librarian. She kept her place, then."

Sun Wolf took the indicated chair—like the divan, of heavy, gilt-trimmed ebony—looted fifty years ago from the Governor's Palace and recently reupholstered in a local red wool. The King's solar was a big room, built out of the end of the Hall, and lined with windows on two sides. The ever-present storm shutters had been thrown open, and morning sunlight poured through, dazzling on the glass-smooth marble checkerwork of the floor as if on the sea. Like shaggy islands, the white pelts of mountain sheep alternated with black bearskins and scattered rugs of deep-desert work, bright, primitive mosaics of red and blue. It was a comfortable room for a King who'd worked in the mines as a boy.

"Kaletha tells me that tourniquet of yours probably kept me from being laid up worse than I am. Seems I have to thank you twice."

Sun Wolf shrugged dismissively. "I'd already gone to the trouble of saving your hide; be a pity to have wasted my time, after all." He slouched back in his chair, relaxed but watchful. Under his booming heartiness, the King was on edge; the wine, which Sun Wolf never touched at this hour of the morning, and the tray of white rolls, butter, honey, ham, and dates, which a noiseless servant now brought in, implied more than a man simply thanking another for keeping robbers from making pemmican of him. The King wanted something.

"That's what I like!" Osgard laughed. "A man who does what he has to without a lot of bother and fuss—a fighter, a man of his hands!" He threw a glance after the departing servant and refilled his wine cup. "They say you were the best mercenary in the West—at least you commanded the highest prices, back when we were fighting old Shilmarne and her troops. But by the Three, you delivered the goods! What are you doing ragtagging it like a tinker through the Middle Kingdoms, without the price of a roof over your head? You lose your troop?"

"I gave it up."

"Because of that?" Osgard gestured with his wine cup to the leather eye-patch.

The Wolf shook his head easily. "Just say I gambled high stakes with the gods."

"And lost?"

He touched the patch, the fire-seared socket beneath. "And won."

Osgard regarded him shrewdly for a moment, hearing in his shattered voice the echo of all those reasons and knowing that it was all of them that he would hear. He was silent for a moment, his big, work-knotted hands fidgeting with the stem of the goblet. His eyes shifted away, then back. *Here it comes*, the Wolf thought. Osgard said, "I want to hire you to teach my son."

Sun Wolf considered this for a moment in silence. It was the first he'd heard of the boy, for only the King's daughter had come flying to her father's side last night. The way word went around a small community like the fortress, there was no way the boy could not have heard. But he only asked, "How old is he?"

"Nine." The man's voice turned flinty. "Nanciormis has started him on sword and horses, but the boy's a sniveler. He'd rather run and hide than face his lessons like a man. His uncle has his own duties and can't go after him as he should. It's time the boy learned to be a man."

The tone of hard challenge made Sun Wolf remember his own father. Mistaking his silence, Osgard went on, "I'll make it worth your while, Captain. He's the Heir of Wenshar—the first born Heir in a hundred and fifty years, since the days when the Ancient House of Wenshar ruled this land. He's the foundation of my line, and, by the Three, I want him to be a King that knows how to wield a sword and hold his own!" He drank off his wine and set the cup crashing down on the bronze of the small tabletop, his wide, light-green eyes blazing with the intentness of a man who has always been able to strive for and win what he sought.

"I'm the fifth King of Wenshar since we threw out the governors and freed ourselves from slavery. I fought alongside my uncle Tyrill against the desert bandits and against old Shilmarne's troops and whatever you care to name. When Tyrill died, he named me his heir, the way Casfell Ghru named him, and old Kelden the Black before him. None of those men had an heir, barring Kelden's, who was killed in battle—they all chose the best man they knew as their successor. By the Three, it's kept the land strong!

"But it's different now. My uncle fell when I was young, and I married . . ." He hesitated infinitesimally, and when he spoke again, it was with a quieter note. "I married a lady of one of the Ancient Houses, the last Princess of the old House of Wenshar."

Sun Wolf cocked his head, curious. "Wenshar? From the old city out in the desert?"

"No." Osgard cut him off shortly, and his green eyes flickered for a moment with anger. Then, as if realizing he'd spoken more than he meant, he explained awkwardly, "That is—none of her people had been near there in generations. That city's empty, dead—the armies of the Middle Kingdoms destroyed it when they conquered these parts. But yes, her people used to rule all this country and much of the desert besides. Their house had no power anymore, but they were one of the Ancient Houses, nonetheles. And she was the kindest woman in all these lands and bore me the sweetest daughter a man could want, who's to marry one of the shirdar lords to seal their alliance with us . . . And she bore me a son." He sighed and refilled his cup again, the sunlight blinking hotly on the purple surface of the wine. "The boy's my heir. I want him to be the best man as well. He's got to hold what I've held, after I'm gone."

Sun Wolf sopped a piece of bread in the honey and said nothing. He was remembering the scene in the tavern last night, the little black man, Norbas Milkom, drinking to the Lady Taswind's health, and not to her affianced lord's.

"What's his name?"

"Jeryn." A little too loudly, after a little too long a pause, Osgard went on, "The boy's not a coward. But he needs discipline. He reads too much, that's all. I've put that right, but he needs to be taught by a warrior, a man who can think in an emergency—a man like yourself. They say you used to run a school up in Wrynde for warriors. Is that true?"

"It paid to know who I was getting in my troop."

The King grunted his approval. "And it pays me to know who this country will be getting as King. Your woman's a fighter, isn't she?"

"She was my second-in-command. She's gotten me out of places so bad I don't even want to think about them."

"You think she'd take a post in the guard here, if you take it up to teach my boy?"

He paused in the act of smearing butter on his bread. "Depends on what you'd pay her, probably."

Osgard laughed. "There's a mercenary talking," he said with a grin. "A silver eagle every fortnight—and you won't find purer coin anywhere in the Middle Kingdoms. Why should we water our silver? We dig it out of the ground."

"Sounds good." Sun Wolf knew that as currency went, Wenshar's was, indeed, one of the best. There were cities in the Gwarl Peninsula where the silver content of the coinage varied from week to week.

"And the same for you, with board in the Hall and a room here for the pair of you—and the knowledge that you'll be helping a man who's worked hard and fought hard all his life sleep easier nights."

The boy's got him worried, Sun Wolf thought, leaning back in the gilded-ebony chair and considering the big man before him, who pushed so impatiently at his bedrobe and blankets. As a battlefield physician himself, he was perfectly well aware that Osgard's steady consumption of wine would drive his fever up by nightfall; but he'd learned long ago never to attempt to separate a half-drunk man from his cup. If Kaletha had the nerve to attempt to do so, he had to approve of her courage, if not her judgment.

In many ways the King reminded Sun Wolf of his own father, though he was sandy instead of dark—a shaggy, roaring bear of a man, comfortable with the jostling give-and-take of casual friendship and unwilling to stir the mud at the bottom of his or anyone else's soul. A man who could fight all day, drink all evening, and fornicate all night —or who would die in the attempt to seem to.

A man, Sun Wolf thought, such as he himself had striven so hard to be, all those years.

"I'll talk to the Hawk," he said, "and meet your boy and decide then."

"And you, Starhawk?" Kaletha set down the pottery mug of coffee and looked at Starhawk in the buttercup sunlight pouring through the long south-facing windows of the Hall. "Will you, too, join our company, to learn the ways of power?"

Servants were moving back and forth from the service hatches to the trestle tables set up in the big room with its dark granite walls. There were few of them, as there were few guards—the underservants who ate at the lower end of the Hall fetched their own bread and butter and breakfast ale. Starhawk wondered a little about this. She could estimate within a silverpiece how much a place would yield in money and loot, and the fortress of Tandieras was undeniably rich. Ruling the largest chain of silver mines in the west of the world, they could scarcely be otherwise.

After last night's incidents, she was acutely aware that most of the underservants who brought grapes, coffee, and clotted kefir porridge to the small table which Kaletha had invited her to share were of the shirdar.

If Kaletha had expected surprise from her, she must be disappointed. Away from the antagonism between her and the Wolf, Starhawk's own reading of the woman's character was that she preferred the company of women to that of men, though not necessarily in bed. In her way, Kaletha would have been pleased to show Sun Wolf up by taking from him his lover's loyalty.

Nevertheless she gave the matter some thought before replying. "I'm not mageborn."

"That doesn't matter." Kaletha leaned forward, her blue eyes intent. She was a beautiful woman whose beauty, Starhawk guessed, had kept men from taking her seriously—she wore her severeness like armor. But as she spoke, she lowered her shield to show the woman underneath. "Your Captain didn't believe me, but it is true. I understand the secrets of power. I can raise that power, bring it out of the depths of the souls of even the non-mageborn. That is my destiny."

"It's true," Anshebbeth put in, hurrying over to them from across the Hall. She had entered some moments ago in dutiful attendance upon the Princess Taswind, her own habitual, severe black gown contrasting sharply with the girl's casual attire of boy's breeches, riding boots, and a faded pink shirt. They had been chatting comfortably, but, even at that distance, Starhawk had seen Anshebbeth's eye rove quickly over the tables and find Kaletha at her table, a little apart from the other members of the Household. She had lost no time in breaking off the conversation, taking her plate from the High Table where Tazey seated herself alone, and hastening to Kaletha's side.

"Pradborn Dyer certainly isn't mageborn—he's one of our company, a youth from the town—but Kaletha has taught him, released the hidden strengths of his mind, and he has begun to have visions and dreams, which have come true. He can sometimes see things in the dark and is led to find objects which are lost. And I myself, though I'm not mageborn, I have been studying with Kaletha, absorbing her wisdom, learning the secrets of her arts, for almost a year now. It has helped me, helped me enormously . . ." She glanced quickly sidelong at Kaletha, as if for approval.

If Kaletha was as annoyed as Starhawk at having her conversation intruded upon in this fashion, she didn't show it. She preened herself a little under the praise and gave a tolerant smile, retreating behind her schoolmistress facade.

Encouraged, Anshebbeth continued, "Do you know, it seemed that I knew for many years before the Wizard King's death what Kaletha was, though she never told a soul. But her power always shone out of her—"

" 'Shebbeth—" Kaletha said, a little embarrassed now.

"It's true," the governess insisted eagerly. "Even Tazey—Princess Taswind—felt it when she was a little child." She looked back at Starhawk. "We've always been friends, Kaletha and I. She has virtually made me what I am today, has opened worlds to me I never dreamed of. Others felt it, too," she added, her dark eyes suddenly smoldering with venom. "Like that dirty hag Nexué, the laundress, with her filthy mouth and her filthy mind." She picked up a horn-handled tin knife to butter a roll, and her long fingers trembled a little with anger.

"Impure fornicators," responded Kaletha serenely, "see all things through the slime of their own impurity." She glanced a little nervously at Starhawk. For an instant, the Hawk saw again the human side of the woman, which interested her far more than the wizard and teacher did. "You mustn't be led to think . . ."

Starhawk shrugged. "It isn't any of my business."

Kaletha hesitated, not quite certain what to do with that answer. Anshebbeth, who had gone a little pink at the mention of impurity, was looking away. But, in fact, Starhawk had seen relationships like that of Kaletha and Anshebbeth before, among the nuns of the convent where she had grown up and, later, among the warrior women of Sun Wolf's troop; she knew that, in spite of the witlessly smutty remarks of Nexué and her tablemates, the two women weren't necessarily lovers. It was more than anything else a domination of the personality, based on Kaletha's desire to have a slave as much as Anshebbeth's need to be one.

Across the Hall, Nanciormis had just entered, wearing the plain, dark-green uniform of the guards and flirting with the two servant women who'd immediately found reasons to take them to that side of the room. Anshebbeth forced her gaze back to Starhawk, her mouth bracketed suddenly in hard little lines, and a stain of color lingering on her pointy cheekbones.

"It takes courage to follow Kaletha's path, the path of purity, the path of the mind. But I can tell, looking at you, that you have that."

"Not necessarily." Starhawk poured cream into her coffee and dabbed with her spoon at the swirls of dark and light.

Nonplussed, Anshebbeth opened her mouth, then shut it again. The smug self-satisfaction that had glowed from Kaletha in her disciple's presence faded, and her cinnamon brows puckered into a frown. "You've been a warrior a long time," she said after a moment. "That tells me you don't lack either physical bravery or the courage to go against what people expect of a woman. Do you have the courage to go against what *he* expects of *his* woman?"

Starhawk's attention remained on her cup. "It would depend on what was at stake."

"Freedom to do as you wish?" Kaletha pressed her. "To be first instead of second?"

"That's a tricky one." Starhawk looked up. "The fact is, I am best as a second—a better lieutenant than I am a captain."

"Is that what you truly believe," Kaletha asked, "or only what it is more convenient for him that you believe?"

"Are you asking that out of genuine concern for me," Starhawk returned, "or only to get back at him by having me leave him?"

At this display of lèse-majesté, Anshebbeth almost dropped her spoon. But Kaletha held up a hand to silence her indignant indrawn breath; when her eyes met Starhawk's, they were rueful with the first admission of wrong the Hawk had seen from her.

At least, Starhawk thought, *she doesn't pretend she didn't understand what I asked.*

After a long pause, Kaletha said, "I agree. We both asked each other unfair questions. And I think we're each three-fourths sure we know the answers, both to our own and the other's . . . but only three-fourths." She looked down at the small plate of bread and kefir before her for a moment, then back at Starhawk, a spark of genuine warmth in her eyes. She held out her hand. "Will you join our company only for company, then? I, for one, would be pleased if you would."

The door on the dais that led through to the King's solar opened abruptly, and Sun Wolf emerged, followed immediately by Osgard himself. The King's face was mottled alcoholic red and pasty white, and he was limping heavily, but fended off Sun Wolf's single offer of assistance. Kaletha's brows snapped together; she got swiftly to her feet, black robe billowing as she strode towards him. "My Lord . . ."

He waved her angrily away. "I don't need your damned help, and I don't need your damned advice, either!" he roared. "I'm not a weakling! Hell, back when we were fighting Shilmarne's armies in the passes, I went through six hours of fighting with a shattered kneecap!"

Her voice thin, Kaletha said, "You were thirty then, my Lord, not fifty, and you hadn't been drinking."

"What's my age got to do with it, woman?" he bellowed back. "Or what I drink or how much I drink, for that matter? Where's that boy of mine?"

Frostily, she said, "Your son, my Lord, is not my responsibility."

"Well, you're supposed to be a damn wizard, you should know. Nanciormis . . ." He swung around in time to see the tall commander step easily up onto the dais. "You're supposed to have him for sword practice now."

Nanciormis shrugged. "I presumed other duties called him, for he did not come."

Balked of that prey, Osgard looked around for other and lighted on his daughter Tazey, who was consuming the last of her bread and posset with the swift care of one who proposes to escape unnoticed. "Where's your brother?" the King demanded, and Tazey, who had just taken a bite of bread, looked up at him, startled. "Hiding again, I daresay—in that damned library, most like. Send that . . ." He looked around again, and his eye lighted on Anshebbeth, down at Kaletha's table. Anshebbeth quailed visibly, and her thin hand went to her throat as he roared, "Why the hell aren't you up here with my daughter where you belong, woman? I don't keep you in my household to gossip with your girlfriends."

Tazey rose quickly. "I'll find Jeryn, Father."

"You'll sit down, girl. 'Shebbeth's your governess, and her duty is to keep beside you, not to go wandering off. Now go fetch him, woman!"

For one instant Anshebbeth sat rigid, her lips flattened into a thin line of anger and humiliation; then she got quickly to her feet and disappeared through a narrow door into the turret stair. She wasn't out of earshot when Osgard added to Sun Wolf, "Twitter-witted old virgin's enough to give any man the fidgets."

Starhawk buttered another hunk of bread as Kaletha came back to her, her blue eyes calm and contemptuous. "The man is a lout," the Witch of Wenshar said, "and is raising his son to be a lout as well. I had hoped that, along with weaponry, Nanciormis could teach him graciousness and polish, but I see he's taken the first opportunity to put a stop to that." She seated herself in a swish of heavy black skirts. On the bench at Starhawk's side again "I hope you'll forgive my speaking honestly, but I scarcely find it likely that our future King will learn anything from that barbarian save the breaking of heads."

Starhawk shrugged. "Your opinion of the Chief has nothing to do with me."

"It's obvious that a man like that seeks out teaching in the ways of power simply to aid him in the killing of other men. The rest he disregards. He understands nothing about purity, nothing about the powers of the mind, from which all magic springs."

Starhawk dipped her bread in her coffee and took a soggy bite, far more amused than indignant. "And I'm sure you'll forgive my honest speaking when I say that you have a rather short acquaintance on which to judge him in such detail."

"I have eyes," Kaletha returned bitterly. In her glance, quickly averted, Starhawk read the contempt for Sun Wolf for having a mistress and at herself for being one. Curious, she leaned her bony elbow among the half-cleared breakfast dishes and waited. On the dais, Osgard was breathing stertorously; Sun Wolf, his massive, gold-furred arms folded, wore a closed expression of guarded annoyance. After a moment, Kaletha's stiff back relaxed. She turned back to the Hawk.

"I'm sorry," she said, the words sticking in her throat. "I've judged you, and I shouldn't have. Among people like yourselves, fornication is a matter of course, isn't it?"

"Oh, thanks!" Starhawk grinned, more amused than offended at the assumption of complete promiscuity—and indeed, she thought to herself, there was nothing to indicate to Kaletha that Sun Wolf hadn't lost his eye in a pothouse difference of opinion over some woman's favors, instead of a duel to the death with the greatest wizard in the world.

"About time," Osgard grunted, on the dais, as Anshebbeth came flustering back through the narrow door, which led to an inside stair. "Captain Sun Wolf—my son, Jeryn. Stand up straight, damn you, boy."

If Tazey, seated in apprehensive silence at the High Table behind them, was clearly her father's daughter, with the King's height, his athletic grace, his streaky blond hair, and absinthe–green eyes, then Jeryn was just as clearly a shirdar woman's child. He had the thin, hawklike features, though his unwashed, black curls were cut short and his olive skin was paste-pale from staying indoors. At this distance, Starhawk couldn't see the color of his eyes, for they were downcast, sullen, and shifty, guarding secrets and resentments under puffy lids. He dressed in the formal clothes of court, short trunks and hose, which bagged around his skinny knees; he wore them without pride and looked shabby and unkempt, an orphan who has dressed himself from a prince's ragbag.

"What do you think, Captain?" Osgard's tone had turned bullying. "You figure you can do anything with this boy?"

Jeryn said nothing, just held himself braced in a way that spoke worlds about the kind of treatment he expected from his father. And it was hardly, Starhawk thought impersonally, a fair question. There were enough people left in the Hall that Sun Wolf's refusal would be widely interpreted as an admission that he couldn't make a warrior of the boy, either through his own fault or through Jeryn's. Osgard had undoubtedly meant the scene to hinge on Sun Wolf's pride in his ability to teach. Though the Hawk knew this would not have applied, she also knew that putting Sun Wolf to the choice now, in public, would work because he would not openly reject the boy.

After a long moment, Sun Wolf said, "I said I'd have to talk to my partner."

It was a way out, but Osgard wasn't about to give it to him. "Well, hell," he said genially, "there's no trouble about that, is here?" He turned, and held out his hand to Starhawk. "You got no objections to a post in the guards, have you, Warlady? A silver eagle every fortnight, board and bed? Pardle Sho may not have the fancies you'll find north of the mountains, but there's money aplenty here and places to spend it, if you're not too finicky in your tastes. It may not pay like the mines do, but there's more honor to it and less labor. How can you say no to that?"

Sun Wolf's eye had the angry smolder of a man who has been gotten around in a way that he could not fight without looking like a boor. Starhawk, aware that Sun Wolf had no objections to looking like a boor and was on the verge of making an issue of it, rose, hooked her hands into her sword belt, and said casually, "I can't say no till I've tried it for a week."

It was something the Wolf had taught her—when in doubt, play for time.

In a week, she reasoned, anything could happen.

And, in point of fact, it did.

Starhawk wasn't sure just what woke her. *A dream,* she thought—a dream of three women in a candlelit room, their shadows moving over the painted walls, giving the grotesque images there a terrible life of their own. She could not hear their words, but they sat close together around the candles, combing their hair and whispering. The room had no windows, but somehow Starhawk knew that it was late at night. The scene was an ordinary enough one, yet something about it—the way the shadows flickered over those frescoes whose designs and motives she could not quite make out, the way the candlelight glowed in the dark, liquid eyes—frightened her. She had the feeling of being a child, listening to an adult discussion of smiling hate, a sense of something hideously wrong whose form and nature she could not understand. Though the wavering light penetrated to all corners of the little bedchamber, with its curtained bed and its delicate, jointed shirdar furnishings—though that nervous illumination showed nothing but the three women, with their long black hair and robes of white gauze —she knew they were not there alone.

She woke up sweating, knowing there was something with her in the room.

The moon outside was full. By the angle of the bars of silken light streaming in through the window, she knew it was late in the night. A band of it lay across the bed, palpable as a gauze scarf; she felt that, had she dared move, she could reach across and pluck it up. Beside her, the bed was empty. Sun Wolf would still be with Nanciormis and the King, nursing his beer and telling war lies. She herself had been less interested in getting to know them than she was in going alert on morning duty.

She did not move, but, from where she lay, she could see almost the whole room under the brilliance of the inpouring desert moonlight.

It was empty.

There was something there.

Her eyes touched every black pocket of shadow, every angle of that ghostly radiance, from the spread of the cracks of the floor—like an arcane pattern of unreadable runes—to the hard spark of the buckles on her doublet and jacket, which lay thrown over the room's single chair. The night cold was icy on her face, the smell of the dry mountains filled her nostrils with a clarity too vivid for dreaming.

She wondered if it was watching her and what movement she could make that might do any good.

Years of war had given her an instinct for danger. Whatever was in the room with her, she had no doubt whatsoever that it was utterly evil.

She lay on the inner side of the wide bed, under a black bearskin and two quilts against the freezing night of the desert foothills. In her fear there was none of the child-terror that wants only to pull the covers over the head, secure in the knowledge that the evil will not violate that sanctuary; her fear was adult. To reach the door, she would have to roll across the width of the bed; to reach the window, she must dive over the foot. The sense of evil strengthened, localized; there should have been a shadow there, crouching just beyond the foot of the bed where the moonlight struck the brightest, but there was none.

Outside in the stables, the dogs began to howl.

She felt a tweak and a jerk and saw the blankets move.

Then clear and distant, she heard Sun Wolf's voice, like metal scraping in the cold, still night; and Nanciormis' rich laugh. Nothing moved, nothing changed in that terrible still life of empty moonlight, but she felt the stir and shift of air and heard a sound no louder than the scratch of a cockroach's hard claws on the granite lump of the threshold. Through the open door, she saw dust swirl in the court outside, though no wind stirred the camel-bush just beyond.

She rolled from the bed, pulling the topmost blanket off and around her body. Automatically, she caught up her sword, knowing it would be useless. The court outside was drenched in liquid–silver moonlight that shadowed every pebble, every stone of the little well-head, every leaf of the camel-thorn and sedges clustering around. Not even an insect moved, but the dogs howled again, desperate, terrified; from the stables, she heard the stamp of frightened hooves. She forced herself still, hidden in the shadows of the door. Across the court, an adobe gate made a pale blur in the shadows surrounding the Hold—across that granite monolith, a line of shuttered windows marked the Hall like a row of sightless eyes. Above them, a balcony ran the length of the building, every arched doorway looking onto it rimmed in the silvery glow of the moon. In the checkered maze of shadow between Hall and gate, Sun Wolf's voice echoed on the stone, bidding Nanciormis good night. Though she could clearly see there was nothing by the moonlit gate, still terror filled her. She stepped into the fragile splendor of the moon, cried out desperately, "Chief, look out!" and her voice echoed against the high wall of the silent Hold.

Hating to, but knowing if the Wolf were in danger she must be closer, she gripped her sword and ran forward into the court—and stopped suddenly.

There was nothing beside the gate.

Of course, there never had been anything beside the gate—but it was gone, now.

Slowly, not trusting her instincts, she moved again, her naked sword in her hand, her other hand clutching tight the blanket wrapped around her. Her heart was thudding in her chest, the air cold in her nostrils against the warmth of her breath, the dust chill beneath her feet.

She stood beside the gate. There was nothing there, nor anywhere else in the night.

The soft scrape and rustle in the shadows made her turn sharply, in time to see Sun Wolf drop over the low wall that bounded the empty quarter, some distance from the little gate. He hesitated for a moment, and she signaled him to come. Her arm, where it held the blanket over her, was a mass of gooseflesh—she was trembling, though not entirely with cold.

He had his sword in hand, the moonlight bitter as frost on its edge and point. "What is it?"

She hesitated, not certain what to say. "I—I don't know. I didn't see anything, but . . ."

But what?

He studied her white, sharp face in the moonlight, with her baby-fair hair, flattened by the pillow, sticking in all directions, her gray eyes alert and watchful as a warrior's, but puzzled, troubled. "Tracks?"

She shook her head. She sensed that she ought to feel foolish, like one who had wakened screaming from a nightmare about hens or rabbits, but she didn't. The danger had been real, that she knew. And the Chief, may the Mother bless his balding head, accepted it as such. They had fought shoulder-to-shoulder for a long time and knew that, while their observations might be inexplicable, they were at least not inaccurate. He looked around him at the deserted court, as if scenting the air for some trace whiff of evil, his single-yellow eye gleaming almost colorless in the ripe moonlight. The aftershock was coming over her with the memory of the fear; she was conscious of a desire for him to hold her, for the rough, knobby feel of sword hilt and belt buckle through the blanket, crushing against her flesh. She told herself not to be stupid. In an emergency that kind of activity tied up one's sword arm. Her instincts told her the danger was over, but her mind and the habits of a lifetime of war refused quite to trust.

"Come on," he said softly. "Whatever it is, it seems to be gone." He began to move toward her, then stopped himself and led the way back down the stony path, a sword-length apart, like scouts on patrol. Starhawk felt surprised at how sharply the rocks in the court cut her bruised feet. She had not even noticed them, before. She and the Chief flanked the dark slot of the cell doorway, entered—ready for anything—though both were almost certain that there was nothing inside. And there was not.

While Sun Wolf was checking the room, Starhawk turned to look back over her shoulder at the gate. It stood innocent under the blaze of moonlight, no shadow touching its sand-worn pine lintels, nothing moving the weeds around it. Something white drifting along the balcony of the Hold made her raise her eyes; she could see a figure there, the crystal glory of moonlight glinting in the gold clips that held his long black braids. He was gliding from archway to archway, as if seeking a room—she remembered he and the Chief had been drinking and remembered, also, the telltale tracks of broken veins that at close distance marked the commander's elegant nose.

But even though he seemed to have trouble finding which room was his own, he moved with his usual steady grace. He pushed aside the curtain within one dark arch, and Starhawk thought she heard the soft, startled cry of a woman's voice from within. But no scream followed it; he stepped through into the darkness, and the darkness hid him.

CHAPTER

SUN WOLF'S TERM OF EMPLOYMENT AS INSTRUCTOR IN MANLINESS
to the Heir of Wenshar lasted slightly less than twelve hours—something of a record, even for Sun Wolf.

He had the weedy, sullen boy slathered with herbed grease to protect his virginal skin from the sun, and protesting all the way, out of
the fortress between dawn and sunup, running on the lizard-colored
ranges of scrub and camel-bush that spread out below the black granite knoll of Tandieras. The blue dawn periods between the freezing
cold of night and the breathless daytime heat were brief; though, as
autumn advanced, they would lengthen. *As it was,* Sun Wolf thought
disgustedly when Jeryn stumbled to a gasping halt after a quarter of a
mile, *they were more than lavish.*

"This isn't safe, you know," the boy panted sulkily and jumped
aside, lashing his hand at an inquisitive bee. He wiped at the sweat
tracking through the grease; stripped to a linen loincloth, with dust
plastering his scrawny legs and snarly hair, he was a sorry sight. "If a
sandstorm came up now, we couldn't get back."

"True enough," the Wolf agreed. And indeed, three days ago, on
the ride in from the distant coast, he and the Hawk had been trapped
in a cave in the black cliffs of the Dragon's Backbone by a sandstorm.
He had felt it coming—the breathless rise in temperature and the
throbbing in his head—long before the Hawk had, and that had saved

them, allowing them to reach cover in time. From the moment the cloudy line of white had become visible on the desert horizon until all the world had been swallowed by a screaming maelstrom of wind-driven sand had been literally minutes. After the blinding brown darkness had passed, they'd found the desert littered with the ruined corpses of prairie dogs and cactus owls, the flesh literally filed from their bones by the pebbles and sand in the wind. In Tandieras it was said that even wearing the protective white head veils of a desert rider, a man could be smothered and dried to a mummy in a drift of superheated dust within half an hour.

"But I can read the weather; feel the storms before they hit, before they even come into sight. I know there's nothing on the way."

The boy shot him a look of sullen disbelief from black eyes that looked far too big for his pointy white face and retreated again behind his wall of silence. Sun Wolf had already found that, protest though he might, the boy would never ask for help. Perhaps it was because he had early learned that doing so would only worsen any situation with his father.

Jeryn tried again. "Nanciormis never made me do this."

"And that's why you got winded after two minutes of exercise." Sun Wolf pushed back his long hair—he had barely broken sweat. "We're going to do this every morning at this time, and it's going to be hateful as hell for about three weeks, and there's nothing I can do about that. Let's go."

"I'm still tired!" the boy whined.

"Kid, you're gonna be tired for months," the Wolf said. "You're going to run back to the fortress and lift your weights and work a little with a stick with me, sometime before breakfast this morning. Now you can either do it fast and have time to do other things you'd like, or slow. It's up to you."

The boy's full, soft mouth pursed up tight to hide the resentful trembling of his lips, and he turned furiously away. He began to race back toward the Citadel at an angry, breakneck pace *calculated,* Sun Wolf thought, following with a hunting lion's dogtrot, *to exhaust him before he'd gone a third the distance.*

He couldn't say that he blamed the boy. Since yesterday, he had his own frustration and resentment to chew at his soul.

Kaletha's method of training was entirely different from the brief, exhausting exercise in memorization he had undergone with the witch

Yirth of Mandrigyn and from the dogged routines he had worked out for himself. He had learned to meditate from Starhawk and did so dawn and dusk, but Kaletha's instructions in meditation were more complicated and involved her frequent intervention. "You must learn to change the harmonies of the music of your mind," she said, kneeling before him in the latticed shade of a corner of the public gardens of the town, and Sun Wolf, to whom meditation had always been a matter of inner silence, again fought the urge to slap that smug look off her face.

As an exercise, it seemed unbelievably trivial. But the White Witch's other students didn't seem to think so. In their various shaded niches along the colonnade at the top end of the public gardens where they usually met, they were all meditating with faces furrowed in either concentration or ecstasy— *both,* Sun Wolf suspected irritably, *for their teacher's benefit.* Starhawk meditated alone and had taught him to do the same. The few times he had seen her at it, she had seemed relaxed, almost asleep. *But then,* he thought wryly to himself, *it took more than communion with her soul to disturb the Hawk's marble calm.* He had known her for nine years and was still trying to figure out what it would take.

He could see her, down across the blasting afternoon sunlight of the open court in the indigo arches of shade beyond, talking to the grizzled Norbas Milkom, owner of the Golden Vulture Mine. The black man's scarred face split with a laugh; by their gestures, they were discussing the mountain campaign of eight years ago.

In the afternoons, when the heat of the day had begun to burn itself off and the people woke from their siestas, half the population of Pardle Sho ended up in these gardens. The three acres of rambling walkways—under arbors of grape, jacaranda, and phoenix-vine, or of bare, sandy squares where occasional ancient orange and cypress trees stood but more often simply native cactus—covered the last footslopes of Mount Morian where the land was too irregular for even the builders of Pardle to put houses. Before the Revolt, the gardens had originally belonged to the governors of the slave-worked mines, and the ruins of the Palace formed their southern boundary. But now they were the favorite promenade of the town, where people came in the afternoons to talk, hear gossip, meet their friends, flirt, transact personal business, or listen to the singers who sat in their shaded corners, caps full of pennies before them. It wasn't unusual for itinerant teachers to meet with their students there; at the other end of the colonnade Sun Wolf knew one brisk little man could always be found teaching engineering to a class of one or two.

Kaletha's voice came to him, measured as if each word were a precious thing to be cherished by its lucky recipient. "Purity of the body is the greatest necessity of magic," she emphasized for the third or fourth time that day. She was speaking to Luatha Welldig, a fat, discontented-looking woman of forty or so, dressed, like all of them except the Wolf and Egaldus, the Trinitarian novice, in severe and unbecoming black, but her glance flicked to Sun Wolf as she spoke. "Without purity of the body—freedom from spiritous liquors, from overindulgence, from the crudities of fornication—" she was looking straight at him as she emphasized the word, "—the mind remains a prisoner in the maze of the senses. The body must be pure, if the mind is to be free. All magic rises from the mind, the intellect, the reason."

"That isn't true," Sun Wolf said, looking up.

Kaletha's pink lips lost their curves and flattened into a disapproving line. "Naturally, you'd prefer not to believe so."

He shook his head, refusing to be angered. Slowly, stammeringly, not certain how to explain and oddly conscious of his scraped-out croak of a voice, he said, "The intellect may learn to guide magic, but it doesn't spring from the reason, any more than water is generated by the pipe it flows through."

"Nonsense," Kaletha said briskly. "Reason and the ability to control the base passions are the sole province of humans, and humans are the only living creatures to possess magic."

"But they aren't."

The dark red brows climbed. "Oh? Are you telling me that camels can turn sandstorms? Or house cats can read oracle-bones? Or do you believe in funny little people we can't see who hide in cellars and clean up the kitchens of deserving goodwives?"

Sun Wolf felt the anger stir in him, and with it a deep unwillingness to argue the point. He felt in his heart she was wrong, yet lacked the technical expertise to prove himself right—and lacked, still more, any desire to pick and unravel at the smoky whole of his instincts.

Into his silence, Anshebbeth said timidly, "Kaletha, when you speak of purity—surely there are different sorts of—of physical love." She spoke as if she could barely get the word out of her throat. Sun Wolf stared at her in surprise, startled that she would defect from her teacher's slightest utterance, much less do so to take up his side of the question. In the harlequin sunlight of the vine's shade, her thin, white cheeks were blotched with embarrassed red. "Can't—can't true love be—be freeing to the soul as well as to the body?"

Kaletha sighed. "*Really,* Anshebbeth." She turned away.

The governess fell silent, her thin hand stealing up to touch her throat in its high collar, as if to massage away some dreadful tightness.

Sun Wolf considered her thoughtfully for a moment. She had surely had little to say to him, falling in obediently with Kaletha's contempt. But he remembered the look she'd once given him: covert lust plunging immediately into scalding shame; he'd seen her, too, hungrily following Nanciormis with her eyes. He wondered how that sharp, tense white face would look if it relaxed into laughter, and what the masses of tight-braided black hair would feel like unraveling under a man's caressing hand. But her gaze had already gone back to Kaletha, and she leaned to catch what the White Witch was saying to Egaldus. *No man,* he realized, *would stand a chance of gaining Anshebbeth's undivided attention if Kaletha were in the room—supposing that he'd want it.*

Manlike, he had simply considered her contemptible. Now, realizing what she had all her life given up for the sake of this woman's bare approval, he saw her as pathetic.

Across the court a kingfisher glitter of brightness caught his eye. The Bishop Galdron had joined Norbas Milkom; the two men talked gravely, the white-bearded patriarch with his glittering gold tabard and the tough, scarred mine owner, the diamonds from his rings flashing. Starhawk had left them. A moment later he saw her walking along the colonnade with Nanciormis. Both the Bishop and the mine owner watched the big Guards Commander disapprovingly. If Nanciormis was aware of their looks or their disapproval he didn't show it; he moved like a king, serene and elegant in his slashed red-velvet doublet and flowing desert cloak, his dark hair knotted up on the back of his head against the afternoon's heat.

During their drinking bout last night, Sun Wolf had observed that, although Nanciormis, like most of the men of the desert, tended to treat women with a combination of courtliness and patronage, he recognized the women of his guard as colleagues in the arts of war and only flirted with them with their tacit permission. He wasn't flirting with the Hawk, Sun Wolf could see. Flirtation was an art Starhawk had never understood. She would still occasionally give Sun Wolf a blank look when he complimented or teased her, which amused him. Beneath that lioness facade, she was in some ways a startlingly innocent girl.

And yet . . .

Last night came back to him, the sharp fear in Starhawk's voice as she'd called to him from beyond the moonlit gate. She was not a woman to run from shadows. Her fear had not been the timidity of a woman asking a man's reassurance, but a warrior's fear of a very real danger. There had been neither tracks nor marks in either the yard or the little cell they shared.

Starhawk had not had any explanation, but, with a shiver, he recalled the dead doves.

A shadow fell across him. He looked up to see Nanciormis. "I see you've joined the would-be Summoners of Storm." The big man braced one thick shoulder against the arbor post with its twisting of thick, scraggy vines and looked genially down at Sun Wolf. "A useful skill for a warrior to acquire, now that there's no Wizard King to hunt you down and kill you for it—but your time could be better spent."

"If I were looking for skills to augment war," the Wolf replied, "I don't doubt it. But I have quick-and-dirty wizardry already."

"Have you?" The coffee-dark eyes narrowed thoughtfully. "I know the servants all say you do. I only thought that meant you'd managed to impress the Lady Kaletha in some fashion—not easy, I'll admit. What then do you seek here?"

Sun Wolf was silent for a long time, looking up into that fleshy, handsome face with its high cheekbones and aquiline nose already flecked with broken veins. The dark eyes, with their shadows of pouches and wrinkles, were both wise and cynical, but there was no dismissal in them.

After a few moments he said, "I don't know. If I knew, it would be easier. A man can learn to fight in the streets and taverns, but against a warrior, trained and disciplined, he's no match in a long fight; and he can't use that knowledge for anything else."

Nanciormis' brow puckered. He clearly did not understand. Sun Wolf had guessed already, from the sloppiness with which Jeryn had been trained that he would not, Sun Wolf guessed that in Nanciormis' younger days—and he couldn't be much above thirty-five now, though his portliness made him look older—he had been a notable warrior. But his very abilities, like his natural charm, had spared him from having to learn discipline. Never having had to learn anything beyond what he already knew, he was a man who lived on the surface of things—adept but unimaginative. Having never been defeated, he operated on the unconscious assumption that he never would be. A professional would destroy him.

There was a small stirring among Kaletha's disciples now, as she moved across to speak to Starhawk. Beyond her, Sun Wolf could see Egaldus fade unobtrusively into the shadows. A little to his surprise, he realized the novice was using a cloaking-spell, a means of nonvisibility, to avoid the notice of his master, the Bishop, on the other side of the garden. It was one of the first magics Sun Wolf had learned to use, and the young man did it with considerable skill. Only by concentrating could the Wolf keep him in sight; the shadows of the twisted grapevines lay like a blind over the bright hair and the embroidered blue and white of his robes. Anshebbeth, too, the Wolf noticed, had grown very quiet, gazing down at her thin hands.

Nanciormis beckoned him, and the Wolf rose to follow down the shaded aisle of cracked and uneven tiles. The commander glanced back at Starhawk—leaning against a gnarled wisteria vine, her head a little on one side as she talked to Kaletha—then across at Milkom and the Bishop again. "I'd advise you to be a little careful who sees you here," he said softly. "Witches have a bad name in Wenshar, as I told you last night. Whatever you think Kaletha might give you may not be worth what you'll have to pay for it."

That morning, across the speckled range land, Sun Wolf had seen the dark, jagged line of the Haunted Mountains, guarding the secrets of the ancient city of Wenshar. But Kaletha had grown angry when he'd asked her about it and had spoken of other things. It struck him now that though, with the decline of the day's heat the gardens were filling up with off-shift miners, cattle herders, and young people of the town, no casual strollers came up this far from the gardens below. He had enough experience with human nature to realize that this was not from tolerance. If fear had not kept them away, he thought, they'd be gawking and heckling like bumpkins at a fair.

Fear of Kaletha? he wondered. *Or—of what?*

"I see you managed to catch my nephew for sword practice this morning," Nanciormis went on, his eye trailing appreciatively after a fair-haired girl strolling down the colonnade on the other side of the court until the shadows at its end swallowed her. "What do you think of him?"

What Sun Wolf thought of him was that he'd been very poorly taught. But he only said, "You can't tell anything on the first day. They're always eager to impress you with how much they already know." That applied to himself, he thought ruefully a moment later, as well as to Jeryn.

Nanciormis laughed. "If you do as well tomorrow you'll be lucky. The boy has a certain quickness, but he's lazy and, I suspect, a coward. I've tried to push him into courage, or at least put him in situations where he'd be forced to master his fears, but he's clever at hiding. He can disappear for hours when there's something afoot he doesn't want to do. I've tried to get him onto something a bit more manly than that pudding-footed slug of a pony he's had since he was a toddler—Tazey rides other horses with no trouble, but he won't. And as for venturing even a few yards out onto the desert . . ."

"Has anyone ever taught him to survive in the desert?"

"How, when he won't poke his nose outside the library?" demanded Nanciormis, amused. "In any case, he's so afraid of going out there that he's not likely to need the knowledge. If you can do anything to increase his nerve, we'll all be grateful—his father most of all. His father's never had much use for him."

"Even though he's the first heir born to Wenshar since the Ancient House of Wenshar failed?"

The dark eyes slid sharply sidelong to him, then flicked away. "Osgard's always been in an ambivalent position about Jeryn. He is, as you say, the heir, and Osgard has enough pride in the realm that he wants the boy to be able to hold it after him. But Ciannis died bearing him. I'm told it was a bad pregnancy, and she nearly lost him twice. Osgard saw then and sees now that in some fashion he was obliged to trade a woman he loved for a child who was like a sickly rabbit in his infancy and who turned bookish the minute he learned to read. Book learning is all very well in a ruler, but there are other things, as there are other things besides war—not that the citizen-kings, the war-kings before Osgard ever understood style, beauty, or respect for the ancient ways. But Jeryn's sneaky and furtive as well as cowardly."

"I expect, if my father drank himself maudlin and hated me for killing my mother, I'd be sneaky and furtive, too."

Nanciormis gave him a sharp look. "Osgard never used to drink himself sodden that way before Ciannis died."

"No," the Wolf said, "I don't expect he did." They had reached the end of the colonnade; the lengthening of the afternoon light had shifted the shade of the trellises overhead, and bars of puma-colored light sprawled across the worn tile of the walkway. Across the court, he could catch the faint burring of a mandolin badly played and a nasal voice singing snatches of a popular song. In an hour he'd have to locate Jeryn again for another lesson before dinner and he had the feeling this wasn't going to be as easy as this morning had been. The novelty had definitely worn off.

He glanced back in Kaletha's direction. The Bishop of Pardle having taken his leave, Egaldus was standing at her side, listening to her conversation with his heart in his sky blue eyes. Kaletha asked him something. He gestured with the grace of one trained to the theatrics of Trinitarian liturgy and plucked a ball of greenish light from the air. It shone softly against his fingers in the shadows. Kaletha laid a hand on his shoulder and nodded approvingly. Anshebbeth looked away, her thin lips pursed.

"What about his sister?" Sun Wolf asked. "It would do him good to have a sparring partner. I think she's a sensible girl, and she's enough older than he that he won't feel belittled if she beats him. She looks as if she'd be good, too. I watched her in the war dance. She moves like a warrior."

Nanciormis grinned. "She should. When she was a little girl there wasn't a boy in the town she couldn't trounce in either a fight or a ball game. She can ride anything with four hooves and dances like a bird on the wing. I'm afraid it wouldn't do, though."

"No. The boy doesn't like her?" Sun Wolf guessed.

"Worships her—or at least he did, up until a year or so ago. He tolerates her now, as boys do with older sisters." A gust of swallows swirled down into the central court, perching on the stone rim of the nearly dry fountain there to drink. Bees were coming out as well, dipping down to the water that was fed by springs welling from the harsh stones of the Dragon's Backbone. Sun Wolf guessed there would be water in these fountains year-round.

Nanciormis went on, "No, it isn't a problem with Jeryn. But as you know, Tazey's going to be married to Incarsyn of Hasdrozaboth. He'll be here tomorrow for the final negotiations. And while among my

people there is the occasional warlady, it certainly would not do for
their lord to marry one, or for Osgard to—shall we say?—foist one off
upon him as a wife. Nor would Incarsyn want such a woman—certainly his sister would not and she's the true ruler of the Dunes. The
marriage is a political expedient to tie these—" He paused, catching
himself up over some epithet he had been about to apply to the sons of
slaves imported from the north to work the silver mines, who had
taken the best of the foothills land from the Desert Lords and pushed
them deeper into the wastes of the K'Chin. Then he concluded the
phrase. "—these new realms to the Ancient Houses, even as his own
was. But, as with Osgard's marriage to my sister, there can be romance
in it as well. Incarsyn is young and comely, but he is a man of the
shirdar and not apt to take to a woman who is too adept in wielding a
sword."

Sun Wolf glanced along the colonnade. Like sheets of opaque gold,
the sunlight lay between the arbor pillars now, blinding and stiflingly
hot where it struck. The contrast with the twisted shade of the vine-
sheltered bay where Kaletha and her small group of students sat was
dazzling. Their dark robes blended with the shadows, the faces only a
white blur like cutouts from paper. Kaletha was speaking to them all,
her voice a soft, hypnotic drone, whispering hidden secrets of magic
and power. Beside them, leaning on the pillar, Starhawk stood listening, the shearing brilliance of the sunlight lying dappled over her
square shoulders and close-cropped hair like wind-scattered petals.

He smiled a little to himself and said simply, "That's his loss."

"Captain."

Sun Wolf, whose single eye was good enough to distinguish in the
polished brass of a shield on the armory wall the reflection of the man
who stood in the doorway shadows said, "My Lord?" before turning.
"Keep at it, boy," he added, as Jeryn automatically lowered his sword.
"An enemy's not going to give you time to rest your arm, so neither
will I."

The red-lipped little mouth tightened angrily, but the boy turned
back to the ironwood hacking-post. His strokes against it barely splintered the wood. Down, backhand, forehand—down, backhand, forehand—each blow with its laborious windup and finish was a separate
action, with no carry-through of momentum from one blow to the
next. Sun Wolf turned to face the King.

"I'd like a word with you."

"You're paying for my time," the Wolf responded, walking over to the broad arch of the door. The faint, uneven *tup . . . tup . . .* of steel on unyielding wood echoed softly in the stone vaults of the round room with its high-up ring of windows, a muted percussion behind the words they spoke.

"Damn right I'm paying for your time," Osgard said. He stood foursquare, his shoulders broad in their straining doublet of dull bronze, the wide gold chain over his shoulders catching little chips of light on its S-shaped links. As usual, the King's neck ruff was undone and lay in limp disorder under his chin; also, as usual, he smelled faintly of stale wine. "And what I'm not paying for is to have it said that my son's being taught by witches."

Sun Wolf hooked his thumbs over the broad leather belt of his war kilt. Salty droplets of sweat hung from the ends of his thin, wet-dark hair and trickled down through the gold rug of hair on his back. His rusted voice was soft. "Who says this?"

"Are you denying it?"

"No. I'm just curious to know who says it."

"I have that carrot-headed bitch in my Household out of respect to my dead wife and because I'd rather, if we do have a witch in Wenshar again, that she was under my eye rather than scheming in the pay of the shirdar lords or the Middle Kingdoms. But I've told her to keep her distance from my children. I'm not having talk start about them, and, God knows, there's been talk enough, with that sleek little tomcat Egaldus sneaking here from the Bishop's palace and Galdron all in a snit over it. Well, I won't have it, I tell you!"

His face was scarlet with its mottled network of broken veins; his voice, in the stone vaults of the room, was like thunder. The chop of sword against wood had ceased.

"Nobody in my life ever asked me what I'd have or I wouldn't have," Sun Wolf replied, his single eye narrowing, "and I'll lay odds nobody ever asked you, either. Now, you can push your son into being what you want him to be, but what I am and who I spend my time with is no affair of yours."

"I'm not pushing anyone!" Osgard roared. "Don't play the sophist with me! I get enough of that from Kaletha and that damned Bishop! My son is my affair, and my Household is my affair, and I won't have it said there are witches teaching the Heir of Wenshar!"

Goaded, Sun Wolf snapped, "I'm teaching him swordsmanship, rot your eyes, not poxy divination—I couldn't teach him divination if I wanted to!"

"I'd better not hear of you keeping company with that damned woman again . . ."

"If you don't want to hear of it, then you'd better stop gossiping with your laundry women!"

The guess was evidently correct, for the King's face went redder, if that were possible, and Sun Wolf set himself for a side step and a blow. But the King only drew deep ragged breaths, his thick, liquor-scarred face working with rage. "Get out of here."

Forcing down his own anger, Sun Wolf turned in silence and went. Aside from the fact that it was a stupid quarrel, he knew that calm acquiescence would be more annoying to Osgard than reciprocated wrath—and he was right. As he walked past him into the trapped heat of the stone corridor, Osgard bellowed, "GET OUT OF HERE!" The shout rang in the groins of the roof like beaten steel. A moment later he heard the singing clatter of metal and knew that the King must have strode to snatch the boy-sized sword from his son's hand and hurl it in rage against the wall. But he did not look back to see.

In the little adobe room on the edge of the empty quarter he left a note: *Gone to the hills.* Then he singled his own dappled gelding from the palace cavy, saddled up, and left Tandieras as the sun touched the broken edge of the Dragon's Backbone like a phoenix settling to rest.

CHAPTER

*F*OR HER PART, STARHAWK WAS NOT UNDULY DISCONCERTED BY Sun Wolf's disappearance. She had long experience with his habit of storming off in a rage to be by himself for hours, days, or sometimes a week or more—and she had her own suspicions about where he had gone. From the open watch-station on the highest tower of the Citadel of Tandieras where she stood guard duty, she could look across the flatlands to where the isabelline scrub country faded into the vast plain of blackish, pea-sized gravel called the reg—treeless, waterless, life-less, stretching away to join the ergs, the dune seas of the south. Though the sun had barely cleared the shoulders of Mount Morian, the desert had already begun to shimmer with the heat. Through the wavering air could be seen, like the dark spine of a half-buried skele-ton, the Haunted Range, which guarded the dead city of Wenshar at its feet.

With Starhawk this morning was Taswind of Wenshar, the dry wind flicking at her tawny hair as it stirred in the turban of white veils that Starhawk, like the other guards, wore to protect her head from the desert sun. Instead of her usual boy's riding clothes, Tazey wore a gown of rose-colored wool; following the girl's absent gaze, Starhawk could guess why. Around the tower, the Citadel lay spread out like a peasant's counterpane of blackish grays and maroons and a dozen faded hues of homespun buff, stitched here and there with the dull green of dusty bullweed and cactus. The square block of the Hold lay almost directly underfoot—the Hall, the King's solar and his bedchamber beyond, the long balcony which connected the rooms of his Household, the sprawl of Women's Hall and Men's, and the brighter quadrangle of the kitchen gardens.

From up here, Starhawk could see the small cell where she and the Wolf had stayed and the little gate that led from the empty quarter to the dark, granite courts beneath the balcony of the Household. The empty quarter beyond lay like a picked skeleton—a jumbled chaos of adobe walls, five and six feet thick, decaying back into the mud of which they were formed, a tangle of shadows over which doves stirred like windblown leaves.

Starhawk, neither sentimental nor concerned about proving her courage to herself or anyone else, had slept last night in a bunk in the Women's Hall with the laundresses, scullery maids, and female guards, and had slept well.

Where the stables ran into the vacant quarter there was a harshness of new yellow wood and unweathered tiles. A row of old shops and halls had been converted into stabling for the white horses of the shirdar lord, Incarsyn of Hasdrozaboth, and quarters for his servants and guards. Elsewhere, more repairs marked the rooms where he himself was housed. A scrap of red bunting from yesterday's welcome stirred in the tepid morning wind like a strayed hair ribbon. It was to these rooms that Tazey's eyes were drawn.

"New earrings," Starhawk commented after a moment, not adding that Tazey had also done up her hair differently to complement the tiny, lustrous teardrop stones. "Were they part of his groom-gift?"

The girl's face went pink like a deep-desert sunset. "No," she said, and shyly met the Hawk's eyes. "He sent these to me this morning all on his own, not because he had to—I mean, they weren't heirlooms of his house or anything. He bought them new in the market, just for me. They're sand-pearls."

Starhawk studied the odd, pearl-like stones found so rarely in the wasteland stream beds. "And, if you'll forgive me for being crass," she said, "not cheap."

Tazey blushed still pinker, recognizing that Starhawk understood the compliment their cost implied. The Lord of the Dunes had arrived yesterday with his retinue, and, in the ensuing twenty-four hours, Starhawk had seen Tazey undergo a transformation from an unselfconscious girl to a young lady who knows herself to be not only wanted, but desired. It was a role she was not used to, but the very novelty, at the moment, gave her a sparkle of untasted delight. Whatever else could be said about Incarsyn of Hasdrozaboth, at least he knew the proper way of dealing with a bride who had been given no choice of her groom.

The girl shook her head, took a deep breath, and met her eyes. "Warlady, listen," she said. "I—I need to talk to you. I think I need help, but it can't get to Father. Will you promise?"

"No," said Starhawk calmly, and saw the girl's tanned face fall. She looped back a trailing end of her white veils. "Your father pays me for my loyalty—I can't promise not to tell him something I don't know, when it might touch the safety of his realm. But I do promise I'll give you as much as I can."

Tazey looked relieved and nodded, understanding the distinction. Starhawk had time to think obliquely, *She isn't pregnant and she hasn't learned some invasion plan of Incarsyn's* . . . before the girl said, "It's Jeryn. He's gone."

"When?"

She shook her head. "This morning—maybe last night. I don't know. You know Father had a fight with Captain Sun Wolf."

Starhawk shrugged impatiently, "The Chief fights with everyone he works for. It's nothing. He'll be back."

"Jeryn . . ." Tazey hesitated. "Jeryn asked me the night the Chief left if he'd gone for good. He said he didn't think so, since you were still here. And I said, I—I thought he might have gone to the old city of Wenshar."

Starhawk's eyes narrowed. "Why did you think that?"

The absinthe green gaze avoided hers. "It's the sort of place he might go if—if he were interested in magic and wasn't afraid of the stories." Her face still averted, she hurried on, "And then this morning, I went to Jeryn's room because—because he'd been upset yesterday. Uncle Nanciormis said something to him at his lessons yesterday—you know Uncle's back teaching him? I think he called him a coward . . ." She looked back at the Hawk, grief and hurt in her face at what she could neither control nor repair. "And he isn't a coward, really he isn't. Only . . . Anyway, his bed was empty. And I'm afraid he's gone after the Captain."

Starhawk considered this in silence for some moments, wondering how much of the obviously fabricated tale was based in truth. Tazey's gaze had fallen—she was an appallingly poor liar. Her hands, long and slender like Nanciormis' and presumably her mother's, though they were burned brown as a cowhand's by the sun, pleated nervously at the silk-fine folds of her skirt.

"You realize it's far more likely he's hiding somewhere because it's time for his lessons? Especially if your uncle's been calling him a coward."

Tazey's face flushed, and she shook her head emphatically. "I—I've looked in all his usual hiding places. He's not in the Fortress. I know it."

Starhawk forbore to ask her how she knew, knowing she would only get another evasion. She glanced out across the reg toward the crumbling black line of the Haunted Range, hiding behind its curtain of heat dance, then back at the girl. "I'm not free until after breakfast." By the angle of the shadows that lay across the face of the Binnig Rock, the giant granite half-dome which loomed above the jumbled shoulders of the Dragon's Backbone where they crowded close to Tandieras knoll, that would be fairly soon. "After this long, I don't think an hour either way will make much difference to Jeryn." She added, "You know it can't be just you and me."

The girl swallowed apprehensively. "I go riding all the time without 'Shebbeth."

"That's not what I mean and you know it," the Hawk said, her voice gruff. "Could you trust Incarsyn?"

There was a long silence while Tazey struggled between what she knew to be true and what she wished to believe about the man she was required to marry. Then she shook her head. "He wouldn't understand." She groped for a way to phrase the fact that the Prince, who, she wanted to think perfect, in fact had very little in common with her. "He wouldn't think it proper that I go. I mean, that I ride a horse . . ." Miserably, she added, "Among his people, noble ladies all ride in litters."

She broke off, looking away again, fighting off the tightness in her throat that was not in keeping with the romance of the Prince's ardent wooing. *The worst of it was,* Starhawk supposed, *that Incarsyn would never understand.*

But there was nothing she could say; to avoid anything worse, she stuck to the matter at hand. "We'll find some of the guard who'll keep their mouths shut. You probably know them better than I. Be thinking about that between now and breakfast.''

"All right." Relieved not to have that open wound sympathetically prodded, Tazey smiled, gathered up a handful of skirts, and picked her way carefully down the ladder to the tower room below. A few minutes later, Starhawk could see her as a foreshortened oval of rose pink and straw, hurrying from the door at the tower's base towards the Hall.

A good and dutiful daughter, she thought, with ironic pity, doing her best to meet halfway a bridegroom whom she had no choice but to accept. And what choice *had* she? She had not even the freedom to choose, as Starhawk had once chosen, the solitary mysticism of the convent over a life as some man's cherished brood mare and bedmate. The alliance with some Desert Lord not quite powerful enough to be a threat had to be made—the dowry had already been paid. Had the girl been able to make one good, cogent argument to her father against the match, she might have had a chance. But she could not, even to herself, allow the joy of her own freedom as a reason. Why give up a man who bore all conventional resemblance to the prince of your dreams on the grounds that you would never be able to ride again?

Starhawk shook her head. The inconvenience of believing in the Mother—or the Triple God of the Trinitarians, for that matter—was the belief that events had some kind of universal meaning. Sun Wolf, at least, was secure in the knowledge that the spirits of his departed ancestors were no more able to control the random events of this world than he was—though, being dead, they could see them coming. She herself had long since given up trying to guess good from ill and let them all move in the Invisible Circle as they would. But her heart hurt for the girl, nevertheless.

Starhawk saw Prince Incarsyn an hour and a half later, when she came to her late breakfast in the Hall. A few years younger than she, he was dazzlingly handsome, with the graceful vitality of a man who thinks with his body rather than his intellect. The clothing of the desert added to the feral beauty of his movements—loose trousers and half-boots, a tunic of dark indigo silk, thick with gold embroidery, and, over all, the flowing white cloak of the shirdar. Like all the folk of the desert, he had a complexion of sun-dyed bronze and black, curly hair, clubbed back from his temples in jeweled pins and falling almost to his waist behind. He paused in the act of handing Tazey graciously

down from the dais to bow to Starhawk as she entered, and Tazey
wavered, her hand still in his, torn between excusing herself from him
to speak to Starhawk and prolonging his attentions to her.

It didn't help, of course, that Incarsyn had absolutely no doubt that
she would accompany him.

Starhawk said, "Let me get my breakfast, and I'll see you in a few
minutes," and the girl nodded, grateful to be spared the awkward
choice. Feeling Tazey to be shy as he conducted her toward the Hall
door, Incarsyn chivalrously carried the weight of the conversation,
clearly attributing her confusion to himself. His soft, well-modulated
voice was lost among the other mingled voices echoing in the high
ceiling of the Hall as Starhawk made her way to Kaletha's small table.

"I don't like it," Norbas Milkom was grumbling at the High Table
beside the King. He reached into the dish of ham before him, a splash
of rainbows dancing from a diamond the size of a rabbit's eye on his
gnarled black finger. "I told you before and I'm here to tell you again
—I don't like it, and the miners don't like it. This marrying into the
tribes! Why can't the girl be let to wed her own kind, eh? One of my
boys or Quaal Ambergados' son. The Three Gods know we're as
wealthy as any Desert Lord skulking about the sands with his handful
of followers and goats—money we came by honestly, digging it from
the ground with our hands, not plundering it from traders."

Nanciormis, sitting at the King's other side, said nothing, but his
pouchy eyes glinted at this slight to his people. Starhawk saw Anshebbeth—in hovering attendance on Tazey and her betrothed, but close
enough to the High Table to be eavesdropping as usual—turn and
glare back at Milkom with smoldering indignation.

*Was her anger for the sake of the shirdar—Anshebbeth's own people, though
she worked in the King's Household and had given up going veiled as the deep-
desert women did?* Starhawk wondered, *Or could it be for Nanciormis' sake?*
It had not been lost upon Starhawk that, while she should have been
keeping an eye on her charge, Anshebbeth's glance kept straying to
the commander's broad, green velvet shoulders.

"Kings must marry their own kind, Norbas," Osgard said patiently.
"If she did not wed one of the Desert Lords, it would have to be the
son of one of the Lords of the Middle Kingdoms."

"Why must it?" Milkom demanded, the old tribal scarring on his
face flexing with his frown like braids of rope. On Nanciormis' other

side, the Bishop Galdron leaned forward amid a glitter of bullion embroidery and jeweled sleeve borders.

"I confess to a certain apprehension for the welfare of the Princess Taswind's soul," he said in his mellifluous voice. "The shirdar are pagans, remember, worshiping the djinns of the desert. As a woman of an Ancient House, she will have to be initiated into the cult of the women of the family. There are evil influences there . . ."

"The old beard-wagger sees evil influences under his chamberpot." The voice spoke almost in Starhawk's ear. She swung around, startled, to the place she'd thought vacant at her left—*dammit*—she'd turned her head a moment ago and *seen* it vacant. The novice Egaldus sat there, a cup of coffee cradled between his well-kept hands, smiling in discreet triumph at her and Kaletha's astonishment.

"Not bad, eh?" he grinned, eyes dancing like the boy he still mostly was.

Kaletha's back seemed to lengthen. "Scarcely a seemly use of your powers."

"Kaletha . . ." He reached across Starhawk, to put a hand over the Witch's cold, white fingers. Kaletha made as if she would draw away, but did not. "I'll have to be in attendance on him this afternoon. Perhaps if I came later?" The bright blue eyes were ardent with hope. Kaletha averted her face, but her hand remained where it was. "I have power—you raised it in me," he coaxed softly. "You're the only one who can teach me. Please."

He certainly knew how to ask, Starhawk thought, amused. *No wonder Sun Wolf annoyed Kaletha.*

Old Nexué's voice croaked out, "Well, it's her Little Majesty!" and Starhawk glanced up to see Tazey had come back into the Hall. "Been giving you a wee taste of the wedding-night beef?" Tazey, blushing furiously, hurried over to where Starhawk sat as the old woman and the gaggle of laundresses with her, hooting with lewd glee and making gestures and comments as old as woman and man, pushed their way out the kitchen door and back to their work. The King and his party had risen and left; the High Table was empty now save for Nanciormis, who sat alone, long fingers stroking the silver wine cup before him, his dark, curving brows pulled together in thought. Anshebbeth, lingering on the dais in some private reverie, jerked about at the old woman's first cackle and stamped her foot, calling furiously after her, "Stop it! How dare you, you filthy hag!"

But by that time, Nexué had gone.

" 'Shebbeth, don't," pleaded Tazey, though her own cheeks were red as if burned. "She didn't mean any harm."

As she and Starhawk climbed the dark inner stair to her rooms so that she could change to riding clothes and head veils, she added "She —and Kaletha, who just burns up inside about it—should know by now that Nexué *always* gets worse about something if you show you're upset over it."

At the corrals they were joined by two young guards named Pothero and Shem, who, Starhawk guessed, had been childhood friends of Tazey's. As they came near, Shem, who was the taller of the two and black, said, "Jeryn's pony, Walleye, is gone."

Tazey flinched, startled, then recovered herself and nodded. "Yes, I —I know," she stammered—but she hadn't known. *If she had,* Starhawk thought, adjusting her veils, *she'd have brought it in as evidence. She knew he was gone, but wasn't about to tell me how.* With the uneasy sense of edges not matching, she mounted the stringy yellow dun the boys had saddled for her and followed Tazey through the Fortress gate and down the knoll, swinging through the steep rocks and out onto the desert floor. The two young guards brought up the rear, head veils fluttering in the dry mid–morning heat.

The stillness of the air increased Starhawk's disquiet. The horses' hooves were a swift splatter of sound, like thrown water on the hard, dusty earth; the electric quality of the air prickled against her exposed cheeks. It was autumn, the season of the killer storms—the season of the Witches, they called it in Wenshar. She knew there was no telling when such a storm would strike. They were riding across the open palm of fate.

"Why do you think Jeryn went seeking the Chief in Wenshar?" she asked, as the jutting, dark mass of Tandieras knoll, the Fortress, and the looming, eroded shoulders of the Binnig Rock dwindled to ragged darkness behind them. Ahead, the ground lay hard and speckled dun, studded with widely spaced tufts of wiry grass and an occasional waxy-leaved camel-bush. In spite of the nearness of the winter, it was still stiflingly hot; heat dances, turned the air to water, concealing the broken line of dark, glazed sandstone mountains far ahead. "And don't say you don't know," added Starhawk quietly, and Tazey bit her lip.

For a while, the girl only concentrated on the barren landscape before them, her gloved hands sure and steady on the reins. Then she ducked her head a little, as if ashamed.

"As I said," she murmured, "Wenshar is where a mage would go. Because of the Witches."

"Who?"

Her voice was barely audible over the soft thud of hooves on stone-hard earth. "The Witches of Wenshar."

Starhawk urged her horse up beside the girl's thick-necked bay, so that they rode knee to knee. "I've never heard of them."

"Father doesn't like them talked about." Tazey glanced nervously at Starhawk, then away. "There used to be a saying—there still is, in the town—'Wicked as the Witches of Wenshar.' Only sometimes it's 'Wicked as the Women of Wenshar,' because all the women of the Ancient House of Wenshar were witches. Their souls were damned because of it, the Bishop says. They could summon the sandstorms, or dismiss them; they could part the winds with their hands, or call dark-ness in broad day just by combing their hair, or summon the dead. They were cruel and evil and they ruled all these lands along the foothills of the Dragon's Backbone, before the Lords of the Middle Kingdoms came and took the lands away and dominated the other Desert Lords. I suppose it's why Father was so angry when he found out any teacher of Jeryn's was mageborn."

"Because of the reputation they gave the mageborn in Pardle Sho?" Starhawk asked, puzzled.

Tazey turned to look at her, green eyes wide in the gauze frame of rippling veils. "Because of Mother. She was the last Princess of the Ancient House of Wenshar. Father is afraid—has always been afraid—that people would say the evil is in our blood. And it isn't," she added earnestly, as if worried that Starhawk would think so, too. "Jeryn can't stand Kaletha. I—"

Starhawk raised a hand, silencing her, and reined in. "Stay back," she ordered the others sharply, already swinging down from the sad-dle as Tazey drew rein beside her. "Don't foul the ground."

"What is it?"

They had reached the harsh, stone plain of the reg, a landscape that made the desolate scrub closer to the foothills seem a pleasure garden. Here nothing grew, nothing lived. The seeds which slept elsewhere in the desert soil, awaiting rain, had long ago died in their sleep; the eternal carpet of pebbles lay hot, black, and utterly lifeless underfoot.

Starhawk felt the burn of it through the soles of her boots, through the buckskin knee of her breeches where it touched the ground, and through her gloved hands. The storms could turn the reg into a flaying hail of rock—the riders had stopped twice already, to pick the small, vicious stones from their horses' feet. Now Starhawk picked up a small stone and held it to the hot afternoon sun. On its upper edge was a faint smudge of blood.

She smelled it, then wet her finger and touched the dried patch of brown. "Last night, it looks like." She tossed it down.

"Look, here's more." Pothero sprang down a little further on. The smudge on that stone was smaller, barely a fleck.

"Not drops." Starhawk squinted out over the bleak, stony carpet of the reg. In the heat—shimmer, eroded columns of sun-blackened stone rose from the barren pebbles, some singly, others in ragged lines. Tsuroka, the shirdar called them—guards posted by the desert djinns to keep watch on the dead land. "How much did Jeryn know about horses, Tazey?"

The girl shook her head. "Not much. He hated riding. He always got sunburned because he'd never do it enough, and it made his bottom sore. And Father and Uncle Nanciormis were always making him ride horses too strong for him—to build up his courage, they said."

Starhawk cursed without heat.

Tazey went on, "Walleye used to be my pony; he was just a fat, old slug Jeryn could ride on when he was about five. But he always liked the pony best because he wasn't afraid of him."

"*Is* he afraid of horses?"

The girl hesitated, thinking about it. "Not horses in general," she said after a moment. "But of the horses Uncle gives him, yes. And they are pretty high-spirited." She smiled. "This one I'm riding is really his."

"Your father," began Starhawk, looking at the jittery, restive bay. Then she sighed, and let the observation go unmade. "Fan out," she ordered the guards. "Looks like poor old Walleye picked up a stone. See if you can find any more traces."

There was more blood, further on. When, a mile and a half later, they came to a wide patch of gray sand left by last week's storm, even the eternal sweep of the desert winds had not been able to eradicate wholly the marks which indicated that Jeryn had still been riding his pony. Starhawk cursed again—the visceral oaths that only worshipers of the Mother can contemplate.

"He doesn't know any better," Tazey pleaded unhappily.

"Then he shouldn't have charge of a defenseless brute," Starhawk retorted. "He probably thought the poor thing's gait was out because of the gravel."

She straighted up, to scan the hot, southern horizon for the fiftieth time that afternoon. But the earth lay silent. The dividing line between black and blue was sharp and clean as if cut with a knife and a rule. The shadows lay over toward the east, kohl-dark and lengthening. They had come nearly twenty miles from the foot of Tandieras Pass, with nearly ten more to go toward the shallow inward curve of the eastward cliffs of the Haunted Range where the City of Wenshar had lain.

Uneasily, Shem said, "We're not going to find Jeryn in the ruins before dark."

Beneath his veils, Pothero's dark eyes shifted. *Stories,* Tazey had said. *What stories, concerning a city a century and a half dead?*

"He'll know we'll be looking for him," Shem offered encouragingly. He unwound his veils a little to take a drink from one of the waterskins. His teeth flashed in an uneasy grin. "Hell, he'll probably be waiting for us on the edge of the ruins, or be starting back, lame pony or no lame pony. He won't want to be in that place when night comes any more than—"

"If he made it that far." Starhawk walked a few paces forward and picked up something from the ground—a single thread of white muslin, but bright as a banner against the leaden gravel. She held it up. "He must have torn up his headcloth to tie around the pony's foot. That's worse than stupid—he can't have known he shouldn't let the sun get to his head—but it's my guess he'd make for the nearest shelter." She glanced up at Tazey. "He isn't stupid, is he? Just ignorant as hell."

The girl nodded wretchedly.

"Those rocks?" Shem pointed toward the north, where a weathered gray flatiron of rocks broke the sand like a beached ship half-heeled over in heavy seas.

Starhawk considered them, then looked away to the southeast, where, some five miles off, stood three tsuroka, crumbling, cinder-colored columns dyed maroon by the afternoon glare. "I think he'd have turned back first, figuring he could make it back to Tandieras. By the time he realized he couldn't, he'd be closer to those. You boys ride north—we'll check south. Send up a smoke if you find him."

It was Starhawk who found him when her horse whinnied as they neared the decaying heaps of talus and rubble that surrounded the tsuroka and was answered by a faint, neighing reply. Jeryn was curled in the long purple shadows of an overhanging boulder. His bare face was sunburned red and blistered in spite of the coating of the Wolf's sunburn grease, tear-tracks cutting the dust and slime like water runnels on the desert's face. He was asleep, but woke up, crying, when Tazey called his name and came scrambling down the rocks to him; brother and sister clutched each other desperately, and Starhawk could see the boy was dehydrated and feverish from the sun. He kept sobbing, "Don't tell Father! Promise not to tell Father!"

"We won't," Tazey whispered reassuringly, as the hot, desperate hands clutched at her shirt sleeves and veils. "We're all sworn to secrecy, you know we are . . ."

"I didn't make it," Jeryn sobbed. "But I'm not a coward—Uncle said I was a coward not to fetch him back, if I didn't like the way Uncle was teaching me. But I'm not—I'm not. Is Walleye going to be all right?"

Starhawk, aware of the priorities, had already checked the miserable pony's split and bleeding hoof. She caught the beast's hanging head and dumped most of her spare water down its throat, knowing that, though Jeryn might have remembered to take water for himself, he had undoubtedly forgotten that horses drink, too. "I don't know," she said roughly, still angry about the pony's suffering. "He'll need one hell of a farrier to fix that hoof."

"I did as best I could," the boy sobbed miserably, still huddled in his sister's arms. "He can't die. . . . It's all my fault . . ."

Starhawk opened her mouth to deliver some well-chosen words about ignorance which had in times past raised blisters on the hides of toughened mercenaries, then shut it again. Whatever else could be said, Jeryn, having gotten his poor pony into this mess, hadn't left him in it; and considering how frightened the boy must have been, there was a good deal in his favor for that. So she only said, "If we can get him back to Tandieras, he should be all right."

She glanced back out at the hot, black flatness of the reg, then at the two children, the boy sobbing, his burned face pressed to Tazey's shoulders. "And I think your uncle deserves to be horsewhipped, and your father as well. This wasn't brave—it was criminally stupid."

"Uncle didn't mean—" began Tazey, more frightened by the mercenary's perfectly level, conversational tone than by all her father's roaring bluster.

"Your uncle," returned Starhawk, with quiet viciousness, "never means much of anything by what he says or does. Most people who sow harm don't. He's like a nearsighted man, seeing clearly only what he wants and not much caring to think about the rest." She scrambled out of the shadowed cleft, the rock burning through her boot soles as she returned to the horses and collected a broken handful of mesquite and acacia branches tied to the back of the saddle. She'd gathered them at the edge of the reg, knowing that, if a signal was needed, out there she would find nothing to burn. *It is just soldier's luck,* she thought, hunkered over a handful of bark peelings and cracking flint and steel, *that the sun is just past the strength required to use a burning-glass.*

When she'd coaxed the spark into a smoldery thread of smoke, she looked back. Tazey had pulled off her veils, soaked them from the waterskin and wrapped them around her brother's swollen face. "You know your father will be searching by now."

The girl nodded miserably. Jeryn, clinging to her waist, broke into frightened, half-delirious sobs. Starhawk checked the southern horizon again, gauging the tiredness of the horses, her recollection of the look of last night's moon, and the state of their water. The skyline was clean, unblurred by the telltale line of dust, but her hackles prickled at the sight of it. Across the reg to the north, the sun gilded a plume of dust as Shem and Pothero rode back toward them.

"Come on," she said softly. "We've pushed our luck already. It's a long way back."

The storm appeared on the southern horizon when they were seven miles from the rocks. Starhawk had sensed the growing uneasiness of the horses, the heat, and the close, pounding feeling in her head and had turned her eyes, again and again, to the blank southern quarter of the sky. Now she saw it, a deadly glitter like gold tumbling in a hopper, darkness and lightning underneath. Her horse flung up its head, terror overriding its weariness. She twisted its face back into the wind, and heard Shem cry out and the clatter of retreating hooves even as she yelled, "Make for the rocks!" Through a blur of dust and the wind-torn ends of her veils, she saw he'd been thrown. The cloud before them swelled with unbelievable speed, the oven-heat of the storm surrounding them, and brown darkness began to fall.

The horses were frantic, even the lame Walleye fought to escape and run before the storm, though they could not hope to outrace it. Pothero tried to pick up Shem, and his piebald gelding threw them both and went galloping north amid a stinging whirlwind of flying sand and stones.

The air was laden with dust, hot and smothering. Flying gravel tore at Starhawk's face as she wrenched her horse to a stop. Electricity tightened like a vise around her skull—in the howling fog of approaching darkness, she could see the dry lightning leaping from earth to sky. She swung down from her saddle, trying to yell to Tazey, "We can kill the horses for a windbreak!" knowing it to be a last resort and nearly useless. The scream of the winds ripped her words away. She dimly saw Tazey's horse rear, overbalanced by the two children on its back. Something black and huge, the flying trunk of a deep-desert acacia tree, she thought, came whirling out of the gloom like a malevolent ghost and struck the horse broadside. They toppled, Tazey dragging her brother clear. In panic Starhawk's horse jerked its head, snapping the reins in her hands. Then it, too, was gone.

Darkness covered them, a black wing of death. An uprooted cactus came flying out of the darkness to strike her, the spines tearing through the steel-studded leather of her doublet as if it were silk. But worse than that was the heat and the dust, winding them already in a baking shroud that would drain the moisture from their bodies and leave them mummified. Shem and Pothero stumbled to her, heads wrapped in their veils like corpses, blind with dust. Jeryn grabbed her from out of the darkness, sobbing something about Tazey . . .

Her head throbbing unbearably, her body aching already with desiccation, Starhawk squinted through the flying black fog of smothering dust. A flicker of dry lightning showed her the girl's dim outline, walking into the storm, her unveiled hair flying back as she raised her hands.

For the first instant, Starhawk thought it was to protect her eyes from the dust. But a second burst of ghostly light outlined Tazey's hands as she stretched them into the wind, fingers pressed together like a wedge. And, as if they had been a wedge, the winds parted around them.

In her first, bursting glare of enlightenment, Starhawk's chief thought was, *So that's how she knew where her brother would be.*

The force of the storm curled back from Tazey's hands like waters breaking over a rock, leaving an arrowhead wake of stillness. In that eerie wake, only tiny puffs and eddies of wind touched Starhawk's face, but she could see the dust on either side in heaving curtains and hear the screaming keen of flying sand over gravel. The two young guards stared, dumb with shock and horror, at that blade-slim figure in the choking gloom; but when one of them opened his mouth to cry out something obvious, Starhawk, Jeryn still clinging to her waist, strode over to him and said quietly, "Don't say it."

The young man stared at her, blood from blown gravel and debris trickling down his face, staining his veils. "But—"

"You break her concentration, and we're all dead."

Starhawk had dealt with wizards before; the two youths had not. They turned horrified eyes back to the girl they'd grown up with, as if she had been transformed before them into some dreadful monster. Like theirs, her face was scratched and torn, matted with dust. In the ghostly darkness, Starhawk could barely distinguish her features—her eyes shut, her lips moving occasionally, her hair tangled with blown twigs and gray with dust, her outstretched hands bleeding. She seemed locked in some dreadful trance, focusing all her mind, her soul, her life, upon turning the winds, as she had been told witches could do. The pony Walleye, reeling like a drunken thing, had staggered into the wedge of stillness behind her and collapsed. The young guards, staring at her, seemed to waver between doing the same and taking their chances with the storm.

Seeing the horror on their faces, Starhawk added grimly, "And you had damn well better keep your mouths shut about this afterward as well." She turned and led the stumbling Jeryn back close to his sister. After long hesitation, the two young guardsmen followed.

It was almost dawn before they returned to Tandieras, but nearly the whole of the Fortress was grouped by torchlight around the gate. Runners from the search party that had found their small fire after the storm died had carried rumors as well as demands for water and medical attention. Starhawk, her body hurting from dehydration and sheer weariness, saw from afar the carpet of firefly lights against the charcoal bulk of the Fortress knoll and cursed.

She reined the horse she had been given by the searchers over close to Tazey's makeshift litter. Jeryn, in exhausted sleep, stirred fitfully in her arms and sobbed, "I promised not to tell . . . I promised . . . don't tell Father . . ." Starhawk tightened her grip around the boy's scrawny body and reflected, with calm anger, that, beyond a doubt, some officious fool *had* told his father.

The men of the search party had all been very quiet. Tazey herself, though she had seemed only very dazed after the passing of the storm, had not spoken at all and now, under the light of the searchers' torches, seemed to have drifted into a vague sleep. Starhawk remembered how, once during the past summer, Sun Wolf, driven by frustration and rage at his own impotence to tap the wellsprings of his power, had worked at calling the lightning throughout one northlands storm. Perhaps he had thought that, like the physical skills of which he was such a master, the power could be increased with violent and steady use—and perhaps, if the wielder knew what he was doing, it could. He had lain in a fitful half–trance of black and hopeless depression for days, as if his soul as well as his body and his power had been drained.

Rest would cure it, the Hawk thought. *If, that is, she were allowed to rest.*

The crowds by the gate were very still, as the rescuers had been, when Shem and Pothero whispered of what they had seen.

In the cold dawn light, the yellow torch glare altered the faces of the crowd—awed, frightened, confused. Starhawk saw the Bishop Galdron, lips pressed in arctic anger, as if Tazey had chosen to be mageborn instead of desperately hiding her suspicions about her powers. Beside that small, glittering figure, Egaldus was keeping his thin face carefully expressionless, but he radiated barely concealed triumph and glee—glee that on Kaletha's face was transformed into smug satisfaction as she tried to push her way forward through the crowd in the broad court before the steps of the Hold. Starhawk, knowing Kaletha saw herself already as Royal Instructress in Magic, felt a twinge of weary anger. Anshebbbeth, closely buttoned as usual despite the earliness of the hour, wore a tight expression, her genuine concern for Tazey's injuries fighting with naked jealousy, as if what the girl possessed had been taken away from her.

Between the torches that flared on either side of the doors into the Hall, Osgard, Nanciormis, and the handsome young Incarsyn stood, their faces a study in shocked noncommitment. Incarsyn, particularly, looked simply confused, as if struggling to select the most appropriate emotion out of a rather small natural stock.

Starhawk dismounted. None of the guards seemed eager to go near the litter, so she helped Tazey to stand. Dusty, scratched, her blond hair hanging like a dried broom around her scorched face, the girl wavered unsteadily on her feet, and Jeryn, stumbling, staggered to support her other side. In dreamlike weariness, they moved through the haze of torchlit dust toward the steps, where a bloodshot, tear-streaked Osgard waited, his untidy doublet smeared with liquor stains. The silence was absolute, but Starhawk could feel it around her, worse than the weight of the storm.

Then into that silence, old Nexué's voice cawed like canvas ripping. "A witch! She's a witch!"

Tazey raised her head, her green eyes transparent with horror. "No," she whispered, pleading for it not to be so. Then her voice wailed, crackling *"No!"*

Kaletha had started to bustle forward, but Nexué pushed before her, skinny finger pointing. Tazey could only stare at her, blank with shock, a rim of white showing all around her pupils in the torchlight. There was triumph and distorted glee in the old woman's face, as if the damnation and ruin of the Princess were some kind of personal victory. "A witch! A—"

With a kind of calm rage Starhawk turned and backhanded the old woman across the mouth with her closed fist, knocking her sprawling to the dirt. She was too late. Tazey whimpered again, "No . . ." Covering her face with her hands, she slowly collapsed. Osgard, Nanciormis, and Incarsyn all hesitated to step forward, and it was Starhawk who caught the fainting girl in her arms.

CHAPTER

FROM THE WINDOW OF THE TEMPLE, SUN WOLF COULD SEE THE lights bobbing in the canyon below.

He had seen them last night, when he had looked out into the black violence of the killer winds. Later, when the rock-cut palaces of the vanished city, carved from the very sandstone of the canyon walls, had lain cold and colorless under the ghostly moon, they had been there still. They flickered at him now from empty doorways, from black eye sockets of wide square windows, and from the shadows of the peach-colored columns of the carved facades. The whisper of their bodiless voices braided into the wail of the desert winds.

He knew what they were.

In the north, as a child, he had seen demons, the only person he had ever known who could do so. His father, he remembered, had beaten him the one time he had spoken of it—for telling lies, he'd said. Sun Wolf wondered now whether it had actually been for telling what the old man did not want to accept as truth. He had wanted a warrior son.

In all his years of hearing tales about demons, the Wolf had never heard that they could hurt people much. He knew their thin, whistling voices called from the hollow places of the earth, luring men to their deaths in marshes or over gullies in the dark of the moon. But they fled men and bright lights. No man who knew what and where they were should be in danger from those cold, incorporeal spirits.

Yet he knew himself to be in danger, though danger of what he did not know.

He had scribbled in the dust of the rose-hued sandstone temple he had taken for his quarters the few patchy demonspells Yirth of Mandrigyn had taught him and drawn all the Runes of Light on the doorpost and on the sills of the great upper window.

And still he did not feel quite safe.

They moved below him through the monochrome darkness of the canyon, faint lights that shone but did not illuminate the smooth pillars, the filigree turrets, or the winding stairs cut at intervals in the fantastically eroded rock faces of the canyon wall.

The City of Wenshar had been built where the tawny sandstone cliff–face of the Haunted Range—black with the baked mineral patina of the scorching sun—curved inward to form a shallow plain raised above the level of the desert and sheltered from the cruelty of the winds. There, three small streams flowed out of the broken mountains to lose themselves in the farther desert. On the raised plain, the City of Wenshar had spread out around its gardens of date palms and cypresses—until the invading armies of the Middle Kingdoms had crushed the Ancient House of Wenshar and taken its lands and its mines.

Time and sand had nearly destroyed the few walls war had left standing. But up the three canyons lay a twisting maze of wadis and cuts—of square, isolated blocks and towering stone needles, valleys as wide as a street or so narrow the Wolf could span them with his arms —lit only by bright ribbons of sky three hundred feet above. Here the wealthy nobles of Wenshar had carved gem–like palaces and temples from the living cliffs themselves. Sheltered from the sun, their fantastic sandstone facades had not been darkened by the desert heat. They shone peach and amber and rose, softly banded yellows, citrine, honey. Here, time had ceased, dammed behind the enchantment of the stone.

Sun Wolf had always loved rocks, their strength and the personality of their shapes. On the road and in Tandieras, he had missed having a rock garden in which to meditate and spend time. Hearing nothing more of Wenshar than its evil reputation, he had been awestruck by this fairy-tale beauty.

Yet from every shadow, in every niche and doorway, he sensed the presence of demons. The city crawled with them, big and little; in the three days he had wandered here, he had felt them watching him. Sometimes it seemed to him that he had only to press his hands to the ground to hear their voices. But that was something he feared to do.

By day he never saw them, though occasionally, in those palaces cut deeper than a single chamber into the cliffs, he heard their flitter and murmur, like dry leaves blowing over stone floors that neither wind nor plant had touched in generations. But two evenings ago, in the shadows of the central canyon, he had glimpsed them, no more than a flicker out of the corner of his eye, massing in the shadows before him as he tried to leave. He had doubled on his tracks to take a narrow wadi that rejoined the main way lower down—the mountains here were split into great, free-standing blocks in places, which enterprising ancient nobles had hollowed into whole palaces. But the demons had been waiting for him. The sun had disappeared by then from the brilliant stream of blue overhead, its rays only edging the topmost rim of the rocks. He could sense a soft, evil chittering in the shadows.

When he'd doubled back again, he'd realized he was being driven.

There was no lore of demons in any of the jumble of things Yirth had taught him, nor had he ever found any in his search for wizards. He knew they rose out of rocks and swamps, out of water sometimes. If they were in this land, the magic of the old Witches of Wenshar would have held them at bay until, with the Witches' destruction, they had seeped forth like oil from the ground.

They had no strength. Being bodiless, he doubted they could physically hurt a man much. Nor could he think of a reason they would want to, needing no sustenance. Yet in places the canyon floors were heaped with broken piles of animal bones, mouflon sheep and gazelles, driven to their deaths from the ledges above even as men were lured into marshes by the demons of the north. The bones lay whole and undisturbed.

Standing there in the growing azure dimness of the evening, listening to the crooning whisper of the demons massing like lightning bugs in the shadows before him, he had suddenly wondered why.

He had turned again, seeking a way out. The canyon had widened before him into a long space where a line of eroded stone needles, narrow columns as high as the canyon walls, towered gilt-tipped against an opal sky. Twisted cypress trees, a recollection of vanished wells, stood about the needles' bases, gray trunks weathered and contorted as if they sought to swallow their own branches. Entirely across the rear of the canyon stretched the longest palace facade he had yet seen. Amber steps led up to level upon level of peach and salmon columns, fragile turrets, and strange spires, all glowing in the last of the light. But as Sun Wolf stood in the black shade beneath the undead cypresses, he'd heard, voices crying out to him from the dark arches of that vast edifice, sweet as the voices of children who live upon human blood.

He had been afraid then, unreasoningly, and had fled back down the canyon, heedless of the whistling gibber in the shadows through which he passed. He had gone to his own temple headquarters in the westernmost canyon and scrawled the ghostly scrim of runes, invisible to any eyes but his own, over the windows and doors behind him. He had no way of knowing whether they would, in fact, keep the demons from passing. He had sat awake through that night and every night since.

Outside, they moved in the darkness still. Faint, deformed bodies drifted in shells of light, seeping in and out of the rocks, floating in the air like drifts of vagrant mist. He knew that what he saw was their true being, as a mirror will reflect the true being of a wizard cloaked in illusion, and what frightened him was that he could not tell whether they were ugly or beautiful. He could hear them whispering to one another in their piping, little voices and knew that, if he allowed himself to, he would understand—or think he understood. But that, too, he feared to do.

Why did he feel that they would come if he bade them?

Why this strange sense, in the inner corners of his heart, that he knew their names?

They had tried twice more to drive him into that open space at the end of the central canyon where dark cypresses grew at the feet of the needles—tried to drive him into the cantaloupe-colored palace that lay beyond. He had gone there once, the day following the first attempt, curious as to what they wanted of him. He had chosen the hour of noon, when the burnished sun beat straight down on the gravel that covered the carved roadways and dry stream bed—the one hour when he felt safest.

From the top of the steps he had looked into a shadowy hall, a huge, square space whose walls were covered to the height of his shoulders in places with the fine gray sand that drifted between the columns of its open facade. The room went back far deeper than any he had previously seen, its nether end hidden in shadow, and, unlike any other he had seen, its walls had once been plastered and painted. The dim shapes of the frescoes there were almost unrecognizable, yet something about their posture, the activities implied in the stiff, shadowy outlines which were all that remained, troubled him. To his right he could see a small black rectangle of shadow, an inconspicuous door to some inner chamber from which no window opened to the outside. And from that dark door, softly and distinctly, he had heard Starhawk's voice say, "Chief?"

After that he had not dared to go into the central canyon at all. In the heat of noon he slept; in the few morning and evening hours he searched the city, looking for any sign, any book, or any talisman that the Witches of Wenshar might have left, searching for some trace of their power among the crowding mazes of rose-colored cliffs. Only that day he had heard the desperate, feeble crying of a baby and had followed the sound to the entrance of that central canyon. He had stood there a long time, listening to that starved wailing before turning his back and walking away.

By night he watched, and the demons watched him.

Two nights ago, while the storm had screamed overhead and the canyons had been filled with a ghostly haze of hot dust that stirred with eddying winds, they had gathered hundreds thick outside, drifting close to the window where he stood, heart pounding, to stare at him with empty, glowing eyes.

Now the sky above the canyon rim was paling. In an hour it would be safe for him to sleep. He prepared himself to meditate, for it was for this as well as for other things that he had come here. But as he settled his mind into stillness—sharp and clear and small as in a dream—he became aware that Starhawk had entered the city.

Like an echo in his mind, he seemed to hear the strike of hooves along the crumbling walls that spread out beyond the canyons. As he sometimes could, he called her to mind and saw her sitting her horse amid the faded tesselations of the old market square's broken pavement, the stir of dawn wind moving in her white head veils and the horse's flaxen mane. Then he saw her turn her head sharply, as if at some sound.

Very quickly, Sun Wolf descended the curved flight of buttercup sandstone steps to the wide room below. Beyond the spell-written doorsill, the canyon was filled with blue silence; the hush of the place was unnatural, for, in spite of the water in its few stone tanks, birds shunned the place. His feet scrunched on the drifts of sand and gravel as he hastened down the old road. In the hours when the demons still walked, it was too dangerous to take his horse.

As he'd hoped, Starhawk's good sense had kept her in open ground. She sat a sorrel nag from the Palace cavy at the mouth of the narrowest of the three canyons, turning her head cautiously, listening for sounds. The first light of the desert dawn lay full over her, glinting in the silver mountings of her dark green guards' doublet and jerkin and on the steel of sword hilt and dagger. Even as Sun Wolf saw her among the scattered ruins of waist-high walls and fallen pillars of shattered red porphyry, she leaned forward in the saddle, as if trying to catch the echo of some faint cry up in the canyon before her. Nearby, there was a sharp cracking noise, like stone falling from a great height upon stone, and her horse flung up its head, rolling a white, terrified eyed, and tried to bolt.

Starhawk was ready, and the Wolf guessed it wasn't the first such incident since she'd entered the ruins. She reined the frightened animal in a tight circle at the first skittish leap. Framed in the white veils, her sunburned face was impassive; but even at this distance, she looked stretched and taut, as she did when she'd been on patrol too long. As soon as she had the horse under control, he stepped from the shadows of a dilapidated archway and called out to her, "Hawk!"

She looked up, started to spur in his direction, then reined again. Holding in the nervous horse with one hand, she fished in her jerkin pocket for something, and the new light flashed across glass as she angled the mirror in his direction. Only then, satisfied, did she nudge the horse and trot through the drifted sand and bull thorns of the street to where he stood.

"What is it?" She would never, he knew, have come seeking him without reason.

"It's Tazey," Starhawk said quietly. "You'd better come."

"So she's been in a coma since then." Starhawk held her horse in, fighting its not unnatural eagerness to put large expanses of the reg between itself and the harsh, maroon-black cliffs of the Haunted Range's outward face. "Kaletha tried to get in to see her last night. Osgard won't hear of it, and it was all Nanciormis could do to keep him from throwing Kaletha out of the Household entirely." There was no change in her soft, slightly gruff voice as she added, "I think she's dying, Chief."

He glanced sharply over at her. The cuts on her face from the sand and rocks of the storm still glared red and ugly; her gray eyes were fixed ahead of her on the dark notch of Tandieras Pass, barely visible across the lifeless plain of black gravel. Nine years of fighting other peoples' wars for money had taught them both that it is difficult to ride or fight while in tears. Tears were for later.

Sun Wolf squinted with his single eye at his horseback shadow on the pea gravel underfoot, calculating the angle of the sun. "What time did you leave there?"

"Midnight. Osgard and Kaletha were still fighting."

"Wonderful." He pulled the end of his veil up over his mouth against the dust. "I can tell he's going to be thrilled to death to see me."

The shadows had turned and were beginning to lengthen again when they rode up the trail to the dark stone gatehouse of the Fortress on Tandieras Pass. "No sound of mourning," was Sun Wolf's laconic comment. Starhawk nodded. They were both thinking like warriors of the next thing at hand—a cold-bloodedness they understood in one another. Sun Wolf felt no obligation to express his genuine fears for the girl, of whom he'd become fond in the few days he'd known her— nor did he assume Starhawk's enigmatic calm to spring from unconcern. If Tazey died, there would be time enough for grief.

After three days of parched silence in the Haunted Range, it seemed strange to him to see people moving around and to smell water and cooking meats, stranger still to realize he could believe in the reality of what he saw. As they rode in under the gloom of the gatehouse, a small, waiting shadow caught his eye. He reined in, letting Starhawk precede him into the dust-hazed confusion of the stable yards. The shadow stepped forward, pitifully small and thin in his dark doublet and hose and the sorry white ruffle at his neck. The pointy white face looked pleadingly up at him through the gloom.

"How's your sister?" the Wolf asked quietly.

For a moment he had the impression Jeryn would run away. Then the boy ducked his head and mumbled, "You've got to help her. What's wrong with her is magic, isn't it?"

"It is." Sun Wolf dismounted and stood looking down at the skinny, furtive little boy. "And I'll do whatever I can do—but only if *you* get yourself back into bed. The Hawk tells me you caught one hell of a sunstroke coming out to fetch me."

Jeryn colored slightly. "I'm better."

Sun Wolf put his hand under the boy's chin and forced the head up to look critically into Jeryn's face. "The hell you are," he replied evenly after a moment's study of the too-white countenance under its short black curls. "A man who doesn't rest his injuries isn't just a fool —he's a liability to his commander, because they'll never heal properly and, sure as pox and blisters, they'll act up when he's needed most." He passed his hand roughly over the boy's hair, as if patting a dog. "I'll take care of your sister."

"Captain . . ." Jeryn hesitated, then swallowed hard. "I—I'm sorry. It was all my fault to begin with but—but Uncle Nanciormis said I was a coward for not standing up for you to Father. He said if I didn't like the way he taught me I should have tried to keep you here. And I—I'm *not* a coward," he insisted, with the wretchedness of one who knows he will not be believed. "It's just that . . ." He stopped, his lips pressed tight. Then, embarrassed to show his tears, he turned to flee.

"Jeryn."

Though it spoke so quietly, the rusted voice stopped him. He turned, fighting desperately not to cry.

"I never needed proof you were brave," the Wolf said. In the white frame of veils, his face seemed dark in shadows, with its unshaven jaw and single, panther-yellow-eye. "And I never saw any reason to think you were a coward. What's between your father and me is something you don't have to concern yourself with. It has nothing to do with you."

"No, sir," Jeryn whispered. "I'm sorry, sir."

The boy turned and started to run away when Sun Wolf asked, "Your dad with Tazey?"

He stopped again and turned back. "Yes, sir," he said. Then, matter-of-factly, "He's drunk, sir."

Sun Wolf nodded. "Fighting drunk or passing-out drunk?"

"Fighting drunk, sir."

"Wonderful." The Wolf sighed. "Thanks, Scout. Now you get to bed."

"Yes, Captain." And the boy was gone like a shadow.

"You have to hand it to the King for stamina," Sun Wolf grumbled, unwinding his head veils as he and Starhawk climbed the sand-drifted path up from the stables toward the black, square towers of the Hold. "A man's got to be tough to stay fighting drunk for over twenty-four hours without moving along to the passing-out stage."

"I used to work for a man who could do it," Starhawk commented, as they mounted the outside stair. Sun Wolf checked his step as if she'd pinked him with a dagger in the back.

"That was different!"

"*Different* was one word for it," she agreed mildly.

Sun Wolf growled, "That's the damn thing about falling in love with your second-in-command," and resumed his stride up to the balcony with its row of arched doors, Starhawk unsmiling at his heels. "They are with you too long and they know you too well."

"Yes, Chief."

Jeryn and Taswind occupied the last two rooms along the balcony shared by the King's Household. The brazen sun slanted along the dark granite curve of the building's southern face, hurling the shadows of the two partners like an inky scarf into room after room. Anshebbeth, sitting in one of them, sprang up with a nervous cry, her hands reaching out, her face pale and hollowed with sleepless strain. When she saw who it was, she sank back and resumed twisting her hands.

Even out on the balcony, Sun Wolf could hear Osgard's braying voice.

"I won't have it, I tell you! That foul-mouthed nag Nexué's been all over the town, and there isn't a man who isn't saying my daughter's a witch!"

"Although I take exception to the connotations of the word *witch*," Kaletha's caustic voice said, "you cannot deny that what happened has proved that Taswind *is* mageborn."

"The hell I can't deny it!" He turned to loom furiously over Kaletha as Sun Wolf pushed aside the patterned curtain that led into the outer chamber of Tazey's rooms. "She's no more a witch than her mother was! A sweeter, dearer, more obedient girl never walked the face of the earth, do you hear me?"

Kaletha only stiffened and looked down her nose at the bloodshot, unshaven, sweaty giant before her. As usual, her dark red hair was pulled back in braids and loops as intricate as potter's work and her plain black homespun gown spotless; her very fastidiousness a scornful rebuke. "She is mageborn," she insisted stubbornly. "You owe it to her to let me teach her the ways of power."

"I owe it to her to keep her the hell away from you! I won't have it said, and I'll personally take and thrash you if you go near her with your sleep-spells and your weather-calling, and your filthy, stolen books! What man's going to want to marry her, Desert Lord or no Desert Lord, if lies like that go around?"

Her protuberant blue eyes blazed. "They are not lies, and there is no shame attached to it."

"You uppity hag! She'd die of shame before she'd be what you are! Get out of my sight, before I—"

"If you will admit me instead of that useless, whining Bishop—"

"To have her be your student?" Osgard roared, losing what little remained of his temper.

"She needs a teacher, and as I'm the only one—"

"What my daughter needs is a husband! I'll have the man crucified who says she's a witch—or woman, too! I tell you this—she'll never be a student of yours! Now get out!"

The inner door curtain moved, its woven pattern of reds and blues like a wind-stirred garden where the edge of the sunsplash hit it. The Bishop Galdron stepped through, white hands folded before his belt. Though minus his brocaded ceremonial tabard, he still reminded Sun Wolf of an overdressed doll, robe and stole and surcoat all worked with a blazing galaxy of jeweled hieratic symbols. His cold blue eyes touched Sun Wolf and the Hawk, still standing in the arched doorway, then moved to Kaletha. Sternly, he said, "Yes, go. You have done harm enough by your mere presence. Better Taswind had died than had damned her soul with witchery."

"She's no witch!" Osgard roared, livid.

"She is a witch." The old man's red lips folded taut within the silky frame of mustaches. "And as a witch, she is damned . . ."

"Get out off here, both of you!" Osgard's face was scarlet, a tear-streaked mess of graying stubble and broken veins. "You should talk about witchery, you stinking hypocrite, when your own acolyte has been keeping company with Kaletha for months!"

Galdron turned, startled and deeply shocked, and Kaletha could not repress a smile of smug and vicious triumph at his discomfiture. Then she swept past Sun Wolf and out onto the balcony. Galdron, face pink with anger, hastened at her heels. The curtain swirled in the backwash of their wake, then settled over the folded-back storm shutters once more.

Sun Wolf remained, facing the King.

"You . . ." Osgard's voice was thick and slurred. "You—it's your fault. My son ran away to see you . . ."

"Your son ran away because he was too scared of you to speak for me, and your daughter was too scared to ask your help." Sun Wolf folded his arms, his whole body relaxed into battle-waiting, a deceptive, hair-trigger readiness. "Now will you let me save her life, or are you going to have her die to prove yourself right?"

Osgard's face went white with speechless anger; Sun Wolf wondered clinically if he would suffer a stroke on the spot. Then, with a bellow like an exploding furnace, he roared, "I'll have you crucified for that! Guards!" In a swirling gust of stale wine fumes the King sprang for Sun Wolf's throat.

Reflecting in the split second between the King's attack and his own reaction that his father had been right when he'd cautioned him, in the name of all his ancestors, never to mess with magic or argue with drunks, Sun Wolf sidestepped the attack. He blocked the outstretched hands with a swipe of one forearm and used the other hand to deliver a neat, straight punch to the stubbly jaw that the King walked directly into.

Osgard went down like a felled tree.

Sun Wolf stepped back from the unconscious King just as Nanciormis and half a dozen guardsmen came bursting through the door that led down to the inner stair from the Hall. For a moment the Wolf and Nanciormis faced one another across the slumped body, the guards clustering at his back and clutching their sword hilts in readiness for anything. Then the commander turned to the guards and said gravely, "His Majesty is fatigued. Take him to his room."

He stepped aside as they bore the King out past him and down the stairs, watching inscrutably until they turned the corner down into the Hall. Then he glanced back at Sun Wolf.

"I see I was wrong about the uses of magic," he said quietly. "Do what you can for her. I'll see you're left alone."

"I'd call that magnanimous of him," Starhawk remarked softly, as the commander passed through the wide arch out onto the balcony and thence, presumably, to his own room down at its farther end.

"Except that he waited until he was damn sure nobody was around to hear him say it."

"Maybe." Sun Wolf watched thoughtfully as the vast curtain settled back to stillness once more against the hard glare of the arch. "He's a politician, Hawk—and as a politician he deals with the way things are, not how they're supposed to be. Whatever else can be said about him, he's enough of a shirdar lord to know that magic has nothing to do with the Bishop's threats of Hell."

He turned for the inner door to Tazey's room, and Starhawk said quietly, " 'Shebbeth should be here."

He stopped, a little surprised, knowing she was right. For all she was a soldier, the Hawk had a woman's acute sensitivity to social usages. "If you think she'd be of any use, you're welcome to go look for her," he said. "Though it's my guess Osgard turned her out—and no wonder."

Starhawk paused, remembering the governess' tear-streaked face and hysterical hand-wringing, glimpsed through the balcony door, and said no more on the subject.

The windows of Tazey's small bedroom faced northwest, toward the harsh chaparral desert and the rugged mountains beyond. At this time of the day, the room was flooded with sunlight and, with the windows tightly shut in accordance with good medical practice, unbearably hot and close. The air was heavy with the smells of burned herbs, sickly after the dry movement of the desert air from which Sun Wolf had come. Tazey lay stretched out on her narrow bed; but for the movement of her young breasts under the sheet, she might have been dead already. Her tan stood out like a bad coat of paint against the underlying waxiness of her flesh; from the corners of her shut eyes ran the dried tracks of tears wept in her sleep.

Hesitantly, Sun Wolf knelt beside the bed and took the girl's hand in his. It felt cold. He counted the pulse, when he found it after long search, and it was leaden as a stream choked with winter ice. A lifetime on the battlefield had given him a certain skill at rough-and-ready surgery; later, Yirth of Mandrigyn had shown him the spells to hold the failing spirit to the flesh until the flesh had time to respond to medicines. But this was not a matter of the flesh at all. The symptoms resembled, if anything, those of freezing and exhaustion.

He had no idea where to start. He had healed warriors with warriors' means, but this was different. In the last nine months, he had done a very little healing by means of the few spells Yirth had taught him and had always been astonished when they worked. He looked down now at the girl's browned face against the pillow, the scattered, sun-streaked hair, and the blue smudges of exhaustion that shadowed the tensed eyelids. For the first time, he released his hold on a warrior's readiness and felt grief for her, grief and a terrible pity for what had befallen her.

He remembered her in the war dance—the light, buoyant strength of her movements, the joy in her eyes at being only what she was. In the few days he'd been in Tandieras he'd become fond of her, with a virile middle-aged man's affection for a young girl, that odd combination of paternalism and a sort of nonpersonal lust. But she was, he understood now, a wizard like himself, perhaps stronger than he. And she would be as terrified of her powers as he was of his. *The sweetest daughter a man could want,* her father had said of her. No wonder she was terrified to find herself, against her will, the thing he most wanted for her not to be. No wonder that knowledge drove her power inward, until her very soul was eating her body with guilt and grief and shame.

He let go of her hand and rose to open the casements of the windows, letting in the dry smell of the desert—the comforting mingle of stables, sage, and sky. Voices drifted to him—Kaletha's short and defiant from the courts below, the Bishop's full of querulous rage. Closer, he heard Anshebbeth's sobs, muffled, as if against bedding or a man's shoulder. Taking a stump of chalk from his pocket, he drew on the red-tiled floor around the bed one of the Magic Circles, a precautionary measure against evils that Yirth, when she had taught him this one, had been unable to define clearly. After a moment's thought, he also traced the runes of wizardry, of life, of strength, of journeys undertaken and safely completed—marks that would draw to them the constellations of influences and could help to focus his mind. It was all done by rote—he had never used them before and had no idea how to do so, but went through the motions as he would have undertaken weapons drill with an unfamiliar piece of equipment. There was no sense neglecting his teaching simply because it meant nothing to him yet.

He returned to the bed and took Tazey's hand.

He wondered if it was imagination, if it felt colder than it had. He drew three deep breaths and settled his mind to meditation. Clumsily, hesitantly, he pushed aside all the crowding worries and resentments, the random thoughts that the mind flings up to disguise its fear of stillness. He gathered light around him and, as if sinking into deep water, he sought the Invisible Circle, where he knew he would find Tazey hiding from herself.

She woke up crying. For a long time, she lay with her face turned away from him, sobbing as if everything within her body and soul had been torn out of her—*as indeed,* Sun Wolf thought, almost too weary for pity, *it had been.* He himself felt little but an exhaustion all out of proportion to the short time he felt he had meditated. Then, gently making her roll over, he rubbed her back as he had seen market women rub babies to soothe their wordless griefs.

Only after a time did he notice that the room was cool. The air outside the broad window had been drenched with light and heat when he had sunk into meditation; it was dark as pitch now. Listening, he tried to determine from the sounds in the building below how late it was, but that was difficult, for Tazey's illness had cast a pall of silence over the Citadel. Someone—Starhawk, probably—had kindled the two alabaster night lamps that rested on the carved ebony clothes chest, and molten lakes of light wavered on the ceiling above.

He felt weak and a little strange, as if he had swum for miles. His legs, doubled up under him, were stiff and prickly as he shifted position. For a long time, he was content to remain where he was, only rubbing the girl's back to let her know she was not alone. He had found her in the desolate country that borders the lands of death, wandering, crying, in darkness; he knew, and she knew, that she had not wanted to come back with him.

After a long time she turned her head on the pillow and whispered, "Is my father very angry?"

She was a mage like himself now, and he could not lie to her. Moreover, in the shadowlands of the soul there is always a bond between those who have sought and those who have been found. He said, "Yes. But you can't let that rule you anymore."

She drew in a quick breath and held it for a few seconds before letting it go. "I didn't want this," she said at last, her voice very thin. She lifted her face from the pillow, ugly, swollen, cut up with the violence of the sandstorm and crumply with tears. Her absinthe-green eyes were circled in lavender smudges, the eyes of the woman she would one day be. "I tried . . ."

"Jeryn knew enough to ask you where I was."

She nodded miserably. "I used to find things when I was little and he was just a baby. Once when he got lost in the old quarter of the Fortress I found him just by—by shutting my eyes and thinking about him. That's how I knew you were in Wenshar and how I knew he'd gone after you. But later I—I tried not to do it anymore." She sniffled, and wiped her reddened nose. "Does this mean that I'm damned?"

"It means that Galdron will say you are."

She was silent for a time, digesting this distinction, then said, "I didn't want this. I don't want to be a witch. Witches are . . ."

She paused and looked up at him.

"No one's asking you to decide right now," Sun Wolf said quietly. "But I, for one, want to thank you, with all my heart, for saving the Hawk's life. You saved Jeryn, too, and your friends Pothero and Shem."

"But they're afraid of me now," she murmured, and another tear crept down her puffy cheek.

"Probably," he agreed. "But I don't think Jeryn is, and I know the Hawk's not—so it isn't everybody."

Her voice was distant, wistful, as if she already knew she was speaking of someone else. "I don't want to change. I mean—I might not like what I'll become."

Tenderly, he brushed aside the snarly rats of her dust-laden hair. "Then don't change tonight," he replied. "You can't change at three in the morning anyway, nobody can . . ." Her sob caught on a laugh. "Sleep now."

"Will you . . ." She swallowed, embarrassed. "Do you think you could—could stay with me for a little while? I had dreams. . . . When I was asleep, before you found me, I dreamed . . . awful things. The Witches . . ."

"I'll be here," he reassured her softly, weary as he was from the long day's ride and from last night's watching. (He had been known to sit for longer than this in all-night watches on some enemy camps.) He held Tazey's hand, large and strong and warm now in his own, while her soft breathing evened toward dreamless sleep. Detachedly, he studied the smudgy, chalked circles around the bed—the Circle of Light, Yirth had called one, and the Circle of Darkness, though why they were so called she had not known. He shook his head. *Kaletha was right,* he thought. *She would have to be taught,* and he knew that neither he, nor, he suspected, Kaletha, was equipped to do it.

Another thought crossed his mind, and he frowned, wondering why it had not occurred to him before—not only for Tazey, but for himself.

Tazey murmured something, stirred in her sleep, and then lay quiet again. Though she still slept lightly, he could see no dreams tracking her discolored eyelids. Soundless, as if on patrol, he climbed stiffly to his feet and crossed to the curtained door.

"Hawk?" he said softly into the dimness beyond.

There was no reply.

He stepped past the curtain to the candlelit outer room. Muted radiance played over the carved wooden armoire, the oak chairs with their red leather seats, and the little round corner fireplace. On the polished sideboard, a couple of candles in silver holders shed soft rings of brightness. The heavy curtains had been drawn over the archway to the balcony—a stray gust of dry wind stirred them, a ripple of reflected flame danced along their gilt borders. There was no one there.

He walked to the other doorway, which led to the inner stair down to the Hall. Through it he could see torchlight and shadow from the hall below playing across the stone vaults. A muffled clamor of voices came to him, rising and falling, agitated but unintelligible. *If Galdron's making more trouble for her,* he thought grimly, *or Nexué . . . If Kaletha's carrying on again about her poxy rights . . .*

A shadow swept across the red glow from beneath, and a moment later he heard a cat-soft stride on the stairs that could only be Starhawk's.

"What is it?" he asked when she appeared in the doorway.

Her face inexpressive, she said, "Nexué the laundress."

Sun Wolf's single yellow eye glinted dangerously. "What's the bitch been up to now?"

"Not much," said Starhawk calmly. "She's dead."

CHAPTER

7

W ITH QUIET VICIOUSNESS, ANSHEBBETH SAID, "I CAN'T SAY I'M
surprised to hear it. Sooner or later someone was bound to wring that
filthy old woman's neck." She stared into the fire with dark eyes that
smoldered like the logs crumbling there.

"Don't talk like that." Kaletha shot her an angry sidelong glance; in
her black homespun lap, Sun Wolf observed that her hands were shaking.

The governess looked up at her, hurt at the rebuke. "You—" she
began, and Kaletha cut her off.

"Hatred is an impurity of the soul as foul as the fornications of the
body," she said too quickly. "If I've taught you nothing else, you
should have learned that."

Her dark eyes filling with wounded tears, Anshebbeth nodded, her
hand stealing to her tightening throat as she mumbled that she had not
meant it. Annoyed, Kaletha looked away. Egaldus, talking quietly
with Nanciormis, the Bishop, and two shaken-looking guardsmen
down near the door, raised his head at the shrillness of her words; but
after a moment's hesitation, he stayed where he was.

Quietly, Sun Wolf moved to the wine cabinet at the far side of the
dais from the dim glow of the hearth where the two women sat, and
filled two silver goblets of wine.

"That's your answer to everything, isn't it?" demanded Kaletha as

Sun Wolf's shadow fell over her. "Drink—like that pathetic sot Osgard . . ."

"My answer to everywhere is having you relax, woman."

"I am relaxed, and I don't need your wine, nor does Shebbeth." Anshebbeth stopped her hand in mid-reach for the goblet, then obediently folded it with her other in her lap.

Nanciormis left the little group beside the arched vestibule doors and strode the length of the Hall to the dais to put a gentling hand on Anshebbeth's shoulder. In the wavery glow of the sconces on either side of the hearth, his curving black brows stood out sharply, as if, beneath the bronze of his tan, he had gone pale at what he had heard.

"Perhaps Anshebbeth should go up and sit with Lady Taswind," he suggested softly. "I need to speak with the Captain alone for a few moments." To Sun Wolf, in private, he had made any number of crude jests at the governess's expense, but part of his charm lay in his knowing when to say the right thing.

Shebbeth's anxious glance shifted from Nanciormis to Kaletha, but Kaletha, still irrationally annoyed with her subservience, looked away in pointed disgust. That she would have been still more annoyed had Anshebbeth not immediately agreed with her, as she had done in the public gardens when the subject of physical love came up, evidently had no bearing on the matter. Anshebbeth, with the tight misery on her face of one who knows she can do no right, gathered her dark skirts and hastened away up the winding stair.

"At least that gets *her* out of our hair," Nanciormis murmured, taking one of the goblets from Sun Wolf's hand and leading him away from the carved bench where Kaletha now sat alone. "How is Tazey?"

Sun Wolf shook his head. "Sleeping all right, now," he said softly. "She'll live—but I tell you right now, she won't be the same."

The commander let out his breath in a sigh. "Dear Gods—" He used the shirdar word for gods. "Never in a hundred years would I have thought Jeryn would try to go after you. Frankly, I didn't think the boy had it in him—but it was a stupid thing to say, nevertheless."

"What did you say?" The Wolf paused in his step and regarded the commander curiously under the harsh doubled light of a pair of torches on the wall.

The gold rings that held his braids flashed as Nanciormis shook his head. "I no longer remember exactly, though I should. He'd been whining all afternoon—that Sun Wolf hadn't made him climb ropes and Sun Wolf hadn't made him do tumbling and Sun Wolf hadn't made him lift weights—which I knew perfectly well you had. At last I lost my temper and said that if he preferred your teaching, he should have had the nerve to stand up to his father for you. That's all. I *never* meant that he should go after you." He took a quick gulp of the wine; some of the color was returning to his heavy cheeks. "And now this . . ."

Sun Wolf glanced along the Hall to the guards, still grouped in a whispering cluster around the dark archways to the vestibule. "What happened?"

Nanciormis took another drink and shook his head. "It must have happened sometime late last night," he said quietly. "Whoever did it has to have been tremendously strong. Nexué was literally hacked into pieces. I don't know what they used—an axe or a scythe, perhaps . . ." He swallowed, still shaken by the memory.

He had seen war, Sun Wolf thought. *This was different.*

"A strong man can do a lot of damage with a sword." He turned his own untouched cup in his hands, watching the torch-glare flash on the dark wine, but not drinking. He had eaten nothing since their nooning stop at the edge of the reg, and he knew his capacity for wine was not what it once had been. "And this happened last night?"

"Or early this morning. She was found in one of the old workshops in the empty quarter—by the blood trail, she'd been pursued there . . ."

"What was she doing down there?"

Nanciormis let out an ironic bark of laughter. "There's a servants' privy near the wall—by the look of it that's where she was bound, though she could have been going anywhere. Nexué was a sneak and a spy as well as a gossip—there wasn't much going on in the Citadel she didn't know about. The empty quarter's been used for assignations before this."

"And she wasn't found until *tonight?*" Sun Wolf's tufted eyebrows plunged down over his nose, making the worn eye patch shift.

"What with . . ." Nanciormis hesitated. Even with Osgard snoring in his bedchamber, he was reading softly. "With the uproar over Taswind, no one noticed her absence until this evening when the wind turned."

"What about the dogs?"

"Dogs?" Nanciormis looked blank.

"There are dogs all over this Fortress. You're not telling me they weren't at the corpse."

The commander frowned suddenly, seeing the anomaly. "They weren't," he said after a moment. "Nor were the raverns, now that you speak of it, and there are always a few of them hanging around the kitchen middens. Now why . . . ?"

"I'd like to have a look at the place."

Nanciormis nodded. Sun Wolf glanced back—Starhawk was sitting on the bench beside Kaletha with her arm around those slender, bowed dark shoulders. The Bishop being out of the room, Egaldus was hunkered down before the White Witch, holding her hands and speaking soft words of comfort to her. Kaletha sat rigid, shaking her head stubbornly again and again.

Though Sun Wolf said nothing, Starhawk looked up at him and, with a final, gentle pat, rose from Kaletha's side. As she joined him and they began to walk toward the door of the Hall, Sun Wolf paused and looked back at Nanciormis. "Osgard know?" he asked.

The commander's full-lipped mouth quirked with scorn. "Would it do any good if he did?"

"You'll have to be gone by daybreak," Starhawk said as she and the Wolf wound their way through the small courts around the Hold's long southern side toward the little gate that led to the empty quarter. "Osgard gave me the word I could stay—apparently they really need guards because working in the mines pays twice what the King does— but he made it damn clear I'd better not mention how I happened not to get killed by the sandstorm."

"What's his alternative explanation?"

She shrugged. Even with the moon on the wane, its light was strong enough to cast shadows beneath the small adobe gateway. Looking back at the Hold, the Wolf could see the glow of the night lamps in Tazey's rooms, turning the curtained arch to a dully glowing gold like a banked oven. He didn't remember who all else those rooms belonged to, save for the one with the rose reflection of candlelight, which must be Jeryn's. He paused in the small gateway, looking down at the sloping path across the little court beyond, and an odd shiver went down his spine at the sight of the black door to the cell he and the Hawk had shared.

Matter-of-factly, Starhawk went on, "I don't think he has one, not even for himself."

"He'd better," the Wolf growled. "She's got to be taught."

She glanced up at him in the ivory–yellow moonlight. "Who taught Kaletha, I wonder?"

He grinned. Starhawk might not be mageborn, but she understood more about how magic had to work than anyone the Wolf had ever talked to. "It occurred to me to wonder that myself when I was up with Tazey. I've been thinking Kaletha sprang her 'destiny' on the other people here in Tandieras cold, but . . . There has to have been somebody, even if he never declared his own powers for fear of Altiokis. Beyond a doubt, he or she is dead now, because we haven't heard of any other wizard—but there could have been another student. If we can find out who that wizard was and back-trail him . . ."

"I don't know," the Hawk said doubtfully. "I've listened to her teach. Now, when you taught back at the warrior's school in Wrynde, it was always, 'My father always said . . .' or 'The captain of Queen Izacha's bodyguard showed me this . . .' But she hands it all down as if she'd invented it."

Sun Wolf paused, realizing what it was about Kaletha's teaching that had rubbed him the wrong way. "In other words, she wouldn't say." He leaned his wide shoulders in the broken adobe of the gateway. The moonlight, where it touched his hair, turned it to wan and faded gold. Across the court a pack rat slipped from the door of their cell, ran a few paces, stopped to sit up, sniffing cautiously at the cold air, then dashed in a tiny skiff of thrown sand to the camel-bush beside the old well. "She's close with her power," the Wolf went on slowly. "She wants to stay the teacher, to hold her disciples to her—she likes the power it gives. If there is competition for the post, she's not going to let anyone know. But in a place like this, you can't hide the kind of relationship teacher and student have to have. It takes years to learn, Hawk—if she'd been that close to someone that long, somebody would know."

" 'Shebbeth," Starhawk said promptly. "She's been here at least ten years. Jealous as she is of anyone who's Kaletha's friend, you bet she'd know."

"And she'd probably tell," the Wolf said, "if only to run them down." He looked back over his shoulder to the amber warmth of the archway at the top of the outside stair. "She'll keep," he said. "She's with Tazey now and shouldn't be leaving her. Come on." He shoved himself off the wall with one shoulder and moved out into the cold moonlight of the court, the sandy gravel scrunching under his boots. "There's a lot to do and not much left of the night."

They found Nexué's tracks easily—Starhawk could have done so herself without Sun Wolf's ability to see in darkness. Even the scrubby, wire grass and camel-thorn cast frail shadows by the brilliance of the westering moon. The path to the servants' privies out beyond the stable hugged the wall, but, since the storm, no one had crossed the little court itself. A single line of smudgy marks veered sharply away from the packed earth of the path, first back toward the gate, then away past the cells into the empty quarter.

"She must have seen someone standing about there in the shadows of the corner of the wall," the Wolf guessed, studying them. "Or heard something . . ."

"Heard, most likely." Starhawk picked her way carefully through the drifted sand left by the storm. "There are no marks in that shadow."

Sun Wolf grunted to himself. He could see where Nexué had changed direction and run, not back toward the gate, but across the court to the mazes of crumbling adobe walls and barred black moonlight of the empty quarter. Circling, he kept his eyes to the ground, moving cautiously so as not to foul other marks. But even with a wizard's vision in darkness, he saw no print, no mark, no reason that would have caused the old woman to do so.

Someone on the path, perhaps? In the ensuing twenty-four hours between the incident and its discovery, scores of servants had taken this route to the privies. *Still . . .*

Drift-sand from the storm lay deep in the court, poured in little dunes through the door of the abandoned cell. Nexué's tracks were only a desperate shuffle—her run must have been slow and scuffling, with sand and pea gravel kicked back in sloppy crescents behind her. If someone had run in her tracks, the footmarks were only blurred dents, tangled with hers.

Yet something made the Wolf uneasy. The empty quarter lay silent as death around him as he stalked the trail to its obvious and pitiful conclusion—the first drippy smattering of blood, where some swung weapon had made its contact with flesh, then the hand mark where Nexué had stumbled, caught herself, and fled desperately on through the parched, empty courts. The blood had dried during the intervening day, but the old dye shop where she had finally fallen reeked of it still. Looking around him at the dark stains lying like shadows where no shadows should be, Sun Wolf felt a kind of thankfulness that it was now the coldest part of the night and there were no insects.

Nexué had been a gross and dirty-minded old woman, he thought, *but still . . . By the amount of blood, she must have run about here for a long time.*

What was left of the body had been taken away. The ground was a scuffed muck of confused tracks of the guards, Nanciormis, and the Bishop. Impersonally, Sun Wolf cursed them all.

"Not a single damn killer's track," he muttered as he and Starhawk retraced their route back through the empty courts and the walkways whose roofs had been stripped away by decades of autumn storms and whose shattered rafters slanted down amid the sand drifts to impede their steps. Somewhere in the stillness an owl hooted; there was the swift skitter of sand, a shadow passing soundlessly overhead, and a faint squeak of pain. Sun Wolf's boots slid heavily in the drifted sand between two walls, then ground on the harsh gravel beyond. "And if they had the wits to run along the tops of the broken walls, they could have gotten clean away without leaving so much as a mark. There's a dozen dry wells and pits where a weapon and bloodstained clothing could have been dropped . . ." He paused, frowning, his single eye glinting like transparent amber in the zebra shadows. "I don't like this, Hawk."

She nodded, understanding what he meant. Around them, the empty quarter was silent as death.

"Could you have done it?"

"Physically?" She shook her head. "Oh, maybe with one of those big two-handed swords like Eo the Blacksmith used to use—the kind that, even if she hit you with the flat of it, would break your back. But there wasn't room in some of those corridors to use something like that, and you sure as hell couldn't do it running. No." She folded her arms, looking around her at the silent mazes of sand and half-fallen adobe. "I can understand someone wanting to kill her to shut her up about something—the Mother knows she was a spy as well as a gossip and spread her filth around like a monkey. But—they found her literally in pieces, Wolf. Someone chased her through those courts and walls for nearly a hundred yards. What they did to her was more than just murder—and I can think of only one person who was big enough and strong enough to cut her up that way and who wanted to shut her up."

Sun Wolf nodded. Before them, the bulk of the Hold was mostly dark now as the final commotions of magic and murder lapsed into exhausted repose. The light still burned in Tazey's room at one end of the long southern balcony. At the southeastern end of the jagged block of crenelated granite, another rectangle of wine gold showed where a lamp still glowed in the King's solar.

The Wolf said slowly, "We can't know he was the only one, Hawk. There could have been others, for other reasons or maybe for the same reason. But yes—I'd sort of like to know where Osgard was around this time last night."

When Sun Wolf ascended the stair that curved up over the Hold's southern face, the rooms along the balcony were silent. Below and around him, the velvet darkness had turned to ash; eastward, the slag-colored bulk of Mount Morian loomed against the first stains of dawn. Like candlelight caught on a needle's tip, the spire of the cathedral below glinted with wakening gold. Pinpricks of light across the mountain's feet showed where men and women were already rising to breakfast in darkness before going on shift in the mines. Standing on the balcony, the Wolf sensed all the furtive movements of the night winding to a close—foxes and coyotes in the empty mile between town and Fortress trotting back to their burrows in the rocks, licking the last dabs of blood from their whiskers, wrens and wheatears waking to whistle their territories in the dark.

In Tazey's room, the candles still burned. Sun Wolf, hidden in the fold of shadow and curtain, softly called Anshebbeth's name, remembering how sound carried against the long southern face of the Hold, but got no reply. Stepping soundlessly across to the inner chamber, he saw Tazey tossing restlessly in unquiet sleep; there was no sign of her governess. He cursed the woman for leaving her and crossed to the bed to lay his hand over the girl's fingers. They felt hot. Her face looked flushed and swollen, as if with fever; when he bent over her, she turned her head away, whispering desperately, "I won't! I won't!"

With a touch astonishingly light for such massive hands, he brushed aside the snarly hair from her face. "You don't have to, Tazey," he murmured, though he could tell she was deep asleep.

She gave a little sob and quieted; he remained kneeling beside the bed, where he had spent so many hours that afternoon, until she appeared easier in her dreams. It seemed incredible to him that this was part of that same night.

When her breathing had settled into evenness again, he got to his feet and moved softly through the outer room once more and out to the balcony. As Tazey's governess, Anshebbeth should have a room near hers, though privately he suspected she was with Kaletha, wherever Kaletha was. 'Shebbeth was genuinely fond of her charge, but he'd seen her abandon Tazey any number of times, when she should have been playing chaperone, to go scurrying to the Witch's side. *And overwrought as she had been down in the Hall earlier,* he thought, *Kaletha just might have asked it of her.*

But he was wrong.

The curtains were drawn shut over the next arch, but a strip of roseate light lay like a petticoat hem on the tiles beneath. He listened for a moment, but heard no sound, then gently pushed the curtain aside.

Anshebbeth startled up from the divan. "My love, what . . . ?" she began, seeing his dark shape against the night; then, as he stepped into the light, her sleep-flushed face scalded crimson, then drained white. She hastily pulled her unfastened gown across her narrow breasts, shaking fingers tangling with the unbound swatches of her black hair as she clutched the collar up to her throat. Her shoes lay separate, fallen, on two sides of the divan; the warm air redolent with the pungence of sex.

His whole mind one giant, astonished question, Sun Wolf only said, "You should be with Tazey. She shouldn't be alone."

"No—of course not—" she twittered inaudibly, fumbling at buttons, her huge dark eyes cast down. "That is—I came in here to—to lie down. I was so tired—the news about Nexué . . ."

He looked from the rucked cushions of the divan to her narrow white toes, peeping, somehow obscene, from beneath the crumpled skirts. Starhawk, he thought, would be vastly interested, as he was himself—it came to him in a burst of enlightenment why 'Shebbeth had spoken out in favor of carnality and called down Kaletha's scorn on her head.

"It's none of my business," he said quietly. "But I have to be gone from here at dawn, and there's something I want to ask you."

She turned back, her narrow face suspicious as she finger-combed her thick hair back, her black eyes darting over the tiled floor in quest of hairpins. They were strewn everywhere, as a man's plucking hand would leave them scattered. Sun Wolf picked up two and walked over to give them to her. He had never considered her a pretty woman, though physical beauty meant less to him that it once had; more than her thin, pointy plainness, her obsessive clinginess repulsed him. The cruel jests Nanciormis made of her were not entirely unjustified. She took the hairpins from his hand without touching his fingers; her eyes did not meet his. "What?" she asked.

He did not sit on the divan, knowing she would have shrunk from him. "It's to help Tazey," he said gently, and she relaxed a little and looked up into his face. "And she's going to need help."

Anshebbeth drew in her breath and let it go in a tense sigh. She was taut as wet rope, as if holding herself in. Sun Wolf fetched a chair from against the wall and sat opposite her; he saw her relax a little more, now that his physical size did not tower over her. Shrilly, she said, "Kaletha is more than willing to help. But that—that pathetic sot of a father of hers won't let her." She brought out Kaletha's words pat. "He'd rather see her die than admit she was born with the power."

"I know," said the Wolf. "That's what I need to talk to you about. Tazey's father and Kaletha don't get along—I think that's one reason he's refusing to accept her help or the help of any of her students."

"He's just being unreasonable," she returned, speaking rapidly, still not meeting his eyes. She pushed one hairpin in, but dropped the other nervously. It glinted in her sable lap with the coppery gleam of the lamp. "He's a stubborn old drunkard who won't see Kaletha's power, her skill, her destiny—"

Sun Wolf held up his hand. "I know that. But neither you, I, nor Kaletha, can help what he is."

"He can admit he's been wrong . . ."

"But he won't."

"He should," she insisted stubbornly, and Sun Wolf felt a surge of sympathy for Nanciormis' cruel jokes.

"And he may—but maybe not early enough to help Tazey." Anshebbeth started to make a comeback to this, and he went resolutely on. "All we can do is deal with the situation as it is. Osgard doesn't believe Kaletha, doesn't credit her power, I think partly because he's known her all her life. But another wizard might have a chance."

"It's Kaletha's right to be her teacher." The thin white hands clenched in her lap as she leaned forward. "It's her destiny."

"Maybe," said Sun Wolf, wondering how Anshebbeth could go on championing the cause of a teacher who he had seen treat her like an importunate dog. "But if there's a fight over it with Osgard, it's Tazey who's going to suffer."

Anshebbeth's mouth tightened, as if she would protest Kaletha's rights in the matter yet again, but she did not. She looked down at her long, thin hands, turning the fallen hairpin over and over again in her lap, and said nothing.

"Who was Kaletha's teacher?"

She raised her eyes at that and answered immediately, pride in her voice. "Oh, she didn't have one."

Sun Wolf frowned. "What do you mean, didn't have one? You don't just . . . just make up spells. Someone has to teach you."

The governess shook her head, the expression on her face the smug, proud look of a girl who is friends with the prettiest girl in school. "Kaletha didn't need a teacher. And, in any case, there was no one— since the destruction of Wenshar, there has been violent, unreasonable prejudice against the mageborn throughout these lands. Her destiny led her to books of magic, lost for centuries, but she had the power before then. I knew it even when she was just a young girl and I first came here to be Taswind's governess. It glowed out of her, like the flame in an alabaster lamp." Her face changed as she remembered that imperious red-haired girl; soft eagerness suffused her voice. "She was seventeen, beautiful, proud, and pure—even then—as if she knew her destiny. And there were many men who—who—who would have dishonored her purity, if they could. But she was strong, disdaining such abasement . . ." Her voice faltered, and color mounted again in her pale cheeks. She hastened on, "Right from the beginning, though I am the elder, it was she who was my teacher, not I hers. She—"

"What books?" He had heard her on the subject of Kaletha before. Osgard's words came back to him, *your filthy, stolen books* . . . "Where did she get them?"

"She would never say." Her hand fidgeted nervously at her throat, but she looked glad to speak of something other than Kaletha's idea of purity. "I never saw them, myself. But if it had not been the books, she would have grown in her powers in some other way. And it is much harder," she added nervously, "to achieve that kind of skill simply from books without a teacher. All that she has, she has striven for herself—with meditation, self-denial, and—and her own mind. She is one of those people who cannot help but be great. I . . . ." Her voice trailed off. Nervously, she stroked the disheveled cushions of the divan, her black hair spilling down, all wrinkled from its braids, to curtain her crimsoning face. "I will never be great. My honor is—has always been—to help her. She knows this. We understand one another."

She understands you, anyway, the Wolf thought, with cynical pity. *You poor deluded bitch.* But he only said, "Where are these books?"

But Anshebbeth would only shake her head, unwilling—or unable —to say.

Starhawk was waiting for him at the bottom of the stairs. He tried to think when she must last have slept, before riding out to Wenshar to fetch him—and, that, after the sandstorm and all that had happened since. But as usual, she gave the impression that, if he had suggested immediate and bloody battle, she would only have asked in which direction the enemy lay.

He sighed. He himself felt utterly weary, the tiredness coming on him suddenly, like the rising tides of the distant sea. Daylight and darkness memories telescoped together: bluish lights wavering among pillared shadows upon which they cast no brightness; Osgard's thick, slurring voice raised in anger; and a single line of desperately stumbling footprints through the drifted sand of an empty, moonlit court. The moon stood now over the Binnig Rock, a baroque pearl on the gray silk sky.

"You'd better go." Starhawk leaned her elbow on the smooth granite of the balustrade, the line of her body reminding him of a lioness in its easy strength. He saw now she'd washed and changed clothes at some time during the night; she was always as clean as a cat when she wasn't up to her elbows in other people's blood. "They tell me you can make a pretty decent living as a miner—the pay's twice what guards get."

Sun Wolf looked up at the line of dark archways on the balcony above—the balcony where he remembered Starhawk saying she'd seen a man slip into one of those rooms, and heard a woman's startled cry, on the night he and Nanciormis had come walking back from drinking with the King. He remembered, too, Starhawk's voice that night, calling out to him from the frosted moonlight of the court, warning him of danger whose existence she could not prove.

Then he glanced back toward the dove-colored bulk of that gate.

Nexué had passed through it, on her way to what had turned out to be her death. He wondered if the birds in the empty quarter had been silent that morning, as they had been when he had found the slaughtered doves.

"I don't think I should leave, Hawk," he said quietly.

Her tone was judicious. "King's gonna be sore when he sees you in the Hall for breakfast."

He didn't take up her jest. "Smuggle me some. I'll be a couple of courtyards into the empty quarter." Even as he said it, he felt a shiver, remembering again the blood-splattered adobe, the sifted gray dust untouched by tracks. Beyond the little gate he could see the maze of walls and rafters and courtyards filled with drifted sand and broken tiles—the unburied corpse of a fortress. The woman beside him straightened up and tucked her hands into her sword belt, a stance she had picked up over the years from him. The first glow of dawn glinted like cold steel dew on the studding of her jerkin. She regarded him with eyes the color of the gray-winter sky, not surprised. But then, the Hawk was never surprised.

"Why ever Nexué was killed, that butchering wasn't the act of a sane man. And maybe it wasn't the act of a man at all. There's a stink about this, Hawk, a stink of evil. I don't know who's going to need protection, but somebody sure as hell will."

CHAPTER

*T*HROUGHOUT THAT DAY AND THE NEXT, SUN WOLF LAY HIDDEN in the empty quarter. When he went to earth there in the dawn after the finding of Nexué's body, it was with a certain uneasiness, but he slept dreamlessly in one of the long dormitories, which still retained its roof. He took the time to scratch the Circle of Light and the Circle of Darkness in the dust around him, not knowing whether they would work against a supernatural danger and not knowing what that danger might be. It was only an edge, a possibility—like covering his tracks. Waking with the noon sun glaring through the holes in the roof where, over the years, storms had blown tiles loose, he saw a camel-spider the size of his out-spread hand trundle determinedly over the uneven curves of the dirt-covered floor, stop at the edge of the outer Circle, then skirt it as if it were a pool of water.

During the day, Sun Wolf remained indoors and under cover. Too many windows and battlements of the Fortress overlooked the sprawl of those decaying walls. In his heart, he did not really fear Osgard's threat to have him crucified if he ever showed his face in Tandieras again . . . but that was Osgard sane.

Someone had cut Nexué to pieces, and Sun Wolf was not about to make the mistake of thinking that drunken yelling was all the King might do in his rage.

When darkness fell, he moved out of the few roofed buildings and looked for tracks. Even in a desert climate, adobe structures decayed very rapidly once they lost their roofs; the maze of the empty quarter consisted of many walls only a few feet high as well as cells, chambers, and dormitories, whose roofs had but recently fallen but still retained their semblance of being rooms. Drifts of sand, gravel, and broken roof tiles lay everywhere, stitched with tracks: the ladderlike marks of sidewinders, the feathering of lizard tracks, light bird prints like the ancient shirdar runes he had seen carved in the butter-colored sandstone of Wenshar. The adobe walls were five feet thick and more—it was easily possible for a human killer to have run along the tops of them, leaving no marks on the sand below. But nowhere around the blood-splattered dyer's workshop did he find signs of a man's weight having passed along the top of the walls.

Like the foxes that slept in their holes all day, Sun Wolf prowled the maze of shadows in the checkered moonlight. In the northern courtyards he sensed a trace of magic, the uneasy scent of spells in the darkness. As he had when scouting beneath the walls of an enemy city, he sank close to the ground, putting himself below a standing man's line of sight, aware that the indigo velvet of the shadows would be no concealment from mageborn eyes. He followed the magic, like a thread of perfume. Oddly, he sensed no danger, but a moment later saw a scorpion, barbed tail held high, veer suddenly out of its way and go scurrying off in another direction. He remembered again how the birds had fallen silent the morning he had found the dead doves.

Cautiously, he slipped forward; as he looked over the sill of a decapitated wall, he heard a woman moan.

The man and woman in the cell beyond lay twined together, the moonlight that poured through the broken roof covering their legs from the thighs down like a cast-back silken sheet. Where it struck the clothes on which they lay, Sun Wolf could see the glitter of bullion embroidery against black homespun, the tabard written over with the holy runes of the Trinitarians. In the shadows, his wizard's sight picked out the soft surge of the full breast and the young man's arm, white as the body of the woman he clasped. Gold hair tumbled, mingling with unraveling coils of smoky red.

It was none of his business, he knew, as he moved back with all the silence of those hundreds of night-scout missions. But it did occur to him to wonder whether, after all her talk of purity, Kaletha had ever seen Nexué spying on her here.

* * *

For Starhawk it was an interesting time. She had always enjoyed watching people, taking a deep and satisfied delight in seeing her friends behave exactly like themselves, whether for good or ill. She had always done this, and it had never earned her popularity. Neither her brothers and their sweethearts, the nuns in the Convent of St. Cherybi where she had grown up, nor the other mercenaries of Sun Wolf's troop had felt particularly comfortable under the nonjudgmental gaze of those calm gray eyes. Perhaps this was because, as an outsider, she was frequently amused by what was going on and, often at the same time, felt deep and genuine concern.

In two days of quietly standing guard and attending Kaletha's lectures in the gardens of Pardle Sho, she sometimes had the impression of lying on the bank of a water hole, watching from a blind as the animals came down to drink.

Tazey remained in her bed, for the most part only lying and looking at the ceiling, though occasionally she wept. It had cost Starhawk little to leave her family and enter the convent, but she still remembered with agonizing clarity the single long night she had spent trying to decide whether to remain there quietly among women she had known all of her short life or to follow the dark and violent path of a man she had spoken to only once, a man who had touched off in her soul a powder keg of longings which, in her heart, she knew could never again be quenched. Her greatest fear, she remembered, had been that she would turn into someone she did not want to be—someone she would not even want to know. But she had known, from the first moment she understood that Sun Wolf would admit her into his troop, that there was no way back. She would either go, or know forever that she had not gone.

Whatever lay beyond the silent wall that guarded the future, Starhawk's heart ached for the girl and her lonely choice.

It would help, she thought with impersonal anger, *if they would simply leave Tazey alone.* But of course they did not. Her father came, sober, grave, his sweat smelling of last night's liquor in the dense heat of morning, and talked gently to her, calling her his little girl. Tazey agreed with what he asked her but when she was alone, she wept hopelessly for hours. The Bishop Galdron put in his appearance, too, speaking in measured, mellifluous tones about the Nine Hells and predestined choices. Starhawk, meeting him on the stairs coming down from the balcony of the Household, informed him that if he ever spoke so to Tazey again she would personally slit his nostrils.

"The man is a bigot and a hypocrite," Kaletha said primly, folding her hands amid the jagged sun-splashes that fell through the arbor onto her black homespun knees. "He cannot possibly sincerely believe that the use of one's wizardry automatically condemns one to eternal damnation. But even so, a threat of physical violence, however much you may not have meant it, reflects badly on us all."

Starhawk shrugged. "If I were a wizard, or even wanted to be a wizard," she said evenly, "you might have a point—always supposing I accepted your right to judge my conduct." Kaletha started a little, but hastily got her first reaction in hand and did her best not to show her surprise that any one in her company would not automatically accept her dictates. *In her more human moments,* Starhawk thought obliquely, *Kaletha has the grace to realize the hubris of that assumption.* Around them, the public gardens of Pardle Sho were somnolent under the heat; its few spiky cacti and dark boulders, which were all that graced this particular high court, reminded her for some reason of the Wolf.

Starhawk went on, "And yes, I did mean it. Tazey has to make her own choice in this. Whether she decides to turn her back on her father and a potential husband or hurt for the rest of her life pretending that sandstorm never happened, it's *her own choice,* and Galdron has no business waving Hell under her nose. Either way, she's going to have enough hurting to do as it is."

"The man is a boor . . ." Anshebbeth began, looking up from a meditation upon which she had clearly not been concentrating.

"No," Kaletha corrected. "He's very civilized—it's what makes him dangerous."

"It makes him believable, at any rate," Egaldus added thoughtfully. He was seated on the granite bench in the latticed shade beside Kaletha; the bench was only large enough to seat two comfortably, but Anshebbeth had crowded onto the end of it under the pretext of needing to speak to Kaletha and had gone into her meditation there rather than moving to another bench. It automatically included her in any conversation, and Starhawk, having watched her find reasons to follow Kaletha from where they had formerly been sitting, guessed that changing seats again probably would not shake her.

The young novice's face settled into a curiously adult line as he went on, "My Lord Bishop has the gift of always having a plausible answer, always having some alternative possibility. You know he's coming up to the Fortress tonight, with a scheme for sending Tazey to an outlying nunnery in the foothills near Farkash on the coast. Disinheriting her, in effect, but also exiling her."

Kaletha's face flushed with anger. "He can't! In any case, sending her away from any possibility of being properly taught won't make her any the less mageborn!"

"No," Egaldus said drily. He stood up, the sunlight tipping the thick masses of his fair hair like a soft, sparkling halo around his face. "But it seems to be Galdron's current panacea." His blue eyes looked gravely down into those of the woman before him, and he sighed. "He's talking about doing it to me as well."

As if her throat had been cut, the White Witch's high color ebbed to wax. Not quite aware of what she did, she reached out to take his hand.

The young man went on, "He's learned about . . ." He glanced at Starhawk, Anshebbeth watching them with devouring black eyes, and the other students—Pradborn Dyer, Luatha Welldig, and Shelaina Clerk—meditating or chanting quietly to themselves on other benches along the uneven, latticed walk. "About my being your student," he finished. "He speaks of sending me to Dalwirin or even to Kwest Mralwe."

A little numbly, Kaletha said, "He is your mentor. You told me yourself he looked upon you as his chosen novice, his eventual successor."

Egaldus nodded. "That's what he can't forgive. That after he's favored me, I'd dare find the spark within myself and come to you to kindle it to flame. It's why I have to learn from you all I can before I go, if I'm to be on my own."

Her face changed at that. Starhawk felt it, almost like a physical cooling of the air as Kaletha's hand slipped away from his, and her body settled back just a fraction on the bench. Egaldus felt it as well. His blue eyes had an odd, calculating glint as he regarded her, his head tilted a little to one side. Very softly, he asked, "Or are you still going to keep it all to yourself?"

Turning, he walked away.

He had gone five or six paces when Kaletha started up. "Egaldus . . ."

"Kaletha . . ." Anshebbeth's timing as she turned and laid her hand on the younger woman's arm was far too precise to be accidental. Egaldus rounded the corner at the end of the walkway. The brazen sun seemed to ignite his embroidered tabard in gold and azure fire against the parched sand as he strode down the garden. As if oblivious to all that had passed before, Anshebbeth said, "Since I *will* be able to speak to Tazey, perhaps if you told *me* what to say to her, or gave me some instruction to pass along to her . . ."

In a voice like watered poison, Kaletha said, "I'm afraid you'd scarcely be qualified."

The older woman's mouth pinched tight. A blotch of sunlight, falling on her face, caught the sudden twist of wrinkles around her hungry eyes. "Perhaps if you spent as much time teaching me as you do teaching Egaldus . . ."

"Egaldus is mageborn."

"You said before, you could make me mageborn, too." Anshebbeth's shrill voice cracked. "You said I—"

Crushingly, Kaletha said, "That was when my teachings—my efforts to release the powers hidden within the human mind—were your first priority, Anshebbeth. That was when you were willing to devote yourself to purity of the body and exercises of the mind. I'm not sure that's true anymore."

Anshebbeth was still holding onto her arm. Kaletha turned her wrist to shake off the possessive clutch of those long white fingers and walked after Egaldus, her voluminous black robes billowing behind her in the glare of the autumn sun.

"That wasn't exactly fair."

Kaletha averted her face, pretending to be looking out across one of the smaller courtyards near the bottom of the gardens. This one was well watered, with a couple of orange trees pregnant with fruit in its center. The smell of them mingled thickly with that of the roses growing in little craters of packed gray-brown earth at the four corners, the ever-present harshness of dust, and the sticky warmth from the vendor of cinnamon buns on the opposite walkway.

"If she'd quit hanging onto me, maybe she'd be pushed away less."

Starhawk had spotted Kaletha alone here on her way out of the gardens to return to her duties. Anshebbeth was still looking for her higher up. Whether Kaletha had overtaken and spoken to Egaldus or not, Starhawk guessed the result was pretty much the same. She leaned her shoulder against the coarse, shaggy wood of the arbor and looked down at that white profile beneath its auburn swags of hair. "If you pushed her all the way away," she remarked, "she would have gone."

"You don't know 'Shebbeth." Kaletha remained resolutely staring into the garden, the harsh light showing up the small wrinkles in the delicate skin around her eyes. Above the tangle of bare wisteria vines and old walls, the shadows had begun to slant across the face of Mount Morian and to dye black the eastern cliffs of the distant Binning Rock. "She elected me as her mentor and teacher and someone to tell her what to do and be when I was seventeen. And the Mother knows she needed it—an awkward half-caste provincial from Smelting with enough shirdar nobility in her background to get her parents to send her to finishing school in the Middle Kingdoms and make her discontented with everything around her. Neurotic, whining, clinging . . ."

"But you've known her for a long time."

Kaletha paused. The beautiful shoulders under their black gown tensed as she presented the back of her head to Starhawk's unemotional gaze. Then she sighed, seeming to read in the Hawk's uninflected voice the unspoken observation that, had she truly wanted Anshebbeth never to bother her again, she'd had ample time to say so. Some of the stiffness went out of her. "I know," she said.

She looked up at Starhawk, the defenses of the one whom she made herself to be in front of her disciples lowered, hesitantly, like the shield of a warrior who doesn't quite trust the cry of "friend." "And I was . . . unfair. But—I don't know."

"Well," the Hawk said judiciously, "I admit that when someone walks around all day with 'Please don't kick me' written on their back, the temptation to kick them can be almost overwhelming."

The White Witch started to stiffen with indignant denial of any sentiment so unworthy of her, then caught the glint of understanding in those calm eyes, pale in the sunburned face.

Starhawk went on, "And her timing wasn't the best." She came around and sat on the other end of the bench, facing Kaletha in the hot, spotted shade. "But it's still no reason to be cruel."

Kaletha sighed again and nodded. With a gesture oddly human after her rigid, self-controlled serenity, she pressed her fingers to her eyelids, smudged brown with sleeplessness. Her face looked suddenly older, with the struggle not to admit, even to herself, that she was jealous, that she was frustrated by the King, and that she could not quite control all those around her. "Maybe it's for the best," she said wearily. "Egaldus being sent away, I mean—if he *is* going to be sent away. He might have just said that to . . ." She paused, then changed her mind about what she was going to say and went on with something else, her tone calm as a frozen lake. "He is very—eager. Too eager, like your friend, though of course his teaching is far more advanced than Captain Sun Wolf's is, and I believe he has more potential because his mind is better disciplined. He's like a man trying to pour water into a basin which isn't dug deep enough. He doesn't understand when I try to tell him that some of it's going to spill on the ground."

Are you going to keep it all to yourself? he had asked. Starhawk leaned her back to the arbor post behind her and remembered Sun Wolf's words about Kaletha and her power. Looking across at that pale, controlled face, Starhawk wondered suddenly how much of Kaletha's desire to teach Tazey stemmed from the fear that she might be surpassed in power by a girl younger than herself. A couple of young girls strolled past them, each with a miner on either arm, the girls all done up in bright cotton and glass-bead finery, flowers and sweet grass braided into their long hair.

For a moment Kaletha's lips hardened in a disapproving sneer. Then she went on, still behind her wall of pedagogical calm, as if Egaldus was truly the issue. "It takes years of preparing the mind, of disciplining the body. I know, I studied in silence, in darkness, for years . . ." She stopped again and looked quickly at Starhawk, as if remembering her closeness to Sun Wolf. Then, bitterly, she twisted on the bench and looked out into the dry garden again, keeping her secrets clenched close within. "All magic springs from the mind," she said after a moment. "How can power spring from a dirty and undisciplined place? It requires study and purity . . ." She hesitated over the word.

"Not to mention," Starhawk said softly, "the Great Trial."

Startlement broke Kaletha out of that rigid mold. There was genuine puzzlement in her voice. "The what?"

"She'd never *heard* of it?"

Starhawk shook her head. She had come down to the empty quarter as soon as it grew fully dark. It was a restless night, full of the movement and dry, electric whispers of the wind. Far out on the desert Sun Wolf could sense a storm, but it was traveling elsewhere, and the foothills would only feel its farthest hem fringes. The moon hung over the black hump of Mount Morian like a trimmed coin.

Last night Starhawk had not come to him, knowing it was possible that she would be watched. Before they had become lovers, Sun Wolf had occasionally wondered about his second-in-command's habitual self-contained calm—off hand, soft-voiced, capable of an animal's logical cruelty. He had trained with her and fought sword-to-sword with her too often not to suspect fire lay under that gray ice. It was her vulnerability which had surprised him. It was good, beyond anything he had known, not to have to hide the needs and fears of his soul from her behind an unbreakable wall of strength.

They coupled in fierce silence in the cell that had been theirs, close enough to hear the music that drifted from the Hall. Afterward, spent, they lay in the darkness, warming one another under the meager blankets Starhawk had left for him with last night's food, taking pleasure only in the touch of one another's skin. It seemed like half the night before they spoke.

"She asked me what it was," Starhawk said from the hollow of his shoulder where she lay. "I told her. I have a feeling she meant to go through it in secret, so no one would know she hadn't done it already, until I told her how it was done."

Sun Wolf shivered. The hallucinatory poison which could bring a wizard's powers to fruition invariably killed the nonmageborn—*and perhaps,* he thought, *some of the less strong among the mageborn as well.* The old man who had whispered of it to Starhawk once had spoken of preparation for the Trial, but no one knew anymore what that preparation had been. He himself had only survived it because he had a trained mercenary's physical strength. The agonized screaming was what had destroyed his voice. The memory of the pain would follow him to his grave. He knew down to the depths of his heart that if he had not been given the poison for other reasons—if he had known he would have to take it to achieve a mage's full powers—he would never have had the courage to do it.

But then, like Tazey, he had never wanted to be a mage.

"Tazey will have to go through it."

Starhawk's short, baby-soft hair moved against his chest. "I know."

"She'll need a hell of a lot of teaching first."

She nodded again. "You know the Bishop and Norbas Milkom have come up here to try and talk Osgard into sending her to a convent," she said. "The Bishop because he's afraid for her soul—I think Norbas Milkom because he sees it as a good way to break up her marriage with a shirdar lord and maybe later, just coincidentally, talk her around into marrying one of his own sons."

"They'll never do it." Sun Wolf's hand smoothed the skin of her shoulder absently, yet delighting in the feel of it, like silk under his palm, broken by the delicate trapunto of an old knife scar. "It hinges on Osgard admitting that Tazey's mageborn—that she isn't the perfect little princess he's always wanted. Galdron's going to be lucky if he gets away from the palace without a flogging for even bringing it up."

But evidently the Bishop went unflogged, for three hours later he came, in silence, to the base of the outside stair that led up to Tazey's lighted room. The night had grown cold, the terrible electric quality of it ebbing as the distant storm died away over the desert. The music had long since ceased from the Hall, but the light in the King's solar continued to burn, and an occasional soft-footed servant had come and gone from the curtained archway of Tazey's room. The curtains were orange and scarlet desert work; with the lights in the room behind them, they rippled like a rainbow of fire. A reflection of that dim and far-off luminescence sparkled on the Bishop's embroidered cloak as he gathered up his robes like a lady's skirts, glanced surreptitiously around him, and started to ascend the stair.

"It's a bit late to be going calling, Galdron," said a soft, even voice from the shadows of the stair.

The old man stopped with an apoplectic snort. Midway up the stair, a rawboned figure unfolded itself from the shadows; the sinking moonlight brushed a few ivory strands of short-cropped hair and the glint of steel studding on a green leather jerkin such as the guards wore. The Bishop blustered, "They said that the Princess sleeps ill of nights and that, if she was still awake, I might speak with her." But like her, he kept his voice low. A sharp word spoken anywhere between the stair and the little gate that led from the court to the empty quarter would wake every sleeper on that side of the Palace.

"They probably didn't mean at three hours before dawn."

"I have been speaking with the King," the Bishop replied with dignity. "I thought . . ."

"You thought you might be able to talk Tazey into wanting what you want for her? Give her a few choice nightmares to think about before she sees her father at breakfast?"

"Whatever nightmares the witch's guilty conscience might visit upon her," Galdron said sententiously, "they are well spent if they will save her from the eternal nightmare of Hell by causing her to repent."

"Repent what? How she was born? Saving four people from dying? You have a beautiful voice, Galdron; you can probably persuade people into believing anything." The dark figure began to descend the stairs toward him, and there was a sudden flash of moon-silvered steel as a thin knife appeared in her hand. "I think it would be a whole lot less persuasive with your nose slit clear back to the sinuses."

Galdron backed down the stairs so hastily that he nearly tripped on the flowing satin of his crimson robe. He stammered, "I shall call—"

"Call whom?" a rich, deep voice asked softly from the courtyard shadows. The Bishop looked back irritably over his shoulder. In the shadows, eyes gleamed white in a dark face above the pale blur of a collar ruffle. "The guards, and tell them you tried to talk your way around Tazey when her Daddy had already told you no? I told you it was a fool idea. Let's go back to town."

Galdron hesitated for a moment. In the moonlight Starhawk saw his face purse with frustration. Then he looked up at her where she stood on the stairs, his white beard like streaks of ermine among the dark fur of his cloak collar. "Don't believe that I have given up," he said, still softly. "The girl's soul is in danger. I have told her father so, though that . . ." He hesitated and glanced at Norbas Milkom, who had materialized beside him in the shadows. He amended, ". . . though her father will not believe me. There is too much witchery in this Palace already. She must be removed, or evil will come of it."

And turning, he vanished into the night. Laughing softly to herself, Starhawk slipped her knife back into her boot and went up the stairs.

The following morning Tazey was pronounced well enough to make her appearance in the Hall at breakfast.

Sitting in her usual place at Kaletha's table, Starhawk eyed the girl worriedly, as Tazey was ushered in by her father and her uncle. Her dust-blond hair artificially curled, her broad, straight shoulders framed in a profusion of cantaloupe-colored silk ruffles, she looked washed out and miserable, hopelessly distant from the gay and beautiful girl who had so joyfully danced the war dance. Years of friendship with Sun Wolf's various concubines had given Starhawk the ability to spot make-up carefully applied, in this case to cover the ravages of sleeplessness and doubt. The King, in puce damask that accentuated the broken veins in his nose and cheeks, held his daughter's hand with possessive pride, his weary, bloodshot green eyes darting over the faces of the unnaturally large crowd at breakfast, daring any to speak.

None did. *However and why ever Nexué's strident gossip had been silenced,* Starhawk thought, *the silencing had been effective. There was a good chance that the whole affair would be scotched.*

And what then? she wondered. *The gorgeous and somewhat woodenheaded Prince Incarsyn would marry Tazey and carry her off in splendor to his jewel-like little city deep in the dune seas of the south. She would eat candied dates, ride in palanquins, bear his babies, and try to forget what it felt like to part the winds with her hands.*

As the King conducted his daughter to her place at the High Table, Anshebbeth came hurrying down to where Starhawk and Kaletha sat. The governess, in her high-necked velvet gown, looked as if she, like Tazey, had spent a night either sleepless or ravaged by hideous dreams; her thin hands twitched as she kept glancing back toward the King. Though her place was with her charge on what was clearly an official occasion, she perched nervously on the chair at Kaletha's other side.

"They came last night," she fretted. "The Bishop and Norbas Milkom . . ."

"Starhawk was telling me," Kaletha replied, a little spitefully, as if to lay emphasis on Anshebbeth's exclusion from the prior conversation.

The governess threw a hunted look up at the High Table where Osgard was irritably ordering Jeryn to sit up straight. The boy, just up from his own bout with sunstroke, looked like a lizard in molt, wan and exhausted and peeling, his white hands with their bitten nails toying listlessly with his food. Her voice sank to a whisper, "Do you think he will—will proclaim your banishment?"

"*Your* banishment?" Starhawk asked, surprised.

Kaletha's lips compressed with barely stifled irritation. Anshebbeth explained hurriedly to Starhawk, "We were told, Kaletha and I, that the real reason Galdron and Norbas Milkom came last night was to demand that—that Kaletha be sent away! Only because of her power, only because her excellence would be a temptation to the Princess— only out of spite, and jealousy, because of Egaldus becoming a wizard! They hate her, Galdron and Milkom . . ."

"Stop it, 'Shebbeth!" Kaletha said, embarrassed.

"It's true," the governess said eagerly, trying too hard to make up yesterday's lost ground. "You know they hate you."

Kaletha pushed at a forkful of beans on her plate. Still without looking up, she said, "I wish you'd stop taking every backstairs rumor your lover whispers into your ears as sacred truth."

At the viciousness in Kaletha's voice as she pronounced the word *lover,* Anshebbeth's pale face turned the color of paper, her hand clutching nervously at her throat.

Coldly, Kaletha turned to face her. "You don't think I know you've been playing the slut with Nanciormis? The man gossips like an old woman and sneaks and spies worse than Nexué did. No wonder I've never been able to raise the smallest powers in you, as I have in Egaldus. All you think about is yourself."

Not at all to Starhawk's surprise, Anshebbeth hung her head. There were tears perilously close to the surface as she whispered, "I—You're right, Kaletha. I have—I have thought too much of myself—not enough of your welfare, or that of others. If I haven't achieved power yet, I realize it's my own fault . . ."

Kaletha opened her mouth to say something else, but Starhawk, realizing that nothing encourages cruelty so much as subservience, broke in with, "I think you'd better get back to the High Table, Anshebbeth, or Osgard *will* think about banishing Kaletha."

The governess started, throwing a stricken glance up at Osgard's irritated face. She gulped, hastily wiped her eyes, and gathered up her flowing skirts, to scurry back and take her place at the bottom of the High Table, dropping flustered curtseys to everyone there, even as a stirring around the Hall door marked the entry of Incarsyn of Hasdrozaboth, Lord of the Dunes.

He looks, Starhawk thought, *his usual gorgeous self in the full panoply of the shirdar lords.* He had all Nanciormis' grace and beauty, unblurred by the lines of sensuality and indulgence which had long ago eroded the commander's handsomeness. In his white cloak, his baggy trousers and soft boots with their stamp-work of gold, his flowing surcoat, and strings of scarlet and blue amulets, he looked like a young and graceful hunting cat; whereas the commander, though he had the same hawk-like shirdar features and the same thick braids of black hair, more resembled a somewhat spoiled tabby who has long ago decided that mousing was beneath him.

Osgard rose, leading Tazey by the hand. The girl's face had the set, desperate look it had worn, Starhawk realized, when she had first stepped forward to face the darkness of the storm.

With slightly rehearsed grace, Incarsyn bowed and smiled. "It is better than you know, my Princess, to see you well again."

Tazey took a deep breath, released her father's hand, and stepped forward. Reaching up, she removed the small, gleaming droplets of the sand-pearls from her ears. Her voice was small and steady and like the clink of a dropped dagger in the enormous silence of the Hall.

"Thank you." She faltered for one instant, glanced desperately back at the King, then went on. "You've been too good to me for me to want to pay you in false coin. What you've heard is true. I'm mageborn." And she put the sand-pearls into his hand.

In that hideous instant of silence, Starhawk's interested glance took in all the faces at the High Table—Osgard's engorging with blood as his hand came up involuntarily as if he would strike her, and Jeryn's dark eyes blazing to life with the first expression of soaring joy Starhawk had seen in them at his sister's courage; Nanciormis was smiling. *Why smiling?* Beside her, she was aware of Kaletha smiling, too, with triumph at having thwarted the King and with anticipation at being, after all, Tazey's teacher.

For one shocked instant, Incarsyn looked as taken aback as if Tazey had confessed to selling her favors in the Pardle bazaar.

The silence seemed to last for minutes, though Starhawk calculated it was in fact twelve or thirteen seconds. Then Osgard found the breath to gasp, "You—"

Incarsyn lifted a stilling finger. Reaching forward, he took Tazey's hand, turned it over gently, and replaced the sand-pearls in her palm.

"It is a poor lover," he said softly, his liquid voice carrying to all corners of the Hall, "who abandons his betrothed because she cuts off her hair, or changes its color, or decides that she will learn to play the war pipes. What you have told me is no more than this. If you will have me, Lady Taswind . . ." Graceful as a panther, he sank to one knee and, closing her fingers around the pearls, pressed a kiss upon her knuckles. ". . . I will still be your true lord."

The applause rang like a thunderclap in the rafters, shouts of approval and toasts in weak breakfast wine. Osgard, stayed in his stride forward to shake Tazey until her teeth rattled, stepped back, his broad face wreathed in a smile of startled surprise at this magnanimity. But Tazey, Starhawk saw, looked stunned, shaking her head in confusion as a tear tracked down her hollowed face.

"I think it was beautiful," Anshebbeth sighed dewily, coming to join Kaletha's table a few minutes later.

"Do you?" Nanciormis walked quietly up behind her, a half-drunk vessel of wine in hand, pressed there by the King to toast the betrothed couple. His pouchy eyes glinted with cynicism which could not quite conceal furious anger.

Anshebbeth flustered, confused about what she might have said wrong and even more confused by Nanciormis' presence, *as if,* thought Starhawk, *she can not make up her mind whether to stand next to him or Kaletha.* "Well—that is—after what people have been saying . . . though of course there's nothing wrong with it . . . But Incarsyn—"

"Incarsyn," said Nanciormis bitterly, "would have said the same thing were she a humpbacked leper and still the daughter of the King of Wenshar. I know." He looked somberly at Kaletha, and even her cool reserve relaxed a little, under his warm brown gaze. "I met him late last night, coming back from the brothels in town. 'Does it matter to me if the girl's a witch-bitch?' he said. 'I rode north to marry her whatever she looked like; if she boils toads and couples with snakes for her pleasure, what is that to me? It could be worse—she could play the war pipes.'"

Anshebbeth went white with shock and disillusionment. Kaletha's nostrils flared in anger, but there was no surprise in her face as she threw a bitter glance at the High Table, where Tazey, rigid with desperate composure, listened to the Prince's light glow of blandishments that spared her the effort of stammering a reply. "So he'll take her away with him after all," she said bitterly. "And her father will be spared having to think about her 'disgrace.'"

"It's what he came here for."

With soft and bitter violence, she whispered, "Men," and turned her head suddenly, going back to her breakfast in arctic rage.

After a moment's hesitation Anshebbeth gathered up her long skirts and sat beside Kaletha, offering the comfort of her presence, but she threw one look quickly back over her shoulder at Nanciormis, as if asking his permission. Nanciormis said nothing, but his dark eyes warmed for a moment with complicity; with that Anshebbeth smiled, uneasily content.

"Then it's been a sham all along?" Starhawk asked quietly, looking up at the commander.

"By no means." Nanciormis shrugged, started to drink from the cup in his hand, then grimaced, and put it down. "She's a beautiful girl, after all. But she's my niece—I care about her happiness." He looked back toward the High Table, a very real anger in every line of his thick shoulders beneath their snowy cape. He was a politician, as Sun Wolf had said, for all his relatively minor post as commander of the guards; Starhawk knew him to be skilled in dissimulation, seldom showing his true thoughts. But his anger in this situation was genuine —*and so it might be,* thought Starhawk. She herself had never seen that side of Incarsyn—in fact, had never seen him being other than a shirdar gentleman: not very imaginative, but doing his best within his limits to be kind.

Nanciormis went on bitterly, "He cares less for her than he does for his horses—I've heard him say two or three times that he wouldn't trust any woman on them . . ." Kaletha's back stiffened at that, and she turned from her barely touched plate to look up at him again. "He despises the mageborn—I won't repeat to you some of the things he's said about you, Kaletha, and your followers. But he has better sense than to say them to a girl who can get him related to the mines of Wenshar and maybe out from under the control of that sister of his. But of course, I can't say so to her."

"Since she had no choice in the matter," Starhawk remarked softly, "what would be the point?"

Down at the end of the High Table, a sudden movement of red and black caught her eye, and she saw Jeryn sit up, looking toward the doors with sudden brightness lighting up his thin face for the second time. At the same instant, she knew that Sun Wolf was looking for her; turning, she saw him standing in the archways that led to the shadowy vestibule, scanning the crowd.

As if she had called out to him across the great, sunshafted hall, he turned his head and met her gaze.

Perhaps because they had been together last night, she felt for one split instant the strange tangle of her love for him pull her daytime mind—a passionate caring that was both physical and maternal, a need for his happiness that was so deep it shamed her . . .

And then, between one eyeblink and the next, the soldier in her realized he wasn't supposed to be there.

But he was walking foward toward the dais, and so happy was Osgard with his alliance with the shirdar secured that he lofted his cup in greeting and called out, "Hey, Captain!" before he remembered why he'd ejected the Wolf from his court.

A look of truculent suspicion clouded his face, and he stood up. Starhawk had already begun to move toward the Wolf, reading in his silence, the way he held his body, that there was something very wrong. Under a layer of dusty beard-stubble his face looked drawn, as she remembered it looking sometimes when he would look on things that had been done in the sacking of a city, in the cold light of the following day. His leather eye patch was blotched with moisture, his faded hair sleek and wet, as if he had dunked his head in a horse trough to clear his mind. Starhawk thought, *If he tries to stop the match now, we're going to have to fight our way out*, touched her sword hilt, and gauged the best route to the closet window.

Osgard must have been thinking the same thing, for he demanded roughly, "I thought I told you to stay the hell away."

"You did," the Wolf said. "I just came to tell you the Bishop Galdron and Norbas Milkom are dead."

CHAPTER

9

"**W**HEN DID YOU SEE GALDRON?"

Starhawk held tight to the reins as her horse tried to throw up its head, made nervous by the stench of blood. "About three hours after midnight." The sun, already well above Dragon's Backbone at breakfast time, was now hot; the air in the little clearing among the boulders where she and the Wolf had first rescued Osgard from the disgruntled shirdar seemed alive with the low buzz of insects. Used as she was to day-old battlefields, the place made Starhawk's stomach turn. "Milkom was with him. I got the impression they were heading straight back to town."

Standing beside her near the little cluster of horses at the road's edge, Sun Wolf nodded. "They must have been. I was wakened by something about two hours before dawn, but all I heard was every coyote in the hills howling. It wasn't till daylight that I smelled the blood."

From the mouth of a little wadi that wound away back into the rocks stumbled one of the band of Trinitarian priests who had met the posse from the Fortress at the place; he was an oldish man, bareheaded even in the rising heat, his robes like an incongruous bouquet of orchids against the lead-colored rocks. He leaned against a boulder and vomited as if he had been poisoned. Even at this distance, Starhawk could see the rim of scarlet along the hem of his robe.

Sun Wolf scratched his moustache and continued, "I went on into town to the Cathedral and got Egaldus and a bunch of the priests to come out here to keep an eye on the place, but I had a look around, first. You see anything odd about this?"

She looked around them at the small space of open ground. In places dark mud had dried to crusted puddles, soaking into the dust; she noted automatically that the ground underfoot was dust and pebbles, not sand, and covered like a lunatic quilt with back-and-forth stitching of tracks—the priests', the posse's, those of the onlookers that had already begun to gather and were being held back, rather unsuccessfully, by Nanciormis and a couple of his guards back on the road.

"You mean, besides two men and two horses dismembered?" she remarked, glancing back at Sun Wolf.

"Besides that," he agreed, folding his arms.

She scanned the road: the gravelly dip and the surrounding rocks; Egaldus with his blond hair like a thick halo in the hot sun, speaking with gentle authority to the older priest; and Osgard, some distance away, sitting on a boulder, his face buried in his hands. Softly, she said, "I'm trying to picture how it was done, Chief, and I can't. The area of the kill's huge—it starts over there where one of the horses came down . . ." She pointed to a churned-up patch of black mud on the slope down from the road. Tracks zigzagged frantically away, passing within feet of them—pointed-toed slippers. She'd noted them on Galdron, pearled tips poking coyly from beneath the crimson hem of his robe. One of them, with the foot still in it, lay halfway under a boulder near the mouth of the wadi, swarming with flies. So far the priests had missed it. "Milkom's body was over in those rocks there, but the first blood starts only a few feet from here." That, by the look of it, had been an artery. She was astonished the little man had been able to run so far. "Two trained assassins on good horses could have done it, *maybe*. But . . ."

Her glance slipped back to the Wolf. His sunburned face looked dark against the white frame of his head veils; his single eye, yellow as a lion's, was narrowed in thought. Knowing his answer already, she said, "There weren't any tracks, were there?"

"No," he said.

For a time they were both silent. Across the open ground, Osgard's voice rose in a despairing shriek to no one in particular, "I'll have the bastard crucified! I'll have the skin flayed off him and leave him for the ants! I'll get whoever did this—I'll get him!" Nanciormis came hurrying down from the road toward him, leaving the guards to deal with the gaggle of neck-craning miners and cattle herders. Incarsyn, standing closer to the King, holding the bridle of his own horse—one of the famous white mares of the desert—didn't move. He looked dazed and shaken, like the man in the legend who had bargained with the djinns for his worst enemy's head in a box and, opening it, had found his own.

After a little while Starhawk said, "While I was getting ready to ride with you, 'Shebbeth came to me, in tears because Galdron had never liked Nanciormis, and she was afraid people would think he had something to do with it. She said Nanciormis was with her last night . . ."

"Was he?" Sun Wolf asked, more out of curiosity than anything else.

"Oh, yes." She nodded. "I was on the balcony for at least two hours after I saw Galdron. Nanciormis came sliding out of 'Shebbeth's room close to dawn."

Her dark brows twitched together for a moment as she remembered the narrow, rather gloomy confines of the Women's Hall, with its unmade beds, abandoned by the underservants when they went to see Tazey's reinstatement at breakfast, and the grayish shafts of filtered light that came in through the windows that overlooked the wide quadrangle of the kitchen courts. Anshebbeth had clutched desperately at her hands, her face skull-like, sleepless, and her hagridden eyes huge, begging the Hawk not to tell anyone. She would be ruined, utterly ruined, if the King found out. Starhawk, knowing the standards of propriety necessary in a Princess' chaperone, had to agree with her there. But she would testify to anyone, she said, if necessary, that Nanciormis had not been abroad that night . . .

She looked across at the commander now. He was kneeling on the ground before the King, graceful as a tiger in spite of his bulk, every gesture he made lambent with beauty and power. For this man, poor Anshebbeth was risking not only her reputation—no small thing in a community as tight knit as this one—but her position, Tazey's reputation, her friendship with the person dearest to her, and her own hopeless dreams of sharing Kaletha's magic; and for thanks, Nanciormis tumbled her as he casually tumbled the laundry women, making jokes about her behind her back.

It was all none of Starhawk's business, but she was conscious of a wish to see the commander prey to some kind of comprehensively disfiguring skin disorder for a number of weeks.

Quietly, she went on, "The damn thing is, it would be nice to have to worry about it being Nanciormis, or Osgard . . . or anyone."

Sun Wolf nodded. The wind turned, blowing a little skiff of dust over the dark splatterings of the blood trails; Egaldus and two of Incarsyn's shirdar bodyguards emerged from behind the rocks, carrying something between them wrapped in a blanket. One of the horses whinnied and shied. Overhead, the vultures rode the thermals, curious but staying unnaturally high.

Like the hoarse, stripped scrape of metal, Sun Wolf's voice went on. "I had a feeling about Nexué's death, and this time, I'm sure. Whatever killed those poor bastards, Hawk, it was nothing human. I think the time has come for me to have a little talk with Kaletha."

"You have no right to ask me about my power!" Kaletha almost spat the words at him, like an angry cat. In the slatey shadows of the small chamber just off the Women's Hall, her face was like a white mask, floating above the dark, heavy folds of her gown.

"The hell I haven't, woman! Two men have been murdered, and a woman also, if I'm right. You're a wizard . . ."

"Just because you can find no sign of a killer, you accuse me?"

Sun Wolf's eye narrowed. "I'm not accusing anyone. But you have books of magic that could tell us—"

"So!" The word came out like a trumpet of bitter laughter. "I thought we'd come to them, sooner or later. You'll take any excuse to get your hands on them, won't you? You are greedy, like Egaldus, but without Egaldus' discipline and respect."

Sun Wolf held his temper with an effort, but his harsh voice was thin. "I don't give a tin damn if your way of holding power over your students is to deny them knowledge—"

"Power has nothing to do with it! I *share* my knowledge!"

He didn't take that bait, but went inexorably on. "—but right now we need to know what killed those men, what *could* have killed them. You're the wizard around here. I know there are demons in Wenshar. There could be other creatures in the desert as well, creatures we know nothing of . . ."

Kaletha scoffed, "Who told you that old tale? That old tattler Nanciormis?"

"I've seen them, dammit!"

"More lies," she said, her voice cold. "No one has ever seen these so-called demons—nor, for all the superstitions about them, has anyone ever been hurt by them. They're tales to keep children good and to give men an excuse for punishing wives who meddle. But magic is entirely the product of the human mind, purified by self-sacrifice and reason . . ."

"If it's entirely the product of the human mind," said the Wolf, "then it has to be fouler than a cat-house latrine."

"Don't you use language like that to me."

"Don't you understand?" Sun Wolf took a step toward her, and the tall woman fell back before him, hate and resentment in every rigid line of her body. Through the wide window that overlooked the kitchen garden, doves could be heard, and the soft chatter of women walking the paths between the dusty herb beds. The smoke of the kitchen fires, already heating up for that evening's dinner, drifted like an acrid whiff of far-off battle on the shift of the wind. "Magic is born in us, because we're children of the earth. It isn't we who produce it. Its presence doesn't make us better or holier people. Magic can be as pure and true as a man giving up his life for people he doesn't even know—may his ancestors help the poor clown—or as foul and petty as the things lovers say to each other when they tire of love."

"That's another lie!" The smoky red braids swung against her cheeks with the sharp turn of her head.

"How would you know?" he demanded. "What do you think the Great Trial is? What do you think it does? It breaks open the crust we grow over our souls because we can't stand the sight of what's down at the bottom. It makes us see and understand."

"That may be true of your magic, may the Mother help you," Kaletha said, her voice shaking, "but it isn't true of mine. Don't play the wise man with me, giving yourself airs because you thought some barbarian rite of passage would give you all you wanted. You can see it didn't. You have neither wisdom nor purity—every word you say makes it plainer to me that you should never be allowed to touch the books of power that are in my custody."

"Who put them into your custody?"

"Fate!" she lashed at him. She strode from him, diagonally away across the small, sparsely furnished stone room, with its virginal bed in its niche and the tall-legged reading desk beside the open window.

Beside the desk in the slanting bar of yellow light, she swung passionately back.

"They are mine." The blaze of her intensity could be almost physically felt where he stood near the door. "Magic has all but died in the hundred years of Altiokis' tyranny and repression. It has become soiled and filthy with superstition, dirtied from the handling of men like yourself, who see it only as a tool to further their own greeds and lusts."

Softly, he said, "You're quick to say what kind of a man I am and what I want."

"My power has made me quick." Contempt dripped from her voice like honey from a rotting tree. "And it is up to me to teach magic, to refound it among the worthy and the pure."

"Like Egaldus?"

Her breath caught, her nostrils flared, and her lips clamped shut as if sealed. For a moment there was no sound in the room but the hiss of her breath in her nostrils. Even the passing tread of feet in the garden outside had ceased.

He went on, "Now, I don't care if you couple with him in the empty quarter—hell, it wouldn't matter to me if you had him in the Hall at breakfast time. But don't try to tell me what I am. Don't look down on me for loving the Hawk, nor on the Hawk for loving me."

Stiffly, she said, "That isn't the same. Your love for her is founded in the flesh alone and debases you both. But mine for Egaldus grew first from our purity, from his admiration and regard. Only later did it . . . blossom. Though I don't expect you, or anyone else, would understand that it is different from the loves of other people."

"So it's like demons," Sun Wolf said softly, "that I can see and you can't. I need to see those books, Kaletha."

"No." Her voice was flat as baked clay.

He walked over to the window, to stand near her in the rectangle of the light. "Don't you understand?" he said, his voice quiet now, without anger. He looked across into those beautiful blue eyes, hard with suspicion beneath the cinnamon lashes. "If the killer was a—a being, a ghost or a devil—" Her lip curved with scorn. "—they might contain some mention of it, some way to track it, to fight it . . ."

"Something *you* might believe," she returned. "They contain the usual superstitions, the interpretations of those ignorant of the true sources of magic."

"All right," he said. "If the killer is a wizard, using magic, at least we could trace him or her. Where did you get the books, Kaletha? Who wrote them? What other wizard gave you your knowledge? You can use your power to find the true culprit."

"You think I haven't thought of that?" She swung away from him, scorn jeering in her voice. She paced, a restless red eagle caged in the narrow room. "You think just because I'm not a soldier like your precious mistress I have no brains? Yes, I'm going to use my power to find the true culprit—my power, yours, Egaldus—the latent powers hidden deep in the souls of Luatha and Pradborn, 'Shebbeth and Shelaina. Haven't you, with all your wisdom—" the word rolled caustic from her tongue, "—seen the obvious means of finding the culprit? I'm going to ask the Bishop Galdron."

Sun Wolf stared at her, shocked and cold as if she had unexpectedly driven a dagger of ice into his heart. For a moment he couldn't think of anything to say. In the silence, he heard the clink of Starhawk's spurs on the tiled walk outside, her voice asking some question, and Anshebbeth's answering.

He finally whispered, "Galdron's dead."

Kaletha's nostrils widened a little at the obviousness of the remark. But she only said, "He and Milkom died late in the night, a few hours, at most, before dawn. It has not yet been one full cycle of the sun. When we call his spirit, it will answer."

"That's necromancy." The horror he felt went deeper than his memories of his childhood—of the village shaman making his stinking conjurations with the fetid remains of enemies' hands and ears— deeper than conscious thought.

Kaletha said calmly, "It has been called so, yes."

"You tell me I'm an evil magician," the Wolf said, stunned that Kaletha would contemplate such a thing, "and then you stand there in cold blood and tell me you're going to conjure the spirits of the dead . . ."

"Of the Bishop of Pardle," Kaletha corrected him. "It is not the same thing. I will conjure him because, for all his hypocrisy about magic, he was pure in both mind and body. We should have nothing to fear from the spirits of the pure."

Sun Wolf's voice was hoarse. "The dead are dead."

Her lips pursed up like a nursemaid's at the stubbornness of a stupid child. "No more than what I would expect," she said, "of a barbarian.

Your superstitious dread of the dead, like these 'demons' you claim to see . . ."

"Would you stop calling me a barbarian?" He took a deep breath. "Yes, I'm a barbarian, and yes, I fear the dead, and yes, I fear demons, and with good reason. They're things you can't tamper with."

"Only if your magic is impure," Kaletha responded evenly. "You do well to fear, Sun Wolf—it shows prudence. But I assure you it has been done before, safely—even routinely. Men like yourself misunderstood it, fearing and hating. They slandered those who had the power to do it. But those who understood what they were doing came to no harm. Tonight, when we make the conjuration, you will see."

"I'll see nothing, Lady." Sun Wolf stepped back, filled with a loathing fear that a lifetime of bloodshed had never brought to him.

"Don't be silly," she snapped. Carnelian glints flickered in her eyebrows as they snapped together. "I need all the power I can raise. There must be seven of us."

"You can find your seventh elsewhere. And if you don't, better still."

"Now who's obstructing whom in finding the killer?"

"I don't know." Sun Wolf backed toward the door, fearing, and not even much caring that she clearly thought it was her that he feared. "But if you summon enough power to call the spirits of the dead, the killer may not be what you find."

Later, when he went up to the library, Sun Wolf wondered what it was about the idea of summoning the dead that filled him with such unreasoning horror. Yirth of Mandrigyn had warned him against it—scarcely necessary, since among her spells and incantations there had been no means of doing so. He could see her stern, narrow face again now, with its jade-cold eyes and the disfiguring birthmark like a smutch of thrown filth over her mouth and chin. Low and soft as a rosewood flute, she had said, *As for the calling of the dead, they say that no matter how good the purpose of the callers, nothing but evil has ever come of it . . .*

Behind that memory, the images of his childhood swam—the shaman of his village in the bitter north, Many Voices, laying out by firelight the Circle of Bones to summon the voices of the ancestors. Even then, the hair had prickled on the back of his neck, for fear that he might see pupils gleam once more in the sockets of those dead, smoke-stained skulls.

Of course he hadn't. Many Voices had been a thoroughgoing charlatan, but the best the village had possessed at the time. The little man
had shown signs of living to a ruinous old age—so perhaps he was up
there still.

At least, Sun Wolf thought, as he entered the first of the several
quiet, shadowy rooms above the solar, with storm shutters folded
nearly to and black ranks of books sleeping in the dimness, *Many
Voices had been harmless.* He had made his conjurations against the
storms that had regularly soaked the village, *cast his curses against cows
which had continued to chew untroubled cuds in the meadows* which lay like
deep pockets of velvet among the rocks of the cold moors, guarded
closely the secrets of his ignorance, and never promised to do anything of critical importance. *Kaletha . . .*

Sun Wolf frowned into the dimness of the room. *Kaletha.*

Her books had come from somewhere, he thought. *If wizards enjoyed such a
foul reputation in Wenshar, it would be no surprise that, Altiokis aside, some
earlier mage had kept quiet about his or her power. Even now, that mage's
other pupils might be abroad.*

To help? he wondered. *Or is it one of them whom we're looking for,
casting this magic at us from afar? Or . . . What?*

He remembered the demons in Wenshar, the blue-white gleam of
their skeletal light, and the sense of terror, of danger. Danger of
what? No one had ever heard of demons physically harming a man,
and Milkom and the Bishop had been literally ripped to pieces.

Without any real hope of finding anything, he began to walk along
the doorless cabinets of blackened oak, looking at the books within.
By the shape of the cabinets he guessed that this room had been the
original library and archive of the Fortress. The chamber beyond, with
its wide, south-facing windows looking out over the desert, had clearly
always been a scriptorium. The books had undoubtedly been mostly
ledgers then, paybooks and quartermasters' reports, stacked on their
sides behind locked cabinet doors, along with paper and ink. He could
see the holes in the oak cabinet fronts where the doors had been
removed and the marks where the height of shelves had been altered,
to stand the books upright in the new fashion; he saw also where new
shelves had been added to accommodate acquisitions over the years,
first here and then in the scriptorium and the other small room to his
left. There were both new and old books there—enormous tomes of
yellowed parchment, reeking of dust and lanolin, their crackling

leaves scattered with illuminated capitals, as if someone had spilled a flower basket over them—and dense, cramped volumes of paper, printed on smudgy new presses like the ones they had in the universities of Kwest Mralwe and the Gwarl Peninsula.

He took one of the old books off the shelf and opened its worn and dirty red leather covers. It was a treatise upon the divine interrelationships between the Three Gods, at unnecessary length, in the queer, intricately inflected dialect of the realms of the eastern steppes beyond the Tchard Mountains. Further along he found a romance in the florid old style of the Megantic Bight. Sun Wolf could read most permutations of the old language of Gwenth, though he could write only the choppy book hand of the north and the runes of his own childhood tongue. He replaced the romance, after running a quick, critical eye over its pages:

> So evil was the countenance of the creature
> that Wintessa did faint, and Grovand held her
> in his arms and, despite the danger of the
> monster leaping at them, was lost in the beauty
> of her curls that lay like a river of spun gold
> upon his breast, and her lips pale as sea shells
> in the shining moon of her face . . .

I'd have dropped the silly bint, spun-gold curls and all, Sun Wolf thought dourly, moving on. He tried to picture Starhawk fainting in his arms at the sight of a monster leaping at them, no matter how evil its countenance. She'd probably have grabbed a broom handle and tripped the thing while he, Sun Wolf, was still unsheathing his sword.

He picked up a small, black-bound book from a table and found it in a tongue unknown to him—even the letters like nothing of the alphabet of Gwenth.

"That's in the shirdane."

Turning sharply, he saw Jeryn leaning in the doorway of the smaller room to his left. He tried to remember when he'd seen the boy last—a glimpse of him, slouched in his chair at the High Table at breakfast that morning, when Sun Wolf had broken the news of the Bishop's and Milkom's deaths.

"The shirdar were never in the Empire, so they never read and wrote the way everyone else does. People talk about them as if they were barbarians, but they're not, you know." The boy hesitated in the doorway, a fat book tucked under one scrawny arm, as if unsure of his welcome.

Sun Wolf folded his book shut. "I know," he said. He looked around him at the dark ranks of silent knowledge. "These seem to be from all corners of the world."

Jeryn nodded, his dark eyes looking wide in his pinched, thin face above its formal little ruff. "I didn't know you could read, Chief."

"Well, people talk about me as if I was a barbarian, too."

The boy grinned, a little embarrassed, and ducked his head.

Sun Wolf leaned back against a corner of the shelves, turning the volume over in his big, scarred hands. "How well do you know the books in this place?"

Jeryn shrugged. "Pretty well." Finding his ease again, he came in and took a tall-legged, spindly stool from a writing desk to climb up and unerringly replace the tome he carried on a high shelf. "I can read most of them, but some of them are hard—the writing's little, and they talk about things I don't understand. But this one's one of the good ones," he added, holding up the volume before he slid it back into place. "It's about rocks and jewels and smelting gold. Did you know that, instead of breaking up the silver rock with hammers, they could probably make a machine to do it, and run it off a mule-tread-mill?"

"And to think they want to waste your brains turning you into a dumb warrior." The Wolf sighed. "Is there any other place in the Fortress where somebody could hide books?"

The boy thought for a moment, then shook his head. "I don't know. In their rooms, maybe. How many books?"

Sun Wolf glanced at the shelf near him. The smallest volumes would have hidden under his hand, the bigger ones were longer than his forearm. He had taken a quick glance around Kaletha's cell-like room —it had been bare as a nun's. "I don't know."

"I bet we could find out." Jeryn climbed down from the stool again and pulled ineffectually at his black hose where they twisted around his skinny calves. Sun Wolf estimated it was the time when the boy should have been at afternoon sword practice, but didn't say so. He was no longer a teacher, so it wasn't his business. Besides, from what he'd seen of Nanciormis' teaching, he guessed the boy was better off as he was. Having no talent for dealing with children, the Wolf simply treated Jeryn as he would have treated another man—in this case a man who had knowledge of the libraries of the Fortress.

"They have a record of the books here." The boy led him into the small chamber from which he'd come—like the original library, dim, close, and smelling of paper, ink, and the dust of storms, which had been left to accumulate on the thick granite of the window sills around the joints of the shutters. "They write everything down. They have to," he added, pulling the fat ledger from the shelf and glancing back at Sun Wolf. "If you don't write everything down, you'll never know if it disappears."

Sun Wolf grinned. "You should try keeping track of a troop of mercenaries during the winter, if you want practice writing things down so they don't disappear." He set his book on the corner of the table as Jeryn opened the ledger, and leaned over the boy's shoulder to look. "We want books of magic—books of power. I don't know where they came from, how many of them there were, or when they came in, but it was at least a couple of years ago, probably more. But they came in from somewhere, and I think Kaletha got her hands on them and stashed them someplace."

"The empty quarter of the Palace?" Jeryn suggested promptly, keeping his place in the long, cramped columns of titles with one delicate forefinger as he glanced up.

"I would have thought so," the Wolf said, after a moment's consideration. "But most of those buildings are pretty unprotected. The ones with the roofs off are decaying badly already. And people go there sometimes, looking for lost chickens or a quiet place to fornicate . . ." *Oh, well*, he thought a half second later, as the dark eyes flicked up to him and then away, suddenly a boy's again and startled to hear a grownup just come out and say it. "I don't think she'd risk it."

"There are cellars under the empty quarter, you know," Jeryn said after a moment. "Cut down into the rock, some of them. They used to store grain and things down there during the season of storms, back when this was the Fortress and they were under siege all the time. Most of 'em are real dirty," he added fastidiously, and went back to perusing the cramped columns of book hand before them.

"*Black Book of Wenshar?*" Sun Wolf squinted down at the unfamiliar handwriting. "Sounds promising."

"They only call it that because it's got a black cover," Jeryn supplied. "It's a big book with the family trees of the Ancient House of

Wenshar, one of the books Mother brought with her in her dowry. It says here, 'Writ in the shirdane.' "

"Well, that won't do us much good."

"Oh, I can read the shirdane," said Jeryn. "Kaletha taught me, back before she became a wizard and started teaching magic. Later some of the scribes helped me. That book there . . ." He pointed to the little black-bound volume Sun Wolf had set down, ruinously old with its crumbling pages in slanting, flowing characters, their ink faded almost to nothing, "It starts out . . ." He opened it, studied the last page for a moment, then explained, "The shirdar do their books wrong way 'round. This says, *A Treatise on the Use of Cactus and . . . and . . .*" He struggled with the word, then said, "I don't know this one. Cactus and something, anyway, *in Healing.*"

"Aloe, probably," Sun Wolf guessed, looking down at the boy with a kind of admiration. "Does your father know you read this?"

Jeryn fell silent at the mention of his father. After a long moment he said, "I don't think so. I told him I could, once, and he—he said I shouldn't waste my time."

Sun Wolf stared to say, *A man who spends twelve hours a day pickling himself in brandy has a lot of room to talk about wasting time*, but shut his mouth on the words. The boy had enough troubles without being reminded of what was undoubtedly as great a shame to him as his bookishness was a shame to his father. Instead he simply said, "Well, I'm telling you it's not a waste of time—not in a King who's going to have to deal with the shirdar all his life. Was this part of your mother's dowry?"

"I think so," said Jeryn, turning the small volume thoughtfully over in his hands. "She brought a lot of books, and some of them were pretty old."

Sun Wolf scanned rapidly down the list before him. "This one isn't listed here, though—not in your mother's things."

"That's funny," said Jeryn. "Because I thought all the shirdane books were Mother's. In fact, I know they were, because it doesn't say anywhere else that they're in that language."

"So there are books here that weren't listed." Sun Wolf weighed the alien herbary in his hand, remembering something Starhawk had told him Tazey had said, an idea slowly taking shape in his mind. "Where are the others in the shirdane?"

Jeryn hurried back out to the larger room, to one of the cabinets which still retained its door. As he unlatched and swung it open, he said, "They keep them all together, because nobody can read them except a couple of clerks."

Some were almost new, others ancient and filthy, their leather covers blackened with smoke and dust and the oily grip of hands long turned to clay. Sun Wolf counted them—there were twenty-five. "And there were only seventeen on your mother's dowry list." He turned back to the boy, his single eye glinting in the hazy gleam of evening sunlight that diffused through the half-closed shutters. Reaching up, he took one of the oldest looking and balanced it on the edge of a shelf for the boy to look at.

"*The Book of the Surgeon*," Jeryn read out the scrolled, faded symbols laboriously. "Oh, look, there's a skeleton!" he added eagerly, opening a few leaves in.

"And not a very good one," Sun Wolf added, gazing down over his shoulder. "His elbow bends the wrong way—look. I don't remember this on the list, either."

Jeryn shook his head, puzzled.

"Is there an inventory of things that were here when the Fortress was taken over during the rebellion?"

"There should be," Jeryn said slowly. "I mean, if I were a rebel captain and took over an enemy fortress, I'd want a list of what was there so I'd know how to use it against the enemy."

By the time they located it, the sun had long since sunk behind the mountains; all three still, dust-smelling rooms had gone pitch dark, and both searchers were smutched from head to foot with the stirred grime of ages. Sun Wolf was objectively conscious that he was both tired and hungry. In the furor over Milkom's and the Bishop's deaths, Osgard had not had time to order the Wolf from the Fortress, but he'd missed breakfast and wasn't sure if his welcome would hold for dinner —always provided there was anything left by the time he and Jeryn got down to the Hall. But all weariness faded beneath an unaccustomed, scholarly elation as he and Jeryn sat cross-legged on the book-scattered floor, surrounded by the blue-white pool of magelight that illuminated the crackling pages of the old ledger that rested on Sun Wolf's knees.

"Here it is." His hand cast wavering cobalt shadows over the faded page as he pointed. "Thirty volumes of accompts, six large skins for the working of covers and forty skins of parchment . . . dried ink

. . . ink pots . . . *twenty-six Books of the Witches of Wenshar.* I thought as much, when Kaletha talked about the summoning of the dead."

"Twenty-six," Jeryn said, his small hand resting lightly on Sun Wolf's shoulder as he looked around his arm at the page. "And if Mother brought seventeen," he said, "and there's twenty-five there now . . ."

"That means that somewhere in this Fortress are eighteen books," Sun Wolf said, his voice low and his single eye gazing thoughtfully into the darkness, "written by the Witches of Wenshar."

CHAPTER

∽ 10 ∽

*D*ARKNESS LAY OVER THE FORTRESS OF TANDIERAS; HIDING in corners from the yellow torchlight in the Hall, but walking, alive and sniffing, through the empty quarter. Pale starlight rimmed the broken tiles of the old weavers' courtyard with frost, but did not touch the sable blackness inside the long building there. By the wavering sulfur glow of the requisite seven bowls of fire, Kaletha gathered her followers for the summoning of the dead.

Clear and silvery, her voice lifted in the invocation to the Mother. "We ask her aid, having done all that we can . . . We have purified ourselves with fasting . . . We have cleansed this room with fire and herbs and water . . ."

Standing between Anshebbeth and young Pradborn Dyer, Starhawk flexed her aching hands. She hadn't swept floors since her convent days.

". . . We have circled ourselves with Darkness and with Light . . ."

A spurt of gold flame from one of the bowls made the deep-scratched lines of the pentacle seem to bend and lengthen. It sprawled over the earthen floor like a dead bird; the smell of the dry ground where it had been cut mingled with that of the adobe walls, of must and crushed herbs, of the cloying incense, and the electric dustiness of the wind. A gust groaned through the walls of the empty quarter which lay just beyond the court, making the flames shudder; Starhawk could not repress a quick glance over her shoulder, to the darkness that seemed to wait just outside.

Wreathed in smoke and incense, Kaletha moved from point to point of the pentacle, taking care never to step across its lines. She touched, in turn, the water in the dishes at its valleys and passed her hands above the bowls of fire; the shadows of her fingers caressed the faces of those who stood in the narrow zone between the inner pentacle and the outer Circle of Light.

"We have drawn the Circle of Light about us, to ward off all creatures of darkness; we stand before you defended against all that would do us harm . . ."

Except ourselves, thought Starhawk, as the cold hands of those on either side shut around hers. *Except ourselves.*

"I don't like it," the Chief had said, when she'd spoken to him earlier that evening down in the Hall.

She hadn't asked, 'Why not?' If he had anything to go on but his animal instinct for danger he would have said as much. Instead she had asked, "How dangerous can it be?"

"I don't know. I don't know how powerful Kaletha is or what kind of magic she's learned from those books of hers. I don't know how much power she'll be able to raise from those of her following who have power of their own—Egaldus and Shelaina." This had been a few hours ago, when Starhawk had come down to the Hall and found Sun Wolf and Jeryn devouring a belated dinner of fried cheese and porridge. Their hair and faces glistened from what looked like a hasty wash in the nearest horse trough, and their shirts and doublets were gray with old dust and cobwebs. "According to everything I've heard from Tazey and Nanciormis, the power of the Witches of Wenshar was just about always used for evil. It wasn't a question of some of them being good and some of them evil—they were all a bad lot, no matter how good they were to start with."

When Starhawk looked doubtful of that, Jeryn put in, "It's true." The branch of candles, used at supper and relighted by the errant pair as they'd come from their mysterious investigations in the library, shone in his dark eyes as he looked up at her. "It's why Tazey was so scared—why Father's so angry, too. It isn't just that Tazey didn't want to turn into a witch and be damned. She didn't want to turn into someone who'd deserve to be damned. And they did."

The supper things had long since been cleared away, and the folk who remained in the lower end of the Hall, sewing or mending harnesses or sharpening weapons, talked in muffled tones. Beneath the door of the solar, a thread of light was visible. For a time, Osgard's pacing shadow had crossed it, back and forth, back and forth, as if he imagined he could outwalk pain and loss. Some time ago this had ceased. Now there was only the muted clink of a solitary wine cup on the little bronze table.

Starhawk had frowned, her gaze going from the big, lion-colored barbarian with his eye patch and his scarred forearms under their tangle of sun-bleached hair, the brass of his grimy doublet winking softly in the candlelight, to the fragile boy beside him, his black curls mussed and usual shabby primness thrown to the winds. "Is that possible?" she'd asked. "For magic to be intrinsically evil?"

"It shouldn't be," the Wolf had said. "But then, by all rights, it shouldn't work at all. But it does. We still don't know *why* magic works, Hawk, any more than we know what lightning is or what life is, for that matter—why a woman should be able to bring another human being alive out of her belly, a person who never existed before and who could raise empires and ride the wind . . . Why women?"

"They're smarter," Starhawk replied promptly and with a straight face.

The Wolf had grinned back—it was an old jest between them. Then he'd sobered and said, "We don't have to understand a thing, or even believe in it, to be killed by it, Hawk. And after going for years believing magic had nothing to do with me, I'm not about to start thinking I understand it. I *don't think* magic should—or could—automatically corrupt those who wield it; but on the other hand, there's a certain amount of unreliable evidence that in this case it *did*. And in any event, I've been warned against necromancy before. Kaletha may not need to intend evil for evil to come of it."

"She needs seven," the Hawk had said slowly, propping her boot on the bench beside him, her elbow on her thigh. "I'm the only other person she trusts. And in an odd way—I don't exactly trust her, because she's irresponsible with her power and with her influence over other people. But . . . in a way I understand her."

He had looked up at her for a moment from his half-devoured meal, puzzled, as if he had not quite expected her to form a friendship or a liking where he had none. Not that it was against his will or even his expectations—merely, that he had not thought about the possibility since they had become lovers.

Finally he'd asked, "Pox rot it, Hawk, don't you feel it?"

"I feel there's danger, yes," she'd said. "But I also think one or the other of us should be there. And if she's going to call power out of whichever of us it is, it should probably be me because I don't have any."

He had nodded, accepting her logic. But the sense of danger came back to her now, a nervous prickle; a warrior's indefinable awareness that the situation, for reasons she could not precisely define, stank like carrion. She had spent the hours between her talk with Sun Wolf and the approach to midnight meditating, and perhaps it was for this reason the night around her seemed alive, and the darkness filled with half-coalesced entities, waiting only to be named.

She was the only one in the Circle who neither was nor wished she had been mageborn. As they joined hands and Kaletha formed the final link in the glowing ring of human energy between Circle and pentagram, she looked at the faces of those around her: Luatha, her fat face creased in concentration, which did not quite eradicate the lines of sullen discontent around her mouth; Shelaina, wraith-like and with-drawn, looking at Kaletha with her face transfigured by the half-trance in which, under Kaletha's guidance, she could light fires from cold wood; and Pradborn, his eyes tight shut and his lips moving as he muttered to himself one of Kaletha's spells of self-hypnosis. Beside her, Starhawk was aware of Anshebbeth, her whole thin body tense as the fist of a frightened amateur around a knife hilt, her face a white mask with its sleepless, dark-circled eyes. Through her palms, clasping Anshebbeth's long, cold finger bones and Pradborn's chubby flipper, she felt the stir of power, an almost palpable crosscurrent of moving energy, different from the deepening stillness of the Invisible Circle in which the nuns of St. Cherybi had meditated. Or perhaps, the practical part of her mind said, it was only her knowledge of the tensions which divided that little band.

At Kaletha's signal, Egaldus' musical tenor rose to lead the chant-ing. The words were unfamiliar to Starhawk except for one earlier rehearsal, an ancient invocation whose hypnotic sonority numbed the mind. Kaletha's eyes were shut. Outside, the wind muttered distant rumors of storm.

We are children of Earth, thought Starhawk, her mind beginning to sink under the drone of the voices and of her own participation in the archaic ritual, her thoughts slipping down beneath the weight of the incense toward the point at which they would be completely stilled. *Deny it though the Trinitarians might, our minds are born of our bodies, clay informed by living fire; from this comes the power of what we are, not what we do.*

As her mind blended with the chant and the drug-like sweetness of the smoke, the part of her that remained a warrior tingled like a cat at sunset with the sense of power growing in the darkness beyond the protective Circle of Light.

By starlight, the empty quarter of the Palace had the disjointed appearance of a beast's skeleton, rib and femur and tibia tracing where the walls had lain, amid a scattering of random vertebrae. The fragile whiteness picked out bleached edges and corners of wall and stone and the silken curve of miniature dunes whose crests frayed in the searching wind. Shadow swathed empty doors and windows and filled the mouths of a hundred courts and alleyways like black curtains of cobweb. The air was livid with electricity and the sulfur stench of power.

If he struck flint, Sun Wolf thought, standing in the sand-strewn court just inside the gate, the ether itself would explode.

Methodically, he began to quarter the ruins.

He carried no light, nor did he summon the fox fire of the mages, not wanting to confuse his eyes with what they saw in light and shadow. He was aware that it would be difficult in any case to see what he sought. Kaletha would have concealed the place from the casual eye, casting spells around the entrance to the cellar—if cellar it was—that would cause the glance to slip over the place, as it habitually slipped over so many things in common life. From his experience scouting and using scouts, Sun Wolf was well aware how few people could name every item in a room or tell whether a door opened outward or inward; most people, if asked, would be surprised to learn of the door. He had learned also how easy were the spells to make this happen.

So he walked through the empty courts carefully, marking with a little scribble of light each empty doorway through which he passed—temporary marks, which would fade with the sunlight and be gone. He counted on his fingers the four corners of every roofless cell he entered—old workshops with desiccated shards of benches tumbled where the sandstorms had left them along the walls, *their corners deep in sand and shattered roof tiles,* the dark rafters overhead murmuring with the voices of sleeping doves; what had once been kitchens, with foxes' messes in their round little fireplaces; and roofless stables and byres filled with a whispering harlequin of shadow and the furtive scurry of nervous desert rats. The ones farther in had roof beams fallen down across them; nearer the inhabited portions of the Fortress, the beams, scarce in that treeless country, had been taken away. Even in the rare rains of the foothill winters, the thick walls, five and six feet wide at the base, were beginning to melt to shapeless lines of mud.

He made himself walk to every corner and touch the drifted mats of wood chips and sand there, knowing how illusions could make him think he had seen each shadowed corner look like every other. He knew that it was in the minute and singular checking of every detail that good siegecraft and good generalship—and, incidentally, good magic—lay, so only those with a certain methodical patience could master them.

Yet through it all, he was conscious of the magic moving in the night. The air seemed to grit upon his skin, as if all his body were a raw wound; the magic-laden silences picked and chewed at his taut nerves until even the sliding of his long hair over his scalp in the movement of hot, restless desert winds was enough to make him start. He could sense Kaletha and her disciples raising power from the bones of the earth, calling it forth from the ambient air; he knew that his own magic partook of it, drawing strength from the strength that walked free and restless in the darkness. He had visited the dyer's workshop with its shallow, crumbling vat pits, where Nexué's body had been found the day after her murder. But now, when he walked its four corners again, looking with particular care at the hideously stained stones of its fallen walls, he could feel the echoes of the malice and horror that had been enacted there still lingering in the ground. The bass strings of a harp will speak if the wind passes across them; so crumbling ghosts of magic vibrated around him there as he passed, a shadowless shadow in the night. In another place he felt it again, like a weak afterwhisper of sound. It took him a few moments of gazing at the black stripes of rafters overhead against a blacker sky to realize that it had been in this cell that he had found the massacred doves.

* * *

Hand knit to hand; flesh to flesh. Starhawk was aware, through the strange sparkling darkness of what was almost like meditation, of the power passing through the meat and sinew from the innermost marrow to the innermost marrow of the knotted bones within. She had never before partaken of this pooling of power, but she could sense the energy moving around the circle, greater than Kaletha's power, or Egaldus' fast-growing strength. It seemed to her that the flames that burned over the herbs and the incense had sunk, that shadow moved over the faces of the seven, that the lines scratched in the earth to define the pentacle and the Circle were faintly glowing, and that the faces themselves, which she had known throughout the last ten days, had changed, different and yet not unfamiliar, as if she had always known what they looked like underneath the skin.

She was chanting, repeating over and over the meaningless syllables of the unknown rite, the sound itself washing over her mind like the rhythm of sea waves; she was aware they had all begun to sway with the movement. She had no idea how long they had been chanting, nor did she care; as when she mediated, it seemed to her that time had settled and stopped, and she would have been neither surprised nor upset to walk outside and discover that the stars had not moved at all or that the sun was rising. But in meditation, she was conscious of all things, like the silence of deep water. In this, she was conscious only of the chant, the steady beat of its strength in her mind, and the scarcely controlled power slipping from hand to hand. It was like sleep, but moving sleep. The mind was released, she thought dimly—the mind that lay like a shield over the dark well beneath, from which the power came.

And just before her own mind surrendered to the chanting, she realized why all of the victims had been attacked when they were. *But if that's the case* . . . she thought, and fear hit her as suddenly as if she had stepped off a cliff.

Like the whisper of wind, she heard Kaletha's voice, though whether inside her skull or outside she could not be sure. "Don't break the Circle . . . Don't pull your mind from the power . . ."

The others were relying on her. For a panicked instant she wanted to release the hands she held, flee to the empty quarter and find the Chief, tell him, warn him . . . But the disciplines of meditation were strong. She let her thoughts sink back into the nothingness of the chant, and, as if she had opened her hand, the knowledge raveled away into the dry flicker of the night wind.

Sun Wolf put his hand on the loose dune of sand-covered rubble, which dissolved before his eyes into insubstantial shadow. He saw almost at the same moment that his fingers touched it, the iron of the grillework that the spell had concealed, and he jerked his hand away in terror, as if burned. He fell back a step, the muttering dryness of the desert wind making cold the sweat that suddenly stood on his brow, his heart slamming like a smelter's hammer . . .

But there was nothing to be afraid of.

His mind told him that, even as his breath raced from his lips. *Not even instinct,* he thought, *no clue, no sign. Just fear itself.*

His father's harsh teachings had managed to make him forget for nearly forty years that he had been mageborn, but it had never quite eradicated his curiosity. The old man had said a hundred times, "You're too nosey for a warrior, boy," usually followed up by a clip on the ear. He stepped forward again.

He could see the spell marks now on the iron. That delicate frieze of signs, invisible to the human eye, could only have been written by Kaletha. In the living horror that whispered in every shadow of the night, he still felt fear of them and of this place, a deserted kitchen in the midst of the old quarter; but he was aware now that not only the grille, but the remains of the tiled floor and the crumbling adobe walls, had been written with fear-spells. The power that walked the night picked them up and made them resonate in his mind like the ghastly images of nightmares.

He wiped the sweat from his palms and fished in his doublet pocket for a wax writing tablet and stylus. It was only the spells of the night, he told himself, forcing his hand steady as he copied the signs as well as he could, to study them later. There was no danger . . .

Or was there?

He clicked the tablet closed and pocketed it once again. Just because his fear was induced by a spell didn't mean that there was no reason to fear.

Kaletha would be on the lookout for a spell mark near her hideaway; but, at a guess, she had no woodscraft. He marked the corner with three bricks, to find it again in case of some spell that confused the memory of directions, and walked out into the court.

The fear lessened as he stepped beneath the broken door-lintel. Outside, the wind was stronger—not the hard, tearing forerunner of the storms, but the shifting whisper of dry voices, playing tag among the ancient stones, like the demon voices in the canyons of Wenshar. In a corner near a dry well, he found a couple of dusty cottonwood saplings, seeded in a wet year from the old tree in the next court. They were half-dead, and it was no difficult thing to tear one of them up by its shallow roots. His nape prickling like a dog's at the queer, rising tension of the night, he pulled his knife from his belt and began stripping the sapling into a pole, listening all the while, though for what he did not know.

He wondered if Kaletha would be able to summon the voice of the dead.

More than any artificial spell of hers, laid on this place to keep intruders away, the thought terrified him.

Cautiously, he reentered the darkness of the ruin.

The sapling was nearly seven feet long, brittle as only dry cottonwood could be. He worked its end through the metal of the grille and levered sideways. The metal grated on stone; like the swish of silk on dust, he heard something move sharply in the pitchy darkness underneath.

The iron was heavy, but no earth had settled around it—it was nearly clean of rust. He tipped the grille out of its sunken bed and reached gingerly over to topple it aside. Then he looked down into the hole beneath and felt the skin crawl along his scalp.

The pit below was alive with snakes.

Most of them were the brown-and-gray desert rattlers. When his body bulked dark against the night above them, they set up a dry buzzing as they raised their horned noses skyward. In the darkness, he could see among them the slender lead-colored rock asps and, like gross, flat-headed slugs, the big cave mambas, as long as his arm and half again as fat. Even as he watched, he saw another one slither forth from a hole in the wall of the pit, to fall with a soft, sickening plop to join its brethren. The sandy floor of the cellar below seemed to glitter with black, watching eyes.

They must have been drawn by Kaletha's spells from all over the empty quarter, he thought, *since first I came near the place.*

He felt a sudden rush of sympathy for the local attitude toward the Witches of Wenshar.

Well, pox rot you, he thought. *Two can play that game.*

He hunkered down on the rim of the pit, sapling pole in hand. The vicious buzzing of the rattlers rose again; in the darkness he could make out sinuous movement and the dozenfold flicking of forked, black, questing tongues.

Reaching out with his mind, he felt the prickling of those stupid alien angers, a shortsighted rage to strike at warmth and the smell of blood. Never taking his eye from the snakes, he caressed the cottonwood pole with his big, sword-scarred hands, as if to work magic into it as he would work a lotion. He imparted his smell to it, the heat of his flesh, and the shadow of his bulk against the night. The darkness all about him seemed charged with power, intensifying in his mind the smell-feel of the reptile instincts below that woke such disturbing echoes in his own thoughts. He could feel the spells that worked on them, that had drawn them there, and that would turn them to attack a man. Those spells, too, he worked and turned into the wood, while taking into his own body the illusion of coldness and stasis and the smell of the ancient stones.

He addressed a brief prayer to such of his ancestors as might be listening and flung the pole down into the corner of the pit below.

It bounced; at the movement, the snakes were upon it, striking again and again at the spell-written wood. There was absolutely no time to lose and none to think, but it did cross Sun Wolf's mind, as he lowered himself by his hands and dropped the few feet remaining to the sandy floor of the pit, that it was perfectly possible for him to have gotten the first part of his spells right and muffed the second.

No, he thought. His body bloodless, smelling of stone and dust was cold to the tongues of the snakes. He was a dead thing; it was the pole that was alive and must be killed.

They continued to strike the pole.

The cellar was clean, about a dozen feet square, and low-roofed, smelling of earth and stone and of the dusty fetor of the snakes. The air there was dry and still. No dust drifted its corners—the walls above sheltered its entrance from the prevailing winds. A short ladder lay along one wall, where it could be lowered and dropped from above. In the darkness, Sun Wolf could make out a table, a reading stand, and a tall-legged stool. Beyond them, a niche was cut out of the far wall, a low ceiling beam sheltering a sort of hollow there. Deep inside it he saw two small chests of iron-bound leather, neither of them larger than a woman could carry by herself. There were no lamps. To nonmageborn eyes, even by day, the place would be dim and shadowy, and by night, a Stygian pit.

But even in the darkness, he could see the skittery movement swarming along the lids of the chests.

He threw a quick glance back at the crawling heap of loathsomeness around the pole. His instincts told him that wouldn't last much longer; it was a fight to keep his concentration on the illusions that kept them attacking the wood and blocked their awareness of the heat of his own veins. He understood then why meditation was so essential, strengthening and freeing the concentration. He knew he could maintain two illusions at once, but never three.

The lids of the chests were crawling with scorpions.

Slow with loathing, his hand went to the pocket of his doublet for his gloves. But even as he did so, movement caught his eye on the overhanging beam and on the earth and stones it carried. He'd have to duck his head under it to reach the chests. Even as he watched, a scorpion dropped down from the beam into the niche—one of the big, shiny brown ones, long as a man's hand, whose stings could pierce all but the toughest leather. The sweat was cold on his face as he passed his hand nervously across the back of his neck, and he understood then that he couldn't do it. The boxes were locked. Given time, he could force a lock, but he could not pick up a trunk that size, filled with the weight of books, without crawling halfway under that lintel.

Kaletha had defeated him.

Anger and resentment surged up in him, but the sensible part of him, the strategist that had come more and more to the fore as he grew older, told him not to be stupid. He had been in situations where he would rather have died than admit that a woman had defeated him, but the stupidity of the acts to which he had let himself be driven in that kind of rage had never been worth it. She had power. Though he could feel that his own powers were heightened with the sorcery stirring through the night, something told him not to push his luck.

His hyperquick hearing picked up the stir and swish of movement behind him. Turning, he saw the snakes had finally realized that what they bit was dead wood. For the most part they were still milling, but a mamba as big around as his leg was crawling toward him like a swollen, dirt-colored worm.

Snakes would strike at sudden movement; he glided away from the chests, glancing everywhere and cursing his blindness on his left side. It might have been the heat of his anger at Kaletha that shivered the wall of illusions that covered him, merely the cumulative pressures of maintaining the spells, or the uncanny power that filled the night like hallucinatory flame—he did not know. But other snakes swung their heads toward him, tongues flicking. He flipped the ladder cautiously over with the toe of his boot, and a single scorpion—the small, whitish- gray kind whose sting was no worse than the sting of a bee— darted to safety in a corner. He jerked his foot aside as the mamba struck at his boot heel and he shoved the ladder into position. If he panicked, he knew the spells would crumble. Before the snake could strike again, he was scrambling up out of the pit, to the wind and shadows above.

When he reached the top, his hands were shaking so badly he could barely push the ladder down through the hole again and replace the grille.

"And when was that?" asked Starhawk, her voice quiet in the gloom of the little cell beyond the stables.

Sun Wolf shook his head. They lay together in the makeshift bed of pine poles and faded quilts, flesh against chilled flesh, but neither had moved to make love. Their kisses had been those of comfort against fears and thoughts neither could quite define, and they held each other, not as lovers do, but like brother and sister, frightened of the dark. "I don't know. I came back here; it was at least an hour before you did." He moved his head, to look down at the browned, delicate face in its short frame of ivory hair, where it lay on the hard pillow of his pectorals. "Why?"

Her gray eyes seemed transparent in the thin glow of the magelight that burned like a lamp around the tip of one bedpost. "Because I— I'm not sure, but I think that's when there was a break in the power of the Circle. It's like—I can't tell what the Circle was like. Like a tug of war, maybe, or—or rising to the climax of lovemaking. I don't know. But there can be no break in it, no slacking. The power has to feed on itself."

Sun Wolf nodded, understanding. "What you may not be strong enough to get from yourself, you can achieve by combining many minds—if you can get those minds to pull together. Yes. But if one stops pulling, they all slack."

"And they all did," said Starhawk. "It was like a harness trace breaking, or like falling out of love. Kaletha tried to recover it, but . . . we never did, completely."

She moved her weight slightly against him, hard muscle and hard bone, the ridges of scars breaking the silk of the flesh.

He asked, "Did Galdron come?"

Starhawk shook her head and moved again, pressing closer to him under the mottled, sand-colored homespun of the worn quilts. By the witchlight, he could see the deepening of the scratchwork of fine lines around her eyes; through his arm around her body, he felt the tension of her muscles.

"What is it?"

"I don't know." She shook her head again, and Sun Wolf, sensing not only her fear but his own, drew her tighter yet against him. "The concentration broke, or it never peaked. Nothing. But I could feel it —" She looked around her at the darkness crowding onto the blue witchlight and the velvet night beyond the window, charcoal black and still with the predawn drop of the wind, as if all the world held its breath. "And I feel it still."

"I know," the Wolf said softly. "So do I. And I'm wondering why. Power was built up, Hawk—it's still here, hanging over the empty quarter like a miasma. Something . . ."

She frowned suddenly, as some word of his tugged at her mind.

"What is it?"

"I don't know. Something you said . . . Something I thought during the summoning . . . it was important, but damned if I can remember what it was or why. Only . . ."

Something beyond the windows snagged the corner of his vision. His head whipped around, and the Hawk, feeling the sudden flinch of his muscles, was silent, as he killed the blue glow of the witchlight and they lay together, staring out of darkness into the dark.

There was movement in the empty quarter.

He rolled silently out of bed and walked naked to the window, holding to the velvet density of the shadows around the wall. The air was freezing on his flesh. Like a ghost, Starhawk joined him, the quilt thrown over her shoulder, carrying her sword.

Neither spoke. Around them the power was palpable in the night, the hideous tension that had grown, not lessened, as those who had formed the Circle had sought their beds.

Sun Wolf was not sure, but he thought he saw the bluish flicker of demon light among the labyrinth of skeleton walls.

Silently he turned away and found his boots, war kilt, and sword. As he pulled them on, Starhawk joined him, locating her own clothing as she had located her weapon by touch in the dark. By the time she was ready, Sun Wolf had gone to the door and was looking out across the little court toward the empty quarter. He was sure of it now. There were demons there.

This is none of my affair, he told himself. But he felt his heart quicken with the same fear he had felt in the carved canyons of Wenshar, a fear unlike—deeper than—a man's fear of death or harm. *Fear of what?* the calm, detached portion of his mind wondered impersonally. *It has nothing to do with me.*

But in a queer way he knew that it did.

His hand tightened around the greasy old hilt of his sword. The Hawk was like an armed shadow behind him as he moved silently across the starlit court.

In the labyrinth of the old courtyards, the presence of the demons was stronger. He could sense them, feel their malice prickle along his skin, and hear their thin, piping voices calling to one another among the stones. *Why here?* he wondered. *Why tonight?* Did they follow the smell of power, gravitating to this place for the same reasons that they haunted the ruins of Wenshar? Was that what they wanted of him when they had hovered through those moonless canyon nights outside the window of the rock-cut temple, waiting for him? Was it the revived power of the old Witches that drew them now, like vultures to the stink of dying things?

He could hear their voices, sometimes little piping cries or a low crooning, like a child singing over and over to itself the only line of a song that it knew. For an instant it crossed his mind that it *was* a child, lost somewhere in the mazes; then he shook his head and thrust the thought aside. Like their voices, it was only bait in a trap.

What kind of a trap? he wondered. *A trap for whom and why? Except for the occasional biting-demon, they couldn't harm humans—could they?* As in the ruins of Wenshar, he felt cold with fear of them, fear not for his body, but fear of he did not know what. He wondered suddenly about the Witches of Wenshar and about what had become of those who had refused to use their power for evil—or if they had ever had a choice.

Faint and confused among the walls, he heard a voice calling, "Kaletha! Kaletha!" *Egaldus,* he thought . . . *or a demon's voice that sounded like his. Had Kaletha run to check her cache, as soon as she could rid herself of her disciples? Was that why the concentration of the Circle had given way when she had somehow felt his spells against her snakes?*

"Kaletha!" he bellowed, and the echoes mocked him, *Kalethakalethakaletha* . . . "If you can hear me, stand still and call!" *call . . . callcall . . .* "

"Kaletha!" came the other voice, like a desperate echo.

Sun Wolf strode forward, his eye sharp along the ground before him, the tops of the walls, and the few remaining buildings on all sides. They crossed through what had been a stable court, then hurried down a roofless colonnade where the sand drifted knee-deep along the back wall. Through an eyeless window gap, he saw the flicker of something bright and moving, a discarded insect-chitin of light, save for those greedy, unhuman eyes . . . then it was gone. He realized that he still had his sword ready in his hand and that Starhawk did, too, though neither weapon would do them the slightest good. The very air seemed weighted with evil, ready at a word to take shape . . .

Why did he feel that, in the back of his mind, he knew that word?

"Kaletha!" he roared. "Egaldus!"

Farther off now, but recognizable as the young acolyte's, the voice called out, "Kaletha? Kal . . ."

And then the word turned to a scream.

CHAPTER

11

*"T*HE DEMONS WERE THERE. I KNOW, I SAW THEM."

"Are you saying you think they did it?" Incarsyn asked from his place on Osgard's left.

Nanciormis sneered, "Don't be an ass, man."

Osgard's bloodshot green eyes narrowed. "If you saw them, they couldn't have been demons, Captain. Demons are . . ."

"Invisible," Sun Wolf finished, slouching back in his black oak chair at the fireplace end of the High Table and studying the three men facing him across the length of the dark board. "I know." Through the line of tall southern windows the sun slanted in hard bars of horizontal gold, but around them, the Fortress of Tandieras was unwontedly quiet. Not until sunup would any man or woman of the guards venture into the empty quarter to fetch forth Egaldus' remains, but the rumor had swept the place like a chaparral fire after a dry summer. Sun Wolf could hear the murmur of it, breathing like wind in the corners of the servants' halls; he could feel the silence as he or Kaletha passed.

He went on, "I don't know why I've always been able to see them, but I have. It may come of being mageborn . . ."

"Kaletha can't," Nanciormis pointed out promptly. "Nor, to the best of my knowledge, can . . ." He just barely broke off the word *Tazey* at a furious glare from the King.

"It is said among my people," Incarsyn put in, "that those who can see demons do so because they are themselves demon-spawned."

"That's rubbish," the King snapped.

"So there are those among you who can do it?" Sun Wolf asked thoughtfully, raking the Lord of the Dunes with his single golden eye.

The young man nodded, but he didn't look comfortable about the whole subject. Since yesterday, he had the pale, shaken appearance of one in the grip of some heavy and unaccustomed thinking.

At Osgard's invitation, the Lord of the Dunes had come to this council, but Sun Wolf, feeling the subpulse of politics between the three men, sensed that the request had been a false one. He had sat there through Sun Wolf's recital of his second investigation of the empty quarter last night and of the finding of what was left of Egaldus' body, looking handsome and exotic and a little puzzled in his gold-stitched tunic and snowy cloak. Neither Nanciormis nor Osgard had much to ask him—he was there simply, Sun Wolf guessed, to remind him that he was still pledged to become Osgard's son-in-law, no matter what afterthoughts might be now churning through his mind.

Nanciormis said, "In any case it's foolish to believe it was demons. They are incapable of harming man."

"Not necessarily," the Wolf said. "There have been biting-demons, stone-throwers . . ."

"But certainly none capable of doing that kind of damage."

Incarsyn folded one white hand upon the other and appeared to study for a moment the circle of glinting fire thrown by the facets of his ruby ring. Then he looked up again. "Among my people, it was said that such things happened to those who ran afoul of the Witches of Wenshar."

"Old wives' tales!" Osgard's voice was harsh as the crack of a whip in the warm blaze of the morning heat.

"Were they?" Sun Wolf asked softly and turned to look at the young Lord of the Dunes. "Tell me, Incarsyn, were all the Witches of Wenshar evil? Was there none among them who used her power for something other than selfishness and lust?"

The young man frowned and shook his head. Obviously the concept of a good witch had never crossed his mind. Perhaps in the shirdane in which he thought, such a concept was linguistically impossible. In the crystalline brilliance of the morning sunlight after the sleepless alarms of the night, his youth and hardness contrasted even more sharply with Nanciormis' slack cheeks and double chin—the more so because of the racial similarity of those two hawk-boned sets of features framed in the flowing darkness of their braided hair. "None," he said simply and then smiled a little, lightening up his face. "They were, you understand, women. A woman will, by nature, put first in her considerations, the things that immediately affect her whether they be material goods or satisfaction." He spoke as one who forgives a simple-minded child for soiling itself, and Sun Wolf suppressed an unexpected urge to get up and knock his handsome head against the wall.

He started to retort, but Osgard's heavy voice drowned them both. "The Witches of Wenshar have nothing to do with it!" he thundered. "It's clear as daylight what happened! Egaldus was tampering with heresy and magic last night with that bitch Kaletha, trying to raise spirits, they say, and got what was coming to him. They both had every reason to wish Galdron ill, since the old hypocrite was threatening to exile him—"

"And so he raised up a spell that backfired on himself?" Sun Wolf demanded. "Talk sense, man."

"Kaletha and Egaldus were lovers," Nanciormis added scornfully, but his dark eyes, regarding Sun Wolf, were narrow with thought. "She'd never have harmed a hair of his golden head."

"Which isn't necessarily true," remarked Starhawk later, when the Wolf was sitting cross-legged on the parapet of the watchtower, a hundred feet above the granite courts of the Hold, peeling an orange. "Just because you love someone doesn't mean you can't fear and hate and resent them as well."

"People couple for all kinds of reasons." In the stifling stillness of the desert air, the orange's perfume was shockingly sweet. "You can lie with someone you hate, if it gives you a chance at them."

"True, but that's not what I mean." Starhawk turned her gaze from the brazen emptiness of the desert. Framed in the white veils, her face had a stripped look—bones, scars, and ice-gray eyes like a man's—but for the softness of the lips. "Love isn't an easy thing to define. You can resent people you love—enough to want to kill them, or at least hurt them badly. People do it all the time. Not the least reason is because they hold that power over you."

Sun Wolf was silent for a moment, thinking about that and wondering if the Hawk spoke from personal experience on that score. He offered her a segment of the orange, and she shook her head—she never ate on duty, he remembered, even if it was only watching the dead landscape of the desert for motion that never came. From up here, the Haunted Mountains were visible, a stained and broken knife blade over the heat shimmer of the reg. Had she resented him—hated him, even—in the years she'd been the second-in-command of his mercenary army, loving him and watching him bed a steady parade of eighteen-year-old concubines? In those days he had seldom thought of her as a woman. Perhaps neither had she.

But looking up, troubled, he met the smile in her eyes, so he asked instead, "You think Kaletha resented Egaldus enough to kill him?"

"You're a teacher." The Hawk made a sweeping scan of the desert horizon, then turned her eyes back to him again. "Would you train a student who was strong enough to defeat you? Not just to give you a good fight—but to whip you, crush you, kill you maybe?"

Again Sun Wolf fell quiet for a time. The sun, warm on his own loose-draped veils and the leather of his shoulders and thighs, had lost its summer intensity, but the air still felt thick and electric, charged with storms. At last he said, "I never have done so. I don't know." He hesitated, then added truthfully, "I'd like to think I'd have more pride as a teacher than I would have vanity as a warrior, but . . . I don't know."

Starhawk smiled a little and resumed her steady watching, presenting him with the smooth line of her profile, somehow delicate in spite of the high cheekbones and too-strong chin. "And you're forty now and a wizard," she said. "I can lay you money you wouldn't have when you were twenty-eight. Would you have trained me to be able to defeat you?"

The words were slow and hard to say. "I'd like to think you could." But even as he said them, he knew he didn't, not really.

You are greedy, like Egaldus, Kaletha had said. And to her Egaldus had said, *You still wish to keep it all to yourself.* He had held Kaletha in contempt for doing it—it wasn't a particularly pleasant thing to realize about himself.

"But you're pretty sure I wouldn't," said Starhawk, her voice gentle. "I understand Kaletha, Wolf. And in spite of herself, I rather like her. I think she's wrong to be hoarding the books of power, but I can understand why she's doing it—why she keeps her disciples under her thumb the way she does—maybe why she let Egaldus seduce her. She knows she's never had proper teaching; she knows now about the

Great Trial, which she didn't know about before. Whatever she says about it, she knows you've gone through it and she hasn't. She's fighting to hang onto her power—over you, over them, over Egaldus."

"You think she'd have killed him to keep him away from the books?" Then he frowned, his blunt fingers pausing in mid-motion, sticky with red orange juice like droplets of blood. "But I went after the books, too. Hell, I went down into the pit. Nothing happened to me."

"It may not have been an impersonal trap," Starhawk said quietly. "Whatever destroyed Egaldus . . ." She turned back to him, dark, level brows tugging down over her nose. "*Could* Kaletha have summoned up that kind of power, specifically? Or . . . ?"

"I don't know!" Sun Wolf swung his hand in frustration. "Incarsyn said the Witches of Wenshar did, but . . ." He looked up and saw the woman's face suddenly puckered with a far-off look, as if she listened for some sound beyond the range of hearing. "What is it?"

She shook her head. "I—I can't remember." She leaned on the battlement, a rangy cheetah-shape of dark green leather and white shirt sleeves against the endless speckled dustiness of barren scrub land. "It's on the edge of my mind, something about how the power was summoned . . . I don't know." She made a wry face. "I'll remember it in the middle of the night sometime." Even those words seemed to catch a loose thread in her memory, and she paused again. Then her eyes turned back to the desert, and all concentration on dreams or half-memories vanished in sudden sharp alertness.

Sun Wolf slewed around on his precarious perch on the battlement to follow her gaze.

On the hard desert horizon a gray plume of dust floated, glittering in the morning air.

"It can't be a storm." Tazey shaded her eyes and gazed out over the desert. She was still dressed, as her father had ordered, in girlish ruffles and curls for the benefit of her suitor; pinks and lavenders that looked garishly incongruous around the strained and hagridden face.

"Of course it can," Kaletha snapped, glancing sidelong at her. "I have sensed one on its way since morning . . ."

"If it's a storm, it's got a damn narrow base." Sun Wolf turned, as Starhawk and Nanciormis appeared on the thin flight of stone steps that led down to the courtyard below the gatehouse balcony where they stood, both with brass spyglasses in their hands. "The winds won't hit till this evening."

Kaletha's nostrils flared with tired loathing at this contradiction of her words. Like Tazey, she looked rather white around the mouth, though Sun Wolf could not see from her eyes if she had been crying. She looked haggard, as if the magic that had weighted the air last night had been drawn from her veins. Sun Wolf found himself remembering that Egaldus had died calling her name.

The Witches of Wenshar, he thought, and realized that the three of them standing there on the gatehouse, gazing off across the desert toward the advancing column of dust, were the only witches in Wenshar now.

Starhawk handed him his spyglass, made by the best instrument-maker in Pergemis; he unfolded it with a snap as Nanciormis extended his own and set it to his eye. In the dust and heat haze, the shapes of horsemen and dromedaries were clearly visible, as were the white burnooses of the shirdar and the brightly dyed curtains of a swathed litter. He took his eye from the glass at the sound of footsteps on the stair behind him in time to see Osgard, Incarsyn, and Anshebbeth hurriedly mounting the stairs to crowd onto the gatehouse platform.

Anshebbeth hurried straight to Kaletha. "You shouldn't be out here," she fussed. "You should be resting, you've had a terrible shock."

Kaletha shook her off impatiently. Snubbed and hurt, the governess turned to Tazey. "And you, dear—You were awake all night, practically . . ."

"*Please*, 'Shebbeth . . ."

Nanciormis handed his spyglass to Incarsyn and said, "Is that who I think it is?"

The young man stood gazing like some beautiful statue, the loose sleeves of his crimson tunic flattened to his arm muscles by the hot eddy of wind which rolled the knot of curls at the nape of his neck. A crease of consternation appeared on his brow. "The Hasdrozidar," he said at last. "My own people." He lowered the spyglass from his eye, the curves of his mouth set tight with apprehension.

Nanciormis said silkily, "They will be led, I believe, by your sister, the Lady Illyra."

Even at this distance, Sun Wolf could now make out unaided the swaying shape of the great litter in the midst of its circle of mounted outriders. They were moving fast. Either they, too, sensed the onset of the storm that would hit the Fortress a few hours after nightfall, or they simply had the desert dweller's instinctive uneasiness about being in open ground in the season of witches. Beside him, he was aware of the look of sick fright on Tazey's face and of the slow flush of anger to Osgard's.

Incarsyn's voice was tight but steady. "So it seems." He hesitated for a moment, as if figuring out what his next action should be, then turned and placed a comforting hand on Tazey's shoulder. "Have no fear, my Princess. She is only a woman. She cannot separate me from the wife that I will have." He bowed with his usual lithe grace, then strode away down the stairs.

Osgard rumbled, "She'd damn bloody well better not," and followed after, his white surcoat billowing in the hot winds that had begun to shift along the Fortress's parched granite walls.

Tazey still stood looking out across the desert, her face like something boarded against storms worse than that which she had parted with her hands. Her fingers, where they rested on the parapet, were shaking.

"Only a woman," Nanciormis quoted derisively. At a glance from him, Anshebbeth fell back from her protective hovering at Tazey's side. The big shirdar lord's voice was soft, but carried clearly to those who remained on the parapet beneath the tall shadows of the Hold. "When that young man decides he wants the alliance with Wenshar's silver mines, there isn't much that shakes him. Don't be deceived, Tazey. He knows your esteem will only pave his way."

"Let her alone," Starhawk said quietly.

Nanciormis glanced at her, impatient. She had stood where the shadows fell most densely, without saying anything, her hands tucked behind her sword belt—it was easy to forget she was there. "I don't want my niece deceived into something she'll regret," he said roughly. "Incarsyn cares less for her than he cares for his horses. He's told me that."

Tazey did not look at him, but Sun Wolf could see in the burnished sun-glare the swim of tears in her eyes. "I haven't been deceived," she said in a small, steady voice. "I've been pushed and bargained for and cozened and threatened with everything from a good beating to eternal damnation . . ." Her voice shivered, but did not break. "The only thing that's helped me to bear it is that he's been kind enough to try and deceive me."

"In Pardle Sho," her uncle retorted with smooth brutality, "there's a woman who raises rabbits for meat. She goes out every morning when she feeds them, picks them up, pets them, cuddles them, and calls each by its own name, so that they will come to her and she doesn't have to chase after them at slaughtering time."

Tazey swung around, looking up at the tall bulk of the man beside her. The sun glimmered in the tear that lay on her face and on the pink opalescence of the sand-pearls dangling from her ears. She whispered, "I hate you." Turning, she gathered up her absurd, ruffled skirts and ran after her father down the narrow steps.

The sun slanted over toward evening; the wind began to rise. It talked to itself in thin, whistling sneers around the corners of the Fortress, in and out of the thick, decaying adobe walls of the empty quarter; it smelled of sand and electricity and burned the sinuses with dust. Tempers shortened as the grip of the drying air crushed brains and nerves; people too often spoke their minds or acted without considering consequences; small hatreds and angers flared. In the courts of the cordillera towns, a storm was considered mitigating circumstances in cases of assault and murder.

The caravan from the far-off oasis city of Hasdrozaboth had arrived. Its hundred or so lean, sun-hardened riders had stabled their horses and camels in the hastily fitted dormitories on the edges of the empty quarter and joined to crowd the bodyguard, already formidable, of their Lord. From his little cell near the stables, Sun Wolf could hear them talking to one another in the lilting singsong of the shirdane and smell their cook fires and the spiced greasiness of their meals as he unrolled his armor from its wrappings.

"She'll know if you aren't at supper," Starhawk said quietly. She folded her arms and looked out past the half-furled window shutters to the sulfurous light in the little court. A man dressed like a groom, his black, curly hair proclaiming him one of the shirdar—though he had, like most of the Wenshidar, cut off his braids when he had gone to work for the new rulers of the land—passed along the path from the gate, heading for the privies. Starhawk saw him glance nervously at the parched, silent walls of the empty quarter and hurry his steps.

"It's the only time I can be sure where she'll be." In the long heat of the afternoon they had made love and slept, though in his dreams Sun Wolf had seen again the cold, bodiless eyes of the demons. A little uneasily now he unrolled the shirt of chain mail he hadn't worn since the seige of Melplith a year ago and checked the buckles and leather. The weight of it was strange in his hands after so long, the harsh, musical jingling of its rings both foreign and familiar to his ears. There was a bright patch where it had been mended on the breast—a sizeable rip, but he could not for the life of him remember what had done that or when.

"If she can kill at a distance," Starhawk said, "that might not matter." Behind her, a dust devil scampered across the court; a chance gust of wind groaned around the walls. From the stables nearby, Sun Wolf could hear the horses stamping nervously in their stalls. "Always supposing Kaletha is the killer."

Sun Wolf nodded, not surprised. That thought had crossed his mind as well. "You think there might be someone else. Someone who's hiding the fact they're mageborn. Someone who might, at some time in the past, have had access to the books."

"Something like that." She braced her shoulders against the window frame, the slice of light angling through, shining white against her hair. "A witch would have to be awfully stupid to go around killing people by magic in a community where there aren't lots of witches around, but we've both seen stupider things. Remember that apothecary in Laedden who poisoned his neighbors' wells? It might almost be—I don't know—some kind of elemental force, like a beast, killing at random. It's hard to picture someone inflicting that kind of butchery deliberately."

"I found it hard to picture a couple of boys killing their own mother to get the family savings to buy their way out of a besieged city," the Wolf remarked. "We live and learn. They sure as hell offered me the money to let them through the lines at Melplith." He pulled the heavy leather chaps he'd borrowed from one of the horse wranglers from beneath the bed, laid them alongside the mail shirt, studied the ensemble, and tried to judge whether the protection offered would be worth the limitation of his movements. The chaps would certainly protect him from the snakes if he moved fast enough, as the thick leather gloves he'd acquired would protect his hands from the scorpions. As for meeting anything else . . . they might keep him from being hamstrung and brought down on the first slash, but after that, nothing would prevent the whirlwind violence that had destroyed Egaldus and that had scattered pieces of the Bishop Galdron and Norbas Milkom over a dozen square yards of sand from shredding the flesh from his bones.

"Do you think you can keep Kaletha busy for the next few hours?"

If he was attacked, he reflected, hefting the stiff guards in his hands, there would be nowhere to run anyway. Feeling Starhawk's silence, he looked up.

"Chief," said Starhawk slowly, "I'd rather not."

Once, he knew, he would have demanded why, quick and rather indignant. Now he let the silence lie; after a long moment she sorted out her words.

"I'll watch her if you want and try to stop her or get word to you if she comes into the empty quarter. But I won't use her friendship with me—her trust of me, in spite of what she knows about me and you— against her. I want to keep her friendship with me separate from my love for you."

Her voice was, as usual, calm and uninflected, giving nothing to anyone, not even to him. But in the years he had known her, and especially since they had been lovers, he had come to listen beneath its cool tones. He remembered her on the tower, saying, *But you're pretty sure I wouldn't,* and he realized he had asked her, unthinkingly, what he had no right to ask.

In the first half second he felt anger at himself and annoyance at her for doing that to him . . . and a little, he realized, for choosing Kaletha's rights over his whims. That pushed him back to sanity, and he nodded. "All right," he said. And then, though he saw no change in the gray eyes still resting on his face, he added with a kind of stiff unfamiliarity, "I'm sorry. I shouldn't have asked you that."

She concealed her relief and her somewhat unflattering surprise equally well and only said, "I'll do what I can."

As it happened, the entire question became academic anyway.

Starhawk left him to look for Kaletha; the night drew on. The groan and mutter of the winds fell still, the silence even more terrible, hot and thick over the fortress on its knoll and the dusty town beyond. The night was pregnant with storm. Sun Wolf, sitting on the splintery wooden doorsill of his cell waiting for darkness, watched the shutters being put up in every window of Tandieras. The sun sank, turning the Binnig Rock to the color of old blood and flashing like threads of fire on the spires of Pardle Cathedral. He knew there were lamps being lighted in the Hall and in the line of archways on the balcony of the Household, but not even a sliver of brightness illuminated the dark bulk of the Hold. It seemed to him a dead fortress, silent as the rocks. Even the birds were hushed, seeking their own hiding places. The stillness was eerie, too like that of the dead City of Wenshar.

He tried to relax and center his mind, tried to keep it on the spells he knew he would have to work, but it strayed again and again to Starhawk. It had startled him that she would refuse to go against one of her other friends for his sake, and he was aware that he felt miffed about it, as if she should feel loyalty to no one but himself. It was unfair to Starhawk, and he knew it.

He sighed and shook his head at himself. His ancestors would die of shame. Going soft, his father would say—yielding where he should grasp tighter for his own survival. He had survived forty years by hanging on. His life had been a fist which let nothing go. It was difficult to open it to other things.

As a warrior, he had known what he was. Here, in this baked landscape of black rocks and demons' whispers, he was seeing what he might become; and like Tazey, he found that it terrified him.

The hardness of that dreadful, motionless sky softened to a scrim of dove-colored silk. The smell of the storm was in his veins, pricking and hissing at his mind. It was not quite dark, but if he was to finish, it was best that he go now. With all the windows of the Hold shuttered, it was good odds no one would see him. He carefully closed up the windows of his own little cell and, in the semi-dark, stripped off his leather doublet, the chill startling against his ribs through the worn homespun of his patched shirt.

It wasn't until the approaching footfalls were very close to the doorway that he realized it was not Starhawk returning. He looked up as a shadow blotted what was left of the light. Against the dusk he saw two of the white-robed shirdar, their hands on their sword hilts, motioning silently for him to come.

"So you are Sun Wolf." The veiled woman's hands moved on the arms of her jointed bronze camp chair. They were strong hands, white, like Incarsyn's, moiréd with a lace of shadow in the shuttered chamber's flickering dusk. "The barbarian mercenary."

"My Lady." He inclined his head and felt the scrutiny of those remarkable dark eyes. "And you are the Lady Illyra, chief of the people of the Dunes."

Her mouth was hidden beneath the indigo veils which shrouded the faces of all deep-desert women, but the heavy lids of those dark eyes lowered. At their corners he saw the brief crinkle of appreciation at what he knew to be considerably more than an idle compliment. But she said, "It is not the way of our people that a woman should rule. It is my brother who is Lord of the Dunes." Her voice was low and harsh, and in it was the authority of one who had never asked any man's leave. By the dry, leathery folds of skin around her eyes, Sun Wolf guessed her age at close to his own—forty. Since her teens, according to rumor, she had ruled for her baby brother Incarsyn, commanding the armies of Hasdrozaboth without ever removing her modest veils. The thin, dark fabric puckered with her breath as she went on, "The women ruled Wenshar, and there was nothing but grief for the shirdar, for all the years of their ruling and for all the years after. I speak merely as ambassador for my brother, who has heavier tasks at hand."

Sun Wolf considered her for a moment—the tall, rangy body, muffled in robes and veils of black and indigo, the nose that crested out beneath the gauze of the veil, and the brilliant eyes, cold as a rattlesnake's, on his. He wondered whether she were beautiful or ugly beneath those layers of gauze and knew that it did not matter, neither to her nor to anyone else. He said, "Matters like courting a woman of Wenshar?"

"He will not marry her."

"He said that he would, knowing what she is."

There was scorn in the deep voice. "He does not know what she is. He thinks magic is what the women do with feathers and herbs, to make this man or that love them or to make barren the other concubines of their husbands. He thinks it is an amusement, like dancing or zhendigo, the arts of touch, and practiced for the same reasons—to please men." The movement of her body breathed a musky perfume which mingled with the pungence of the incense-scattered charcoal in the braziers behind her and the sting of dust stirring from the shutters of the windows. "So think all men, when first they say, 'I will take to me a woman who knows magic.' For this is all the magic that they will allow women in the desert. I know," she went on softly. "I have ordered the death of more than one witch among my people."

She took a bell from the table at her side and rang it, a tiny, piercing sound in the gloom. Sun Wolf, relaxed but battle-ready and still not certain where this interview would lead, moved a hand casually to his sword hilt as a slave came in, a good-looking young fellow with the beardless chin and soft fleshiness of a eunuch. Kneeling, the slave laid a cushion of red, embroidered wool by Sun Wolf's feet. As he settled upon it, sitting on his knees after the fashion of the desert, Sun Wolf automatically checked all possible entrances to the room. Most of them had been curtained against drafts, which lifted the hangings uneasily, like the dark shrouds of passing ghosts. He was particularly aware of the one directly behind his back.

"Why?" he asked her curiously. "You know what it is to be a woman and to fight for power."

"For that same reason," she replied. "I know what I did to win the power I hold. Our ways are not the ways of the north countries, Lord Captain. The desert is harsh. It does not forgive even well-meant errors. Our ways have lasted for a hundred generations of men. They work. When one crosses a desert, one does not leave the straight path from water hole to water hole, even though people cry, 'There is water over that dune there.' " A gust of wind bellied a curtain in the shadows beside her and stirred at the gauze veils covering her face and hair. "To change the old ways is to risk becoming lost. So the Witches of Wenshar proved."

"Tell me," Sun Wolf said, "about the Witches of Wenshar."

"The rumors that brought me here to halt this match of my brother's," she said, "noise that you are a witch yourself. Is this true?" The word she used, with its dialectical inflection, lacking in the less formal speech of Wenshar, tugged at something in his thoughts.

He nodded slowly, unwilling to use that word, that inflection, for himself. "It is."

"Good." The lines around her eyes flexed again, though he had the feeling that, beneath her veil, the smile on her lips would not be a pleasant one. "Very good. Listen to me, Captain Barbarian. My brother is anxious to make this match with the daughter of the King of Wenshar, because we are a small people among the Lords of the Desert. We have never been great among the tribes, and some of our neighbors are very powerful. Particularly, we, like all the tribes, are threatened by the great lords of the north, the Middle Kingdoms beyond the mountains. They have told me that the Wizard King who held all the world in subjugation is now dead, and I have lived in the desert long enough to know that, when the great lion dies, there is much fighting among the jackals for his flesh. My people have need these days for strength."

Sun Wolf remembered all the petty wars which throughout the spring and summer had wracked what was left of the Wizard King's empire. "This is so."

The hands, long and strong with their hooked nails, folded around the chair arms. The Wolf found himself wondering whether this woman had ever been married, as all women of the shirdar by custom must be, and if so, what had become of the poor bastard.

"Yet I say that my brother will not marry a witch, even though she is the daughter—and will be the sister—of the King of Wenshar, and that King, her brother, a sickly boy of no great strength. It I let the marriage go forward and permitted her to live afterwards, she would grow in strength, not having learned, as all our women do, to speak softly and in fear of men. In time she would challenge my powers, and those others who object to me would gather around her. Whether I was right or I was wrong, there would be dissensions in our people, and for those dissensions many, perhaps all, would die. If she married and died soon after, that would be worse, for her father, her brother, or her uncle, who casts his eyes on the power in Wenshar, would take it as a reason to ride against us, and again many would die."

"And if she married and did not die in spite of your best efforts," added Sun Wolf, "the situation would be worse still."

The slow smile once again shivered the corners of her eyes and crept like poisoned syrup into her voice. "I see we understand one another."

"I understand you, woman," said the Wolf. "But I still don't understand what you want of me."

"No?" The level, dark brow tilted at one end, vanishing under the low band of dark silk. "Without this girl, my people still need some power, some weapon against those who threaten us. Indeed, as a witch, if she weds one of these sons of slaves who make up what passes for nobility here, we shall need it still more. And like my brother, I would not be averse to having a mage among our people, particularly one renowned in the arts of war."

Sun Wolf's mouth twitched a little beneath his ragged moustache. "Just so long as he's a man."

She nodded equably. "Just so. You would be no challenge to me, Captain. They say, even in the deep desert, that you are a man who is loyal to those who pay him and not a whore to take pay from this man and that, not caring. You are a fighter and a wizard, not a ruler of men —for if you were a ruler of men, you would have found men to rule ere this."

Sun Wolf was silent for a time. He could feel the storm very close now, like the edge of a knife against his skin. Dimly, he heard men calling to one another outside and the snorting and stamping of the prized white horses of Hasdrozaboth, against the rising groan of the wind. After some moments he said, "I do not know what I am, Lady. When I hired myself to others to do their fighting for them, I knew what I was selling. I don't know that anymore. I can't say, 'I'll do this' or 'I'll do that,' because magic . . ." He paused, knowing that whatever he could say about magic, she would not understand, because he did not understand it himself. He shook his head. "Tell me about the Witches of Wenshar. What is it that walks in the ruins of Wenshar?"

Illyra rose from her chair and paced around behind it, her big hands resting on the small, flat circle of its back. Behind her the embroidered red-and-blue hangings over the windows had begun to belly and ripple with a continuous movement, as if evil things scurried invisibly behind them. Sun Wolf felt the electricity in the air crackle along the hair of his arms and begin to pound in his temples. Illyra considered him for a moment with wise, dark, cruel eyes.

"You have been there, then?"

"Yes."

"And what did you see?"

"Demons," Sun Wolf said. Resting easily on his folded-up knees on the red wool cushion, he looked up at the veiled woman before him. "The demons that rise out of the earth."

"That was all?" she asked, and he nodded.

The woman sighed and paced a few feet from him, then turned back. "In the desert," she said, "all the men revere and fear the djinns of the sand and the sky, the spirits that dwell in the rocks. But the women of the Ancient Houses have their own cults, each to its House. Each cult guards its own secrets. So with the Women of Wenshar." Her hands rested like a vulture's claws over the chair back, pale against the dark knurling of the grain.

"It was a poisoned cult, they say. They handed its secrets down generation after generation. They chose whom they wished to marry to their sons and brothers, to bring into the cult, and took what men they would to couple with, as men take concubines. It is said that they called up demons out of the earth and coupled with them as well. They practiced necromancy and called the spirits of the dead. Any who opposed the Witches were torn to pieces, as they say were the Bishop, the King's friend Milkom who hated the shirdar, this priest who was the White Witch's lover, and the old washerwoman who slandered her. They say also that any woman who betrayed the cult met a similar fate. Certainly it fell upon any man whom they hated."

"And did this magic corrupt any who touched it?" asked the Wolf.

Illyra studied him curiously, heavy lids masking her eyes, as if asking what lay behind the question. A gust of wind took her enormous veil, swirling it so that its end nearly brushed Sun Wolf's face where he knelt before her chair, and made the flames of the brazier twist like snakes seeking to escape the incense-strewn coals. When they subsided, the room seemed darker than before.

"So they say." Her voice was hard and bitter. "Any girl who, seeing the rites of power, refused to embrace them, perished—but it is said that such was the skill of the Women of Wenshar in choosing and guiding their initiates that few refused.

"Thus they ruled all of Wenshar and much of the desert round about through fear. And thus it was that, when the Lords of the Middle Kingdoms rode down over the passes to destroy Wenshar and slaughtered these women with fire and sword and magic of their own, none of the Desert Lords would help the Witches, for all had suffered by their arrogance, greed, and senseless destruction."

She began to pace again like her brother, moving with a leashed, animal grace. "The fools. They let their enemies pour out the wine that they themselves had to drink. The northern lords held the passes of Wenshar, and from there it was a simple matter for them to conquer the desert as well." The anger in her voice was as harsh as if the women who had wronged her had done so personally and were still alive, not generations dead and turned to ash. "And so the Witches brought ill upon us all. And even when the northern lords were destroyed, it was not the same as it had been before. Their power was taken by the sons of slaves, the scum of the mines, who know nothing of this land and care less—dispossessing us, the shirdar, from our rightful rule. They only want its silver, like a man who buys a horse, thinking only to eat it and not of the grace of its legs, the softness of its muzzle, or the speed of its shadow over the land. They are pigs, their noses flat from pressing them to piles of gold . . ." She turned back to him, somber eyes dark with ancient rage. "And they hire what armies they will, to destroy what is good and beautiful and turn it only into money, which is all they understand. There is not a shirdar lord who does not feel this at heart—for they destroyed not only our power, but the order of things as they should be."

As if suddenly aware of how far her anger had brought her, she halted in her pacing and looked down at him again, cold and withdrawn once more. "So I tell you this," she finished quietly. "My brother will never marry the seed of that doubled evil, the offspring of witches and slaves. Not for all the alliances in the desert, nor all the silver which they can grub from the ground."

Her eyes narrowed, returning to him. "And you, Sun Wolf," she said. "If you do not serve me, whom then will you serve?"

He shook his head and said, "Lady, I do not know."

CHAPTER

 12

W *ITH THE FINAL SINKING OF THE SUN, THE WIND HAD RISEN TO* nearly gale velocities; Sun Wolf had to fight his way along the rope stretched across the court of the shirdar, his hands and face torn by sand and flying pebbles like stinging insects. Even in the shelter of the small courts and pillared colonnades on the west side of the Hall, visibility wasn't much better, the thick haze of hot, gray dust adding to the blackness of the night. Ghostly flashes of dry lightning illuminated the murk, but gave no clear light.

In the Hall, most of the Household was still at supper or lingering over its remains. The moment he entered the big, shadowy chamber, Sun Wolf felt the tension, the smell of barely masked fear—the sense of being in a plague city, where no man knew which neighbor's chance touch might end his life. Torchlight, blurred by the dust in the air, skittered over the faces of guards and servants, retainers, gentlemen, and ladies-in-waiting who, in ordinary circumstances, would long have retired to their rooms. To this and to the keyed-up tension of the storm was added also the baking dryness of the air. Men were drinking more heavily than usual, and their voices grated against the uneasy hush in the Hall.

In spite of the unusually large number of people in the Hall, the gap around Kaletha's table was noticeable. The White Witch sat, staring ahead numbly, a plate of untouched eggs and greens before her. Anshebbeth, at her side, was talking gently to her, trying to draw her out of herself with a patience the Wolf would scarcely have expected from the twitchy old maid. With a mercenary's usual practicality, Starhawk was downing her dinner, but Sun Wolf didn't deceive himself into believing her oblivious to those covert glances and fearful whispers all around.

Kaletha looked bad—drained and shaken and ill. *She might have killed her lover to preserve her pride and her power,* the Wolf thought unwillingly, *but she had loved him.* Some of the Hawk's words came back to him, and he wondered what it would do to him, to lie, against his better judgment, with someone, not out of caring, but solely in order to keep his power over them—to make, in essence, a whore of himself for power. Would he then kill the person who had done that to him?

Could she? Starhawk had asked.

He now knew what he had formerly only suspected, that indeed she could. And, moreover, if the magic of the Witches somehow corrupted those who used it, she very likely would.

As Egaldus had done when the Bishop had sat at the High Table, Sun Wolf cloaked himself in shadow and illusion to cross the Hall. As he did so, he wondered obliquely whether Kaletha would have killed Galdron to protect Egaldus, if she were already jealous of Egaldus . . . or if, when dealing with love, any logic mattered.

Starhawk looked up at him in surprise when he sat beside her. Since Kaletha and Anshebbeth were far too wrapped up in one another to do so, she spooned him up stew from the common dish and poured him some ale, which he drank thirstily. At the High Table, Osgard took no notice.

This was hardly surprising, since the big man had obviously been drinking all afternoon and showed no signs of letting up now. His harsh, blustering voice boomed out over the frightened murmur of muted conversation around him: ". . . white-livered little coward. He lied about you, Nanciormis. D'you know what he said? What the hell's gonna come to this country with a lying little coward for a King?"

Nanciormis, fastidious and elegant in his pearled black doublet and lace ruff, turned his head slightly to regard his brother-in-law with veiled disgust and contempt. Beside the sprawling, wine-soaked giant, Jeryn sat in crushed silence, his unwashed hair and untidy clothes a sorry sight. The Wolf remembered Illyra's scorn for the sons of slaves and wondered suddenly whether Nanciormis, last scion of the Ancient House of Wenshar, felt it, too. Tazey, on her brother's right, put down her small fan of ornamental feathers to reach across and touch the boy's arm, as if to tell him he wasn't alone.

In the unvoiced whisper scouts use on night missions, Starhawk murmured, "What did you find?"

The Wolf shook his head. "I didn't go. Had an assignation with a lady instead."

"I hope she bit you. You want some bread?" She broke a loaf and handed him half. It tasted faintly of dust—there was a skin of dust over the head on the ale, which gritted in the Wolf's moustache.

"If she had, I'd be the rest of the night cauterizing the wound. Anything happen that I should know about?"

"Two fights between guards and Incarsyn's shirdar, one between a laundress and a scullery maid, and rumors of a strike down at the Vulture Mine in Pardle Sho."

"It could just be the storm."

"No. They say the miners are afraid to go down the pithead, for fear of meeting whatever's been doing this killing. Yes, it's stupid— but this business is going to come to blood fast, Chief." She wiped her fingers neatly on a piece of bread and reached for one of the oranges in the yellow pottery bowl on the corner of the table. On her other side, Anshebbeth's gentle, comforting voice ran on. Against the shadows, Kaletha's ravaged profile was motionless, white as carved bone.

Quietly, the Wolf said, "It's just a question of whether the right person's gets shed." In a soft voice, he told the Hawk of his interview with the Lady Illyra. "Incarsyn may talk as if women are nothing in the shirdar—and maybe they aren't, in the things the men lay claim to, like riding and dancing and worshiping the wind—but it's damn certain *some* of them can hold power."

"Maybe," Starhawk said quietly. "If you've been raised to know how to finesse for it and if that kind of power is what you want."

A gust of wind from outside made the torch flame swirl and leap and the massive shutters rattle as if in shock. There was a commotion around the outer doors of the Hall; in the dark arches from the vestibule, Incarsyn stood framed, dust streaming in gray threads as he unwrapped his veils. His white-cloaked warriors were like a silent company of sand djinns behind.

"My Lord." Osgard heaved himself to his feet and gestured with his cup to the empty place on Nanciormis' left. "We feared we'd not see you." His bass voice drawled with wine.

Lithe as a puma, the shirdar lord made his way among the benches. Anshebbeth started unwillingly to rise from her place beside Kaletha to be with Tazey as propriety demanded. But Incarsyn stopped short at the foot of the dais and inclined his head, his braids swinging forward like gold-bound velvet ropes.

"My Lord," he said. "It grieves me much to say so, but my esteemed sister has brought me messages of great urgency from my people. It is necessary that, as soon as the storm subsides, I and my men make immediate preparations to return to them as quickly as may be. Please forgive us this unpardonable breach of civility and rest assured that the memory of your hospitality will remain with us, as the memory of campfire light upon a night of cold."

In the long moment of silence, the King's red face flushed still deeper crimson. There was no one in the room unaware of what the young Prince had really said. Osgard's voice thickened with an intoxicated rage that knew no diplomacy. "And my daughter?"

The movement of Tazey's feather fan froze, her brows stood out black on a face suddenly ashen.

Without a word between them, Sun Wolf and Starhawk slid to their feet and began to make their unobtrusive way to the dais.

Once more Incarsyn bowed, but he did not meet Tazey's eyes. His voice was unwilling but still smooth. "I fear that the messages that my sister has brought have made it impossible for me to wed your beautiful daughter, my Lord."

Osgard surged to his feet. "You mean you won't have her—is that what you're saying?" he bellowed. "*My* daughter, the Princess of Wenshar . . ."

"Father . . ." Tazey began pleadingly, and Nanciormis, alarmed, started to get up.

Face purple with rage, Osgard hurled his chair aside. "You lousepicking, pox-rotted, djinn-worshiping horse kisser! My daughter . . ." He lunged for the young man, hands outstretched to kill. Nanciormis, taken entirely by surprise, leaped after him and caught him from one side, as Incarsyn stepped back, his hand going to his dagger hilt. Sun Wolf and Starhawk got the King's other arm just as Nanciormis buckled from a booted kick to his thigh that nearly broke the bone. As he stumbled back, Sun Wolf grimly held onto the heaving, swearing drunkard, reflecting that all the commander's fighting had obviously been done, sword in hand, on battlefields. He himself had gone through more tavern brawls than he could count and had dealt with enough drunks to constitute a more formidable army than many small cities could have mustered. He and Starhawk dragged the clawing, cursing King backward over the ruins of the chair toward the door of the solar, which Jeryn, the only person at the table who seemed to have retained his wits, dashed ahead of them to open.

The minute they were out of sight in the darkened solar, Sun Wolf pulled a hand free and slugged Osgard a hard blow to the jaw to knock him out. It took him three tries and left both him and Starhawk covered with bruises, spilled wine, and fingernail scratches, before they shoveled the King's inert body onto the divan.

"Mother!" Starhawk swore, as Sun Wolf flexed his bruised hand. "I've seen you coldcock a *horse* for a bet, Chief . . ."

"It was a sober horse," the Wolf growled. Still shaking his knuckles, he turned disgustedly to the door. When they emerged from the solar, the dais seemed to be jammed with people: servants all talking excitedly and guards looking at one another, wondering whether they should arrest Sun Wolf for lèse majesté. Nanciormis was standing with Incarsyn, who had not moved from his place before the High Table; his beautiful voice, too low for them to catch the exact words, was smooth and rapid, every beautifully wrought gesture speaking of conciliation and apology for a father's very real, though regrettable, anger for what he felt, however wrongly, to be a slight upon his daughter . . .

"And he was picked as King by his predecessor?" Starhawk wondered quietly, glancing back at the sodden, snoring form in the chamber behind them. "It's a wonder they haven't been at war continually for years."

Sun Wolf shook his head. "Drinking like that grows on them, Hawk," he said softly. "He probably hasn't been like this for more than a year or so. I'd bet a week's pay it takes less now to set him off than it did, and he'd tell you himself he's had more reason these days . . ." Still rubbing his aching hand, he glanced down to see Jeryn at his side within the solar door. "You always that quick, Scout, or you been in tavern brawls before?"

Jeryn gave a cracked laugh and looked away so Sun Wolf wouldn't see him sneak a hand up to wipe his eyes; the Wolf dropped a casual hand to the boy's quilted velvet shoulder. At the foot of the dais, Nanciormis seemed to be making headway. Sun Wolf caught the shirdane word for storm. Around the clustered backs of shirdar and green-clothed Fortress guards, Incarsyn could be seen to be nodding, unwilling but mollified. In the strange dust haze of the lamplight, Anshebbeth was at Tazey's side, holding the girl's hand, furiously protective and nearly in tears herself. Tazey, fan trembling in her shaking fingers, looked gray around the mouth, as if she were about to be sick.

Again he caught the word for storms in the babble of the shirdane and the phrase, *the season of witches*. Glancing down at the boy beside him he asked softly, "How's your etymology, Scout?"

Jeryn looked up at him, surprised.

"Can you tell me the difference between a wizard and a witch?"

"Sure," Starhawk remarked. "A wizard is what they call you when they want to hire you, and a witch is what they call you when they're getting ready to run you out of town."

Nanciormis and Incarsyn made deep mutual bows. The Lord of the Dunes turned away. Her face set and white, Tazey rose from her place, handing her fan to the startled Anshebbeth and slipping through the crowd toward the two Desert Lords. In the grimy orange torchlight she looked older, haggard, and shaken; when she stopped before Incarsyn, Sun Wolf could see by the tremor of her girlish gown how badly her legs were shaking.

She began, "My Lord Incarsyn . . ."

The Lord of the Dunes turned away from her without meeting her eyes. With his retainers behind him, he strode the length of the smoky, silent room and out the door. The wind swirled in their white cloaks, tearing at the torch flames. Then they were gone.

Only then did the noise rise again, the muted voices like the *brush* of the sea.

Nanciormis walked over to his niece and put a comforting arm around her shoulders. She jerked away from him, the color that had flooded her cheeks an instant earlier bleaching away again, her eyes filmed with blinding tears. After a moment's stillness, she, too, walked from the room.

"Having met the Lady Illyra," the Wolf remarked softly in the brown gloom of the shadowed dais. "I think Tazey's well out of it."

Starhawk rubbed the bridge of her nose, as if seeking to crush out the dry ache within her skull. "She was always well out of it," she replied. "She never wanted it."

Beside them, a sharp, tiny noise and a gasp of pain made them turn. Anshebbeth stood staring down at her bleeding palm, where the furious clench of her hand had broken the delicate ivory sticks of Tazey's fan. With a muffled sob of embarrassment, the governess fled the room, leaving the broken fan lying on the floor, its feathers dabbed in blood like a slaughtered bird.

"You've got to admit," Sun Wolf said later, "that Incarsyn did the most tactful thing he could. The business about 'messages from my people' was all my granny's second-best mail shirt, but as a reason for leaving, it would pass. If Osgard hadn't been damn drunken fool enough to push it, people would have gotten used to the idea in six or ten months that he wasn't coming back to wed Tazey, without ever having to insult Tazey by saying it out loud." He picked up his cards. "Isn't there anything in that deck below a nine?"

"Stop complaining; you dealt this hand."

"Bloody Kaletha's taught you how to hex decks."

"Yeah. And if you'd hung around with her long enough, you'd have learned it, too. How's that for a crib?"

"Damn Mother worshipper."

"At least I don't worship sticks and old bottles, like some barbarian ex-commanders of mercenaries I could name but won't, because they're present. Fifteen two, fifteen four, and a pair is six plus those are all the same suit . . ."

"I see 'em."

". . . and two for thirty-one . . ." She moved the peg neatly around the cribbage board in the flickering ochre firelight.

Sun Wolf grumbled again, "Damn Mother worshipper."

It was growing late, but few people had left the Hall. The storm still howled around the walls; the hot air was thick with dust and electricity and heavy with the unventilated stinks of torch smoke, cooking, and stale sweat. Underservants had taken up the trestle tables, but at least half of those who had eaten supper were still there. Now and then their voices would rise, sharp and angry, as the crackling air shortened tempers and made speech careless. Then silence would fall again as they all realized once more their unwillingness to leave, and the wind would moan among the rafters like the grieving damned.

It would be a long way, Sun Wolf reflected, down those dark corridors to rooms where they'd lie alone, listening to that wind and wondering whether Nexué and Egaldus had seen anything of their killer before they died. Even the lower servants and guards, whose dormitories opened off the main Hall, clustered still around the hazy pools of muddy torchlight, perfectly prepared to wait out the storm. Contrary to custom, the doors of both the Men's Hall and the Women's stood open. Upper servants—the chief cook, the dancing master, musicians, and clerks—who had their own chambers, nodded sleepily over games of cards and backgammon; the chief scribe was curled up, unabashedly asleep in a gloomy corner.

Sun Wolf stared moodily out past his unsatisfactory collection of fives, sixes, and unmatched royalty, wondering if it was the same in those halls on the fringes of the empty quarter which had been given over to Incarsyn and his retinue. He'd sized them up when he'd been taken through to Illyra's quarters and knew them as hardened warriors who feared neither man nor the desert's cruelty.

But this was different, this death which could be neither fought nor fled. The demons of Wenshar returned to his mind, the moony, phosphorescent forms that had flicked in the corner of his vision in the silence of the empty quarter, and the way those cold, glowing shapes had clustered during the storm, thick as bees at swarming time, beneath the windows of the temple in Wenshar.

He wondered where Kaletha was and exactly when in the confusion she had slipped from the Hall.

Starhawk was looking inquiringly at him over her flat-folded hand of cards, the slight crease of pain more marked on her forehead. He laid his own cards down quietly. "I'm going out to have a look around. The storm's fading," he added, as she started to protest. "The heart of it's off south, anyway."

"Be careful." She said it casually, but in her eyes he saw she didn't mean the storm.

He shook his head. "I feel—I don't know. I don't sense any danger —not like last night. In any case, it's not midnight yet, or anywhere near. The other attacks were all between midnight and dawn. I won't be long."

"I seem to remember hunting you for two or three months after the last time you said that," Starhawk remarked, collecting the cards and shuffling them competently. "But have it your own way." She was laying out a hand of solitaire as, cloaked in shadow and illusion, he drifted for the vestibule.

The wind nearly jerked the great outer door from his hands as he opened it a crack to slip through. Outside, the bulk of the Hold and the courts and walkways around it offered him some protection; but even so, the force of the gale made him stagger. Like a man fighting to wade through a riptide, he thrashed his way to the pillars of the colonnade and, wrapping his arms around the nearest one, held his body tight against it. Sand-laden wind clawed his long hair back from his face and ripped at his skin with talons of gravel. The hot dust clogged his nostrils and the electricity in the air throbbed in his brain.

He could sense the moon riding high over the roiling wall of dust and chaos. With his eye squeezed shut against the savagery of the storm, he let his soul dip toward the silence of meditation, listening— seeking the Invisible Circle in which he would be free to walk everywhere in the tempest-torn citadel.

Slowly he became aware of the various currents of the searing wind streaming like water around the towers, of the weight of stone and tile on the balanced stars and chevrons of the roof beams, of nightlamp shadows beneath them, and of the open eyes of two royal children staring awake at the raving darkness. He felt the lightning flare and die between the Binnig Rock and Mount Morian and off the Cathedral's dry, glittering spikes. He sensed how the hurricane savagery ripped and swirled around the walls in the empty quarter. Sand was scouring the broken tiles of the floor, the dust was burying the smells of decaying blood there, the snakes in their holes were dreaming of ophidian hates, and the doves in their crannies were dreaming of nameless, walking fear . . .

Above the wind, he heard a scream.

The sound wrenched him from his contemplation. Even as it did so, his sense of it was lost, swallowed up in the demented fury of the winds. His warrior's instinct told him to rush back at once to the Hall for help—the wizard in him forced him back into the silence of his meditation, casting through the wind-scoured halls for the direction of the sound.

Another scream and another, above him and to his right. The balcony of the Household.

He swung around and ran for the Hall door.

As he fought it open, he heard the scream as men would hear it, surging in terror over the howling of the fading storm, directionless, from nowhere, terrifying in its uncertainty. Rising like an echo behind it, he thought he heard a second scream of horror and despair; but with the wind hammering in his ears as he heaved the door to, he could not tell. By the time he crossed the vestibule, Starhawk, sword in hand and a dozen scared servants at her back, was halfway up the interior stairs.

The little hall that ran behind the upper rooms of the Household was a vortex of winds. He flung a glowing ball of blue light before him, and it showed him all the doors tight shut. He was aware of others clambering up the narrow flight behind him: Osgard, in night clothes stinking of stale wine and vomit; two guards, ashen-faced with fear; the chief cook with a cleaver; and Incarsyn, naked under a silken bedgown, sword in hand. A door jerked open near him, and Anshebbeth ran out, fully dressed, her black eyes wide with horror, clutching the black billows of her skirts. She gasped, "On the balcony! I heard . . ."

Sun Wolf leaned into the wind as he plunged through her room and out through the open shutters to the darkness and storm.

Up on the long balcony, the violence of the storm was terrific. Had it not been for the crenelations of the wall, the Wolf would have been swept from his feet; but feeling himself skid under the sweep of the powerful blast that scoured the south wall, he dropped to his knees and grabbed for the stone of the wall. After a moment, he put forth his strength against it, turning the main force of the blast enough to struggle to his feet. The dust in the air threw back most of the witchlight, but he could make out which of the archway shutters had been forced open from within. The great inner curtain flapped like a torn sail in the slip stream. Staggering to the parapet, he looked down.

The dark, irregular lump of a body could just be made out, huddled at the foot of the wall. Eddies of the storm, broken by the courtyard walls, rippled at the dark sprawl of bloodied robes and stirred the black, half-unraveled braids of the jeweled hair.

"Did you see it clearly?" Osgard handed Nanciormis a cup of wine.

The commander hesitated for a long moment, dark eyes traveling from Osgard's face to Sun Wolf's. Then he shook his head and gasped as Kaletha rinsed down the abraded wound in his arm with a scouring concoction of wine and marigolds. "But believe me, I didn't stay for a close look."

Sun Wolf folded his arms and leaned his back against the tiled mantel of the solar. The last, spent whispers of the storm were dying down. In the silence, Anshebbeth's sobbing was jarringly loud. When they had carried the unconscious Nanciormis inside, she had collapsed into hysterical screams. Kaletha, appearing out of nowhere, her carnelian hair streaming disheveled down her back, had struck her disciple across the face and cursed her, from jealousy or impatience or merely the burn of the storm along her overstretched nerves. Ignored and hurt, the governess now whimpered wretchedly in a corner.

While Kaletha was ascertaining that Nanciormis was in fact still alive—due to his falling first to the roof of a small colonnade and only from there to the ground in the shelter of the wall—Sun Wolf and Starhawk had run lightly back up the inner stairs and along the narrow corridor to Nanciormis' room. Not surprisingly, they had found nothing there. A chair had been overset, and the jointed bronze table thrust violently aside. An open book sprawled on the floor. Sun Wolf picked it up; it was a treatise on falconry. Against the stone wall, a burned patch and a ring of amber shards showed where the lamp had been hurled, the flame killed almost at once by the dust-laden violence of the wind. Dust and debris were everywhere, from when the shutters had been opened. Sun Wolf had closed and locked the door behind him, and only Starhawk's presence at his side had prevented him from glancing repeatedly back over his shoulder at the darkness until they were in the torchlight of the solar once again.

"I don't know what made me look up," Nanciormis was saying quietly. "I couldn't sleep, though, on the whole, storms don't bother me. But there was something—some sense of evil in that room . . ."

He glanced quickly up at Sun Wolf again and then at Kaletha, silently tidying up her poultices and dressings. A frown creased his brow.

"What is it?" the Wolf asked, and Nanciormis looked quickly away.

"Nothing," he lied. Even having his heels sniffed by death didn't seem to have shaken his sangfroid. He looked pallid and bruised from his plunge over the parapet; but in the frame of his half-unraveled braids and dusty, open shirt collar, his fleshy face had already regained its usual sardonic lines.

Incarsyn, standing beside Osgard, his unbraided hair hanging like a woman's to his waist and their earlier quarrel passed over now in this crisis, asked softly, "Did it speak?"

The commander looked up at him, his dark eyes half puzzled, as if searching for the right words for a memory of terror and chaos. "I—I don't exactly know. I think . . ." He passed a hand over his mouth. "It—when it moved toward me I realized—I knew I was in danger but it was like a nightmare. But when it moved I flung the lamp at it . . ." He hesitated, glanced at Sun Wolf again, then away. Having seen Nanciormis' slowness to react to Osgard's drunken attack on Incarsyn, Sun Wolf was a little surprised that the commander had gotten away at all and mentally noted that whatever it was—spell, demon, djinn— evidently it did give sufficient warning to escape, if there was anywhere to escape to.

Anshebbeth, rocking back and forth, covered her eyes with her hands and whispered, "Oh, dear Mother . . ."

"Anshebbeth, *shut up!*" Kaletha's voice cracked. Sun Wolf observed with interest that, although Nanciormis had quickly recovered, Kaletha's hands were shaking uncontrollably. She dropped the scissors and picked them up again, her eyes downcast.

"How did you know what to do?" Osgard poured himself another cup of wine, but it was only an automatic gesture; his face was pale with shock, and he looked cold sober and ill.

"The last scion of the Ancient House of Wenshar," Incarsyn said softly, "would know."

Kaletha glanced sharply at Nanciormis, who only shook his head. "I —I don't know, exactly." He pulled up his white silk shirt once more over the bandage. Under it, the muscle of his body was still discernible, like rock half-buried in soft mud. "But yes, the stories I had heard said that—that men had escaped the Witches by running out into the storms. They were often killed that way, too, of course; it was only chance that I fell on the sheltered side of the wall."

Sun Wolf frowned, sifting this in his mind. He guessed that Nanciormis' account might not be entirely trusted, yet saw no reason for the commander to lie about his escape. He was, as Incarsyn said, the last scion of the Ancient House. The Wolf wondered what the commander was hiding.

Osgard wiped his stubbly face. "You'll sleep the rest of the night here," he said. "It—it doesn't seem to strike when people are together . . ."

"It struck Galdron and Milkom together," the Wolf pointed out, leaning one arm along the tiled mantelpiece. "Though it may only have been meant to kill one. But it's also only happened between midnight and dawn before. Now it's getting earlier. And we have no guarantee it won't have a second try. It's a long way yet till day."

Anshebbeth groaned and covered her face with long, skeletal fingers. Kaletha began "Really . . ." Starhawk, with a glance at her that would have frozen a millpond, went over to rest comforting hands on the governess' shoulders.

"I can't stand this," Anshebbeth whispered brokenly. "I can't stand it . . ."

"Now, Anshebbeth," Nanciormis began, looking embarrassed and uneasy at the prospect of another full-blown bout of hysterics. *And well he might,* Sun Wolf thought sourly. *A man might be bedding a woman in secret and still shrink from openly admitting it, particularly a woman as unprestigious as Anshebbeth.* For her part, desperately as she might need comfort, the governess clearly knew better than to seek it publicly in his arms. "Perhaps you'd better go back to your room and get some sleep."

"No!" 'Shebbeth wailed. "I want to stay here."

"It might be better," Starhawk put in tactfully, "if you stayed with Tazey." She glanced at the King. "We should probably move Jeryn in there for the rest of the night as well. I'll keep guard."

Anshebbeth looked desperately at Kaletha for comfort, but she, too, was looking the other way, hastily gathering her things to depart. As Sun Wolf followed her more slowly out into the Hall, he heard Nanciormis say to the King, "I think I'd better have a word with you, Osgard . . ."

The wind still sobbed in the narrow stair as Sun Wolf ascended. The noise almost masked the slithery swirl of a silk nightdress around the turning above him and the sticky pat of a bare foot on cold stone fleeing into darkness. When he reached Tazey's room, the lamp flames were still shuddering with the wind of a body's hasty passage, but the girl lay on her bed, rigid and pretending sleep, her hands pressed over her face.

Sun Wolf walked the darkness of the empty quarter until dawn. He sensed no evil, no danger there, yet his every instinct of a warrior prickled that there was something amiss. In the shifting sand drifts among the broken walls, he sought for signs of Kaletha's passing, but found none. That meant nothing—the nervous after-eddies of the storm would have eradicated them. Kaletha had looked shaken to the marrow. Because Nanciormis had seen something she preferred to believe did not exist? Because it was becoming clear that the spells of the Witches of Wenshar, so casually tampered with, might contain things beyond her knowledge or control—might even turn her evil against her will? Or merely because someone had survived an attack?

Why Nanciormis? As last scion of the Ancient House of Wenshar, he might know things . . .

Or was there a why? Sun Wolf was uneasily aware that, as a wizard himself, he, too, might know too much, but he had not been attacked.

And the cool, detached portion of his mind retorted, *Yet.*

The cold stars turned against the black sink of the sky. The night circled toward morning. Blazing with lights against the darkness, the Hold towered above him; behind it, black and silent, loomed the bulk of the Binnig Rock. Standing on a platform of crumbled adobe wall, he spread out his arms and sank into meditation once more, tasting, smelling the night. But there was nothing, save the breathing of the serpents and the dreams of the doves.

When he returned in the cool yellow brightness of dawn, it was to find Starhawk, Anshebbeth, and Jeryn all deeply asleep, and Tazey's bed empty.

A note lay rolled on the pillow.

It was superscribed, "Father," but he tore off the pink hair ribbon that bound it. Beside him, Starhawk slumped against the side of the bed, eyes sealed in stuporous sleep—Starhawk, raised to the all-night watches of convent vigils, who had never been known to sleep on guard duty in her life.

The note said:

Father—

I made Starhawk and 'Shebbeth fall asleep, please don't be angry with them.

Incarsyn was right to put me aside. Sun Wolf and Starhawk are right. I am a witch and the Heir to the Witches of Wenshar. It is all my doing—Nexué, and Galdron, and Norbas Milkhom, and Egaldus, and Uncle Nanciormis. I know this now and I swear to you, it won't happen again. Please, please forgive me. And please don't look for me. Don't blame anyone—I'm doing this by my own choice. I don't want to become like the Witches of Wenshar, and I know that's what would have happened to me.

I love you, Daddy; please believe that I love you. I never wanted this. I never wanted to be anything but your daughter and to love you. Please just tell Jeryn that I've gone away, and that I love him very much. I love you and I'm so very sorry.

Good-by,
Tazey

CHAPTER

⤳ 13 ⤳

*U*NDER THE CRUEL BRILLIANCE OF THE LATE AFTERNOON SUN, Wenshar lay like an elephants' graveyard of houses that had somehow crept to the base of the blackened cliffs to die. Wind sneered through the crumbled stone walls, unbroken even by the buzz of a rattlesnake; dust devils chased one another like lunatic ghosts. The few portions of houses still boasting roofs watched the two searchers from windows like the dark eyepits of skulls.

Starhawk's mare started for no apparent reason, throwing up her head, long ears swinging like leaves in a gale; the woman leaned forward and stroked the sweating neck. But she made no sound.

Listen as he would, Sun Wolf could hear nothing—no echo from any of those three twisting canyons or the rock mazes beyond.

But he knew they were there, waiting.

They had been waiting for him since he had left.

Wind thrummed in his ears as he turned his horse's head toward the wide mouth of the central canyon. Starhawk followed without a word; the blue shroud of shadow covered them as they passed the narrow gate of its mouth. In the stifling heat of the canyon, the rocks stank of demons.

Neither spoke. They had ridden together too long to need words; they both knew that whatever happened, she must not lose sight of him.

A short way past the canyon mouth, a narrow trail led up its wall, to a sort of lane above the first levels of the pillared facades fronting it. The last time he'd been here, Sun Wolf had explored it. At points along the main road up the canyon, bones were heaped, where mountain sheep, gazelles, or straying cattle had fallen from above. Near the foot of the trail lay a little pile of horse droppings. A grain-fed horse, Sun Wolf saw, pushing them apart with a twig, not a mustang scavenging on sagebrush. He pulled his head veils closer around his face and began to lead his own mount up the narrow way. Farther up, they found the tracks of shod hooves.

He felt neither surprise nor triumph at having guessed correctly. In a way, it was the only place Tazey could come, even if her only intent was to destroy herself. Though neither her mother, her grandmother, nor her grandmother's grandmother had known the demon-haunted city, she knew herself to be its heir.

"She could be above or below," the Hawk said. Soft as she spoke, her voice echoed hideously from those narrow, gaudy walls.

"There's half a dozen ways down to the bottom of the canyon." Sun Wolf glanced over the edge to the tilted pavement, half-hidden under shoals of pebbles, winding along the parched course of the old stream. "We'll stay up top."

Starhawk nodded. There was no question of splitting up— not in Wenshar.

Afoot and leading their nervous horses, they moved up the trail.

Sun Wolf knew from his earlier explorations that the trail was neither narrow nor intrinsically dangerous. Rose-colored spires and cupolas, cut in openwork like lace, towered above and around them; here and there, stairways arched to pillared doorways under canopies of stone vines. They led their horses to the trail's edge and looked across the canyon to the shadowed folds of rock, the sightless doors, and down to the dead oleanders by the sterile wadi and the white heaps of bones.

"Why?" Starhawk asked softly. "Demons aren't creatures of flesh, are they? They can't eat what they kill, if they kill it."

Sun Wolf shook his head. Glancing back at that calm, immobile face in its white frame of veils, he knew she couldn't be feeling what he felt. She might sense herself watched, but not have that terrible awareness of being known. At the edges of his hearing, he could detect the demons' whispering, like the canyon wind that turned locks of his

horse's mane, the words just too soft to make out. He feared to listen
more closely. His hand tightened on the reins he held; under the veils,
clammy sweat crawled down his face.

"I don't know what they are, Hawk," he replied. "I know there are
biting-demons, so they can do some physical harm. Everyone knows
demons lead men to their deaths in swamps or in the desert, but . . .
no one's ever said why they do it."

The shriek came at the same instant that his dappled gelding flung
up its head in panic. The leather of the rein cinched around his hand,
and he caught at the cheek piece of the bridle. From up-trail the echo
of hooves splintered the close, shadowy air. Fighting to keep his own
panicking horse from bolting, he could not turn to see, so the little
sorrel mare was upon them before either he or Starhawk could get out
of the way.

He saw the mare from the tail of his eye, bearing down on them
with flaxen mane streaming and blood pouring from her flanks. It all
happened in instants—he barely slid out of the main impact as she
crashed into his gelding, white eyes rolling in mad terror, flecks of
foam from her muzzle stinging his face, tangling him between the two
heaving bodies in a desperate thrash of hacking hooves. With his
hands full of bridle and ears and his mouth choked with dusty mane,
for a moment he could do nothing but hold onto his own horse's head.
Starhawk, who could be capable of great brutality when in peril, had
twisted and levered against her horse's bridle and threw the frenzied
animal to its knees against the jagged canyon wall to their right. Half-
crushed and lifted off his feet, the Wolf could glimpse her through a
frenzy of veils and dust. The mare was on his blind side; so was the
cliff edge to the rocks below. The bridle-leather cut his hands, and he
braced his feet. A second later he heard a skittering crash, rocks falling, the mare's frantic scream, then a crash, somewhere down the
canyon below him, and another.

Then nothing.

He released his grip under the gelding's chin, and the beast threw
up its head with a wild snort, but made no further moves to fight or
run. It stood trembling as he pushed his veils back. He was still on the
trail itself, not even near the raised brink. Starhawk came hurrying up
to him, still leading her stumbling horse. Had she let go to help him,
he knew they'd certainly have lost her mount and probably the mare
as well. In spite of the part of him that felt piqued that she hadn't come

to his aid, he realized grimly that Starhawk was never one to lose her grasp on essentials.

"You all right?" she asked.

He looked down at himself, covered with dust and filth and, he now saw, daubed with great, uneven splotches of the mare's blood, all mixed with sweat. He wiped his face. "Haven't felt so good since the last time I got mauled by bears."

"Glad to hear it." She led the way to the edge of the cliff.

The mare lay dead on the rocks below. Something like heat shimmer seemed to dance over her twisted body; but even at this time of the afternoon, the canyon's shadows were deep. She lay on her back; a thin sprawl of white veils fluttered out from beneath.

In spite of the fact that he knew that by no stretch of the imagination could Tazey's body be covered by that of the dead horse—even had she not, as any rider would have, fallen clear in the fifty-foot drop onto the rocks—he felt a shudder deep within him. He glanced quickly across at Starhawk.

She shook her head. "The saddle was empty."

He looked back down at the mare. Blood ran down her flanks, lathered by the dust and sweat until her body was almost coated with it. The smell of it rose to them, on the dust-choke and the incongruous dry sweetness of the sage. Then he raised his head and saw Tazey, standing about twenty feet away.

She stood just where the trail turned around a rocky bulge in the amber stone of the canyon wall. Her hands were pressed to her mouth, her honey-colored hair was hanging in unveiled tangles over her faded pink shirt, and her boy's breeches and boots were dusty and scratched. As he saw her, she turned to run.

"Tazey!"

She stopped, her face a blurred white oval in the blue shadow of the rocks. Her voice shook. "Please go away."

Sun Wolf straightened up and handed his gelding's rein to Starhawk. "Don't be stupid."

"I can't . . ." She swallowed hard. Her eyes, in the dust and the circles of sleepless shadows that ringed them, were almost transparent. "I don't want to hurt you."

"I doubt you could, Tazey." He walked toward her, slowly so as not to frighten her, but she did not flee him. The brooding silence of the city pressed on his consciousness, like the dead watching open-eyed from their graves. With it, he sensed the queer, terrible prickling of another warning that he had been aware of since noon. "There's another storm coming late tonight, you know that . . ."

"I know," she said softly. "I thought . . ." Her voice cracked. "It started with the storm. I should never have tried to stop it."

"Since you saved the Hawk's life as well as your own, I'm glad you did." He reached her side. He could feel her whole body tremble as his hand touched her shoulders. She was so different, so changed from the beautiful girl who had done the war dance, that his heart ached for her. "Why would you hurt me, Taswind?"

She shook her head wretchedly. Tears tracked slowly down through the dust on her face. "I don't know!" She wiped at them and pushed back the tangles of her hair to look up into his face. "I don't want to, not—not consciously. The Witches of Wenshar . . ."

"Have you seen Kaletha's books, then?" Starhawk inquired matter-of-factly, coming up with the two horses on lead.

That stopped the girl. Puzzlement took the place of desperation in her haunted eyes. She shook her head. "No. I . . ." She swallowed, and the fear and grief rushed back; with them came knowledge that no girl of sixteen should have to endure. "The Witches of Wenshar— Uncle Nanciormis used to tell me about them. He knows about them, as Mother did, a little. He said that in the cult, the coven, of the family . . . They didn't always know it was them, you see. People they hated, people who crossed them, people who got in their way, would die, but they . . . but they didn't know at first that it was they themselves doing it. They didn't know they had the power. Only later, when they accepted it and used it . . . But it would start with dreams . . ."

She drew a deep breath, trying to steady herself, and wiped her face again, smearing the sweat, tears, and dust into brown smudges across her cheeks. Her fingers shook; she clasped them together, locked tight to keep them still. "I was afraid that was what was happening when— when the Bishop . . . and Father's friend just happened to be with him. I had nothing against Egaldus, nothing at all, but there was such power in the air that night, such . . . such violence. You felt it. You know. It could have been anyone. I dreamed horrible things . . ."

Green eyes stared up into his. "I don't want to become like the Witches of Wenshar. I never wanted to. And then Uncle Nancior-mis—"

"If you ask me," Starhawk remarked dryly, "Uncle Nanciormis is the only one who deserved what he almost got."

"Don't say that!" Tazey whispered franticly. "Don't—"

Gently, Sun Wolf said, "I thought you liked Nanciormis."

Her voice strangled to a thread. "I do." She pressed her hands to her mouth. "I did. I don't know. He . . ."

With careful firmness, Sun Wolf put his arm around her shoulders. There were no house fronts at this point on the trail, and, in any case, it would have been unsafe to go into one; but near the vast, jutting nose of eroded rock, a bench had been carved in a niche beneath a garland of stone lilies. He sat down, cradling her against him, until her shaking stopped.

At last she managed to say, "Uncle Nanciormis—came to me after —after Incarsyn—last night." She looked up and shook the hair from her eyes again. "He—he said things to me. He—he—he—" The words choked in her throat.

"About being a witch?" She shook her head violently, *too quickly,* Sun Wolf thought.

"But I—I hated him after that. That same night—just hours later . . ." She shook her head again, her hair hissing dryly against his unshaven face, tears trickling down her filthy cheeks. "It's growing in me, Sun Wolf, and I don't want to be that way! I'm so afraid. Everybody gets angry at people and hates people, sometimes. I do. But since the storm, since I've been a mage . . ." She clutched at him desperately, sobbing into the dusty head veils that lay in a tangle over his shoulders. He stroked the girl's heaving back, rocking her as he would have rocked a child, waiting while her sobs subsided.

At length he asked, "Tazey, tell me this. Were you aware of directing your hate? Or do you just think it's you because you happened to hate some of the people who died?"

She brought her head up from his shoulder, her eyes ravaged. "Uncle Nanciormis . . . You don't have to know. You don't have to do it consciously. You don't even see it in your dreams, not at first, he said. It has to be me. It's only happened since the storm."

"No, it hasn't," Sun Wolf said quietly. "The first morning I was in Tandieras, I found some dead birds in the empty quarter. There was something growing even then, before you'd touched your powers." He looked down into her face and with one dirty thumb wiped the smudged tears from beneath her eyes. "It was little then—it couldn't hurt a human. Later, I think Starhawk felt something, maybe directed at her, or me—maybe just wandering loose in the dark. But now it's grown." He stroked back the tangled curls from her face. "Tell me one thing, Tazey. Did your mother know about the inner cult of the Women of Wenshar?"

For a long time, she sat quiet, her eyes never leaving the brass buckles of his doublet. But his words about the dead birds and the thing Starhawk had felt by the gate that night appeared to have their effect. When she spoke, her voice was very small but calm. "I don't know. Mother died when I was seven. Uncle told me that—that girls in the family weren't initiated into the cult until they'd had their first period. So I don't know."

"Do you think she knew?"

There was another long silence in which the wind boomed softly down the canyons and the horses twitched nervous ears. At last Tazey said, "Mother was—like Father keeps saying—Mother was sweet and good and kind. But . . ." She raised her eyes to his. "I don't know if it's the same way with men as it is with women. But we . . . I know we—women—can be two or three things, I mean really *be* them, sincerely, at the same time. I know what I am deep inside, and it's—it's not how I try to be with people. And the things I think and dream and want at night aren't the things I want in the daytime."

She fell silent. Sun Wolf gathered her to him again and held her like a child, but his mind moved now on other things. The wind bore the burning whisper of dust, the prickle of the far-off storm, and the sweetish back-taste of the dead mare's blood that still blotched his clothes. During the Great Trial, he had seen the depths of his own soul, and the glimpse of what lurked there had been enough to convince him that there was no such thing as an act impossible to conceive.

Curled in his arms, Tazey whispered, "We should be going. We can make it back to Tandieras before the storm comes, if we leave now. I —I don't have a horse . . ."

"You can share with the Hawk," the Wolf said softly. "Whatever is happening, the key to it's here, in Wenshar." He glanced up at Starhawk, who stood silently with her shoulder to the carved sandstone pillar of the niche. "The killing isn't going to stop until we know why it started. I'm staying the night."

* * *

The preparations for return across the desert were made quickly. Starhawk and Tazey's going would be slower with only a single horse between them, and the storm would come, Sun Wolf thought, before midnight.

While Tazey was filling the waterskins at the rock tanks near the canyon's foot, Starhawk walked back up to where the Wolf sat on the eroded stump of a broken balustrade, carved like the tsuroka from the sandstone of the cliff. He glanced up at the sound of her boots on the gravel.

"What is it?" she asked softly, and he shook his head, not even certain in his own mind what it was that he had listened to in the hushed-wind murmurs around the rocks. The air already had the feeling of evening to it, though, above the high canyon rims, the sky blazed like polished steel. Perhaps the sounds had been, in fact, only the wind.

She hunkered down at his side. "Chief," she said in her quiet voice, "I have a bad feeling about all this."

He did not glance down at her, keeping his single eye up-canyon, but he felt the touch of her shoulder against his thigh. "My guess is the heart of the storm's going to be south again, over the desert," he said. "Even if you don't make it back to the Fortress, Tazey should be able to keep you both safe."

"It isn't that. You remember the time we got caught in the seige of Laedden, when the plague broke out in the city? You remember the mob in the square, lynching that dim-witted boy who used to draw chalk pictures on the pavement, because somebody said it was his fault?"

Sun Wolf nodded. He'd ordered his men to stay out of the fray when two of them had wanted to rescue the boy, knowing even then that the action could have triggered all their deaths. They'd been staying in a boarded-up tavern. The contents of every bottle on the shelves hadn't helped him much.

Starhawk went on quietly, "It felt like that in the Hall last night. If Nanciormis knows about the Witches, it's a sure bet other people do as well."

The polished glare of the desert came back to his mind, the sandy harshness of the wind flickering around the gatehouse walls, as he, Kaletha, and Tazey stood watching the white dust column advance from the south. *The only witches left in Wenshar*, he had thought: himself, the woman, the girl.

"All the more reason," he said slowly, "for you to keep an eye on Tazey, once you get back."

Starhawk nodded; she'd thought of that already. "When you return," she said after a moment, "don't come to the gates. Work your way around through the empty quarter; there's old gateways through the back. Wait for me in the cell behind the one we've been staying in. It's close enough that, if there is trouble, we can collect our things and the money we've stashed behind the loose brick there and get out."

He turned his head and considered the woman hunkered at his side, ranginess folded compactly to balance on booted ankles, brown hands resting one over the other, as long as a man's, but narrower. Her face was, as usual, expressionless, save for the shift of thoughts behind the pewter-colored eyes. "You think it'll come to that?"

"I have no reason to, no," she replied. "But there's no sense taking chances." She straightened up in one single, graceful motion. She would follow—and had followed—him to the Cold Hells and back, but he had long since given up the notion that she would ever display anxiety for his safety. "You think staying the night here will tell you what's behind this?"

"Maybe not. But it'll sure as hell tell me something."

Twilight came early to the canyons, filtered gloom deepening in the mazes of the split rock walls while the sun still blazed on Starhawk and Tazey's retreating dust. At the foot of the central canyon Sun Wolf found a small temple whose inner sanctuary could easily be barricaded with rubble and thorn. He spent an hour marking it with every spell he knew, the Circles of Light and Darkness and all the Runes of Ward. He did not know whether what he did was correct, but he worked slowly, carefully, concentrating all his powers upon their formation. He felt tired when he was done, as if he had accomplished some physical labor, and it disturbed him, when he looked up at the fading slit of brightness high overhead, to see how much time it had taken. He watered his horse in one of the broken tanks in the westward canyon, fed it, then hobbled and tied it in the sanctuary, barricading the door and scribbling sign after sign upon the barricade—of guard, of illusion, and of light.

In the half darkness of those silent corridors of rock, he walked along the central canyon to the palace at its end.

Nothing whispered to him now from the black sockets of empty doors and windows; only silence waited in the eternal dark under the deformed cypresses. In the deepening shadows, the carved facade that stretched across the canyon's end seemed the color of dried and ancient blood.

He climbed the steps. Here, alone in the silent city, had the conquerors from over the mountains done more than simply break doors to loot. A double line of crouching statues, lions and leopards it appeared, had guarded the stair. Their heads and forepaws had been deliberately smashed off—not only smashed, but pulverized, for no broken pieces littered the sand-drifted steps. One beast still retained part of a paw. Sun Wolf saw that it had been a woman's hand.

There was no question in his mind where in the palace he must go. The small door to the right of the great entry hall beckoned to him, like the mouth of a tomb one sees in nightmares, knowing it for one's own. He had heard Starhawk's voice calling to him from its hoarded night. Now there was only silence, save for the faint reverberance of his footfalls and the distant muttering of the canyon winds.

As a wizard, he could see clearly in the interior darkness of the corridor beyond, but he summoned witchlight anyway. From the faded frescoes on the walls, women's eyes looked down at him—dark, knowing, amused. A room opened before him, and he stopped on the painted threshold as the stench of the evil there smote him in the face.

I shouldn't be here, he thought, as his heart lurched and began to slam heavily into his ribs. *I should go away QUICKLY and draw the Circles around myself . . .*

But it was foolish. If he did that, he would learn nothing, either about Tazey or about that eerie sense that it was him they wanted . . .

Wanted for what?

The room stretched before him. Every foot of its barn-like emptiness lay bare. Under the blue-white radiance of the magelight, it seemed to say, "See? There's nothing to fear here." Yet the smell was there, as sharp and terrible to him as the smell of blood.

His breath fast and light and the instincts of thirty years of war tearing at his guts, he moved slowly into the room.

At the far end, a door was tucked into one wall, barred shut and ruinously old. Halfway down the long chamber, a stone altar had once stood, but only the stump of it was left. Like the statues outside, it had been violently broken; but forcing himself to step closer, Sun Wolf saw that even those who had done the thing had been too afraid to remain in this room long enough to finish. Fragments of its frieze were still visible. He shuddered and looked away.

The Lady Illyra had said nothing of the customs of the inner cults of the shirdar Houses, but, without being told, he knew that this room had been their temple. What they had done had been done here.

In front of the altar a trench, six or seven feet deep, had been cut to the bedrock, though the gravel and debris of decades now littered its floor.

Here, Sun Wolf thought, hating it, drawn to its lip, almost against his will. *Here.*

He knelt and made sure of the strength of the edge. Then he took a deep breath and dropped lightly into the pit.

As if it had been a well filled with invisible water, he felt the presence of the demons. Through his boot soles he could sense them underfoot, could feel them moving like glowing fish within the rock walls all around. When he knelt to press his palms to the gravel on the floor, his soul cringed from it, as from red-hot iron.

Through his hands he felt their whispering in his mind, meaningless noises like the guttural murmur of the wind beneath the earth. His understanding flinched from them, holding back, like a lover holding back from some too-intense ecstasy. Then he bent his head, and his long, thinning hair fell forward around his face. He forced himself to relax, to hear.

As he had suspected, they knew his name.

It was only a touch; he slammed shut his mind against them and stood up quickly, shaking as if burned. Looking down, he could see a filthy glow rising like ground water through the gravel beneath his boots. He sprang up, caught the rim of the pit, and swung himself up and out. Somehow the magelight all around him had failed, but it seemed now that every fissure in the rock of the temple wall and every twisted shadow of the broken altar glowed with what was not light. Below him he could see them clearly now in the pit, seeping up out of the earth, staring at him with cold and empty wisdom in their eyes.

He fell back a few paces to the altar, wanting to run but aware in the calm corner of his mind that it was far too late. No Circle he could make would be strong enough now.

Like the crystal skeletons of ghosts, they drifted into the air above the trench. Gibbous laughter flicked at the edges of his consciousness. It seemed to him he heard in it Kaletha's scornful voice, his father's hoarse bellow, and the drink-slurred mumble of Osgard. Other voices threaded through it—the giggling of Altiokis, the Wizard King, and Sheera of Mandrigyn's caustic laugh. Like black liquid bubbling to the surface from the darkness of his dreams, he felt the old hates, old angers, and past resentments welling up within him at the sound.

The demons glowed brighter. Their ring around him closed.

Other things went through his mind, a pestilent ooze dripping from the walls of his thoughts—dark lusts and the memories of women raped in the fury and triumph of sacking a city in the aftermath of battle. Things came back to him, things that he knew he had done, cruel and stupid and bestial—things he had done because in the fighting he had come within kissing distance of death, and his mind had craved power as a dying man's body craves the water of life. But now he saw these things, not with the horror of what he had done to other human beings, but with an animal's savor at the taste of blood.

Looking up, he saw the eyes of the demons all around him. They were yellow, like his own remaining eye.

They had been cold, but now, as they gathered closer and closer about him, those shrunken, spider limbs glowed with the reflection of warmth. No longer fully transparent, the frail ectoplasm showed pale, bleeding colors, like watered paint filmed on glass. Their mouths opened, and he saw all those ghostly red teeth, as if they had been tearing at living flesh.

Like sound re-echoing from a thousand hollows of polished bronze, he heard them whisper, *Take it. It is yours.*

Power surged like the pulse heat of lust in his flesh—the power to crush and tear, the power to wield the winds. He saw himself smashing Osgard across the face only for the pleasure of watching him cringe; felt the hot desire to take and keep that slut Kaletha's books, not because he wanted them, but because she did; to have her and cast her away like the cheap trull she was; to bring down a city if he wanted it and have its fat bourgeois snivel to him with offers of gold, of women, of more power—power for its own sake, to warm his blood like brandy—the power of the mageborn.

He managed to whisper, "No."

Those fragile fingers touched him. The hunger for power clutched him, belly and loins and mind, and the demons screamed it back at him a thousandfold. They were starved, and their starvation kindled in his flesh like fire in dry tinder.

Feed us, they whispered, *and we will feed you*.

He cried again, "NO!" And this time his hoarse voice, raucous as the broken caw of a vulture, echoed against the stone roof and down all the painted corridors of darkness. He turned from the broken altar stone and fled back into the darkness of the room, smashing blindly through the inner door, stumbling into the black corridor beyond, with the demons rushing in a glowing mist at his heels, like greedy dogs sniffing at the smell of his fear.

He sensed them everywhere in the darkness around him. Even as he fled from them, his heart trip-hammering with terror, Sun Wolf kept that cold battle calm that had more than once saved his life. He was aware that he had to turn left and work his way back to the vast entrance hall; and, as he fled through silent chambers and corridors painted with queer, stiff scenes of animal-headed women tearing apart fawns and rabbits with their hands, he was aware again that he was being herded.

Voices piped at him from the darkness, voices that blended eerily into those that he knew—Starhawk's, Tazey's, Jeryn's. Other voices whispered and laughed to him from the frescoes of the walls, the Queens and Princesses of the Ancient House of Wenshar jeering down at him, with their bare white breasts and streaming hair, from the painted immortality of the walls. There were other things in the darkness as well—evil that clotted in the corners and filled some hallways like a miasma of blood—but he closed his mind and plunged through, knowing that, above all, he must not be driven into a corner. If it cost his life, he must avoid the touch of those skinny, fleshless fingers and the warmed honey of the demons' power.

Gasping, he plunged into open darkness; starlight gleamed between pillars, barely to be seen in the Stygian gloom. The desert night, usually so cold, was treacly warm on his skin, and dust stung his nostrils.

The storm, he thought, despairing, even as he plunged across the open darkness of the floor. Like a rotten pomegranate spawning flies, the darkness spawned demons around him.

They rose from the floor before him and materialized from the walls. The colors of their flesh glowed as they drank his fears and were warmed by them. Their teeth tore at his hands and face. In the starlight, as he plunged outside, he saw the black glitter of running blood.

He had denied them the right to feed upon his power. To them he was now no more than the mare that they had driven over the cliff to feed on its fear and pain.

They were capable of killing; that much he now knew. The riddle of Wenshar fitted together in his mind with horrible clarity—what it was the women had done in their cult, and how its power had been reawakened. He plunged down the steps, running as he had never run before, with the storm heat of the night burning in his lungs, knowing there was no escape.

Still he ran, stumbling on the broken roadway in the ghostly shadow of the stone needles and the black cypresses, hearing the faint chitter of their laughter at his heels, and breaking every sinew of his body to buy minutes, seconds . . .

He remembered Nanciormis lying in the shelter at the bottom of the wall and Incarsyn saying, *"The last scion of the Ancient House of Wenshar would know . . ."*

His mind reached out and found the storm.

It came like a stampede of wild horses, apt to the power of the mageborn and greedy to answer his call. He felt its direction, searing out of the west, and knew he had to make open ground. Here in the canyons it would be only an eddy of wind. The demon glow flickered bright in the tail of his eye, and something ripped his arm like a comb of thorns; the muscles of his thighs and knees burned, his chest seemed filled to bursting with hot salt, and the ground a loose carpet of potholes and rolling rocks beneath his pistoning feet.

The black weight of the storm dinned in his head. He thought of the tearing stones, debris, and choking dust; he thought of what would happen if he missed the shelter of the ruins below the canyon mouths. But Nanciormis had been right to fling himself over the battlement; Tazey had been right; and weirdly, old Galdron, stroking his silky beard in self-satisfied righteousness, had been right. It would be better to die than to do what the Witches of Wenshar had done.

Now was the only chance he had to escape.

The demons were waiting for him in the canyon mouth. He bellowed the ancient battle cry of his tribe as he hit the narrow place at a dead run. He felt the teeth of the demons fasten on his neck and jaw, felt claws clinch around his arm and rip through his sleeve and the flesh beneath. They drew on the heat of his blood, and the shock of it was like falling naked into icy water. His knees buckled, but he forced himself not to fall, as he had forced himself in thirty-one years of battle and carnage. The only thing to do was keep running, running into the sand-laced winds . . .

Pain shot through his leg, and he went down. Gravel tore at his flesh as he buried his face in his arms. Like razors, teeth ripped his shoulder and raked his back; claws scrabbled at the hand he'd clapped over the nape of his neck. Then hot wind twisted at his hair and clothes and the rage of the storm struck him—searing, tearing, choking.

He felt the demons loosened from his back, like burrs ripped from a dog's coat. Almost sobbing with relief, he dragged himself up to one elbow, then to his feet, his legs shaking so badly they could barely obey his will. Wind-blown debris savaged him, adding to the blood already running down his face and arms. It took all the strength he had left to push the worst of the burning dust aside.

Like a blind and wounded animal, he began to crawl toward the shelter of the ruined walls of Wenshar.

The sun woke him, and the pain of his stiffening wounds. He rolled over, aching; sand and debris slithered grittily from his legs, which lay partly outside the shelter of the half-collapsed brick kiln into which he had dragged himself. He looked down at his hands; blood and filth clotted the semicircular tears in the flesh. His whole body hurt. He had remained conscious long enough to twist the worst of the baking shroud of dust from him, but he still felt parched with thirst, feverish, and strange.

He crawled out of his shelter, blinking in the brightness. When he stood up, sand, pebbles, and twigs poured from every crease of his torn shirt and doublet and from his breeches and boots. His hair, the stubble of his beard, his moustache, and even his eyebrows were stiff with grime, matted into place with blood; sand gritted in the empty socket of his left eye beneath its leather patch. He coughed and spat the dust from his throat.

Before him in one direction lay the whitening bones of the city, half-hidden now under gray drifts of sand; beyond them lay the black reg and the ghostly sentinels of tsuroka, already shimmering in the day's heat. He turned. A couple of chimneys and the corner of a wall rose through the sand like the ribs of an animal. Around his shelter, the dune was broken by a dip, the print of the spells which had saved his life. Everything else was buried under ash-colored dust. In the new light, the decayed and blackened cliff face of the Haunted Mountains wore a brooding, waiting look, as incongruous and horrible as a thoughtful frown on the brow of a half-rotted corpse.

He had outwitted them and had learned their secret. But the demons of Wenshar were far from finished.

It took a good deal of courage simply to go up the canyon far enough to get his horse. He was rather surprised to find the beast unharmed where he had left it behind the barricades in the honey-colored temple. In the exhaustion-drugged depths of his unconsciousness, he had felt the storm ebb and had felt the demons go seeking other prey. The echoes of their triumph when they had found it, the terror and the blood of their prey clung in his throat with the back-taste of the dust. He had assumed he'd be walking back to Tandieras. But other than being crusted with dried sweat from a night of terror and half-crazy with thirst, the beast was as the Wolf had left him. Moving slowly, stumblingly, Sun Wolf led him to the rock tanks, where both of them drank and the Wolf washed the numerous shallow gashes that covered his arms and face. Then he saddled up, wrapped on his head veils, and turned the horse's head back toward Tandieras once again.

He reached the Fortress shortly before sunset and waited until it was dark to work his way around through the dilapidated gates of the empty quarter.

But it was not Starhawk who waited for him in the gloom of the abandoned cells. It was Nanciormis, with Kaletha and over a dozen guards and shirdar warriors, to arrest him for the murder, by means of sorcery, of Incarsyn of Hasdrozaboth and all those who had gone before.

CHAPTER

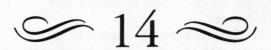 14

"*I*F YOU TELL US WHO PAID YOU AND WHY," NANCIORMIS SAID quietly, "you could spare yourself a lot of pain."

"The hell I would." The shackles that held Sun Wolf's wrists extended out to either side of him clinked faintly against the stone of the wall as he tried to shift his shoulders. About the only thing that could be said for the dungeons under Tandieras—stinking of old excrement, crawling with roaches, foul with smoke from the brazier in the corner of his cell—was that they weren't damp. His single eye glinted in the choking murk. "You know as well as I do that Illyra's going to spare nobody pain who was responsible for killing that wooden-headed brother of hers. Without him she can't go on ruling the Dunes. Confessing would only buy me her hate instead of her suspicion."

The Desert Lord folded his heavy arms, his thick lips pressing taut. "You have more than her suspicion, Captain," he said. "Your bluff is over. We know."

"You *what*?!"

Behind him, Osgard, sober for once, his sweat like pig muck in the close heat of the cell, said, "It wasn't until you came to Tandieras that this started. Nexué didn't die until you'd come back from Wenshar— by the Three, why we didn't realize then it was you—"

"It wasn't me, rot your eyes!" the Wolf stormed. At the angry jerk of his chains, the guards who crowded in the narrow doorway raised their crossbows. Sun Wolf realized belatedly that, as a wizard, his slightest movement could be grounds for death. He sensed already Kaletha's spells on the manacles, like a blindfold over certain parts of his mind. Evidently someone believed in taking precautions, anyway.

Osgard's face reddened at the contradiction, but Nanciormis merely raised one white-gloved hand. "There's no need to maintain the charade any longer, Captain," he said quietly. "I saw you, the night you tried to murder me."

"WHAT?" Even in that first shocked instant, Sun Wolf remembered how Nanciormis had evaded certain questions after the attack, had looked away from his eyes, and had spoken to Osgard afterward. "Dammit, man, I was in the Hall when it happened! A dozen people saw me . . ."

"No one saw you leave," Osgard said, his voice thick. "But a dozen people saw you come running back in, Johnny-Behind-The-Fair, when the screaming started. You seemed to know where it would be, and be damned to the noise of the wind."

"And even had you not," the commander put in, "it is witchery we deal with." He stepped closer, the amber glow of the brazier making pinpoints of fire far back in his somber eyes. "When I felt the horror coalescing in the darkness of my room, when I understood what was happening, I flung the lamp at it. And for an instant, outlined in the flame, I saw it. It had your face, Captain."

Sun Wolf stared at him, shocked into silence. When he could speak, the words came out as a whisper. "It couldn't have." But the demons in Wenshar had had his eyes. And Tazey had said that the Witches did not always know.

Cool even through the shock and horror, he thought, *I would have known.* He shook his head slowly. "No," he began, and Nanciormis struck him across the mouth.

"Do you deny you were in Wenshar last night?" The gloved fingers took him by the chin and forced his head back again; torchlight glanced over the overlapping crescents of dried blood that marked Sun Wolf's face and neck. Close to his own, the Wolf could see the broken veins on that elegant nose, smell wine and mint on his breath. "Do you deny that you had to do with the demons in Wenshar?"

He had to fight the urge to boot the man's testicles halfway up to his solar plexus. "I was in Wenshar, yes. If you'll listen to me—"

Nanciormis struck him again, casually, but with a force that slammed his head back against the wall. Stepping back, he said softly, "They say that all the Witches of Wenshar had such scars, from coupling with the demons in that city. I hope for your sake, Captain, that you were paid to do what you did by the enemies of Wenshar, and that you are not simply a madman acting from his lust for blood. For if you tell us who hired you to destroy all hope of an alliance with the shirdar, you may look forward to the mercy of a slit throat after the torturers are through." He turned and signed to one of the guards.

Exasperated at the man's obtuseness in spite of how shaken he was, Sun Wolf growled, "And don't bother showing me the instruments of torture. I've seen 'em plenty of times, and they don't impress me." *Why?* he thought, his mind racing—*how could that be possible?* But for answer, all he saw were the demons' golden eyes. They didn't always know, Tazey had said. Suddenly, horribly, he understood the girl's secret terror, worse because of what he had learned in the ruins last night.

Nanciormis paused and turned back toward him. "Perhaps not," he said. "You are a strong man, Captain. If you are being paid, I hope it is sufficient."

There was a jostling around the door—the cell had been excavated and lined with stone back in the days when Tandieras was merely the administrative center for the governors of Pardle, and the room wasn't a large one. It was crowded already with Osgard, Nanciormis, two guards with crossbows, the brazier, and the Wolf himself. The other guards who entered, two men and a woman, made it all the worse. The instruments that the woman carried were those of what was called ironically "small torture"—a thumbscrew, an assortment of iron rods, which the woman placed in the brazier to heat, razor-edged pincers, the sight of which always turned the Wolf's stomach, the thin-bladed probe for prying under the fingernails, and tie-frames to hold the hand open while balls of burning cotton and oil were dripped onto the palms.

The two men led Starhawk between them.

Everything within Sun Wolf contracted to a single, cold ball of horror.

Absurdly, he wondered why he hadn't seen this coming. He'd certainly forced enough information from captives during campaigns by the same method. Perhaps because, of the hundreds of concubines who'd filed through his bed, there'd never been one for whom he'd have put a campaign, or any one of his men, in danger. Had one of his friends in the troop been tortured in the same fashion, he'd have felt sorry, but he'd have known that whichever of them it was would understand.

This was different.

Starhawk's face was brown with dust through which tracked runnels of sweat; her eyes seemed the color of white ice against that darkness. A bruise covered half her face, running back under the pale, sweat-matted hair of her temple. By the scabbed edges, it looked like the flat of a sword; that was probably what had knocked her out. Her throat, visible through the open neck of her torn shirt, was marked as well, under a choke-noose of chain. It had undoubtedly been one hell of a struggle.

Nanciormis said softly, "Who paid you, Sun Wolf? The King-Council of Kwest Mralwe?"

"Nobody paid me," he said. The words came out queerly level and quiet. "I had nothing to do with it."

But he knew despairingly it would do him no good. He felt paralyzed, as if he had been knifed in some unarmored spot; his only thought was that Starhawk must not suffer for this.

His mouth felt dry, his lips as if they belonged to someone else. "If you'll listen I'll tell you . . ."

"We're not interested in your lies." Nanciormis' silky voice turned cold. "We know what's happening. We want a confession."

Anger flared in him at this man's stubborn stupidity, like the criminal incompetence which had nearly killed Jeryn, the blind selfishness with which he satisfied his lusts for his niece's governess without any thought to its consequences to her. But he held his rage in check. Whatever he did, the Hawk would be the one who paid.

Carefully, he said, "There's nothing to confess. Unless it was without my conscious knowledge—"

"That's a lie!" Osgard surged forward, face crimson. His hands wrenched at the collar of Sun Wolf's shirt, nearly strangling him. "The Witches all knew what they were doing! It's a lie they use to excuse themselves!"

Beyond the King's massive shoulders, Nanciormis watched the scene in silence. *Of course,* thought the Wolf dizzily, he was too much of a politician to contradict a man whose daughter might be accused.

"My Lord," the commander stepped smoothly forward and put a hand on the King's arm. "I think we can get the truth easily enough."

Turning, he walked back to Starhawk. With the deliberateness of a physician, he tore open her shirt to the waist, pulling the thin rags of the fabric down over her arms. Under the bruises, Starhawk's face was as uncaring as a prostitute's. The two guards holding her arms shifted and tightened their grip; the third, coming up behind her, took hold of the slip-chain and drew it tight around the flesh of her throat.

Sun Wolf twisted against his own bonds, the manacles tearing unnoticed at the flesh of his wrists. "She has nothing to do with this, damn your eyes!"

Nanciormis took one of the metal rods from the heart of the fire in the brazier, its end cherry-red with heat. "Of course she doesn't," he remarked, and twirled it a little in his hands. "A pity, isn't it?"

As the glowing end came near Starhawk's breast, Sun Wolf saw her relax, turn her head aside and, still expressionless, shut her eyes. She was sinking into meditation, fast and deep, like a porpoise sounding in the sea, trying to dive beyond the reach of pain . . .

"Stop it!" The crossbows raised again as he flung himself against the chains, but he scarcely noticed. All he saw was the glow of heat near the white skin of the Hawk's breast, and how the sweat poured down her calm face. "STOP IT! All right, I did it! The King-Council of Kwest Mralwe paid me—five hundred pieces of gold! For God's sake let her go!"

He was shaking, his body drenched with sweat, gasping as if he, not the Hawk, were facing the heated iron. Starhawk's eyes snapped open, shocked—she hadn't been so far into her trance that she wouldn't have felt it. "Don't be a fool, Chief, we haven't been near Kwest Mralwe."

Even as the choke-chain jerked tight around her throat, he roared over her, "They contacted me before we ever left Wrynde, dammit! Shut her up and get her out of here. She doesn't know a thing about it!"

Starhawk was struggling now, fighting for air against the strangling loop of metal around her windpipe. The agony of panic and terror the Wolf felt as he watched them systematically club and strangle her into semiconsciousness was nothing he had ever experienced—something for which he had never even thought to prepare himself in all his years of war. He found himself roaring hoarsely over and over, "Stop it!

Stop it!" His whole body trembled as they finally dragged her from the room. There were tears as well as sweat running down his face, and he was aware of Nanciormis watching his humiliation with interest, disgust, and a certain smug satisfaction, as if this proved that Sun Wolf was not, in fact, a better man than he.

Another time, the Wolf would have felt fury. Now he was too sickened and shaken to care. He was aware he had broken, as he'd broken other men, and that they'd done it by the simplest of means. Some detached portion of his mind was mildly interested in the fact that he didn't care about even that; the rest of him was thinking illogically that Starhawk hadn't made a sound.

The commander's thick lips curled in a little smile.

"So the Lords of Kwest Mralwe paid you to murder the Bishop Galdron and Egaldus and Incarsyn?"

"Yes." He was panting, sobbing, as if he had run miles. *So much,* he thought, with strange detachment, *for the hardened warrior who can take anything his enemies dish out.*

"Why?" Osgard grabbed him furiously again by the shirt-front and dragged his face close. Green eyes like bloodshot rotten eggs glared into his. "And Norbas Milkom died just because he happened to be with Galdron, is that it?" His breath was like a cesspit; the Wolf fought nausea. "A man who'd never harmed a soul—a man who was my friend and the best friend this country ever had!" His big hands tightened as he slammed the Wolf back against the wall. "You stinking, murdering traitor, I took you into my Household—"

"Get out of the way, you fool!" Nanciormis wrenched the King's hands free and shoved him impatiently aside. He turned back to the Wolf, speaking quickly, as if to get this over with. "You did this to cause disruption of the alliance between Wenshar and the shirdar?"

"Yes." Sun Wolf swallowed, grasping for what was left of his thoughts. "I don't know," he amended, realizing this was likelier— *anything,* he thought, *to make them believe.* He had seen torture, seen the torture of women. *Anything,* he thought, *to spare the Hawk that.* "They didn't tell me. They knew I was mageborn, knew I could get control of the demons . . ."

The dark eyes narrowed in their pads of flesh. "So that's how it's done," he murmured. Then, with a glance at the King, "And the King would have been your next victim."

Sun Wolf nodded. He felt drained and strange to himself, emptied

of the pride he'd once held in his own strength. It had all happened so
quickly. He understood then why men who held out through the pain
at the torturers' hands would weep after it was over.

"You stinking traitor." The King's breath hissed thickly in his nostrils. "You took my money, you ate my bread—I entrusted you with
the life of my son." He spoke quietly, his anger coalescing into a
hardness far beyond his usual pyrotechnic wrath. "Witch-bastard—you
have no more pride nor honor than a camel-skinner's whore." Stepping close, he spat in Sun Wolf's face.

Sun Wolf was aware, as the spittle ran warm and slimy down his
chin, that there had been a time when he would have struck at the man
for that, even if they killed him for it. But not even anger was left him
—only numbness and fear for the Hawk. *I would never have hurt Jeryn*,
he wanted to say, but could not. He'd seen the abject and stupid hopes
of men once he'd broken them, clinging to straws of self-deception
and the delusion that if they licked their torturer's boots sufficiently
clean, no further harm would be done to those they loved. He remembered, too, his scorn of such men and what he'd done to those loved
ones out of spite and pique and sheer perverseness, if the victim's
pleas had been too fulsome. There was that, too, in Nanciormis' eyes.

But all of it changed nothing. He felt alien to himself, as if soul and
body had, in less time than it took to put on his boots, been turned
inside-out.

"We'll take his confession and fling it in the faces of those toads in
Kwest Mralwe . . ."

Nanciormis shook his head. "It would do us no good." He fastidiously wiped his face on a cotton handkerchief he'd taken from his
sleeve. Even through the stench of the straw underfoot and the King's
stained and sweaty puce doublet, the Wolf could smell the aromatic
vinegar with which it had been soaked. "They'll only deny it—deny
that they ever knew the sources of the power of the Witches. But as
the ones who broke that power, they very well could have known how
to awaken it again." He glanced back at the Wolf. "As for this one—
we have his confession. We need no more."

He signed to the guards. They raised their crossbows again, and
Nanciormis put his hand on the King's arm, to draw him back out of
the way.

Osgard remained where he was, between the barbed iron points
and Sun Wolf's chest. "After the bill for it is signed," he said.

Nanciormis stared at him as if he'd taken leave of his senses. "What?"

The King regarded him for a moment, green eyes slitted. "After a bill is made out and signed for his death and posted in the city from sunrise till sunset tomorrow," he said. "The fact that he's a witch-bastard and a killer doesn't mean I can break the law to kill him without a bill."

Emotionally emptied, Sun Wolf observed with distant interest that this was one of the few times he'd ever seen Nanciormis taken off guard. Between the velvety ropes of the braids, his face turned tallowy yellow with anger, his mouth squaring hard at the corners. Then he recovered himself, stammered, "We have the man's confession! He betrayed you, would have murdered you in your bed. He slaughtered Milkom like a sheep . . ."

Osgard's voice turned to flint. "Don't talk about Milkom to me," he said softly. "It's only chance my uncle Tyrill named me and not Norbas his successor. It could have been either of us, because we both believed in law. A shirdar lord might have a man's throat slit on his own say-so, in the dark, without anyone's knowing about it, but that isn't how it's done here. I'm the King, but I'm King under laws, something you and your people never got around to making."

"And my people," said Nanciormis, viper-quiet, "are the stronger for it. Among my people, these killings would never have gone on as long as they have."

"Your people," retorted Osgard, his voice equally deadly, "were unable to hold these lands against folk who were united by law, Nanciormis. Remember that."

And turning, the King strode from the cell. Nanciormis stood for a moment, watching his shadow pass across the torch-glare in the stairwell; then he turned back and studied Sun Wolf with considering eyes.

For a long moment he said nothing. Sun Wolf met his eyes through the burning smoke of the brazier that now choked the cell, acutely aware that the two guards still remained, their weapons at the ready. He was utterly weary, body and soul—yesterday's long ride and the horrors of the night mingling with the ache of strained shoulder muscles, the hot, viscous trickle of blood down his arms from the torn flesh of his wrists, and the burn of sweat in his wounds. His only thought was how Starhawk had fought them—silent, desperate—and how in silence she had been beaten unconscious. In the strange, clear corner of his mind that was detached from any personal concerns, he was aware that, though Osgard would undoubtedly promulgate and sign the correct legal bill for his death immediately, by tomorrow there was a good chance he would be too drunk to inquire whether Sun Wolf had survived the night to be executed the following sunset. By the commander's eyes, Nanciormis was thinking it, too. Sun Wolf knew he should be afraid, but somehow was not. He only stood, his head tipped back against the stone wall behind him, watching the commander incuriously. In spite of the almost unbearable heat of the room, he felt queerly cold.

But something of Osgard's sober and deadly quiet seemed to have reached through the commander's contempt for his brother-in-law. At length he signed to the two guards. "Keep watch on him. Remember he's a wizard. Stay alert. If he either moves or speaks, kill him at once. Understand?"

The men nodded. Nanciormis paused for a moment longer, studying Sun Wolf's chained figure, stretched between the torches, the light glancing along the crescent-shaped scabs of the demon bites, gleaming stickily on the perspiration streaming down his chest and ribs. Then his mouth hardened with some private thought; turning, he strode from the cell.

It was a long time before Starhawk found the strength even to move. The fresh pain blended with the ache of bruises several hours old, taken in the struggle when they'd arrested her as soon as the boys on the watchtower had sighted Sun Wolf's horse. Looking back on it, she wondered with dull disgust at herself why she had not suspected the very fact that no one had arrested her upon her return with Tazey. Of course Osgard would be readier to plant the blame on him or Kaletha, rather than on his daughter. She wondered what had finally tipped the scales.

Some circumstance of Incarsyn's murder? She shivered, remembering the screams that had shattered the terrible silence between the end of the storm and dawn. Some piece of proof that Kaletha was innocent? Or was it just that Sun Wolf was a stranger? She cursed herself for not picking a less obvious rendezvous, for not knowing the empty quarter well enough to choose one further in, and for not being ready for a delayed arrest.

She sighed and tried to roll over on the uneven stone of the floor. It was like a cobblestone street, bumpy and filled with little pits and holes where roaches nested under crumbled straw. Its jagged edges cut into her bare arms, and she winced and lay still again.

She had to get him out, if it wasn't too late already. Illyra had threatened the most barbarous and lingering death for the witch whose magic had slain her brother. But in the long hours of the earlier night, while she had waited with hammering heart for the guards to come for her, she had gone over every square foot of the stone-lined room. There was nothing she could use for a weapon or tool.

Sun Wolf had confessed. He might be already dead.

Her body hurt; her soul felt shaken to its marrow.

She had long known that she was willing to perjure her soul and destroy her body for Sun Wolf's sake—it had never occurred to her that he would do likewise for her. Struggling to submerge mind and feeling to the dark silence of meditation, she had heard him cry out, and it had left her stunned. He would not have confessed, she knew, if they'd put the iron to his own flesh.

That he had done so for her sake terrified her. She was used to pain from arrows, swords, and every instrument designed to cut or break human flesh. The tears that slid in such silence down her face were from grief at his humiliation and because she understood now that he valued her above his own pride.

He had said that he loved her. Until now she had not understood that his love was of the same quality as hers.

This is weak, she told herself angrily, *weak and stupid. While you're sniveling over how much he loves you, he could be dying. There has to be something you can do.*

But the tears slid cold down her face. Even had she not been half-dead with exhaustion, she knew there was nothing she had not already investigated before.

Somewhere behind her, she heard a faint, hollow *scritch*.

Her muscles stiffened.

In the long waiting she had become familiar with every sound of these cells—the queer, hollow groanings of the wind in the walls, and the scrabble of rats who hunted the enormous brown jail-roaches in the corners. This was different.

Very faintly, she heard it again—the unmistakable scrape of wood on stone and the soft squeak of a hinge.

"Warlady?"

An unvoiced whisper, a scout's in enemy territory. She moved her eyes to the judas-hole in the door. The faintest glow of reflected torchlight filtered through, but no shadow of a watching guard. She rolled over—every pulled, burning muscle of her back and belly stabbing at her—and sat up, shrugging her torn shirt back up on her shoulders again.

In the blackness of the rear wall, a small square of more velvety black had appeared and, in it, the white oval blur of faces.

As soundlessly as she could, she edged her way to the back of the cell.

Tazey was wearing her boy's breeches and a man's embroidered black shirt, all smutched and filthy now with mud and slime and what looked like soot. Jeryn's usual prim, formal outfit of hose, trunks, and a stiffly braced doublet were as grimy as his sister's.

Starhawk breathed, "Sorry, but we just had the chimney swept yesterday—come back next week." They both put their hands over their mouths to keep from giggling with relief.

She ducked down and crawled through the narrow black slot in the wall; there was the faint scrape of wood as Jeryn replaced the hidden door. Small hands groped for hers in the darkness, and they led her, half stooping, half crawling, a few paces and around what felt like a corner. Then with a hiss and sneer of metal, a lantern-slide was uncovered to show them in a narrow passageway with a sharply sloped roof. Roaches longer than Starhawk's thumb scrambled for cover from the light.

Jeryn whispered, "This runs behind all the cells."

Starhawk nodded. "It's an old trick, if a prisoner turns stubborn. Put him in a cell with his partner and station a man to listen to them talk when they think they're alone. Or if he's a Trinitarian, hide a man here when the priest comes to hear his confession. It looks like it hasn't been used in years."

They were staring at her with wide eyes; Starhawk felt her hair, sticking straight up, all stiffened with sweat and blood, and the puffy, discoloring bruises on her face and half-exposed breast. "I'm fine," she added. "The Chief . . ."

Jeryn whispered, "We heard. We were behind the wall."

Tazey added softly, "Father's gone to sign the bill of execution, but the law states it must be posted from sunrise to sunset before a man can be killed. He—" She swallowed. "He hasn't been hurt."

Starhawk had half guessed, from their lack of panic, that the Wolf had at least a few hours left. Exhausted and shaken as she was, the sudden release from stress made her eyes sting nonetheless and her throat ache. With an impulsive move, she hugged the girl to her, fighting to keep from breaking the armor of her calm. There was no time for it now.

"I—" Tazey hesitated, biting her lower lip. "I can use magic to get the guards away from him. I don't think it will be hard." She spoke swiftly, as if admitting something which hurt her; but once it was said, she relaxed a little. She looked far better than she had yesterday in Wenshar; better even than she had on the silent trip back across the desert—less withdrawn and hagridden. Starhawk guessed she'd used magic to get out of her own room—as their friend she had certainly been watched—even as she had laid sleep-spells on her watchers two nights ago. *You can sometimes un-be what you are*, the Hawk thought, *but you can never unknow that you were it.* Tazey had made her choice. For her there was now no going back, if indeed there ever had been. She went on, "We can . . ."

Starhawk shook her head. Her mind was working fast, running ahead. Her immediate fears for the Wolf were assuaged. She was thinking like a trooper again. "No," she said. "Listen, what hour of the night is it?"

They looked at one another, then Tazey said, "About the third."

"All right." Starhawk drew the children close to her, keeping her voice low, for the tunnel would carry the smallest noise. "People are still awake—they're still alert. We can't make a break-in until two or three hours after midnight, when most people are asleep, and when the guards will be tired and stale—not only the guards on the Wolf's cell, but the guards around the corrals."

Huddled, squatting, in the narrow space beside her, they nodded, accepting her soldier's wisdom. She could see Jeryn tucking that piece of information away in his mind for another time.

"The Chief was right. These killings aren't going to stop until we know why they started. We need to know what the Witches of Wenshar knew. We need Kaletha's books." She looked at them in the upside-down glare of the shaded lantern, two grimy royal urchins sitting with their chins on their knees in the stinking spy-tunnel behind their father's dungeon, dark eyes and green shining through the tangles of their dust-streaked hair. "Are you kids game?"

* * *

"Do you know *every* tunnel and cellar in Tandieras?"

Jeryn glanced over his shoulder at her and flashed her a shy grin. "Just about." There was a trace of pride in his soft, treble voice. Broken out of its habitual sullenness, his peaked face looked more handsome and less pretty than usual. He wiped away the soot that had coated them all on their way through an old hypocaust, leaving a large, pale streak amid the general filth.

Jeryn had crossed the big, musty-smelling kitchen cellar without light, by touch in the dark; he'd flashed the lantern-slide, once, to guide Starhawk across. Long training in night scouting had taught her to take in the cleared pathways at a glance. She'd negotiated the expanse of piled sacks of potatoes and wheat, clay oil jars as tall as Jeryn was, and knobby, dangling fronds of onions and herbs without a sound that might be heard by those whose footsteps creaked over their heads. She could hear Tazey making her way softly now, moving in the dark, as the mageborn could.

The boy's cold, fragile little fingers sought hers. "I used to hide anywhere, when Uncle Nanciormis wanted me for sword practice, or riding. And it wasn't that I was a coward," he added, a crack of hurt suddenly breaking his voice. "That is—it isn't cowardly not to want to do something you can't do if it's dangerous, is it, Warlady? I mean, I'm *not* afraid of horses—it's just I—I can't ride the wild ones the way Tazey does, and I know it. But Uncle . . ." He hesitated, ashamed. "Uncle told Father I was a coward for not wanting to do it and a sneak for running away from lessons. I tried, I really did, to climb ropes and scale walls and things, but I . . . I just can't. That's—that's why I had to find the Chief out in the desert in Wenshar. Because he—he's a better teacher. I mean, it's boring, but he's careful you won't get hurt, you know? Sometimes I thought . . ." He stopped himself, let go of her hand and, by the sound of it, wiped his nose hastily with a sleeve which would leave it blacker than before.

Starhawk felt that knobby small hand in her own, remembered the thin legs, the pipestem wrists. He hadn't the strength that would have gotten him safely through the more dangerous elements of training, and Nanciormis was clearly a teacher who found it easier to blame his pupil's failure on anything but his own careless ineptitude. It was easier, she thought, remembering her own earlier humiliations in Sun

Wolf's school for warriors, to hide from the lessons than to be mocked.

"I did try." Then, as if ashamed of the crack in his voice, he turned toward the small door, hidden behind a wall of wine tuns whose wooden sides were thick with dust. "Through here."

Starhawk paused, as Tazey ghosted up beside them in the darkness. "Wait a minute."

She took the lantern from Jeryn and flashed a quick gleam in the direction of the shelves nearby. As she had suspected, remembering her convent days, in addition to red wheels of wax-covered cheese and bags of ground flour, they also contained empty flour sacks, folded neatly for the myriad purposes of the kitchens. She took one of them, removed the lid from a barrel of dried apples, and collected half a dozen, then borrowed Tazey's knife to cut a substantial chunk from one of the cheeses. After stowing it in the sack, which she tied through her belt, she neatly turned the rest of the cheese toward the wall so the cut would not be noticed until someone wondered why all the mice and roaches in the Fortress were converging on that particular shelf.

"When we run for it, the place is going to be like a polo game with a hornet's nest for the ball," she whispered. Shoving two more sacks through her belt, she followed Jeryn to the little slit of a doorway behind the wine tuns. "I'm not going without something to eat."

As Starhawk had suspected, the empty quarter of the Palace was as deserted as the ruins of Wenshar itself. Even had they known she had escaped, she doubted anyone would have searched there before sunup. Moving like a ghost through the bleached skeletons of the decaying walls and sand-drifted cells, she admitted they had a point. From across the deserted compounds, she could smell the faint, nauseating waft of old blood, like the stench of a three-day-old battlefield, and recalled the horror she and the Wolf had found, all that was left of Egaldus—remembered, too, Incarsyn's blood splattered not only over the walls of the room that had been his, soaking the sheets of his bed where the largest part of his body still lay, but the gore that had dripped down from the ceiling as well. The room lay on the edge of the empty quarter, where Nexué and Egaldus had both died.

Beside her, Jeryn whispered, "Uncle Nanciormis said he—he saw the Chief's face. Could—you don't think—"

Starhawk knew what he was getting at, but deliberately misunderstood. "Could it have taken on the Chief's features?" Jeryn, though that wasn't what he'd meant, nodded eagerly at this more acceptable hypothesis. "I don't know. That's why we need to know about the Witches." She halted, the chill of the night biting into her body through the rags of her torn shirt, stinging the bruises on her face and arms and making her wrenched muscles ache. When she turned her head, the short steel slip-chain around her throat pressed cold into the flesh. "The Chief said it was in a corner of a big adobe kitchen with the roof half fallen in and two ovens, catty-corner to each other."

Jeryn nodded. "I know where that is."

Tazey glanced worriedly over her shoulder. The night wind had fallen, and silence seemed to hang over the empty quarter like the darkness of sleep before dreams begin. Her voice barely touched that hideous stillness. "You don't—You don't think we're in danger?"

Deadpan, Starhawk said, "Two out of three, we're safe."

"Two out of three?"

"If it's you or the Wolf behind it, we've got nothing to worry about."

Realizing belatedly she was being kidded, Tazey grinned shakily. "Oh, thanks."

Save for the faint skiffs of wind playing hide-and-seek in the zebra moonlight beneath the broken roof beams, the dark kitchen was silent. Nevertheless, Starhawk waited a long moment in its doorway before entering. It was in her memory that Egaldus had been killed wandering at night in the empty quarter, and it was probably a safe bet that he hadn't been seeking herbs to harvest in the dark of the moon. But nothing molested her. She raised her hand, signaling the children to come.

When Starhawk and Tazey lifted the grille clear of the pit, scales stirred on sand in the darkness below like the whisper of dead leaves. She slid the cover from the lantern and held it down in that black well. Something twitched in the darkness. As if jet beads had been scattered from a burst sack, the eyes glittered unwinkingly up at them.

Starhawk took a deep breath. Sun Wolf had told her about it; but, as with the fear-spells written on the grille, just knowing was not the same. "Do you think you can do it?"

Tazey wet her lips and hesitated for a long time, staring down into the dark. Then she shook her head. "I don't know how. It's—I know what Sun Wolf and Kaletha say about illusion, but—I can't make them think a stick is something and your body is a stick. I just—I can't feel what they'd feel. I'm sorry, Warlady."

She looked wretchedly at Starhawk, as if expecting to be cursed for her failure—obliquely the Hawk wondered if her father had led her to expect that. She put a comforting hand on the square, delicate shoulder. "I'm certainly not sorry you admit it," she said frankly. "And particularly that you're not willing to try anyway." She squatted on her haunches, hugging her knees, and stared down at the restlessly moving shapes below. The dry buzz of rattlers echoed against the low roof, rising to a harsh crescendo. In spite of herself, she felt her stomach curl with dread. "And even if you could deal with the snakes," she added, "there's still the scorpions."

"Could you make the snakes go after the scorpions?" Jeryn leaned over their shoulders to look down into the pit, fascinated. "Make them hungry or something?"

Tazey thought that one over, and Starhawk swallowed a grin at the practicality of the suggestion. "I don't think so," said the girl doubtfully. "I don't really know how to make them think or feel anything. I don't know how they—how they think or feel."

"So that puts out just making them fall asleep." Starhawk rested her chin on her knees, considering the matter in the light of what the Wolf had told her of magic. "If scorpions sleep in the first place. I know snakes do—"

"Look," said Jeryn abruptly. "Tazey—you stopped a windstorm or made it blow in another direction. Can you do other things like that? With the air, I mean?"

She frowned up at her younger brother, puzzled. "I—I don't know."

Starhawk cocked her head to one side. "What did you have in mind, Scout?"

"Well, snakes shouldn't even be awake at night—neither should scorpions, because it's too cold. Can you make it colder?"

"Yes," Tazey said, then stopped, looking disconcerted.

"You're sure?" asked Starhawk.

She looked a little uncertain, not at her answer, but at her sureness. "Yes. I—It's like the wind."

Not an answer, Starhawk thought, *that would make sense to a non-wizard,* but she had been around Sun Wolf and Kaletha enough to know that wizards spoke to one another in a kind of bookhand, with minimal clues that both understood for things which could never be explained to those who had not felt them.

Tazey edged closer to the brink and rested her chin on her folded hands. Jeryn stepped back, knowing by instinct that he must remain absolutely silent. The girl shut her eyes.

Starhawk did not pretend to feel, as Sun Wolf could, when magic was being worked. All she saw was a young girl in faded old breeches and a black, too-large shirt, her head bowed and her saffron hair falling over her face, sunk in a self-induced trance of concentration. But she saw in the moonlight the faint, cold mist begin to curl into the air above the inky shadows of the pit, like ground fog on a winter morning, and felt the hair prickle on her scalp. Jeryn stepped back a pace, his thin face catching with a fleeting expression that was not quite fear, not quite grief, as he looked at this enchanted stranger who had once been his sister.

Starhawk's instinct was to throw something down into the pit, to make sure the terrible chill had worked its way upon the things below. But from her own early days of meditation she knew how easy it would be to break the girl's desperate concentration. She knew, too, that there was no telling how long she could keep it up. She handed the lantern to Jeryn and tucked Tazey's knife in her belt to force the locks with. With a whispered mental prayer to the Mother and to whatever of her or Sun Wolf's mythical ancestors might be listening, she lowered herself by her hands down into the darkness.

She dangled for a moment, listening for the telltale swish of scales upon dust. Nothing but silence met her ears. *Would the sound of her dropping,* she wondered, *break Tazey's hold on the spells?*

There was, as the mercenaries liked to say, only one way to find out.

She landed lightly, springily, knees bent. The light wavered and staggered over her head as Jeryn leaned down after her with the lantern. Its gleam reeled over scaled backs—black, brown, patterned in sand-hued lozenges or glistening like oil and pearls. One mamba flicked its tongue stuporously. That was all.

The cold in the pit was incredible, slicing through the rags of Starhawk's shirt and chilling her to the bone. Her breasts hurt with it —she was glad of the small warmth of the hot lantern-metal so close to her fingers. Even in the desert dryness, her breath was a cloud of white steam. Tiptoeing so as not to step on any of the snakes, she made her way across the room and remembered to set the light far enough from the niche so that the heat from the flame inside would not revive any of the sleeping vermin. By the time she reached the niche itself, she was shivering uncontrollably.

Scorpions covered the chest and the rafter above them, like metal plates sewn on a garment. Starhawk paused for a moment, rubbing her bare hands, loathing the thought of what she must do. *It's do it or go back out and think of something else*, she told herself. *After the roaches in the jail and the vermin in some of the inns you've stayed at, it's no time to get squeamish now.* With cringing fingers she reached forward and picked a jointed brown body off the lid and tossed it aside. It landed with a faint *plop* in a corner. None of the others moved.

Starhawk supposed she had done worse things in eight years of soldiering—retrieving the chest of gold pieces one sacked township had sunk in the latrine pit behind the town hall came to mind. But shivering in the cold, ensorcelled darkness as she crouched to force the locks, waiting for the breath of warmth that would tell her that Tazey's concentration had failed and that she herself was, for all intents and purposes, already dead, she couldn't think of too many.

There were thirteen books in one chest, five in the other. Two of them were so large and clumsy she could only carry them one at a time, picking her way back through the loathsome carpet of the pit, to hand them up to Jeryn. Her hands were clumsy with cold, barely able to close around the heavy volumes that she passed up to him in twos and threes, hoping there were no scorpions hidden within the bindings that would revive in the warmer air above. It wasn't likely—the chests looked tight against moisture, sand, and the small, glue-eating vermin of deserted places. When she was finished, she closed up the chests again, picked a six-foot diamond-back off the rungs of the ladder, and scrambled out of the pit, her bruised flesh shuddering with considerably more than cold.

Jeryn was looking at her, eyes enormous with awe. As she gently shook Tazey out of her trance, the boy whispered, "You're braver than Uncle Nanciormis—braver than my father."

"I've just had eight years' more practice as a looter," Starhawk said. "Now for God's sake take a look at my back to make sure none of those things dropped on me, and let's get the hell out of here. We've got a lot more to do tonight."

CHAPTER

 15

*F*OR THE FOURTH OR FIFTH TIME, PAIN WAKENED SUN WOLF, JERKing him back to awareness of more pain. He changed his half-waking sob into a curse and braced his knees once again to take some of the excruciating tension from his burning shoulders and back and his lacerated wrists; the guards, on the other side of the cell, shifted nervously and raised their crossbows. It was the squat, blond young man and the dark shirdar girl again, he saw—he had lost count of how many times they'd swapped off with the other pair sitting upstairs in the guardroom playing piquet. His knees trembling, the Wolf felt like telling them that if they were tired of the routine, next time *he'd* go sit in the guardroom for a change.

It would be something, he thought, if he could only summon up the smallest of go-away spells to keep the roaches and the few big, fat, insolent flies away from the raw flesh of his wounds. But the sorceries in the chains did their job thoroughly. All he could do was shake his cramped arms weakly and curse. He was growing too weary now to do either.

It was about the seventh hour of the night. He had the rest of the night to get through and all the hours of daylight tomorrow. The thought was far worse than that of whatever death he'd have to endure afterward.

A draft from the corridor moved the putrid air, and his eyes swam with the smoke. By sunset tomorrow in the desert dryness, he knew he'd be half-crazy with thirst, but now it was lack of sleep that tormented him most—lack of sleep, and the tree of agony rooted in his legs, growing up his spine to his cramped, searing shoulder muscles, and branching out to the red rings of bleeding pain that circled his wrists. Sooner or later his knees were going to give out. And then, he thought, he'd look back on this moment with nostalgic longing.

Wherever they'd put the Hawk, he hoped she was better off than he.

The queer, sinking sensation of panic returned at the thought of her.

She would never have broken as he had.

That might be, he thought ruefully, because it was unlikely that, had their positions been reversed, he would ever have been an innocent victim. But at heart, he knew Starhawk to be both colder and tougher than he was. Since he had come to love her—since he had embraced the magic that was his destiny—he had discovered in himself a widening streak of sentimentality that his father would have puked to behold —puked first and then beaten him till the blood ran.

He wondered if she would despise him for breaking down as he had or if she'd guessed what he knew—that his holding out would have made no ultimate difference.

Why had the demon had his face?

In the darkness of the corridor outside, something moved.

Sun Wolf raised his head sharply, and one guard shifted her crossbow while the other turned, casting a swift glance through the stone arch. The reflection of torches from the staircase above had long since sunk into smoky darkness, but, like a gauzy brush of fox fire, white light danced along the cracks in the stone. Then it was gone.

Exhausted almost past caring, Sun Wolf wrenched his body back away from the door—and that light—as far as he could, forcing himself not to feel the burning scrape of the manacles on his wrists. As he did so, he let out a gasp and molded his unshaven features into what he hoped was a convincing expression of utter shock and horror, as if the light were some threat as much to himself as to the guards, though in point of fact he felt no sense of danger from it at all. The guards looked at one another, then back at him. He threw them a desperate look and hoped to hell they remembered him sobbing and begging Nanciormis for mercy. *If I had to go through that,* he thought grimly, *at least let me get some good from it . . .* Whatever the hell was happening, it would be better than being shot out of hand.

At least he hoped so.

After a moment's hesitation, one guard signed to the other to keep his eye on the Wolf, then stepped cautiously into the corridor to investigate. He saw the girl's shadow on the wall, the dancing phosphorescence leading her away. The other guard braced himself, crossbow leveled, his eyes never leaving the Wolf.

Thus he didn't even see Starhawk as she stepped lightly through the arch behind him with half an adobe brick twisted into the bottom corner of a flour sack. She caught the man before he fell and held onto his crossbow, too, lowering him gently to the rock floor as Jeryn slipped in like a little shadow at her heels.

The ache of joy flooded Sun Wolf, painful as the rush of blood to a numbed limb, to see her alive and, at least by mercenary's standards, unhurt; it was so intense that he could only whisper as she came close enough to hear, "Where the hell have you been?"

She was pulling free the pins which held the wrist chains to the rings in the wall, the rags of her shirt hanging like a beggar's on her rangy frame and a layer of dust gummed to the bloody filth that coated her swollen face. "I leave the royal ball before the dancing is over to come here and rescue you, and that's all you can say?"

He lowered his arm and swore violently to keep from crying out in pain. Starhawk's arms were gentle, solid, and strong as a man's. For a moment their eyes met. Then he clasped her to him, gritting his teeth against the agony the movement cost him, holding her as hard as his shaking arms would permit, his face pressed to her sticky hair and the crossbow jammed uncomfortably between their two bellies. He tasted her blood and his own as their split and puffy lips met, regardless of the pain. Then he whispered, "Let's go." He knew if he didn't let go now, he never would.

Jeryn slipped past them to the darkest corner of the little cell and pushed low down on the wall. A small section of it fell back, and, without a word, the boy ducked in. Chains still dangling from his lacerated wrists, Sun Wolf slipped after him, and Starhawk, ducking through last, crossbow in hand, pulled the door shut behind them.

Tazey was waiting for them with saddled horses beside the old gate of the empty quarter that led down to the pass. Covered with dirt and soot as she was, Sun Wolf took her in his arms. He knew where that luring light had come from.

"Good-by." Her small hands were cold against his back through the holes in his torn shirt. "I wish you could have stayed. I'll need a teacher . . ."

"Rot good-by," the Wolf said shortly. "We may be getting the hell out of here, but I'm not leaving until I know what's behind this."

"You don't—" she began.

"The hell I don't." His single golden eye went from her to Jeryn, holding the horses in the shadows of the broken-down gate. "Aside from the fact that sooner or later Lady Illyra or Kaletha's going to track us down, I don't think that thing's stopped killing. We've got no guarantee about who its next victim's going to be. Since we don't even know what the range is, it could conceivably be either me or the Hawk or both."

From the direction of the main block of the fortress came a distant shout, then a rising clamor and torchlight spinning like mad fireflies along the walls. Starhawk remarked, "Either there's a skunk in the Hall or they know we're gone."

Sun Wolf glanced out through the broken-toothed maw of the gate to the chiaroscuro of velvet and ice that the moonlight scattered over the twisted land. An elf-owl hooted once from where ocotillo threw its shadows like a skeleton hand across the sand-drift near an old wall; the moon gleamed like a rim of frost on the spines of the Dragon's Backbone. "There a place we could hole up in the mountains where the horses could be hidden?"

Jeryn looked blank—he might know every underground tunnel and secret passage in Tandieras, but he'd never stepped willingly outside its walls in his life. Tazey said, "There's a deserted chapel high up in the side of the Binnig Rock—up there." She pointed to the dizzying bulk of the half dome. "The trail's pretty narrow, but it can be done on a horse."

He turned to Jeryn. "You think you can find your way up there tomorrow, as soon as you can slip away? I'm going to need somebody to read pieces of those books to me."

The boy nodded, dark eyes glowing.

"Good. Tazey, stay here and keep an eye on things—best you aren't both missing at the same time." He swung into the saddle. If Starhawk alone had been there, he probably would have groaned and cursed with pain; but as it was, he only gritted his teeth. "And see if you can't smuggle us weapons of some kind—and a blanket." He collected the reins and turned away through the narrow gate to the pewter moonlight of the narrow trail beyond.

Tazey asked softly, "Will you be all right tonight?"

Starhawk said, deadpan, "I think we'll manage to keep each other warm."

"Chief"

He turned his head sleepily to look down at the ivory-fine features of the woman who lay in the crook of his arm. The washy dawnlight turned her hair colorless, the bruises on her face almost black. The air was bitterly cold, so that even the harshness of the sacking and saddle blankets in which they were wrapped was welcome. The links of the slip-chain still around her neck jingled softly as she raised a scarred hand to touch one of the few unbruised portions of his face, with a gentleness no one would have guessed who'd seen her brain a man with a mace in battle.

She said softly, "Thank you."

"Did you think I wouldn't have given them whatever they wanted, told them whatever they wanted, to save you?"

She was silent a long time, while buried thought fumbled its painful way to the surface. The gray light seeping through the chapel's narrow door to lie over the two ragged fugitives silvered her eyes—he saw them flood with sudden tears. "I never thought anyone would," she said at last.

When next they spoke, the light had warmed on the thick tangle of brush and mesquite outside the chapel door, and wavering gleams of yellow and green reflected into the shadowy stone room from the catch pools outside. The slit windows above the little stone altar glowed with the wide nothingness of desert air, five hundred feet above the level of the crumbling talus and rock below. The chapels of the Mother were for those who would fight to reach her, not like the easy, open churches of the Triple God.

"Why'd you ask Jeryn about his etymology? About the difference between a witch and a wizard?"

Drowsing on the edge of sleep, Sun Wolf almost laughed. Only Starhawk's logical mind would bring a question like that out of the afterglow of lovemaking.

"What is the difference?"

Starhawk considered the two words for a time. "In the dialect of the north it's a difference of—of kind of magic," she said at last. "A wizard is an academic; the word 'witch' implies earth-magic, granny-magic sometimes—intuition. In the dialect of the Middle Kingdoms, and here along the cordillera, I've noticed that 'wizard' is masculine and 'witch' is feminine—the way 'God' is feminine in the singular and masculine in the plural."

"Close," he agreed, and sat up, shivering a little at the touch of the chill air. "But in the shirdar there's a different connotation, a pejorative one—the implication that the magic wasn't yours to begin with. The shirdane is a language of nuances. In it, like in the north, a wizard is an academic, one who studies, a scholar or an engineer. But the shirdane word for 'witch' is someone who buys her power, usually in trade for her soul. When they speak of the Witches of Wenshar, they aren't describing power—they're speaking of how power was acquired." He sat cross-legged under the ragged blanket and pushed back the faded strands of thinning hair from his scabbed, unshaven face.

There was something ironic, Sun Wolf thought, in his utter comfort in this bare stone cell. When he was the wealthiest captain of mercenaries in the West, he'd never have believed he would one day delight in being a ragged, filthy fugitive this way, sitting in a bare stone room with nothing but a half interest in a saddle blanket and four saddlebags full of stolen books to his name. *Nothing like a quick glance down into the Cold Hells to make you pleased with life on damn near any terms.*

"It's the demons of Wenshar that were the source of the Witches' power," he went on. "They traded their power, their service, to the Witches—became their servants."

"Are you sure?" Starhawk raised herself on one elbow and pulled the saddle blanket awkwardly over her bare shoulder. "Demons are—immortal. And immaterial. There are old legends of people controlling them, but why would they allow themselves to be controlled? We have nothing they'd want."

"Don't we?" His hoarse voice was soft in the watery gloom. "Think about it, Hawk. Demons have no flesh, as we know flesh; no blood; no passions. They are cold creatures, ephemeral, entities unattached to bodies. They can never die—and so they never live. I felt their minds all around me in Wenshar, Hawk; I felt their cold, that seeks after warmth." He leaned forward, resting his elbows on his knees.

"They crave heat—not heat as we understand it, or at least not as we understand it consciously, but the heat of the soul, of the blood—the heat of fear, for which they drive beasts and men, if they can trap them, to panic deaths, so they can drink it as it spills out of them; the heat of lust, which leads them to couple in dreams with men and women, feeding their partners the images that they crave, to warm themselves by that mortal fire. And the heat of hate, which is the best of all, because it doesn't fade with time.

"The demons in Wenshar became addicted to hate, the way men become addicted to dream-sugar. The Witches of Wenshar fed them, using their magic to open the channels between their minds and the demons', and the demons found they liked that food. There are earth-demons in many parts of the world, but mostly humankind avoids them, as they avoid humankind. Originally the House Cult of Wenshar may only have sought to control the demons, because their city was built where they lived. But later they sought to bend them to their bidding. Afterward they found there was a price to pay. That was the secret power of the Witches of Wenshar—that the demons would kill whomever they hated. But in return, they had to go on hating."

Starhawk glanced over at the untouched books, piled at the foot of the bare stone altar. Sun Wolf shook his head.

"It's only my guess," he said. "But the demons knew me for mageborn the minute I entered their city. They tried to get me to take that power, to use it as the Witches did. The Witches gave their hate to the demons, to feed on and to act on, but in doing so they gave them a taste for it. Corrupted them, if you like. Demons are immortal. While Altiokis dominated this part of the world, people would not admit to being mageborn, not even to themselves. Demons have been living in that city for over a century, like roaches, feeding on the piled rot of old hates. They're coming out of a long starvation."

In the glowing blue-green cleft of the doorway, a tiny rock-mouse paused, whiskers aquiver, silhouetted against the colors of leaf and stone. A flurry of doves swept past the entrance like a skiff of blown snow. Starhawk looked down at her hands for a long time.

"The kids say Nanciormis saw your face on the demon that came for him."

Sun Wolf nodded, remembering how, in the darkness of the temple in Wenshar, the demon eyes had glowed golden, like his own. In that moment, when their minds had touched . . . ? He hadn't forgotten the dead birds found after his own first night spent in this country.

"I can't explain it," he said slowly. "But I think I'd have known."

"According to Nanciormis, via Tazey, they didn't, always. That cuts both ways," she added after a moment. "The fact that you found the dead birds before the storm doesn't mean it couldn't have been Tazey herself. She may well not have known. In the north I've heard of knocking-demons, and there's always a young boy or girl somewhere involved. And she is mageborn."

"So's Kaletha," the Wolf said. "And if Kaletha's thirtyish now, she must have been in well into her teens while Queen Ciannis was alive —old enough to have been initiated into the cult, if Ciannis was its last survivor. Particularly if Ciannis was as frail as Nanciormis says and might have suspected she wouldn't survive a second childbirth."

"Maybe," Starhawk said. "It could account for Kaletha wanting as badly as she did to get Tazey into her teaching, if her own vanity didn't. But there was no change, nothing new happening with Kaletha that could have triggered all this. Why now? Why not nine months ago, when Altiokis died?"

"You're arguing as if the killings made sense. They may not." Sun Wolf heaved himself to his feet and gasped at the agony of his back and legs.

Starhawk pushed herself more or less upright also, moving as if she were in pain but not showing it on her face. "Don't get excited," she said in her usual calm voice. "It's going to be lots worse tomorrow. Let's see what the books have to say about all this."

Of the eighteen books, seven were in various forms of the old tongue of Gwenth, as it had been spoken in the Middle Kingdoms in the centuries before. Together, Starhawk and Sun Wolf limped to the rock-pools below the chapel and watered the horses and bathed in the freezing, shallow water. Sun Wolf shaved with Tazey's dagger and bound the messy, abraded flesh of his wrists with part of what was left of his shirt. It was fully light when they returned to the chapel and settled down to read.

"I don't like this," Starhawk said softly, looking up from the faded and grubby pages of the Book of the Cult. "Nanciormis was right. They didn't always know, especially not at first. But their mothers and sisters and aunts would watch for the signs, if the girl was mageborn, and would initiate her, teach her to control the demons her mind had summoned. It was only five or six generations, you know," she added, settling her bruised shoulders gingerly back against the wall. "That's not a long time in the history of the Ancient Houses. It looks as if there was a family cult before that time, but the demons probably came in when the mageborn streak surfaced. Unless . . ." She paused for a moment, frowning to herself at those words, then began thumbing back through the faded, close-written pages again, with their red and blue capitals, their loops and pothooks where words were abbreviated by a hurried scribe, seeking impatiently for something there which she could not seem to find.

Sun Wolf's yellow eye narrowed. "By my first ancestor, that palace must have been a hell to live in," he murmured. "Have you ever dealt with a knocking-demon, Hawk? Even when they aren't throwing things, or making noises, you can feel them in a place, watching you. No wonder no one would come to the defense of Wenshar when Kwest Mralwe sent armies through the passes."

In the forenoon Jeryn rode laboriously up the trail on Walleye, sweating in his ill-wrapped head veils and starting at every unfamiliar noise. He curled up in a corner of the chapel where a dim sun shaft fell through the weed-clogged roof hole of the rock chimney. While Starhawk pursued her own researches, Sun Wolf sat beside him, following the boy's finger along the scribbled black line of brushed writing. The more he heard, the greater his uneasiness grew.

All those who wrote of demons remarked upon the fact that in dreams they might show the features of those who sent them. Nowhere did it say that they could cloak themselves in the forms of those who had not.

They had known his name, in Wenshar. Could that have given them his form as well? Or was there another explanation?

I'd know it, he thought, over and over, while feeling the stir of fear in his veins. *By my first ancestor, I would sense it, in my dreams if nothing else . . .*

But the boy's voice droned on, over the names of the various demons—hundreds of them—and the obscene and hideous spells of their summoning. Sun Wolf remembered, years ago, a man in his troop who, disturbed suddenly in sound sleep, had strangled his mistress to death, taking several minutes to do it. Waking, he had sworn with bitter tears that he remembered nothing of it—that when the men had wakened him, he had been sitting by her corpse—and could not be convinced that it was not they who had done it and put the blame on him.

In the haunted halls of Wenshar, the painted shadows of the women had watched him from the walls, amusement in their dark eyes. They had initiated one another, the elder helping the younger along, cushioning the shock of that terrible knowledge. What was it to one who had not that help?

After Jeryn had gone and he and Starhawk were settling down to the meal of meat, bread, and wine that the boy had brought, along with blankets and a chisel to rid them of the last of their chains, he spoke of his fears. The Hawk thought the matter over, as if they had been discussing some third person whom neither knew well. "Do you hate Nanciormis?" she asked.

Sun Wolf considered. After what the commander had done to him and to Starhawk last night, he realized he should, but he didn't, really. Perhaps, he thought, it was because he'd done the same thing himself. "I don't trust him," he said at last. "He's too strong and too smart for the position he's in, or he thinks he is, anyway. Osgard seems to have been pretty shrewd to keep him where he is. He looks good, but he's irresponsible—he's a decent fighter, but he couldn't teach a dog to lift his leg to a tree. He could have got Jeryn killed one day, if he goaded him into trying a horse too strong for him. He's a schemer and a user and he gossips worse than an old woman. But no, I don't hate him. And I certainly didn't hate him before the attack."

"Or Incarsyn?" she pressed. "You care about Tazey, and you might say he insulted her."

"There wasn't enough to Incarsyn for anyone to hate." The Wolf took a bite of the tough, harsh-textured bread and stared thoughtfully at the canyon wall beyond the door, where the shadow of the rim lay across it in a slanting line of blue and gold as sharp as if it had been drawn with a rule, inked, and gilded. He added, "Tazey might have."

Starhawk shook her head. "She never wanted to marry him," she pointed out. "She just couldn't say so to her father—maybe couldn't admit it to herself. If he'd died before backing out of the match, maybe . . ."

"You think she wouldn't have feared her father would find some way to revive it, in spite of Illyra? Particularly if Nanciormis had told her what he told us about what Incarsyn had said of her?"

The woman's dark brows went up thoughtfully and she looked down into her wine cup, digesting that idea.

"You're still talking as if the killings made sense," the Wolf said. "They might not have. Tazey might have hated Incarsyn, might have hated Galdron for telling her she was damned—evidently she believed she hated Nanciormis enough, after whatever it was he said to her, for it to be her. That still doesn't explain Egaldus' death."

"Unless we're dealing with two killers," Starhawk said quietly. "Kaletha may very well have had reason to hate Egaldus, if he was trying to get her books away from her. She certainly had reason to hate Galdron."

"And Nexué?" the Wolf said. "For all she was a vicious old gossip, Hawk, she was pretty harmless. The way you deal with someone like that is to cast spells to make her hair fall out or her sciatica act up, not strew her guts over fifty square yards of ground."

"If you're sixteen, you might." Starhawk finished a piece of bread, tossed the crumbs to the threshold where three little black wheatears swooped down to fight over them. "And then, we don't know what Nexué knew. She was a spy as well as a gossip. If she'd seen Kaletha and Egaldus coupling like weasels in rut in the empty quarter, Kaletha might just want her dead to preserve that purity she's always throwing up in everyone's face. It would kill 'Shebbeth to find out her precious teacher is less than perfect. As badly as Kaletha sometimes treats her, she isn't anxious to give up that devoted a slave."

"You've changed your mind about her, then?"

"No." She leaned back against the dressing stone of the lintel. "I'm just arguing both sides. It doesn't sound like Kaletha—but it doesn't sound like you or Tazey, either." She frowned again, scouting the thought, then let it go. "As I said, there was no change in Kaletha's life, except one, which argues more than anything else that it *wasn't* her."

He cocked his head, curious.

"You," the Hawk said. "A rival, a barbarian, a boor. She hated you from the beginning. You should have been the first. A potential book thief . . ." She gestured towards the dark volumes, stacked at the foot of the altar, threads of reflected light gleaming dully gold and pewter on their bindings. "Also, you're the one with the greatest chance of figuring out what's going on. But there hasn't been an attack directed at you."

"Hasn't there?" The Wolf studied his bandaged wrists for a moment, the flesh around them bruised brown and stained now with the poultices he'd concocted to cleanse the wounds. "You know what was odd about that attack on Nanciormis? It was the only one to take place early enough in the evening for people to be around."

"You know," Starhawk said, "I thought there was something strange about that. Something—I don't know. During the calling of Galdron's spirit . . ." Her dark brows came together for a moment, as if she searched for some lost thought, then she shook her head. "But not only was the attack on Nanciormis the only one reasonably early enough to expect witnesses, but it was the only one which the victim survived."

Sun Wolf dusted the crumbs from his hands. "I don't think Nanciormis was the one who was supposed to die as a result of that attack," he said quietly. "I think it was me."

"Could Kaletha have done that?" she asked. "Sent an illusion which felt like the coming of a demon, with your face?"

"She might have," he said. "I can't think of a neater way to get rid of someone in a position to expose her without drawing blame to herself by killing me and narrowing the field still further. If she'd been dealing with demon magic from these books, she would have known what one felt like and put it together. Particularly if she was afraid to send the real demons after me, for fear I'd take them and twist them to my own will."

He got painfully to his feet and limped to the door. Outside, the narrow rock-cleft, sun-touched for only a brief hour at noon, was sinking again into cool green gloom. From here, he could smell the water and hear the sounds of the birds and beasts who came down to drink, so unlike the untouched, sterile catch-tanks of Wenshar. "In the Dark Book our little Scout read us this afternoon it said there always came a point at which the Witch realized her power, realized it was she who was causing the deaths of those she hated. I think Kaletha might have reached that point with Egaldus' death. She certainly didn't shed a hell of a lot of tears over it."

"Not where you'd see them, anyway," Starhawk put in softly.

"But Nexué, and Galdron, and maybe Egaldus, were all her enemies—and when Egaldus died she must have realized there were people who'd guess it. And she had to shift the blame. There was no—no *smell* of evil in Nanciormis' room after the attack. That might just have been an effect of the storm, but I'm not so sure."

"And Incarsyn?"

He glanced back at her over his shoulder, his one eye darkening with concern. "I don't know," he said. "That worries me. Maybe by that time the demons had begun to touch Tazey as well. Maybe . . ." He half turned back, drawing closed the clasps of his worn old sheepskin doublet, which had been part of Jeryn's contribution that afternoon.

The southern-window slit above the altar was dimming now, as darkness settled on the desert. Through it, nothing of the Fortress was visible, nor the town—only the endless planes of air and sand, marching away into a flat infinity, broken by the single whitish plume of dust where one of Nanciormis' scouts cantered back towards Tandieras after an unsuccessful day of search.

"So what are you going to do?"

He sighed heavily. "There's no way I can prove my innocence, or Kaletha's guilt. And if the demons have begun to touch Tazey's mind . . ." He turned back. Starhawk, her big hands clasped around bony knees, sat watching him in the blue glow of the witchfire. "I think if Tazey could get away from this place, she'd be all right," he said. "But I can't see her father letting her go, not to get the teaching she'll need. And untaught, God only knows to what channel her powers will turn." He leaned his powerful shoulders in the stone lintel. "We'll have to stop them both at the source."

Starhawk glanced again at the books. The witchlight, gleaming on the sand-polished jewels and the queer, twisted silver shapes that clasped them shut, seemed to impart a glowing half-life to them, as if they had spent the centuries, like the demons, dreaming in silence of alien longings. "Do you think you can?"

He nodded, though he felt by no means sure. "There are spells in the Demonary that provide for the binding of demons into a rock, or a tree, or an altar stone," he said. "The Book of the Cult lists all their names. If I can make a Circle of Darkness wide enough and draw them into it, it would keep them long enough for me to work such a binding, to hold them to the stones of Wenshar for eternity."

The woman who had been for years his second-in-command and who never failed to pour the cold and lucid water of her logic onto his strategies regarded him with those enigmatic gray eyes for a moment, then said, "If it works."

Sun Wolf nodded and tried to ignore the chill curl of dread at the thought of standing once more in that haunted temple. "If it works," he agreed.

CHAPTER

∾ 16 ∾

ORDINARILY IT WOULD HAVE TAKEN THEM UNTIL JUST AFTER noon to reach Wenshar from the tiny chapel on the Binnig Rock, but they were delayed, searching for certain herbs and stealing a bull calf from an isolated foothills ranch. By the time they entered the ruined city, the shadows were already beginning to slant over, the sun blinding but curiously heatless in the crumbled mazes of the lower town, a glaring line halfway up the chromatic rocks in the canyons. It took them a few hours to water their horses, stable them in the rear chamber of the temple Sun Wolf had used before, and to barricade them in. As he drew the Circles of Light around the door this time, Sun Wolf was interested to see how close his own half-learned, half-guessed defenses had been to the Circles as described in the Demonaries. Whatever happened, they knew they could not afford to lose the horses.

He thought with brief regret of the small cache of his and Starhawk's money, hidden behind a loose brick in the dusty little cell where they had slept and talked and made love. When this was over and the demons bound to the rocks of Wenshar for all time, they would have to flee; a dozen pieces of silver would come in handy, perhaps make all the difference, somewhere along the road between capture and escape.

But more than that, there was a sharp ache inside him as he realized that it would be years, if ever, before they would see Tazey and Jeryn again. That, too, was a sensation totally unfamiliar to him, as unfamiliar as the pain and terror he had felt for Starhawk's safety—as if, loving her, some wall within him had been irreparably fissured, and he had had thrust upon him the capacity to love others as well. He had come to look upon those two children as if they had been his own; his deceased ancestors were the only ones who might have kept track of the bastards he'd fathered over the years. Odd that the first children for whom he should feel responsible should be some other man's.

But if nothing else, Tazey would be safe. If he could not engineer her happiness, at least he could give her that.

"I don't like this, Chief," Starhawk said softly, as she watched the Wolf trace the final signs of the Circle of Light around her on the smooth-swept temple floor. The bleached smudge of daylight that lay like a rumpled carpet by the nearer door was fading. The gloom seemed thicker beyond the wavering rings of a dozen small fires whose smoke, in spite of the old air shafts hidden in the darkness of the ceiling, stung and burned the eyes. It would soon be night.

Sun Wolf sat back on his knees and used the ragged hem of his torn shirt to daub loose charcoal and ochre from his scabbed fingers. "I don't like your even being here," he retorted. He wiped sweat from his face with the back of his hand, leaving long smudges of black and rust. The vast silence of the dark temple around them picked up the echoes of his broken voice. "But I'd like it a hell of a lot less if you were where I couldn't see you."

"I didn't mean that."

Looking across the lines of the Circle at the thin, strong face, with its old scars and rock-crystal eyes and sun-whitened hair, warmed to honey by the light of the small fire enclosed with her in the enchanted ring, Sun Wolf knew too well what she did mean.

They had both been a dozen times over the rite of summoning in the Demonary and the Book of the Cult of Wenshar. Near the lighter doorway into the entry hall the bull calf lowed plaintively, as if it knew it had reason to fear the slow gathering of darkness.

The central canyon, as they had walked up it, dragging the unwilling calf between them, had been dead silent. The crunch of their feet on the gravel, the slip and scrape of the calf's hooves, and its frightened bawling, had echoed in that horrible stillness, prickling the hair on the Wolf's nape with the sensation of being watched. Now and then, from the tail of his eye, he had glimpsed movement. Several times he had turned his head, knowing there would be nothing when he did so. And there was not. Familiar as he had come to be with the haunted canyons and the not-quite-empty black eyes of the stone-cut houses, still his heart thumped hard against his ribs, and the sweat crawled clammily down his backbone at those soft, scritching movements and the touch of those unseen eyes.

What little light filtered into the temple from the entry hall was fading.

He and the Hawk, working together and as swiftly as the unfamiliar rituals would let them, had swept and ritually cleansed the temple. Sun Wolf had repeated the archaic spells learned from the Demonary as he had drawn the runes in the temple's four corners, first slowly and clumsily, checking the moldering black book to make sure they were right, then with more certainty in his harsh, scraped voice. It would take him longer to form and consecrate the greater Circle, which was his ultimate goal, without her help—longer, as the weariness grew on his stiff and aching arms and tired mind; but he was not having her unprotected once night came.

His back and arms smarting all over again, his mind fighting the strange sleepiness of concentration held too strictly and too long, he paced and marked out the biggest Circle of all, encompassing the stone altar and the pit before it in the floor. Meticulously, he drew the signs on the stone floor with lumps of charcoal, with sticks of red ochre, and with thin lines of powdery white sand like the finest sugar —Circle within Circle, Darkness within Light, points oriented like a compass rose to the corners of the universe, long curves sweeping to enclose power within. Instead of marking the rune circle on the outside of the defensive points, he marked the runes on the inside, to imprison rather than repel. And deliberately, he left two of the runes unwritten.

He flinched, and looked up. He'd left his doublet and head veils crumpled in the corner near Starhawk's small Circle, and the chill air crept through the holes in his bloodstained shirt to touch the damp hair on his back. It was now utterly dark. Repeating the words of the rune-spells over and over to himself, he had let his mind slip into the trance of concentration. He had no idea how much time had passed.

Outside, the canyon lay submerged in chilled obsidian darkness. Of the half-dozen little fires lit around the temple floor, all had died but the one small blaze in the Circle with Starhawk. By the dim throb of that orange light he saw the glint of her eyes, the pale blur of her shirt-sleeved arms still wrapped around her drawn-up knees. In the utter silence, he could hear her breathing, steady and calm. Then the calf bleated again, desperate fear in the sound.

Sun Wolf got to his feet, like a man startled by some other sound than that. His stiff back muscles stabbed like a hidden stiletto. He was aware of his own hunger and thirst, the stink of his unwashed body, and the dark heavy odor of spent wood smoke, the smell of the rock, of dust, of . . . incense? Through the darkness, for a moment, it was as if he smelled myrrh burned two centuries ago, like scents caught in women's hair. Through his skin he was aware of a sandstorm, building somewhere out in the darkness of the desert. Though cold, the air felt suddenly stifling, hushed with expectation. In the terrible silence, he nearly jumped out of his skin at the whisper of one breath of wind, trailing over the stone like the hem of a woman's silk gown.

Brimming with shadow, the pit lay before him. He turned from it, and his own shadow brushed over the mottled sides of the broken altar. Why had he thought, for just that moment as he glimpsed it from the tail of his eye, that it stood whole again? Outside the frail glimmer of Starhawk's little fire, the darkness seemed thicker, clotted in the corners of the vast room like the vapors of old decay which would never be cleared away.

The demons lay in the stone, like sharks below the surface of the sea, and watched.

The calf bellowed again, desperate with fear.

He hated what he knew must come next.

Starhawk had not understood it and had only been repelled when Jeryn had read in his cool little alto voice how the Witches of Wenshar had summoned their demons. Very few of them had used animals in the pit, once they'd realized more demons would come if the victim were a human child. Even back then, it seemed, orphans were cheap in the poor quarters of the city. Some of the Witches, the Book of the Cult had said, could summon the demons without sacrifice; but when Starhawk had suggested trying to do so, the Wolf had categorically refused. The book had not said it, but he had sensed what he would have to be projecting with his mind—filth and hatred and the unholi-est of urges—to bring them. He'd rather kill a calf, even in the grue-some way prescribed.

It took more nerve than he'd thought it would to walk to the edge of the pit. He wasn't certain what he feared he would see there, with his wizard's sight, in the swimming blackness below. But it contained only a little sand drifted in the corners, and the skeleton of what looked like a dove, white as a bit of lace dropped upon the loose gravel of its floor.

He wondered why the sudden thought of how deep that gravel might lie over the bedrock repelled him like a nauseating smell.

Turning back, he kindled the little heap of aromatic woods he had left on the bare stump of the broken altar and from it lit two fire-bowls which he set in place of the two missing runes on the inner Circle. Stepping carefully between them, he walked out of the Circle and over to where Starhawk sat beside her little fire.

Without stepping over the protecting barrier, he said softly, "You all right?"

She nodded. She had been silent for hours, watching him, gray eyes inscrutable. He had been totally absorbed in his task and wondered now what she had seen in the darkness as it had closed around him. All his nerves prickled, his mind screaming to him to beware in this vast darkness where the dry rustle of gowns and hair seemed to have only just that moment stopped in the black beyond the fire's light.

"Whatever you see," he said quietly, "whatever you think is happening, don't step out of the Circle. Once it's broken, it will be no protection to you."

She nodded. "I know."

"They shouldn't be able to get in at you." Of that, at least, mercifully, he was now sure. "Once I draw the last two runes and complete the great Circle, they shouldn't be able to get out. With them trapped, I should be able to work the binding-spells to hold them to the rocks of Wenshar forever."

She cocked her head a little. The smudgy firelight deepened the shadows of her hollowed eyes and the lines that fanned backward from them on the unswollen side of her face and scored deep marks from her nostrils to the soft corners of that calm mouth. "How long's that going to take you?"

He muttered a curse at her for seeing what she saw: the marks of fatigue on his face; the dark ring of weariness around his single eye and the bruised look of the lid; the taut mouth beneath its straggly mustache; and the strange pallor under the stubble of his golden beard. He was close to the edge and he knew it, nearing the point where the cumulative stresses of flight and concentration would begin to cause mistakes. Even the smallest break in his mental barriers could be fatal in dealing with the demons of Wenshar. "Until just after dawn, rot your eyes, and what the hell business is it of yours?"

"And the sandstorm? Will that break before you're done?"

The Wolf hesitated. The sandstorms, as he and Nanciormis both had learned, would scatter the demons on their winds—but as they both had known also, where the demons were able to walk during the killer winds, they walked more strongly. They fed upon violence, even the violence of the air.

As if she read his answer in his silence, she said, "Can you send it away? Or delay it?"

He shook his head. He could feel the whisper along his bones, a crawling tingle as if his nerves were being drawn from his flesh one fiber at a time; it was coming and it was strong. His hoarse voice quiet, he said, "I haven't the strength to spare, Hawk. Not from what I have to do. By dawn . . ." He shrugged and spread his hands. "We may have time. An hour would be all we need."

Dark wind licked the tiny fire; Sun Wolf swung around as the bull calf bellowed again, in despair as well as terror. The poor creature was jerking wildly at its rope, its bound feet bouncing and threshing, its eyes gleaming in the faint reflections of the fire. Sun Wolf was aware again of how dark it was in the temple, how the shadows seemed to creep forward, curious, questing fingers seeking to probe his body and his soul. He shifted his aching shoulders again, his heart beginning to pound at the thought of what lay ahead.

Softly, the Hawk said, "Good luck, Chief. May the spirits of your ancestors lend you a hand."

"The spirits of my ancestors would disown me for messing with demons," he replied, the levity he had intended hushed from the raven-croak of his voice. "They at least had brains." He wanted to reach across, to touch her, like a man drawing luck from some talisman of dark-stained ivory and gold, but even that would have broken the Circle and negated the forces of protection held so tenuously in the tingling air. The little fire before her feet was sinking, and he could not even spare the power to summon witchlight to brighten that ghastly darkness for her. He wondered, as he turned from her and walked toward the terrified calf beside the door, how much of what was going to happen she would even see.

It was going to be a hideously long night.

The calf fought Sun Wolf's grip on its stubby horns as best it could, bracing its bound feet, writhing as he half dragged, half carried it toward the Circle. The ghost-whispers of wind murmuring in the ventilation shafts echoed like an eerie chanting. Had they chanted, Sun Wolf wondered, as two or three of their number had dragged some poor terrified child to the altar? Chanted to summon the demons, to hold their own powers of protection against them?

He remembered again the painted eyes of those worn frescoes and the dark cynicism of their ironic regard. A slashing hoof cut his shin; slobber from the calf's muzzle slimed his hands and stung in the half-scabbed demon bites; its rough coat abraded the skin of his side as it flung its weight against him. In his mercenary days, he'd tortured men and taken pleasure in torturing them, if they'd hurt or betrayed him or some member of his troop. Why did slaughtering this bull calf, who'd have ended up dead at cattle-killing time before the onset of winter anyway, make his soul cringe as it did? Why did those huge brown eyes, white-rimmed with terror, seem so human, staring up into his? He dragged the animal between the two fire pots and the calf bellowed again in fear of the flames . . .

And from the corner of his eye he saw movement.

A glow that illuminated nothing flickered in the darkness behind him.

They were coming.

He was battered and aching in every muscle of his tired body by the time he got the calf wrestled up onto the uneven altar stone. The beast flopped like a landed fish, its pitiful, frantic bellowing for its mother turning the vast stone darkness into a ringing sound-chamber whose echoes went through Sun Wolf's skull. He roped its hind feet together, and then to its already-bound forelegs; sweat ran down his ribs and back, sticking the torn rags of his shirt to his body and burning in the abrasions of his wrists within their filthy bindings. He worked from the front side of the altar rather than the back, hating the open, silent mouth of the pit at his back, but preferring that, for the moment, to the alternative. Where he stood now, panting, smelling the warm animal smell of the calf, the dirt, and the aromatic woods of the small fire beside the altar steps, he could look between the two fire pots into a Stygian corridor that seemed to run back far past the rear wall of the temple in its concealing shadows, a corridor extending into the blackness of the earth, into realms he had never known and never wanted to know—into time.

He could see them now, far back along that corridor, bobbing like marsh-lights over swamps long dry. He could hear the whisper of their chittering laughter. The fire beside the altar seemed to wink in the glinting reflection of their eyes.

The knife hilt pressed like an arm bone into his hand. With deliberate brutality, he slashed the tendons of two of the calf's legs, one fore and one hind. The poor beast cried out with pain as well as terror, the smell of the blood on the knife mingling with the smoke, filling the darkness of the room. Something cold brushed Sun Wolf's shoulder. Whirling, warrior's muscles honed by terrors of his own, he almost cried out himself at what he saw, inches from his own face—the skeletal countenance of a demon, its head the size of a calf's, brown eyes bulging from sockets of terror, complete even to the fringe of white eyelashes—the calf's eyes. Under them, the unspeakable mouth smiled.

Turning back swiftly, Sun Wolf slashed open the calf's belly, blood pouring hot and slippery over his hand. He felt the prickle of cold claws in his back, the thin, bodiless muzzling of teeth against the skin of his neck; he forced himself not to look, not to think, not to panic. In the split second before the hot fumes of the blood and the smell of the sagging entrails choked him, he remembered being buried alive in a collapsing sapper tunnel at the siege of Laedden, remembered the torture pits of Elthien the Cruel, and remembered the floating flame speck whirling in the darkness of the dungeons of the Wizard King Altiokis, the pain of it lancing into his left eye . . .

He hadn't panicked then, and he had lived.

The blood smell pierced his brain. His head throbbed with the frantic lowing of the tortured calf. His mind felt locked, clamped in a crystal grip that he dared not open. *The Women of Wenshar had all done this*, he thought dizzily.

But they had enjoyed it.

As if he were someone else, he watched a demon like the glass skeleton of a serpent twine down his outstretched arm, to lick the blood from his hand with a human tongue. The edges of the altar were thick with demons, seeping from the stone, floating down through the air, and whispering and giggling in straw-frail descant to the agony cries of the calf. One of them smiled at him with a mouth like Tazey's, except for the fangs. Another had breasts like Starhawk's, even to the scar. Their cold pressed all around him, teeth like chips of broken glass chewing at the bandages on his wrists. Worse than the cold was the knowledge, from he knew not where, that it would only take a slight giving of his mind to feel that cold as warmth.

He dragged the calf from the altar, demons swarming and crawling over it, bouncing weightlessly free and floating in the air, limbs dangling, like monster wasps over a rotting peach. He cut free the calf's feet and shoved it over the edge into the pit, averting his eyes from what he half-saw swarming below. The calf bellowed in agony and terror, staggering from side to side in the pit, crippled, bleeding, dying, unable to escape the things that had now begun to tear at it. Through the glittering, crawling swarm of demons, Sun Wolf could see the dusty hide matted with blood, as Tazey's mare had been. In the darkness of the pit, demons flashed like starlight on glass, colors deepening their skeletal shapes, blood spattering them, and their eyes the dark eyes of women.

The Witches of Wenshar had summoned demons so—and not with animals.

From the sticky trail that led from altar to pit, he daubed up enough blood to mark the last two runes, as he knelt between the rune circle and the outer boundary of the Circle of Light. He then traced in the last markings, the calf's blood mingling with his own where the demons had ripped the bandages from his wrists.

The Circle was finished. It would hold the demons—for a time.

And for a time, he could only crouch on his knees outside the Circle, his blood-slimed hands pressed together over his mouth, shaking so badly he was unable to stand, like a small child exhausted by fleeing to safety from that which whispers in the dark. He felt cold, empty, sick, and weary unto death. Yet he knew he had a night's work ahead of him, to bind the demons permanently to the stones . . . And he must start at once, before the sandstorm, whose approach bit and whispered at his nerves, gave them its electric strength.

He raised his head, and saw that Starhawk's Circle of Protection was empty.

Shock jolted him like a fist driven into the pit of his stomach. He stared for a moment at the tiny glow of its smoky fire and the dark flower of points, curves, and runes on the stone floor, all with the inner glow of magic gone.

"Chief!"

He swung around. She stood beside the darkness of the temple door, face and throat and her one bare shoulder and arm white against those horrible shadows. With her was Tazey.

Somehow, he managed to get to his feet. The two women started to come toward him, and he waved them violently back. In the peripheral vision of his single eye, he could see the cloudy swarm of corpse-light weaving and billowing above the pit, like hornets over a burning nest. The women had no business coming anywhere near.

He stumbled to them across the patterned sandstone of the floor. Reflected in their eyes, he saw how he must look—bloody, scratched, with the filth on his face and the dark line of the eye patch standing blackly against the pallor beneath. Starhawk put out her hand to his neck, and he flinched—for the first time he was aware that the demons had bitten him, shallow scratches, like love bites. He remembered what he had read of the Witches of Wenshar, and the simile turned him ill.

"They came, then."

The Hawk had, of course, seen nothing. Even now he could see her looking toward the altar and the pit; in her eyes he could see no awareness of the evil lights floating above the glow of the pit. He fought a hysterical urge to laugh. "They came."

But by the horror on Tazey's face as she stared toward the pit, he knew she saw something and he wondered obliquely if their forms looked the same to her.

She tore her gaze from it and looked back at his face. "You have to flee," she said quietly. "Nanciormis and his men are coming. Kaletha's with them. They saw Jeryn coming back and followed his trail. I got the fastest horse I could. If you can get even a little ways away from here before the storm comes, it will cover your tracks."

"And you?" Starhawk's arm tightened around the girl's slim, straight shoulders.

"I'll—I'll wait it out here."

"The hell you will," the Wolf rumbled. "That Circle isn't going to hold the demons forever . . ."

"You could draw one around me," she offered, clearly frightened but not about to obligate him to help her by admitting it. "I wouldn't be in any danger then."

Sun Wolf put his hands on her shoulders, the blood on his fingers leaving sticky red blots on her faded pink shirt. "You'll be in danger as long as you live, if those demons aren't bound to the rocks that spawned them here and now," he said quietly. "So will everyone in Tandieras—everyone in Pardle. Whoever has been calling them . . ." He hesitated and looked away from that absinthe gaze. "It isn't only danger from them. If the Hawk and I ride on, and there's another killing, you may very well take the blame. I'm sorry, Tazey. I know what they did with the Witches . . ."

She flinched—evidently Nanciormis had told her that, too. But she only said, "It's what they're going to do to you."

"How long do we have?"

She shook her head. "I don't know. I rode as fast as I could. I could see their dust behind me and their torches after it got dark, but I lost sight of them when I came into the ruins. An hour, two hours, maybe. They'll be hurrying," she added, "because of the storm."

It was close. He could feel it turning, far out in the desert—dust columns like mountains, black-bellied anger holding night and blotting dawn. His struggle to keep his mind locked against the probing lusts of the demons had left him shaky with fatigue; he had little enough power left to complete the binding-spells. Within the enchanted Circle, he could hear the demons chittering furiously over the fading wails of the dying calf.

"I can't turn it," he said softly. "In any case we may need it . . ." He hesitated. They would need it for escape, from Nanciormis and his men, perhaps from the demons, if it came before the binding-spells were done . . .

There were too many variables, pressing upon his aching mind like the collapsing weight of a tunnel roof. He could sense the anger of the demons now, as they began to scratch and whisper at the rune-circle that held them in. The light of Starhawk's little fire, far back in the vast cavern behind them, was going, and he knew he had no strength to spare, either to make witchlight or kindle the ashes again. His hoarse voice low to hold it steady, he said, "Take care of the fire, Hawk. I'll do what I can to finish and get us out of here, but it can't be rushed." If the demons got out, the Hawk and Tazey would be in danger, too.

She said softly, "I know." Tightening her arm around Tazey's shoulders, she led her back toward the dying glow of the flames. Sun Wolf stood for a moment, willing strength back into his numbed muscles and shaken mind, as he had willed it on a dozen occasions in the camps of war throughout the years, rallying his men to fight or his own bruised body to haul himself out of some peril or other . . . They all seemed so trivial now, compared to what he must face.

He could smell dawn coming, hours away. If there was even a little daylight between the retreating hem of night and the coming of the storm, it would help, but he sensed now there wouldn't be. Whatever happened, it was going to be close.

The awareness of the storm grew on him as he dragged out the small pack of implements he had assembled and the battered black Demonary with its crumbling leather cover. The storm's electricity chewed at his bones as he drew further signs on the floor and repeated the words, marking the runes and the great curves of the power-lines, digging strength and the last glitters of magic from the marrow of his bones to summon and fix the power of the ritual in the air.

As he had in the snake pit, he cursed his own sloth in pursuit of Starhawk's meditations, cursed his arrogance in refusing to believe entirely what Kaletha had grudgingly tried to teach him, and felt the power slip with his concentration, even as he cursed. He brought his whole mind back, to center on his work—runes drawn, softly shining in the air, and the sweet resinous smells of the aromatic herbs, the search for which had further delayed their arrival in Wenshar earlier that day. He relaxed into the ritual, willing himself to see the reality of the light-runes that flickered into shape between his hands—the clumsy, heavy-knuckled hands of a warrior, nicked with scars and gummed, like a butcher's, with blood. He forced each gesture to be calm and unhurried and precise, sinking his mind and thoughts into the soft chant of the words, unfamiliar at first, then stronger as his tongue caught their alien rhythm. He forced his mind not to be caught in wondering contemplation of the glowing ritual itself. That was perhaps the hardest of all.

He repeated the names of the demons, as they had been known and written over the years by the women of the cult, summoning each, binding each, holding it to the honey-yellow sandstone beneath his feet with the ritual mix of herbed wine and blood, commanding it never to depart from this place, never to walk upon the air, never to seek surcease of its cravings in the dark warmth of men. He felt their anger and their rage shimmering from the pit as he walked the outer perimeter of the Circle and repeated their individual names. And he felt his own exhaustion twist his sinews as he dredged and scraped power from his heart, like a starving man scraping the scum of rice-boilings from the rim of an empty pot.

He couldn't let himself stumble. He couldn't let his cracking concentration break. The demons were swarming against the glowing barriers of the Circle of Darkness now, their arms edged with color and their cold, chitinous bodies burning with smoky phosphorescence, whispering in thin voices that stole like wind through the chinks in his soul. It had grown hot in the temple, the air close and thick with the coming storm. Gluey wind kissed his cheek as he passed between the Circle and the doors, the hot electricity of dust . . . then, sharply, the smell of horses.

Starhawk had gone to the door. It was a small entrance, narrow and tucked away; she'd be able to hold it . . .

He dragged his concentration back. He could not even permit himself to speculate on how long the ritual would last, could not let that break the silence he held like perilously friable armor around his heart. The demons; the storm; Tazey sitting near the broken protective Circle, feeding twigs to the little fire, her absinthe gaze dark with horror as she saw the ragged heat-swirl of the demons and sensed the tearing cold of the demons' minds seeking a way into his. The far-off call of voices touched his consciousness, the rattle of weapons, the scuffle near the door, and the smell of new blood. He heard the chittering of demons and the weak groaning—by his ancestors, he'd never have thought the calf would have lived that long in the pit. Arms aching, he traced the signs in the air again, his numbed mind repeating the formulae, thanking all the spirits of his ancestors that the magic took most of its strength from the building power of the rite, not from his own emptied reserves.

There was another cry from the door and the hiss and clash of swords. He pulled his mind back again as his warrior's reflexes twitched. There were too many of them for her, even in that narrow way. The demons swirled up like rags of fire above the pit—a glowing holocaust breaking against the ceiling—screamed at him in voices he knew he alone could hear, and reached skinny arms for him. He raised his hands again, his back muscles a twisting spine of flame.

Then in the darkness deep at the back of the temple, where the second door was, he saw the glint of a crossbow bolt—not aimed at him. Without turning his head he knew where Starhawk stood, sword in hand, silhouetted now against the black rectangle of the narrow entrance, a dead man and a wounded one at her feet.

He yelled, "DROP!" the second before the iron bow whapped, hideously loud in the echoing temple. Spinning, he was aware of all that fragile creation of magic and light that hung in the air around him shattering like kicked glass. Rocketing iron clashed on stone; footsteps thundered, racing across the temple floor toward him from the inner door. He swung to meet the two men who fell upon him, bearing him backward. The sacrificial knife was in his hand as he made a despairing dive inside the reach of one attacker's drawn sword. At the last second he twisted, springing aside from the second man's sword . . .

And he felt it, when the next thrust drove him backward over the Circle of Darkness.

He screamed, "NO!" as he hit the stone floor, and for an instant the demons swirled like hornets around him, a rending glitter of claws. Then the two men in the green leathers of the Tandieras guards were on him. He tried to get up. The knife fell from his bleeding hand as his back struck the stone of the altar; the weight of human arms and bodies twisted him face down on the stone. Edged metal pressed up under his jaw.

For a moment there was nothing but the smell of blood on the stone where his face pressed it and the thin, sharp push of his pounding veins against the pressure of the razor edge. Then from somewhere Nanciormis' voice said, "Is there anything in the pit?"

The soft vibration of boots through the stone under his cheek. No sound.

Then, "Dead calf, sir. Fair tore to pieces it is. He was sacrificing, right enough."

"Anything else?"

"No, sir."

More footfalls. Closer now, Nanciormis said, "So. It is as we said. He is the witch."

Sun Wolf raised his head from the stone, the blade against his throat giving back slightly as he did so. The commander stood at the pit's edge, looking down into it; his full lips thinned in an expression of disgust and horror, but every line of that thick, muscular back reflected satisfaction like a smirk.

And well he might feel so, the Wolf thought bitterly. His accusations were borne out beyond the shadow of any man's doubt. Beyond in the darkness he glimpsed the shapes of Starhawk, standing between the black-robed Kaletha and half a dozen guards, and of Tazey, shivering tearfully in the uncertain arms of the faithful Anshebbeth.

In all the silent blackness of the temple, there was no other movement. On the floor, his own footmarks and those of Nanciormis and the guards scuffed through the lines of the Circle. The smell of blood and smoke hung on the air like the stink of a battlefield, but the demons were gone.

CHAPTER

∽❧ 17 ❧∽

"*T*URN THE STORM?" KALETHA'S SHORT LAUGH REEKED BIT-
terness, like sweat in a beggar's rags. "You'd put it to better use if you
tied that barbarian thief hand and foot and pushed him out in it. It
would save Illyra's torturer the trouble of flensing the meat from his
bones." Her white hand, like a spider in the darkness against its black
homespun sleeve, stroked the rotting cover of the Demonary that she
held like a child to her full breasts. "Both of them," she added spitefully, glancing across at Starhawk, who sat, hands bound, in watching
silence. Starhawk met her eyes calmly, without apology. It was Kaletha
who looked away. From where he lay Sun Wolf could see her fingers
tremble with anger.

He sighed and let his head drop back to the patterned amber stone
of the floor. He was glad only to be out of that haunted temple,
though this wide oval chamber deep in the center of the palace maze
wasn't much of an improvement as far as he was concerned. Most of
the doors in the old palace had been battered from their hinges by the
invading troopers of Dalwirin a century and a half ago; to escape the
fury of the storm, whose voice had begun to rise in the canyons outside, it had been necessary to come deep in. The absence of drifted
sand and debris had told them that this inner chamber was a safe
refuge.

From the storm, Sun Wolf amended, watching how the torches flickered nervously in the crossing drifts of wind from the ventilation shafts. *From the storm.*

Anshebbeth wet her lips and glanced across at the Wolf. "Are you . . ." Her voice sank, an exaggerated whisper above the conspiratorial murmur of the wind in the shafts. "Are you sure he's *safe?*"

Annoyed, Sun Wolf rolled to a slightly more comfortable position on his back, his shoulders and his arms, bound behind him, piercing him with sharp pain. He'd long ago learned that, when one is tied up, there is no such thing as a comfortable position. "Hell, no, I'm not safe," he growled. "And none of us is, in this demon-haunted hell hole."

"Be silent," Kaletha snapped. Everyone was on edge. The heat and electricity of the storm plucked and teased at the nerves and set up a throbbing in the brain. Impatient and contemptuous, she went on, "There are no demons. The only thing to fear is your killer's mind and your stolen magic, and those, yes, are safely bound."

Anshebbeth, sitting huddled beside the silent Tazey, looked little comforted, but Sun Wolf could have told her that even without the spells laid on his wrist chains, she had nothing to fear from him. He felt emptied, as if after long sickness or starvation, like grass burned to its roots. In a way, that troubled him more than the binding of his powers. The demons had been summoned, their appetites whetted, not satisfied. They were still abroad in the storm-hot, hazy darkness of the painted halls.

"You've bound my magic, Kaletha, but not my mind. The demons in this place are real."

"If you are not silent," she said, low and perfectly steady, "I'll have one of the guards come over here and cut out your tongue. Do you understand?"

One of the little cluster of frightened guards glanced up from their huddle around a small fire directly beneath a vent shaft, then looked quickly away, pretending he had not heard. They might be under Nanciormis' orders to obey Kaletha, Sun Wolf thought, but they weren't at all happy about it.

A gust of wind kicked at the blaze, sending sparks whirling up. Sun Wolf shivered, seeing again how the demons had whirled above the pulsing glow of the pit. The guards drew nervously together—young men and women recruited from the cordillera mining towns, trained to fight, perhaps, but only to fight what they could see. In the unsteady light, their shadows writhed over the honey-colored sandstone pilasters circling the walls and lent to the painted figures on the plaster a subtle and furtive life.

Though the storm winds did not blow here, the air was curtained with fine dust, which lent a ghastly, muted quality to the firelight and made Sun Wolf's head ache. In that hideous haze, nothing seemed quite as it should be. All around the room they watched, mocking, from the faded walls—mother and daughter, grandmother and daughter-in-law, crones and girls with dark eyes and too-knowing smiles. He felt them, like ghosts, listening, staring down at the last Princess of the House who sat head bowed, beside her governess, not daring to raise her eyes. Kaletha, too, seemed to feel the pressure of those ironic gazes, but she remained straight-backed as a queen, as if daring them to show themselves.

And he was troubled with the thought that they might.

Somewhere the wind sobbed in the corridors; Anshebbeth slewed around to face the empty door from which the sound seemed to come, then edged closer to her teacher. With thin, shaking hands she plucked at the red-haired woman's sleeve.

"Please," she whimpered. "Can you—Can you do anything? This is a terrible place, Kaletha. I know it, I can feel it. We shouldn't be here. The Captain is right, it is haunted."

Kaletha jerked her arm away and rubbed her temples, as if doing so could crush out the splitting pain of the storm-ache within. "You're the one who's haunted," she snapped irritably. Her eyes darted to the door and back again. "Haunted by your own fears, which he plays upon like a common charlatan."

"No . . ."

"There are no demons." Her mouth was suddenly rigid with rage. "Even you believe his lies now, as everyone does."

Anshebbeth stammered, "No—"

"Then why are you afraid?" Kaletha cut at her. "He used my magic, stole it, twisted it to work evil out of his own greed and vice. His greed has given wizardry an evil name that shall never be eradicated, leaving me—*me*—and all who come after to suffer for it. That's all there is. The power comes from the mage, from the mind, not from some—some desert legend or djinn of shirdar superstition."

"But what if he's right?" Anshebbeth's eyes, black and liquid, shirdar eyes, flickered from one empty socket doorway to the next.

She was shivering as she tried to draw nearer for comfort, and angrily Kaletha moved away. "There were demons in the temple where we found him: I sensed it, felt it. And I felt them . . . the night Egaldus—"

"Will you stop whining!" Kaletha swung around, blue eyes blazing in the firelight. "Don't you speak to me of Egaldus! What would you know about demons or anything else?"

Spots of red flared on Anshebbeth's white cheeks. "Just because Egaldus was a more apt pupil than I doesn't mean I know nothing—" she began shrilly.

"Apt!" Kaletha's laugh was like a dog's bark, harsh and false. "You don't know what you're talking about!"

"Don't I?" Anshebbeth's thin nostrils flared, her black eyes widening with a long-pent boil of fermented rage as the storm triggered her temper as it had triggered Kaletha's. "And whose fault is that? Because you'd rather have taught him than me . . ."

"He had more promise—he had the power—"

"He had you!" Anshebbeth almost screamed. "Again and again, for all your talk of purity! I heard you tell the Captain that, through your window—I heard it! You taught him because he was a man, because he'd lie with you and pretend he loved you!" Tears flooded the dark eyes. "*I* love you! *I* could have given you everything he did . . ."

"When? While you were playing the slut in Nanciormis' bed?"

The tears spilled over, creeping down the blotched, swollen cheeks. Starhawk, sitting unnoticed by the wall, watched the scene with head tipped a little to one side, gray eyes suddenly sharp with interest. Hysterically, Anshebbeth cried, "At least he cares for me for what I am—which you never have—never . . ."

"Oh, for God's sake, don't snivel!" Kaletha turned away and pressed her hands to her head again. Anshebbeth fell back, her hand rubbing nervously at her throat, her face working with stress and grief.

Tazey reached out to touch her comfortingly. "Don't. She doesn't really mean it. Everyone loses their temper during a storm." But at that moment footfalls rang in the darkened hall. With a sob, Anshebbeth flung herself to her feet and, as Nanciormis came through the dead socket of the door beside her, fell desperately into his arms.

For one second Sun Wolf thought the commander would thrust her off him. His thick face, doughy-looking with strain, twisted in revulsion as Anshebbeth's skinny arms clutched at his shoulders. The two guards behind him went on into the oval room with carefully averted eyes, not wanting to look at their commander and his hysterical, middle-aged mistress; that, too, showed on Nanciormis' face. He patted her heaving back perfunctorily while she ground her flat breasts and running nose into the soft green leather of his doublet, but the Wolf could see in his face only the desire to get this over with and get her off him as quickly as he gracefully could. Sun Wolf supposed he should have thought better of the commander for taking even that trouble, but suspected Nanciormis would have shown less forbearance without the presence of an audience.

He turned to trade a glance with Starhawk and saw her gaze, not on Nanciormis, but on Tazey. The girl was watching her uncle and her governess, nauseated cynicism in her eyes.

"That's right, go to him!" Kaletha jeered viciously. She had not forgiven the public revelation about Egaldus. "You'll never see, will you? If I was never able to touch magic within your mind, it was because your mind wasn't willing—because you had other fish to fry. It was you who lied, not I!"

Anshebbeth was sobbing miserably. "No! No!" Nanciormis, with the exasperation of an insensitive man who finds himself facing a scene, shoved her aside and strode over to the Witch.

Very softly, under the cover of the commander's angry bluster, Starhawk said, "Tazey?"

The girl turned her head. Through the blurred apricot haze of dust, tears glinted in the shadows.

"What did Nanciormis say to you?" asked the Hawk. "What made you hate him so much that you thought it was you who had summoned the demons? *Was* it about your magic?"

Even in that strange gloom, Tazey's face went first scalded pink, then white with shame. In a stifled voice she said, "No. He . . . He tried to kiss me." She moved over closer to them, her face looking old and drawn with fear and shame at the memory. After a moment she corrected, "He did kiss me. I used to think it was sort of sweet, that he would be in love with 'Shebbeth. Now I see it—he only wanted to—to get near me. I—He—" She looked pleadingly at Starhawk and the Wolf, revulsion clear on her face. "He's my *uncle!*"

"He's your uncle," Starhawk said softly. "Your mother's brother. Except for Jeryn, the last Prince of the Ancient House of Wenshar."

Something in the way she spoke, the half-detached, half-speculative tone of her soft, even voice, made Sun Wolf look up at her suddenly. Her eyes looked as they had in a hundred pre-dawn conferences on battle lines and siege camps, adding up a thousand tiny details and coming up with . . .

"Taswind!"

Tazey looked up at Nanciormis' voice. Her uncle strode over to her, his white cloak billowing, his eyes oil-dark and hard.

"Come away from them."

She did not move. The big shirdar lord hesitated for a moment, indrawn breath waiting on his lips, then changed his mind. He came to where she sat, against the wall at Starhawk's side, and squatted before her. She tried to pull her elbow away from his gloved hand, and the silk and leather grip tightened.

"Don't be a fool," Nanciormis said softly. But now, listening for it, Sun Wolf heard the caress behind the hardness of the words. He saw by the angry stiffening of the girl's mouth that she heard it, too, and resented it like a too-familiar touch. "They've played the friend to you, yes. Up to this point men can still be gotten to admire your loyalty, even if it is misguided. Don't you see?" He leaned closer to her, put his hands on her strong, slender shoulders, where the Wolf's grip had left sticky fingermarks of blood. His voice softened further, urging, coaxing. Tazey's face was like stone.

"The proof is sure. If it wasn't with the apparition that attacked me, what more can men need? He's been seen to have sacrificing as the Witches of old used to do. You have to disassociate yourself from them. I can protect you . . ."

Tazey pulled her body from his grasp. "Get away from me," she said softly. Sun Wolf could see her tremble. "Just get away."

Nanciormis glanced sharply from Sun Wolf to Starhawk and back to Tazey, and the glint in his dark eyes was an ugly one. But he turned, to summon Anshebbeth—and saw that the doorway where she had stood was empty. His brows plunged down over the hawk nose; he muttered angrily to himself, "Damned bitch . . ."

Starhawk said quietly, "It's a dangerous game you're playing, Nanciormis. It's you she'll be hating next."

The commander slewed around, as if at the sudden whine of a drawn sword. After a second's shocked immobility he lunged to his feet, dragging Starhawk up by a handful of ragged shirt, his hand raised to knock her back against the plaster of the wall. And in that second, as when he had turned his head from the bleeding calf to see the demon grinning over his shoulder, Sun Wolf understood.

He thrust himself back against the wall and so to his feet, oblivious to the stabbing pain in his legs. "I wouldn't," he said, his hoarse voice like the faint scrape of metal on rock. Nanciormis stopped. For a moment he stood, even as his guards, half-risen around the fire at the commotion, waited immobile, fearing to tamper with a wizard even to aid their lord. The firelight glistened along the sweat on Nanciormis' face.

Very softly, Starhawk said, "Magic isn't the key, is it? I think that's what I understood, what I realized and forgot during Kaletha's summoning of the dead—that it didn't have to be magic. And that's what scared me—that if it didn't have to be magic, it could be anyone. No wonder they call the time of storms the season of witches. Because the key isn't magic. It's hate."

"I don't know what you're talking about." He didn't raise his voice loud enough for the guards, or for Kaletha, to hear.

"Don't you?" Her cool gray gaze shifted to Sun Wolf, as if they sat in a tavern with all the evening ahead of them to converse. "You called Kaletha a fool when you first met her, Chief," she said. "Why?"

Slowly, Sun Wolf said, "Because of her claim to be able to teach anyone magic—to make a mage of anyone. At the time I called her a fool because I thought she couldn't. Now I think it's because she could.

"Magic . . ." He hesitated, groping for words to explain the core of fire in his soul. "Maybe magic does come, as Kaletha says, from the mind. But the mind is a deep darkness. Magic wells out of depths the nonmageborn can't penetrate, can't even comprehend. It's as if there were a cover over that pit in their minds. In the mageborn, that pit is uncovered. We can control what flows out of it. That pit is where we descend, during the Great Trial."

Nanciormis said nothing, but in his thick face, the dark eyes shifted.

While the Wolf was speaking, Kaletha had come over to them, in her blue eyes an intensity he had never seen there. In the gloom her hair seemed braided out of smoke. "Yes," she said. "It is that cover I sought to remove."

"But removing the cover wouldn't give the person the ability to control what came out, would it?" the Hawk said. "Or what went in, to feed on the power there." In the darkness of the hallways beyond the gaping doors, wind groaned like a soul in pain, and below the wind was a faint chittering that raised the hairs on Sun Wolf's nape. Starhawk went on, "I'm not mageborn—for me, the pit of my soul is covered over. But in meditation, I've been able to listen to the sounds on the other side of that cover and to make guesses about what's down there."

Tazey said softly, "The demons . . ."

"There are no . . ." began Kaletha, but another moan of wind silenced her, and she did not finish. Under the cinnamon darkness of her looped braids her face turned chalky, as she faced, for the first time, the possibility that there were indeed matters with which she was not qualified to tamper.

"When we formed the Circle to call up the soul of the Bishop Galdron," the Hawk said, casually leaning her back and her bound hands against the painted plaster of the wall behind her, "I could feel the power moving through it, from hand to hand. You, Egaldus, and Shelaina Clerk, a little, could summon power up out of that pit in your souls at will. I couldn't—not until I sank into a trance from the incense and the chanting. Not until I lost myself in dreaming. And now I remember realizing that all the killings had happened in the deep of night, as if the mind that wielded the demons had to be asleep before they would go free. That meant that the killer might not know who he was, might not even be mageborn. The storms do that, too—make everyone less careful about controlling their rages. Later, when you said you'd never heard of the Great Trial, I knew it couldn't have been used by the Witches. That meant they wielded power without having passed the Great Trial—that like you, they could teach anyone, mageborn or not, to wield that same power. I checked through the books myself, later. Nowhere did it say all the Witches were mageborn—but it did remark that many of the killings took place in the deep of night."

"And just as many took place in the day," Nanciormis snapped. His eyes went from face to face and then darted swiftly to the small knot of guards still warming themselves by the fire. He seemed to feel their curious glances and kept his voice quiet, as they had all kept their voices but for his single outburst of rage. "Everyone in Tandieras was certainly abroad and awake when I was attacked."

"Of course," said Sun Wolf. "You needed witnesses to the fact that you had nothing to do with the killings."

Nanciormis' face flushed. "I don't have to listen to this . . ."

"I want to listen to it," Tazey said unexpectedly. In the tangle of lion-colored hair, her face was pale and set.

"The man's mad—a tramp wizard who's confessed himself in the pay of our enemies. You can't—"

The girl's voice was cold. "As Royal Princess of Wenshar, I *can*." She turned back to Sun Wolf. "Go on."

There was a moment's deadly silence, during which Nanciormis stared at his niece with hate in his dark eyes—hate, and considerable surprise.

"That must have grated on you like a broken tooth, mustn't it?" the Wolf said, his hoarse voice low. "Knowing you were born of the house that had ruled Wenshar and seeing it in the hands of a blustering drunkard whose parents were outlanders and slaves? Knowing it would pass to a scholar brat who could barely lift a sword, for all that he knew the language and customs of the shirdar as no king had for three generations? Osgard never trusted you enough to give you real power—he kept that for his friend Milkom. And if I'd been jumped coming home by a bunch of shirdar, I'd be a little careful, myself. You know, that attack on the road the night we met Osgard never did seem quite right to me, but as a Prince of an Ancient House, you'd be able to arrange with the shirdar to do it. And as the Prince of an Ancient House, you'd have known about the demons. And you'd have known there was no way it could be traced back to you."

"Naturally it can't," Nanciormis said derisively, but his hand, still closed over Starhawk's shirt, clenched nervously, a ripple of tendon and bone beneath the embroidered leather of the glove. "Because it was nothing to do with me. It's a good try, my barbarian witch," and the Wolf heard the shirdar inflection in the word, the meaning of one who copulates with devils to buy power. "But your attempt to discredit me will be no more successful than your attempt was upon my life. I certainly had no reason to hate half the people who died."

"No," Starhawk agreed calmly. "But the ones you did hate, you made damn certain Anshebbeth did as well."

In the terrible silence that followed, Sun Wolf could hear the storm winds groaning like souls trapped forever in the haunted labyrinths of the palace. Within, eddy and counter-eddy scurried through the halls, stirring the murky curtains of dust on the air in the dark rooms where the painted frescoes stared open-eyed into the eternal night. He was aware of them now—a shrill skitter of sound, a skeleton flicker of light far down a corridor that none of the others seemed to see. Sweat crawled down his arms to the manacles and the chewed, dirty bandages on his wrists.

Starhawk went on, "We always thought it sounded like two killers, didn't we, Chief? Not counting, of course, the attack Nanciormis faked on himself, which even at the time looked like just a means of getting you out of the way. But it was only one man wielding a weapon—a weapon that sometimes went and killed on its own."

Kaletha's lips moved; though she made no sound, Sun Wolf could see she whispered, "Anshebbeth . . ."

Starhawk's gray eyes went to her ashen face, and something softened a little in her voice. "She never was mageborn, was she? And you were never able to wake magic in her at a conscious level. That meant that she couldn't see what was happening. But you broke that cover over the pit of her soul, nevertheless—and it was to her that the demons spoke. There was a cauldron in her of lust and hate that refused to look at itself . . ."

"No." The word came out strangled and dry, but Kaletha's eyes suddenly swam with grief and utter horror. As if to convince herself, she stammered, "There are no demons. Only the mind, the powers of the mage . . . It was my destiny to teach, to help others realize . . . Dear God, what have I done?"

"Nothing." Nanciormis thrust Starhawk from him and turned angrily to face the Witch. "You've done nothing. Neither this bitch nor her demon lover can prove anything. They're lying to save their skins."

"How else would you explain Nexué's death?" Starhawk asked, catching her balance easily. "You knew the signs before that time, though, didn't you, Nanciormis? The signs the Witches used to look for, when one of their adepts was first becoming acquainted with those dark dreams of power and hate. Did she tell you of them? Was that when you went to her room on the balcony that first time, woke her out of that first dream of hate against me and the Wolf? She was the ideal weapon. You fed her lies and gossip, played on her love for Tazey, her fears for Kaletha's safety, knowing Milkom would be riding with Galdron—Milkom who would never have countenanced your offer for Tazey's hand. And you did offer, didn't you, as soon as Incarsyn was out of the way?"

Nanciormis said nothing, but Tazey's smoldering green eyes answered as clearly as words could have.

Starhawk went on, "At that point Incarsyn should have been safe. But you'd already planted the seeds of hate for him in Anshebbeth, with your gossip of what he'd said of witches, and how he'd treated Tazey. Whether any of it was true or not—the poor bastard always seemed pretty harmless to me and he had the decency to be kind to her—that hate couldn't be erased. And besides, he still might have wanted the Kingship of Wenshar enough to have gone against his sister's bidding."

"Kingship?" Tazey's dark brows startled down over her eyes. "But I'm not the heir. Jeryn . . ." She stopped. In the hush, Sun Wolf heard it again: the whispered chitter, a slither like a woman's gown passing over stone. He looked quickly around the oval room, wondering if he had truly seen a shadow moving retrograde across the restless jitter of the flames.

Tazey's face darkened with rage from which all fear of her uncle had departed. She said quietly, "You pig. No wonder he was afraid to take his sword lessons with you. No wonder he spent all his time hiding. No wonder he'd risk his life to get another teacher."

He put a firm hand on her arm, and she wrenched away from it as if it had been smeared with dung. "You're letting this man's lies run away with you."

"Am I?" Tazey said harshly. "I know my brother's not a coward. He knew it, too, until you started telling him—and telling my father— he was one. Until Sun Wolf came, he would have done anything to prove it, like riding the horses you gave him which were too strong for him, or going out in the desert. You told him to do that, too, didn't you?"

"As the last Prince of the Ancient House," Starhawk said, "your marriage to her would have made you the logical heir, when the inevitable accident finally did happen. But I'm sure you know that."

"What I know," Nanciormis said, "is that you and this man, by his own confession, were sent as agents from Kwest Mralwe to spread confusion and dissension in Wenshar, and now you have succeeded beyond even the King-Council's wildest hopes. You have shattered the alliance between the shirdar lords and the Lord of Wenshar; you have discredited me, the only man capable of ruling in the stead of that pathetic sot on the throne"

Furious, Tazey lashed out at him. With a warrior's quickness, he caught her wrist before her palm connected with his face. His grip like steel on the slender, browned flesh, he went on softly, "You have spoiled all chance for the only logical union that would save the kingdom." He turned his head back to look at Sun Wolf. "You've earned your pay well. As for that slut Anshebbeth . . ."

He looked around. The guards, who had been huddled in low-voiced conversation over their fire, looked up now, as if at some sound. Their faces, male and female, bearded and unbearded, were drawn and strained in the jittery light, their eyes darting nervously from door to black and gaping door. Neither Kaletha nor Anshebbeth was anywhere in the room.

Starhawk's face went white under the bruises. "She's gone after her." She twisted past Nanciormis like a cat through a half-closed door and started for the rectangle of peaty darkness. "Kaletha!"

Furious, Nanciormis caught her arm, and flung her back against the wall with all his strength. With the nearness of the demons like acid on his nerves, Sun Wolf lunged at him, kneeing him in the groin even as Nanciormis twisted to avoid it. The commander went down, white-faced with pain, and Sun Wolf made a dash for the empty eyepit of darkness.

Galvanized into belated action, the guards were upon the Wolf like a dog pack, bringing him to the stone floor even as he writhed and kicked against their grip. A boot connected with his ribs, and he felt at least one break, stabbing like a knife in his side. He twisted in time to catch another brutal kick on the outside of his thigh and heard the sharp whine of drawn steel, and Nanciormis' voice, thick with pain and rage, yelling "Kill him!"

Sun Wolf turned his head as much as he could in time to see Starhawk drop through the grip of the single man who held her, somehow grab his knee with her still-bound hands and rise again to dump him backward. Her roundhouse kick broke the wrist of the woman guard whose sword was sweeping down toward Sun Wolf's neck. The weapon went ringing, the guard cursing in pain as others dragged Starhawk back and Tazey's voice sliced through the confusion. "I forbid it! Let them up!"

"Don't listen to her!" shouted the commander. Sun Wolf could see him, staggering to his feet and fighting with all his strength not to hunch over. "She's under this wizard's spell."

"I thought Kaletha's bonds rendered his spells harmless," Starhawk retorted, and Nanciormis slapped her with furious brutality. Blood trickled from her lip, but she raised her head to meet his eyes nevertheless.

"Kill them both."

"No!"

He caught Tazey as she tried to spring forward and held her in a grip of iron. The guards hesitated, weapons in hand, their edges glinting in the shaken firelight. Sun Wolf, panting, his every breath now as if a knife were being driven into him, tried to move, and one of the several guards on top of him twisted his arm and ground his cheek against the stone of the floor. Through his agony, even then, he sensed the demons, whispering a name.

Nanciormis said, "Do it."

Sun Wolf felt a knee crush his back and a hand take a killer's grip of his thin, sweat-soaked hair. Then he felt it, like fire along his mind, driving out even the death that would come in the next instant—the rush and whisper of the demons, the surge of horror and power. A woman screaming—for an instant he believed he was the only one who heard.

The weight pressing his body to the floor flinched, then slacked, frozen. The knife dropped past his face, clattered unnoticed on the stone.

The screams went on, reverberating through the mazes of that haunted labyrinth, but no one in that firelit hall moved. Above the shrieking he thought he could hear other things: the shrill chittering of the demons, a soft whisper of terrible laughter like an echo from the end of a lightless corridor. He wasn't sure, but he thought he could hear a second voice, somewhere distant, screaming, too.

Then Tazy said softly, "Let them up. Cut them loose. We're going to need whatever magic we can get."

CHAPTER 18

THEY FOUND ANSHEBBETH, SITTING ON THE ALTAR WITHIN THE fragments of the broken Circle of Darkness. The air here was hot, thick with filtered dust, and reeking of smoke and fresh blood. Anshebbeth's gown was matted and dabbed with it where she sat on the stone, and, by the faint witchlight he and Tazey were able to summon between them, Sun Wolf saw finger-runnels of it marking the woman's white cheeks under her half-uncoiled tangle of hair.

She turned her eyes toward them, huge and luminous in the shadows, as they stopped in the inner doorway of the temple. Sun Wolf saw that she was mad.

"Come in," she said, and smiled, as the demon had smiled when Sun Wolf disemboweled the calf. "Come in."

Nanciormis and the guards hung back, but Sun Wolf walked forward into the shadowy temple, his steps putting soft fingerholes in the silence. With a cat's fastidious tread, Starhawk followed him. A moment later, Tazey shook free her uncle's staying grip and moved out also, her breeches and boot tops, like the stained rags of the Hawk's shirt, mere blurs of white in the gloom. Everywhere now, Sun Wolf could sense the demons, smell them, and feel their greedy expectancy, half-slaked but craving more to satiate. The dust caught the bluish-white glare of the witchlight, filtering it into a ghostly fog; in places it seemed to glow, though he could see nothing further—reds and a certain shade of blue that reminded him of Kaletha's eyes. Beyond the altar, the pit radiated a rotted light which permeated the darkness and dust; against it, Anshebbeth's thin, dark shape stood up like a corroded spike.

"She's dead, isn't she? Kaletha."

The blood trail, sprayed over walls and floor, had wound for almost a hundred yards among the twisting corridors and painted rooms. "Yes," the Wolf said. "She's dead."

Anshebbeth moved convulsively, clapping her hands over her face. When she took them down, tacky-dry blood smudged her eyelids and the sides of her thin nose. "I had to," she said in a strangled voice. "She was jealous of me. She only wanted me to—to follow after her. She said I should come to help her carry her books back. She didn't trust anyone else. She didn't care that there was danger here, that I'd be afraid. But I'm not afraid anymore."

She smiled again, like a skull. "Now I can make other people afraid."

"If that's what you want," he said. He stood with his arms at his sides, the rough golden hair on them prickling with the hot weight of evil in the room. They'd taken the chains from his wrists, but the magic in him was kitten-weak. He was aware of that more than of anything else, staring into the madwoman's dark eyes.

"Now Nanciormis will have to love me." She dangled her feet from the altar, kicking them back and forth, as a child might, and twisted a lock of her straight black hair into a sticky ringlet with her forefinger. "I can give him whatever he wants. I saved him from Galdron's hate and plotting. Now he doesn't have to marry Tazey. Now he'll marry me."

"Anshebbeth . . ." Tazey began, and her governess turned toward her, pointy face blazing with spite.

"I will marry him!" she insisted furiously. "You don't want him! I saved you from having to marry Incarsyn, after all those cruel things that Nanciormis told me he said about you! You're just jealous of me!"

"No," the girl said quietly. The witchlight slipped like electrum along her thick curls as she shook her head. "No, Anshebbeth, I'm not jealous of you."

"Well, you should be!" The thick air sifted with the dry whisper of demons. Light flicked in the corner of Sun Wolf's vision—he turned his head quickly, but there was nothing there. At the same moment Nanciormis and his small knot of guards stepped quickly away from the dark door, as if they had heard something in the blackness of the corridor behind them that they feared more than they feared the haunted temple ahead.

Anshebbeth stretched out her hands, thin and white as bone. "Nanciormis," she whispered, and the sibilance of it was picked up by echo and shadow.

Sun Wolf could see the white rim of terror all around the irises of the shirdar lord's dark eyes. The last Prince of the House of Wenshar knew the tales of what had taken place on that altar and what had happened to the men afterward.

Anshebbeth's face clouded. "What's the matter?" she asked softly. "You don't need to be afraid. I won't hurt you."

In the corners all around her, the demons stirred. Sun Wolf moved his head again, sharply, but that skeleton flick of light was gone. *They know your blind spots,* he thought, *and stand in them . . .*

He saw Tazey whirl like a startled fawn and look back at him with frightened eyes. Still Nanciormis did not move.

"I love you," Anshebbeth insisted, hurt in her voice. "I did it all for you." Then the note in her voice changed, and there was a sliver of anger there. "It was all for you."

The glow behind her changed into a kind of shivering glitter, and the Wolf thought he saw bright flecks of color begin to swirl in the air above the pit like sparks over a fire.

"Come to me!"

His face a mask of marble, Nanciormis stepped forward. He stopped, swallowed hard, and cast a quick glance of terror and pleading at Sun Wolf.

All his life, the Wolf thought, Nanciormis had never thought of long-range consequences to himself or anyone else, except where they served his ends. Now he was like a man wading in the ocean who steps off the underwater cliff to find himself suddenly struggling in deep water, fearing the things that swim in it beyond his knowledge. He whispered helplessly, "Please . . ."

"You're afraid of me," Anshebbeth said softly. "You don't need to be afraid of me." In the frame of her disheveled hair, her blood-marked face was horrible, the rage that had come easier and easier to her in the last weeks flaring suddenly in her eyes. "Say you love me!"

He was fighting desperately to keep face and to grip his slipping hold on even the pretense of self-command. Barely audible, he whimpered, "I—I love you, Anshebbeth."

Her face contorted again. "Liar! You lied to me!" Terrified, Nanciormis fell to his knees, raising supplicating hands. *He knew,* the Wolf thought through the pounding of his head and the dagger-thrust of each indrawn breath, *just what she could do.*

"You all lie to me!" Anshebbeth swung around, staring with wild, mad eyes at them all. "None of you loves me! You all love each other." Tazey had stepped almost unconsciously into the protective circle of Sun Wolf's arm, sensing the horror that was gathering in the corners of the temple. Starhawk, typically, had moved off to the left, widening the target distance between them and giving herself more room.

Anshebbeth's voice broke with self-pity. "But no one loves me! And no one ever will."

Hands uplifted, Nanciormis gabbled, "Of course we love you, 'Shebbeth. We all love you."

"It's hard to love hate, Anshebbeth," the Wolf said, like a thin swirl of sand in the darkness. In the face of her rage, the blue glow of witchlight over his head had dimmed to a small, flat pearl, like the sun on a foggy day; he could see the demons now, melting out of the ghostly blur of dust. Their eyes were the dark eyes of shirdar ladies, their lips like women's lips running with blood. "You've become addicted to hate, even as the demons are. It warms you, as it does them."

"It isn't my fault!" she screamed. Her skinny finger jabbed out, and Nanciormis shrank back from it, his fat face tallow-colored, as if he were about to vomit with terror. "It's his! He did this to me! He made me like this! And now no one will love me ever!"

She buried her face in her hands again, the white fingers twisting her hair as her whole bony body shook with sobbing. His nerve breaking, Nanciormis turned on his knees and crawled, scrabbling over his stained white cloak, for the dark doorway back into the labyrinth of the palace. But as he reached it, he stopped, and the sickly magelight showed the sweat pouring down his face between his hanging braids. The guards were already crowding farther from the door, pressing into the wall in a tight little group, back to back, their weapons pointing outward. The fat man scrambled ungracefully to his feet, stumbled toward them for protection, and the corpse-light glow flashed on the sword points as they turned toward him. The wrath of the demons clung like the stink of plague to his flesh and his garments. None of them was willing to let him come among them. "Sun Wolf, help me!" He turned his tear-streaked face back toward the dark figure on the altar, fighting for an echo of his former mastery. "Anshebbeth, I—I didn't mean to. Truly. I'm—I'm sorry . . ."

"You made me do it!" she screamed. "I wanted to be mageborn, so Kaletha would love me, would treat me as her equal! But you made me hate people! You whispered to me and whispered to me about this person said this and that person said that. And then I'd dream about them—dream about their deaths, and when I heard about it the next morning I'd be glad . . ."

Nanciormis covered his face, giving at the knees and crumpling, as if his whole body were rotting with terror. Anshebbeth rose to her feet, her face working, the winds stirring the eldritch shimmer of dust around her, flicking the darkness of her dress and hair. The adepts did not always at first know their power, Sun Wolf remembered, but there was always a moment when they did. What ritual had they used, what final twisting of the soul, what dreadful self-justification, to temper and seal and harden the girl into their numbers? Had many of them had resisted and cried out as Anshebbeth was crying now?

Tears were streaming down her face, tears of fury and utter wretchedness tracking through the gummy blood. Shrill and barely human, she sobbed, "I feel them here—I hear them whispering. It was like my dreams, but I wasn't asleep! Kaletha—Kaletha—"

She turned on Nanciormis like a rabid weasel, and he buried his face in his arms and groaned. "You made me be this! You made me hate!"

The air seemed to burn around Sun Wolf's flesh. Wind that came from nowhere knifed in his hair and the rags of his shirt and fingered Nanciormis' cloak and long braids as he lay groveling on the stone. Tazey gasped, her hand tightening on Sun Wolf's bare arm, as glowing shapes began to pour up out of the pit, flowing along the stone floor, around the altar, and over Anshebbeth's feet. They drifted dangle-footed in the air, like monster wasps with Anshebbeth's eyes. Nanciormis scrambled to his feet and started to back away, batting blindly at the air around him, then screamed as one of them laid his arm open to the bone.

"No!" he shrieked. "Sun Wolf! Anshebbeth! I'm sorry! I'll do any-thing—please, help me!"

Hate doesn't stop, Sun Wolf thought, strangely calm. *When it's done with him, it will take us all.*

Swiftly, he disengaged Tazey's hands from his arm and strode empty-handed toward the altar where Anshebbeth sat. He felt the tiny slip of light that glowed above his head die. Only the dim glint of Tazey's power shimmered across on those blue, skeletal backs, and on the halo of greedy fangs surrounding the dark shape of the Witch.

Nanciormis screamed again, running desperately as the demons be-gan to harry him around the room as they had harried the calf in the pit. Flesh gleamed opal white, bulging through claw-rents in his clothes, bouncing almost comically as he ran; blood oozed, glittering down his trouser legs and boots. He was sobbing, tears of terror pour-ing down his cheeks.

Sun Wolf seized Anshebbeth by the arms, and she looked up into his face, startled, so intent upon her hatred that she had not seen him come. Her countenance was scarcely human, streaked with tears and snot and blood; from a frame of coarse black hair that flowed down over his hands, she stared unseeing. "No one makes you hate, An-shebbeth. They can only ask you to. You can always say no."

"It isn't like that!" She was gasping, clutching at her throat as if it were strangling her. "I love him, and he did this to me, made me like this . . ."

Darkness closed on them, a vortex of power and terror whirlpool-ing into those stretched black eyes. Sun Wolf shook her, violently, furiously, trying to break that rigid centeredness of hate, and her head lolled on her shoulders, her mouth open in a soundless shriek. In the blackness, he knew the demons were around him and he felt the soft nibble of fangs against his neck. "Do you love him?" he demanded. "Or do you love your hate more than him?"

"I don't!" she sobbed. Then something broke in her, and she gasped, "I don't want to!"

Pressed to the stone of the wall, Nanciormis was screaming, beg-ging as he fought with the bleeding air.

"Say it!" the Wolf commanded.

Anshebbeth stared up at him like a hysterical child, unable to speak or draw breath. He shook her again, her neck snapping back like a white, corded stem in the black wrack of her hair. A sob ripped her, as if it would tear her body in two. He saw the madness retreat from her eyes and knowledge take its place—knowledge and horror at what she knew she had become.

As though torn from her with a knife, her scream rent the air. "I don't want it! Let him go! I don't want this!"

Nanciormis shrieked again, huddled against the wall as the glowing ring closed around him. In Sun Wolf's grip Anshebbeth's body felt as fragile and skeletal as theirs.

Despairing, Anshebbeth screamed, "I can't let it go! I can't let it go! I want to but I can't . . ." She twisted away from him, burying her face in her skeletal hands.

Then she screamed—not the tense, tight shrillness of her strangled shrieks before, but loud, aching, louder and louder as the torrent of freed sound seemed to rip apart the containing flesh. Like startled hornets the demons rose from Nanciormis, shining horribly in the dark air. Sun Wolf flung himself aside as they descended upon the altar in a whistling swarm, knowing he had been too late. Anshebbeth did not raise her head, but screamed on and on, rocking like a hurt child, as if some last rag of sanity had slipped finally from her grip. He caught a glimpse of Starhawk running toward him, as he turned back weaponless, magicless, to face the phosphorescent storm of death.

Anshebbeth's scream scaled upward, twisting the darkness as the demons settled over her. In a flash of terrible enlightenment, Sun Wolf understood that she had regained, rather than lost, her sanity. She knew what she had done.

Blindly, striking with her hands at the glowing fangs that ripped her flesh, she ran forward, the demons driving her into the pit. Starhawk reached the Wolf's side at the same moment that Anshebbeth fell, the glowing ghost shapes swirling down after her, shriek after shriek ripping the air.

It took her twenty minutes to die. When it was over silence settled on the dark temple, as it had lain for a hundred and fifty years.

"You awake, Chief?"

Sun Wolf started to roll over, then ceased with a gasp of pain. Vaguely, he remembered Starhawk wrapping a makeshift field dressing over his cracked ribs as he was sliding into sleep in the sickly yellow post-storm light, but the recollection was cloudier than the dreams that had followed. He felt chilled, sticky, and bone-tired, hurting in every limb, with dust gummed in his eyelashes, moustache, and the stubble of his beard.

He felt someone bend over him, light and very swift, and lips touched his. Opening his eye, he saw Starhawk just straightening her body where she knelt beside him.

"Well, that fairy tale does work after all," she remarked.

She was wearing the dark-green leather doublet of the Tandieras guards over a black shirt which made her sun-gilded fair skin shine like ivory. She had bathed and looked clean, calm, and, except for the black handspan of bruise on her face, utterly unruffled. Squinting past her, he saw over the broken wall of the ruined house in which he'd slept, the cliff faces of Wenshar, blackish maroon in the polished sunset light, guarding their treasure of rose and apricot within. Like strange and far-off music, he heard the hushed voices of Nanciormis' guards and the comfortable nicker of horses.

The storm had ended shortly after noon. In spite of an exhaustion so deep that he could barely stagger, Sun Wolf had insisted on moving down from the canyons to the piled debris and crumbled walls of the Lower Town before he would sleep. It had taken him and Tazey two hours to work all the binding-spells to hold the demons forever within the rocks of Wenshar; exhausting, nerve-wracking hours, while he had listened, with as much of his mind as he could spare, to hear the demons wakening again from the pit where Anshebbeth's mangled body lay.

They had not wakened. Like drunkards, they were satiated, wallowing in the afterglow. He hadn't wanted to expose Tazey to the full knowledge of what the demons were and of the terrible powers necessary to hold them to the stones, but he had had no choice. He had been simply too weary, too drained, to pass through the ritual a second time alone. Later, the girl had been very silent as she had walked beside him down the sand-drifted canyon in the after-hush of the storm, but he suspected that she was less shocked by the vileness of the demons than she would have been even twenty-four hours ago.

With the demons bound to the rock that had given them birth, it would have been possible to sleep safely, even within the temple, but Sun Wolf had not wanted to risk the dreams that might come.

He mumbled, "What is it?" By the color of the light, he knew he'd slept four or five hours.

"Riders on their way," she said. "Still a couple hours out on the desert, but my guess is it's reinforcements."

"Good." He sat up. Starhawk, as usual, refrained from helping him; he didn't know whether he should be miffed or pleased with the implied compliment of superhuman stamina. The jab of the hardened dressing was almost as bad as the cracked ribs underneath. "They can take Nanciormis back."

Starhawk shook her head. "He's gone," she said. "You'd started the binding-rites already when his guards took him out of the temple. He was cut to pieces, you know, and bleeding like a flayed steer. For a long time he just cried in a corner. . . ."

"Don't tell me," the Wolf said wearily. "They thought the poor bastard was pretty harmless where he was."

Starhawk shrugged. "After what went on in the temple, they weren't anxious to search the canyons for him. I'd have the lot of them flogged, myself, but it's not my business."

Sun Wolf sighed and sat quietly, his back to the crumbling house wall. Dry wind curled across his naked chest, bearing the smell of dust and horses.

He wondered why, in spite of everything—the memory of his humiliation at the commander's hands, the beating they'd given Starhawk, the pain in his wrists and side—his only anger toward the man stemmed from what he had done to Anshebbeth and what he had tried to do to Jeryn—not even so much trying to murder him, but planting in his mind the fear that he was a coward and turning his father against him.

He still found it difficult to hate Nanciormis. After seeing Anshebbeth's death, he found it difficult, at the moment, to hate anyone.

Thinking back, he realized that he always had—and in that he was like Nanciormis himself.

"He was only playing the game, you know," he said after a time. "It was only selfishness and greed, with no hate in it. He couldn't have summoned the demons if he'd wanted to, and maybe he knew it. There was nothing personal in it at all. None of them, not Tazey nor Anshebbeth nor Incarsyn, was real to him. Only himself and his wants."

"It's what tipped me off, you know." The Hawk settled back on her heels, a bar of sunlight slanting through the broken roof, turning her hair to platinum but leaving that cool, scarred face in shadow. "You

saw Nanciormis as a man, but I saw him as a woman sees him. He was
a man who used women. He used other people, too—their hates, their
loves, their fears—and their magic. In a way, his evil was deeper than
Anshebbeth's hate or Kaletha's vanity and irresponsibility with what
she'd found in the books that had lain forgotten for centuries in the
library. And, of course, poor Ciannis knew less of the cult than Nanciormis did. If she had known, she might have warned Kaletha about it
—if she ever knew Kaletha had found the old books at all. But Nanciormis simply didn't care."

Sun Wolf nodded. "The worst of it is," he said quietly, "that it was
my evil as well. That was what being a mercenary was all about. Like
killing that poor calf—you do what you have to do, like an animal
eating. I don't know how many people I've killed, not for a kingdom
or for love or pride or for anything, really—just because some politician was paying me to take a city they happened to be living in."

The corner of her mouth moved slightly, less ironic than simply
rueful. "Yes, I know," she said. Their eyes met. In hers he saw the
understanding that he had done evil and that she had known it for evil
at the time and had still followed him into battle as his second-in-
command. It was, he understood then, what Nanciormis had done to
Anshebbeth. It was how she had known.

It was some time before he could say anything. When he did, it was
only, "I'm sorry, Hawk." In her eyes he saw that she knew for what.

She only shook her head. "It's history," she said, meaning it. "Like
Anshebbeth, I had the choice. Unlike her, I don't hate myself for the
choice I made." He remembered that she had remained Kaletha's
friend.

"You understood that?"

"Oh, yes. She knew in the end what she had become—and the one
she most hated was herself. I suppose it's what happened to all the
girls, when they came to an understanding of what was happening to
them." She uncoiled her whipcord body and rose to her feet, watching
with her usual mild detachment as Sun Wolf agonizingly followed. "It
was only the evil ones that survived."

"I can't say that I blame those that didn't," he said.

They passed through a gap in the wall, which might or might not
once have been a door, and walked across the trampled, dusty side of
a sand dune toward where one of the old rain tanks hid in the niche of

a rock, away from the prevailing wind. "Would you have done the same in her position? If you learned it was you?"

Sun Wolf glanced up at the dark, eroded cliffs of the Haunted Range, guarding their rainbow labyrinth of evil within. "I'd like to think I would."

There was water in three of the old tanks; Sun Wolf bathed in the shallowest of them; Starhawk joined him there and later on the spread-out blanket that he'd worn flung over his shoulders like a cloak. "No wonder soldiers' women have to be versatile and creative," she commented, when he flinched at the pain of his ribs.

In time they both dressed in the clothes that were part of the bundle Tazey had brought to Wenshar with her to further their escape. The bundle also contained some food, their weapons and mail, but not the little cache of money. "Cheer up," Starhawk said, slipping various hideout daggers into her boots with the air of one resuming a much-loved garment. "With the demons laid for good, they'll have to give us *some* reward—an exorcist's fee if nothing else."

"Bets?" the Wolf grumbled.

They rode out of Wenshar as darkness began to fall and met, an hour and a half later, the oncoming party from Tandieras in a circle of torchlight on the pebbled desolation of the wind-scoured reg.

As they got close, Sun Wolf could see Osgard's coarse blond-gray hair by the torchlight and, beside his great horse, the fat, trotting figure of Walleye and his small rider. Tazey cried out, "Daddy!" and spurred her buckskin gelding, riding like a mad antelope to throw herself into her father's arms.

"It seems I've you to thank that I'm not going to find scorpions in my blankets some night." By the campfire's windblown light, Osgard looked sober and better than he had since the Wolf had come to Tandieras. The veils that swathed his coarse, stubbly face were pushed back, falling over his sand-colored cloak behind. With his rough shirt and battered boots, he might have been just another range hand, as he had been before his warrior-uncle had made him King. "Oh, I knew he was dangerous, but . . ." He hesitated, then looked into the amber heart of the fire, his thick mouth pursing with embarrassment. "I suppose I was like the owner of a dog trained for killing. You get careless."

Sun Wolf nodded. "I know." On the other side of the campfire, a guard told a joke, but the laughter was subdued. Out on the asphalt blackness of the reg, it was less easy to dismiss the demons and djinns of desert lore as mere superstition, no matter what the priests of the Triple God might say. "He did, in a way."

"He always was careless," Osgard said. "He was a good fighter, but irresponsible—he never thought anything could touch him. I'm not sure being publicly broken and turned out like a beaten dog in the desert wasn't something to which he'd have preferred death. He had a conceit of himself, besides liking his pleasures. But I wouldn't have let him put a hand on Tazey . . ." He paused, and the bluster died out of him again. Off by the other campfire, Tazey and Jeryn sat together, conversing quietly with Starhawk, their arms around her. Past Osgard's shoulder, the Wolf could see Jeryn's dark eyes shining with a boy's gruesome enthusiasm as Tazey spoke of what had happened in the temple.

The King sighed. "But God knows I'd have sworn I'd never have let matters go this far. Damned witches with their stinking magic . . ." He stopped again, looking over at the Wolf, as if he'd spoken slightingly of sand in the tents of the shirdar.

Sun Wolf shook his head. "Magic had nothing to do with it," he said. "Nanciormis was the kind of man who'd have used any weapon. He'd made attempts on your life—and Jeryn's—before he learned Anshebbeth's mind had been touched by the demons. Her power was just the readiest weapon at hand. If she'd been mageborn and not simply the victim of her own and Kaletha's vanity, she'd have understood what was happening to her and been able to control it. I felt it— I think Tazey did, too. If you have power, you must face it, touch it, and learn to use it, or it rots within you like an abscessed wound." He fell silent, regarding the King across the campfire, and Osgard, knowing his thoughts, looked away again.

He muttered, "I—I know." Unwillingly, his eyes returned to the Wolf. "But you can't blame me, can you? I wanted a daughter I could be proud of . . ."

"Good God, man," Sun Wolf said angrily, "you've got one of the finest natural wizards I've ever heard of for a daughter and a son who'll politic and finesse and treaty-make rings around the shirdar and the Middle Kingdoms, and all you can do is complain because they're not a brainless brood mare and a beef-witted ox like you and me? I can only think of two things in my life that I wouldn't trade for those children of yours. Can't you be proud of them for what they are and not for what you want them to be?"

Osgard stared into the fire, rubbing his big, sword-scarred hands over one another, as the Wolf remembered his own father used to do. Then he looked up again and grinned, a little embarrassed to admit it. "Jeryn is a clever little bastard, isn't he?"

"It's men like Jeryn," Sun Wolf said, "who hire men like me. Let 'em be what they are, Osgard. They're going to get hurt bad enough swimming against the stream as it is."

The King sighed and rubbed his stubbly chin. "I know it," he said quietly. Then, after a long pause, "Where should I send Tazey?"

She'd been willing, Sun Wolf remembered, to give up everything she wanted to please him. He remembered the fauve torchlight on her hair as she danced the war dance and the pride that had glowed so visibly from Osgard as he'd spoken of her—*the sweetest daughter a man could want.* Beside the nearby campfire, she and Jeryn sat huddled in their quilted jackets and head veils, their eyes bright as they talked to Starhawk, reunited for this last brief time.

"You could send her to Yirth of Mandrigyn," he said at length. "She's just about the only wizard I know qualified to teach." He added, seeing her father's face thicken at the thought of how far away Mandrigyn was, "But if Tazey prefers, I could stay here for awhile first, teach her what I know. It isn't the teaching she'd get from Yirth, but it would tell her what to look for later. And it would give her more time here."

"No." Osgard sighed. "Tazey can't stay here. And neither can you." A half-burned log broke in the fire; he picked a branch from the slender bundle of wood they'd brought in from the far edge of the reg and pushed the fallen chunks back together. The spurting flame showed deep lines in his unshaven face—annoyance and shame.

"You don't know the temper of the people in Pardle, Captain. They're a superstitious bunch, when all's said, and the mageborn have always had a foul reputation in Wenshar. I wouldn't have cared if you'd been lynched on the way back, but when I heard Illyra's men were out hunting your blood, I thought I'd better come and make sure Tazey got back all right. The miners and the Trinitarians being on one of their witch hunts is one thing, but Illyra . . ."

Sun Wolf felt his face flush with anger. "I didn't have a damn thing to do with the murders."

The King held up his hand. "That doesn't matter," he said. "And I think you know it doesn't matter."

The cruel vulture-eyes of the Lady of the Dunes returned to Sun Wolf, and the keyed-up tension in the Hall, the night Nanciormis had staged his attack. And it was gold pieces to little green apples that Nanciormis had spread the story of his confession from the Fortress to the town. Anger surged like a core of heated iron in him, but he knew Osgard was right.

"I think you'd better ride on tonight."

Osgard collected all the spare food and water from his troop of guards, and Jeryn and Tazey helped them load it on their horses. "We can hold off Illyra for a while," the King said, as Sun Wolf finished tying the latigos that held the slender bundle of his possessions to his dapple gelding's cantle. "But you'd better ride straight north and get across the Backbone as soon as you can."

"Easy for him to say," Sun Wolf growled, as the big monarch went striding off to give some direction or other to the little knot of dark-clothed guards. "You know every copper we have is still behind that brick in our cell in the empty quarter?"

Starhawk regarded him, amused, by the faint glow of the ball lightning that flickered over his head. "You want to risk meeting Illyra to go back for it?"

Sun Wolf grumbled an impious wish concerning Illyra's future sex partners and tightened the gray's cinches. He added, "I never should have promoted you from squad captain."

"You always said a warrior had to be versatile."

"I wasn't talking about sweeping floors and feeding pigs from here to Farkash."

"Chief?" The bright flicker of magelight danced in the night; the black gravel of the reg crunched underfoot as Tazey and Jeryn came back from the baggage piles, carrying sacks. It was not lost on the Wolf that the guards looked askance at the soft light that surrounded the girl, and gave her wide berth. "These are all the Demonaries and books of magic that weren't in the shirdane."

Sun Wolf hefted the sack experimentally, then opened it and removed the three largest volumes. These he handed back to Tazey. At her inquiring look, he explained, "They're too big to grab up in an emergency. I'm not going to have them destroyed by accident just because I want them with me on the road. Take them to Mandrigyn with you, along with the others. You and Yirth between you can work out translations of the shirdane ones."

She nodded, hugging the books to her breast. Her mouth flinched a little, and she looked away; he saw the witchlight glisten in her eyes.

Gently, he reached out and put a hand on her shoulder. "You'll like Yirth," he said softly. "She's a good lady." Then, grinning, he added, "You say hello to Sheera of Mandrigyn for me, too."

"And be prepared to have her spit in your face if you do," Starhawk added irreverently.

Jeryn, who had been doing something over by Sun Wolf's horse, came back into the double ring of fox-fire light, and the Wolf could see in his face, too, the grief of parting.

Tazey asked hesitantly, "Will I meet you again?"

"Not if we keep getting thrown out of every kingdom we visit."

Sun Wolf ignored his second-in-command. "One day, yes." He hugged them both, the daughter and the son that he would never father, and felt Jeryn's thin arms around his waist in a tight clutch and the sting of Tazey's tears against his unshaven chin. Neither mercenary captains nor wandering wizards could afford to raise children. It was the first time he had been conscious of regret for what he had been or for what he was.

It was the first time he fully understood what it was he had given up.

The wan glow of Tazey's witchlight was visible for a long distance across the reg as they rode away.

"It's going to be hard for her," Starhawk said after a time. "Hard for them both. But she never really wanted to be mageborn, you know. She really wanted to be what her father wanted her to be—a beautiful girl who dances well, rides anything with four legs, and eventually marries some handsome man and lives happily ever after. There was a time when she could have turned aside from what she has and gone back to lying to herself about it. She gave that up for us."

"No." Sun Wolf glanced back over his shoulder at that will-o'-the-wisp, a marsh light in the flat, black desert of stone. "You can never turn aside from it, nor lie to yourself about it. Not ever."

The moonlight dusted her uncovered ivory hair as she moved her head. "Do you want to?"

He thought about Tazey and Jeryn again, their years of learning to

be what they would be, years in which he could have no part. "Sometimes."

His horse stumbled a little on the harsh gravel, making him curse as
his cracked ribs pinched him, and something tied to the saddle horn
jogged against his knee. Curious, knowing he had hung nothing there,
he reached down and brought up a little wash-leather bag that jingled
softly as he opened it and dumped its contents into his hand.

"Well, I'll be go to hell."

Starhawk drew her rangy bay mare closer, to look over his shoulder
at the handful of silver gleaming softly in the dusky moonlight. "It has
to have been Jeryn," she said.

Sun Wolf laughed, with relief and triumph and delight. "Nine years
old and already he knows you don't turn your hired troops off without
pay!"

"Yeah?" Her eyebrows went up. "And how long do you think his
daddy's troops are going to cover our tracks against Illyra once they
realize he's gone through and rifled every pocket and saddlebag in the
camp?"

Sun Wolf shuddered and shoved the money into the pocket of his
sheepskin jacket. "Kid's going to be hell on wheels when he takes
over Wenshar," he said. "Let's ride."

"And just think," Starhawk mused as they nudged their horses into
a canter, north to the distant, jagged line of the mountains under the
sand-colored moon. "The next teacher you find may be even worse."

A B O U T   T H E   A U T H O R

At various times in her life, Barbara Hambly has been a high-school teacher, a model, a waitress, a technical editor, a professional graduate student, an all-night clerk at a liquor store, and a karate instructor. Born in San Diego, she grew up in Southern California, with the exception of one high-school semester spent in New South Wales, Australia. Her interest in fantasy began with reading *The Wizard of Oz* at an early age and has continued ever since.

She attended the University of California, Riverside, specializing in medieval history. In connection with this, she spent a year at the University of Bordeaux in the south of France and worked as a teaching and research assistant at UC Riverside, eventually earning a Master's Degree in the subject. At the university, she also became involved in karate, making Black Belt in 1978 and competing in several national-level tournaments.

Her books include *Dragonsbane; The Ladies of Mandrigyn; The Silent Tower;* THE DARWATH TRILOGY: *Time of the Dark, The Walls of Air,* and *The Armies of Daylight;* and a historical whodunit, *The Quirinal Hill Affair,* set in ancient Rome.